Pass in Review

HONOR

Brian Utermahlen

Brian Utermahlen

May 16, 2013

For I am a man under authority,
having soldiers under me:
and I say to this man 'go' and he goeth,
and to another 'come' and he cometh...

- Matthew 8:9

Cover art provided by Jeff Sanson
Sanson Illustrations, Houston TX

DEDICATION

To my Dad

who was one of those special young guys in WWII who
came off the farm, from the factory or out of the classroom to fly in the Air Corps,
and did so very well against an experienced enemy once upon a time
in the skies over the Mediterranean, Europe and the broad Pacific

ACKNOWLEDGMENTS

Thanks to the surviving members of the 14th and 82nd Fighter Groups (P-38) from WWII who spent time with me re-living the era when they and other young pilots won the air war in the Med

Thanks to Dixie Sloan, Dick Willsie, Ben Mason and others of the 82nd FG (WWII) who spent the time to share their incredible life stories with me at 'Wings Over Houston' and elsewhere

Thanks to all the surviving members of the 49th Fighter Squadron – the HANGMEN of WWII especially, those who shared their memories with me at their San Antonio reunion – BW Curry, RT 'Sparky' Sparks, Frank Mullinax, Jack Lenox, Cliff Bailey

Thanks to the friends who encouraged me as I completed this 2nd installment of PASS IN REVIEW

Thanks to Brian Carpenter, Dick Steiner, George Considine, Sue Schmidt, John Scanlan for their proof reading, suggestions and overall support in both DUTY and HONOR

Thanks to Jeff Sanson of Houston for an extraordinary piece of cover art that captured the story and the characters beyond my wildest expectations – Again!.

Most of all, thanks to my wife, Dianne, for EVERYTHING these past forty-eight years including her proofing, editorial critique, encouragement and 'tough love' toward the first two installments of the PASS IN REVIEW trilogy

This is a work of fiction and all fictional characters are the product of the author's imagination and have not been patterned after any person living or dead.

The historical characters in this saga are portrayed as they have been presented and recorded in history and with rare exception in positions they held at the time and place they held them.

Dialogue between historical personages and the fictional characters is the product of the author with attention, however, to the political and military views they are recorded to have held and in keeping with their own views, language, and personal circumstances known to history.

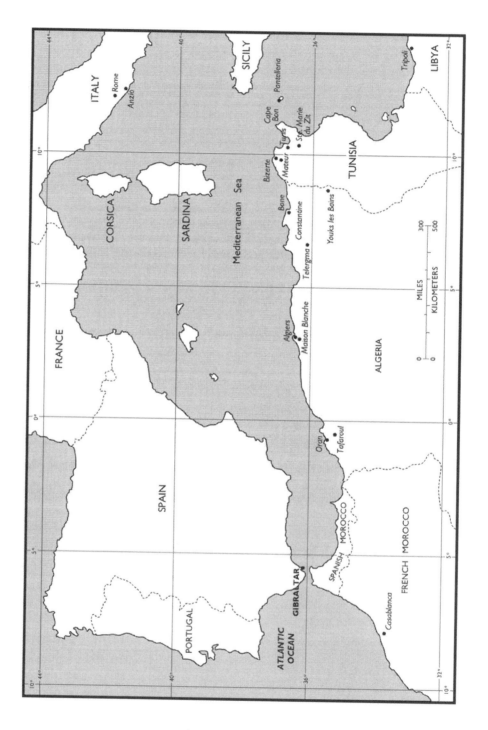

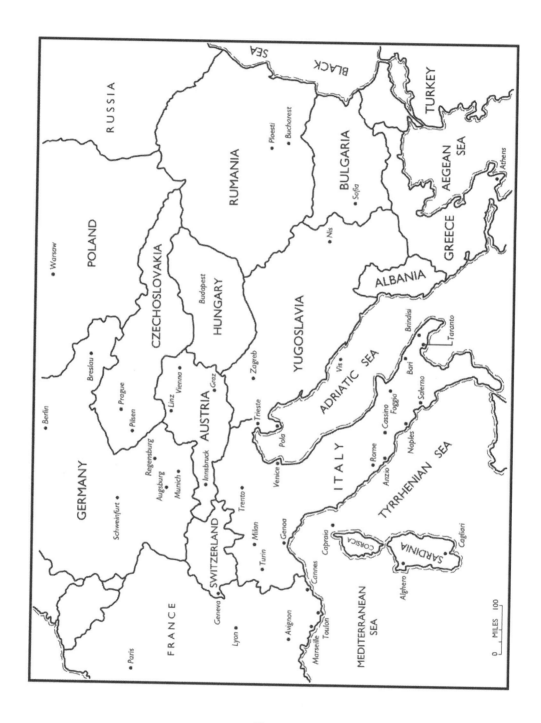

As sacred to us as our Alma Mater is our Honor Code.

It is not just a set of rules made to make relationships at the Academy more effective - it is the code of the fighting man.

In fact, it is more to the Army than a code; it is almost a religion. As such, all its principles cannot be put on paper but must exist in the minds of the men of West Point.

Bugle Notes - 1950

.

PROLOGUE

New York City - May 31, 1940

It was late Friday afternoon as Dave Nolan entered the ornate lobby of the St. Regis Hotel four blocks south of Central Park. He had the bell captain call ahead to William Donovan before stepping into the open elevator for the ride up to a deluxe suite his old friend kept for those times when he passed through the city. After a long ride of bumps and grinding gears up through the hotel's floors he got out and knocked on the large wooden door down the hall.

The entryway was immediately flung open revealing 'Wild Bill', America's chief of worldwide intelligence, dressed in a red silk smoking jacket over wool trousers and a white dress shirt; he held a drink in one hand and looked pleased.

"Damn good to see you again, Dave," he said motioning Nolan inside, leading him into the formal sitting room with a white fireplace at one end. "How about an old fashioned? Not as good as the one your Denise makes but it's as close as I can come to duplicating perfection." Donovan busied himself at the small bar along the wall away from the window as Nolan looked around at the large multi-room suite, again wondering at the wisdom of accepting his old wartime commander's invitation.

"How's your pretty bride these days?" Donovan asked easily, handing him the drink and taking a seat across from him on the sofa.

"She's worried."

"That you're seeing me?"

"Shouldn't she be?" Among other things, Denise still blamed Donovan for the debacle of their trip to Berlin in October '38 when Dave was briefly assigned as military liaison to chaperone Charles Lindbergh around Nazi Germany. "She still hasn't forgiven you for getting us sent to Berlin."

"Well, a lot of water has gone under the bridge in the year since I last saw you two at your summer cottage. What I told you then has come to pass. And I'll tell you this, too – America will be in another war before the next year is up. You can count on it. That's why you and I need to talk."

Apprehension sifted quickly through him as it had many times over the years because of Donovan. "Bill, I was serious the last time you tried to recruit me."

"I know, but the planet has shifted and all the rules have changed. The world we knew then is not the world we live in today. You have to admit that."

"That means my work is now more important than ever," Nolan pointed out.

"What Barrett Enterprises is doing is more important today than it was a year ago, but your own role is diminishing."

"Not from where I sit. I'm busier than ever." Yet even as he said it, he realized his major contribution toward re-inventing his father-in-law's corporation into a leaner, meaner, more profitable version of Kaiser Industries had just about run its course. He'd planted and watered; now the corporation was shifting into the reaping of benefits with his role changing to managing the organizations he'd trained to execute the overall plan.

"You need to listen to me and come on board this time." Donovan sipped his drink and stared hard at him with his intensely blue eyes – an intimidating look Nolan knew only too well. "A year ago I thought you'd be perfect as one of the key lieutenants in my intelligence organization. When you turned me down, I found somebody almost as good as you. I'm actually glad you stuck to your guns back then because what your country needs now is even more important. Here's why:

"A week ago, an agent of British Secret Intelligence arrived here in New York with a letter from Admiral Blinker Hall and a message from Winston Churchill. He has two critical missions to accomplish – first, to obtain from the U.S. Government destroyers, battleships, aircraft, plus military equipment and supplies to replace those left at Dunkirk by the British Expeditionary Force. It's obvious to all of us that France will fall under the German *Blitzkrieg* in a matter of weeks. By July 4th the only thing separating Britain from extinction will be twenty-five short miles of English Channel. England is the last free European domino standing… the question now is – for how long?"

"And the second mission?" Nolan asked.

"To influence the president and Washington policy makers to support England, economically at first, but militarily in the long haul. I told him I'd do everything I could – and that I had someone who would help me." Donovan gave him a deep, penetrating stare. "If you turn me down again, Nolan, I'll find it hard to pray for your sin-sick, shriveled up soul."

"Bill, I told you before I am *not* getting drawn into another escapade involving government lawmakers or bureaucrats," Dave Nolan said with harsh conviction. "Twice in one lifetime is enough."

"Listen Dave, none of us have the luxury of sitting on the sidelines. The war we fought back in '18 was terrible, but it was nothing compared to what's coming. This next war will be far worse and manifestly more consequential. It's not going to be another intramural squabble between royal families limited to less than ten percent of the earth's surface. What's on our doorstep is a global clash of civilizations and ideology to be fought everywhere on the planet."

"And you think someone who retired from the Army as a lowly major after almost twenty-three years, who failed miserably on two separate occasions at similar political assignments is going to be some kind of help to you now? I think you need to go back to being a teetotaler."

"Perhaps. But I'm in good company. Even before I thought of you, Winston Churchill had already asked for you by name."

"I don't know what to say, Bill. I'm astounded. He's only been Prime Minister for three weeks, and in that time his country has been at war with the most potent military machine in history. How could a manager in some obscure corporation an ocean away warrant even a second's worth of attention from a man in his position? Makes no sense at all."

"Churchill had access to your observations while you accompanied Lindbergh around Nazi Germany. I gave your reports to him when he was a backbencher railing about what he saw happening in Germany and the inevitability of war despite – or maybe because of – Chamberlain's shameless appeasement of the Little Corporal. He was impressed with your insights and conclusions. I've always said you were one of the keenest observers of the human condition I've ever known, and Churchill recognized the same talent I came to appreciate in you. That's point one. Point two is Brigadier Henry Smythe-Browne."

"Brigadier? The last time I saw him he was a newly promoted lieutenant colonel." The Englishman had been the British Military attaché to the Berlin embassy reporting directly to their ambassador, Sir Nevile Henderson. He'd first encountered Smythe-Browne at Allery, the huge American hospital complex near Chalons-sur-Saone where they had both been sent in the fall of 1918 for surgery along with rehabilitation and recovery. Some years later in Berlin, Henry, along with Sir Nevile, had tried recruiting him as a back channel to Washington around the American ambassador who the Brits saw as a hindrance and worse, a Nazi sympathizer.

"Smythe-Browne has done well for himself in their Army," Donovan was saying, rising to take Nolan's glass and moving to the bar to refresh their drinks. "He positioned himself as the personal assistant to Sir John Dill, Chief of the Imperial General Staff and he's found favor with Anthony Eden because of his work on the evacuation from Dunkirk. In addition, he just happens to be an old school chum of Churchill's private secretary, John "Jack" Colville. That's how your name got in front of the new prime minister. Smythe-Browne suggested you and I be invited over on a "business trip" to see firsthand what's happening. They're hoping we'll return and convince Roosevelt to throw in with them against the Hun. The Brits are in big trouble, and they know it."

Dave Nolan listened to everything, remaining calm on the outside but roiling inwardly. This had all the same markings as two previous fiascos generated by the politics of Washington – his military intelligence trip to Russia in early 1919, and his month long tour of Germany with Charles Lindbergh almost twenty years later. The first one ruined his planned marriage to a woman he'd never completely gotten over, and the second had been the proximate cause of his resignation from an Army career in which he'd invested his entire adult life.

"How can you possibly think I'm a fit for something like this?" Nolan asked. "I'm definitely not a politician and I darned sure don't have connections or stature to affect anything of consequence in Washington."

"I'm not asking you to be a politician. I'm demanding you be a patriot doing your duty, Nolan – honoring a vow you made to this country two dozen years ago. I don't recall there's a sunset date on your oath to protect and defend the Constitution." Donovan leaned toward him and their eyes locked. "I've never known you to back away from any commitment you made. This would be a really lousy time for you to start."

"Bill, you're asking me to do something I don't necessarily understand as defending the Constitution. And, I haven't asked for the job nor do I want it."

America's chief of worldwide intelligence looked squarely at Dave Nolan, remembering the many times during the Great War when as a junior officer the Pennsylvanian had frustrated him. "Life would be a lot easier for all of us if we got to pick and choose our duties and obligations. Whether you like it or not, this is a duty that came looking for you."

Nolan took a deep breath and slowly shook his head. "I still don't see how I could help you. Being a friend of Henry Smythe-Browne and having a few insights into a handful of the top ranking Nazis isn't a sufficient résumé for someone who's going to convince the president one way or another about anything."

"You'd be surprised at how much cachet you have. I don't want you because you were the best small unit commander in the AEF, or because you used to hunt at Karinhall with Hermann Goering. You're a businessman now, and a damned good one from what I hear. That business perspective is something our government – and President Roosevelt in particular – wants explored. We must know if the British manufacturing base has the ability to sustain the war effort needed to halt the German military. If so, for how long? I don't have the expertise to answer those questions." Donovan handed him a typed sheet of paper. "This is an initial list of queries from Edward Stettinius, the new advisor to the Council of National Defense."

Nolan knew of Stettinius – he'd once been chairman of the board for U.S. Steel, and he traveled in some of the same circles as Edgar Barrett, Nolan's father-in-law and current boss. Dave had met Stettinius once, right after resigning from the Army. "He's a solid business man with good instincts," Nolan observed offhandedly as he quickly scanned the questions.

"Those issues are ones you observed and reported on from Germany years ago. That's why I need you and why the president agreed to Churchill's request that you accompany me."

Dave took several minutes to read through and digest the implications of the questions. The Council wanted information about England's industry, but beyond that, this was also information on vital matters upon which America's own industrial mobilization might come to depend. He thought about the Christmas holiday gathering at Edgar Barrett's estate a year-and-a-half earlier when he first realized that the aristocrats of American business were less prepared for a future worldwide conflict than even the woefully undermanned and outgunned Army.

"These are good questions – a good place to start anyway," Nolan offered when he was finished reading the list. "How long do we… do you have to do all this work?"

"That's a question for which I don't yet have an answer. But it has to be soon, before there's no Great Britain left. If England falls, America is completely isolated – alone against the Nazis, and eventually, I and others believe, against the Nipponese in the Pacific as well. Time is of the essence."

Nolan thought about this silently, looking now and then at the list of questions. "If I do let you rope me into this, I need three things. First, your assurance I'll have a say in how this is done. I won't be held hostage to some scheme of a politician or bureaucrat in Washington who doesn't have a clue about what he's saying. Second, if I decide this is another cockamamie scheme like that Russian fiasco after the War, I'm free to walk away with no strings attached. I will not sign or work under the restrictions of any government-mandated agreement. My word has to be an acceptable bond. I'll need your personal assurance on those two."

"You have it. And the final thing?"

"I have to get agreement from Edgar Barrett before I commit. He has a big investment in me and what our corporation is doing. I also want him to look at these questions and add some of his own. He's a man who's very good at reading the tea leaves and is willing to take significant risks when the potential reward warrants."

"Assuming that falls into place, can you be ready to go within the next three weeks?"

He thought about his calendar for a moment. "I could be available between July 8 and the end of that month."

"I also need you in Washington all next week to flesh out these questions with the National Defense Council while I meet with the State Department and the Joint Chiefs on intelligence matters and military issues."

"I can't make it all week. That's right in the middle of June Week at West Point, and it's the only one my son will ever have. I can be in Washington Wednesday afternoon and Thursday morning only. That's it… but I haven't agreed to anything yet."

"I'll need your decision by tomorrow night."

Dave Nolan shook his head. "Not possible. Tomorrow afternoon is Mitch's last baseball game for Army – I'm not going to miss that. Denise and I are going down to Annapolis by train early in the morning. You'll hear from me Sunday evening." Nolan looked quickly at his watch. "I'd like to stay and chat some more, but I have to go. I've got an hour-and-a-half drive to the Academy. There's a reception for parents at the Supe's quarters, and barring mishaps I should be able to make it. Another black mark for you with Denise if I don't get there on time."

Donovan relaxed and chuckled. "Wouldn't want that. Go on. Get out of here. And Dave... it was good to see you again. My best to your boy. I hear he graduated high in his class and was some kind of exceptional ball player," Donovan said as he walked Nolan to the door and opened it. "And my best to your pretty wife as well. Put in a good word for me with her."

"I seriously doubt it'll do you much good, Bill."

A few minutes after Nolan had gone and the last sounds of the creaking elevator faded away, there was a knock on the door of Donovan's suite. He opened it and let in William Stephenson – a Canadian in British Secret Intelligence.

"I heard everything," Stephenson said, once the door closed. "Do you think he'll do it?"

"Yes. He's already decided. His problem now is to break it to his wife. She's very strong-willed, and she doesn't like me much. She was a nurse at Allery during the last war and was trying to get Nolan sent home to the States, while I needed him to command a battalion in my regiment. He left the hospital early to return to the unit. The last time we talked it was clear she still hadn't forgiven me. She's not a problem, but Nolan might be. He's absolutely fearless and independent as hell, so I can't guarantee he'll be sympathetic to Britain's cause. We'll get a completely candid evaluation of the English manufacturing base, but that may not necessarily be what you want."

Donovan could tell he'd worried Stephenson; while that hadn't been his intention it would put the Brits on notice.

"Your people had better be primed to explain to him every detail of their manufacturing processes and the economics behind them. When he was one of my combat commanders he was easily the biggest pain in the ass I had in my entire command, but more often than not he was right. Everything, including business, is a contact sport with him...

"Consider yourself warned."

- CHIMERA -

Chapter 1

"The official opening for the completely refurbished Ellington Field outside Houston is a little more than three weeks from now, on June 26," Dave Nolan said, gazing around the conference table at the sixteen well-dressed men taking in this information with detached, studied indifference. "The Air Corps is already flying into and out of the facility. Victoria Air Corps Base One will be ready for operations by September 15 and we break ground for the airfield in Waco two weeks after that."

The elongated table made of Columbian mahogany was freshly polished and reflected the early morning sun filtering through the floor-to-ceiling windows. A thin haze of cigar and cigarette smoke hovered like a low summer overcast above the conference room table in the dark paneled executive board room of E.W. Barrett Enterprises, Inc. while the Board of Directors listened to the latest presentation from their corporate Operations Director.

"Your interim report on the Ellington job indicated we're paying a six percent premium for engineers in the Houston area and a four percent premium for field labor in Victoria," Bernard Hanson was saying as he thumbed through the document in front of him. "That cuts deeply into margins. Are you going to do the same to us in Waco?"

Nolan took a deep breath and again looked around the room. *What a waste of time*, he thought. *Leave it to old Hanson to find the dark cloud instead of a silver lining.* "Actually, sir, paying a premium increased our margins an extra eleven percent for Ellington and should be a good twelve percent at Victoria. We more than covered the higher salaries in both instances."

Hanson gave him a hard look, and was about to say something when Hollis Dickerson, the accepted financial accounting expert on the Board, interrupted him.

"I thought it counter-intuitive myself until I had our accountants over at *Haskins & Sells* put a pencil to it. Edgar sent over copies of the final cost sheets and your contract," he said, looking at Nolan. "Our people confirmed your numbers and thought the performance clause very ingenious – imaginative was the operative word, as I recall. How did you do it, Dave?"

"The military is always willing to sweeten the pot if they can get facilities delivered ahead of schedule," Nolan explained. "A half percent for each day under the promised date doesn't sound like much sitting at a negotiating table, especially when our competition is turning in cost overruns and delivering late."

"Every time we get a new contract for engineering design and construction management, we get a percentage point or two more efficient on managing costs," Edgar Barrett added, "just like we do when building our own manufacturing facilities. Our architects, engineers and most importantly our accounting people are really sharpening their pencils these days. The results are detailed in the report."

"And how many of these contracts for training bases is the military sending out for bids?" James Nally asked. He had been the chief financial officer for Continental Oil in Denver and now retired, sat on this and two other boards.

"Right now there's one in Corpus Christi that should go out in the next six months, another in San Antonio, and one in Bakersfield, California," Nolan replied. "If America should get drawn into war before then, that could double or triple overnight. Because the military must train year round, the deep South and Southwest are where all the new bases will be built and the old ones refurbished."

"But California?" Hanson asked. "Isn't that a little far afield, Nolan?"

"Actually it's not, sir. The model we're using for full service engineering and design, plus construction management is one that *isn't* dependent on location, only on our ability to hire local talent. We've proven to ourselves and the Army it works fine."

"But Kaiser Construction is very strong in that area." Hanson continued.

Nolan smiled. "True. They're pretty well entrenched, and they have a good reputation, but they're a little slow-footed." Nolan looked over at William Stanley, the retired Corps of Engineers two-star. "General, what does the military say about our corporation?"

The crusty old soldier gave a wry smile. "The Corps' main office in D.C. and the branch offices along the Gulf coast and up the Mississippi think of Barrett pretty much in the same league as Kaiser – smaller, but more nimble. Nolan and his team talk their language and produce on time. That's worth a lot."

"We don't have the corporate overhead Kaiser does," Nolan added. "The equipment and labor we require for the construction business are rented for a finite period of time, not part of our company inventory so they're not a fixed cost. They're an operating expense we can write off as a cost of doing business."

Hanson grunted, but appeared satisfied. "You got an answer for everything, don't you son? Got all your bases covered."

"All the bases and his own ass," General Stanley chuckled.

There was a long silence in the room. Edgar Barrett took his time extracting a cigarette from an ornate wooden box in front of him and lit it as the men around the table looked at one another. Finally, he asked if there were any more questions, and when there were none he said, "Well, gentlemen, we thank you for your participation and input yesterday and today. I think we've accomplished everything we laid before ourselves to deal with, and… there being no further business, you've all earned dinner this evening at –"

"Excuse me, Edgar," Bradley Herberger interrupted. The former Chief Financial Officer of Goodyear tapped the ash from the end of his cigar, and nodded toward Dave Nolan. "There's one more piece of business we haven't addressed."

"You're right, Brad. My apologies." Edgar Barrett looked quickly at his son-in-law. "Dave, we're going to have to ask you to excuse yourself at this point. We'll be done in just a few minutes."

Nolan looked around at the men seated at the table, each gazing back at him benignly. He felt the awkward silence in the room and at last he said, "I don't think it would be wise for me to leave just yet."

Edgar Barrett looked mystified. "Dave I assure you…"

Nolan shook his head and finally said, "I'll stay, thank you."

"Dave, we really do have to ask you to leave," Hollis Dickerson said. "It's protocol…"

Nolan looked back at the financial expert, and then at the retired general. Each man in the room had been at or near the top of his chosen profession before coming on Edgar Barrett's board. They had been, and still were, movers and shakers among former colleagues and their own successors, and they'd spent entire careers unaccustomed to having their directives questioned, even when couched as friendly requests.

"Gentlemen, I know what you're planning," Nolan replied, looking around the room. "So, to ensure you don't do it, I'm going to stay."

"Dave," Edgar Barrett implored, looking a little flummoxed. "You've earned this."

"I won't let this board do something for me I can't do for my people. There's a shared sense of hardship and sacrifice among my crew that's making all this work right now. At the moment, we can't afford to pay everybody what I think they're worth. This *is not* the time to increase the salary of the CEO's son-in-law." After another look around, he stood slowly, and retrieved a sheet of paper from his brief case. "But since you're in the mood to spend some money, I suggest we pay bonuses to these people out of the performance windfall from the Ellington project. We could take two to three percent and spread it among the men on this list who were the ones who actually made that happen. A little pat on the back goes a long way, doesn't it, General?" He passed the typed sheet of paper to Edgar Barrett, thanked them for their consideration, and left.

When the door closed behind him, the men in the room all turned and looked at General Stanley who, after a few seconds simply shrugged his shoulders.

"Spoken like a troop leader. He's not going to sit still for us raising his salary before he can do it for his troops. I told you that's what he'd do, didn't I? Anybody smart enough to figure out the cost structure of Kaiser Construction and use it against them wasn't going to have too hard a time figuring out what a bunch of geezers like us was up to. He's taking care of the people working for him. That fella may be drawin' his paycheck from Barrett, Inc. but I'm telling you the young man never left the Army."

A half hour after the Board of Directors departed Barrett Enterprises headquarters, Dave Nolan stuck his head into his father-in-law's office.

"Got a minute, Ed? There's something important you need to know."

Edgar Barrett looked up, and waved him into the elegantly appointed office as he finished signing a few documents.

Dave sat in a high-backed leather chair across the large desk from his father-in-law and looked around, remembering a similarly decorated office in Washington where two decades earlier a young general named MacArthur had unexpectedly changed the course of his life and career with an assignment order and then a speech he was rehearsing for Congress about the future of West Point. Barrett's office felt similar but was much more elegant, with its original art work, expensive appurtenances, and the large old wooden desk. It was rumored to have been made from the timbers of the *HMS Gannett*, the sister ship to the *Resolute* which had provided the wood for the desk that now sat in the Oval Office.

"Sorry about all that, Dave," Edgar Barrett said at last, affixing a final signature and placing a last sheet inside a folder. "The paperwork is never done. But it's not as bad as the Army, is it? General Stanley tells me there's a requirement that everything has to be done in quadruplicate, two copies of which must be legible. That true?"

"I never argue with my superiors, especially generals."

His father-in-law laughed aloud. "Of course not. Anyhow, great presentation. And you handled old Hanson exceptionally well this time. Don't take his criticisms personally. He's doing exactly what I'd hoped he'd do when I asked him onto the Board. He's my corporate curmudgeon – somebody who can think up every reason imaginable why what we decide won't work. He's worth every penny I pay him. Figuring out the workarounds is what I pay you for, Dave. None of them can fully comprehend what you've been able to accomplish in the short while you've been here. I sometimes find it a little hard to believe myself."

"Necessity is the mother of invention. I'm beginning to believe that."

It had all started with an obstinate contractor named Chambers who had made the crucial expansion project of the original corporate plant a monumental headache two years earlier.

With costs out of control and management of subcontractors making everyone's life miserable, he'd fired Chambers and set up his own general contractor operation and a shadow contract management team reporting to him. The old military maxim that *nothing gets done unless the commander inspects it* proved out and suddenly he realized the company not only possessed the minimum requisite skills, but Piersall – his first contracts manager – and his team actually enjoyed it. For the first time in the history of E.W. Barrett Enterprises a project came in ahead of time and under budget. He put Piersall's team to work on expanding the Detroit plant with even better success.

With General Stanley's help, they bid on a job in Maryland to refurbish parts of old Camp Meade using their model and suddenly they were not only a success, but on the list of qualified contractors with the Corps of Engineer's regional office in Baltimore. Within six months, they were in demand by the Corps in New Orleans and along the Texas Gulf Coast and were now thinking brashly about challenging Kaiser on their home turf. People in the home office were whispering among themselves how much happier Edgar Barrett was these days.

"If you'd listened to my daughter and come on board twenty years ago, this corporation would own General Motors and I'd be richer than Rockefeller. So would you."

"I'm doing just fine, Ed."

Barrett sat back in his chair, resting his elbows on its arms, interlocking his fingers and looking quizzically at him. "I know you are. Maybe a little frustrated with a certain member of my board, but I don't expect that would be reason enough for you to quit and go elsewhere."

Nolan frowned, wondering why Edgar Barrett would say that. "You've talked to Denise."

"A phone call from West Point yesterday noon after you left to come here for the board meeting. You have a way of – how should I phrase this?… a way of unsettling her. I guess you know that – and I've seen you do it from time to time over the years just to clip her feathers. Not that it's a bad thing, mind you." Barrett smiled, trying to hide his amusement. He'd learned his son-in-law could deal with difficult people, including his own headstrong daughter.

He'd first recognized it when the young cadet had shown up at the summer home on Long Island, invited by his daughter for the remaining six weeks of his first vacation away from West Point. Denise had intended he'd be a quick teenage summer romance, like others she engaged in – tease the boy, lead him on a little and cast him off at the end of the vacation. She tired of boys quickly back then. Easily the prettiest girl in her crowd, she'd learned she could walk all over any young man – until that summer.

Without talking with him, she scheduled their time together, filling each minute with the things she liked to do on the Island with her friends. He had torpedoed that on the first day by telling her he planned to spend five or six days a week at the plant learning something about the business world while making a few dollars. Denise's outburst was loud enough to be heard halfway out to Montauk Point and it was the first of many interesting interludes woven into an otherwise typically humdrum summer at the cottage. Her summer fling turned into a two year romance that left her inconsolable when he graduated without asking her to marry him.

Two years later as a volunteer Red Cross nurse, after searching for and finally finding him badly wounded in a military hospital in France, she was again heartbroken when he went back to his unit instead of returning home with her as she'd planned. Then, after almost a year of silence, from out of nowhere he came to see her at the cottage. She was livid, determined he could spend a very long time in a very hot place as far as she was concerned. Edgar Barrett remembered the day well. And he remembered the look on her face as she stormed out of his office at the plant on the way to a showdown on the shores of Long Island Sound. Somehow in the course of that spring afternoon, Nolan had talked his daughter out of marrying the man to whom she was engaged and marrying him instead.

Later, Barrett reminded himself that if Nolan could do that, there probably wasn't much he couldn't do once he'd set his mind to it. The decision to let him run with the construction contracting idea was easy, though there were some long, sleepless nights when the operation's payables outstripped its accounts receivable. But they'd made it all work out in the end.

"Denise said you'd been to see Bill Donovan," Barrett was saying. "She's worried."

"She's afraid I'm going to throw a monkey-wrench into her life again."

"According to her you have a habit of doing that."

"She's right. I do. I need to talk to you about this, Ed. Unlike the last time, I'm inclined to go along with Donovan on this. But, I told him the only way I'd agree was if I got the approval from both you and Denise. I owe each of you a veto vote on this. You invested a lot of time and money in me and what we're doing in the construction business. And, I owe Denise more than anyone because I dragged her around to some of the world's worst backwaters in my time with the Army. She's just now starting to enjoy some real stability and financial security. For her sake I can't and I won't threaten that."

Barrett nodded, understanding. "What can you tell me?"

"I'm assuming you know what Bill Donovan has been doing for the past twenty years."

"You may be assuming too much. Everyone conversant in New York politics knows at least a little bit about him. I know that after the War he was appointed U.S. District Attorney for Western New York, and he was a gangbuster during Prohibition. I heard he lost a lot of powerful friends and made a lot of influential enemies. He's a delegate to the Republican Convention in Philadelphia at the end of the month – he's supporting Wendall Wilkie over Governor Dewey. Donovan rubs shoulders with a lot of people in high places in both parties."

"Last week he asked me to work with him again."

"Knowing what I do about your relationship with him over the years, I'm not surprised he's come after you again," Barrett replied. "This is the third time in as many years, isn't it?"

"Yes. And the fourth overall, if you add the time he recruited me to take one of the companies in his battalion during the War."

"So, what does he want this time, Dave?"

"He wants me to go to England with him to take a close look at Britain's industrial base to see if the Brits have the manufacturing capability to stand up against the Nazis. And if so, for how long. He thinks I have enough background in the business world to do that. It's something he doesn't personally have, and he trusts me." Dave reached inside his coat pocket, pulled out a typed sheet and slid it across the desktop. "This is an initial list of questions from Edward Stettinius down in Washington, and Donovan wants me to spend three or four days in D.C. with others in the government who want to add areas of interest and other questions."

Barrett read the list quickly, making notes now and then on a separate pad at his elbow.

"Good man, Stettinius. We did a lot of business together when he was at U.S. Steel. Did some fine salmon fishing in Maine back then, too. He's a very young man – younger than you. You two share a meticulous, almost obsessive, attention to detail and what I'd call a nearly terrifying sense of responsibility. He's driven. Started out as a stock clerk at General Motors back in '26 and went to the very top... When do you go to England?"

"I haven't yet decided that I'm going to say 'yes' to Donovan."

Edgar Barrett lowered his head and peered at him over the top of his reading glasses. "That's the first statement you've made since coming to work here that I don't believe."

"No, I'm serious. If you or Denise veto this idea, I walk away from it."

"But you think it's the right thing to do... it's important and, you really want to do it."

"Yes and no. I owe Bill Donovan a lot, but I owe you and Denise more. That's the truth. You're right – I want to do it because I know it's important and I also know I *can* do it. But my first priority is to family – to Denise and our kids first; you and this corporation second."

"How long would you be gone?"

"Three or four days total this month in Washington. In Great Britain, three or four weeks immediately following, depending on a raft of problems I haven't begun to think through yet."

Edgar Barrett took a deep breath, contemplating as he looked out the window over the New York skyline toward Brooklyn. "You have my vote – do it."

"You're sure?"

"First rule of marketing, Dave – when you make the sale, shut up."

"I still have to talk with Denise." Nolan shook his head and smiled at his father-in-law. "I'm sure you can imagine why I'm not really looking forward to that."

Barrett's eyes lit up and he chuckled knowingly. "I'm going to make this easy on you. I'll talk to her. You go back to West Point this evening for the rest of June Week. This afternoon before you get there, I'll call her to finish the conversation she and I started yesterday."

"First rule of marketing notwithstanding, I'm still concerned about tying up a lot of loose ends – the Ellington details, the final inspection at Victoria and the Waco startup. There's the bid package for Corpus and –"

"All of which are covered by your operational teams in the southwest. You made sure nobody, including you is indispensable to the operation now. Believe it or not, thanks to you and General Stanley, the board understands 'chain of command' and 'contingency planning'. And they appreciate how you handle it as much as the profits you've booked. That's why they wanted to give you the bonus. Are you telling me now you don't believe what you were trying so hard to convince us of last night and this morning?"

"I should invoke rule number one, right?"

"You should. Now, I've got some work to do before lunch. You get back to that school and enjoy your time with my grandson. Where's he going for his first assignment?"

"Flight school at San Antonio – he's dead set on flying. Mitch is probably crazy enough to be good at it."

"I'm really proud of that boy. We'll be up for that formal dinner the evening before he graduates. I'll see you then." As Nolan rose to leave Barrett handed over the original list of questions and a sheet from his pad with a half dozen more. "I assume what we talked about is strictly secret. Dave, if you want to talk more about this inspection tour you're going on, I'd be glad to." Barrett squinted and furrowed his brow. "What you're being asked to do over there is more important than either of us can imagine right now, and when you get back we'll continue this conversation. For now, you just go enjoy my grandson's June Week."

*   *   *   *   *   *

Afternoon was quickly sliding into evening as Dave Nolan stood with his back to the broad emerald expanse of the Plain, looking at the statue of Washington on horseback in front of the great granite structure that was now the Cadet Mess Hall.

Washington Hall was new since the days when he'd been a cadet but the resonance from every pore of this timeless enclave on the Hudson had changed little since the first day he'd seen it. He rememberd well that day after the long train ride from New York City to the solitary little train station sitting close by the river, beneath the towering granite ramparts of the school.

He'd been around the world since then – seen the hell of battle in French fields during the Great War, the scorching summers of Texas and Arizona, the constant rain of the Great Northwest and the tropical paradise of the Philippines. There had even been a short winter stay in the vastness of Russia, and time in Hitler's Germany chaperoning Lindbergh and trying to keep him out of trouble with the press and President Roosevelt. But none of those places had touched his soul like this ancient highland redoubt. Strangely, it felt like home, even more than little Duncannon on the shores of the Susquehanna where he'd grown up.

Now he'd been back to watch his son walk across the stage set up on the east side of Michie Stadium and receive his diploma. It had been a bittersweet moment, sitting there looking at Lusk Reservoir and beyond to the Hudson River and the medieval-style campus below; just off to the northeast sat the Cadet Chapel, dominating the heights above the parade ground. The whole place was saturated with memories.

Cadets began filtering out of North and Central areas into dinner formation facing the Plain. He remembered standing in that same spot for the first time a quarter century earlier, scared to death and wondering what in the world he'd gotten himself into.

Yet, this June Week had been a pleasant surprise. He'd renewed acquaintances with a number of old friends – like Doc Hanley who had been fresh out of med school when he delivered both Mitch and his sister Erika at the post hospital on Thayer Road. He and Doc had both been assigned to the Academy when MacArthur had been superintendent right after the War, along with Andy Fauser, his cadet roommate who was now a department head.

One morning at the Hotel Thayer, he'd run into Ed Timberlake, who had been a class behind him. They had sat out on the back patio one evening long after dark, drinking bourbon and rehashing the 1914 football season when both of them had lettered and the team had gone undefeated to win the National Championship. It seemed every place he turned there was a memory or an old friend, and as the week came to an end, he was surprised to find himself sorry to see it over. Tomorrow, after Mitch played the role of best man for his roommate at the Cadet Chapel, they would all pile into the car and head home, and maybe that would be the final chapter closing the book on his association with this old place.

"A penny for your thoughts, soldier," a familiar female voice said from behind him.

He turned, looking at his wife, feeling that same excitement he'd felt the first time they had met on that winter night many years ago, not far from where they now stood. "Not a soldier any longer, Denise," he replied evenly. "Got better things to do these days."

She smiled at him and slipped her arm under his and rested her head on his shoulder. "Do you really mean it?"

"How many times do I have to say it?"

"Every time I ask." She looked up at him with hooded eyes. "Just checking."

"Oh, ye of little faith."

"It's just that I know you. There's a part of you that will always be a soldier, Dave. Tell me that's not true."

"You're beginning to sound weirdly psychological."

"Like you that time down in Texas at the little ranch house when we met the old Ranger? What was his name?"

"Applejack Dawson – how could you forget that?" he asked, exaggerating his surprise.

"I have a lot more to worry over now than remembering names from a distant and best forgotten past." She squeezed his arm. "Mitch is going off to fly airplanes and Erika still has it in her head she wants to move to Washington. And you?"

He took a deep breath and saw the worry behind her eyes. "It's not the Army."

"But it is the government. You said you'd never get involved in that kind of thing again. You've already more than done your duty." She gazed at him sadly – a melancholy look he had seen many times over the years and it now tugged at his heart. "Running off with Donovan again means you'll be away a lot."

"Not any more than I have been in the last couple years working for your father. And once it's over, it's over. It's not like being commissioned in a military service and accepting that as my whole lot in life. I wouldn't even consider it except I can see the need and I think this time I better understand what's required. I made it clear I'd opt out if and when things stop making sense to me. I couldn't do that before."

From across the broad green expanse of the parade field, a trumpet sounded the first notes of Evening Retreat, piercing the quiet evening. The sound echoed through the ragged granite mountains. Their eyes went to the base of the large flagpole on Trophy Point, framed against the Hudson. The cadet companies were called to attention and 'present arms', and then the cannon next to Battle Monument fired. The report rumbled through the hills like a long drum roll followed by the haunting trumpet notes, quick and urgent, as the flag was lowered.

Denise saw from the corner of her eye that Dave had instinctively begun to salute before stopping himself. *Always the soldier*, she thought. Of all the officers she'd known over the last twenty-some years, he was still the most authentic, even out of the uniform and out of the Army. As much as she wished it wasn't so, nothing would ever remove that from him.

"We should head back to Bear Mountain for dinner and then pack for the trip home tomorrow morning," he said, as the final notes of Evening Retreat sounded. When the last cadets had marched into the mess hall, they strolled down the sidewalk, past the first divisions of barracks. As they passed by the French Monument across the street from the arched granite sallyport leading into Central Area, he leaned toward her and asked, "Remember what happened here when you came up to see me for the first time after we met?"

"Not everything. Why?"

"That was the first time you slapped me. I told you the folklore of the monument. Legend has it that whenever a virgin walks by this statue the ground will shake and rumble. And I commented how everything remained utterly calm when you passed by."

She poked him hard in the ribs. "Are you trying to start another argument?! That never happened! You were too smitten to say anything that outrageous to me. I wouldn't have let you get it away with it." She hugged his arm close to her and smiled up at him. "I don't know what I saw in you back then. You never did have any social graces – still don't."

"Socially clubfooted you used to say. But I had an eye for beauty." He put his arm around his wife and pulled her close, kissing her on the lips. "Even Harrison Reeves gave me credit for it that Founders Day when we were all assigned here after the War. Remember?"

"I remember," she said as they continued toward where he'd parked the car on the Thayer Road. She recalled the moment in emerald clarity – it was the night she'd met both he and his wife for the first time. It had been the strangest evening – a preview of many more very much like it through the years at different posts around the globe. She had never grown completely comfortable around either of them – Harrison, with his condescension and his quick temper was naturally hard to like or trust. But Michelle? What was it about her? Denise still couldn't put her finger on it – even now, almost twenty years later.

"What a great June Week this was," Denise told him as they crossed Thayer Road near the library. "It's been at least four years now since I've seen some of my friends. Catherine's two oldest are out of college and Muggs's boy just started at Georgetown. Nita Haggerty's son finishes high school next spring and hopes to enter Maryland in the fall. It all makes me feel old. Tell me I'm not really getting old, Dave."

He was only half listening. *Her friends.* Their friends, actually, he reminded himself. But some of their husbands were still in the Philippines. *In the mouth of the dragon,* he thought to himself. If war did come – no, *when* it came – they wouldn't have much chance if they were still in the Islands, he'd decided.

At Command and General Staff, when he was still in the Army, he'd studied the Pacific situation and written three staff studies on American defense of the Philippines. With classified sources unavailable to him before or since, plus his own intimate knowledge of MacArthur's plans for the Islands, he'd seen the precariousness of the situation.

All those esoteric discussions with Ike Eisenhower and Andy and Cole Alford over drinks at the Officer's Club in Manila about what could and should be done had seemed just so much alcohol-induced drivel. But later, removed from the immediacy of daily training schedules and field maneuvers, the fact became clear to him that the Philippines had only one chance in ten of adequately withstanding the Japanese if they decided to attack – and they would. He was certain of it. Surely Washington had figured that out, too! Now from the safety of his present circumstances it all seemed so far away.

But he had friends still there – Cole, Judd Haggerty, Dick Sherrill and Digger Dawson. And well over half the officers and enlisted men from his old battalion in the regiment, soldiers he'd come to know and admire. All of them dangling out there like some kind of bait on a number three hook. Andy had been transferred to West Point twenty months ago – to his great relief – but Cole's cavalier response to his letter written just before his trip to Germany to babysit Lindbergh had bothered him.

"… and Erika's just not old enough to be going down there to Washington and doing this on her own," Denise was saying, looking at him crossly. "You haven't heard a thing I've said."

"Sure I have. You were the same age, or a couple years younger when you traveled alone to Annapolis to watch us play baseball that time."

She looked at him and frowned. "It's not the same…and your mind *was* elsewhere."

"I was thinking about Cole and Judd still out there in Manilla," he replied, "I wish there were something I could do. Always thought of Cole as a little brother."

"Well, he's not, and he's not your responsibility. But your daughter is, and she's gotten it into her mind to go work in Washington. You need to talk to her."

"I will," he said absently, still worrying over his troops in the islands, especially Alford.

He'd taught Cole everything he could think of about being a combat platoon leader, and felt a certain sense of pride remembering the day Alford led his platoon up that narrow little erosion ditch to knock out a German machine gun position on the Ourcq Heights. It had been the young lieutenant's first combat and he'd pulled it off like an old veteran. He remembered overhearing some of the older men in his company talking about the brand new lieutenant – saying he'd been a good fighter and might make a decent officer some day if he'd learn to stop walking like he had a broom handle up his butt.

But they really weren't his troops now, he tried to tell himself. Not anymore. He had other, and some would say, more important issues over which to say grace – including a headstrong daughter who seemed bent on bedevilling her mother.

A name crossed his mind, and an idea took form.

Barton Scarborough.

Chapter 2

"Well, Senator, I think your Committee on Foreign Affairs, and this government, need to ask yourselves a question: What is the obligation that a government owes to the men it calls upon to fight its wars?" Wild Bill Donovan replied to the question posed to him by the panel of senators arrayed on a raised dais in the small, crowded chamber.

It was chaotic in the Senate committee room and everyone except Donovan seemed oblivious to the question and answer session being conducted between the senators and his old Rainbow Division commander. What Dave Nolan saw as he sat halfway back in the room was confusion, listlessness and disrespect toward Donovan and the Burke-Wadsworth Selective Service Training bill under consideration. *This is important to the men who will have to fight the war that's coming!* he wanted to stand up and shout to everyone involved in this charade.

"As one who has had to fight in one of this country's wars," Donovan was saying over the muted buzz of activity, "I think the government owes to each of these men first and foremost a fair chance for his life, so that, prepared as he is to make the ultimate sacrifice, he shall know that he doesn't throw away his life uselessly. To give him that fair shake, he must not only be physically conditioned but he must also be given the best and newest weaponry plus the training necessary to use them properly in a fight."

Nolan thought back to the chilly morning when as a newly promoted captain he'd taken command of an unruly and slipshod company in Donovan's battalion – he'd said essentially the same thing then to those men after he'd inspected their equipment and put down an open attempt at insurrection. Being a company commander had been exceptionally difficult, and oftentimes through the years the memory of all the good men he'd lost was a burden he felt unable to bear. Still, he was convinced that commanding Company A of the old Irish 69th in Europe was the most important experience of his life.

"The committee thanks you, Mr. Donovan, for the excellent brief and oral testimony you supplied for our consideration this morning," the Senate committee chairman said over the increasing buzz of conversation in the room.

Dave heard Donovan's short reply and stood, moving into the aisle as the room began to empty. From the back of the chamber a young man in a hurry bolted forward and ran into him. Without stopping to apologize, the man moved quickly through the crowd to Donovan and handed over a small envelope as he leaned in and whispered into Wild Bill's ear. Donovan quickly opened the note, read it and motioned for Nolan.

"Our lunch plans just got scuttled," Donovan offered, quickly placing his folder of notes into a leather briefcase. "You and I have been summoned to a meeting."

"Sir, I was told to deliver this note and provide you a ride back to the White House," the messenger said quickly, a little distressed. "There was no mention of a second party."

"Well, son, where I go this friend of mine goes. I have an idea what this is about and I'm sure the president would agree with me to include him."

"Sir, this is a very high level meeting."

"All the more reason to bring Mr. Nolan along. Can't keep the president waiting."

The ride through midday Washington traffic from the Capitol building to the White House was slow and tedious and at times Nolan wondered why they just didn't get out and walk. But Washington and its ways were new to him and so he bided his time rehashing with Donovan what he'd done in the past few days.

When the limousine stopped next to the guards' gate at the head of the long driveway to the White House, Donovan looked up from scratching out some notes. The driver announced the two passengers through his window and the guard looked at his listing with a frown and then went inside the guardhouse to make a phone call.

"I'm sorry Mr. Donovan, we don't have a clearance for your Mr. Nolan," the guard said through the back window when he returned. "I'm afraid I'll have to ask him to step out."

"Dunlop – that is your name, right?" Wild Bill asked after looking at the man's nametag. "Listen, I've been through this gate to visit the White House a half dozen times already this year. You know who I am. Now, the president just called me away from testifying on Capitol Hill to attend a meeting in the Oval Office and he expects me to be there. I can't go into that meeting without my assistant here. His name is David Nolan and he's the chief operating officer of E.W. Barrett Enterprises out of New York. I personally vouch for him. You clear us both in now, or tell the president you won't let me through without his personal intercession on my behalf. I'll wait as long as it takes, but I'm not sure the president or the limo behind us will." Donovan went back to his notes as the guard hurriedly talked on the phone.

"Look, Bill, don't go causing a commotion on my account," Nolan said.

"Well, it *is* on your account. France just fell to Hitler and my guess is the White House wants to parlay about moving up our trip. You made a big to-do three weeks ago about being part of the decision-making on how this mission goes down. Here you are, important enough to ruffle some feathers over. Besides, it's not the president causing us to cool our heels in the summer heat – it's the functionaries who only have the power to say 'no' to things. You've probably already discovered that the only way to get things done in this town is to talk to somebody high enough in the chain-of-command to have the power to say both 'yes' *and* 'no'. This won't take long, wait and see."

And it didn't. In less than a minute the guard was waving them through.

As he stepped from the back seat of the car and looked at the brilliant white of the old building, the perfectly manicured lawn and grounds he was at once overwhelmed. It suddenly struck him he was really entering the White House and in a matter of minutes he'd be in the presence of the most consequential figure in the country, and probably the entire western world. *Nolan, you're a long way from High Street in Duncannon, Pennsylvania.*

"Impressive your first time isn't it?" Donovan whispered. "I know – you're dumbstruck. Best you get over it and get your wits about you. These people inside know you only by name but they're going to be closely taking your measure. They want to know what you're made of and if you're up to the task. They also want to see if I have the ability to pick the right man for the job – this one, and others in the future. If anything, I'm more on trial this afternoon than you are. Don't let me down."

"I don't know that I ever have."

"Not yet, and don't let this be the time you start. And don't let that make you nervous. Remember – you know more about what you're being asked to do than anyone in that room, so don't let them rattle you. I remember when you whipped a German tank battalion outside the city limits of Rheims one morning with a half strength infantry company. Fending off a bunch of old gray-haired politicians should be duck soup for you after that."

Their travel through the labyrinth of the White House was a blur to him. There was something altogether *other* about the place, the way he imagined it must be inside the Vatican, or the Louvre in Paris or Buckingham Palace. He kept trying to tell himself this was just another meeting, like all the others so far this week; but, when the door opened into the president's inner office he realized he'd utterly failed to prepare himself.

Franklin Delano Roosevelt in shirtsleeves, sat behind the large, imposing *Resolute* Desk with a cigarette in a long holder clamped between his teeth. The normally jovial president was grim-faced. Around the room sat men he'd only read about and whose pictures he'd seen in the papers and on *MovieTone News* in the theatres – Secretary of State Cordell Hull, Secretary of War Henry Stimson, Secretary of the Navy Franklin Knox. Two other men rounded out the meeting; one he knew only in passing – Edward Stettinius. The other he knew as well as his own father – William Howard Payne, senior senator from Pennsylvania and the chairman of the

Senate Appropriations Committee. Senator Payne had appointed both he and his son, Mitch, to the Military Academy.

"So good of the two of you to come on such short notice," the president said to Donovan. "I trust your testimony on Capitol Hill went well. And Mr. Nolan – it's good to finally meet you. Senator Payne has told me about your career at West Point and service during the Great War. I wish we could chat about both but time and circumstances work against us I'm afraid. We few assembled here share a responsibility unlike any in our nation's history. We find ourselves responsible for determining and then executing a response to horrific events across the Atlantic. France, our nation's oldest ally, has fallen to the onslaught of Nazi Germany, and our nation's closest ally and friend, Great Britain, is in danger of imminent collapse. I must confess this government is in the dark as to exactly what is happening at the moment on the far side of the ocean. We are currently, I'm afraid, like a group of blind men. William, you and Mr. Nolan are our only hope for determining what is happening with our British friends."

"We are prepared, Mr. President, to do whatever you ask of us." Donovan replied.

"What we need is for you two to do the task originally envisioned," Secretary Knox said, "sooner and with greater urgency. Can you be ready and depart within two weeks?"

"Yes, sir, I can," Donovan replied without hesitation.

Nolan quickly envisioned his schedule and thought about Denise's likely reaction. She would not be happy with accelerating his departure – there was an important social event she wanted to attend in Oyster Bay hosted by the Hunt Club, and they still hadn't agreed on how to deal with their daughter Erika's decision to move to Washington, a bidders meeting in Texas, and the problem with contractors putting in a new dock and seawall at the summer house...

"And you, Mr. Nolan?" the president asked, turning his head to look directly at him. "Can you also be ready to depart for England in the same time frame?"

"Sir, I'm at your disposal. As soon as I can obtain clean clothes and a suitcase to put them in, I'm ready."

"Very well." Roosevelt pursed his lips and nodded slowly. "We must know two things immediately. First –"

There was a sharp knock on the outer door and it opened quickly. Roosevelt's secretary entered with a single sheet of paper and handed it to the president who thanked her and quickly scanned it before placing it at his right hand on the desk.

"As I was saying," the president continued, "the first thing we must know is whether or not Churchill is capable of infusing new spirit into the British nation. Secondly – are the British capable of defending themselves and do they have they the means? If so, for how long? These are very complex questions, gentlemen. Only after we have the answers can we approach the issues of the best way to insert ourselves into this latest war on the Continent."

Dave Nolan sat quietly, listening to the president. It dawned on him that Roosevelt had already decided, contrary to his public pronouncements, that America would enter the war in Europe on the side of Great Britain against Nazi Germany. The issue was no longer 'if' but 'how' and that was a significant departure from his public rhetoric. Looking around the room he saw the hardly noticeable nods of these key Cabinet members. Two of these men – Knox and Stimson, both Republicans – had taken on their positions a week earlier, on June 20. It was obvious this was a signal of bipartisanship on the part of the Administration, a move applauded on both sides of the political aisle.

Knox had served in the Rough Riders at San Juan Hill, and had been an artillery officer in the Great War, reaching the rank of major; he was a part owner of the Chicago Daily News and had been Alf Landon's vice presidential running mate in 1936. He had the reputation of being strong on defense and a proponent of a powerful two ocean Navy.

Stimson, a thin aristocratic looking man with a narrow but full mustache was now serving his second assignment as Secretary of War. He reminded Nolan of his old friend Henry Smythe-Browne. The secretary was a lawyer, a Republican Party politician and a spokesman on foreign policy. He'd served as Secretary of War for two years under Republican William Howard Taft just prior to the Great War and had now returned to that job in a Democratic administration. He was seen as a leading hawk calling for war against Germany.

"It would be helpful," Secretary Stimson asserted, "if we could learn how the Nazi fifth column operated in Denmark and France so we can monitor and hopefully prevent their operations within our own borders."

Each of the secretaries had detailed questions and Nolan recorded them in his notebook as the meeting wore on. Edward Stettinius handed over two additional sheets of typewritten questions from the War Resources Board, but said little. He was striking in appearance with prematurely white hair and dark eyebrows, blue eyes and a well-tanned face. Most of the time he sat across the room staring at Dave Nolan, evaluating his every move and infrequent words.

After more than a half hour, the various cabinet members had exhausted their lists of questions and the president announced an end to their meeting.

"I think we've made a good start on commissioning our two emissaries," the president said, looking at the sheet brought in earlier by his secretary. He looked up and fixed his gaze on Dave Nolan. "When you return from England, I would like to hear more about your days at West Point, especially your time after the War, as Douglas MacArthur's special aide. I understand you were quite helpful to him."

"I was just a lowly lieutenant, sir, doing as the general told me. It was a privilege to serve under him a second time." As he answered, Nolan wondered if he'd said the right thing or not. What if MacArthur was on the Administration's excremental list? Quite possible with George

Marshall now Chief of Staff of the Army and Roosevelt's chief military advisor. MacArthur had treated Marshall badly years earlier and maybe it was payback time. *Come on, Nolan. You're thinking like a damned politician. Knock that off!* he shouted at himself. "I've been privileged to serve under many good commanders in my lifetime, sir."

"Including one William Donovan, I see."

"Yes, sir."

"He's a good man, this Wild Bill, but a Republican, unfortunately. He's going to their National Convention next week to choose a nominee to unseat me in the coming election," the president said with a smile, an obvious attempt to lighten the moment in the Oval Office. "What do you think of that?"

"Haven't given it a thought, Mr. President. I'm not a politician."

"But your father-in-law is. At least he's active in raising money and staffing the New York Republican delegation – has been for years. I assume you're also a Republican."

"Actually, I'm neither Republican nor Democrat. I'm my own man when I cast a vote, and I choose to vote for the person best able to lead my country. Party affiliation isn't a consideration. As I look around at your cabinet, Mr. President, it seems that's the same way you choose those who work most closely with you."

Roosevelt seemed pleased, his eyes lit up and he smiled even more broadly. "Are you sure you're not a politician, Mr. Nolan?" The president chuckled and looked at Senator Payne. "Will, I see what you mean about this young man carefully choosing his words,"

"My observation from the first day I met him when he came looking for an appointment to that military school, Mr. President."

Roosevelt gazed slowly around the room. "Henry, I'd like you to spend time this afternoon with Bill Donovan. I hadn't thought about a threat from a German fifth column until you mentioned it. That should be right down his alley. Perhaps you'd want to alert Hoover and get some cooperation from the FBI. Edward, likewise with Mr. Nolan. I'll have my secretary arrange lunch here in the White House in one of the small conference rooms."

"I think it would be wise, Mr. President, if I also sat in representing Congress," Senator Payne offered. "There have been some rumblings, unwarranted though they may be, about the legislative branch being bypassed and ignored."

"Fine." The president looked at Donovan and Nolan with a most serious expression on his face. "We're asking you two to take on a considerable assignment. Your task is to observe and evaluate the British resolve and their ability to stand against what appears to be the most potent military machine in the world. At the same time you're also confidential ambassadors representing me personally to Prime Minister Churchill. You cannot promise him too much, nor should you encourage him too little. Assure him of the great concern felt by the President of the United States and this administration.

"It's my strong conviction that upon the outcome of this mission rests not only the fate of Great Britain but also the fate of this country of ours. I wish you well."

*   *   *   *

On Saturday Navy Secretary Franklin Knox took his first cruise on the *Sequoia*, the official yacht assigned by the Navy for his use. Donovan, Dave Nolan and Knox's Assistant Secretary, James Forrestal, accompanied him for lunch and a cruise down the Potomac.

Two days earlier, Cordell Hull had wired Ambassador Kennedy in London that Donovan would be making a trip to London along with a business man from E.W. Barrett in New York, ostensibly for the purpose of establishing business contacts between U.S. industry and British manufacturing. Their actual purpose, according to the note, was to investigate Nazi fifth column activities in England to determine how to counter such actions in the United States. Kennedy was warned not to reveal this to the British or anyone else except, of course, embassy personnel with Top Secret Clearances. The note also said that Donovan was making his own arrangements and setting up his own meetings so as not to interrupt normal embassy activities.

The next day – July 12 – Ambassador Kennedy wired a reply:

> *I will render any service I can to William Donovan whom I know and like. My staff here is convinced it is getting all the information that can possibly be gathered, and to send a new man in here at this time, with all due respect to Secretary Knox, is to me the height of nonsense and a definite blow to good organization in the Embassy.*

"Looks to me like somebody's nose is out of joint," Donovan said after reading Kennedy's note and handing it to Nolan.

"Exactly what the president said when I showed it to him," Knox replied, leaning back in his afterdeck lounger. "I think he realizes some of the problems we have with the embassy in London. Kennedy also telephoned the under secretary of state and told him your trip will likely cause a lot of confusion within the British government, and that he had things well in hand with his current military and naval attachés."

"Is he going to be a problem, Frank?" Donovan asked.

"Not at all," Forrestal said, looking first at Donovan and then Dave Nolan. "Anderson and General Miles already sent messages through secret military channels to Captain Alan Kirk – the naval attaché – and Brigadier General Ray Lee. They've been told to cooperate with you completely without including the ambassador in either the planning or meetings they're now arranging with top British intelligence officers. And that includes the industrialists and manufacturing planners Dave will meet with. Roscoe Hillenkoetter, our naval attaché in Paris is also scheduled to meet with you. Right now we really don't know what to do with him. It's awkward with this Vichy government the Germans are installing to run half of France."

"Did Kennedy actually say what they printed in the *Globe* last week?" Donovan asked, taking another glass of iced tea from the Navy steward circulating around the group with a tray of full glasses.

"Apparently so," Knox replied.

"What the hell was he thinking?"

"The same thing he always thinks."

Joe Kennedy, America's ambassador to England, had told a Boston Globe reporter a week earlier that 'democracy was dead in England.' And then he'd added an exclamation point by pronouncing it was nearly dead in America, too.

"Why in the world did he say that?" Dave Nolan asked the group. "How does somebody in his position get away it?" He'd been in positions twice in his own lifetime – once in Russia after the War and twenty years later in Berlin working out of embassies in foreign countries – and on both occasions had been recalled for nothing more than doing his job too well, or for doing what the ambassador had essentially ordered him to do. "I don't understand why he said it, or why he's not standing at attention in the Oval Office right now getting his ass chewed."

The Navy Secretary looked at him and said, "You're not the only one frustrated and asking those questions. The truth is that socially and temperamentally Kennedy is drawn to a coterie of upper crust defeatist Brits who think Britain should accommodate Hitler to save England from the devastation and certain horror of a coming war."

"Then why doesn't the Commander-in-Chief just recall him?" Nolan demanded.

"It's knotty, I'm afraid," Knox replied self-consciously.

"What he's doing is contrary to British and U.S. interests." Nolan looked at the Navy Secretary, at Forrestal and then at Wild Bill. He thought of the morning he'd taken command of A Company in Donovan's battalion when O'Grady and a handful of his friends had openly defied him in front of the entire company. It had surprised and shocked him at first, but he'd exercised his authority as commander. He had confronted the offenders, restored order and eliminated an unhealthy situation in the unit. If a lowly infantry captain could reinstate and maintain control over a mutinous group of enlisted soldiers, then certainly the most powerful man in the country could ride herd on a single ambassador.

"It's complicated. More complicated than we know," Knox said.

There's some big league dirty politics involved here that he can't or won't reveal, Dave Nolan surmised. *This is why you told yourself not to get too close to Washington, Nolan. But you're in it up to your chinstrap now, and it's probably not going to get a whole lot better. Maybe you should have listened to that pushy gal you married...*

"It's starting all over again isn't it, Dave?" Denise had said as he rummaged through his dresser looking for socks and underwear to pack for the trip to Washington.

"What do you mean, it's starting over," he asked offhandedly, still searching through the drawers. "Is this all the dress socks I have?"

"You're not listening to me, Dave," she said brusquely, standing across the bedroom with her hands on her hips and frowning at him. She walked over to the dresser and opened the bottom drawer. "A half dozen new pair of socks and seven shirts starched and folded. Now will you listen to me? Don't tell me you don't have time, either. You've never been late for anything in your life – and even if you missed the mid-afternoon train the *Royal Blue Line* has another an hour later." She closed the top of the large suitcase and sat down next to it. "Will you please stop for five minutes and pay attention to me?!"

"All right," he said at last, putting down the clothes in his hands and leaning against the chest-of-drawers, his arms folded across his chest. "What is it?"

"Don't make it sound like I'm some kind of extraneous annoyance. I'm your wife and you haven't talked to me in almost three weeks, and now you're going off again for what? – a month, or more?"

"I've been busy."

"You're all wrapped up – in the business, in that foolishness in Washington and now Bill Donovan has shanghaied you into some *Terry and the Pirates* adventure in England."

"Terry and the Pirates is set in the Far East, and –"

"I know that! What I'm saying is that it's starting all over again, isn't it? And don't tell me it's not!"

Denise was working herself into a full blown confrontation as she had frequently over the decades – beginning in the years they'd dated while he was a cadet. For a brief instant as he looked at her face now, he was reminded of a long ago September night when they had dined alone by candlelight on the outdoor porch of Jeanne-Marie Villamoyanne's little inn in Chalons-sur-Saone. They had argued more fiercely than at any time before – or since. It had been the greatest of fights and the most incredible reconciliation in all their time together.

"Winston Churchill and the president asked me to go," he said evenly.

"They're politicians, Dave. You can't trust people in politics."

"You're father's in politics."

"He's not *in* politics, he's on the outside looking in and doing everything he can to try to keep it all somewhat on the up and up. That's why he works on getting other people into office, people with moral standards and ethics. He hates politics, but he knows he has to get involved in some way to keep the wolves from the door. What he really wants is for Washington to leave him alone to run his business like they used to years ago. I remember when we came back from Germany and stayed with them. He told me over cocktails one night before dinner that he really wasn't afraid of the Nazis in Germany, or the fascists in Italy, or even the communists in Russia. The people he was afraid of are the Washington crowd on Capitol Hill, because they were the only ones who could really hurt him – and they did it routinely."

"I know how he feels about Washington. We've talked about it. But I'm not in D.C. Nor do I want to be. What I'm doing is something the country needs."

"It's what certain politicians need. And you like doing it."

"I like doing things that are important. That's why I was away these past few weeks negotiating a contract that'll bring a lot of money and a certain cachet to the corporation."

"And what status will this trip to England bring the corporation? There is none is there? You're doing this because it's a thrill – because you crave excitement. That's why you walked out on me at Allery that time, and that's why you're going to Europe. And right now I need you here, and so does your daughter. I should have listened to my intuition from the start of this."

He was suddenly angry. "First of all, you know very well I didn't leave Allery to go chasing after some thrill. I had a duty to those men and I told you that very clearly. And secondly, Erika doesn't need me right now. She's made up her mind what she wants to do and she's done a pretty darned good job of making things work out."

"But she's so young, Dave. And going to work for a Congressman is foolish."

"She's almost exactly the age you were when you decided to chase across France as a Red Cross volunteer nurse during the War. What you did was a lot more dangerous than what she's doing. If she was going down there to work for anybody other than Senator Payne, I'd be doing everything I could to keep her here. But she's chosen wisely. Our daughter did her homework – she investigated all the possibilities, talked with your dad first, then to me and you, and then to the Senator. He told me she 'bushwhacked' him like an unarmed paymaster's car at our summer place after June Week. Our little girl has grown up – she's a young woman now. A very bright and attractive and headstrong young woman. Look at her – she's you at her age. Maybe that's the reason you're having trouble with this."

"As a psychologist you're a terrible flop, and you're no help."

He shrugged his shoulders. "It is what it is."

"I hate when you say that! It's like you're announcing the end of discussion because nobody could possibly disagree with you because –"

" – they wouldn't have a leg to stand on."

"You are so vaudeville, Nolan."

"So you've told me." He sensed Denise's fury had run its course. He took her in his arms and kissed her. "I understand you're worried. I am, too – a little. But she's got the best of all possible situations going for her. She's going to be working for the most decent man in the Congress. A real statesman. She'll learn a lot just being around him, and he'll keep an eye on her. She'll be staying in a Georgetown home owned by Harrison and Michelle Reeves and have for a roommate a woman who has worked in Payne's office for twenty-some years. The Senator told me he's coerced his daughter into spending even more time in his office, and Michelle has promised to keep an eye on her. With the recent gentrification of that Georgetown neighborhood by a number of people in FDR's administration, I can't think of a safer place for her to be."

Denise looked skeptical but remained silent as she looked deeply into his eyes.

"I still don't like the whole idea of this trip of yours. Everything about it seems wrong. I know you trust Bill Donovan, but I never have. I'm convinced he's playing you for some kind of fall guy like he has in the past."

Dave Nolan shook his head from side to side. "Next to your father and Senator Payne, he's the man I trust the most on this planet."

"More than Andy Fauser?"

Nolan smiled at her. "After all the lies he's told about me? Yeah, I think so."

"Doc Hanley put him up to most of it, egged him on to make those stories more fantastical with each retelling."

"Doc's real low down on the list, too, for the same reason."

Dave stopped to think about these two friends of theirs, and many others they'd known over the course of more than two decades in the Army. It left him with a formless melancholy, a sense that perhaps the best days of his adult life were behind him. She was right about his love of the thrills he'd sought after while in the service – the next set of orders arriving to send them to something or someplace new and exciting. There had been many disappointments over those years, punctuated briefly and infrequently with the most rewarding, pleasant experiences. And the people. Most of all the people.

It reminded him he needed to touch base with Andy to see if he'd been able to find something – anything – for Cole Alford and Judd Haggerty back in the states.

"Dave, this trip still worries me. I don't like it, but it seems I can't do any more to change your mind than I can Erika's. All the decks are stacked against me."

"I'll be fine. There's not that much happening in the way of combat operations on the British Isle right now. My chance of getting hurt is probably less than my chance of getting abducted by one of those villains from outer space in the Flash Gordon movies."

"I'm not as worried about your physical safety as I am your mental well-being. You're dealing with a lot of people who in my opinion are petty, self-centered egoists who would just as soon ruin you as look at you."

"That's too harsh, Denise."

"And the fact that you would say that worries me even more…"

A uniformed Navy steward approached and announced lunch would be served in the interior dining room. Knox and Forrestal went inside while Donovan stayed behind with Dave to finish his drink and talk briefly.

"Nolan, there are some things you need to realize before we leave tomorrow. Frank Knox is a long time friend. When he was appointed to his job he immediately asked me to take the post Jim Forrestal has now as his undersecretary. I declined – reluctantly. What you need to know is that he's doing everything imaginable to get rid of Joe Kennedy. None of us like him sending those reports to everyone about the chances of Britain's survival. If Knox could get rid of him tomorrow, he would. In the black and white world of the old Irish 69th, you and I could avoid the shades of gray – Frank Knox can't."

"That's hard to believe. A man in his position, having the ear of the president like he does, should be able to be tactfully blunt about what looks like treason to me."

"It's even worse than you know. Kennedy has convinced Army intelligence the Royal Air Force won't last two weeks as an effective fighting force – maybe less than a week. He's got the military intelligence organizations so misinformed and confused that the Chief of Naval Intelligence – a rear admiral named Anderson – just told the Senate he has no idea at all what is happening in Europe and our mission is the *only* way to find out the truth."

"Even more reason for people like Knox and Hull and Stimson to pressure the president to relieve him of his duties in London."

"The president can't." Donovan said emphatically, sounding irritated. "Joe Kennedy is planning to come to the U.S. to mount a challenge within the Democratic Party against Roosevelt by putting his hat in the ring for the nomination."

"You're saying that Roosevelt wants to keep him in London as ambassador, spewing this negativity and confusing our intelligence gathering organizations because he doesn't want Kennedy to challenge him for the Democratic nomination?" Nolan was incredulous. "That's insane. We're talking the survival of Western democracy and he's worried about his personal re-election? This is what you and I are working for?"

"The president can't move against Kennedy just yet."

"Not yet?! If not now, when?"

"As soon as he can get more on Kennedy. The president needs more time for J. Edgar Hoover to assemble a file on him."

Nolan looked away and rolled his eyes. "You're telling me the fate of England and perhaps the United States hinges on whether or not Roosevelt can get enough dirt on Kennedy to keep him from mounting a challenge in the upcoming election? This is pure politics – ugly, disgusting politics. That wasn't part of our deal. Remember what I said before about cockamamie schemes? This is beginning to sound like Russia all over again! I didn't sign on to be part of anything like that."

"No, you didn't. Neither did I. But this is what we've been handed and we'll deal with it. In the war, we didn't sign on to fight under the generalship of weak and timid men like Joffre and Foche and Petain – we fought it to protect our country and the soldiers under us. You and I are undertaking this assignment, not to support or protect Roosevelt but to do the same thing we tried to do in the last war. We do this to protect the United States. You gave your word of honor once upon a time to defend and protect the country. I believe you meant it then and that you'll you do it now. And I know you've given me your word you'll be on that Pan Am Clipper tomorrow afternoon.

"I'd be greatly surprised and disappointed if you weren't."

Chapter 3

The following wind had been howling for over four hours, whipping up mountains of whitecaps and ominously deep troughs between waves as Mitch Nolan implored the gale to abate, the clouds to part and the sun to rise by the sheer force of his personal will.

For him, it had been one terribly long, tense night in the middle of the dark Atlantic.

He continued gripping the helm's large wheel tightly, constantly making small heading corrections as the boat continued to shift and slide beneath him. The stern of the sailboat lifted again and the bow of the thirty-nine foot Bermuda rigged sloop corkscrewed itself into another twenty foot trough. Large dark clouds hugged the horizon ahead as the sky just above them gradually turned various shades of orange. He'd been at the wheel when the squall overtook the sloop just before three in the morning, and he'd been soaked through completely by the sudden onslaught of slashing horizontal rain before he could slip on the top to his oilies.

The bow rose and again plowed into an oncoming wave and salt spray cascaded over the entire length of the boat, pelting him and the afterdeck like a sandblaster. He shivered, wiped the droplets from his face and squinted over the rolling, plunging deck. As he'd done many times over the past few hours, he cursed the sea, the wind and his own stupidity.

"What on earth was I thinking!" he yelled at the top of his voice, but the wind carried the sound away so that he couldn't even hear it himself. And then he laughed out loud. *Now THIS will be some story if I live through it!*

A face – sleep-numbed, unshaven, and looking horribly hung over – emerged above the top step leading inside to the cockpit.

"Nolan! How long's it been blowing like this?"

"About four hours!" Mitch yelled back to make himself heard.

'Marvelous Marv' Crosley was suddenly sober and wide awake as he jumped out on deck, looking at the mast and the sails and catching a heavy spray of saltwater from the bow's next downward plunge. "Four hours?! We should be lying ahull rather than running under full sails. Why didn't you reef the mainsail and drop the jib?"

"Because I don't know what that even means!"

"We're lucky to have a mast or any sails left in this gale. Four hours?!" Crosley leaned below deck and yelled for the other passenger on the sailboat, Roy Lindquist, who emerged shortly looked even more hung over and disheveled than Crosley. He looked around as if dazed, and then his face went ghostly white.

"For cryin' out loud, Nolan! You trying to kill us all?!"

Mitch continued to hold onto the big round wheel as he watched his two partners lower the mainsail most of the way down the mast and tighten the smaller sail.

Long, tense minutes later Crosley and Lindquist sat down next to him looking like death warmed over and as soaked as Nolan.

"Damn, Nolan, why didn't you come wake us? We could have lost the mast, the mainsail and who knows if she would have turned turtle or foundered." Crosley looked shaken as he said it – maybe because it was his father's boat, or maybe because he was afraid of dying in the murky Atlantic at night. "We were way over-canvassed for that wind."

"I yelled my head off for an hour when the wind came up, Marv, but you guys were too drunk to hear me. And you, Roy… you earned that nickname this morning – you're lucky to be here at all."

For four years at the Academy, Roy Lindquist had been known as 'Lucky Lindy' for surviving semester after semester academically at or very near the bottom of the class. He'd been not more than a tenth of a grade point from being 'found' and dismissed from the school; he finally graduated as the class *Goat* – the bottom man academically. At graduation, he'd gotten a standing ovation after receiving his diploma, and by tradition a silver dollar from every one of his classmates. He was famous. And there was also a rumor floating around the class of '40 that Lindquist had engineered, during his stay at West Point, a number of the outlandish pranks still unsolved by the military police and the Tactical Department. Everybody on post was certain he'd masterminded the coup of removing the reveille cannon from Trophy Point and installing it in the Superintendent's flower garden one fall night of their senior year – but nobody could prove it, yet.

"You came up on deck about five this morning to puke your guts out and almost went overboard," Mitch Nolan was saying. "I barely caught your belt before you went ass over tea cup into the briny deep."

"That wasn't a dream?" Lindquist moaned.

"No, it wasn't."

"Yeah, but still you should have lowered that sail or at least come down and got us up," Crosley said over the wind.

"I was too scared to leave my post at the wheel. I told you guys not to drink so much celebrating our one month anniversary." Nolan glared at his classmates, but he felt the release of knowing they had survived a real trial. There was a certain rush and satisfaction in it as if some crucial rite of passage had been met and mastered. It was like the day in the Philippines at age sixteen when Pug Johnston had told him to pull off to the side of the grass airstrip and crawled out of the back seat of the little tail dragger. 'Time to solo, Mitch,' the Navy pilot had said. Suddenly the safety net was gone and he was on his own, feeling wholly alone with nothing or no one to catch him if he failed. He'd made the three circuits around the airfield, clutching the control stick with a death grip, but exhilarated beyond explanation.

"Man, oh man!" Lindquist said after awhile, his eyes glazed over. "We almost became the three best pilots the Air Corps never had."

"Oh ye of little faith," Mitch said, feeling better now that the sun was high above the horizon and the wind seemed to be backing down. "You should have known nothing serious was going to happen with Captain Nolan at the helm."

It was a night he'd always remember in a summer he'd never forget...

After graduation from the Academy and a few days at the Nolan's summer cottage, they had all gone to Monmouth for Pauly Burns' wedding, and then down to Camp Meade for 'Jeff' Jeffers' marriage to that cute brunette half the class had fallen in love with their last two years at West Point. The three of them had fully enjoyed impressing bridesmaids at both weddings with their new uniforms and swagger befitting future fighter pilots.

Crosley's father offered them his sloop for the summer and they began with cruising the Chesapeake, eating Maryland crab cakes, oysters and steamed clams at shore-side restaurants, and fishing for rockfish in Eastern Bay. The liquor locker on the sailboat was overstocked and the Bay was filled with fish and interesting places to explore. Marv had sailed the boat with his father from the shipbuilders yard in Maine when he was a sophomore in high school; the month before entering the Academy, he and his father had sailed it to Bermuda and back.

Lucky Lindquist had also grown up sailing the Chesapeake and so the three of them set off for the last six weeks of their graduation leave exploring the rivers and creeks feeding into the nation's largest estuary. They sailed the Kent Island Narrows, Rock Hall, and St. Michaels on the Eastern Shore. Later they visited Hart Miller Island, and the Patuxent River on the Western Shore, until one day in early July while tied up next to the crab factory on Tangier Island Marv threw out the idea of sailing to Bermuda.

Marvin Simpson Crosley – known to his teammates and friends for four years at the Academy as 'Marvelous Marv' – played first base and occasionally came in as the left-handed relief pitcher on the Army baseball team. He was lanky, taller than Mitch, and hit left-handed with a stooped shoulder stance that made him look like a flamingo perched on one leg. At first glance he appeared terribly awkward, but he'd led the team in hitting two years in a row, and he'd never made a fielding error around first base. Mitch had given him the nickname 'Marvelous' halfway through their second year and it had stuck. Roy Lindquist had been in the same company as Mitch in the Corps and came from Maryland, as did Crosley, whose family had lived in Annapolis for generations.

"How big is that island?" Mitch wanted to know.

"Bermuda? It's not one island, it's dozens of little ones real close together – all told it's about twenty miles long and maybe a couple of miles wide," Crosley said. "It's absolutely beautiful, like a necklace of rough cut emeralds laid out on a blue velvet tablecloth – crystal clear waters, pink sand beaches. Real British. Nothing like it on the planet."

"How far?" Mitch asked.

"Six hundred nautical miles, give or take."

"Six hundred miles?! How in the world are we going to find a tiny little island like that in the middle of the Atlantic?"

"Nothing to it," Roy Lindquist offered. "… it's the only island out there."

They had no trouble convincing Mitch it was not only reasonable but a once in a lifetime adventure not to be missed – an opportunity to sail to the little British island in the middle of the warm, clear Gulf Stream. They sailed down to Hampton Roads, provisioned the boat for a two week trip, and anchored overnight in Willoughby Bay. Early the next morning, without a worry or a care in the world they set out under a cloudless sky with a fair breeze...

Soon the wind backed down from the previous night's blow and in a little while they were once again traveling under full sail. Mitch went below for coffee and a breakfast biscuit and immediately fell asleep on one of the bunks until noon when Linquist stuck his head below decks and called out, "Land Ho, Nolan! See, told you – nothing to finding this place. Get up here. You don't want to miss this."

The ocean was calm and the wind was a light following breeze when Nolan shook off his sleepiness, came out on deck and looked around. Directly ahead he could see the distant faint outlines of low hills. Soon outlines of tiny houses painted in various light pastels emerged from the deep emerald hills. A shoreline formed just north of east. As they drew closer to land, the water became an even lighter shade of blue; in a half hour they slipped between two points of land into a crystal clear bay.

"Ireland Island off to our right," Marv Crosley said casually, standing at the helm behind the big, spoked steering wheel. "We're just now entering the Great Sound, and Hamilton is off to the southeast between those two small islands. Lucky, run up that Annapolis Yacht club pennant – the red one with the diamond shaped yellow and black cross-hatching like the Maryland flag. Maybe they'll honor that and not charge us a docking fee while we're here. Never hurts to try." Crosley started the motor and had Lucky lower the sails. "Nolan, fix us drinks to celebrate our arrival and be quick about it. Royal Bermuda Yacht Club cocktails. There's a bar guide below somewhere."

"After last night, not sure I trust you with a drink in your hand," Nolan shot back.

"Captain's privilege. Lashes at the mast if that drink fails to pass muster."

Mitch went below and a few minutes later came back on deck with the drinks. Before making one for himself, he shaved and put on a shirt he'd bought in St. Michaels a week earlier. He made himself a drink and went up on deck to enjoy the view. Off to the southwest a crew on a small launch was putting out buoys in a long straight line running through the center of the Sound.

"Guys, our timing couldn't be better," Crosley observed. "That launch is setting up a landing zone and clearing a sea lane for the Bermuda Clipper. You're about to witness something special."

Lindquist scanned the western sky with binoculars and was the first to spot the large, high-winged Clipper.

Nolan was struck by the size and grace of the seaplane as it descended at a steep tail low angle. This was not one of the big Boeings that decorated the Pan Am posters he'd seen – it was a Sikorsky, a smaller plane, yet from the deck of the sailboat it seemed huge. Close to the surface, the plane stopped its descent and seemed to hang suspended above the sea lane as if dangling at the end of some great unseen string. It floated above the Sound and then finally touched the water, skipping once, and then in an explosion of sea foam the hull of the seaplane plunged into the water like a greenhead mallard landing to decoys. The hull sank deeper into the clear water and the spray seemed to vanish miraculously. The plane coasted away from them, floating easily on the surface as if it had been sailing the calm waters all the time.

"I bet that's one fun ride," Lindquist mumbled. "We need to catch up with the guys flying that thing and get a tour."

They motored past the chain of small islands into Hamilton city's protected harbor, ringed by little verdant hills covered with bright flowers and tiny houses. A few minutes after entering the calm, clear waters they slowly approached the dock at Albuoy's Point, behind which sat an imposing two story building painted pink with white architectural accents and black shutters. They tied up at the outermost pier and waited while Crosley went inside the clubhouse to negotiate a berth.

In the middle of the harbor a launch motored toward them, followed by another and larger one, each crowded with people seated in the shade of a flat canvas cover. They could make out the dark uniforms and white hats of the Pan Am crew, and learned from an older man working on the Yacht Club pier that the boats were headed to the quay on the next property.

Intent on talking to the pilots of the Sikorsky seaplane, Mitch and Lucky walked down the street to the British airways site and waited while the launches docked. As the passengers debarked, Nolan noticed a young girl – a *pretty* young girl he amended when he got a closer look. She appeared to be traveling with her parents who left her on the dock with their luggage and went into the terminal building. Mitch approached the girl while Lindquist talked to one of the Pan Am pilots, trying to get a tour of the Clipper. Her back was to him as she looked around the harbor from beneath a small white parasol.

"I was wondering what it was like to fly in a Clipper," he said to the girl. When she turned and looked at him apprehensively, he added, "Professional curiosity. I'm a pilot myself, but I've never flown a seaplane."

"How interesting," the girl said indifferently, sounding not at all interested while gazing at him with her hazel eyes. She had the fine, aristocratic facial features of the world's favored, was of average height and slightly built. Her chestnut brown hair was pulled back and held in place by an ornamental hair clip.

"My apologies, I should have introduced myself. I'm Lieutenant Mitch Nolan, U.S. Army Air Corps. I just sailed in from Annapolis." He pointed across the water toward Crosley's boat. "That's my sailboat over there tied up at the Yacht Club. The fella talking to the Pan Am pilot is one of my deck hands. The other is inside the club negotiating a temporary tie-up at the club pier."

The girl cocked her pretty head and looked at him dispassionately, quickly running her gaze up and down. "That's a really pretty boat. What kind is it?"

"It's a sailboat," Mitch answered nonchalantly, but something about the girl's attitude set off a warning alarm in the back of his mind.

"Interesting," the girl said again. "How many sails does your sailboat have, mister…"

"Lieutenant Nolan. It has two."

"Two sails?! Is it a special kind of sailboat then, if it has two sails?"

"No, not really. It's just a plain old sailboat."

"Just a plain old sailboat? Are you sure?"

She asked a few more questions and seemed to find the idea of sailing boats fascinating. The more she probed, the harder he tried to change the subject and was glad when her father returned with a teenage boy at his side who picked up some of the luggage and headed toward the line of cabs.

The man looked warily at him, then at his daughter.

"Kathleen?"

"Father, this is Mr. Mitch Nolan. He just sailed in from Annapolis. That's his boat over there," she said, pointing toward Crosley's boat.

"I see. Sailed it here yourself?" the older man asked.

"No, sir. I'm here with two of my friends. We just graduated from West Point and were sailing around the Chesapeake until we got the wild idea to come to Bermuda."

"Nice little trip. It can be troublesome though if the weather decides not to cooperate. Do you have much sailing experience?"

"A lot more now than when we started. Got caught in something of a blow last night, but made it through."

"Ah, yes. Heard about that from Pan Am. For awhile I thought we might not fly from Baltimore this morning ourselves. So you fellas sailed through that. Good seamanship I expect." He looked around the dock as he spoke, his mind occupied elsewhere.

"More like good luck, sir. Hope we don't have to go through that again."

"He says he's also a pilot, Father, in addition to being a seasoned sailor. Isn't that so, lieutenant? But I wonder how he can be an Army pilot if he just graduated from that West Point school. How is that possible, Mr. Nolan?" she asked innocently.

The alarm in his mind was ringing loudly now. She *was* yanking his chain – he'd thought so before, but now…

"Well Miss… I'm sorry, I didn't catch your name."

"Stroud."

"Well, Miss Stroud, it's all very easily explained," Mitch said solicitously. "You see, I soloed – that means flying by oneself without an instructor – years ago in Manila. My father was stationed there in the Army before I was appointed to the school." He was about to explain that Manila was located in the Philippine Islands but thought better of it. "I haven't been able to fly much these past four years – I was too busy with school work and parading around and playing baseball."

"You're a ball player?" her father asked, looking at him, more interested now.

"Yes, sir. I was a catcher for three years on the varsity."

"I used to play some ball myself. Ever heard of Lefty Grove?"

"What fan hasn't, sir?"

"He and I were on the same pitching staff for three years – two years of sandlot ball in Baltimore, then a year in D level ball when we got called up to the Martinsville Mountaineers." There was a sudden animation in the older man's eyes. "So, you played catcher. Tell you what – we're staying at the new hotel on the South Shore at Elbow Beach. Why don't you stop by sometime this week and we'll have a catch. I'll show you the pitch I taught Lefty that made him famous."

"I'm sure Lieutenant Nolan has better things to do than reminisce with you about bygone days of athletic glory," the girl interjected, looking at her father with a stern sideways glance.

"Not at all, Miss Stroud," Mitch said easily. "I love talking about the game with guys who played back in the day, like your father and mine. Sir, it would be my pleasure to have a catch with you."

The older man thought for a brief moment, furrowing his brow and looking pensive. "You say your name's Nolan… What's your father's name?"

"David. David Nolan."

"I met your father… He's with E.W. Barrett Enterprises out of New York. He played ball too and attended the Academy years ago," Mr. Stroud declared. "I dined with him one night early last year when we were negotiating against one another for a construction contract at Camp Meade, Maryland. Your father beat us out on that contract. We never did figure out how he could bid as low as he did and still make money. How does he do that?"

"I don't know a thing about his business, sir."

"Well, the next time you see him, you tell him that Roland Stroud is still interested in representing his corporation, when I'm not engaged by *Stillman and Dolan* of course. And son, I'm going to be greatly disappointed if you don't stop by to see me this week."

Mitch smiled and nodded at the man, catching a glimpse of his daughter out of the corner of his eye. He suspected she wasn't as eager as her father to see him again.

But he reckoned he could change that.

Chapter 4

At the time of Dave Nolan's arrival at *Claridge's* on the corner of Brook and Davies Streets in London's Mayfair district, a German air attack was in full-throated fury.

In typically British understated response to crisis, the hotel manager and staff calmly welcomed them – Donovan, in particular, as a frequent guest – while the crunch and explosion of bombs not far away interrupted casual conversation. Wild Bill was exhilarated at being close to the action again and at the realization that the lobby was as elegant as always and virtually unchanged since his last visit. *Claridge's* hosted only the most important visitors to London – foreign royalty and heads of state, and of course William Donovan.

"The rattle and clatter of musketry," Donovan mused as they signed the register. "Brings back memories, eh Nolan?"

"If and when we hear musketry that's when we'll know the fat's really in the fire. What we're hearing is the sound of indiscriminate bombing and since early '18 I've always hated it."

They had spent a good part of the morning and half the afternoon on the train to London after flying through the dead of night from Lisbon to Whitchurch on board an Imperial Airways plane that skirted the French coast far out over the Atlantic. While the Clipper flight to Lisbon was as comfortable as it was elegant, the last legs aboard the British airliner and train had been especially miserable. By the time they arrived in London, Nolan was certain international travel was not his personal cup of tea.

A youngster who looked ten or eleven hoisted their luggage onto a hotel cart and led them to the elevator; arriving at tenth floor, the boy removed Donovan's oversized suitcase and started down the hall, struggling mightily with the load.

"Let me give you a hand with that," Donovan said, reaching out for the suitcase's handle.

"Thanks, but no, sir," the boy said. "I started my job and I'll thank you to let me finish it. I'll get stronger as I go, and I'll never quit. Never."

Nolan and Donovan exchanged glances. "Bill, I think we have our answer about British resolve – this boy just about said it all."

Since entering the business world, Dave had developed a practice of tipping bell boys and breakfast waitresses considerably beyond custom because he realized their lot in life. He gave the youngster two one-pound notes, and was just beginning to unpack when the phone next to his bed rang. The front desk advised that he and Donovan had visitors.

Exiting the elevator, he saw two young women in the deep blue uniform of the RAF's Women's Auxiliary Air Force standing near the front door, across the crowded lobby. The concierge caught Nolan's eye and nodded toward the two WAAFs just as Donovan arrived. The two women walked briskly over and one of them spoke.

"Mr. Donovan, Mr. Nolan. I'm Sergeant Dyer and this is Corporal Glendenbrook. We are your drivers for the duration of your stay. We hope you didn't find our earlier visit from the Luftwaffe terribly inconvenient. They can be something of an annoyance."

Nolan looked at the young corporal and wondered why she looked familiar, but marked it off as his personal quirk of seeing the similarities between ordinary people and well known celebrities. She was of medium height, attractive, with long brown hair that came to the top of her shoulders. Her posture was perfect, he noticed, and she seemed quietly reserved or perhaps a little sad. There was a slight, barely noticeable, cleft in her chin. *Who was it she looked like? A teenage Kathryn Hepburn? Maybe.*

"I fear we haven't given you any time to rest, sir," Sergeant Dyer was saying to Donovan. "I've been instructed to bring you straightway to Buckingham palace. The king insists on seeing you at the very earliest moment." She leaned forward and whispered. "A cipher originating in Berlin is now in the hands of our government. It is most urgent you come with me immediately." Dyer turned to Dave Nolan. "Sir, I must apologize and tell you your accommodations will not be here in *Claridge's*. Brigadier Smythe-Browne insists you lodge at his estate in Upper Kent. Corporal Glendenbrook will escort you there. My apology for any inconvenience, but the brigadier is insistent."

"No apologies necessary. Henry and I are old friends and it won't be the first time I've stayed with him." He looked at the corporal, still puzzled by the nagging question about who she resembled. "I'll be down as soon as I can get my luggage."

Fifteen minutes later, he'd loaded his bags into the boot of the Austin 10 staff car.

"I'm sorry, sir, but you'll have to ride in the back seat," the young WAAF said when he bypassed the door she held open and began to climb into the left front seat.

"It's hard to talk to somebody's back, and it may even be a distraction to you. I'll sit up in the front seat, thank you."

"Sir, I'm afraid that's just not done."

"Corporal, for a quarter century I went to a school and then served in an Army that too often chose to do things by tradition without being hampered by progress or common sense. And this is a small thing, really. Like I said, I choose to talk to people face to face rather than to the back of their heads. Are you and I going to have a problem over this?"

The corporal cleared her throat and stiffened her back, raising her head as she looked down the length of her nose at him. "We shan't, sir." He looked into her eyes as she stared at him on the edge of defiance until at last she opened the front door.

When they'd left *Claridge's* and gone a few blocks, he finally said, "You're Henry's daughter Aynslee, aren't you? We met very briefly one evening a couple of years ago at your father's home. My wife and I were just arriving and you were in a hurry to see the young man you were engaged to. A pilot as I recall, flying Hurricanes from Biggin Hill, wasn't it?"

"Yes, sir. We're married now and I have a daughter."

"Congratulations. I suppose your father shanghaied you into this assignment – chauffeuring an old man like me instead of staying around home enjoying yourself with your husband and child. I'll talk to him. See if we can't work something out."

Her chin came up a little, that same almost imperceptible sign of defiance he'd seen from her once already. "That won't be necessary, sir. I should think all of us are in for a rather tough go for awhile. No more grand holidays sitting about cabbaging all the day, topping up our tans and drinking cocktails – at least not until the war is over."

"This isn't your normal duty though, is it?"

"No, sir. My duty station is RAF Hornchurch, sector E. I work in the controllers room, sir, as a plotter. I'm one of the crowd that controls RAF fighters out of 11 Group in Essex – Debden, Biggin Hill, and Hornchurch primarily, but I've worked the lads from most of the airfields of the Group."

"Perhaps you can show it to me some day."

"Perhaps, sir. I'll ask my father to clear it with Stuffy… I mean the Air Marshal."

Nolan smiled at Aynslee's slip of the tongue. *So Marshal Dowding is known among his troops as 'Stuffy" – that's interesting, and maybe telling. A small piece of the puzzle we're trying to put together. Is the man overtly conventional, old-fashioned or maybe hidebound? Why is the leader of Fighter Command called that by his troops in a job requiring maximum flexibility and risk-taking? Have to talk with Donovan about what this means – one of us should spend some serious time at Bentley Priory, and soon.*

He was still thinking about Dowding and others with descriptive nicknames he'd known throughout his own military career when they left London behind and entered a world of green fields and manicured lanes in Kent. It was late afternoon and the sun was beginning to cast long shadows. Outside his window became one of those landscapes painted by a master – lush fields, well defined wood lines, white picket railings at entranceways along the road and stone boundary fences running through the middle of pastures. It seemed impossible as he looked at the serenity of the countryside that a war raged on the continent and was now spilling over into this idyllic panorama. The two lane road straightened out for a mile before disappearing into the far woods.

They had gone halfway to the wood line when suddenly a few hundred yards to their left front, at an altitude of a hundred feet, two twin-engined Messerschmidt Bf-110s suddenly appeared. They were painted a mottled green and gray camouflage with yellow spinners around the props and a large black cross outlined in white halfway back on the fuselage.

"Stop the car!" he ordered abruptly, as if barking a command at one of his own troops. Aynslee's panic stop threw them against the dashboard and the car slid into the left ditch. "Get to cover off the road!"

Suddenly it was November 1918 again, and he was in a small abandoned French village wrecked by the havoc of war; a flight of German biplanes was headed toward him and his men, stitching the road and the buildings with machine gun fire, chewing up his command almost at will. Someone - Father Duffy, or was it O'Grady? - was yelling to him that Higgins was shot and lay dying inside a nearby building...

The -110s were firing now and the clods of dirt being kicked up from the shells were coming toward the staff car. Nolan saw the young WAAF frozen in the middle of the road, staring at the winking flashes from the fighters' guns. Rising from the ditch, he ran to her, grabbed around her waist and picked her up. Turning he saw the shells chewing up the pasture in front of him, and he jumped into the ditch, throwing her face down and flung himself on top of her an instant before the planes roared over them. He saw two bombs hung beneath the second plane's fuselage, and both tumbled free. Nolan covered the girl with his body and placed his hand over the back of her neck as he tensed waiting for the explosions.

They never came.

Long seconds later he raised his head to look around and saw a white snowstorm of paper floating in the air, much of it scattered across the road and caught in the brush lining both sides as if a brace of garbage collectors had decided to spoil the scenery by dumping a daily trash collection. He turned and saw the planes climb in formation and then wing over as if intending to make another pass at the staff car, until they abruptly stopped their turn and headed away, diving behind a shallow ridge to the south.

"Are you all right, Aynslee?" he asked, but her answer was cut short as a flight of four Hurricanes passed directly over the car not fifty feet above the ground.

"Are you all right?" he asked again as she rose to her feet, brushed the dirt off her uniform and looked around for her hat.

"Nothing appears broken, sir," she replied. Looking at the white sheets of paper floating in the air, Anynslee was clearly annoyed. "What is this bloody mess?"

"Propaganda from der Fuhrer probably. Thank goodness it wasn't a bomb or we'd have had it. We need to collect some samples and get them back to Intelligence. Get a handful." He quickly went down the road and picked up several of the pieces of paper. Standing alongside the two lane road, he read the printed words of the flyer:

A LAST APPEAL TO REASON

It was in fact a German propaganda leaflet appealing to the English people to rise up and overthrow the British government, or else convince their leaders of the foolhardiness of resisting the German Fuhrer's offer of peace. It was a difficult read on several levels, primarily because of Hitler's confused feelings toward England. The leaflet was a convoluted maelstrom of resentment and fury against the British government for refusing his offer of peace while at the same time admiring the English people as brother Aryans. It explained in bizarre circuitous reasoning why the two Anglo-Saxon nations should actually unite to rule rather than fight one another. The impression was one of reading the ramblings of a lunatic.

Soon they were back on the road, and as they continued on to Smythe-Browne's estate, Dave thought through what he'd read in *Mein Kampf* on the Clipper during the long trip over. It was deeply disturbing and frustrating, not at all like the volumes from Sun Tzu and other oriental thinkers he'd read on the long voyage to the Philippines years earlier.

Nothing he'd read in Hitler's jailhouse tome advocated a war against England. Hitler had spoken of his admiration of the British Empire, the necessity for its existence and the order and civilization it had brought into the world. Poland had been invaded for racial reasons, France for the sake of revenge and the necessity of ridding Europe of a weak populace and culture. But England would be spared if they would only listen.

Nolan made a mental note to listen nightly to Dr. Goebbels' broadcasts from Berlin.

The staff car finally turned off the road and passed through the gate of Smythe-Browne's property. The sun cast a warm golden glow over the quiet country estate and he was glad Henry had 'rescued' him from all of *Claridge's* elegant overindulgence.

"David, old boy!" Smythe-Browne said as he descended the short set of steps from his front door to the circular gravel drive after Aynslee had parked the staff car behind a gleaming black Bentley. "So good of you to come."

"Didn't know I had a choice. My driver was markedly persuasive and she made it sound like an order, not a request."

"And we had a spot of bad luck on the way," Aynslee told her father nonchalantly. "Two ME-110s strafed our car once and were coming around for another go at us when a flight of four Hurricanes from 111 Squadron out of Croydon happened by."

"Well, sounds rather more like a spot of *good* luck," Smythe-Browne said casually.

Henry had aged since the last time Nolan had seen him just three years earlier in Berlin. He was still thin, tall and ramrod straight, but his hair was now mostly gray. Dave remembered thinking back then the Brit looked like he was born to wear a uniform. Smythe-Brown looked every bit the gentleman he was – a man with inherited wealth, land, and the aloof air of royalty. Denise had enjoyed tweaking his stuffy self-confidence at the parties and dinners in the German capitol, as she had during the War while his nurse in the hospital complex at Allery.

"I can't tell you how good it is to have you and Donovan visiting England on behalf of President Roosevelt. Every department of our government is at your disposal. I am particularly grateful you're here, old friend," the Englishman offered, smiling and grasping Nolan's hand. "Above all, the prime minister is well-pleased."

"I hope Bill and I don't have to disappoint him – or you. But we can talk about that later. Actually, I'm glad you rescued me from *Claridge's* this evening. I was hoping to get a few hours of your time tonight somehow and here you've solved my problem. I expect your nightly rates to the U.S. government are a little lower than the hotel's," Nolan said, glancing at the Rolls Royce, "unless you're still making payments on that."

"You like the new Bently? It was my last major purchase before war broke out."

"It's a bit too much for me, but yes, it's a nice looking machine."

"Well, then, we'll take it for a spin tomorrow morning early. I'll even let you drive if you can convince me you understand the notion that while you Americans drive on the right side of the road, we English drive on the proper side."

"I'll work on that, Henry."

The Englishman carried one of his two suitcases into the house, showed him his room in the east wing of the estate house, and waited while he washed up and changed into casual clothes. All the while the Brigadier kept up a constant commentary of the German air raids that had begun a little more than a week earlier. And then Henry took him to the kitchen.

"David Nolan," Maud exclaimed, wiping her hands on an apron, and giving him a hug. She was not high born, Henry had told him their last time together, and she was still as unpretentious as back then. She and Denise had quickly become friends. They spent a few minutes catching up on the events in New York during the summer – Mitch's graduation and Erika's departure for Washington to work for Senator Payne. "I so wish Denise had been able to come with you. But this damnable spat with the Nazis has ruined everything I suppose. I'm preparing chicken and dumplings the way she taught me the last time. I've been practicing all your American dishes she showed me the week you two were here and I fear I've worn out poor Henry. Dinner's in an hour, but I have much to do. Rather than hanging about underfoot in the kitchen, why don't you have a drink before supper. I believe Aynslee is already in the study getting a head start on you."

The young woman had changed out of her uniform and was sitting in an overstuffed chair playing with her daughter when Nolan and her father entered. Dave watched her for awhile when Smythe-Browne fixed them both a bourbon on the rocks. Aynslee was the same age as Erika and watching her gave him a strange awareness that he was at that age and time in life to be a grandfather. *No. Forty-five is way too young*, he thought. He remembered his own grandfathers well; they had both been old... very old. And wise. He felt he was neither.

"Henry, I need for you to do two things now that you've gotten me here," Dave said after sitting down and sampling his drink. "I know you put the bug in Churchill's ear to get me to England, so here's what I require for my itinerary." He reached into his sport coat pocket and retrieved a thick envelope which he gave to Smythe-Browne. "This is a list of people I need to talk to; the second page is a list of plants I need to visit. Your staff will have to set up my itinerary and arrange for the key people at the indicated plants to be present. As much as I'd like to stay here each night and drink your bourbon I don't have that luxury. I want to spend the majority of my time interviewing and investigating, not riding around the British countryside in a staff car. I'll give you two days to arrange all that. If there's anything or anyone else I should see or talk to, add them. Include in my itinerary overnight lodging as necessary. The third through the seventh pages are questions I have to answer for the government in Washington. That's going to be the outline for my report back to the president and his cabinet. Please provide that in advance to the people and places on my list. I don't want to waste a lot of their time and mine while clerks and secretaries search through files for information, or some manager looks for somebody who can answer my questions."

"That's quite a task, but I'm confident we can do it. Actually, many of those on your list are the very people we wanted you to see, so some appointments are already in the works. Tomorrow afternoon you'll have tea with Lord Beaverbrook and a meeting afterward."

"An excellent way to start," Dave replied swirling the ice cubes in his drink and looking at Aynslee. "I'd like to get away early tomorrow morning – a quick trip to Bentley Priory for starters. Just an informal visit without fanfare or briefings. Then over to Hornchurch mid-day to observe operations and maintenance. That'll help me get some grounding right out of the chute before meeting Beaverbrook."

"I'll make arrangements this evening, sir," Aynslee replied.

"Now Henry, let's get down to serious subjects. Straight up, I'll tell you the fundamental object of this mission is for me and Donovan to ascertain if your government is earnest about this war… and to determine if you're worth supporting. So, what the hell is *really* going on?"

"Horns and all?"

"Wouldn't have it any other way. I'm looking for the British view of the current military situation and what you see as future direction of the conflict. I need that as context to determine if the current manufacturing base is up to supporting those military plans now and in the future. Bill Donovan and I will compare notes before we deliver our reports so we'll spot any inconsistencies in the various stories we're told. He's planned a series of informal breakfasts and luncheons with all our military and naval observers in London including Navy Captain Alan Kirk and Army Brigadier General Lee."

Smythe-Browne looked a little flustered at the news concerning Kirk and Lee. "I was told the American embassy would not be in the loop, as you colonials like to say."

"The Ambassador and his primary staff aren't, but Lee and Kirk are outside that inner circle at the embassy – they report directly to military intelligence in Washington. We do have to pay Joe Kennedy a courtesy visit at some point but don't worry. Neither Donovan nor I have any use for him on this mission. That's all I'm going to say. I know from our time together in Berlin how you feel about his politics, but he's not a factor in our determination. Please pass that on to the prime minister to assuage his worries. Your real concern should be Britain's intentions."

Smythe-Browne sipped his drink and replied. "We stand completely alone against the Nazis. Of course we have the resources of the Commonwealth behind us, but after Dunkirk there is little on the ground between us and the Germans and little with which to oppose a landing on our shores other than the RAF. Our intelligence indicates the Nazi military has enough planes to land 150,000 paratroopers in southern England."

"That sounds like an awful lot, Henry," Dave commented. "Do they have that many paratroopers trained and ready to go?

"We're not absolutely certain, of course. But a coordinated air and sea invasion right now would be game over if it gained a foothold on our soil." Smythe-Browne took a deep breath, looking at the ceiling and obviously weighing an important decision. He looked quickly at his daughter, then back at the American. "Very few people in England know what I'm about to tell you, David. I trust you'll be discreet. Shortly after Dunkirk, I accompanied Sir John Dill and Anthony Eden to a meeting in York with the senior officers of formations based in the north of England. At that meeting, Eden directly asked the assembled commanders whether troops under their command could be counted upon – regardless of circumstances – to carry on the fight against Nazi Germany."

Nolan watched the tension growing on his old friend's face, and sensed his inner turmoil as he related that moment.

"An audible gasp arose from every man there, including me," the brigadier continued. "It seemed incredible, impertinent even coming from a man as esteemed as the eminent Secretary of State for War. I wondered how he could ask such a question of these military commanders. He explained that in the circumstances of the moment and the potential – and likely event, one must admit – of an invasion on our southern shore, it seemed to the government unwise to throw in badly armed men against an enemy firmly entrenched on our soil. It seemed to the government that would be a futile effort to save a hopeless situation.

"Eden then went on to ask the obvious subsidiary question whether the troops would, if called upon, embark at a Northern port still in our hands for transport to Canada to carry on the fight from there. You see, Nolan, without a nucleus of trained soldiers from the home country, the prime minister's policy declaration of carrying on the fight from overseas would be infinitely more difficult. We discussed quite openly the likelihood of our current forces to carry on the fight from overseas. "

"What did your commanders tell you?"

"I shan't bore you with the details, but to a man, our senior commanders told us that all units would stand and fight on British soil. They were quite candid, however, in saying that the men would likely not carry on if ordered to evacuate our home island and leave families behind. At the end of that meeting we were unanimously of the opinion that we have no other alternative but to make our stand here on England's ground. So there we are my friend. Our Agincourt, our St. Crispin's Day is in the offing. By the grace of God, and perhaps the aid of our American friends, we will attain a victory to rival that of Henry V. For the moment our fate lies in the hands of RAF pilots stationed in the south, and factory workers in Birmingham and Liverpool and numerous villages scattered about. We need your help in these dark days."

Henry Smythe-Brown looked at his daughter and then back to Nolan. "I'll tell you much more after dinner. I'll answer every one of your questions and lay out everything I know. I don't want to burden my daughter with the weight of it all. She has enough to worry about with a husband flying Spitfires and a daughter to raise."

"You're right, Henry. These are very dark days."

Smythe-Browne finished his drink and placed the glass on the table next to him. "You said earlier you had two things you needed for me to do. Your second request, old friend?"

"Get me another driver," Nolan said, "because I'm going to fire the one I have."

*   *   *   *   *

With the wind in his hair, the late morning sun beating down, and the motorbike purring seductively beneath him, Mitch Nolan thought things had never been better in his entire life…

Along with Lucky and Marv, he had ventured into Hamilton that first afternoon to scout the town and figure out how to get around Bermuda. They walked along the harbor frontage, looked into store windows like tourists, and talked with the stiff British Bobby directing traffic from inside a small white gazebo in the middle of Front Street. Finally they found *Chittenden's Bicycle Shop*, a place that rented out motorbikes, mainly to tourists. When they inquired about rates, the owner told them everything he had in his inventory that still ran was already spoken for. Mitch counted eleven motorbikes sitting alongside the shop; when they asked, the owner told them his mechanic returned to England a month earlier claiming 'island claustrophobia' and he hadn't been able to keep all his machines running.

"Would you mind if I looked at your bikes, sir?" Mitch quickly said. "I might be able to get some of these back working for you – for a price."

"Take a look around. I'd be willin' to pay a fair wage if you can," the owner said.

"We can talk about that if it turns out I can fix them. I guess you started having bike problems early last week."

"About that, I'd say. How'd you know?"

"A *James* is a good bike, but requires taking care of. I've worked on these before. I'll look over your machines and let you know if I can help."

Mitch walked through the repair shop out back, and then inspected one of the bikes. He pulled a short length of narrow diameter hose off the motor and held it up to the light to look through it, then took the top off the carburetor. He turned to Linquist and shook his head, smiling. "My little brother found an old *James* like this in Manila. This bike is probably a year or two newer than my brother's, but it looks the same. These fuel lines have to be cleaned out about once a month and the carb adjusted or else they foul and won't run. It's not hard and all a mechanic needs is a flathead screwdriver and a foot long length of sixteen gauge wire to keep these things running. That and a gapping tool to check the plugs. This bike needs about ten minutes of cleaning to get it back running."

A half hour later, he had the first three bikes running again; by supper time he had all of them back in service. The owner was ecstatic and opened his wallet to pay him.

"Mister, I'll make you a deal – if you let me and my two friends each have a free rental for a week, I'll show you how to keep these things running and how you can do it yourself without having to hire a mechanic,. You have eleven bikes in service you didn't have this morning. It won't take you long to make up the revenue lost on the three rentals."

That night, as the sun was going down, the three would-be Air Corps pilots started off on their first tour of the islands…

Mitch turned into the long flower-bordered drive leading up a slight incline to the hotel at Elbow Beach, and almost ran head first into a taxicab.

Damned Limey southpaw way of driving, he cursed under his breath as he swerved and barely missed being splayed across the hood of the small black sedan. The late morning sun was hot, but a southeasterly breeze was blowing in, moderating the temperature. Mitch parked the motorbike, grabbed the beach towel from the luggage carrier and trudged through the hot sand toward the surf, looking for someone in particular.

Kathleen Stroud lay on an oversized white towel tanning herself.

"Miss Stroud?" he said, sounding surprised while spreading out his towel next to her in the sand. "I was told this is one of the best beaches on the island and the one with the pinkest sand. I had to come see it for myself. And here you are! Small island, isn't it?"

She shaded her eyes and looked up at him, frowning.

"We met yesterday."

"Are you sure?" she asked, looking puzzled.

"Mitch Nolan. We talked on the Imperial Airlines dock, next to the Yacht Club."

She frowned again and finally said, "Now I remember. You're the one who sailed that sailboat all the way here from Annapolis through a monstrous storm, aren't you?"

"That's right," he said, smiling confidently. "It's a sloop – a thirty-nine foot Bermuda rig… or Marconi rig if you prefer."

"You didn't know that yesterday." She pushed herself up on an elbow, cocking her head and smiling prettily. "Do you do that often – pretend to be something or someone you're not?"

The look in her eyes said she'd caught him.

"Only when trying to make an impression on a pretty girl obviously above my station in life. Even a peasant can try to impress a princess, can't he?"

"You're very glib. And obvious, Mr. Nolan."

"Mitch. And I wasn't pretending to be something I'm not. I really did sail that boat from Annapolis to Hamilton – maybe not as the captain of the ship, but I did sail it for four hours the night before last in the worst storm I've ever been in. That should count for a something."

She shielded her eyes and said, "You really didn't come here just to see if Elbow Beach has the pinkest sand, did you?"

"No, I came to see if I could find you."

"Should I be pleased, or thrilled – maybe grateful for the privilege of being the object of your attention?!" she asked sarcastically.

He took a deep breath and smiled, then sat on the beach towel next to her. "I'd be willing to accept 'somewhat glad', maybe even 'guardedly pleased' for starters and work from there."

"And your intentions?"

"My intentions? To start with you at 'somewhat pleased' and arrive at 'thrilled' by showing you the best time you ever had on a summer vacation. I don't have any firm plans just yet, but I'm working on it."

"So, you're just looking for a good time."

"For starters. Who knows where it might go from there?" She looked away nervously, and Mitch wondered if he'd been too abrupt or if she was simply shy and inexperienced. She was obviously young, and maybe hadn't dated much. That could make things interesting. "Let's do this – spend a little time here swimming and tanning, then we'll take my motorbike out along the south shore road and do a little sightseeing."

"I've never been on a motorbike," Kathleen admitted, sounding hesitant.

"Really? Then if nothing else comes of today, you can tell your friends back home you met a guy in Bermuda who will one day become a more famous pilot than Lindbergh and he showed you the best time ever."

"Somehow I doubt that very much."

"I say why not give it a try. It'll be fun – for both of us. We've got a whole week; maybe more. A beautiful tropical island with thousands of nooks and crannies to explore."

"Will you promise to keep me out of trouble?"

"On my honor."

"You don't sound like as much fun as you promised." She said seriously, then laughed.

They spent the early afternoon swimming in the clear waters, walking along the beach, and lying in the sun at the water's edge under a high clear sky. Later he took her on a ride on the back of the motorbike along the south shore where they could see the light blue waters of the shallows and the darker blue running out toward the barrier reef. The shoreline was dotted with small beaches in tiny coves, and in places the sand came right to the roadway's edge. They went all the way to where the south road ended on the point of Ireland's Island at the entrance to the Great Sound. The hours flew by and before they realized, it was dinnertime. Her parents were coming back from the beach when he and Kathleen pulled into the parking lot.

"We've been looking for you for an hour!" her mother said, looking them over and gazing disapprovingly at the motorbike, then at Mitch. "Where *have* you been?"

"Along the shore and all the way out to the end of the road, to the very tip of the island," Kathleen said. "It's the most beautiful place ever!"

Her father examined the motorbike and after a short while looked at Mitch and said, "I had a surplus Army Indian motorcyle right after the war. It was a Powerplus that would do sixty when tuned up. The first time I rode that thing I thought I was the next "Canonball" Baker. How fast does this bike go?"

"Not even half of what your Indian would do twenty years ago, sir. I think it tops out at about twenty-five if you're going downhill with the wind at your back. But it's reliable and easy to maintain. My little brother had one of these when he was eleven and rode it all over Manila when my family was stationed there."

Mr. Stroud looked at the James again. "It's been almost twenty years since I've ridden one of those. Where'd you get this?"

"Henry!" Kathleen's mother said, giving him a warning glance.

"Margaret, these things aren't dangerous if a guy knows what he's doing. They're a lot of fun. And if it only does twenty-five..."

"I rented this one from a shop in Hamilton," Mitch offered. "This morning they still had seven left for rental. I have an 'in' with the shop owner, and if you'd like, I'd be glad to talk to him about setting one aside for you. But I'd have to get going – he closes in a half hour."

Mrs. Stroud warned her husband again.

"Margaret. Once a person learns to ride a bike he never forgets how. And I'm not *that* old." He turned to Mitch and looked pleased at the idea. "Tell you what. You have dinner with us on the patio and we'll talk. But right now, let me take a short little spin on this bike to see if old 'Canonball' still has anything to worry about from me. If it's still as much fun as it used to be, tomorrow morning will be early enough to check that shop."

Dinner with Kathleen and her family on the hotel's broad patio facing the ocean turned out to be more enjoyable than he'd expected. He listened to Stroud's stories of playing baseball on the sandlot fields of Baltimore with Lefty Grove and the year they were teammates in the Blue Ridge League. They swapped information about motorcycles. Mrs. Stroud finally seemed to loosen up when he told them about his mother's family and the social life on Long Island where she'd grown up.

They were all interested in his time at the Academy and his views on whether or not the U.S. would enter the war now raging on the Continent. While he admitted a non-political approach to world events, he answered their questions about the relative strengths and weaknesses of England and Germany. They were amazed at his grasp of current affairs and his knowledge of aviation. The fact that his father had once chaperoned Lindbergh around Nazi Germany and had taught Herman Goering the finer points of wingshooting at *Carinhall* in the Schorfheide Forest clearly impressed them. By the end of the meal, Mitch was pretty certain he had passed muster with both of Kathleen's parents.

After dinner he and Kathleen sat side by side on lounge chairs overlooking the beach, watching the nearly full moon rise above the Atlantic.

Not long after her parents had gone back to their room, she suddenly turned to him and said, "Take me for a ride in the moonlight."

"What?" He looked at her in disbelief. "Refined girls from Bryn Mawr don't go riding around strange places at night on the back of motorcycles with guys they just met."

"Aren't you just the soul of honor," Kathleen said, mocking him and laughing merrily. "They won't mind as long as I'm with you. You're a smooth talker and you finessed my parents during dinner when it was clear both of them were at least cautiously skeptical. You could do it again if you had to."

"I wasn't being deceptive, or manipulative."

"Maybe a little?" she retorted.

"Not the least bit. Do I want to have a good time? Sure. Am I leading you on? – or your parents? No. That's not me." He looked into her eyes and said, "But... if you want to go for a ride, I know a great place I can show you. Remember, you asked me."

They sped down the long entranceway to the hotel, turned left onto the south road and rode in darkness with only the dim headlight of the motorbike to light the roadway. A quarter hour later, Mitch turned off the main road, traveled slowly on a narrow path another few minutes, and finally stopped. "We're here."

"Where is here?"

"Follow me and I'll show you."

He took her hand and led her down a gradual slope on a wide passageway beneath the trees that blocked out much of the moonlight and left a dappled canvas on the sandy path. A few minutes later they emerged on a wide beach where the waves lapped quietly onto the shore. The moon was higher in the sky now casting their shadows on the sand.

"What is this place?" she asked, looking left and right. "It looks like most of the other beaches we saw this afternoon."

"Ah, but it's not. We'll see if it's like any other beach you've ever seen." He took her hand and led her to the large outcropping of ancient lava now covered in places with a thick grass and short, stubby bushes. By the time they reached the top and sat down a hundred feet above the shore, she was out of breath. "This is Horseshoe Bay. Isn't this beautiful?"

"It is. It's one of the most beautiful scenes I've ever seen. How did you find it?"

"One of my friends, Marvelous Marv - the one who's father owns the boat - brought us out here last night. He's been here before and remembered it. When I saw this, I knew I had to find a way to show it to you. A scene like this needs to be shared with someone special."

"Is this a line you use with all the girls?"

"You're the only one I've ever brought here. And it's not by chance."

"This *is* a line."

"No, it's not. I'm dead serious. The two of us being here was meant to be. Honest."

"Meant to be? Come on, that's silly – I don't for a minute believe in predestination."

"Look at all that had to happen for us to be sitting here now," he retorted. "This is my first trip to Bermuda. Our boat survives a really bad storm that puts us hours ahead of schedule and places us in the Great Sound at exactly the moment the Clipper from Baltimore lands. You and I meet on the dock. A motorbike shop owner needs help to get his bikes running – I have that experience and happen by. He gives me the transportation to get around. I use it to find you at the beach and bring you to this place. There's a reason for everything – nothing ever happens by chance. I didn't plan or manufacture any of this. Who knows why all that worked out, but it seems like destiny to me."

"That's the goofiest thing I ever heard." She looked at him in the brightness of the moonlight and wondered. *Nothing happens by chance… Is he right?*

She'd found him mildly interesting the previous day at the dock in Hamilton, and had thought about him the next morning as she lay on the beach. The afternoon had been fun and exciting. Even dinner with her parents, which she dreaded, had been curiously amusing.

He was a fount of knowledge about current affairs. He'd told them he read the *New York Times* every day as a cadet and was a student of history, like his father apparently was. When her parents had probed about his background he'd pointed out his mother's family and his father's friendship with Wild Bill Donovan with whom he was now with in England. Without overdoing it, he'd made his own childhood sound as exciting as a Saturday afternoon serial at the movies yet he made himself out to be simply an average Army kid.

"You got high marks from my parents during the interrogation session over dinner," she said, as they sat on the hill looking down at the beach illuminated by moonlight. "I hope you weren't too offended."

"It wasn't half as bad as the grilling I'm going to give to any guy who wants to date *my* daughter." He turned his face toward her and she saw he was smiling. "I'll guarantee that when I'm finished cross-examining one of them he'll think twice about dating my little girl."

"So, that wasn't a show just for the benefit of my parents?"

"I told you before it wasn't." He looked back down at the distinct, curved line of beach and the gentle waves lapping at the shore. "I've only been here for a day and haven't seen much of Bermuda, but what I have seen is beyond description. I can't wait to see the rest of it. And what makes that so special is I'm going to be discovering it with you." Once again he turned toward her looking deeply into her eyes. "A beautiful place. A beautiful night, and a girl more beautiful than all if it. I'm one very lucky guy."

Her breath caught in her throat and she wanted to say something witty or sarcastic to break the tension she felt, but the look in his eyes caught her up short. Out of the blue, she leaned quickly toward him and kissed him on the lips, and just as quickly recoiled from him, gazing wide-eyed at his face. He looked neither stunned nor anxious.

"You were expecting me to do that!"

"Hoping, but not expecting."

He manipulated this whole scenario to get me to make the first move! Abruptly she was furious at him. Unable to think of anything to say she kissed him again, hard on the lips this time while grabbing the back of his head and drawing him closer. She held him tight and kissed him for long seconds; at last she released him. *What do you think of proper Bryn Mawr girls now, Lieutenant Mitch Nolan?!* she said to herself, pleasantly surprised that he seemed flustered and momentarily speechless.

"You shock me," he said at last.

"You think you've been stage-managing the whole day and directing everything toward that moment."

"I'm really not that clever," Mitch replied, smiling at her. "But I take it as a compliment that you think I am."

"I didn't say *I* thought you were clever. I said that *you thought* you were stage-managing the whole day."

"I'm not that devious, either. This is really interesting. I like your spunk, Kathleen and –"

"Kathleen is way too formal. My name is Kate and that's what I'll allow you to call me. All my really close friends call me that. I'll admit I'm beginning to like, just a little bit, the cut of your jib, lieutenant. The jib is that smaller sail up front on your Marconi rig, which I'm pretty sure you still don't know."

"The cut of my jib?" He tried to appear deep in thought. "All right, I'll accept that. Maybe you're not the typically uptight private school type after all. We can work with that."

"I do like having a good time, but I have limits. There are things I won't do."

"Obviously your limits don't keep you from riding on the back of a motorbike. How about we take a ride out to the Swizzle Inn?"

"Is that a bar? I don't smoke and I don't drink liquor."

"You're a sophomore in college and never had a drink?"

"Not everybody is as worldly as you," she said.

"I don't know if that's a compliment or an accusation, but I'll let it pass, for now. I promise not to let you go too far past your limits. I won't let you have more than one drink, if that much. But I want you to try a little beverage I invented last night while I was there with my friends. I call it *A Dark and Stormy Night.*"

"After Bulwer-Lytton?"

"No, after the night I spent at the wheel of a sloop in the middle of a rainy gale. It's Caribbean Rum, a spicy sweet ginger beer made here on the island, and some lime juice. "

"I don't know," Kate said, tentatively.

"Come on, Kate… this'll be a lot of fun. Trust me."

She rolled her eyes at him and looked away. "No girl in her right mind says 'yes' to anything proposed by a guy who says 'trust me.' I've learned that much."

"All right… Kathleen," Mitch said, shrugging his shoulders.

"Very funny." But this was suddenly fascinating, maybe a little rebellious.

She had not wanted to come to Bermuda. How boring, she'd thought back when her father proposed it. But now… She'd never met anyone quite like him – a pilot who fixed motorcycles and hunted wild animals and had lived in a half dozen exotic sounding places before graduating high school. And halfway good-looking. Maybe more than halfway. She'd made up that business about being called Kate to impress him, and he seemed to like it. She smiled at that and thought, *this vacation is turning out better than expected.*

"All right, lieutenant. I'll try one drink – but that's all!"

"You won't be sorry," he said, smiling broadly at her. As he started to rise she grabbed his arm and pulled him close to her and kissed him passionately, her breath coming in quick short gasps. He pulled her down on top of him and she ran her fingers through his hair. She looked into his eyes, kissed him quickly and rested her head on his chest.

"Tomorrow. We'll try your drink tomorrow," she whispered softly. "This moonlight was made for better things."

Chapter 5

"This is going to be a long, awkward ride over to Hornchurch if we don't talk to one another," Dave Nolan said, looking across the front seat of the staff car at his WAAF driver. "Let me explain myself, Aynslee."

"No explanations necessary, sir," the girl said stiffly, jutting out her jaw and continuing to peer straight ahead. "You're well within your rights to ask for a different driver. After yesterday afternoon I fully understand. My apologies for putting you in danger, sir."

Nolan took a deep breath and looked out the window of the staff car as they exited through the gate at Fighter Command headquarters. He wished Henry hadn't done this to him – or to her. It was unfair to both of them; worst of all, it was simply unnecessary. And it had created a conflict for him with a young girl he wanted very much to get to know because she was, in a way, much like his own daughter. He sighed deeply again.

"I said what I did last night because I think your father put both of us in an awkward, untenable position. What he did was unnecessary."

"He had his reasons, sir."

"I'm sure he did. I'm also sure he was completely off the mark." When she remained silent, he continued. "Your father assigned you as my driver in order to spy on me so he could know what I'd learned. He planned to use you as the undercover agent. If he didn't tell you that, I will. You would have been subject to a full scale interrogation each night when you got home wanting to know everything about every conversation and every inspection I conducted. It wouldn't surprise me if he might not even ask you to sneak a look at my notes."

"You can't be certain of that, sir. I'll have you know my father regards you highly."

"As I do him. But I also know him from the time we spent together in the hospital during the last war and from the time a few years back when we were both assigned to our respective embassies in Berlin. He's not above playing politics – he once tried to get me to pass along some unflattering information about certain U.S. officials to my own state department through back channels. I say assigning you as my driver was unnecessary because I'm going to give him everything as I go along, as well as a first draft of my final report to the president. He doesn't need to have you or anybody else looking over my shoulder. All he had to do was ask and I would have told him – I planned to until you showed up at *Claridge's* and I figured out what he was up to. I'm going to let him stew for a few days before I tell him. I ask you to keep that under your hat until then."

Aynslee's expression never changed as she glanced quickly at him and then glued her eyes back on the road.

"Concerning yesterday – you didn't put me in danger, it was those two Messerschmitt fighters. I've been through a lot worse, and yesterday didn't faze me in the least. But it did make me think about you, especially last night when I held your little girl."

"Being a mother doesn't mean I'm not fully capable of doing my duty, sir."

"But driving me around isn't your duty. Your duty is being a controller at one of the 11 Group Sector stations. I saw that yesterday when you talked about it, and I saw it in your face and heard it in the comments from the controllers at Bentley Priory that know you. They were all thinking: *what a bleedin' waste for Aynslee to chaperone that old bloke around.*" For the first time that morning he saw her face relax and the corners of her mouth turn up just a little.

"That's not what they were saying, sir. And that's not the way they would say it." She glanced at him quickly again. "Your accent is awful, sir, and you're not all that old."

"I'm more than twice your age, and that makes me old... old and grumpy. Your father's worse. That's why I'm going to make him sweat awhile. But you should be where you do the most good – that's at Hornchurch plotting and controlling, at home when you can with your daughter and, whenever possible, with your husband. None of that is going to happen while you're driving me around. They should have assigned me an old taxicab driver or a young soldier without a family or girlfriend. Doesn't that make more sense?"

"Put that way it does, yes, sir. I thank you for telling me that."

He looked over at her and asked, "Have we cleared the air? Are we on good terms now?"

"Yes sir, we are," Aynslee replied, and then she turned her head to look directly at him. "You're right about his intentions. I could see he was becoming a nosey parker about your trip, and I'm glad to be off the caper. He's been a bit narky the last month, even with mother. But he's been under a great deal of pressure since Dunkirk. Don't be too harsh on him."

"I won't. He's still a good friend. How far to Hornchurch?"

"Twenty or twenty-five minutes."

"I'm going to grab a few winks. I didn't get much sleep last night."

"Time change, sir?"

"Not really." He was about to tell her it was her mother's dumplings, but thought better of it. Both he and Denise loved Maud to death but she had never learned to cook, and when dinner was over he felt like he'd swallowed one of Admiral Nelson's cannonballs.

Nolan looked through the windshield toward Dover where he could barely make out the white contrails that filled the sky. Dowding had referred to the airspace above the coastal town as 'Hell's Corner' and with good reason. "Sorry to hear your father's so irritable. I'll keep that in mind. We all might get through this war if we keep our sense of humor and work our butts off. But we can't go spying on each other. Wake me when we get to Hornchurch."

It had been known as RAF Suttons Farm during the last war but was now called RAF Hornchurch reporting to 11 Group at Hillingdon House on the opposite side of London. It was home to a number of Spitfire squadrons, with an auxiliary airfield at Rayleigh. Nolan awoke as they turned off the main road onto a dirt path leading to an open grassy meadow circumscribed by an irregularly shaped concrete taxiway. He was surprised at the number and sizes of the buildings; it seemed to him unwise to build and occupy a military facility so close to the front lines. But wasn't everything in Europe closely packed together? They were now only eighty miles from German held France – fifteen minutes flying time for a Bf109. The world had grown a lot smaller since he'd last been to war.

Earthen revetments ringed the grass airfield and small wooden dispersal huts for squadron headquarters were scattered amongst them. Two large three story hangars sat on the east side of the open field, each with large sliding doors on both ends and tall glass windows above bricked sides. Tiny medical huts with brownish green ambulances parked alongside dotted the area. The field was devoid of airplanes as Aynslee parked in front of the field headquarters building. They went inside and Nolan introduced himself to the airfield commander – a major named Hawkens with aviator wings over his breast pocket and crutches propped behind his desk.

"Lost a piece of the leg early on when we were in France," the major explained when he saw Nolan eyeing his crutches. "But the Linseed Lancers are making me a piece to tie to my stump so I can likely fly again. Been a base rat too long already, I say. We have more busses than pilots at the moment and I'm ready to do another turn at the Hun." The major smiled broadly at him while trying to keep his balance behind the desk. "I'll ring down to the hangar and tell the maintenance chief you're here. Bentley Priory said you'd be along to look over our maintenance and supply status. Right now, we seem to have parts enough, and the replacement planes are steady arriving, but like I said, it's the pilots we need – *trained* fighter pilots. Thank goodness near half of our lads seem to make it back if they get shot down. We've even had some of you Yanks with experience show up to give it a go. Canadians and Poles, too."

Aynslee led him to the hangar where a man in his mid-thirties met them and showed him around the facilities and the half dozen Supermarine Spitfires in for repairs. His time in Germany as Lindbergh's 'batman' had taught him more than he'd realized about aircraft design and maintenance. He found the mechanics long on experience but short in number and they were stretched pretty thin after nearly a month under the withering German aerial onslaught. But the first impression was positive.

RAF Hornchurch was everything he'd expected to see at a senior sector airbase: barbed wire, pillboxes with machine guns ringing the perimeter fence, the Army's armored vehicles and personnel guarding the base round the clock. They were walking from the maintenance hangar to the supplies and storage building when the first flight of several aircraft returned.

Four Spitfires in ragged trail formation flew a wide downwind pattern to the east of the field, the first plane trailing a long plume of dark grayish smoke. Sirens sounded and men ran to ambulances and fire trucks. The wheels of the smoking plane came down as it turned to final approach; the canopy slid open emitting a huge cloud of smoke. The airplane dropped to the ground hard, bounced twice and slowed enough for the pilot to guide it off the field onto the concrete taxiway. In a matter of seconds the plane was being drenched with water and ground personnel were helping the pilot out of the cockpit, down the wing and away from the aircraft.

The aviator, a tall young man wearing a white silk scarf around his neck and an RAF dress uniform casually walked away as the plane erupted in flame. The pilot turned toward where Nolan stood and he heard Aynslee gasp.

Three airplanes landed in quick succession, bouncing on the hard turf and quickly slowing then pulling off toward the far side of the airfield and taxiing into revetments. More planes came toward the field; as one of them touched down, the one following it flew over less than a hundred feet up, pulled up sharply and did a roll as it climbed out and then winged over, did a tight left turn as its wheels lowered and then it too landed. In a matter of twenty minutes the field was assaulted with loud engine noise and a flurry of activity as a dozen and a half aircraft landed and taxied to parking spots around the field.

Nolan stood on the ramp in front of the hangar amazed at the level of activity.

Planes were shutting down as crew chiefs and mechanics swarmed like invading insects over the machines, pulling open engine cowlings and inspection panels. Fuel trucks raced across the field and began refueling operations while armorers inspected machine guns and reloaded onboard ammunition boxes. Pilots walked to the dispersal huts and flopped into chairs as maps were mounted on tripods and debriefings began. Aynslee closely watched one of the dispersal huts until at last she ran across the close-cropped grass toward the far side of the field.

By the time Nolan caught up to her, she had wrapped her arms around the neck of a tall, smiling pilot with a blackened face.

"Bit of smoke, that's all my dear," he heard the young man say nonchalantly. "Not much worse than enduring one of those odious cigars my father smokes. And you would be the Yank my Aynslee is chauffeuring about. So good to make your acquaintance old boy," the aviator said, offering his hand. "Leftenant Glendenbrook. Royal Air Force, seventy-four Squadron flight leader. Malcolm Glendenbrook, but the lads call me Muck."

... but the lads call me Muck, Nolan thought as he shook the pilot's hand. He was reminded of a darkening afternoon just days before the end of the last war when another young Brit said something similar to him and died seconds later. *I wonder what Danny Brotheridge might have made of himself if we hadn't met that day?*

"I say, Nolan. A word in private, if you please." The aviator placed his hand lightly on Nolan's arm and guided him to the back of the dispersal hut. Glendenbrook blithely removed a cigarette from an engraved silver case, lit it and inhaled deeply. "When I talked with my wife last night on the telephone she was in something of a snit about your looking for another driver. I just wanted to say, sir, that I agree with your decision but my Ayns seems a bit put off over it. I'd appreciate your not changing your mind on this."

"Don't worry. We had a little talk on the way over this morning and we're past all that." *What is it about these Brits that make them talk down to us all the time,* he wondered.

Glendenbrook's face lit up. "Jolly good, old boy. Takes a load off my mind, I tell you. Especially after the dust up she had yesterday with the two Messerschmitts. I was wondering if you'd be better served with a bodyguard than a driver in any event."

"I'm not a spy, and I don't know any state secrets either. I'm just a business man."

"Well, sir, whatever you are," the young man said, "I do appreciate your letting my wife return to sector duty so she can stay nights with me or her parents and see after our daughter."

"My thinking exactly." Nolan looked across the field at the smoldering wreckage of the Spitfire. "What happens to you now without an aircraft? How long before you can fly again?"

"The maintenance chaps will requisition another. I'll fly one of the spares in the hangar. That's the second plane I've lost. The first time I had to bail out near Hawkinge and get a ride back with a farmer. When you lose a plane, they run you through a short debriefing, check your pulse, assign you another aircraft and, *Bob's your uncle*, you're on the next sortie out that same day." Glendenbrook smiled broadly. "Rather much easier than before the war broke out."

Soon the pilots gathered around a map, covered in clear plastic and written on with markers. There were arcs in red indicating the range of various German fighters, arcs in yellow showing the range of bombers. A captain went through a series of questions, writing down answers. The squadron's total claim was a Focke-Wulf 190 destroyed and another damaged, three Bf109s downed along with two Heinkel He-111s. But they had lost three of their own.

"I saw both Pemberton and Waterbury go down," one pilot said responding to the debriefer's question. "Each of their chutes opened. Pemberton floated into the channel about five kilometers out but Waterbury made it to land two or three kilometers north of Folkestone."

"And Fletcher?" the operations officer asked. "Anyone see Fletcher go down?"

No one had. The debriefing went on for twenty minutes while the pilots munched on sandwiches and offered observations on the numbers of German aircraft and the targets they were after. There were questions about the accuracy and timeliness of any intelligence from controllers at Bentley Priory and the precision of direction steers from sector controllers.

"Anything else?" the operations officer asked, looking around and finally acknowledging Lieutenant Glendenbrook. "What is it this time, Muck?"

"Air sea rescue, captain. There is none, and if one of us goes down in the channel, we're never heard of again. I say the RAF is doing a bloody poor job of snatching the likes of Pemberton out of the water. If he's lucky, the Luftwaffe will pick him up with that little white Dornier seaplane of theirs. Then all he has to do is survive a POW camp until the war's over. But chances are he's drowned. I think you should pass it up the line to Stuffy and ask him not to steer us out over the water until there's some kind of plan to pick us up when we get wet."

The captain looked a little annoyed. "Sorry Muck, but I'm afraid there's little left but to bash on. Perhaps you should draw a life raft from supply."

"My head's already touching the top of the canopy. If I have to sit on a life raft in addition to my parachute, I won't be able to close it."

"Old Muck always did have a big head," one of the other pilots offered in a loud stage whisper. "Descended from royalty I hear."

"Better than being related to gypsies, Turner."

The briefing broke up shortly before noon. The last of the petrol trucks finished refueling, and the mechanics were beginning to close engine cowlings and making notations in aircraft logs. The pilots wandered away, some filtering into the dispersal hut and others going back to their planes. Glendenbrook sauntered up to Nolan and Aynslee.

"Sounds like your commander wasn't too high on the idea of passing your suggestion up the chain of command," Dave said to the pilot.

"He knows what I meant. And he knows I'm right. I'll chat him up over a pint tonight at *The Good Intent*. It's our little unofficial mess and informal bar. More real business gets done in there than in Whitehall I dare say. But that's for later. I'm hoping it's a quiet afternoon for us. Weather over the channel was looking a bit 'iffy' about the time we were relieved by 54 Squadron at Hawkinge. We stage out of there since it's close to the channel. So far activity has been surprisingly light – German fighter sweeps and dive bombing of radar towers by Stukas. Once in a while we get into a donnybrook, like this morning. They're just feeling us out at the moment. The real fighting has yet to begin."

Nolan walked around the airfield and talked to mechanics still working on aircraft and to the armorers who worked on guns or rearming. The .303 shell looked awfully small to him and he wondered if it had enough power to do real damage even with the eight gun bank the

Spitfire carried. One plane was having two of its guns replaced and Nolan asked about the availability of replacements and their quality. After grilling the sergeant for a while he decided to return to the supply building and finish what he'd started earlier. He later took a cursory look at the motor transport section and equipment buildings.

Aynslee took him by the Sector Station control room and he was given a brief tour by the commander of 11 Group who had flown his personal Hurricane into Hornchurch mid-afternoon. Air Vice Marshall Keith Park was a New Zealander, Nolan was surprised to learn, and he admitted to hurrying over to Hornchurch when word got around that Nolan had shown up unannounced at one of his sector stations.

"Whilst I was going in to refuel at Hawkinge, Fighter Command called to say a high ranking American chap was on an inspection tour unchaperoned. They thought I might want to espy his intentions," the Air Marshall said to Nolan while glancing quickly around the room from an upper level. "What *are* your intentions, Mr. Nolan?"

Before he could answer a flurry of activity erupted below where they stood.

The room had three levels – the bottom level had a large map table with the outline of southern England, the Channel and the northern coast of France. WAAFs wearing headphones and holding long thick tools like shuffleboard paddles stood around the table occasionally moving the markers. At a second level was a tier of mixed WAAFs and RAF officers seated at desks also wearing earphones and communicating now and then by telephone. On the third tier stood the Group Commander, another senior officer – apparently the Sector Commander – along with Dave and Aynslee. The sudden burst of energy in the room caused the movement of numerous blocks on the table, indicating radar sightings of inbound German planes and the movement of Spitfires to intercept.

"Here," Keith Park offered, handing him a set of earphones. "You might be interested in how this all works. And it does. So far, anyway. The Luftwaffe really haven't tested it yet, but small incursions like this help us fine tune our procedures."

Nolan put on the earphones and suddenly knew he was back in the middle of something desperate, only this time it was fifty miles away and thirty thousand feet in the air. Communications between the ground controller and the pilots were crisp and surprisingly matter-of-fact from what he heard in the headset. Over the next few minutes, markers on the board were constantly moved. More than a dozen people were talking on telephones, and the unseen young Spitfire pilots were methodically and calmly going about the business of trying to kill other young pilots in Luftwaffe uniforms. He was amazed at the composure of the fliers talking to the ground control and the relaxed tone of commands from 'Red Flight Leader' to his section leaders. Nolan wondered what the woman he heard in the earphones meant when she told the pilot to 'Buster.' Over the airwaves came the sound of machine guns firing during brief radio communications, and now came the sound of scared voices calling out '*on your tail, Blue three, turn to port now!*' or '*White four, come in White Four… anyone seen Paddy?…White leader to White Four, come in White Four.*'

Nolan found it impossible to grasp what was actually going on, to visualize and feel it at a visceral level. He'd led men by the hundreds into battle, had seen destruction at its worst and death of both friend and foe as close as the end of a bayonet – that had been horrific for him as a commander, but this seemed substantially worse. At least in close combat the leader could take some kind of personal action, but here in the sterility of the electronic command post there was nothing the Air Vice Marshall could do but worry, and maybe pray. The strain showed in the deep lines of his face and the worry that crept out from behind the mask of Brit stoicism.

The battle continued on for fifteen minutes and then just as suddenly as it started, it was over. There was a brief assessment of damage done and a report of the enemy turning back toward France, and the leader announced returning to refuel and rearm.

"In 11 Group's area we've been averaging ten or twelve skirmishes like that a day. This morning 74 squadron had a bit more of a dust-up near Folkestone." The Air Marshall grimaced and looked around the control room. "Dowding's system works well so far. We'll see when the Germans get serious – they outnumber us more than three to one in aircraft, and if we're to win, our boys will have to shoot down their boys at a rate of four of theirs for every one of ours. If we had pilots as experienced as the Luftwaffe's that would be much easier. Some of the young men in 54 squadron have less than twenty hours in a Spitfire. Things could get dicey."

Nolan talked to Park for a while afterward, testing what he'd heard from the maintenance people about quality and availability of parts. Finally, as the first call for supper came, he and Aynslee got into the staff car and motored out of the airfield.

"An informative day," Dave said, making a note on one of the pages he'd written. "Not what I'd planned, but very informative. I'd like to visit some other air bases to compare with what the people at Hornchurch told me, and then go north into the industrial heartland to work back to the source and see if I get the same answers. Where else would you recommend?"

"Debden, Kenley, Martlesham Heath. Possibly Northolt or Manston," Aynslee said, as if thinking out loud. "You'd get a good mix of Spits and Hurri's and even some old Defiants if you went to West Malling."

"None of those places were on the itinerary I first ginned up. After today, I'd say it would take at least two days per airfield to really find out what's going on at the end of the supply line. I've planned time at Army and Navy supply depots and at some of the major training bases, but this has all the makings of a longer trip than I expected." He furrowed his brow and tried to think through what that meant to his plan developed with Donovan before their departure. This was not going to work out the way he'd hoped, and if it was extended by as much as he thought now it might, Denise would not be happy.

"This was a really good day, Aynslee," Nolan said after a time as they traveled through farm country. It reminded him of Duncannon. In the middle of the summer the corn would be shoulder high and tomatoes would be holding on the vine. Carrots would be up as would lettuce and cabbage and squash. He wondered what the Brits raised over here. And that prompted another question – would the British be able to feed themselves? That was as important as whether or not they could produce the war material needed to keep planes flying and tanks rolling. That wasn't his worry – at least no one back in D.C. had brought it up in the many long briefings he'd had. Maybe that was Donovan's responsibility. *Got to ask him about it*, Nolan thought. *Can't believe I just now thought of that!*

Now, as Nolan looked out of the window at the quiet farmlands of shallow rolling hills and neatly manicured woods, he thought about the upcoming meeting with Joe Kennedy. Donovan had planned to meet with the ambassador soon to get the courtesy call out of the way.

Politics. How he hated the dishonesty and backstabbing. He wondered about the motivation of the ambassador and questioned why he would openly side against the British and his own country. He couldn't imagine himself involved in politics and wondered how Senator Payne, as decent a man as he'd ever known, had survived almost seven terms in Washington.

He'd seen some office politics and duplicity in the business world and often longed for the straightforward, no nonsense honesty in the ranks of the companies and battalions he'd commanded during his twenty-three years on active duty. Sure, there were the politicians, like that lieutenant colonel in Philippines Command... *what was his name? Rybicki.* There was Harrison Reeves who'd always played politics, and others he could count on the fingers of one hand. They were the exception rather than the rule. But for every Reeves there was an Andy Fauser, an Omar Bradley or a Barton Scarborough, and dozens more like them – the uncompromising line soldiers who kept it all together and upheld the honor of the profession. There was a time he liked to think maybe he was one of them.

"I enjoyed meeting your husband" Dave said after awhile when the silence seemed awkward. "How'd he get his nickname? Do you call him Muck like the fellas in his squadron?"

"No, sir. I find it rather offensive, but vulgarity seems a by-product of flying, soldiering in general perhaps. Especially when the lads have had too much to drink or they're in the ringer during a mission."

"I didn't hear any of that over the radio today."

"They were on their best behavior, because the word was out about you." She turned and smiled at him, for the first time since they'd met he thought, and he realized she was more attractive than he'd at first believed. "It isn't every day that –"

Her face went ashen as she looked out the window past his shoulder.

A half mile away and closing rapidly was a Messerschmitt Bf109 with flames coming from the right wing root and trailing a long streamer of dark gray smoke. As the plane pulled up to clear a tree line, one of the two Spitfires behind him let loose a burst of machine gun fire and the German plane shuddered, hit the ground hard and slid a hundred yards until coming to an abrupt stop. The nose dug into the earth and the tail section came up almost vertical, hesitated momentarily, and then slammed back down into the soft ground.

"Aynslee, pull into that lane!" he shouted, pointing, and when they'd gone a couple of hundred yards she stopped near the smoldering wreckage. He ran into the field and onto the wing of the German fighter almost before she got around the car. He was yanking on a lever at the bottom of the canopy and turned toward her. "Bring the tire iron!"

He managed to pry open the canopy, swing it over and pull the pilot free after undoing the shoulder harness. The German was unconscious and bleeding from a gash in his head; he'd been wounded in the left leg and his left sleeve had been cut in several places. Nolan pulled him down the wing and onto the ground and laid him on his back after dragging him thirty yards away. While Aynslee went to the staff car and retrieved an emergency aid kit from the boot, he ran back to the airplane to search the cockpit for maps and other intelligence until the flames drove him away. He returned to the unconscious pilot and checked for a pulse.

Nolan stood up and turned toward a group of a half dozen farmers who were walking down the gentle slope toward the plane. They were carrying tools – one had a long-handled shovel, two others had pitchforks, one had a scythe and the others carried oversized rakes with heavy metal tines. They looked angry.

Nolan stepped between them and the pilot.

"An' who might you be?" the oldest in the group said. He was medium height and stocky, and he was clearly unhappy.

"My name Nolan. I'm an American businessman. The WAAF is Corporal Glendenbrook, my driver for now."

"A Yank, eh? An' what gives ya the right to pull the Nazi outta 'is burnin' plane instead of lettin' 'im fry in it?"

"My driver and I are going to turn him over to the military so they can interrogate him," Nolan replied looking slowly at each face in the unhappy crowd.

"We got a better idea. You just turn him over ta us an' we'll take care of 'im."

"I don't think so. This is a military function, and the corporal will take care of him." The older man took a few steps forward him and Nolan held his hands in front of his chest to stop him. He took a deep breath and looked at the other faces – they all looked intent, suspicious and short on patience. "Let's not do anything foolish here, gentlemen."

One of the younger men laughed derisively. "Gentlemen you say?! Ain't no gentlemen 'ere, mate. Just us farmers. We all of us got buds or family in the Army and ever one 'ere knows someone what didn' make it back from Dunkirk. Just you hand over the Nazi and be on about your business."

"Afraid I can't do that. You see –"

"Sir!" It was Aynslee behind him, and when he turned he saw the German had gotten to his feet and had pulled a pistol, pointing it at his back.

Nolan turned slowly, raised his hands waist high with his palms open and stared into the eyes of the German pilot. Out of the corner of his eye he saw the band of farmers take a few steps back but none turned to run. "Aynslee, just slowly back away toward the car. Get out of his line of sight. Everything's going to be all right."

"What do ya think now, mate?" the older farmer said.

"He's scared, that's all. He's not going to shoot any of us. Stay where you are." Nolan continued gazing at the pilot and finally spoke in German. *"Surrender mein freund …* surrender friend, there is no way to escape. These men want to take you and do who knows what to you. I'm an American and not your enemy. I will see that no harm comes to you. But you have to put the gun away."

The pilot was less than enthusiastic. He looked as if he didn't necessarily trust Nolan and had even less faith in this band of farmers who appeared bent on killing him.

"Listen at that will ya?" one of the men behind him said. "The bloke is one o' them, talkin' that goose-steppin' gibberish and all. I say we take 'em both. Use the Yank as a shield and get the gun from the Nazi. He can't hit us all."

Nolan turned quickly toward them, pulled a large automatic pistol from beneath his suit coat and pointed it directly at the head of the older man who appeared to be the ringleader. "He might not get all of you, but I can… and I will. You men walk away now, and go on about your farming while the corporal and I get this prisoner to the authorities. Go!"

"An' if we don't?"

"You'll regret it, and so will your widows."

The men looked furtively at one another and finally the leader said, "Ya can't get us all and I'm bettin' you won't even try if you're a Yank like ya claim."

Nolan pointed the pistol between the man's feet. When it went off, the sound assaulted his ears and kicked up a large clod of dirt. He immediately raised the pistol and again pointed it at the man's forehead. "It's the largest caliber handgun my country makes. It holds seven rounds in the magazine and one in the chamber, so there's still plenty enough ammunition left. I've used this pistol for over twenty years and I'm an expert shot. If you make a move toward me, I'll assume aggressive intent and protect myself. I can fire three aimed shots in well under two seconds. You *do not* want me to demonstrate. So, go… now."

Slowly, the crowd stepped back and stopped, still looking at the pistol pointed at them.

"Please you men, leave us," Aynslee said in a loud voice. "This man is a special envoy from the U.S. President sent here at the request of the Prime Minister. He's here to determine if the Americans should come help us fight the Germans. If he goes back with the message that we are all a bunch of killers no better than the Nazis, we will be left without their help."

"The bloody hell you say," the older man said, trying to hide his fear of this crazy Yank with the big bore gun. He looked at Nolan disgustedly and said, "Bugger off, Mr. Nolan. We don't need no bleedin' heart allies who would rather shoot Englishmen than Nazis." With a shrug, he turned away and walked back toward the small wooded rise a half mile east with each of the men in his group looking back at Nolan and the burning plane.

Nolan finally de-cocked the pistol, returned it to the shoulder holster and looked at the German pilot. "Now, my friend, hand over your weapon and let's take a look at your wounds."

"I could escape now, you know," the wounded pilot said in his native tongue.

"You wouldn't get far on foot. Even if I allowed you to take our car, you'd stand out with all the crazy traffic rules on this island that you'd violate. Suppose you made it to the coast – how would you get back to France? Swim? and you need medical attention. Give me the gun and let us bandage you up before you bleed to death." Nolan held out his hand and finally the German pilot handed over the pistol.

Aynslee began bandaging the cut on the German's forehead and said, "You really wouldn't have shot any of those farmers."

"Question or observation, Aynslee?"

"Both probably, sir."

"Tell you the truth, I'm not sure. They would have murdered this guy if we had let them. Mistreating prisoners is serious business, I know. And murdering one is an international crime – which doesn't make a difference if England wins the war. No, I probably wouldn't have killed them, but I darned sure would have disabled 'em."

"I didn't know you were carrying a weapon, sir. I'm surprised."

"I'm surprised that you're *not* carrying one. In a war zone only twenty minutes away from the German front line, it only makes sense. If the RAF has machine guns and other security set up around its bases – like Hornchurch – why shouldn't everybody be armed? Do you think the Germans are going to invade?"

"They say they are. Perhaps you have a point, sir."

"You can count on it."

Aynslee looked at the tall American as she wound the bandage around the German pilot's forehead. Nolan was examining the Luger, inspecting it like a jeweler appraising a fine gem, removing the magazine and opening the jointed arm breech.

He was different than she'd expected. Her father had told her he was one of the most decorated soldiers in the American army during the first war, and that he'd escaped from the large hospital where they'd met in order to return to his unit. That was all well and good in the abstract, but the brief and violent episode with the farmers had been all too real. He clearly didn't shy away from conflict or personal danger. Yet, he was self-effacing and had a sense humor. A regular bloke.

"It was a very brave thing you did, sir," Aynslee said when she finished her first aid on their prisoner.

Nolan opened the action on the pistol and wryly smiled at her. "Not so brave, really. Look in there. What do you see?"

"I don't see anything , sir."

"That's the point. This elite member of the *Master Race* didn't even have a round in the chamber. What kind of soldier fails to load his weapon when defending his life?" Nolan shook his head. "Where's the closest military facility where we can unload a prisoner?"

"There's a small training garrison up the road a bit. Six or eight kilometers, sir."

"That'll do. I'll ride in the back with Baron von Richthofen here."

As she started up the car, she looked in the rear view mirror and saw Nolan showing their prisoner the empty pistol and heard him lecturing in German. When his reprimand ended with the word *dummkopf* she thought it was the funniest thing she'd seen or heard in donkey's years.

Chapter 6

Harrison Reeves was described in many different ways by a variety of people.

He viewed himself as shrewd, driven, and admittedly opinionated, but only as much as was required by his discerning instincts and deeper purpose.

Those above him in the Army's chain of command called him brilliant and ambitious – a young general who got results and set the pace for the Department of the Army staff in Washington. To those who worked directly for him, he was extremely demanding, often petty and prone to take the credit for the best work of his subordinates; they knew him as an officer who showed one face which he played up the chain, but another when dealing downward.

His superiors called him well-studied, calm, assured, and given to serious contemplation concerning every assignment and any question put to him. His subordinates, on the other hand, considered him short on command experience, dismissive of those who had served time in the trenches during and after the war in Europe, and prone to jumping to conclusions. His peers viewed him as vain, narcissistic, and essentially untrustworthy.

That he had few friends – which had been the case from middle school through his cadet years at West Point – didn't bother him. What friendships he'd had throughout his life were rare, short-lived and always ended abruptly when he no longer had need of them. He was the first in his class to attain his first star, which didn't terribly surprise anyone who knew him.

Even his marriage to Michelle Payne, the only child of Pennsylvania's senior senator, had likewise been to him a calculated arrangement of convenience. She was still exceptionally attractive and made a stunning companion at the high visibility social and political events he attended. Her father's good offices and his vote in the Senate were essential to Reeves getting his first star as a brigadier general and would be similarly necessary for the ones to follow.

One thing everyone agreed upon was that as the Army's Deputy Personnel Chief, he was showing the strain of being bombarded with the demands being placed on him with the war in France having come to an ignominious conclusion. It appeared obvious to those in the War Department that the president would one day soon have to abandon his stance on American neutrality and go to the full bore support of England. That would mean an explosive increase in the size of the Army virtually overnight. Much of that burden would fall on the shoulders of Brigadier General Harrison Gibson Reeves, West Point class of 1916. That was all true, but it wasn't the reason for General Reeve's grim and infuriated look on the late July afternoon when he returned home from his fourth inspection tour of training bases in the last seven weeks.

Two people, both civilians, were the reasons for his blood boiling: one was a classmate and the other a contractor.

Harrison Reeves could hold a grudge, and he had been nursing one against Dave Nolan most of his life. His West Point classmate had gained Reeves' wrath and everlasting enmity years earlier during a Saturday morning plebe boxing class. In an instant of pain and embarrassment suffered at the hand of an 'inferior' from an unknown river town in Pennsylvania, a lifelong animosity had been born in Reeves' heart.

Reeves had ensured a serious charge of mistreating German prisoners was made against Nolan during the war; he'd made certain a number of awards for valor for which Nolan was recommended were rejected. Then, at the conclusion of the European conflict, Reeves had married the woman to whom his classmate had once been engaged. Reeves always looked upon it as the 'great trifecta' and had continued to subtly bedevil Nolan and work against his career until his resignation and retirement from military service a few years earlier.

The problem was that now the man had somehow recovered and instead of being able to continue gloating over besting this classmate, Reeves had returned home to learn Nolan was now in London with William Donovan acting as the president's personal envoy to Prime Minister Churchill. *That* made him angry.

The other person adding to his bad temperament was the Baltimore contractor who had parked his beat up truck in his circular gravel driveway and was sitting in his living room along with a man in a suit holding a briefcase.

"Why is Langer sitting in my parlor rather than working on the gardener's cottage," Reeves angrily demanded of his wife, as he entered the kitchen and dropped his suitcase in the mud room. "And who is that in there with him?"

Michelle looked up from the built-in desk where a stack of papers sat in an untidy pile. "That's the greeting I get after you've been gone almost three weeks?"

He looked at her impatiently. "As if you wanted something pleasant or inviting, dear one. Just tell me what that thieving builder wants this time."

"He wants his money. And he's brought his lawyer. If Mr. Langer doesn't walk out of here with what you owe him, he's going to stop work permanently and the lawyer is going to leave behind a contractor's lien on the cottage, and this house."

"What?!" Reeves asked irritably. "What kind of nonsense is this?"

"It's the kind of nonsense that happens when you don't pay your bills, Harrison."

"That's insane. I don't owe Langer any money."

Michelle got up from the desk, walked to the kitchen table and picked up one of the stacks sitting there. She shook the sheets in front of his face and said, "This says differently. And so do the rest. These are all bills overdue for payment I found in your office among all the trash piled on top of your desk. It took me all morning to sort through everything and put it some kind of order. For crying out loud, Harrison, you haven't touched anything in there for almost two months, some of it longer."

He scoffed at her and rolled his eyes. "I've been busy."

"You've been traveling almost constantly. I know that."

"And I'm leaving again Monday with Colonel Scarborough for a swing down the eastern seaboard to inspect our training facilities there."

"Barton Scarborough? I thought you canned him and sent him off to the Gobi or the Sahara or one of those other deserts months ago for some crime you imagined or engineered."

"I was going to, and I will eventually, but for the moment he's useful to me. Don't try to disrupt my train of thought," he said irritably, walking to the sink to draw a glass of water before sitting down at the kitchen table. "How can we possibly owe Langer anything?"

Michelle placed a stack of bills in front of him. "These are four bills on the cottage he's submitted dating back to the middle of May. One is for materials, another for the stone mason, the third for the tumbled stone and finally the labor to install the walkway and porch. All of these are past due, and I found them thrown in with other bills for the completion of this house, which are also overdue. Be glad I was able to convince him not to issue that lien on our property until you got back. He and his lawyer have been here for hours."

"I've never seen these bills," Reeves replied, sifting through the papers.

"I don't doubt that," his wife replied sarcastically. "But there they are."

"The man is perpetrating a fraud. I won't stand for it."

"You tell him that. Meanwhile, I'll go upstairs, pack and then call your father or mine and see if I can stay with them for the next few months while you and our lawyers try to work this out." She frowned, disgusted and distressed. "This is embarrassing, really embarrassing, Harrison. And it's all because you're so perfectly disorganized when it comes to our finances. This isn't the first time something like this has happened. Remember that fracas at Benning over payments on our little farm there?"

"An oversight, my dear, quickly remedied and soon forgotten, except for you it seems."

"How about when we were at Belvoir? Was that another oversight?"

"That was the fault of the bank or the investment firm, or more likely both."

"Sure, it was their fault you didn't tell the firm to move money into the account so you could write a check that wouldn't bounce. It's always somebody else's fault, isn't it, Harrison?

Now you'll probably blame me for this one, but the truth is, I don't handle any of the money because you won't let me."

"You certainly seem to spend enough of it," he replied spitefully, rising and going to the cabinet where he kept a bottle of scotch. "I'll have Langer give us an extension until I can get back in two or three weeks and move some money into the checking account to cover those bills. I hope you saw to it my extra uniforms are cleaned and pressed. I'll need one for tonight, and another for the trip Monday."

"Of course your uniforms are ready, but you need to understand there are more bills than just the ones from the contractor."

"What do you mean, more bills?" he asked.

"There are some things around the house that need taking care of – the gutters got pulled away from the front of the house during a thunderstorm. There's a tree down on the south side of the house that needs to be cut up and hauled away. And a few other things with the plumbing and the electricity need repairing."

"So? Tell Luther to get on them. You don't need me to tell you that."

"No, I don't. But –" She paused and took a deep breath. "You know, Harrison, I hate the way you talk down to me all the time. I would have told Luther, but he and our cook quit last week. So, if you want meals from now on, you're going to have to fix them for yourself. They quit because they needed money. When was the last time you paid them?"

Harrison Reeves looked even more angry than when he first entered the house. He poured Scotch into his glass and drank. "Honestly, I don't remember. It's been a very busy couple of months what with the war in Europe and all that could mean for us. I have *responsibilities*, and I can't be terribly worried about the hired help."

"Luther and Mildred both have families. They can't wait until you have time to get around to paying them. People like them live hand to mouth – they have kids to feed and they can't float loans to people like you simply because you're busy."

"People like us you mean."

"No, Harrison, I mean people like you. I would have paid them, and paid on time because I know exactly what they're going through, and I care about them. You don't. You don't even think about them enough to pay what you owe when you owe it. Why don't you let me take care of the household finances? Do you trust me that little?"

The truth was he *didn't* trust her, and never had from the time they first met at his father's Christmas party three weeks after the Armistice ending the last war. But more than that, allowing her the freedom to run the household would loosen his grip on her, and the one thing he would not easily give up was the pleasure he derived from making her ask for everything she needed or wanted. It galled him now that she was back working part time for her father training that Nolan girl and making sure she was set up in the little D.C. townhouse. The pleasure she got from that frustrated him and he'd ordered her not to get involved. But she'd done it anyway, and his absences had not allowed him the opportunity to put a stop to it. One of these day he would.

"Maybe it's a good thing our housekeeper and maintenance man left since Langer and his attorney are going to put a lien on this place. At least they can find other jobs now. You understand, don't you, that by placing a lien on our property they can keep us from living here or using any of it until the disagreement is settled? How embarrassing that would be!" She shrugged indifferently. "Maybe I'll go live with Erika and Megan in town until you have the time to get it all straightened out."

He looked at the bills submitted by Langer and then started to read the multi-page legal document from a prestigious Baltimore law firm. Lawyers. He hated them as much as he despised Scarborough and Nolan and that Arkansas hillbilly, Andy Fauser. *Life would be infinitely more pleasant if one didn't have to deal with the likes of them*, he thought. Looking at his watch, he realized both his financial advisor and the family lawyer would be long departed from work and since it was Friday afternoon wouldn't be back until well after he was on his way to Georgia on the Monday morning train. For a fleeting instant, he allowed himself the indulgence of anticipating dinner tonight in Annapolis with the buxom redhead from the Navy personnel directorate.

"All right, Michelle," Reeves said finally, exasperated and worried about running late for dinner. "I'll set up a checking account so you can run the household. But that's all it's for. Satisfied? What do you need to run the household?"

"I'll need fifteen hundred a month at least."

"Fifteen hundred?! That's crazy!"

"You're right – it's more like two thousand with utilities and upkeep on the cottage," she said and looked beyond his shoulder, counting on her fingers. "What about the lien?"

"I'll write a check to Langer for the total amount of these four bills and –"

"Look closer, there's seven total. Four for the cottage and three for the addition for the main house you decided on at the last minute."

"All right, for all seven. But I'll have to post date them for Tuesday. You'll have to go to Steele at the investment firm and get him to move money to my checking account."

"Actually, that's two checks. Mr. Langer wants it divided between the cottage and the house for his personal bookkeeping. Apparently he has his own accounting system and problems. I told him we'd be willing to do that."

"Fine," he said impatiently. "Fine. Whatever makes him happy at this point."

"His lawyer also has some papers for you to sign. They're acknowledgements of the contract obligation to pay upon receipt and the advisement that the next bill payment we miss will result in immediate filing of a lien against the property. What do I do about trying to hire back Luther and Mildred? I really would like to get them back, but if I can't I'll have to look for other help. In any case, we still owe them back pay. Give me a letter for the bank so I can set up an account for the house, and a letter for Mr. Steele to move some money into it."

"Sure, sure," Reeves answered, looking at his watch and realizing he was cutting it close to get to Annapolis before his dinner at eight. "Type up the letters and I'll sign them. Get my checkbook so I can write the checks."

"I can't do the letters before you leave tonight. You'll have to sign them this weekend before your next trip. When are you leaving?"

"Very early Monday morning. I'll have to stop by the office tomorrow or Sunday, at any rate; sometime before I catch the train. I'm meeting myself coming and going any more." He sighed, as if woefully overburdened. "I wish I didn't have to go to this dinner tonight."

Sure, welcome home, Harrison, she thought, wondering if any others in his traveling entourage had planned a late dinner on their first night back from an extended trip.

Michelle retrieved the check book from Harrison's office, wrote the checks and got him to sign them and the multiple pages needing his signature before he headed upstairs to shower.

When she entered the living room, Mr. Langer and the lawyer rose and thanked her for the coffee she'd made for them; after giving them what they had been patiently waiting for, Michelle escorted them outside to their vehicles.

"I guess I'm still a little confused, Mrs. Reeves," the contractor said after getting into his truck and starting the engine. "I appreciate you getting me payments for the cottage, but like I said, there wasn't any reason for me to stop work on it this week. And who was that lawyer?"

"A friend of my father's. He's doing me a favor."

"All right, Mrs. Reeves. We'll be back out Monday morning bright and early."

"I'll look forward to seeing you, Mr. Langer."

She watched him turn down the driveway toward the heavy wrought iron gate down the shallow hill at the end of the lane. *How pretentious this damned place is,* she thought, looking first at the gate and the gatehouse and then around the forty-five acre estate. It was just a little larger than his father's – and it was newer. But it wasn't quite finished yet, two years after beginning the project. Harrison was a terrible project manager; always waiting until the last minute to change his mind and then getting in the way. It was a good thing the contractor had the patience of Job.

Her husband had no idea what he'd asked for or when, or the cost involved. Like most men who'd grown up accustomed to wealth, he had little appreciation for money and no concept of his own finances. He was like a child in many ways, thinking there would always be money available as if all that was necessary to fund his whims was to call the brokerage firm or the bank or the family lawyer and quote a figure and magically it would appear in his account.

The details of financial management bored him and that was why it was so easy to convince him that he'd woefully mismanaged the finances of the construction and the household staff. She wasn't about to dissuade him of that – not yet.

Michelle watched the lawyer get into and start his car. He was a young man two years out of law school who occasionally stopped into the office to see her father over his committee business. Now, with the arrival of Erika Nolan, his visits seemed to be more frequent. He pulled forward and stopped next to her.

"He signed it," Randall Ashby said, winking at her. "I'll complete the document and notarize it tonight. By tomorrow morning you'll have his durable power of attorney."

"You sure you're all right with this?" Michelle asked.

"I am. Absolutely. Just you be careful."

"I will," she replied and stepped back.

She had finally done it. After twenty-two years of a debilitating marriage she was going to fight back against all the public slights and private degradations. He would pay for the verbal abuse of her mind and physical violence against her body... and his infidelities – beginning on their honeymoon in the Aegean after the War.

Michelle was determined she was no longer going to be his doormat.

For the first time in a long while she felt magnificently free.

Chapter 7

A sudden gust threatened to blow Kathleen Stroud's straw hat into the marina's waters.

The westerly breeze blew in across the Great Sound, and entered the cozy confines of Hamilton's inner harbor. She stood on the Pan Am dock with the morning sun at her back looking over the forest of masts at the Royal Bermuda Yacht Club. This last week had been the most incredible time in her life.

He'd filled her days with forays around the island on his motorbike or swimming in the small secluded beaches along the south shore. He'd wined and dined her most evenings in one of Hamilton's restaurants or at one of the hotels. Afterward, he'd take her to a club to jitterbug or listen to a steel drum band.

On an afternoon ride, they discovered Fort St. Catherine outside the old 17th century town of St. George. They spent the afternoon in a small pub overlooking Tobacco Bay drinking a bottle of wine while listening to the songs of an old sailor – a white haired Portuguese man strumming his mandolin and singing sailing ditties he had learned as a boy from his father and grandfather. And each night they returned to the outcropping of rock set high above Horseshoe Bay. It was her favorite place and she never tired of going back there with him.

He was so different from the young men she'd dated from Penn or Temple, or Drexel. Their awkward approaches at the end of a date seemed juvenile compared to this would-be pilot who knew how to kiss a girl.

One afternoon he dared her to swim with him out to the barrier reef which he said was closer than it really looked. She was terrified but did it, and was glad she had when it was over.

Now as she looked across the harbor toward where the small square houses brightly painted colorful pastels of blue and yellow and pink, she felt overwhelmed by a melancholy she couldn't define. Her vacation was coming to an end and with it an episode which she knew could never be replicated.

She wondered whether or not he would show up, and hoped these past few days had been as important to him as they had been to her. As much as she wished it were otherwise, she was afraid that this brief interlude had meant little or nothing to him.

"I've been watching you pace back and forth, looking over the yacht basin and trying to keep that hat of yours from blowing off into the water."

Her heart jumped and she turned quickly when she heard his voice.

"You were spying," she said. "I don't know that I like being secretly observed."

"I did it all the time these past few days and every time you caught me you smiled. Are you saying you don't like guys looking at you?"

"Some guys yes, some no. Are you trying to start an argument?"

He looked quickly at his wristwatch then over his shoulder down towards the Imperial Airways terminal building at the end of the dock. "The answer would be yes if I thought we had enough time before your parents came back to go over to the boat and make up."

She blushed and quickly turned away so he wouldn't see her smile. It was the kind of remark she had grown to expect from him. One night after dinner at a restaurant down on Front Street in Hamilton they had gone back to the sailboat for an hour until his two friends came back and banged on the locked door leading below decks. "I'd like that," she said quietly.

"So would I. But I don't think that's going to happen today."

"Will you come by to see me in Annapolis?"

"I don't know that I can. I have to get back up to New York to see my family before I go off to flight school down south. I'm cutting it pretty close as it is."

"But you'll write," she said, making it sound like a settled fact rather than a question.

"As soon as I possibly can. I really don't know what happens at flight school. Most military schooling begins with a long period of hazing that seems woven into the fabric of our training. When I was a plebe at the Academy the first two months were called Beast Barracks. And I don't remember either receiving or being allowed to send a letter those first eight weeks that summer. "

"And you think you'll have to go through that again? That sounds awfully silly – doing that to officers who graduated from that school."

"It's tradition. A friend of my father's likes to say that it's years of tradition unhampered by progress. I don't see anything in the military mindset changing that."

"You're saying not to expect a letter from you anytime soon, is that right?"

"As much as I wish it weren't so… but *I will* write – that's a promise."

Kathleen looked away, disappointed. When she looked back at him tears danced along her lower lids and she tried to blink them away. "This has been the best summer vacation of my life," she said softly. "I wish this didn't have to end so soon."

"Me too," Mitch replied earnestly. "You're quite a gal, Kate. I don't think I've ever met anybody quite like you, and I doubt I ever will again. I wish we had had more time."

"Oh, Mitch, please come back with me. My father says the plane isn't full and he said he'd be glad to loan you the money. How many times did you tell me that you always wanted to fly on a Pan Am Clipper?"

He looked away and slowly shook his head. "As tempting as that is, I just couldn't do it. Seventy-five dollars is a lot of money to a brand-new second lieutenant, and at my pay level it would take me years to pay back. Wasn't it Emerson who said: *neither a lender nor borrower be...* That also has to be the motto of a junior officer in this man's Army. And I don't take charity – my father drummed that into me all my life." He took both her hands in his and gazed into her eyes for a silent moment.

"Is this the end of it? Is this all there is?" she asked. "I don't want it to be. I pray it's not, but the look in your eyes and the tone in your voice tells me it is."

"Kate, I really don't know. You have three more years of Bryn Mawr and I have nine months of flight school and who knows where I'll go after that. There's a war going on in Europe and across the Pacific rim. Nobody really knows what the future holds for people like me, and I'm not a prophet or the son of a prophet. I have to take each day as it comes and see where it leads me. I can't make any promises, as much as I'd like to, and as much as I'd like to make them to you." He looked westward, his face troubled. "My father's a business man, and from what *your* father tells me a pretty decent one. He always told me it was best to under promise and over perform."

"Promise me again you'll write."

"I'll promise. But it could be a long time before I can." He hugged her and whispered in her ear. "I'll never forget you, or the moments we shared here in this place."

"I won't either... oh, Mitch. I've been wondering for years where all the really good guys went. And when I finally find one, he can't or won't commit."

"Life isn't fair... I've also been wondering for years where all the beautiful and extraordinary women were. At least I can say I know where one of them is. Kate, whatever you do, don't change. If our paths do cross again, I want to know you're going to stay that same wonderful girl I spent so many amazing moments with in this place."

She kissed him, then stepped back as if recoiling from him, looking over his shoulder. "My father," she said quietly, looking down for a brief second.

Mitch released her, turned and said, "Mr. Stroud, Kathleen and I were just saying our goodbyes, I'm glad to be able to say bon voyage to you and your wife as well."

"Sure you don't want to fly back on the Clipper with us?" the man said. "I was hoping to be able to pry out of you during our flight home your father's contracting secrets. But it seems you're just as cagey as he is."

"Not at all, sir," Mitch replied, extending his hand. "Like I said, my father always has been tight lipped about his business so I really have nothing on my piece of paper that I can share with you. But one day I hope to hear more stories about you and Lefty Grove in the minor leagues and about that drop ball I never could get the hang of throwing."

"I'll take you up on that." He shook Nolan's hand and helped his wife into the Imperial Airways barge for the short trip across the harbor.

"When will you get back to Annapolis?" Kate asked him as he gave her a hug.

"Probably another week," Mitch replied. "My friends want to stay here another day or two before heading back. I'd just as soon leave today – without you here there's not much I'm looking forward to doing."

She looked up into his face and smiled bravely. "The rest of my summer is a waste of time. You have really messed up the remainder of my vacation, Mitch Nolan."

Kate threw her arms around his neck pulled his face close and gave him a quick hard kiss. Then she turned abruptly and descended the short walkway. The barge was almost at the far side of the Royal Bermuda Yacht Club basin when she at last turned and gave him a short wave just as the boat went out of sight.

Mitch stood on the Imperial Airways dock and watched the Inner Harbor for a few minutes after Kate and her family had gone. Finally, he walked to where he had parked his motorbike, and rode east until he passed the small white gazebo in the middle of the road that marked the beginning of Front Street. Just up ahead sat an ocean liner so close to the road that it looked like a great beached whale hovering over the town. He parked the motorbike across from the ship where he saw Lucky and Marv waiting.

"You got here just in time," Marv said. "They finally got that thing docked. We hear this might be the last cruise ship to stop here until after that situation in Europe gets straightened out. This could work out just fine for guys like us."

Soon people began to emerge from the ship, strolling down the walkway and stepping into the bright early-morning Bermuda sun. There were quite a few younger women; Mitch looked over towards where Lucky was pointing and saw the three girls immediately – one of them caught his attention.

She looked Latin or Mediterranean. She was gorgeous, and she was smiling at him.

The Bermuda Clipper passed directly overhead. He looked up and fleetingly thought about the girl from Annapolis.

"Lucky," Mitch said, "you guys are on your own. I'm going for a ride."

Chapter 8

Wild Bill Donovan detested Ambassador Joe Kennedy.

Nolan knew that truth unambiguously from their conversations in Washington before the long flight over, but when they breakfasted at *Claridge's* before finally meeting with the ambassador, it seemed his old commander's adamant dislike of the man had grown. Years of observation had left Nolan's wartime commander with a profound contempt for Kennedy's nasty spirit and bad-tempered personality.

"The man has no objectivity and even less integrity," Donovan told him over breakfast. "The more I've learned on this trip the less I like about him. And it hasn't helped that he's tried to derail everything you and I are doing over here. I told you his comment about Edgar Mowrer, didn't I?"

"Something about not needing a newspaperman to make an investigation for the government and it being a further embarrassment to him and the country."

Edgar Ansel Mowrer was a reporter, a good one with contacts all over the continent and at the highest levels within the British government. The reporter also had frequent contact with Allen Dulles back in D.C. Donovan had hired him to do his own independent investigation with his own sources; that had been a tipping point for Kennedy. In addition to touching base with all his contacts, Mowrer had dined already with Churchill, inspected some defense facilities, and had dinner with Donovan the night before to share observations.

"Kennedy also sent word back to Washington that you and I should be recalled and this mission should be canceled. But he's not going to be very effective in that. If he doesn't know it yet he'll soon find out. He may have been close to Chamberlain and the Cliveden set of British appeasers but Churchill has no time at all for him. He still keeps trying to shut us down because he's afraid that one of my recommendations when I return to Washington is that he be fired."

"Is that going to be one of your recommendations?"

"No. I already told that to the State Department before we left. Besides, I have a lot more important things to tell the people back in Washington. I've had lunch with Winston Churchill, twice, I inspected the hastily thrown up defenses on the south coast, the Dowding system – which I understand you looked at as well – and even spent some time in the underground nerve center of the British government in London. At least somebody was clairvoyant enough to set that up a few years back. I've had more than one briefing from Rear Admiral Godfrey's intelligence people in London, and several with the military staff. I keep my reports and my notes in the hotel safe, but I've had a copy made for you. And I appreciate the drafts of your own reports that you've been sending me. Good information in there Nolan."

Dave looked casually around the room. "I still don't understand why we have to go to the embassy and spend time with Kennedy."

"Protocol. It would be bad form if we didn't. That's all there is to it."

After the comments made by Henry Smythe-Browne while they were in Berlin together years earlier, Dave had done some of the research on his own into the life and background of their Ambassador to England. He had been amazed and appalled. Joe Kennedy was one of the richest men in the United States. He had supposedly made his fortune in the stock market, in movies, and through various illicit means including bootlegging during Prohibition.

"Did Kennedy partner with organized crime during Prohibition?" Dave asked.

"There's some evidence of that. Not enough to prosecute in court. Why do you ask?"

"Just curious. I wondered how a man with no real business to run made so much money that he could dabble in the movies or play the stock market to make a fortune. Why would the president associate with such a person?"

"He made substantial contributions to FDR's presidential campaigns but the president never has trusted him. He never offered him a cabinet position; however, Roosevelt did allow himself to be successfully lobbied to make Kennedy the ambassador to England." Donovan shook his head and looked disgusted. "So far, Kennedy's made himself roundly disliked in England for his defeatism and cowardice. He leaves London before dark to spend his nights at a country estate he's renting, and he's sent his wife and family back to Boston. And this is what get's me: I'm convinced he's engaged in profiteering from this war. He's been commandeering valuable transatlantic cargo space for importation of British scotch and gin to his export-import company back in the States. Once a rum-runner, always a rum-runner."

Nolan was shocked. "Protocol or not, I say we skip this."

"Sorry, can't do it," Donovan replied uncomfortably "I hate to drag you into this today, Nolan. It won't be fun and old Joe will likely be confrontational. He's not going to confront me directly but he'll try to lean on you. I hope you're up to it. Are you?"

"If you don't know the answer to that, you're not the same man I served under in the 69th during the last war."

Donovan suppressed a smile. "Just checking. All right, tell me more about your trip to Hornchurch. I hear you stirred up some trouble with the locals. After we leave the embassy we're going directly to Whitehall to brief Churchill, and he has some questions for you."

"Questions?"

"He wants to know why he's getting angry letters about an American pulling a gun on British farmers. Know anything about that?"

Dave nodded slowly. "I had to keep a crowd of men from killing a prisoner of mine. I'm real sensitive about how German prisoners are treated and I think you know why."

"A little incident in Cirey?"

"The very one." It wasn't surprising the incident should come to both their minds.

He still had bad dreams about the episode in a little French town when he commanded a company in Donovan's battalion. He had been accused of mistreating German prisoners his company had captured in a night raid and three day occupation of a village which happened to be the headquarters of a German infantry regiment. The allegations were untrue of course, and the investigation by a colonel in the 82nd Division had exonerated him completely but he remembered very clearly the initial thoughts that went through his mind when he heard the charges. The false allegation had gotten a life of its own and it had scared him. He wondered what the Prime Minister of England had actually heard, and where this might lead.

"All right Nolan, finish up and let's to do our duty call on the ambassador."

They were driven across town by Donovan's driver and dropped at the front door of the U.S. Embassy. They introduced themselves to the ambassador's personal secretary and were asked to have a seat in the anteroom and wait until the ambassador was ready. They cooled their heels for a quarter hour until Donovan finally walked to the secretary's desk.

"Please tell the ambassador that we appreciate his willingness to speak with us, and we understand the demands of his schedule. However, Mr. Nolan and I also have tight schedules and we're very busy people. We'll take our leave now, thank you."

They were halfway down the hall when the ambassador caught up to them, apologized profusely for the delay, and ushered them both into his nicely appointed office.

"I'm so sorry William," Joe Kennedy said apologetically. "I'm sure you know better than most how difficult these times are and how much demand is placed on the diplomatic corps."

"I do, Mr. Ambassador," Donovan replied evenly. "These are difficult times for us all and you're certainly correct in pointing out everyone's busy schedule. We won't take much of your time. It seemed appropriate to visit with you and inform you that our mission has gone well and is nearly complete."

"Excellent. Excellent. That's good to know. I'd love to hear more." Kennedy sat in his big leather chair behind the desk and said, "Tell me, William, what will you be reporting to the president?" The ambassador appeared strangely nervous, frowning and glaring at them through the small round lenses of his wire-framed glasses.

"I can't divulge the findings of our inquiries just yet, Mr. Ambassador."

"Really? Not even to the president's ambassador to England? That's unusual, don't you think?" Kennedy said. "I'm surprised you're unwilling to share with America's top diplomat in this country the findings of a diplomatic mission."

"Actually, Mr. Ambassador, this is not a diplomatic mission but an intelligence mission, a military mission and an industrial mission. The State Department will forward you a copy of our final report." Donovan was stiff and formal in a way Nolan had never seen before. "But I can tell you the thrust of our recommendations – America should make every effort we can to help England. And it doesn't help their cause or ours for people representing the United States to keep telling the British they can't and won't win in a fight against Hitler's Nazism."

Kennedy looked displeased and his face grew even more tight and pinched. He glowered first at Donovan and then at Dave Nolan. "Tell me Mr. Nolan what is your official standing in all this? I don't find your name listed anywhere on the rolls of the State Department, War Department, the various intelligence agencies or any other agency of the federal government for that matter. So why are you here?"

"I'm a businessman. I'm here to assess the British production capacity and capability for Mr. Donovan and for my own company, Barrett Enterprises."

"That's all?" Kennedy's tone seemed to carry a mild rebuke and a trace of incredulity.

"That's it," Dave replied easily, with a slight smile, all the while bristling over the clearly condescending reproach. It was a feeling reminiscent of the anger he'd felt at the comments made by the French officers at General deBazelaire's headquarters the day they had presented him the *Croix de Guerre* for what he'd done during a nighttime patrol in the last war.

"Are you in agreement with Mr. Donovan then that details of diplomatic missions such as yours are not to be shared with your nation's top diplomat in England?"

"Well sir, I can't remember a time in my life I ever disagreed with Wild Bill Donovan," Nolan replied, "and I certainly don't now. Both he and I were given very specific instructions in Washington concerning our chain of command and our responsibilities to those in it. I'm afraid, sir, that you aren't a link in that chain."

Kennedy clearly didn't like that answer. "Why have you decided I'm not in that chain of command, Mr. Nolan?"

"I didn't decide that, Mr. Ambassador. Somebody much higher than me who is more well informed and more intelligent than I made that decision."

"So what you're saying is that I've been intentionally bypassed. Why would that be?"

Dave was very uncomfortable with the direction of this line of questioning. "Sir, I think that's a question for somebody in the office of the Secretary of State or perhaps the Oval Office. I'm sure you have your own suspicions."

Joe Kennedy looked back and forth between Donovan and Dave Nolan. Finally he said, "Well gentlemen, it appears then we have nothing to talk about. You've done your duty call to the embassy – not that it meant or accomplished anything. You're free to go. I'm sure you can find your way out."

When they were outside waiting for the driver to pick them up Donovan said, "He's worried, and he should be. He'll be gone before the fall elections."

Nolan raised his eyebrows and looked sideways at Wild Bill. "You know that? How?"

"Friends close to the president. FDR has access to the ambassador's tax returns through J. Edgar Hoover and ol' Joe has IRS problems."

"That sounds worrisome – and frankly, it also sounds un-American."

"That's Washington, where they play politics with a hardball."

The car arrived and they climbed into the back seat for the short ride to Whitehall. Nolan thought about what he'd heard and seen in the last few minutes. He found himself in a different world, populated by harsh people and even harsher realities, and he didn't like the feel of it. There was an absence of the ethical code he'd learned to expect in the Army – when an officer gave you his word, you could count on it, with only a few exceptions. Harrison Reeves came to mind, but he was more politician than soldier. Nolan decided when this task was over, he'd get far away from politics and politicians – as fast as he could.

Beneath the treasury chambers in Whitehall the British had converted a labyrinth of centuries old vaults, dungeons and tunnels into an underground command post. The passages through this rabbit's warren of a maze extended from Whitehall, to the home office, Downing Street, Waterloo Station, and even Trafalgar Square.

The Cabinet war room was imposing and Nolan felt a certain sense of important history as he walked through some of the passages and into the place where the prime minister held the meetings that everyone in government called the 'Midnight Follies'. It was like stepping back into an original stage production of a just-penned Shakespearean play. They descended the spiral staircase into the war room where Churchill and his personal secretary, Jack Colville, greeted them warmly.

"This is where I'll sit if the Nazi invasion ever comes," the British prime minister said in his gravelly voice. He looked directly at Dave Nolan said, "Right here. This is my place until the Germans are driven back or they carry me out dead. I will not surrender. Never."

"I believe you, sir," Nolan replied, strangely at ease in the presence of this imposing figure. "Our first day here at *Claridge's* a boy about ten or eleven showed us the same attitude. It seems you've infused it into all of your people – at least the ones I've met."

"I imagine you'll find we English are a crotchety lot. And I hope we're a lot more than that if an invasion comes. We won't give up this little island of ours very easily, and I think on the whole you'll find us a very tough crowd in a fight – every last one of us."

"I believe that too, sir. In fact I got a taste of that my second day in the country. I understand you've heard of it already." *Might as well pull the blanket off of this incident, put a spotlight on it and put it to bed*, Nolan thought. He saw Churchill's face draw down into a frown as he chewed vigorously on a cigar.

"I have," he said sullenly, and let the silence linger.

"Brigadier Smythe-Browne's daughter, Corporal Glendenbrook, was driving us back to her father's estate after visiting Hornchurch. We'd gone a few kilometers when a German Bf109 crashed in a field very close to us. We went directly to it, pulled the pilot out of the plane and took him prisoner. A group of five or six farmers in a nearby field came up and demanded that we hand over our prisoner to them. It was clear they had no intention of taking him to the military authorities but were going to take care of him themselves. They said as much. It wasn't hard to figure out exactly what they had in mind and I couldn't allow that to happen. Is that about what you heard, Mr. Prime Minister?"

Churchill frowned at him. "Essentially, yes. Perhaps with a few more details."

"Probably about my pulling a pistol and pointing it at them."

"Yes, I'm aware of that." Churchill's face hardened and he glanced quickly at Donovan and then returned his attention to Nolan. "This government doesn't approve of its citizens being threatened at the point of a gun. Not by our enemies, nor by an ally."

"I did pull my pistol and threaten those farmers – and I did it intentionally. But they too were armed. I've worked in the fields myself and know what a sickle, a pitchfork or an iron rake can do. I was clear with them about the consequences of trying to take my prisoner, and that I considered their actions a threat against me and my driver. When they insisted they would go through me to get to him, I stopped them from committing a murder. They believed I would do what I said, and that was smart."

The prime minister cleared his throat and looked worried.

"I'm not sure that a British Spitfire pilot would have been afforded the same treatment as a prisoner of war by the Germans. I've been to Germany. I know the Nazi mentality. And I'd be appalled if the British attitude toward prisoners was not exactly the opposite that of the Nazis. I don't believe those farmers were really thinking clearly."

Churchill hesitated. It was clear he was troubled by the incident and wasn't entirely satisfied with the American's explanation, but realized Nolan, in some sense, held the future of England in his hands.

"There's no real harm done, Mr. Prime Minister," Donovan interrupted, giving Nolan a sideways warning glance. "In the heat of the moment, in a tense situation, things get said that aren't really meant. I'm sure Mr. Nolan would not have shot one of your countrymen."

"Yes of course," Churchill said, looking to Dave for confirmation. "You're right. We are not like Hitler's Nazis. In *Mein Kampf* and in some of his statements over the last few years he seems to think that his Germans and my Englishman are very much alike, almost identical. But he is wrong. Very wrong."

"Hitler always sees his relationships with the rest of the world in racial terms," Nolan replied. "He sees Germany and England as members of the same superior race and naturally allies. He views France as racially inferior. I've seen the Nazi propaganda about France taking an honored place in the new Europe, but I'm afraid the French are going to find out Hitler's intentions are to make them another satrapy of the thousand year Reich, little more than a source of food and slave labor."

Churchill seemed to agree but he didn't want to get drawn into any discussion about the French; they had their own problems at the moment and he had England's problems to worry over. Colville, sensing tension in the room, recommended they sit at the large conference table and begin the briefing.

The new prime minister was very much interested in some of Donovan's and Dave Nolan's observations about their aircraft manufacturing, weapons and ammunition factories, and communications developments. It was clear he had been fed the draft reports Dave had been handing over to Smythe-Browne at regular intervals. He drilled down into the specifics of weapons system development, manufacture and maintenance, not so much because he was interested in the minutia of the technical details, but because he wanted to know who best in his government could address the various shortcomings identified in the American's report. Donovan had told him Churchill was closely interested in warmaking, especially the tactics, but not so much the weaponry.

As the conversation wore on and Dave had the opportunity to observe Churchill in conversation with Donovan, he realized the accuracy of many of the observations his friend Henry had shared with him in those evenings when he stayed at the brigadier's estate. Even in casual conversation, Churchill exhibited his considerable oratorical and intellectual powers. Nolan made some mental notes about Churchill that he very much wanted to discuss with his old friend that evening over dinner.

An hour later Churchill signaled an end to their discussion, thanked them both for their service, their candor, and for the things they had done already to further and strengthen an already strong alliance between their countries.

As they rose to leave Churchill took Nolan's hand and looked directly into his eyes. "I must confess I had reservations about you when Henry raised up your name up to take on this assignment. The incident with our farmers also troubled me. I'm glad Henry persevered in championing your case. I've known William Donovan for years, but about you I knew little except from the reports you wrote from your Berlin embassy three years ago. I hope to see more of you in the future, Mr. Nolan."

"That would be my hope also, Mr. Prime Minister. Thank you."

Donovan and Nolan returned to Claridge's and met Edgar Mowrer for lunch in a back corner of the hotel restaurant.

"I tell you, Bill, at the end of these weeks of snooping around England, I think you have a major problem with your embassy here," the reporter observed between spoonfuls of soup. "The fact is everything being sent back to the State Department from the embassy in London is directly contrary to what I see and hear is going on. Kennedy is a defeatist. Why I don't know, but he is. The English under Churchill are going to carry on the fight no matter what, and that crack old Joe made to the Boston paper about democracy being dead in Europe and maybe in America proves it. He even sounded like he was happy about that."

"Don't look to me to defend him," Donovan replied, shaking his head and shrugging.

"What about you Nolan?" Mowrer asked. "Do the British have what it takes to make all this war stuff they need?"

"For the most part yes. It depends on how much damage is done to their infrastructure by German bombing. Most of their necessary manufacturing and assembly plants are beyond the range of German fighters. That's important because the British fighters are superior to those of the Luftwaffe except perhaps the FW-190, and they are totally superior to the Luftwaffe's bombers. That means Leigh-Mallory's 12 Group will knock most of them out of the sky if they venture north of London. That could be the saving grace of British manufacturing capability."

"You're saying they have the necessary plants and raw materials and skilled workers to do what needs to be done," Bill Donovan summarized.

"Not exactly. If the pressure from the Luftwaffe remains at or slightly above what they're seeing now the answer is yes – a qualified 'yes' assuming that British control of the sea can protect their lines of supply of raw materials. Skilled workers they have, not in overabundance but sufficient for current demand and perhaps a ten to twelve percent increase. If it goes beyond that, and what I hear from Bill is that is very likely the case, then they'll need help. I've worked out some scenarios based on a few different intelligence projections."

They looked at one another with expressions that said America had to jump in or live with the consequences of Great Britain's demise.

*   *   *   *

"David old chum," Smythe-Browne offered as he handed Nolan an after dinner brandy, "you've made my daughter a happy bride and her husband a rather cheery fellow for a change. Now that she's back at Hornchurch as a plotter and controller for sector E, they're seeing a lot more of one another than when she was your driver."

"Henry, I'm always willing to contribute to improving your state of mind and if the conjugal bliss of your family enhances that I feel I've enriched our relationship."

"Ah, quite. I remember my personal well-being was always foremost in your mind when we were at Allery together, the British officer said sarcastically." Henry reclined in his high backed leather chair and put his feet up on the matching leather ottoman as he enjoyed a sip of his liqueur. "So tell me, how did your audience with the prime minister go?"

"Had him eating out of my hand. By all appearances, he seems to think I'm the greatest thing since sliced bread."

"I suppose those are two of your favorite Americanized idioms. It seems you've learned little more of the language than you knew during your last stay here with your lovely wife. I say, it is a shame you colonists have so bastardized the language that those of us who speak it properly have a hard time following you."

It wasn't the first time Smythe-Browne had brought that up. It was one of his favorite complaints about the Yanks, and he never seemed to tire of voicing it. "I trust my quaint little colloquialisms haven't intruded on your understanding of the draft reports I've been feeding you these past few weeks."

"Not a-tall old friend. I found them rather enlightening, and very much to my liking, an opinion shared by Sir John Dill and the prime minister himself. I'd say you've made yourself something of a friend in Churchill save for that nasty little gun pointing business on your way back from Hornchurch your first day. I expect the prime minister properly counseled you on the inappropriateness of your behavior."

"Not so much, Henry. I think we came to an understanding, and I'll leave it at that."

"You left him in a good mood, I trust old boy since I have to brief him myself first thing in the morning."

"If I had known you were going to see him that soon after our meeting I wouldn't have mentioned your observations to me about his impatience."

Smythe-Browne's chin quickly receded into his neck as he turned and looked at Nolan wide-eyed. "You didn't?!"

"I thought you Brits had the same approach to commentary that we Americans have in our Army – that you don't say anything you wouldn't want to see headlined on page one of the *Times* or be overheard by your commander. I hope I haven't gotten you into trouble." He was laughing inwardly at the look on Smythe-Browne's face and the color creeping up his neck. After all these years Henry still didn't know how to take him, and Nolan wondered if the Brit would survive even one encounter with Andy Fauser.

"Nolan, your social graces are still very much lacking."

"I've been told." But he knew that was not an opinion shared by his daughter from what Henry had just told him. Having her replaced as his driver had worked for them both.

He had been assigned two people to replace Aynslee: a strapping young paratrooper sergeant as driver plus a clerk from the same unit. It had worked out very well. The sergeant was not only a driver but a bodyguard with a wealth of information about equipment, weapons, military tactics and morale. The clerk was an accomplished typist and editor, having attended college and had worked briefly as a reporter for the London Times. After just a few days both British soldiers grew comfortable with him, opened up and provided key insights into the attitudes and perceptions of both soldiers and civilians alike.

"I hear you at last have an audience with Beaverbrook tomorrow," Henry was saying interrupting Nolan's thoughts.

"I finally got on his schedule – he's even harder to nail down than you are. I can't go back until I fully understand his plans and thinking concerning aircraft production, especially speeding up the delivery of the Spitfire. What can you tell me about him? I got a very brief biography from our State Department but frankly it was lacking."

"How much do you want to know?"

"Everything about him."

"Everything?! I say old chum that's quite the tall order."

"Listen Henry, that's the reason I came over and why I'm putting up with your company this evening. Since you and your son-in-law's father travel in the same circles as Lord Beaverbrook, I assumed you could tell me everything I wanted or needed to know. Frankly, he's probably more important to my part of this mission than Churchill himself."

"I daresay you're correct. The outcome of the battle over our little island is as much in his hands as it is in Stuffy Dowding's." Henry went to the bar picked up the bottle of brandy and topped off both of their glasses. Sitting down he again looked at Nolan and began.

"He's Canadian you know, grew up there and was in business before emigrating to England. The same year he became a member of Parliament for Ashton-under-Lyne. He still runs a newspaper empire. Very influential because of it. His newspapers were not shy with his allegations about the King's pro-Nazi sympathies. He's often at odds with other cabinet members even now – likes the spotlight, he does."

"Sounds like an interesting character," Dave mused, tickled at the look of disdain on his friend's face. "You don't seem to be real high on Beaverbrook."

"If by high you mean approving, or liking, that's not for me to say. He's a close friend of Churchill who appointed him Minister of Aircraft Production, a stepping stone to placing him in charge of overall matériel supply for the entirety of the war effort. I'm told that even in the last month aircraft production and delivery is up to an all-time high, and whether or not that's Beaverbrook's work in evidence, he certainly gets the credit. Of course some say that aircraft production was already rising when Beaverbrook took charge – they and others say that as in many of his investments he was fortunate to inherit something just beginning to bear fruit. Perhaps you might want to explore that with him, David. In any event he is a man with great energy and an even greater capacity for generating ideas, whether good, bad or otherwise. This will be a war of machines, and as such it will be won or lost on the assembly line."

"Not on the battlefield?" Nolan asked, surprised that an infantryman would say that.

"Well, certainly on the battlefield but our soldiers and airmen and sailors must have the machinery of war. If England goes down before the Nazi this year or early next it will not be Lord Beaverbrook's fault, but if she holds up and prevails it may well be his triumph."

"He's that important?" Nolan asked.

"Of a certainty, my friend. I believe history will bear me out on this, that Beaverbrook is already and will continue to be one of the most significant architects of the British response to Nazism. Perhaps equaling even Churchill himself."

"That's a pretty bold prediction, Henry. I've never known you to be one to go out onto a limb like that."

"I don't say that lightly. He's a man you Americans should get to know very, very well, and neither do I say that lightly. I would suggest to you, David, that a single day with our Lord Beaverbrook is not enough for you to make a truly valid evaluation of our ability to produce enough to resist the Germans in the near-term. Can we invade the continent and push the little corporal all the way back to his bunker in Berlin? That is an entirely different question, but another thing you should explore with Beaverbrook."

Nolan leaned back in his chair, gazed for a while at the ceiling and thought about what his old friend had just told him. Smythe-Browne, like most Englishmen, was loath to exaggerate. On the contrary, his normal manner tended almost exclusively to understatement. But that wasn't what he had just heard.

Mowrer had departed for Washington that afternoon and he knew that Donovan was spending this, his last evening at Braddock's, the home of Rear Admiral John Godfrey in Kent.

Godfrey was England's intelligence master and he guessed their conversation that evening would be one of the most interesting imaginable – except perhaps for the dialogue he would have with Beaverbrook. Donovan was leaving the next morning and Nolan was to follow him by two days. He was already more than a week beyond the scheduled return date he had promised Denise. He'd have to deal with that when he returned. Now, and especially after what Henry had told him, he guessed two days with Beaverbrook would not be enough. He could envision being delayed by as much an additional week.

"Henry, I hope you won't mind me camping out here for the next few days. I'm going to need your help extending my use of the staff car and driver beyond the day after tomorrow, and your people will have to get my passage back to the U.S. reworked. I need to get a cable to Denise telling her I'll be delayed another four or five days."

"How do think your Nurse Barrett will react to that?"

"I could become the first American casualty of the European war." Smythe-Browne clucked his tongue and nodded up and down. "Now, tell me the rest of the story about Beaverbrook. I know you've just touched the surface."

"True, old friend. Let me tell you about his idea of flying your twin-engined bombers across the Atlantic instead of disassembling and shipping them on surface vessels. I thought it quite unlikely at first, but he's examined the possibilities thoroughly and it appears not at all to be a chimera as his critics claim. Of course, he assumes you Yanks will "loan" us a sizeable number of your B-25s. You will won't you?"

"That's not for me to decide, Henry."

"But you and Donovan can recommend. Nevertheless, on to the minister himself. Fortunately I have another bottle of this brandy," the brigadier mused. "If you want to know *everything* about our Beaverbrook we shall be here for a long while."

Chapter 9

Far to the southwest the horizon was a narrow black line, and above that billowed ominous dark clouds filled with lightning and rain; the wind had picked up and was now almost a direct crosswind to the grass runway. A half mile south of the strip an open cockpit Stearman biplane was lining up for final approach and landing. A crowd of trainees gathered at the base of the small control tower looked on with a certain awe and jealousy as the first in their flight school class to solo gradually descended toward the training field.

From inside the little blue plane with yellow wings, 2nd Lieutenant Mitch Nolan looked through the tensioned wires and struts at the group of his flight school classmates. This was a moment to be savored. He thought back to his first flying hours in the Philippines with his father's old Navy buddy, Pug Johnston. That had been a lot of fun – but this was even better.

He loved the Stearman – the way it handled, the deep throbbing of the radial engine, and the sense that no matter what you did the plane would keep you from really hurting yourself. *If only it would do more than ninety mph,* he thought.

Left crosswind, stiffening a little, he told himself, taking a second glance at the windsock flying atop the small control tower. *Let's see, Nolan – sock straight out means at least 15 knots, so left wing down into the wind, a little right rudder – but not too much. Take that out just before touchdown. Nothing to it...just a little bit of cross control to keep the nose straight – emphasis on a little bit. Glad now that Pug made me practice crosswinds even when I hated it. Throttle back just a little. A touch more rudder – nose just to the right of the center line. Three hundred feet rate of descent. Half mile to touchdown.* He smiled again to himself thinking everything was right where he wanted it.

And although he was on final approach for landing, the most important part of any flight, he let his mind wander back to that first time he had ever seen an airplane...

He was six years old and was staying with Rosa Morales during the day while his mother worked as the nurse for the doctor in town whose circuit covered much of the Gulf Coast area from Palacios to Aransas Pass. His father had been assigned to Camp Whalen – a dry, dusty, rundown old outpost on the edge of the Texas prairie; he remembered his mother hating it. He recalled liking to stay with Rosa because he loved the smell and taste of her food and the company of her two sons, Estaban and Carlos. They were both a few years older than he and knew all about trapping rabbits among the dove weed patches and catching fish in the ranchers' stock ponds. And, they had a dog he liked – a small, short-haired mongrel pup named *Paco* that was always glad to see him.

The three of them had been checking their traps a mile or two west of the town, along a tree line on the Hewitt ranch. It was late September, an hour before suppertime, as they walked across the north range with the warm afternoon sun on their backs. They were walking down the long, gentle slope toward the stock tank where late afternoon flights of dove circled and swirled. It was the far off, muted buzzing sound that first caught his attention; he remembered wondering if it was one of the beehives old man Hewitt kept. And then, suddenly, it was there, fifty feet off to the right, inches above the tree line. The sight of it took his breath away – the loudest, scariest, most magnificent-looking thing he'd ever seen.

The biplane swept directly over their heads, then climbed almost straight up into the high, clear south Texas sky before winging over pointing directly down at them. The engine thundered and the noise swelled in a deafening crescendo that thrilled him. It swooped so low they all dove to the ground and covered their heads; on the second low pass he could clearly see the pilot's face and his wide smile beneath the goggles. A long white scarf around his neck whipped back and forth, trailing out behind him along almost half the length of the machine. The plane leveled off, pointed toward the town and the pilot waggled his wings twice, waved again and then flew off toward Palacios.

Excited beyond description, he ran all the way to the flat meadow just outside the town where a small crowd had gathered to watch the plane circle and land. When it coasted to a halt and the propeller stopped turning, he was caught up in the crowd that surged forward.

The pilot was a handsome man, younger than his father, with a big, toothy smile that had the young girls gazing at him with a dreamy-eyed look. '*Fifty cents the ride,*' he announced and pulled a five gallon can from beneath the front seat and handed it to Estaban, telling him to run into town and get him some gas. "*Fifty cents the ride!... See the town, and the Gulf of Mexico from Galveston Bay to Corpus Christi from right up there!*" he said, pointing directly overhead.

Fifty cents?! Mitch had thought, devastated. *I'll never have that much money in my whole life... I won't ever get a ride in one of those things!...*

The Stearman continued its slow descent with the radial engine's distinctive throbbing purr drifting across the practice field toward the crowd and the hangar behind them. As the airplane got closer to the ground and slowed its descent, Mitch dipped the left wing slightly into the wind and gave the plane enough right rudder to keep its track aligned with the north-south center line of strip. At a hundred feet above the runway the big nine-cylinder Lycoming engine suddenly roared and the nose of the aircraft turned right as it picked up speed and headed directly at the control tower.

On the ground, the crowd in front of the hangar reacted with a communal gasp of dismay.

In the air, Mitch pushed the throttle to the firewall and felt the plane lunge forward. He lowered the nose of the biplane, gathering speed and dropping his altitude until the Stearman was level with the tower, pointed directly at it; he saw both figures inside moving back away from the edge of the small glass enclosure. The distance between plane and tower decreased rapidly, and his classmates on the ground braced themselves for a crash.

Fifty yards from the tower, Nolan pulled the control stick hard to the left and back. As the bi-wing trainer flashed by the tower in a climbing left turn the tailwheel barely missed ripping the windsock from its mooring. Leveling off, he centered the controls for an instant and then quickly pulled the nose of the plane barely above the horizon and the stick quickly all the way to the right. The plane did a rapid roll around the long axis of the fuselage then quickly returned to level flight. Looking back over his left shoulder, Mitch let out a loud whoop that was lost in the wind and the distinctive sound of the Stearman's prop.

On the ground the flight school class quickly recovered from its shock at an impending crash and most began laughing at the stunt.

"I think our old sailing buddy screwed the pooch on this one," Marvelous Marv Crosley said to Roy Lindquist, looking over his right shoulder. He glanced up at the third story window of the office over the hangar belonging to their training squadron leader. "Yup, I think ol' Lieutenant JJ is going to have a piece of our pal Nolan's hide for that. Wouldn't be surprised if his first solo wasn't his last."

"Think so?"

"Might be. It'd be a shame to wash out of flight school that quick – hope it was worth it."

The remainder of Class 40-7 watched the blue and yellow trainer enter a downwind, turn a tight base leg and then final approach for landing. Engine noise dropped off as Mitch decreased the throttle just before landing; the left landing gear touched the ground first followed almost immediately by the right main landing gear and the tail wheel.

"Damn, almost a perfect three-point landing – and in a pretty good crosswind!" Lindquist observed, nudging Marvelous Marv with an elbow.

"Our boy better hope he gets extra credit for it because JJ is going to ream him good for that flyby."

"Could be… but it was a great show. Our boy can fly a plane, can't he?"

The Stearman continued its rollout and slowed, then taxied to the lineup of other aircraft near the hangar. The pilot swung the tail around with the nose of the biplane facing towards the runway and a few seconds later killed the engine. He pulled off the leather flying helmet and climbed out onto the wing and jumped to the ground. An Army photographer was waiting there for him and took his picture with the cockpit and upper wing of the trainer in the background and one great big smile on his face. The crowd of student pilots gathered around slapping him on the back and congratulating him for surviving his three trips around the pattern and three touch and go landings. From behind the crowd a stern-faced lieutenant named Dan Halbertson – one of the training squadron's instructor pilots – approached the celebration.

"The flight commander wants to see you, Nolan" the instructor pilot said. "You succeeded in doing something I haven't seen in two years – you wiped the smile off his face. That's the dumbest thing I've seen in almost three years of instructing. If I were you I'd say goodbye to my friends right now. From what I just heard and saw in the commander's office you're likely to be off this post before that engine cools."

The crowd of student pilots was silent as Mitch Nolan made his way through them then across the hangar floor and up the stairs at the rear of the building that led to the instructor pilots' room and the flight commander's office. He took off the parachute, hung it on the appropriate peg in the back of the flight instruction room, and then walked down the narrow hallway to Lieutenant Flannigan's office and knocked.

"Enter!"

Mitch Nolan opened the door and saw his instructor standing at a stiff attention in front of the flight commander's desk. Lieutenant J. J. Flannigan looked up from a piece of paper he was writing on and glared at him as Mitch approached the desk and saluted.

"Lieutenant Nolan reporting as ordered, sir."

"Nolan, what do you think I ought to do to you and your instructor pilot?"

"Because of what, sir?"

The sound of Flannigan's fist slamming on top of the metal desk reverberated through the office and down the hall. "Because of what?!... For starters lieutenant, an unauthorized low pass over the control tower followed by an unauthorized aerobatic maneuver – each of which was a gross violation of aviation safety practices and Randolf Field procedures!"

"Sir, I –"

"At ease, lieutenant! As of right now I do all the talking and you and your instructor will do all the listening. Have I made myself clear on that?"

"Yes, sir."

"I don't know who gave you the impression the Army approves of student pilots buzzing the tower. I don't know who you think you are doing that or some half-assed aileron roll that is neither part of nor approved in this phase of training. From my observation of your time here in this training squadron, you have either a death wish or an unwarranted and highly exaggerated opinion of your abilities, neither of which I'll tolerate as the commander." Flannigan turned and looked at Nolan's instructor pilot. "And you, Lieutenant Carpenter, where was your mind when you sent this student up on his first solo after only five hours of training? This is going on your record as a black mark the same way as it's going on Nolan's. I'm going to have to report this, as you know. You'd better hope the Review Board is a lot more understanding and lenient than I'm feeling right now."

"Sir, I never intended to get Lieutenant Carpenter in trouble. He had no knowledge –"

"Damn you, Nolan! When I said at ease and be quiet I meant it! As of this minute, you're confined to quarters until tomorrow morning at zero nine hundred when you report back to this office pending final outcome of an official review of your actions. You're suspended from all flight operations, all instruction, and all contact with your fellow students in this training squadron until the review board decides on your future. Am I clear?"

"Yes, sir."

"You probably just assured for yourself the shortest career in the history of Army aviation. This time next week you'll likely be an infantryman reporting for duty at Camp Benning. I hope you do better pushing troops than you did here learning how to fly." The squadron commander continued to glare at him, and finally dismissed him with a casual backward wave of his hand as if dusting something from the top of his desk. When Nolan left and closed the door J.J. Flannigan looked at Nolan's flight instructor.

"Damn, A.C., what in the world were you thinking?! Only five hours before solo?"

"He's that good, Jim. I know the average for most students is closer to 10 or 12 hours, but Nolan already has a pilot's license that he got when he was living in the Philippines. Some old Navy pilot friend of his father's taught him how to fly and he's got somewhere close to 100 hours under his belt already, and it shows."

"But five hours?!"

"I could've soloed him after his first lesson – he's really that good. I'd put him up for his first checkride right now if I could. He's already that proficient in the Stearman."

"What's he doing flying aerobatics?" the flight commander asked.

"Well, you saw for yourself he does a pretty good aileron roll. Just for the heck of it I showed him one on the third hour of instruction, and the one he did was better than mine. I think we can chalk that up to his time with that old Navy pilot in the Philippines."

"Old Navy guy, eh? I guess that explains all the tight traffic patterns and the short field landings." Lieutenant Flannigan sat down behind his desk intertwined his fingers and looked up at the ceiling as he contemplated what he was going to do. "All right, so he's good."

"Better than just good. He's the most natural pilot I've seen come through here."

"I don't know if I buy that. Even so, we can't let him get away with this; he did violate some rules and that sets a bad example for the rest of the class. Here's what I'm going to do: I'm suspending Nolan from all training for the time being. I'm also suspending you for a week, and I have to report this up the chain. This is going to require a full blown Flight Evaluation Board. He's going to sit and stew over this for awhile. I hope he's smart enough to get himself back on track in a couple of weeks. If he's as good as you say, it's not going to disrupt his flight education. That should put a knot in his knickers and send a warning to the others."

"What about my other two students – Lindquist and Crosley?"

"They're old buddies from the Academy aren't they? Be a good idea to break up that group anyhow. I'll assign one of them to Farquar and the other to Halbertson. Nolan's confined to quarters until you get back. Then I'm going to give him the toughest damned checkride a student pilot ever had – put the fear of God and the Air Corps in him so he won't forget. If he satisfies me and passes my ride, then you can take him one-on-one and see how far he can really go. We'll see just how much of a hot shot pilot this Nolan character really is."

*   *   *   *   *

Dave Nolan looked up from his notes and his mid-morning breakfast at the table along the side wall of the Continental Hotel's restaurant and caught a glimpse of the young blonde girl in her early twenties. He gazed at her as she entered and looked around the room, smiling to himself and thinking how much she looked like Denise at that age. At last the girl saw him, waved and began to navigate across the dining room with the quick, supple grace so reminiscent of her mother.

"Good grief," she said, giving him a quick peck on the cheek, and then taking a seat. "You look like something the cat dragged in."

"Is that any way to treat your old dad, Erika?" he asked sarcastically. "Surely I don't look that bad, do I?"

"Well, not all rumpled or anything, but your eyes are bloodshot and you look like you've been up all night. What gives?"

"I've only been back in the States for twenty-four hours. The Clipper landed at sunrise yesterday morning, and then I had to spend the afternoon listening to your mother complain about how you never call her. At best I got a few hours sleep and then dragged out of bed in time to catch the five o'clock train from New York. As they say down in Texas, I feel like I've been rode hard and put away wet. I was hoping for at least a little sympathy from you."

She smiled at him and patted his hand, her face expressive and her eyes lighting up. "I think that may be the first time I ever heard you beg for sympathy from anybody. Age catching up with you, dad?"

"Age and five time zones." He sipped his coffee, gazing over the rim of his cup at his animated young daughter. "I'm not looking forward to being grilled at the White House."

The trek from England, retracing his steps from the trip over, had been both long and tiring. With the Germans fully in control of France now, the flight from England to Portugal had been protracted, noisy and tortuous as the pilot of the British bomber stayed well out to sea beyond the range of Luftwaffe fighters. The crew flew mostly in the rough weather in clouds under instrument conditions. Boarding the Clipper in the Azores, he had settled down for several hours of rewriting and reworking his notes, especially after the time he'd spent with Lord Beaverbrook. He was glad that Henry had set up a scheduled tour with the minister that had allowed him time, both formal and informal, to get to know the transplanted Canadian better and to listen to some of his more audacious ideas. It had been the most informative part of a very enlightening trip.

Denise's reception at the end of his long journey had been muted.

She was still unhappy with his decision to go to England with Bill Donovan, even if the president and the prime minister of England had personally asked for him. To her, he had broken a promise – or at best manufactured a loophole to slip through – so that he could go off on another adventure. That wasn't true and he'd tried to convince her on the drive out to the summer cottage. His protests had fallen on deaf ears. Her reaction reminded him of the times at Camp Whalen when he'd come back from the field and she was waiting for him on the back porch of their quarters, armed and ready to argue over the futility of his staying in the Army.

He detected now that there was more to it than just her antipathy toward Donovan or a disappointment in him for supposedly welshing on a promise. Mitch had in essence moved away four years earlier, and now Erika had moved on in search of her own destiny in Washington. He perceived she now clung to Glenn even more, not just because he was the "baby" of the family but because he was the last of her brood left. That worried him.

"I heard the senator say something about your leaving England the day of the first really big German air attack on London." Erika was saying. "What happened?"

Dave shook his head slowly. "Sorry kid, I can't tell you. That's for the president and his closest advisers."

"Come on Dad, you know I'm going to hear about it from Senator Payne as soon as he gets back from your meeting. He'll dictate it to Megan, and then I'll have to clean it up and put it in the format of a position paper or talking points for him, so you might as well tell me."

"Have I ever told you you're just as pushy as your mother?"

"Dad!"

"You're not happy until you've found something to argue over with me. It's true, isn't it?"

"It's not! I don't know why you –" She broke off in sudden consternation, her eyes flashing at him like mirrors tilted, full of lights. Erika frowned and said, "I'd be a fool to argue with you, because I wouldn't –"

"– have a leg to stand on," Dave finished for her.

She frowned more deeply and then suddenly laughed. "I remember that's how you always quelled your arguments with mom. I could use a little help in that area myself right about now. She's still not happy I moved down here to D.C. And I know she's going to be even less happy when she finds out that I've met someone."

"Met someone? I don't know how to take that."

"He's a lawyer who works on Senator Payne's committee." All at once her eyes narrowed. "The last thing she told me was to be careful about the men in Washington. I know she's not going to like this development. Can you help me out?"

"All depends."

Erika placed an elbow on the table and rested her chin on the back of her hand, looking innocently at him the way Denise did when she wanted something. "Depends on what?"

"First, on whether or not you're serious about this guy, and most importantly on whether or not he's worthy of you. It's too bad Mitch isn't here to check this guy out the way older brothers are supposed to. Have you told him about this fella or talked to him lately?"

"No. But I did get a phone call a couple of nights ago from that friend of his on the baseball team everybody called 'Marvelous Marv.' You remember him? He stopped by the house a couple of times. It seems Mitch pulled some kind of goofy stunt and it looks like he's going to be kicked out of flight school."

"I hadn't heard." That sounded serious enough. After all the work and focus on flying Air Corps fighters, that would be devastating. "What did he do?"

"Marv didn't say exactly – something about Mitch buzzing the tower in his airplane and then doing aerobatics over the runway – the kind of dumb stuff my brother does all the time."

"And Marv called and told you this why?"

"He still has this crazy idea that he wants to date me. But I'm not fascinated by the idea of being courted by some Academy product. Not interested. Having a brother and a father from there is more than enough exposure."

"But you're interested in this Washington lawyer."

"He's very bright, and both Michelle and her father tell me he's a decent sort. I'm still testing him. He's pretty obvious – everybody says he's been spending a lot more time around our office lately, and supposedly that's because of me. I'm a Nolan, so I'm just vain enough to take that as a compliment," Erika said whimsically, her voice a pleasant warm contralto. "I want you to meet him while you're in town."

"You want him to meet your family already? It's that serious?!" He had an impulse to laugh at the look on her face – and for an instant she reminded him of Denise that afternoon during the War as they shared wine and a picnic basket on a blanket spread out in a field of wild oats and lavender in France, just outside Chalons.

"Not the whole family, just you."

"Give me some more intel on him."

"Dad! This isn't some military operation. I just want you to meet him, that's all."

"Contingency planning, Erika. I might run into him at the Senator's office this afternoon if we end up there after the meeting – you never know what might happen. A wise man prepares himself for any and all eventualities."

"You've been reading *Sun Tzu* again haven't you?" she said accusatorily, looking at him from the corner of her eye, smirking. "No wonder your wife is in a snit half the time any more. There's something really unsettling about your going around acting out the ancient oriental military philosophies of a long dead Chinaman."

At this he gave a low chuckle and peered at his daughter's radiant, expectant face. Their conversation had taken on a familiar back and forth, trading of barbs and slights, little hyperboles meant to tease and test and elicit exaggerated responses. *Now that she's out on her own, she is so much like her mother at her age*, he thought. Thinking about it made him want to be back home with Denise even more.

Denise… As a preemptive peace offering, he'd brought her a Burberry umbrella and a matching scarf, a fine leather purse from Harrods in the royal borough of Kensington and Chelsea, plus a tin of Scottish shortbread cookies. It had taken the edge off her disappointment for a little while. Still, in the back of his mind, it bothered him that he'd been the cause once again of a distance growing between them.

"Dead Chinaman aside, tell me about this young fella," Dave said to his daughter.

"Well, he's good looking, really he is, described as dreamy according to the girl who introduced us. He graduated from Harvard Law last year and had a very nice offer from a New York law firm named Burns and Holloway and somebody-somebody in the city."

"Burns, Holloway, Travelstead and Schwartz," Dave said, completing the name for her. "I know them. Very prestigious. Only the very bluest of blue blood."

After the Great War, he'd returned home intent on two things: resigning from the Army, and finding the girl he'd left behind. Circumstances had seriously interfered with both plans. One day in late May, six months after the Armistice, he'd learned that Denise intended to marry Phillip Ratcliffe, the son of one of her father's wealthy friends, and he'd talked her out of it. The law firm of Burns, Holloway, Travelstead and Schwartz had been on Ratcliffe's horizon, too.

"So he's a dreamy, well-heeled Ivy League lawyer engaged in politics. Does he have a name and can you tell me anything about him I might like?" Dave asked, finishing his coffee.

Erika sighed deeply and looked exasperated. "His name is Randall. Randall Ashby, and he turned down a very nice position with a very nice salary to come to Washington and work for a pittance because he wants to contribute to making this a better country."

"All right."

"You say that like you don't believe it."

"I have no reason not to believe him. I'm just seeking to understand – to figure out what this young man is all about and why you're so interested in him that you want my approval, or my help in getting your mother's approval. Listen, Erika, you're grown and on your own now, you really don't need our approval to date someone. Is it more than just dating? How long have you known him?"

"About a month."

"All right, I'll grease the skids for you with your mother. I have an early afternoon meeting with Bill Donovan at the White House, and after that I don't know exactly how the rest of the day or this evening is going to go. But I'm spending the night here in the Continental and I'm tentatively scheduled tomorrow on the one o'clock train back to New York. Maybe we can work in a late breakfast or an early lunch mid-morning. I'll call you this evening. – if you don't hear from me call the hotel after ten. At worst, I'll leave you a message at the front desk. Tell your friend I'd be glad to inspect him and pass judgment. I've had a lot of practice at that in the last month."

"Oh, Dad," she moaned theatrically. "I'm not asking you to perform a formal guard mount! Mom's right – you really are club-footed socially."

"You think so?"

Erika smiled merrily. "It's the one thing left I think we still agree on."

*　　*　　*　　*

"You may go in, Mr. Nolan," the secretary said, placing the phone back on its cradle and smiling at him. "The president will see you now."

"Thank you," Dave replied, rising and looking at his watch quickly and wondering why he'd been left cooling his heels outside the Oval Office for twenty minutes. *Politicians,* he muttered to himself, thankful he'd be home soon and away from them all.

As he entered, the conversation abruptly ended and they all looked at him. Secretaries Knox, Stinson, and Hull along with Edward Stettinius sat facing Roosevelt off to his left while Senator Payne sat to his right and Donovan directly faced him next to an empty chair.

"Come in. Come in. Sorry to keep you waiting, Dave," the president, in shirtsleeves, said amiably with a smile while the cigarette holder in his mouth bobbed up and down. "Apologies for the delay. This might happen now and then until we get you a Top Secret clearance."

It wasn't lost on him that Roosevelt had called him by his first name, nor did it pass unobserved that the president expected to see him again in the future and with a higher level security clearance. He wasn't sure he liked what that intimated. As he took his seat, Donovan looked over and gave him an almost imperceptible nod; Senator Payne winked. Everyone else, except the president, simply looked unsmilingly at him.

"We've all read the reports you and William compiled," Roosevelt began. "I know you still have to complete your final version including your meetings with Lord Beaverbrook. After we get that and have a chance to read through it there may be some more questions and we hope you'll be readily available to answer them. We have several recent cables from Beaverbrook and Churchill we'd like you to read and comment on before you return to New York tomorrow."

"Yes sir, I can certainly review the cables tonight and make myself available in the future given reasonable lead time," Dave Nolan replied. "I finished editing my final report on the trip back and have my handwritten notes available for typing and distribution."

"Very good," Roosevelt offered. "From what we've reviewed so far and what we've heard from the prime minister and his people, the two of you had a very profitable trip for both us and our friends in England. Both sides of the Atlantic agree it was money and time well spent. What we learned exceeded our expectations."

"From my perspective," Stettinius said, leaning forward in his chair and looking directly at Dave Nolan, "every one of our questions were answered, and many more that we should have asked were covered. The War Resources Board is well pleased with what they got. Going forward we would like to be able to call upon you as a resource or a consultant or in some form or fashion. Is that possible?"

"I'm not sure. It might be, assuming it doesn't interfere with my duties at Barrett Enterprises. Before I commit, I really need to talk with Edgar Barrett, and probably the board."

Stettinius nodded affirmatively and seemed satisfied.

Dave noticed out of the corner of his eye that the president was looking at him closely while the discussion continued to carry on between the other men in the room. Even when the president inserted himself into the conversation, it seemed to Nolan that he kept his eye on him. After nearly an hour Roosevelt took a call on the telephone at his elbow and ended their meeting but indicated for Nolan, Stettinius and the Senator to remain behind.

"Dave," the president began, "I'll get right to it. I heard what you said earlier, but we would like you to consider coming into this administration in a full-time capacity. After reading your reports and the cables received from Prime Minister Churchill and others in England, we think you have an important role to play in our relationship with Britain. It was the unanimous opinion among the senior British officials with whom you met that you're somebody they could work with. And, it was similarly unanimous among those gathered in this office that you're a person with a set of qualifications uniquely suited to being the liaison between the United States and Britain in the area of war matériel."

"I'm honored, Mr. President," Nolan replied, surprised at the offer and also at the knot that had formed in his stomach. "I can't say one way or the other whether or not I'd be interested. I'd have to hear more of what the position entails and most importantly I have to consider the impact on my professional and private life. In all honesty, sir, I've never considered a position in the public sector – in politics, that is. And this position that you're offering is a political appointment I assume."

"It is."

"And to whom does this position report, sir?"

"Directly to Ed," Roosevelt replied, nodding toward Stettinius, "as War Resources Board chair. He and I have been talking about how we might lease or lend to the British matériel and equipment of all kinds. We haven't fully fleshed that out yet but the role we see for you is directly managing that kind of the program, whatever form it finally takes and whatever we end up calling it."

Stettinius added, "Based on the information you provided us and the initial studies we've done internally within the Board, we're talking about managing the production and transportation of hundreds of millions, maybe billions of dollars worth of war matériel in each of the next two to four years. It could be longer, depending on the course of the war in Europe. We need a logician and we think you're what we need."

Nolan thought about that, and the more he thought the more it troubled him.

"Something's bothering you, Dave," the president declared.

"Yes sir," he replied at last, looking at Senator Payne, then Stettinius and finally back at the president. "What you're telling me doesn't seem in sync with what I hear publicly presented to the country or what I see happening within the United States."

"How so, son?" Sen. Payne asked, giving him a concerned look.

"What I hear being said here is that a decision has pretty much already been made that we're going to support England in a significant and material way. That doesn't surprise me. The information Mr. Donovan and I provided supports that decision." He paused briefly, pondering. "But that's not what's being told to the American people. What I saw before departing on this mission, and what I see now, is a country at peace… at peace with lights ablaze at night from coast to coast with a loud and screechy intramural squabble going on between isolationists and interventionists. I see the production of arms and munitions going along at a trickle in this country, and a Congress nearly equally divided over the issue of increasing the size of our military, which at present strength levels is wholly inadequate. I see a country without rationing of food and fuel, unlike what I saw this past month. England - the whole of their population from top to bottom – is preparing for all out war. We're not."

He thought about the comment Aynslee Glendenbrook had made about no more topping off of their tans and no more sipping cocktails by the seashore for a long, long time into the future. That was so alien to what the American population seemed to be thinking at the moment, and so much at odds with what was being presented to them by the administration.

"Now, Dave, it'll take us a while to turn public opinion toward the position the president is laying before us," William Payne said, casting a worried look at Roosevelt. "These things will take time. Tell you what, let's you and me talk about it. This position the president and Edward are thinking of might be able to help that transition. You stop by my place down in Georgetown tonight. We'll do some damage to a bottle of Jack Daniels and figure this out. How's that sound to you, son?"

Dave sensed the tension in the Oval Office and realized his old friend and mentor had fashioned a way for him to gracefully exit a situation where he had spoken out too quickly. "Senator, you know my weakness for a good Tennessee sipping whiskey. I think that may be very helpful to my understanding of what's being proposed here. You're on."

President Roosevelt offered his hand and a big smile across the top of the presidential desk, and soon he was outside the Oval Office giving his home and office telephone numbers to Edward Stettinius and the president's secretary. Long minutes later he was walking alongside Senator Payne down the curved driveway toward the White House entranceway guard station.

"Dave," Payne said leaning close to him and keeping his voice low. "I might suggest you think a bit more before you speak out like that in front of the president."

"You're right. I just said the first thing that came to mind. But what I said was true."

117

"It was, in the main. But I'd say it's the first time in the thirty years I've been knowin' you that you didn't choose your words carefully. It's not like you." Senator Payne looked at him approvingly, slowly shaking his head up and down. "The president is offering you an opportunity the likes of which very few people ever get close to. In the past couple of weeks, your record has been investigated, dissected, explored, probed, scrutinized, scrubbed – and who knows what else – with a fine toothed comb as if you were going to be the pharaoh's resident food taster. Those men in there like what they see. You were left cooling your heels outside because we were talking about you – I guess you figured that out. And if I wasn't late to a committee meeting, I'd give you a little schoolin' on how you talk to a President of the United States. But that'll have to wait until tonight. I don't know how long this meeting is going to last but I should be home by about seven o'clock. You meet me there and we'll have us some of that sippin' whiskey and I'll give you a little education you'll need when you come down here to Washington and start playing in the big leagues. Good enough?"

"I haven't said yes, Senator."

"When I get done with you, you will." Payne slapped him hard on the upper arm, then reached into his pocket and pulled out a key chain. "Here's a key to my little house in Georgetown – you know the address. If I'm not there right at seven, you let yourself in. In fact if you want, you can use the house this afternoon to read over and comment on those cables from the Brits. There's not much in the ice box or the pantry to eat. Maybe I'll pick us up a couple of hoagies for dinner – there's a place not far from there where an old Italian from Philadelphia makes a pretty mean sandwich. Anyhow, I'll see you around seven."

It was almost four o'clock when Dave Nolan arrived at Payne's Georgetown residence.

The house was in a quiet neighborhood, only a block away from where Erika now stayed with Payne's secretary, a dark-haired girl he'd startled and embarrassed himself in front of that last disastrous trip to the senator's office.

Dave settled into the dining room just off the kitchen in the back of the narrow row house, behind the stairway to the second floor. He spread his papers out on the table and got to work. He read through Churchill's and Beaverbrook's cables, made some notes and began composing his thoughts and outlining his responses. Before he knew it, the room had grown dim; when he turned on the lights and checked his watch it was just after six.

He was re-reading his notes about Beaverbrook's concept of flying B-25s and A-28s to England rather than shipping them by surface vessels when he heard the front door open. Looking at his watch, he was surprised to see the senator was almost an hour early. He made a few more notes as he heard the echo of leather heels on hardwood floors and wondered idly why they seemed to sound so strange.

"I didn't expect you this early, Senator," Nolan said, rising and walking into the kitchen. He heard a gasp and then felt his heart jump and the hair bristle on the back of his neck as he looked into the eyes of Michelle Reeves.

They stared at one another for what seemed to him an eternity.

"Hello, Dave," she said at last, her voice soft and hesitant. "It's been a long time."

"Yes, it has," he agreed, wanting to flee the house or look away, aware his face had grown hot and afraid it was now so crimson that it shone like a beacon.

"Four years," she said after another long silence. Her face slowly grew determined; it was a look he'd seen once before – at a 42nd Division Officer's Call a week before he'd shipped out for Europe and the Great War. "Actually, it's been four years and six days since you kissed me good night in the Officers Club parking lot at Camp McKinley. Remember that night?"

"Michelle, please don't –"

"Do you remember, Dave?" She took a deep breath, her chest rising and falling. "I do. I've thought of that night – and you – almost every day since."

"I shouldn't be here alone with you," he said nervously, glancing quickly down the hall toward the front door as if looking for an escape route.

"How do you mean that, Dave? Are you saying the laws of chance preclude the possibility of running into one another? Or are you saying that it's morally wrong for us to be having this conversation now?" She arched her eyebrows at him and tilted her pretty head. "Which is it?"

"I should be going," he replied guiltily, avoiding her question.

Michelle held his gaze as she moved slowly toward him, stopping inches away and placing her right hand gently on his chest. "Since that night at Camp McKinley, I can't hear a Dorsey tune, especially *I'm Getting Sentimental Over You*, without thinking about that night on the back porch of the O-Club with the moonlight spilling over Manila Bay. I can feel your heart beating, like I could that night on Long Island and again that night in Manila." She took his hand and slowly placed it on her chest. "And you can feel mine beating, too, can't you? Two hearts. Two hearts that should have been one. You and I were always meant to be together. You can't deny it."

"Michelle, I'm desperately in love with my wife. I'm a one woman man, you know that."

"I know that no one ever kissed me like you did. I know that the man who kissed me that night four years ago did it with all his passion."

"I was wrong to let it go that far. We were wrong that night and –"

"And what, Dave? That night in the little cottage on the shores of Long Island Sound, too?" Michelle looked away briefly. "I swore to myself that evening in Manila after you walked away from me that if I ever again got the chance to tell you what I was really feeling, I would. All those years, I avoided it – avoided you. And now suddenly here you are. Here *we* are," she said emphatically, and then continued in a low, imploring tone. "Nothing happens by chance, isn't that right, Dave? How many times have you told people that over the years? How many times did you tell me that since the summer day we met in front of our family house in Harrisburg before you went off to West Point? I know you remember."

He could not answer her. *Nothing by chance.* He'd said it so many times to so many people – including Denise, on the day he'd proposed to her.

"I'll never forget," she replied softly. "And I'll never forget that night after the Notre Dame game your sophomore year when you danced the whole evening with me. Or when you walked me to Colonel Perham's quarters around the edge of the parade ground and kissed me there on the front porch. That's another night we spent together I've thought about a lot – every time I visited Elise and Andy Fauser at West Point these past two years. Each time I passed those quarters on Thayer Road or Cullum Hall or Trophy Point, I thought of you. I wish things had worked out differently for us." When she looked at him, little tears danced along her lower lids. "I would have made you happy."

"Don't do this Michelle."

"I'm sorry, Dave, I can't help it. I can't help wondering what my life would have been if your division hadn't shipped out so suddenly, so unexpectedly. What if the Army in all its blissful incompetence had kept to its original schedule and waited until three weeks later to haul you and your division off to France? We would have been married and honeymooning in the Catskills like you'd planned. How differently would things have worked out if, after the war, you'd come back in early April with the rest of your regiment instead of seven weeks later." She looked away and took a deep breath. "I still love you, Dave. With all my heart I do."

Her breath came in short gasps, her mind swirling. *I can't believe this is really happening – it can't be. Not this suddenly, this unexpectedly; not like this. You're making a complete and utter fool of yourself. What are you doing?! Stop! Even if after all this time he still has some feelings for you, he can't and he won't...*

Suddenly, without willing it, her arms went around his neck and she pulled him close, kissing him as she had on Long Island when he was a lieutenant, and many years later in Manila. She was declaring her love for him, covering his face with soft kisses and pressing herself against him, lost in the moment. This was how she remembered the night in the parking lot at McKinley, the evening in the cottage at Eaton's Neck Point and she realized…

Michelle released him and stepped back, looking up, her face filled with surprise and disappointment. Embarrassed, she averted her eyes and said, "I'm sorry – not that I kissed you, but…" They stood in silence for what seemed to her an eternity until at last she said, "You're one of a kind, Dave Nolan. Everybody knows that. Especially me, and maybe Denise even does. I'll put this food away and then I'll go." She quickly put the cans and boxes into the pantry with her back to him, but when she finished and turned to look at him there was a solitary tear running down her cheek.

"Michelle –"

She quickly placed an extended finger on his lips. "No, Dave. Don't say anything. Please. More than once over the years you've said that what we did that night was wrong, that what we did was the cause of the problems and heartaches we each were experiencing. I think now that you were probably right. You've been right about us all along. I won't bother you again, ever. I promise. Like I told you that day outside the post office at Benning, you're one of the good guys. Denise is lucky to have you." The senator's pretty dark-haired daughter was suddenly visibly nervous, frantically looking about. Precipitately she brushed against the table knocking her purse to the floor, spilling its contents.

"Why am I always so blasted… *clumsy*, all the time!" she said aloud, furious at herself. And then she started to sob softly as she got down on hands and knees attempting to retrieve all her articles and put them back into her large handbag.

"Here, let me help you," Dave said, kneeling down, embarrassed for her.

"No! I did this and I can pick this up all by myself – I made the mess and I'll clean it up, thank you very much!"

But he continued picking up items spread across half the kitchen floor – some loose change, keys, a small note pad, a couple of wooden pencils and an expensive Esterbrook pen, a wadded up receipt of some sort; three or four buttons of different color and size. *Why do all women carry half their worldly belongings with them everywhere they go?* he asked himself. He'd broached the subject with Denise once and she'd not answered, just rolled her eyes and shook her head. He'd not asked *that* again.

At last Michelle stood and turned her back to him, stuffing things back into her purse and talking softly to herself.

"You must think I'm a complete idiot," she said angrily, sounding mortified. "This is the most embarrassing day of my life!... throwing myself at you – making a spectacle of myself, acting like a complete idiot and then knocking the contents of my purse all over the house. You must think I'm world's biggest fool, and I don't blame you."

"Michelle, I don't think that at all," he replied, starting to stand. Something nestled under the lower cabinets caught his eye – a piece of heavy thread or string attached to a small chunk of something. When he pulled it out he recognized it instantly and felt a strong surge like the jolt of an electric fence. For many seconds he stared at the small cube of wood with its fine carved lines – for an instant he was back on the tiny porch of a cottage overlooking the Sound at the end of Eaton's Neck Point. The time was evening and a candle flickered in a large storm globe on the table between them; a light breeze was blowing and the western sky was deep lavender and gold. He continued to stare at the small carved lantern, its wood now satiny and smooth as if hand rubbed. At last he looked up.

She was staring at him, her face streaked now and her eyes locked on his.

"You still have this, after all these years?" Dave asked, incredulous.

"Yes. And it's not because of some silly curse like you tried to tell me that night – what? over twenty years ago now? That last evening in Manila, I returned your class ring because it belonged to you. But this lantern, and the memories it holds, belong to me." Michelle quickly snatched it from him and placed it back in her purse. "It's the only thing I have left of 'us'… and despite what you or anyone else might think there really was once an 'us' for you and me." Taking a deep breath she said, "But I know now that's all behind. For good. This really is goodbye for you and me – for us, isn't it? Frankly, I'm glad it's finally over. Really glad."

Her trembling voice and despairing eyes betrayed the words.

Abruptly, Michelle brushed by him, walked quickly down the long narrow hallway and then outside without looking back. Conflicted and perplexed, Nolan watched the door swing shut, and heard the loud noise echo through the house.

Chapter 10

"Last year at this time we had an Army of a hundred and sixty thousand men," General Marshall said, looking around the conference room at his direct subordinates in Washington and their assistants. "That ranked us sixteenth in the world. Our Air Corps numbered twenty thousand men with twenty-two bombers and five hundred fighters – all of them obsolete.

"We have allies in Europe and – no, let me correct that – we have one ally in Europe left standing and an economic giant in the Pacific that has been for some years moving on China, the Southern Resources Area and other places vital to our interests. Men, we are still woefully unprepared – and that's the greatest understatement of my career." He again passed his gaze over the officers. "We're going to work day and night until that's corrected. Are we clear on that, gentlemen?"

Harrison Reeves heard the Army's Chief of Staff listing off the numbers of an inadequate military although his mind was elsewhere. This past week had been mostly frustrating and disagreeable, not only because of the reports coming from the European war and the Japanese expansion in the Pacific but also because of some lingering distasteful news in his personal life.

The work on the addition to his house in Silver Spring was behind schedule and riddled with cost overruns; his new secretary still hadn't got down the routine of the office to his satisfaction. Michelle had moved into a new brownstone in Georgetown to be closer to her work in her father's office, not that it much bothered him, except now he no longer had her to blame for the problems with the Baltimore contractor. And then of course there was the irritation of the latest news about his old classmate from the Academy, Dave Nolan.

Nolan, it appeared, had stolen another march on him and had waggled himself into a position in the Roosevelt administration close to Edward Stettinius and the president. *How galling*, he thought. *The damned dumbgard from Duncannon somehow did it again - got himself bumped to the head of the class by some lucky quirk of fate.* And worse than that, he was in a place untouchable by the Army's deputy chief of personnel, newly promoted Brigadier General Harrison Reeves. At least for the time being.

"This new Lend-Lease program idea is going to put a significant dent in the production runs of the B-25," General Hap Arnold was saying. "The way this new guy Nolan explained it they're going to take more than twenty percent of the production of B-25s and all the Lockheed A-28s for the next twelve months and send them to England. How can we survive that?"

"Increase production," Marshall replied. "It's becoming very clear that the president and this administration are moving toward a position of supporting England, at least with matériel."

"Apparently Nolan and Lord Beaverbrook have worked out a plan to fly them to England," Arnold said. "Can't be done. Not without high loss rates. In a way I can see what they're trying to do, because of all the sinkings of surface vessels. The Brits just had another ship with aircraft we'd consigned to them sunk by U-boats in the mid-Atlantic and there's no reason to believe that German subs won't pick off more. But flying the North Atlantic in the wintertime is about as close to suicide as you're going to find – the weather is just plain awful at that time of year. And that's when they'll begin because by the time they get the planes to Canada, hire the pilots and train them it'll be late October or early November. Weather will have long since deteriorated and my planners figure their loss rate will easily exceed fifty percent. Lord Beaverbrook has convinced Churchill otherwise." General Arnold shrugged and shook his head slowly. "I guess those are the kind of decisions you make when your back is against the wall."

"And their's is," Marshall observed.

"Apparently so."

"General Reeves, give me some good news about recruiting," Marshall said turning his head to the other side of the table."

"Yes sir, Our numbers of recruits are up and increasing. A draft plan for conscription nationwide is in the works," Reeves replied. "Our numbers in the Air Corps are up over 100% compared to this time last year. Ground forces up 49% to slightly more than 240,000 soldiers. Our plans triple the Air Corps to 450,000 and quadruple ground forces in a year. Contingencies are developed in the event the country finds itself at war in the next twelve months. However, those plans will require legislative action from Congress. My visits to training centers around the country over the past two and a half months indicate the biggest issue will be construction of basic training facilities for ground forces and staging airfields for flight training."

"We'll let General Adrian worry over facilities, General Reeves. You're still not up to emergency force levels – about a hundred and ten thousand short according to the report I saw late last month. Keep at it. General Adrian? Facilities?"

"Expansions mainly in the South and Southwest," the tall thin brigadier general replied, pushing a report across the table. "Benning and Bragg getting the most funding earliest. We've had good success with early deliveries of Air Corps facilities in Texas with a new contractor called Barrett Enterprises. New or refurbished facilities at Meade, Ellington Field in Houston, and Victoria all delivered early and under budget." Looking at Hap Arnold, he said, "You mentioned this man Nolan – is he the same one running the construction for E.W. Barrett?"

Arnold nodded. "I'm pretty sure he is."

"One and the same," General Marshall said without looking up from Adrian's report. "He's reporting to the War Resources Board as a part-time consultant for the next six months to help set up this Lend-Lease program."

"And he's also consulting with the Army and Navy Munitions Board in the area of civilian production and scheduling," Charles Hines, another one star general, added. "Apparently he's been to England and picked up some of their best practices and brought them back for us to use."

"Busy man," General Marshall observed, still leafing through the report in front of him. Shortly, he looked across the table at Harrison Reeves. "He's one of your West Point classmates isn't he, Harrison?"

"Yes sir, he is. He retired from the Army two years ago as a major after twenty-three years. From what's been said today, sir, it's good to hear he's found a career at which he can be somewhat successful." He smiled benignly at the Army's chief of staff who appeared not to notice and went on around the table receiving various reports in writing and listening to their verbal highlights. Most of the rest of the meeting was a blur to Reeves as his mind dwelt on the work still to be done on the guest cottage and how irritating it was to hear what he'd heard about Dave Nolan during the meeting. He was still aggravated after the meeting as he was stuffing papers back into his briefcase. A voice intruded into his thoughts.

"General Reeves. May I have a moment?" Harrison Reeves turned toward the voice which came from a junior lieutenant colonel, a quiet and rather colorless man named Shafter who worked in Hap Arnold's shop and dealt with Air Corps training. "Colonel Dunlop wanted me to run something by you since it has to do with Air Corps personnel numbers."

"Go ahead." Reeves answered, glancing impatiently at the aviator.

"Two things, sir. First, a request we just received this morning from the War Resources Board," Shafter replied. "They want us to provide liaison officers on temporary assignment to the Brits in Newfoundland; something to do with ferry flights to England. The Administration wants to ensure an American presence to keep an eye on the operation. That's only ten officers in total, but coupled with what we're seeing as an increasing wash out rate, we're going to fall noticeably short of the requirements for pilots this year. Colonel Dunlop wanted to give you an early warning in case you needed to do something about increasing recruitment aimed at pilot candidates in the fourth quarter."

"What's the problem with the dropout rate?"

"We don't know for sure what's causing the increased rate – maybe its lowered standards to increase recruiting numbers. We're looking into flight school curriculum and instructor pilot qualifications to see if there's something going on there. There also seems to be a rash of disciplinary cases for some reason." Shafter handed over a typed sheet with more than two dozen names; Reeves quickly glanced at the list and one name caught his eye.

Nolan, Mitchell A., 2Lt., 15623

"All right Shafter, I'll tell you what. I'll look into this and see what my office can do to help you out. But I'll need to know the infractions of each one of these officers here and see the original charge sheets. Get them to me by the end of the week and we'll work something out. No need to disappoint General Marshall or get you and General Arnold in trouble."

Harrison Reeves finished stuffing papers into his briefcase.

Maybe the father was out of his reach, but not so the son. He could take care of the disciplinary problem of Nolan's boy, on the surface doing a favor for an old classmate, and send young Nolan to Newfoundland bound for jolly old England across the North Atlantic.

What had Arnold said early in the meeting? - *flying the North Atlantic in the wintertime is about as close to suicide as you're going to find.* If the boy survived the trip, all well and good – David would be indebted to him. And if he didn't?

Well, people die in wars, he thought smugly.

* * * *

The tall, thin British Overseas Airways pilot with the four stripes of a senior captain on his uniform sleeve was announced by Lord Beaverbrook's secretary, Stella, and entered the office where the British cabinet minister stood quietly contemplating a map of the North Atlantic spread over the top of a long table.

"Captain Bennett," the minister said with enthusiasm coupled with a charming smile as he stepped forward and offered his hand. "It is an honor to finally meet you, sir."

"The honor is all mine, Lord Beaverbrook," the aviator replied.

Donald Clifford Tyndall Bennett was a thirty year old native Australian who had already been acclaimed by the British press as 'one of the most brilliant technical airmen of his generation: an outstanding pilot, a superb navigator who was also capable of stripping a wireless set or overhauling an engine.' He had joined the Royal Australian Air Force early in 1930, transferred to the Royal Air Force a year later and then left the RAF in 1935 to join Imperial Airways.

"You, sir are too kind," Lord Beaverbrook said laughing aloud. "You're a national hero, captain, with career achievements most men only dream of. Permit me to be direct. As illustrious as your splendid career has been thus far, what I am about to propose to you will outshine even your brilliant accomplishments. What I'm offering you, Donald, is greatness," Beaverbrook said, moving to a sideboard near the tall windows. "May I offer you a drink?"

"No, sir. Far too early for me."

"Ah, good, Bennett! A pilot should be sober – and so should cabinet ministers. I assure you I am, though you may think you have reason to doubt that shortly." Beaverbrook poured some Irish whiskey into a Rocks glass and motioned for the aviator to join him at the map. "The Germans are winning this war. We have hundreds of planes and they have thousands. We are receiving a trickle of aircraft from America by sea but the numbers are small and the chances of arrival in England are very slight and decreasing daily. Just last week a cargo vessel loaded with ten B-25s was sunk in the mid-Atlantic by U-boats. That was catastrophic, but even worse the next vessel with space for airplanes is yet six weeks away. We need a method of transferring aircraft from America which is more secure and allows for greater numbers. I have a plan to do just that." Lord Beaverbrook swept his hand across the map from west to east and said, "We are going to fly those airplanes from North America to England."

Bennett grew skeptical. "I honestly don't see how that can help us at the moment, Lord Beaverbrook. That would have to be a seasonal operation and winter will soon be upon us."

Beaverbrook laughed out loud. "Of course it's a seasonal operation – all four of them!"

"Sir, I would be glad to critique the details of your operation, but cross-Atlantic flights are still a challenge. No one has ever flown the North Atlantic in the wintertime. Has it been pointed out to you, Lord Beaverbrook, that flying the Atlantic in winter is impossible?"

"Not by anyone I trust. Look, Captain, I'm not asking you to critique this operation, I'm asking you to run it."

Bennett responded with a nervous laugh. "Why isn't the RAF running this? They're not supplying pilots, are they?" Beaverbrook shook his head negatively. "So this plan will rely on civilians – Canadians. Yanks. Brits, and others. It would require pilots, navigators, radio operators, mechanics - all of which are in short supply everywhere."

"All true," Beaverbrook admitted, undaunted. "Greatness requires overcoming great odds and difficulties, something you have done all of your young life. That's why I want you, and that's why I believe you will say yes."

"You would lose at least half your planes in the attempt."

"Even so it would be better than what we have now. Listen to me Donald, this must be done. There is no other option if England is to survive. It's an air war, and we're losing it. Hitler has the planes and while our own aircraft production is increasing, all our projections indicate it is not enough. We must have more."

The tall Australian bit his lower lip as he glanced at the map in front of him, seemingly doing some calculations in his head tracing the arc from Newfoundland to Northern Ireland. He remained silent for some minutes, sometimes frowning sometimes gazing out the window of the cabinet minister's office. At last he turned to Beaverbrook, a scowl on his face and his mouth a thin, determined line.

"As I said my lord, we'll need pilots, radio operators, and above all, navigators – all as scarce as hen's teeth."

The cabinet minister looked back at him, a smile beginning to form on his lips. "Make your list captain, and then quadruple it. I'm not talking about a few hundred airplanes; I'm talking about thousands. I knew you were the man for the job!"

Bennett's eyes returned to the map. "We'll stage at Newfoundland, the biggest piece of tarmac in all of North America. It was built for the trans-Atlantic passenger service rather ahead of its time. It appears it's time has come."

Beaverbrook moved to the sideboard and poured Bennett a drink then handed it to him and raised his own in a toast. "I can see the headline now – 'Hero from the oldest colony saves mother country in time of greatest need.' I still own two newspapers and I'll make sure that headline is seen by the British public when you succeed – of which I am supremely confident." They touched glasses and toasted to their future success.

"Cheers," Captain Bennett said.

"To men of action," Beaverbrook responded. "What you are about to do Captain Bennett will change the course of the war. We have the prime minister's blessing, and his admonishment to quote: *make it work*. We have the support of an American named Nolan who is now well placed in President Roosevelt's administration to help us make this operation a success. And he believes, as I do, that it will be – so much so that he has apparently placed his own son in charge of the American end of our endeavor. The young man is a junior officer in their Air Corps, an aviator himself. It appears he is your first Yank pilot to volunteer."

Bennett nodded. "That is good news, sir. I can already think of several areas in which an experienced military pilot can be useful."

"His father certainly has been a great aid to our cause so far," Beaverbrook replied, refilling his glass. "I'm sure the son will be as well."

*   *   *   *   *

The Mk III Lockheed Hudson had spent most of the last two hours droning through the dark storm clouds shrouding southeast Canada flying solely on instruments, being bumpily tossed about by rough winds of an early fall storm and making Mitch Nolan certain that at any moment he'd throw up all over the instrument panel in front of him.

He was riding in the right seat of the airplane, known to the Army Air Corps as the A-28. And for the last hour he'd been self-absorbed wondering what he'd done to deserve this and whether General Reeves had really been his savior or adversary in working out a way for him to get back into flight school.

"You got the controls, lieutenant. I need to take a look at the map again," the older pilot in the left seat said over the intercom, looking at him and making an overt display of removing his hands from the control yoke of the bomber. He was a civilian, as were all the other pilots in the flight of eight aircraft which had left the Lockheed plant in southern California early in the morning the previous day headed for St. Hubert airport outside Montreal. They had spent the night in Kansas City, Missouri and left there at sunrise, a little over seven hours earlier. Now Mitch found himself at the controls of a twin-engine aircraft, flying by instruments, unsure of his exact location and wishing at the moment that he was doing something other than flying – all of these events were firsts for him.

"We're still locked on the Montreal beam, about two miles short of Saint-Zotique if this radio is accurate and I'm readin' the map right." The older man reached over and pulled the throttles back slowly. "Take it down to two thousand and see if we can't break out. The river should be out your side. Saint Hubert should be at our two o'clock maybe twenty-five or thirty miles. Montreal should be dead ahead. We're driftin' left of the beam – must be pickin' up a south wind. Crank in about ten degrees more right correction."

They continued to lose altitude until the clouds thinned and finally at 3000 feet they could begin to make out objects on the ground. Off the right wing Mitch could see the St. Lawrence River paralleling their ground track; in a few minutes, he could see downtown Montréal in front of them. They leveled off at 1500 feet, skirted the city to the southeast staying over the river. Not long after, he could make out two parallel runways to his right front both running northeast – southwest. The pilot made the call to the tower, received clearance to land on runway 24, and Mitch turned the Hudson to the right and entered a left downwind.

"You want to take it in, captain?" Mitch asked, looking to his left.

"No, you do it. That landing yesterday was a little rough, and you look like you could use the practice. I'll take care of the throttles and the props for you; you just fly the airplane and tell me when to the chop the power at touchdown."

The pilot went through the pre-landing check, set the switches, the power, and made the radio calls to the tower letting Mitch concentrate on flying the pattern and setting the Hudson up for final approach and landing. When the big twin-engine plane finally did touch down the landing was surprisingly smooth and elicited a compliment from the left seater.

"How long did you say you been flying, lieutenant?" the pilot asked as Mitch taxied the twin-engine Lockheed to the ramp adjacent to the hangar where one other of the aircraft in the ferry flight had been parked.

"First solo was in '35 in the Philippines. Haven't flown a lot in the past few years. And to be perfectly honest with you, yesterday and today were the only hours I've ever logged under actual instrument conditions." Mitch was about to tell him that these were also the only hours he had ever flown a twin-engine aircraft, but thought better of it.

A tall thin man, wearing a suit and a gray fedora with a wide black hatband walked from the hangar over to the two parked Hudsons as their engines coasted to a stop. While the captain went through the shut down and post-flight checklist, Mitch unbuckled his harness, got out of the seat and went to the rear of the airplane to open the door; the man approached as he stepped down from the airplane.

"Captain Don Bennett," the man offered, sticking out his right hand while holding onto his hat with the other. "Welcome to St. Hubert."

"Mitch Nolan."

"Ah, quite. So good to make your acquaintance, leftenant." He looked to the south briefly then turned back and said, "Join me for tea inside the hangar while we wait for the rest of your chaps? How was the flight from California?"

"Long. Two very long days – each one seven hours plus, strapped to the seat with enough instrument time to keep it interesting. Let's just say it was more business than pleasure."

"So, you're comfortable with instrument flying," the British Overseas pilot observed as they entered the hangar. He motioned to a seat next to a wooden desk flanked by a large chalk board on one side and student desks on the other, all arranged in a corner just inside the hangar doors. "Sorry, I can offer only China tea, but with a dash of lemon."

"Sounds fine. As far as instrument flying goes, I've got enough now in the Hudson to say it flies well under those conditions. All in all a pretty solid machine in the air and much improved performance now with the new 1200 horsepower Pratt & Whitney engines," Mitch said nonchalantly, trying to sound more experienced than he was. His orders out of Washington had directed him to accompany the aircraft to St. Hubert, turn them over to the British, and ensure proper transition training of the aircrews prior to returning to Randolf Field – no reporting date noted. There wasn't any indication what the transition training encompassed, only that he was ultimately responsible.

So far as he could tell the mission was utterly open-ended, as if whoever wrote his orders didn't really care about its success or failure.

He'd spent two weeks at the Lockheed plant in Burbank arriving there just in time to see the entire assembly of one of the eight planes to be ferried to Canada - it had taken only nine days from start to finish including the initial test flight. During that period he'd been able to spend time with the engineers poring over the design and construction drawings of the Hudson and was able to follow every fabrication step from beginning to end. The assembly crews treated him like a quality assurance inspector and answered all of his questions and even allowed him to assist in some of the minor assembly of systems. By the end of his week and a half at the plant, he knew the Hudson inside out; it was one of the most enjoyable things he'd done since helping Glenn tear apart and rebuild his old James motorbike in Manila.

The ferry flight from California to St. Hubert was somewhat less agreeable.

"Our training is rather slower than I'd hoped," Bennett told him as he placed the cups and saucers on the desk. "We're paying each of these chaps $800 American for this flight which seems to have drawn the attention of quite a few men willing to risk their lives but having precious little experience or expertise in flying. In the last three weeks I've seen more padded logbooks than one is likely to run across in a lifetime. I have a few who are decent pilots but sadly, in the main, they are unschooled and lacking in experience. I'd not been prepared for the level of ignorance concerning basic aviation skills and simple navigation I've encountered. Making matters worse, according to Lord Beaverbrook, we are dreadfully behind schedule."

"How can I help?" Mitch asked. "My orders are pretty open-ended. My job is to deliver these eight aircraft and ensure a proper transition from us to you. I'll help you anywhere, any way I can. During my ground school training I helped about half my class get through aviation basics and navigation. I also have experience in tail draggers like the Hudson, and I know the Mk III systems well enough to troubleshoot and repair them."

Bennett eyed him over the rim of his teacup, and finally asked, "Can you do celestial navigation?"

"No, but I'm a quick study. If you teach it to me, I can help you teach it to others."

"You say you have experience with tail draggers. Have you ever done a ground loop?"

Mitch sat back in his chair and smiled. "Once."

"You're the first one I've met during my time here who told me the truth about that."

"Everyone who's ever flown a tail dragger has done at least one ground loop – anyone who says otherwise is lying to you. But someone who tells you that he's done two is probably not somebody you want flying your airplane." Mitch Nolan took another long sip of tea, set the cup down and looked directly into Bennett's eyes. "I'm prepared to teach your pilots a basic understanding of the systems and the bare essentials they need to do a long cross-country."

"Can you provide flight instruction in the Hudson?"

"And a check ride to ensure you they can handle the aircraft."

"Instrument training?"

Mitch looked around the nearly empty hangar and saw a Link trainer set up near the back wall. "Honestly, no, not if you want me to operate the Link. I'll take them up in the Hudson and put them under the hood, but if you need a qualified instrument instructor or someone to run the simulator, I'm not your man. Other than that, I'll take on just about anything you need to transition these men into the aircraft for your flight. It sounds like you can use the help – I'm here and I'll do whatever you need doin'."

Captain Bennett sat stiffly in his chair, his eyes fixed on the young American. Finally he said, "You're very sure of yourself for one so young."

"The same age you were when you joined the Australian Air Force ten years ago."

"You're only twenty?"

"Twenty-one my next birthday."

"How did you get into your military academy at such a young age?" Bennett asked, raising his eyebrows in surprise.

"My parents started me out in school a year early, and then when we were stationed at Camp Huachuca in Arizona I was the only one in third grade so they put me in with the fourth-graders and I stayed with them until we moved. Academics always came pretty easily to me and classroom work in the military schools was never all that difficult. I stayed ahead of the game all the way through my education." Bennett seemed a little worried now, his face drawn down into a troubled scowl. "Tell you what captain, give me any navigation problem you've given these men of yours, and ask me any question you want that's covered in the operating manual for the Hudson and see if I don't give you the right answer."

Bennett drew back slightly and gazed at him with a thoughtful, cautious look. "You're perhaps altogether too self-assured."

"I prefer confident. And if what you said is true about the level of ignorance of flying in your volunteers, you need someone like me. I've been given an assignment by my superiors that includes providing an adequate transition into this aircraft to help ensure the success of your mission – in essence, to protect the investment of the United States. The way I look at it, I've got as big a stake in this operation as anyone, including you. The ferry mission across the Atlantic is your operation. I know you're the boss… but I'm your damned partner.

"So now, Captain Bennett, let me ask again – how can I help you?"

*   *   *   *

Dave Nolan walked slowly down the broad hallway of the Army's Assignments Branch looking for the office of an old friend and classmate, Colonel Barton Scarborough.

Bart had been in the Army's headquarters, responsible for infantry and artillery branch officer assignments for over three years. At the Academy, Scarborough had been the executive officer of C Company next door in the barracks to the cadet company Dave commanded his senior year – company B. They had been in many of the same academic classes those four years and played together on the Army baseball team. Bart had been a longtime friend; they had stayed in touch by correspondence following graduation. They had attended the same company commanders' course at Camp Benning in the mid-20s, and had even been assigned together for a short period at Camp Lewis in Washington state during the Depression.

It took him longer than expected to find Scarborough's office. He knocked once and entered, finding himself in a small outer office manned by a secretary who looked up from her typing as he walked in.

"Yes, sir, may I help you?"

"I'm Dave Nolan. I called and talked to you earlier this morning."

"Oh, yes sir," the woman said, smiling and looking at him over the top of her reading glasses. "Go right in, he's expecting you."

Nolan opened the door and entered to find Scarborough taking some items from a bookcase covering a side wall and placing them into cardboard boxes.

"Looks like moving day, Bart."

Scarborough looked up from his task and waved him toward a chair facing the large metal desk. "Very observant, Dave. Yeah, I'm moving all right. Got shit-canned by your old friend and mine, Harrison Reeves. He transferred me down to Benning to a lieutenant colonel job pushing basic training troops - essentially the same job you and I did as second lieutenants in our first assignment after graduation."

Nolan frowned but remained silent until Scarborough sat down behind his desk. "Sorry to hear that Bart. How soon?"

"Reporting date is two days before Thanksgiving. Nice of him to throw that in, wasn't it? I've got forty days of leave coming, so I'm taking off just as soon as I can – to get as far away from him as fast as I can. Want some coffee?" the colonel asked, pressing the intercom button. "Charlotte, two coffees please. Both as black as General Reeves heart."

Nolan was surprised at both Scarborough's words and his demeanor. Bart had always been an easy going, happy-go-lucky cadet and officer. The Barton Scarborough sitting across the desk from him now bore little resemblance to what he remembered. "Pretty harsh words, Bart. I don't remember you being like that."

"I never was until I started working around Reeves. Never really knew him when we were cadets – had a few classes with him, but that was about it. He always seemed a little stuck up, a little aloof. I had just started working here – maybe six months before you were sent to Berlin as Lindbergh's traveling companion – when I first began to see and understand what he was really like. The man is devious, manipulative, underhanded, malicious – and those are his good points."

Nolan was uncomfortable listening to Scarborough's diatribe. "Listen Bart, I didn't really come here to talk about Harrison. I was hoping to talk to you about getting some consideration for a couple of friends."

"What does that mean, Dave?"

"A personal favor for me on behalf of their wives." Scarborough leaned back in his chair and frowned as Dave continued. "Two men who were company commanders for me when I had a battalion in the Philippines a few years back – Cole Alford and Judd Haggarty. Both of these guys were in my command in Europe as well as the Philippines. They've been in the islands now for over four years. Their wives have been moved back to the U.S. – seven or eight months now – and they came to me a little over a month ago and asked if there was something I could do or somebody I knew who could help bring their families back together again. I thought about you. And so I'm asking if there's anything you might be able to do for them. They're both really good soldiers, Bart. They're the kind of officers I would fight to keep in my command – and I did. The kind you would go out on a limb for."

"What kind of assignment?"

"Troop assignments. For Alford – maybe even an instructor assignment at West Point. You remember Andy Fauser, don't you? He's head of the Tactics Department at the school and he told me he's short-handed. Both of them could probably be very helpful for you in this assignment that you're going to; they're both excellent trainers of troops. Can you help them?"

Scarborough sat back in the chair, intertwined his fingers in front of his chest and looked up at the ceiling, contemplating. He opened a side desk drawer and extracted a thick stack of paper and began to flip through the pages stopping now and then to run his finger across some of the print before moving on. After a few minutes he stopped nodding his head up and down and looked up at Dave Nolan.

"I can't promise for certainty, Dave, but the answer is probably yes. For you, I'll work on it and do my darndest. Chances look pretty good. I'll have one of my guys pull the records, check their efficiency reports and get them a couple of decent assignments back here in the States so that they can be with their families. Honestly, it'd be nice to do something like that for a change. Would probably even piss off Harrison Reeves and for that alone it would be worth the effort." Scarborough seemed deep in thought for a while and finally asked, "You don't have any dealings with Reeves anymore, do you Dave?"

"No."

"But your son does."

"Not directly that I know of. Why?"

"I just learned about three weeks ago of a meeting Reeves was in where he volunteered to help the Air Corps with some personnel issues. You may not know this, but the Air Corps is operating more and more independently from the rest of the Army. That includes personnel matters. But for some reason Reeves went out of his way to insert himself personally into a situation – one that involved your son. In fact, I assumed that's what you wanted to talk to me about when you called yesterday."

Nolan didn't like the sound of what he was hearing. "We'd heard through a friend of his he'd gotten himself in a little trouble for buzzing a control tower but that was about it. You're telling me there's more to this?"

"A lot more," Scarborough replied seriously, raising his eyebrows and leaning forward on his elbows. "Reeves pretty much took control of the situation and dictated the finding of a flight evaluation board that Mitch be removed from flying status, immediately dropped from flight training and reassigned to the infantry. That's what happened. Immediately after – by that I mean the next day – he directed the Air Corps to offer him a deal. If your son would go on a ferry flight of Hudson bombers across the North Atlantic to England, he would be allowed to remain in the Air Corps and start over in flight school."

Dave Nolan looked into the eyes of his classmate and felt an animate uneasiness sweep through him. "I know the ferry flights you're talking about. I've had more than one long conversation with Lord Beaverbrook about them. I know they're dangerous, like I've always thought all of flying was dangerous. I'm aware that the initial flights will be more dangerous than most, but Beaverbrook and the Brits are confident in their success. He's got one of the world's most competent aviators running the show, and assured me that the initial flight would prove the concept and make the later flights routine and less hazardous. Mitch's flying has always worried me a little bit. And if he ever does go on one of these ferry flights, both his mother and I will be more worried than we probably should be."

Scarborough took a deep breath and looked away, deep in thought for long seconds before he turned to look back at Nolan. "There's some things you don't know, Dave. First – none of the RAF higher ups now think Beaverbrook's idea is worth a damn. He's the kind of guy who thinks that everything he dreams up is automatically a success because so far in his life that's been the case. When he went to England from Canada he set his sights on being a

135

member of the House of Lords – within a year he had a peerage and was no longer Max Aitken but suddenly Lord Beaverbrook. His newspaper business was the same way. Not only does the RAF staff think this is a bad idea, but Hap Arnold's crew in the Air Corps also think it's a suicide mission. The weather over the North Atlantic is so notoriously unpredictable, especially in the winter time when they want to do this first flight.

"Secondly – the way that Reeves had the orders written your son is the one ultimately responsible for the first flight of eight arriving in England. Not Beaverbrook. Not the RAF. Not that hot shot flyer from Australia. But 2nd Lieutenant Mitchell A. Nolan is. My guess is he's probably a lot like you. If that's true, my next guess is that he won't be left behind watching those planes fly off the runway while he waves at them; he'll be in the first airplane flying, leading, navigating, and fixing whatever mechanical problems that happen along way."

"Have to admit that's probably a couple of pretty good guesses," Dave confessed. "Sounds like you know him."

"I don't, but Harrison Reeves is pretty confident that he does. I personally heard him say to some light colonel on Arnold's staff he'd watched your son grow up and even helped him along the way. He's counting on his evaluation of your boy's personality. From what I hear he assumes our Air Corps boys are right about the outcome of Beaverbrook's latest scheme."

Dave Nolan took a deep breath and looked up at the ceiling and thought to himself: *what have I done? Kate Hanley was right about me years ago, that night of our going away party at the officers club at West Point. I stick my nose into places where it shouldn't be, thinking I can fix things by the force of my will. What an idiot I am. Thinking that I was important enough or smart enough to go to England and help them solve their problems so that they could win this damn war against Hitler.*

"Another thing you should know Dave – I was in the meeting the day Reeves scuttled your military career. That business over Lindbergh receiving that German Order of the Eagle when you were assigned as his liaison officer in Berlin, and later when you supposedly interpreted for him and Hermann Goering at a meeting in the American Embassy. General Kruger and the four of us who were his direct reports were called into a meeting to address those problems. Reeves engineered the whole damned thing to put the blame on you and to eliminate both he and I from the discussions. Without him in the meeting, he could never be blamed for anything that came out of it; and with me eliminated from the discussion, there was no one to state your side of the case. It was brilliant. In the end, you were demoted and recalled from Berlin. General Kruger was removed from his position when all the facts finally came down, and Harrison Reeves took his place and got promoted to a one star."

"Why are you telling me all this, Bart?" Dave wanted to know.

"I wanted you to know the truth, Dave. I've always felt guilty about what happened to you and about how you were treated."

Dave thought for some time and finally said, "The truth is that maybe Harrison Reeves did me and my family a favor. My wife has never been happier; we have more financial security than we've ever had, and I have no worries about my future with my current employer. Maybe I should thank him."

"But look what he did to your son."

"No, I can't really blame that on him either. I was the one who did this. It's my fault if something happens to Mitch. I set all this in motion." He stood, walked slowly to the door and opened it before turning and looking at Barton Scarborough. "Bart, don't forget those two soldiers I told you about – Cole Alford and Judd Haggarty. If you think you owe me anything, then get them transferred back to the states and we'll call it even." Nolan thanked his old friend and left the office deeply troubled. He walked down the hall of the Army Assignments Branch worried about one thing.

What have I done to you, Mitch?

*   *   *   *

What have you done to deserve this? Mitch Nolan thought to himself as the Hudson leveled off at eight thousand feet.

Three thousand feet below him was a broken layer of clouds that ran off in all directions through which, from time to time, he could see the ground. Toward the setting sun the cloud layer had formed itself into what looked like a series of parallel hills and valleys stretching out to the horizon. The setting sun reflected off the higher levels of clouds turning them into long, fluffy gold mounds. In the troughs the clouds became deep lavender; beneath the right wing and just ahead of them the cloud formation had settled into a deep bowl now dark blue with only occasional gold colored accents.

Only one time in his life had he seen a sky this beautiful.

"What do you think, Mike. Ready to head back to the barn?" Mitch asked.

"Do we have to, Mitch? I think I'd be satisfied just to stay up here and look at this forever. Have you ever seen anything like this before?"

"Only once –a few years back over Mindanao." Mitch checked his watch and saw it was almost 6 PM. "Ground crews will be wondering where we got to. Time to head back. Know where you are?" The pilot nodded. "All right, head for home."

Mike Seagraves slowly turned toward the southwest and rolled out level.

Mitch allowed Seagraves to continue flying for another thirty seconds and then asked, "Where's the airport from here?"

"Directly off our nose?"

"Is that a question or an answer, Mike?

"Question, I guess."

When Seagraves seemed stumped, Mitch finally said, "I've got the controls. You look at the map and locate the beacon and the airport and then give me a heading that I should turn to taking us back to St. Hubert."

Seagraves opened the map and fumbled with it but finally located both the airport and the location of the AM radio beacon. "The radio beacon is located just to the south of Montréal about five miles southwest of the airport, so we should head northwest about two-nine-zero, or maybe three-zero-five."

"That might get us close enough to locate the airport, but maybe not in this weather. While I'm turning back, I want you to look at the map. The beacon is actually located 3.8 miles from runway six on the airport. The heading from the beacon to the airport is zero-five-seven degrees. So, if we fly to the beacon on that heading – zero-five-seven – and as soon as we cross over the beacon we start the stopwatch and fly for exactly one minute and fifty-four seconds at 120 miles per hour we'll cross directly over the runway. Do you see what I'm saying?"

"I guess so. That kind of makes sense."

It was clear to Mitch that Seagraves really didn't understand what he was saying and that he would have to cover it with him once on the ground.

Seagraves was much like most of the pilots that Bennett had recruited. Only three or four out of the two dozen pilots really seemed to have much flying time or any feel for piloting. No wonder the Australian had been so nervous and defensive when they'd first met. And in the ten days that followed it became clear that not only was Lord Beaverbrook putting a great deal of pressure on Bennett, but Bennett was putting a lot of pressure on himself. There was no way the Aussie could possibly teach all the ground school classes and also teach them how to fly the Hudson, an aircraft he'd never flown himself.

"First thing," Mitch was saying once established on a heading directly toward the Montréal beacon. "We have to lose some altitude. We're way too high for as close as we are to the airport, which is about twenty miles away. What's the pattern altitude at St. Hubert?"

"Twelve hundred feet," Seagraves replied quickly.

"That's right. We want to be about three hundred feet above that when we pass over the beacon headed towards the airport so we can let down slowly and gradually into the traffic pattern. Here's our problem – we have a broken under cast and we have to lose a lot of altitude in a fairly short distance and period of time. Here's how we do that: cross control. "We take the plane out of trim – aileron in one direction and rudder in the opposite direction. That significantly increases the rate of descent. Watch what I'm doing and watch what happens."

Mitch pulled the throttles back while turning the control yoke to the left and applying more rudder by pushing on the right panel with his foot. He pointed the nose of the big Hudson slightly below the horizon aiming it through a break in the clouds where he could see the ground. The vertical speed indicator on the panel quickly crept past a thousand feet per second rate of descent; he made small corrections to keep it at that rate. Soon they could see the city of Montréal just off to the right of their nose.

"Mike, it's your airplane. Take the controls and enter a left downwind for runway two-four. You make the calls to tower and tell me when you want the pre-landing checklist."

Seagraves' landing was a little long and fast but not terribly bad. Mitch had learned through experience over the last six days that the Hudson Mk III was a docile plane to fly but much more difficult to take off and land. Although he had barely more time in the aircraft than the volunteer pilots he was training, he'd discovered quickly the Hudson's idiosyncrasies.

It was almost dark when they finally shut down the engines and the ground crew rolled it into the hangar. After a twenty-minute debriefing with Seagraves, he wandered over to where Bennett sat at his desk going over some administrative details with his "gal-Friday", a tall dark-haired girl named Sheila from Gander, about six hundred miles east.

She had moved to Montréal to make her own way and leave behind the back woods where she'd grown up. Bennett had hired her out of a secretarial pool in the city to do his typing, and to send and receive messages via teleprinter. She was somewhat pretty – a thin girl, anything but shy, and in heels almost as tall as Bennett. She had personally recruited all but one of the two dozen pilots now in the operation – most of them in bars and dance halls in and around the city. She had quickly sized up 'the rather forward Yank' – as she referred to Mitch – and made sure he knew she had a long time beau back home in Gander.

"Well, Nolan, how did today's flying go?" Captain Bennett asked brusquely. Mitch was beginning to wonder if the Aussie ever laughed or smiled or had any sense of humor at all. "I saw Seagraves' last landing was rather long and fast."

"They'll get better with time. That was only his fourth landing ever in the aircraft, and the Hudson's not real tame on takeoff or landing. Whenever you come out from behind that desk and get into the left seat with me we'll see how well *you* do your first time in the saddle." He glanced at the girl who was listening to their conversation with her eyes averted.

"Perhaps tomorrow," Bennett was saying.

"I'll set aside the entire day just for you."

"A whole day? I'm honored." Turning to Sheila and passing her a handwritten sheet the captain said, "Type these lists for me, if you will, Miss Emberley. I've noted the order in the left hand column. Thank you."

Mitch glanced quickly at the list of names and saw Seagraves was numbered twenty-three on the pilots list, next to last. "Your order of rank for selection?"

"At the moment, yes. According to Lord Beaverbrook I've got only until the end of November to deliver the aircraft. Apparently the RAF and the Royal Navy are both chomping at his heels. And so, he's chomping at mine. I've eight too many pilots and six too many navigators – if you call the chaps I have navigators.."

"You've got Seagraves listed too low on your list of pilots. I'd have him at number fifteen, right behind Townsend."

Bennett frowned at him and then slowly shook his head from side to side. "Afraid not. He barely understands the concept of a wind triangle, and has done abysmally in the Link trainer. I daresay your evaluation of him on his first flight would coincide with my own ranking and he's the only one so far to whom you've given a second lesson."

"Because he's trainable."

"In your opinion."

"In my *considered* opinion."

"I shall take that under advisement, Nolan." Turning to Sheila, Bennett said, "That will be all Miss Emberley." Bennett reached into his lower left desk drawer and produced a bottle of whiskey and two glasses. He poured two fingers of liquor into each and handed one to Mitch Nolan. "Let us talk about my first flight in the Hudson tomorrow."

"Actually, I was planning to take the day off," Mitch said, sipping from the glass, "but for you I'll forego it. I'm not really gonna give you the whole day. Maybe two hours right before lunch. To tell you the truth, I need a little time off after six straight days, four flights a day. My backside is wearing out."

"For a while I thought you were intentionally avoiding either me or celestial navigation."

"I was," Mitch answered taking a sip of his whiskey. "I find both rather tedious."

"I see," Bennett replied. "Tedious you say?"

"Believe I did."

"It might surprise you to learn that I find you tedious as well."

"There you go captain, something we can finally agree on." Mitch raised his glass toward Bennett and toasted, "To tediousness."

"On a more serious note," Bennett began.

"We weren't being serious?"

The Australian ignored him and said, "I'm rather surprised at your championing Seagraves as one of our selected pilots."

"Not only is he teachable, he's also loyal. Dependable. I'm impressed with those qualities as well. I believe in another month he'll be one of the top pilots in the group. He's got that kind of work ethic."

"I'm similarly affected with your work ethic, Nolan. Your assessments are clear, concise and surprisingly perceptive for someone of your age and inexperience. You see, I know your circumstances, and frankly I'm greatly puzzled your country would send us someone with your, shall we say checkered, background for such an important mission."

Mitch took another sip of the whiskey, felt it slide fur over his tongue, and grinned tight-lipped at the Australian. "I've been thinking about that myself for a while. You see, there are a lot of people in my government who don't think this is going to work. Your government too, I would imagine. Somebody somewhere higher up in Washington needs a scapegoat, and bagging one is the easiest of all hunting expeditions. So, I'm the scapegoat. That's my theory, has been from the beginning."

"And you still volunteered?"

"They made it worth my while. They dangled the chance for me to redeem myself and here I am having the time of my life. I'm getting fifty hours flying time a week as an instructor– all of that in multi-engine – and the Army is paying me to do it." He finished his drink and poured himself another from Bennett's bottle. "What more could a guy ask for?!"

Chapter 11

"I say Lord Beaverbrook, that's just not possible!"

Mitch Nolan sat across the desk from Bennett, hearing only one side of the transatlantic telephone call but keenly aware the Australian was more upset than at any time he'd observed him in the month since they'd first met.

"No sir! As I've told you before my navigators are just not ready. And they can't possibly be in that amount of time... No, sir, that will not work either. One navigator for the whole lot cannot possibly do. It's unfeasible that these men can fly all the way across the North Atlantic in formation in the type of weather we're likely to encounter along the way... My place is here, sir... No, sir, that's crazy."

Donald Bennett over the past few weeks had grown increasingly less confident in the ability of his navigators, although his trust in Mitch's assessment of the pilots had grown. Not that those evaluations were getting better, but because the captain had flown with a handful of the pilots and confirmed for himself what Nolan had been telling him.

"At the moment, sir, I cannot assure you in any way of the mission's success, and certainly not with the possibility of shortening my training of the crews by that much... That is far too early sir. Lord Beaverbrook I – of course, sir. But Lord Beaverbrook... Sir... Sir... are you there?" Bennett held out the phone and just stared at for many seconds before looking up and giving Nolan a look of utter exasperation. "I can't believe it. I just can't believe it. The man is a bloody fool. He's moved up the schedule yet again – this time all the way to mid-November. Only three weeks and a half from now! He said Archie Sinclair was at his heels like a bloody rabid spaniel and therefore we must cut short our training."

"Who's Archie Sinclair?"

"Sir Archibald Sinclair, 1st Viscount Thurso. He's Secretary of State for Air –a cabinet minister. He and others are pressuring Churchill to pull the plug if we don't get these planes to England very soon. I told him how hard you and I are pushing these recruits but that they are more ignorant than I could have imagined. And you know what he said to me? – that I was a damned perfectionist. Can you believe that? Then he said 'good luck' and hung up on me – just like that! We'll lose the lot of them. Do you know what he recommended just now when I told him my navigators were wholly unready? He suggested I be the one to navigate for the whole lot and that everyone fly formation off of me. How ludicrous!"

Mitch thought about that for a second and shrugged. "Why not do it?"

"Because, Nolan, it's just not done. One cannot expect pilots – even seasoned ones – to fly close formation in the kind of weather we're likely to encounter. With as little time in the cockpit on this particular aircraft as these gentlemen have, it's just not done – not possible."

"Flying the North Atlantic in winter was something *just not done* when you started this. I'd suggest firming up crew assignments now and practicing cross-country formation flying."

Bennett frowned looking entirely dubious. "Even if the pilots can master it – which I'm not at the moment willing to concede – what happens if we're separated by weather?"

"Expect every crew do its own dead reckoning from beginning to the end of the mission, whether in formation or not. That would have to happen in any event. That's the reality, Bennett. Actually, I think the idea of formation flying – a loose formation with you leading and doing the primary navigation – is not a bad idea."

"My place is here recruiting pilots, training them and running the show, not going off and flying across the Atlantic."

"Is that what you told Beaverbrook?" Donald Bennett nodded. "And what did he say?"

"He said that 'crazy' wins, and that's when he hung up. I think I heard him laughing."

Mitch thought for a while as Bennett fumed and scratched out notes on a piece of paper. "For what it's worth, captain, here's what I think. I grew up in the Army, saw my dad handle tough situations and heard from his friends and subordinates how he operated. I heard from a Navy friend of his how they do things in Naval aviation. There's a constant to getting the job done and it rests with the leader. A military flying leader does three things: he flies, leads and trains – that's how he ensures the mission succeeds. Sounds to me kinda like the job you got."

"Perhaps. But I still have the problem remaining with these navigators."

"If the navigators can't navigate, replace them with pilots. The three most useless things in flying are the runway behind you, the sky above you and a navigator who can't navigate. Every one of the pilots can dead reckon, at least to some degree; and they can home to a beacon. Having an extra pilot in the cockpit could come in handy on a long flight like this."

"But we have too much to do to leave in time to arrive by the middle of November. For one thing, from the flights logged thus far we have discovered the fuel consumption on half the aircraft exceeds what we expected. We need larger auxiliary fuel tanks than the ones we now have for the ferry flight. I'm going to put you on that problem. Who would you recommend to lead the formation training flights?"

"Roberson. And you. You need to fly some formation as well, including some time out in the fourth or fifth aircraft to see what happens behind the lead if he isn't careful with power and heading corrections. You'll also see how important the number two aircraft is – he determines how close everybody flies and how large or small the corrections are to stay in formation. That has a big influence on fuel consumption." Mitch looked at the concern on Captain Bennett's face. "We have a lot to do in three weeks, including night formations."

"I shall assign final crew positions this evening and plan on a briefing first thing in the morning and then set out on our first formation flight," Bennett said, sounding almost relieved at the thought of making final decisions and putting plans into action. "Tell me, Nolan, where shall I place you? What do your orders say about making this flight yourself?"

"Actually, as far as I can tell, my orders don't say that I can. Then again, they don't say that I can't. If I were you I'd put me in the number eight slot and let me fly tail end Charlie."

"I was thinking of putting you with me in the lead aircraft."

Mitch shook his head. "I have more time in the Hudson than anybody here, and can monitor how the other aircraft are doing from the tail end of the pack. In the event that something would happen to one of the other aircraft, I could stay with them if they fell behind. Number two, I'm probably not going to get much formation time while I'm out scrounging bigger fuel tanks for the flight."

"All right. Fair enough Nolan," Donald Bennett said, looking over his lists of pilots and navigators, striking lines through some names and making a final count. "I'm going to retain four of the navigators –Wade, Burns, Burnett, and Douglas. And I'm going to drop five of the pilots –Kennedy, Hawkins, Seagraves, Warner and Romero."

Mitch leaned back in his chair and put his hands behind his head, looking past Bennett as he took a deep breath and let it out. "I'd like you to keep Seagraves on as my copilot."

"Why so?" Bennett wanted to know, frowning at him. "It seems to me he lacks confidence as well as ability. I see that in the class instruction that I've given, and I noted your own flying evaluations. He seems to me to be both overly cautious and exceedingly nervous. We can't have either on this operation. I'm sure you'll agree."

"I think he's just nervous around you. And I've seen a lot of improvement in handling the aircraft. You're the boss – I'm the junior partner. But, I'm asking this as a personal favor. I'll keep an eye on him. I promise you won't regret this."

"If I do," Donald Bennett said seriously, "you will, too."

*　　*　　*　　*　　*　　*

"Here we are on the first day of November," Sir Archibald Sinclair said, looking around at the other sixteen men seated at the squared arrangement of tables in the Prime Minister's Cabinet Room deep beneath London. "The snow is by now falling in Newfoundland and still we have no airplanes delivered to us under Lord Beaverbrook's plan. We've not seen one aircraft brought over thus far. I tell you this plan is a disgraceful waste of precious resources."

"Dear Mr. Air Minister, I can assure you your planes are on the way," Lord Beaverbrook said insistently.

"Mr. Prime Minister," Sinclair said turning toward Winston Churchill, "I implore you to put an end to this madness of Lord Beaverbrook's before it is too late."

"It's not madness at all, Archie," Beaverbrook shot back. "It's necessity born of the Navy's inability to keep the U-Boats from sinking all the cargo ships transporting my planes."

Admiral Sir Dudley Pound half rose from his seat, his face growing crimson. "See here, sir! I'll have you know my men have shown the highest bravery in their duties and —"

"It appears their duties include little more than watching my planes as they slip beneath the waves!" Lord Beaverbrook shouted over him. "Your navy can't seem to even begin to stop the wolf packs scouring beneath the Atlantic."

"Gentlemen. Gentlemen. Please," Churchill said forcefully, and then paused, letting silence linger until every eye was on him. "May I remind you our enemy sits across the Channel, not within this room," He took a deep breath, placed his cigar in the ashtray as he looked at Beaverbrook and then at Sinclair. "Archie," he began in a low tone, "I hear your concerns, and they are not without merit. But I also hear the sounds of our people screaming, those who are suffering and often dying in the burned-out rubble of their homes. Our people are resilient; they are solid and they are heroic – they are, but they have a breaking point. We must do something." He then turned to look at Beaverbrook and softly asked, "Where are they, Max? Where are the planes you've been promising us?"

"They are gathering in Newfoundland as we speak."

Churchill stared at him for what seemed an eternity in the still, small room. "Max, this is your last chance. We've waited patiently for the last three months since you first broached this idea. If I don't see those planes on the ground by 10 November, it's off. I'll be forced to call an end to this plan of yours, and I shall also be forced to ask for your resignation."

"And you will have it Mr. Prime Minister; however, the plan *will* work."

*　*　*　*　*　*

The cold west wind howled across the ramp at St. Hubert Airport beneath a leaden winter sky as a three man flight crew deposited their clothing bags into their Hudson, now painted in a light green and brown camouflage pattern with the underside a pale blue. They did their preflight inspections, holding onto their hats to keep from losing them.

Captain Donald Bennett emerged from the hangar and walked briskly to the Hudson just as the crew finished their inspection, gathering them at the plane's rear entrance.

"This is not a joy ride. It's a final pre-crossing assessment flight. The flying time to Gander should be six hours or less and I expect you to record in detail your airspeed, power settings, and fuel consumption on the report forms, is that clear?" Bennett demanded sounding angry, upset. He'd been that way since the phone call a week earlier from Beaverbrook advancing their schedule again. He looked first at Seagraves, then Douglas and finally Mitch Nolan. "You shall also make weather observations every fifteen minutes and record them as briefed. Telegraph me with all your information immediately upon landing. Am I making myself clear, gentlemen?"

"Yes, sir," Seagraves replied.

"When I say immediately upon landing, I mean precisely that. I expect your wire before you begin your drinking," he said, looking directly at Mitch Nolan. "Upon receiving the data, I shall brief the remaining seven crews and we will set out for Newfoundland at sunrise tomorrow morning to join you there later in the day. We will all refuel tomorrow afternoon and set out for Ireland the following day after final maintenance inspections and repairs. Questions? All right then, off you go, lads. Good flying and Godspeed."

Fifteen minutes later they were cleared for takeoff on runway 24 with a right departure turn before crossing the river. They climbed to 20,000 feet on oxygen fed through what looked like surgical tubing they stuck in their mouths. Douglas, their navigator, kept them on track while Seagraves filled out Captain Bennett's forms. At the two hour mark they left land behind and began the two hour flight over the Gulf of Saint Lawrence.

"I can't see anything but water out in front of us," Seagraves said nervously as the land receded behind them. "Never done this before."

"Kinda takes your breath away doesn't it,?" Mitch offered, smiling at him, but feeling an emptiness in his gut and a sense that they were passing over a bottomless pit. "What's that heading again, navigator?"

"Zero-four-eight," Tom Douglas said from the seat behind him where the radio sat bolted to small table and the map lay open to the side of it.

"How long to landfall over Newfoundland, Tom?" Mitch asked him. "If you're within ten minutes either way, I'll buy you a beer when we get to Gander."

Seagraves glanced over at him. "One beer? That's all? If we hit land any time before running out of gas, I'll buy him a whole damned case!"

A half hour before their expected landfall they encountered clouds and Mitch had Seagraves begin a gradual descent on instruments. They broke out at 8000 feet, continued down to 4000 and ten minutes later saw the ragged shoreline of Newfoundland ahead and off to their right. Leaning forward and looking through the windshield, Douglas tapped the two pilots on the shoulder.

"That's disappointing. It looks like I'm going to be two minutes off my time, and a quarter mile off my track," the navigator said sarcastically. "I could've done better if I had a crew that could maintain heading and airspeed."

"Don't push your luck, Douglas," Mitch said, looking at the navigator out of the corner of his eye. "You still have to get us to Gander. Double or nothing on arrival time there?"

"Getting to Gander is too easy. See that railroad track up there? It leads right to the airport – even you two could find it from here." When the large spread of tarmac appeared out of the haze in front of them it seemed like only minutes instead of a couple of hours.

"Okay Mike, it's your airplane. I'll handle the radios and you handle the controls." Mitch picked up the microphone and made the call. "Gander airport, this is Cherokee two-zero-zero-four, fifteen miles southwest for landing."

"*Cherokee two-zero-zero-four, this is Gander tower. Winds three-zero-five at ten. Visibility twenty. Pattern is empty. Cleared to land runway two-four, left traffic. Call final.*"

"Couldn't ask for anything smoother than this," Mitch commented, pulling out the procedures list. "Hope the trip over is this smooth…Pre-landing check… throttles set for –"

There was a loud explosion that seemed to originate from just behind the radio, coupled with an immediate violent yaw to the left as the wing on that side dipped toward the ground.

"I've got the controls!" Mitch yelled over the noise as he leveled the wings and added right rudder. Looking out the window on his side he could see the engine on fire and part of the nacelle missing. Flames licked at the wing and shot out the back of the engine; the noise rose as the engine raced. The vibration in the cockpit shook them so hard he couldn't make out any of the instrument readings…

Suddenly everything around him seemed to slow and become clear.

His father had told him about this once – this thing he called *crystalline clarity*. They were hunting elk near Banff in Canada while the family was assigned to Camp Lewis, and he'd asked the ol' man about what it was like in the War. A stupid question since his father never talked about it. But, his dad had told him how, in the worst of circumstances, a man properly prepared could see and react to things as if they were happening in slow motion.

Crystalline Clarity.

And now he understood it.

He'd spent hours at the Burbank plant sitting in the cockpit running his hands over the controls and switches until he could locate everything in the cockpit blindfolded. He'd read and re-read the emergency procedures in the operations manual for the Hudson until he knew them cold – absolutely cold. It was a confidence builder.

And maybe now a life saver.

His hands seemed to fly over the switches and levers – shutting off fuel to the left engine, feathering the prop, throttling back the right engine just a hair, adding right rudder and aileron, lining up for a straight-in landing on runway six, flaps twenty degrees, gear down, *quartering tailwind-don't forget that…* Sweat ran into his eyes. The tower was calling – *don't bother with them, Nolan, fly the damned airplane*!

He was having a terrible time keeping the nose aligned with the runway centerline – *you're over controlling!* he thought, and forced himself to relax and loosen his grip on the control wheel. Immediately the oscillations decreased.

"Gear down and locked; flaps now thirty; airspeed 105; altitude four hundred; rate of descent five hundred; pre-landing check complete," Seagraves was calling out over the noise, sounding strangely calm in the midst of the chaos.

Mitch looked out at the engine and saw the fire had diminished but the engine still burned brightly, trailing a long funnel of dark smoke. He could see a fire truck with a red rotating beacon on top and a crash wagon moving away from one of the large hangars at mid field.

They passed over the runway threshold at two hundred feet; at fifty feet he began a slow flare, bled off airspeed to ninety, and chopped all power ten feet off the runway. The Hudson hit the runway harder than normal and coasted for a long way before slowly coming to a stop at the middle of the big airport. The fire truck was hosing down the engine and the cockpit filled with smoke as Douglas and Seagraves released their seatbelts and made their way quickly to the back of the plane where rescue workers were pounding on the door from outside. Mitch turned all the electrical and engine switches off, and glanced quickly out the pilot's side window as he released the catch on his safety harness.

He saw Sheila standing on a taxiway halfway between the hangar and where the Hudson sat in the middle of the field; she had been sent ahead a week early by Bennett to arrange hangar space and maintenance facilities. Wearing a dark beret and a long red coat, she stood gazing restively at the burning aircraft with her hands clutched together covering her mouth.

Douglas and Seagraves were already outside and had moved away. Nolan at last climbed through the door onto the tarmac; the fresh air instantly cleared his mind and he realized that he'd left all his aircraft and flight documents in the cockpit. Quickly, he reentered the aircraft, climbed over the aux tanks midway up the fuselage, and retrieved a large leather messenger bag in which he had placed all the maps and the aircraft logbook. He retraced his steps, found the cargo door, and again clambered out. Moving toward his copilot and navigator, he saw Sheila run toward them, hugging first Douglas and then a surprised Mike Seagraves.

"You are the worst of bloody idiots, Mitch Nolan," she said, confronting him, her eyes wide with agitation. "What were you thinking?! Only a fool runs back into a burning building or an airplane still on fire."

He held up the leather satchel toward her and said, "A pilot-in-command never forgets his maps or logbook. I just wasn't up for another one of Bennett's lectures."

"You fool! You absolute bloody fool." She moved within inches of his face and continued to stare at him, her nostrils flared and eyes betraying worry. In the two months since he'd met her, he'd never seen anything like this – it surprised him, and all of a sudden he found it enormously humorous.

"Don't you laugh at me leftenant! You blithering idiot – you could have died in there!"

"I get it," Mitch said laconically. "Yeah, if I died then *you* would have been the one to catch Bennett's lecture. *That's* why you're upset, isn't it Sheila? Not that I blame you. I've seen the Angry Aussie singe your skirts more than once these past few weeks."

For long seconds she continued to stare angrily at him, and then suddenly she flung her arms around his neck, pulling him close as she whispered in his ear. "You're daft as a brush, the most obtuse Yank of the whole lot. You've not even been able to see what's right before your eyes for the last two months."

He was shocked. "What about your beau?"

"I have no one. I said that to keep the others away. I thought you were much brighter than that, leftenant – you were the one bragging that you didn't take 'no' for an answer."

He held her at arm's length. "I usually don't. My only excuse is I don't often find myself doing crazy stunts like flying the North Atlantic, either. My mind was on things other than beautiful women. But I'm going to fix that tonight."

"What about your flight data reports back to Bennett?"

"That's what co-pilots are for," he replied.

*   *   *   *

Mitch Nolan looked at his watch; it would be 4 AM in Ireland, meaning their arrival over the Irish coast should be some time around ten in the morning. They were five and a half hours into the flight, and so far it had gone as smoothly as Bennett had first briefed them; only now as he looked past the captain's lead aircraft the sky looked darker than ever and off to the north he could see occasional lightning.

"You keep smoking those things that fast Seagraves and you're going to run out before we reach the point of no return. You too, Douglas."

"Weather up ahead," Seagraves announced, looking left and right and overhead.

"I would imagine Captain Bennett has his sextant out and is making one final star shot before we get into the soup," Mitch observed.

"Yeah, I can hear it now," Douglas said leaning forward between the two seats on the flight deck. *"You know, lads,* he said, launching into his rendition of an Australian accent, *"every time I unlimber my sextant and do a starry observation, I sense I'm in the very presence of Columbus, Magellan, Vasco da Gama or Amerigo Vespucci or the three Magi from the East."*

They all laughed and Seagraves lit up another cigarette. The white taillight of Bennett's aircraft started flashing intermittently.

"Morse code," Douglas observed. "Q-M-C. Q-M-C-2-2."

"Climb to 22,000," Mitch said out loud. "He's going to try to get above this instead of going through it. I hope we can get on top at that altitude. This thing doesn't have much left above that. Mike, call out our altitude every two thousand feet; when we hit 10,000, Douglas turn on the oxygen bottles and everybody sucks on the rubber hose. Make sure you're strapped in – if we can't get above the clouds it's going to be a long and bumpy ride."

A minute later the lead aircraft started a gradual climb, finally settling on a five hundred feet per minute rate. At 12,000 feet they passed through a thin layer of cloud and found themselves flying between an upper and lower cloud layer. Bennett continued the climb until they again entered the clouds. Ten minutes later, the flight emerged on top of the cloud layer. .

"Seagraves, you've got the airplane," Mitch said a few minutes after they broke out on top and the flying was smoother. "Take it for a a few minutes, will you? That's the longest twenty minutes I ever experienced at the controls. Douglas how are we on fuel consumption?"

"We were running a little bit high."

"Run another quick check, will you?" Mitch thought about their fuel for a while as Seagraves flew the airplane. Back at St. Hubert he had tried to figure out ways to improve fuel consumption. He had an idea but it was not something he wanted to try unless he absolutely had to. A few minutes later the navigator confirmed they were burning about four gallons an hour more fuel than they should be and that would put them in with less than a half hour reserve at landing. Too close for comfort.

"Guys, time to switch tanks - aux 1 to aux 2," Douglas told them.

The mechanics had installed a small square box with a set of two switches between the pilot and copilot seat on the back of the instrument console. When he flipped the right switch there was an immediate loud pop and sparks.

"What was that?!" Douglas shouted.

"A short, and likely a blown fuse," Mitch explained, catching the bewildered glance of Seagraves. "Mike, keep your eyes on the lead aircraft and your mind on flying the plane. Tom and I will work through the electrical problem." Turning to the navigator he said, "There should be spare fuses in the equipment box under your table. Give me one."

Mitch opened the access panel beneath the switch, removed the old fuse and inserted the new one. When he turned the switch back on, the fuse again blew, but this time the lights on the instrument panel dimmed noticeably.

"What the hell was that?" Seagraves wanted to know.

"That was the generator going off-line. We're now running on battery – with all the instruments and lights turned off, the battery will last four hours. Five at the most," Mitch told them, hoping his memory of the electrical system was correct. That means that we can fly with the instrument lights for two hours, or without the lights for four hours. But what it really means is that when we run out of electricity the fuel pumps stop working and we become a glider. That should happen about two hours off the coast of Ireland."

"You're kidding, right?" Douglas said, incredulous.

"That's not something I would kid about." He closed his eyes and leaned his head back on the head rest, willing himself calm so he could think.

What is the problem? An electrical surge probably caused by a cold start. Blown fuse. Solution. Replace the fuse and try again. No go – another blown fuse. Another problem added – generator knocked off-line this time. Solution. Sorry Nolan, no answer. First fuse blew in the new auxiliary pump switch. Second electrical problem has to be in the main electrical bus where the generator is connected. Where is the main bus? Answer – the main bus switch is overhead – a toggle switch.

Mitch opened his eyes, looked up and found the switch that toggled between the main bus and its backup. He toggled the switch forward to the backup position. Nothing happened. He again toggled the switch to the main position and then to the backup position. This time the instrument lights came on.

Seagraves and Douglas let out a whoop and the navigator slapped him on the shoulder saying, "You did it! You did it! You fixed the damned problem, Nolan."

"Not so fast," Mitch said. "What happened is that the main fuel pumps and the lights are now operating on the generator. That's all well and good but we still don't have a way to access the fuel in the auxiliary fuel tanks. We'll still run out of gas if we can't get the aux pumps back on line. Tom, look in the equipment box. Pull out the mechanic's manual and count the fuses."

The navigator pulled out three more fuses, each about three inches long.

"Not a lot of margin for error." Mitch leafed through the manual until he found the electrical section and the wiring diagrams. There was no diagram for an auxiliary tank or pump system, so he guessed the mechanics had taken the path of least resistance and wired it into the main electrical box accessed in the back of the plane. That's what he would've done. "Mike, you still have the controls. Tom, give me your flashlight, a flat head screwdriver, a Phillips head screwdriver, and a pair of wire cutters plus one fuse."

"What are you going to do?" The navigator wanted to know.

"I don't know," Mitch replied. "I'm making this up as I go along. But I'm going to look at the main electrical bus in the back of the ship, check the fuses, and if I'm right there should be only one fuse that's blown. I'll replace that and the one in our switch box. That should work."

"Are you sure?"

"Not really. This is better than nothing, and I think it'll work."

"How are you going to get to the rear of the aircraft and do all that without oxygen?"

"It may take a couple of trips back and forth. If my memory of ground school is right, an average person has five to ten useful minutes of consciousness at twenty thousand feet. At twenty-five thousand , three to five minutes. At our altitude I am going to guess I have three or four minutes to do the work and get back. I'll keep my eye on the watch. You keep your eye on me in case my memory of that isn't correct. Got it?"

Mitch made his way back to the rear of the aircraft climbing over the two large auxiliary tanks. He found the electrical box on the rear bulkhead and removed the cover. All the connections were well marked and legible. He found the one fuse that was blown and was about to replace it when he checked his watch and found he had been gone four minutes. He returned to the flight deck and started breathing oxygen through the tube just as he felt the onset of a lack of orientation. He breathed oxygen for a good five minutes. He was about to return to the rear of the aircraft when he had another idea.

"Give me a pack of your cigarettes," he demanded of Douglas.

"Pack of cigarettes? You don't smoke and this is a really bad time to start."

"I want one of your old packs for the foil wrapper." He took the wrapper, creased and tore it in half, and then wrapped each end of the fuse with the foil. When done, he inserted the foil wrapped fuse into the aux fuel switch box at the base of the pilot and copilot's instrument console. He wrapped a second fuse with foil and said to Douglas, "I'm going to put this fuse in the switch box on the back bulkhead. When I give you the thumbs up signal, toggle the bus switch to *main* and then turn on the auxiliary fuel pump switch right here. If I'm right, the generator will continue to work and the aux fuel pump will come online."

Again, he made his way to the back of the aircraft, removed the old fuse. and inserted the new foil wrapped replacement. Taking a deep breath he gave Douglas thumbs up.

The lights on the instrument panel suddenly flickered and came up full bright, and he heard the auxiliary pump come on. Douglas's mouth fell open; Seagraves glanced over his left shoulder smiling broadly.

It had worked!

Mitch put the last screw into the electrical panel cover, tightened it and took his first step back toward the flight deck when the Hudson hit an air pocket and suddenly dropped. He was thrown against the top of the fuselage, hitting his head and was knocked unconscious.

"What the hell was that, Seagraves?"

"One great big air pocket," the copilot said. "Glad we were buckled in. What about Nolan? Where's he?"

The navigator looked around the back of aircraft and saw nothing of their pilot. "Can't see him from here. I'll go back and check."

He found Nolan lying at the base of the rear bulkhead, tried to pick him up and move him over the auxiliary tanks, and at last gave up. "Nolan's out cold in the rear of the aircraft, he told Seagraves. It looks like he hit his head when we fell through that air pocket. Tried to move him but there's no way I can get him around or over the aux fuel tanks."

"We've got to get down below 10,000 feet, Seagraves. There's not enough oxygen up here for him to survive. You strap in, this is going to be wild."

The copilot pulled back the throttles, lowered the nose, and as the vertical speed indicator began to rise he turned the control yoke to the left and pushed in the right rudder as far as it would go. Within a matter of seconds, the rate of descent increased dramatically and they entered the clouds. As rough as their climb to altitude with the formation had been an hour earlier, this was worse.

"What the hell, Seagraves!" Tom Douglas screamed over the noise of the air rushing by. "I've never seen a vertical speed indicator pegged like that."

He glanced at the gauge now virtually unreadable because of the violent vibration. It made the breath catch in his throat. But as scared as he was, he knew they had to get the airplane down as low as they could as fast as they could to give Nolan a chance. They descended through ten thousand feet. Seagraves, with both hands on the control wheel, gradually brought the aircraft back into trim and slowly pushed the throttles forward to cruise RPM. They were still falling at five thousand feet altitude.

"Level out! Level out!" Douglas was yelling.

At three thousand feet, they broke out of the clouds descending in a shallow, controlled dive toward the roiling, angry ocean. The waves looked huge and there were whitecaps everywhere in every direction. It was the most frightening sight either of them had ever seen.

Seagraves was breathing heavily, like a long-distance runner. But he had the presence of mind to turn toward Douglas and say, "Go back and check on him. Right now!"

Nolan was stirring when the navigator finally made his way back to the rear of the aircraft; he was sitting up with his back to the bulkhead holding his head in both hands. He looked up at Douglas with a blank expression and distant look in his eyes.

"You all right?" the navigator wanted to know. "Look at me Mitch. Are you all right?"

"Yeah, yeah. I'm fine, except my head is throbbing."

"You must've hit it on the side or the top of the plane when we fell through an air pocket. Do you remember coming back to fix the electrical box?"

"Vaguely. It's like I was in a dream, or I'm still in the dream. Who's at the controls?"

"Seagraves."

"By himself? I let him fly the plane by himself?" He got slowly to his feet and with the help of Douglas made his way to the flight deck and slumped into the left seat, with one hand on his forehead. After a while he shook his head looking around the cockpit and then outside at the churning cauldron of the North Atlantic sea. "What are we doing down on the deck?"

"We had to get down to where there was air to breathe, Mitch. Don't you remember?"

"Vaguely… electrical problem wasn't it?"

"It was. You take a rest."

Twenty minutes later he felt a lot better, with only a slight headache and a minor bruise on his forehead. They flew on just below the bottom of the clouds which over the next two hours gradually rose until the eastern sky began to grow lighter. They made the last course correction turning further east, directly into the rising sun.

It was 9 AM in Ireland.

"Time to switch back to the main fuel tanks," Mitch said to Seagraves who was looking through his binoculars hoping to see land.

His copilot hemmed and hawed, and finally looked directly at him. "Well, we've been flying on them for a while."

"This is not good news,." Nolan said. He tapped on the gauges as if doing so might get the needle to indicate more fuel. "Douglas, I think it's time to break Captain Bennett's radio silence and call for a DF steer. It doesn't look like we're picking up the beacon yet."

"We don't have a radio either, Mitch," the navigator told him.. "It must have gotten fried when we had the problem with the aux fuel pumps."

Nolan shook his head up and down and bit on his lower lip.

"Well, you know, it just wouldn't have been half the fun if we didn't have a few little problems on the way over. I've got one little trick left up my sleeve, and I'm sure it'll get us all the way to Ireland."

He winked at Seagraves, wondering if what he had just said was still an 'honor violation' since he was no longer a cadet bound to always tell the truth.

*　　*　　*　　*　　*

"Yes, Lord Beaverbrook," Donald Bennett said into the telephone, "we've arrived with six aircraft. I wish we could say that all have made it but at this moment we cannot. We have one crew yet to arrive or report in."

Donald Bennett looked out onto the tarmac of the airport in Belfast County, Ireland. Six flight crews that had made it now searched the western sky for any sign of the remaining Lockheed Hudson. It was two hours overdue and he'd heard one of the Yanks say something about how the radio silence had screwed Nolan and his crew.

"*Six?! Six planes?! Donald that's incredible. Well done,*" Beaverbrook said over the line. "*It's amazing! Even if we had lost four we would have proven our point. Only one lost – that's miraculous! Good job, man.*"

"Honestly, sir, it seems a rather high price."

"*You're taking this a bit too hard, Donald. I appreciate the sentiment, but we're in a war and sadly casualties are the norm. Again, congratulations, my good man! I'll see you when you come to London.*"

"But sir –" The line had gone dead. Bennett took a deep breath and slowly put the phone back on the cradle. He walked outside to where the rest of the crews searched the western sky looking for any sign of their remaining crew. Gazing through his binoculars he mumbled to himself feeling hugely disappointed. It was not enough to say this was war and that casualties were to be expected, or that their comrades had given their lives in a most noble cause. At the moment those platitudes seemed immensely hollow to him.

An RAF officer walked quickly across the tarmac and approached Bennett.

"Sir there's a call for you in the radio shack."

"Very well." He followed the officer to the communications facility where a sergeant handed him a telephone. "Donald Bennett here."

"*Captain, this is chalk seven reporting in. Everybody else make it all right?*" came the hollow-sounding voice over the line.

"Nolan?! Yes, we all made it. Heavens, man, where are you?"

"*Near Tipperary they tell me, but who cares? Damn these Irish are friendly folks. Everybody else make it okay?*"

"Yes, yes. Every one. You've asked me twice. I can tell you've been drinking, leftenant."

"*Right you are O Captain, my Captain.*"

"Where *exactly* are you?"

"*In the clubhouse of the Ballykisteen Golf Club. I believe your aircraft is on the fairway of the 16th Hole, a rather long, flat par five with a fairway bunker that adds some excitement to an engine-out landing. Your airplane is out of petrol but otherwise perfectly flyable. All it needs is gas and a sober crew, neither of which we seem to have at the moment.*"

"You remain as incorrigible as ever, Nolan."

"*Hell yes I am! Bennett old chum you are the grand master of understatement and odd knowledge. Here's a question for you... Do you know how many people have ever flown the North Atlantic in the winter? I'll tell you – exactly twenty-one... and you're talking to one of them! Hurry up and get here. I think we're about to run out of beer.*"

There was a long silence on the phone.

"*One other thing, Bennett. You owe me eight hundred American dollars. Write out a check to Mrs. Claudia Seagraves in New York City. My co-pilot has her address – it's his grandmother. The only reason he made this trip is because he needs the money to take care of her. Seems like a worthy charity to me. Besides, I don't need cash. The U.S. Army gave me time off to have this little bit of fun and I didn't even have to buy a ticket for the ride.*

"*Is that a great country or what?!*"

Chapter 12

Mitch Nolan thanked the British chauffeur and closed the car door.

As the unmarked government sedan maneuvered down the long drive toward the heavy wrought iron gateway of the estate, he looked around at the manicured lawns and pastures surrounding the enormous old house. The tree-shaded stone dwelling and outbuildings appeared fashioned after an artist's illustration from a bygone age. A shiny new Rolls Royce Bentley and a drab green RAF staff car sat out front in the circular driveway. After a quick inspection of the Bentley, he approached the massive entrance.

It had been a whirlwind twenty-four hours.

After refueling the Hudson, he'd taken off from the Tipperary golf course in front of a large and raucous crowd. Twenty minutes later he landed at the RAF base thirty miles north of Ardoyne near the Irish east coast. From there all the crews were driven to Belfast to catch the ferry to Liverpool and then boarded the overnight train to South Hampton where a troop ship was ready to take them back to Canada. It was all done in secret and none of them, except Bennett, were allowed even one day in London – not much of a hero's welcome. But the Australian had taken Mitch with him into the city to meet with Beaverbrook.

Nolan found the British lord to be somewhat a madcap – a nutty screwball, like a crazy uncle locked in the attic. He was clearly elated over the success of their venture and assured Bennett he'd get a knighthood because of it; he'd even floated the idea Mitch might get one as well which seemed outlandish. But the meeting had been entertaining and an appropriate end to a mission that looked more outrageous now in hindsight than it had in the final preparation just a few days earlier. After a couple of drinks with the cabinet minister and a happy send-off from him, Bennett was driven to the ship, and Mitch was provided a chauffeured limousine to take him to Brigadier Smythe-Browne's estate.

Mitch tapped loudly on the entrance using the large brass door knocker and waited, turning to gaze back down the driveway at the idyllic setting, strangely removed from the bombed and burned out buildings he'd seen in many parts of London. Here, it was as if the war was far away, something happening to someone else – an event reported over the radio, taking place in a distant land. He could have been looking at the rolling hills of the Piedmont plateau in Maryland or Pennsylvania for all he could see now of the effects of the war on Britain. After several seconds, he reached for the brass knocker and again announced his presence. Immediately the door opened and he found himself staring at the face of a pretty girl about his own age. Surprised, his breath caught in his throat and he was briefly rendered speechless.

"Hello," he said at last. "I'm Mitch Nolan and I'm hoping Brigadier Smythe-Browne is available. My father's a friend of his."

"Nolan, you say?" Her pretty face lit up at this and she said, "Of course. I was assigned as his driver for a few days three months ago. It was a most marvelous, and I dare say, exciting four or five days. Yes, I can see the family resemblance now, Mr. Nolan."

"Mitch," he gently corrected, smiling warmly. "Mr. Nolan is what people, mostly older people who don't know him, call my father."

"Ah, but of course."

She was attractive but not ravishing in her deep blue British RAF uniform; yet, there was something magnetic about her rarely encountered in other girls. Her bearing was aristocratic, he thought; a hint of aloofness maybe. It intrigued him. Her smile was polite but not wholly welcoming, courteous without being inviting. Her features were well defined, like those of a model in a magazine advertisement, and he noticed the slightest cleft in her chin which added an interesting accent to her pretty face. Her hair was chestnut, long and dark brown with auburn highlights.

"You know my name but I don't think I caught yours," he said.

"My apologies, Mr. – so sorry... Mitch." She stuck out her hand. "Corporal Aynslee Glendenbrook. Women's Auxiliary Air Force. I am a sector spotter at RAF-Hornchurch and an occasional driver for senior officers and distinguished guests, such as your father. And you?"

"I'm an Army Air Corps pilot who just got into town."

"An officer?"

"Yes, despite the civilian garb." He leaned toward her and spoke in a low conspiratorial whisper. "I'm here on a secret mission, traveling incognito."

"Really?! How intriguing," she said in a collaborator's hushed tone that sounded alluring. "I shan't give you away."

A female voice from inside the house called out, "Aynslee, who is it, dear?"

"A Mitch Nolan – your friend David Nolan's son. He claims to be a spy – should I have MI-5 ensure his bona fides are in order before letting him in?" She winked, looking at him mischievously and giving him a warm smile.

A slim older woman emerged from around the near corner of the long entrance hallway, wiping her hands with a towel, her eyes wide with amazement. Before he could voice a greeting she grabbed him in a full and almost crushing embrace. "Denise's son! By the looks of you, the eldest. How are your dear parents?!"

"Fine, ma'am, the last I saw them. But that was the first week of June." She was still grasping him by the biceps and looking at him up and down as if she were a supply sergeant inspecting a new piece of equipment. "He sent me a letter three months ago and told me how much he enjoyed visiting here this past summer, and that you were on his list of favorite places to visit again some day. I thought I'd check it out myself since I'm passing through town."

"I'm so glad you did young man. The brigadier just arrived home. He'll be positively delighted you came. And like your father, your scheduling is impeccable as there is time for a drink or two before dinner. How is your dear mother?"

Before he could reply, the young WAAF spoke up.

"If you will excuse me, I must be returning to Hornchurch," the girl said. "Duty calls, and the auto is overdue an inspection so I must return it to the motor pool in time to get that done before they close. But I shall be only a phone call away if needed."

"You run along my dear. I expect we shall see you first thing in the morning. Enjoy your evening," the older woman said, smiling passingly and then looking quickly back to Mitch. "Now, Mr. Nolan, do come in. My husband is in the library."

Mitch followed the woman down the long hallway as she recounted an anecdote about his father's visit earlier that summer. She was obviously pleased he'd come by and insistent he stay as their dinner guest. When she learned he had not made any overnight arrangements and that his schedule was somewhat open-ended, she insisted he at least spend the night – and hopefully a day or two longer. She peppered him with questions about his father and especially his mother since it had been three years since she'd seen Denise. When they entered the large library, the tall gray-haired British officer turned from stirring his drink.

"Henry," the woman said, "we have a house guest. This young man is Denise's eldest. He stopped by just now to pay his respects. I have prevailed upon him to spend the night and, perhaps with your influence, several more."

The austere looking man brightened and smiled at him. "You would be Mitchell. Your father told me much about you this summer, as has Lord Beaverbrook in the weeks since. Max is positively giddy about the success you and Bennett had in flying those aircraft across the North Atlantic." The brigadier crossed the room and shook his hand.

"I appreciate the compliment, sir, but really all the credit goes to Captain Bennett," Mitch replied shrugging self-consciously. "What Captain Bennett did in planning the operation as well as training the pilots and navigators is something people will be be talking about for a long time. My role was simply to ensure the planes got to him from California and fly in one of them as a crew member on the way over."

Smythe-Browne looked closely at him and slowly nodded his head. "That's not quite the way I heard it, but I learned years ago never to argue with anyone from Clan Nolan – not your father and – heaven forbid – certainly not your mother. Care for a drink?"

"Yes sir. Irish whiskey on the rocks would be great." Mitch looked around as the brigadier fixed the drink. "So, sir, you learned the lesson somewhere that you can't argue with my mother and win."

"Indeed I did young man," Smythe-Browne replied handing him the drink and motioning toward a leather chair. "Twice as a matter of fact. The first time was in an American military hospital where she was my nurse." He tapped his right leg and continued. "This limb is as good as new because of her. I wasn't happy at the time with the way she conducted my rehabilitation – she was more the stubborn sergeant major than the gracious, compassionate nurse. She fairly well wore me out what with her nocturnal visits to stretch my leg and the thrice daily walks to the front gate she forced on me. But she gave me back the use of my leg. And then there was the time Maud and I were with your parents in Berlin. I shan't go into all the details but your mother and I differed, shall we say politely, on our political views. Though it was clear I was right and she was wrong, still I never won an argument with her."

"I guess that puts you in the same boat as my father then." Mitch smiled to himself and thought: *that's my mom. What was it that dad was always saying about her? – often wrong but never in doubt.* He looked through the window to the land behind the house. "This is really an incredible place you have here, sir. Did I see a stable out behind the house?"

"You did. My daughter loves to ride and so we keep a few horses. As I remember, your mother is something of an equestrienne. Do you ride?"

"I haven't in some time but it would be good to get back in the saddle." He debated asking about the young WAAF and decided to chance it. "I had the pleasure of meeting your driver, sir. I couldn't help but notice how attractive she is."

Smythe-Browne gave him a strange questioning look. "My driver?"

"Yes, I met her at the front door as she was leaving, and I saw her drive off in your staff car. Corporal Glendenbrook. She said she'd been my father's driver this past summer and I was wondering what I might have to do to get her assigned to showing me around while I'm here."

"Oh, you mean Aynslee!" The brigadier chuckled." I hate to disappoint you, but she's already taken. Aynslee is my daughter. By vocation she is primarily a spotter and controller for Fighter Command, and by marriage, wife to one of our more accomplished Spitfire pilots."

"I'm sorry, sir," Mitch replied, glad he hadn't said more and hoping that his face didn't register either the disappointment or embarrassment he felt. "If I spoke out of turn –"

"Not at all, my good man. I understand completely." The smile on the old Englishman's face said that he did. "I was your age once, and believe it or not it wasn't all that long ago. I too had a good eye for beauty when I was young and so I married her mother. Fortunately for Aynslee she takes after her mother's side of the family, not mine."

"Married to a Spitfire pilot you say," Mitch offered, hoping to change the subject quickly. "One of these days I hope to get a chance to fly one. Everything I've heard says that the Spit is a great airplane."

"Indeed. Wish we had a few thousand more. Production has accelerated but we still find ourselves dreadfully short. However, it was our great good fortune in the past two months to have as many as we did. It appears the Hurricane has accounted for more German losses than the Spit, but that's because there are so many more of them. Malcolm – Aynslee's husband – in the last three months has downed fourteen while being shot down twice himself. Fortunately, each time it was near the Devil's Corner but over land, so by the next morning he was back leading his squadron."

"That's quite a record," Nolan observed, disappointed, as if he'd had the wind knocked out of him. *Just my luck. Meet a cute girl, and not only is she already married, but she's taken by a double ace and a squadron leader to boot. Kinda makes that little ferry flight pale by comparison.* "And he's a squadron commander, you say."

"With a fine record indeed, but not altogether unusual in our circumstance. And he finds himself a squadron leader, not necessarily because of ability, but because of simple longevity. He's nearly the only one left from his original group of lads."

Mitch had not been aware that the loss rates were that high in the RAF. *No wonder this Aynslee looked distracted and worried.*

Smythe-Browne finished his drink, poured himself another and refreshed Mitch's. He then looked quickly at his watch and said, "I hate to be the improper host, but you must excuse me. I'm expecting any moment a call from General Sir John Dill. Official business. May I suggest you might want to take a look around the grounds – since you have an interest in horses, you may want to look in on our stables. You might find a thing or two of interest there. The door just to the left of the library entrance leads outside. I suggest you steer clear of the kitchen as Maud will likely press you into service so as to pepper you with questions about your lovely mother and about how to prepare any of a host of American dishes."

Mitch left the house and walked outside toward the stables which sat some distance away from the house. He was disappointed in the news he'd heard about Aynslee and tried to tell himself there were still many fish left in the sea. It didn't seem to help much. Maybe when he got back to the States and returned to Randolph to begin flight school over, he'd have to look up the daughter of the base commander again.

The stable wasn't terribly large. There were four stalls on either side of a wide center aisle; at the main entrance there was a tack room on the right and outside the room were stands holding English saddles. Mitch looked around hoping to find at least one Western saddle but came away disappointed.

Three of the horse stalls were occupied. The first held a bay mare who seemed docile and friendly. She was curious enough to walk up to him as he stood outside and talked to her in a low flat voice. He spent a few minutes talking, rubbing her nose, and patting her along the left side of her neck. The sorrel next to her was a bit more timid but after several minutes he too slowly became curious enough to investigate the low gentle voice. Both of them appeared to be warmbloods and he guessed these were the primary riding horses and may even have been used for dressage or other show riding. On the opposite side of the stable, at the far end away from the other two horses, was a lone white stallion.

This horse was clearly different.

It had the distinctive head shape and high tail carriage of an Arabian but was large for the breed; and Mitch quickly discovered it was neither good-natured nor willing to please. Whether or not it was quick to learn, like most Arabians, was something that piqued his curiosity. For long minutes he stood watching the horse as it eyed him warily from the back of the stall. He began to talk to the animal in the same low, flat voice and slow cadence he had used on the other two horses, but the big white was not seduced by him and would not come to his call.

Slowly, quietly, without any sudden movements, Mitch opened the stall gate, took one slow step inside and stood still.

The stallion reacted as expected – his nostrils flared a warning, he laid his ears back and he raised first one leg and then the other in a clear fight or flight signal. Mitch remained perfectly still with his arms at his sides and said nothing until the horse became totally calm. He then began to speak, once again with a very slow cadence and a very flat voice, never taking his eyes off of the horse. He then took one slow step forward while continuing to speak. Once again the horse reacted with a heightened flight or fight reaction. Over the next fifteen minutes, Mitch continued to slowly but surely close the distance between himself and the horse while talking slowly in a soothing tone and continuing to look into the horse's eyes. At last he was within arms distance of the stallion and there he remained for a full ten minutes without moving while continuing his constant, quiet monologue.

The horse took a tentative step forward, pushed his nose out and touched Mitch's chest. He quickly pulled back, and then a few seconds later, did it again. Mitch slowly raised his arm so his hand was a foot in front of his chest. The horse appeared skittish, but eventually touched his hand with his nose. After a few minutes, Mitch deliberately lowered his hand and slowly backed away until he was outside the stall.

"I'd never have believed it if I hadn't seen it with my own eyes," Smythe-Browne said from behind Mitch's right shoulder. "No one, not even the trainer I hired, was able to do that. And he worked with that horse for almost three weeks. How did you do it?"

"I don't know," Mitch replied shrugging his shoulders as he slowly, quietly closed the the stall's gate. "I just talked and moved slowly and made sure I didn't spook him. I wanted him to know I wasn't afraid of him, and that he had nothing to fear from me even though we were in the same closed space. I once worked for friends of the family, taking care of their horses. What I did in there always seemed to work before; I guess it worked this time, too."

"Amazing. Malcom bought that horse as a birthday present for Aynslee last spring. And since then nobody has been able to get that close without setting him off, much less putting a saddle on and riding him. Young Glendenbrook has a reputation as quite the horsemen, but even he couldn't ride that stallion."

"The horse hasn't been ridden? How does he get any exercise?"

"That's an all day ordeal for two men. Two stout men."

Mitch looked back at the horse which seemed to be studying him closely.

"I'll tell you what brigadier, in return for two days room and board I'll solve those problems with that horse for you and your daughter."

Smythe-Browne looked at him with a slight smile playing at the corners of his mouth. "I don't for a minute think you can do it young man, but I shall greatly enjoy watching you try."

*   *   *   *

Aynslee was troubled as she turned into the long drive of her father's estate.

The German daylight attacks had dwindled to almost nothing but the night attacks of the Nazi bombers on the cities, especially London, had soared. There were just enough day attacks to keep everyone on pins and needles and always alert, and more than enough night attacks to require a full blown effort from Fighter Command day and night. The Blitz was beginning to make her burn the candle at both ends in her job at Hornchurch.

Malcolm was growing utterly exhausted though he was flying less so far in November than he had in the previous three months. But the stress of his being squadron commander was wearing even more heavily on him than the two or three missions a day he had been flying August through October. The war was wearing down both of them.

And they had other problems now as well.

They had had an angry, terrible row the night before. Their daughter Cateline was not doing well in the care of nannies watching over the children of RAF members at Hornchurch. Aynslee had left the airbase just prior to noon under the pretense of business her father had which required her presence. The subterfuge was simply a way to get away from her husband and the war for a few hours. She needed to be more alert for the work that would come that night controlling the few Hurricane night fighters aloft to battle the German bombers.

And the sudden presence of this American in their home was remarkably unsettling.

She had greatly enjoyed those few days she'd spent with the American's father months before. He was, it turned out, one of the more interesting characters with whom she had worked since joining the WAAF. But there was something about the son which troubled her, even though they'd exchanged very few words in a single brief encounter. So, as she turned into the driveway there were a great many things on her mind – deeply disturbing things.

She had gone only a few yards when something out of the right window caught her eye.

Someone was riding a white horse along the far wood line that described her father's property. It was a large and beautiful horse – a magnificent animal with a long smooth stride. She wondered who it could be and why the person had chosen to ride on her father's estate. As far as she knew none of the neighbors owned such an animal. She slowed the car and finally stopped halfway to the house to get a better look at the horse and rider two fields away. The horse came to an abrupt stop and the rider turned to look at her. As she got out of the car, she instantly she recognized who it was.

The Yank.

Quickly he turned the horse and headed directly at her. Halfway there they jumped the five foot high fence, seemingly without slowing, and thundered across the remaining three hundred yards. At the last instant, the rider pulled hard on the reins and the horse stopped immediately, rising up on its rear legs. Mitch Nolan jumped down from the horse with the reins in one hand and walked up to her with a broad smile on his face.

"This is the most incredible horse I've ever ridden," he said, his face flushed red from the chill wind and excitement. "I envy you owning such an animal."

Aynslee's eyes flared wide and she glowered at him.

"How dare you!" she shouted. "Who gave you permission?!"

He was surprised and visibly recoiled from her. "I didn't mean to upset you. I thought –"

"You thought?! I doubt that very much! You thought what?! That I wouldn't mind your coming into our home and assuming you had the run of all things including my property?!"

"I'm sorry, I didn't mean to –"

"Didn't mean to what?! Invade my privacy?! Violate me?"

"Aynslee, I'm really sorry."

"Yes! Yes you are. What kind of moronic manners do you Yanks have, anyway? The Cretans are better behaved."

"Your father said I could –"

"My father has no right," she interrupted again. "You should have asked me!"

"You're absolutely right. I'm very sorry. It was thoughtless, and I should have come directly to you. I thought you'd be pleased if I worked the horse. I have some talent with –"

"You have talent all right, Mr. Nolan. A talent for disregarding the rights and property of others. You're not the man your father is, that's for certain."

Mitch swallowed and took a deep breath. *How did I kick over this beehive?* he wondered. "You're absolutely right, Aynslee, and I don't have a leg to stand on."

"You're bloody well right about that!"

"What can I do to show you I'm *truly* sorry?"

She glared at him for a long while. "You can walk my horse back to his stall and properly brush him down. Then you can leave him and me alone."

"All right, I will." Mitch held her eyes and felt her fury though he couldn't understand the reason behind it. "I'll do as you wish. I'll take care of your horse. And I will never, ever bother you again."

"That will make me inexhaustibly happy," Aynslee said crossly. She turned and walked back to the staff car; with one searing glance over her shoulder at him she got into the driver's seat and slammed the car door. With a roar of the engine, she took off down the drive throwing gravel and dust into the air behind her.

Mitch watched her as she skidded to a stop in the wide circular driveway and stomped up the front steps into the house without a backward glance. The big white Arabian ambled up behind him and pushed Mitch in the back with his nose.

"What do you think, big fella – does she like me or not? Hard to tell, isn't it?" He wrapped his arm under the horse's head and stroked it softly. "Wish I had the Lone Ranger's faithful Indian companion to talk this over with instead of his trusty steed – not that you're bad company or anything."

He sighed.

"If that's what you really want Lady Aynslee Smythe-Browne Glendenbrook," he said, staring down the road toward the estate house, "you'll never see me again, even though I think you really want to... and even though you don't want to admit it to yourself."

* * * * *

Senator William Howard Payne cleared his throat and looked across the top of his desk at the two young people sitting facing him. There were times when one of them frustrated the very daylights out of him. Maybe both of them, now that his staff assistant and his senate committee legal counsel had gotten themselves romantically involved.

"Things in politics are never quite that cut and dried, Erika," the Senator said, trying to sound prophetic in the sense of forth-telling the truth. He puffed hard on his cigar and cast an eye at the young lawyer sitting next to her who knew exactly what he was saying but remained silent and less than helpful with this opinionated, strong-willed young woman.

"Maybe they should be, Senator," Erika Nolan replied. "The economy is just now coming out of the Depression, after eight long years – more than half of which were unnecessary."

"In your opinion."

"In the *considered* opinion of many free-market economists."

Senator Payne smiled at her in his fatherly way. "Ah yes, the freewheeling battle of opinions. The grist of the mill of a healthy democracy."

"No sir, this country isn't a democracy. It's a representative republic, which you know having read my commentary on the administration's latest budget proposal. A democracy is a government based on human opinions and therefore the rule of the majority – purportedly. A republic is a system based on the rule of law; in our case, the Constitution. And the president's latest budget proposal treads heavily all over that document. That's why you and others in the leadership of the Democratic Party have to stand up against this proposed budget in the areas I outlined for you in the review. It's all very clear."

"My dear, two weeks ago, President Roosevelt won over Wendell Wilkie by ten percent. In presidential politics, that is a landslide victory. No one in his right mind is going to challenge him while he enjoys that kind of mandate. Certainly not anyone in the Democratic Party, and certainly not me." He again looked at Randall Ashby for help, but the lawyer looked away and remained silent.

"His own vice president did," Erika pointed out.

"John Nance Garner was a fool to challenge him in the primary. He was easily swept aside, and he ruined his political career."

"He was a conservative from Texas standing up for a conservative America on the basis of the Constitution. He was a statesman."

"He was all of that, my dear. And now he's an ex-vice president unable to do anything for anybody." Senator Payne leaned forward and smiled at the young woman. "Erika, I hear clearly what you're trying to tell me, and I agree that much of it has merit. I value your positions – they are in fact more conservative than my own, and I admit that you've tempered some of my decisions in the past few months since you've been here. Don't back down, don't change. I value your advice and the passion you bring in arguing your positions. I'll review your comments and recommendations again, and over the next few weeks I'll make my final decisions on this budget and the budget process itself. Fair enough?"

"Fair enough." She smiled back at him and seemed to relax. "And I do appreciate your listening to me, even as new as I am. I warned you before you hired me that I wanted to come to Washington to make a difference. That hasn't changed. What has changed though is my realization that it might take a little longer than I expected."

"I've been working on it all of my adult life," Payne replied. "The framers intended for it to be a slow and difficult and frustrating process to bring about change."

"Patience has never been one of my personal behavioral traits. I've seen it in my father and admired him for it, but I've come to realize I'm more like my mother."

Senator Payne laughed aloud and winked at her. "Your mother is a wonderful and lovely woman. Being like her in any respect – and you are in many – is clearly a virtue."

"Thank you, Senator. I'll tell her you said so. We're having lunch together today."

"Wonderful. Please ask her to stop by and chat if she can. I'd love to see her again. Now, I have some committee business that Randall and I must take care of before our next meeting tomorrow afternoon. Please excuse us, won't you?"

"Randall," the Senator began, looking at the young lawyer after Erika had left the office and closed the door behind her, "you're going to have your hands full with that young lady. She's right about being like her mother. She is every bit as pretty, just as independent and equally as opinionated. I wish you good luck. But that's not why I wanted to talk." Senator Payne grew somber, and seemed to age as he sat behind the desk and stared vacantly at the far wall. "I understand you've recently done some legal work on behalf of my daughter. Said legal work skirts along the edge of illegality, and probably well over the line of impropriety and legal ethics should it come to the attention of the Bar Association."

"Sir, I can assure you –"

"Hear me out! I'm not chastising you or warning you off, counselor."

"Sir, I would never do anything illegal, and nothing improper that would in any way reflect negatively on you personally or your position as a United States Senator."

"Damn it, young man, I'm not worried about me. I'm worried about my daughter. I know you obtained for her a power of attorney that she can and has used to establish bank accounts and financial trading accounts drawing on her husband's inheritance."

"She's his wife. There's nothing illegal about any of that," Ashby pointed out.

"Nothing that can be proven, you mean."

"Yes, sir, that's what I meant."

"Good. You keep it that way, understood?"

"I do, sir." Ashby replied.

The Senator opened his lower desk drawer and retrieved two Rocks glasses and a nearly empty bottle of Jack Daniels. "Have a drink with me, Randall."

"I'd rather not, sir. I'm having lunch with Erika and her mother shortly and I'd prefer to be sober and smell like aftershave rather than the devil's cut of hickory-aged bourbon."

Payne nodded, poured himself a shot and quickly downed it, then poured another. "I've not been a very good father to Michelle as I look back on all that's transpired since her mother died – most egregiously, since her marriage to Reeves."

The Senator downed a second shot of the bourbon, quickly pouring another.

"I didn't know it at the time, and didn't find out until the past two or three years what a monster I'd let my daughter marry." Payne looked at the young lawyer with tears in his eyes. "That son-of-a-bitch has made her life an absolute hell all these years and I didn't do a thing to help her out. What kind of father lets that happen to his little girl?"

"Sir, if you didn't know, then what –"

The Senator struck the desk with a clenched fist. "I should have known! Damn it, I should have known. I know his father; we've worked side by side in the senate for thirty years. I saw it in him. I should have known it was also in the son. She doesn't want me to interfere in any way, but this time she's not getting her way. I'm telling you to help her. Help her in any way you can to get away from this evil bully. I will not stand by any longer while he brutalizes her. I'll honor her wish that I stay out of it personally. But know this: as a six term U.S. Senator I carry a lot of weight in a lot of places. If you need help with anything – and I mean *anything* – I can get it for you. Do you understand what I'm saying?"

"Very clearly, Senator."

"Good. Don't you fail me, son." Payne downed the last shot of bourbon, and slammed the glass on the top of his desk. "You protect my little girl, Randall."

*   *   *

Randall Ashby entered *Kavanagh's* and allowed a few seconds for his eyes to adjust to the restaurant's dim lighting. He was recognized by the *maître d* and led to the table where Erika and her mother sat, each nursing a glass of wine as they waited for him. He'd decided to arrive fashionably late to allow them time to do whatever a mother and daughter do when first meeting after a two or three month separation. He'd been made aware by Erika's innuendo that there was some lingering tension between them over her decision to move to Washington and thought it best to stay out of that – for a while at least. The breakfast with her father had gone better than expected and he hoped this luncheon would as well. He approached the table, thanked the head waiter and ordered a glass of whatever Erika and her mother were drinking.

"Mom, this is Randall," Erika said, and Denise extended her hand. The lawyer shook it and took a seat.

"A pleasure to meet you, Mrs. Nolan. Senator Payne sends his regards and asked me to extend an invitation to you to visit at his office this afternoon if your schedule allows."

Denise smiled and nodded. "How nice of him. I think I just might."

"Mom, you really don't have to. It's just an office like any other."

"Now that I've met Randall I might as well meet the other people you work with."

"There aren't many of us. Michelle is usually there. There's me, the Senator and Megan the secretary. That's all."

"What about you Randall?" Denise asked, smiling at him. "Do you always go by Randall, never Randy or Rand or something else?"

"Randall is about as informal as he gets," Erika interjected. "He usually introduces himself to people as Randall B. Ashby."

Winking at Denise he said, "I just liked the resonance of that. Randall B. Ashby. It sounds so antebellum; very southern, gentlemanly – like Rhett Butler or Ashley Wilkes."

"And the middle initial?"

"I usually lie and say it's just that – an initial, because I don't want people to know about my German heritage, especially in the current state of world affairs. Actually, it stands for Bahlinger, my mother's maiden name. Her grandfather came to this country from Hannover, Germany in the middle of the last century. They must've been escaping something because I've tried to trace our lineage back before that year with no luck. My mother says it's because they come from a long line of misfits and cowards."

"You never told me that," Erika commented, frowning a little at him.

"You never asked." He stole a quick glance at the amused look on her mother's face and figured he'd made a good first impression. "Have you looked at the menu yet?"

"Not yet," Denise replied, picking up the small leather folder. "Any recommendations?"

"I'm going to sound like a waiter, but you asked… If you like seafood and want to leave room for dessert there's an appetizer of a Jumbo Lump Maryland Crab Cake with Mustard Crème Fraiche that comes with corn relish. For most people, it's a meal in itself. I'm going to have the Maine Lobster Rolls with their house special coleslaw. The seafood chowder is outstanding and goes well with a house salad and Roquefort dressing. The steaks are good, especially the bacon wrapped petite filet mignon with lemon pepper and garlic butter." He looked at Erika and said, "No garlic butter for you, though. We have a date tonight. Actually, it's really hard to find anything on the menu that anyone could complain about. It all depends on what you're hungry for – seafood or red meat or chicken."

"It sounds like you come here often," Denise observed, turning her menu over to look on the back. "Do you?"

"Often enough, I guess. But, more often to the sister restaurant to this one located in Annapolis. I have good friends from law school who have a sailboat tied up there and we often get together on weekends. The two chefs are brothers and work hard at outdoing one another. I probably know the menu at the other restaurant better than half the wait staff."

"How nice," Denise offered simply. "We have a place on the Sound up in Long Island and it's right on the water. There's nothing quite like a summer afternoon on the beach or on a boat out in the water. Erika's father and her younger brother Glenn spend most summer weekends fishing or digging for clams or tonging for oysters."

"They would really love the Chesapeake Bay then. There are so many good fishing spots and so many places to enjoy just being out on the water. And not far from Annapolis are some of the best areas in the country for catching crabs."

"Sounds delightful," Erika said unenthusiastically. "Personally, I don't dig in the sand for mollusks and I don't put live bait on fishing hooks."

Ashby looked sideways at her. "I can teach you all that in no time."

"I don't do it because I don't like it, *not* because I don't have the ability." She frowned at him. "What are you laughing at?"

They finally ordered and the conversation carried on over the meal – mostly Denise asking Ashby questions about his childhood, where he'd attended school, why he became a lawyer; what motivated him to move to Washington and get involved in politics. The same kinds of questions he had answered for Erika's father. Looking at her and Erika he had to agree with the Senator that they were very much alike – both in looks and demeanor. Erika seemed a little edgy about the grilling her mother was giving him, but it didn't bother him at all. When he turned the tables and began asking Denise about her childhood and then about her time as a nurse in Europe, she seemed flattered at his interest.

By the time the dishes were bused from the table and the waiter had brought them each coffee, he thought the whole thing had gone well.

That was until Denise announced she would be moving to Washington, D.C.

"When and what on earth for?" Erika demanded to know. "Have you talked with dad?"

"Not directly."

"What do you mean not directly?"

"I mean I've floated the idea out, and he's considering it."

"Mother! Why on earth would you want to move out of your virtually brand new house – the house you said was your dream home, and the cottage on the Sound you're always saying you love so much? Why would you leave that to come to a town that you've always held in such low esteem?"

"Plenty of reasons."

"Such as?" Erika demanded in an unfriendly tone.

"Well, your father is here in Washington almost half his time these days. When he's not in Washington, he's most often on the road. If the last five months are any indication, he's only in New York six or seven days in any given month. He tells me that's not likely to change much in the near future. Between consulting with the government and dealing with the Corps of Engineers on behalf of the corporation, he spends more time in Washington than anywhere."

Erika looked and sounded upset. "That's not the only reason is it?"

"Of course it's not the only reason."

"What about Glenn? Are you going to uproot him from another high school right now, in the middle of his sophomore year? That doesn't seem fair."

"It may not seem fair to you, but the truth is the high school he's attending in New York isn't really preparing him for college. If we were to move here he could go immediately into Gonzoga College High School where he would get a much better education."

"But Mom, Glenn doesn't even want to go to college. His grades have never been that good, and he loves being out there on Long Island where he can do all of his fishing and boating and everything else he does on the water."

Denise sighed heavily, obviously growing a little frustrated. "Glenn may not want to go to college right now but he probably will in another year, rather than going into the Army. You probably hear as much or more about the draft as I do. I've already got one son in the Army; I don't need both of them there."

Erika looked at her mother, tight-lipped and taking deep breaths, obviously upset. "Those aren't the real reasons, though are they? You're upset that I left home, and you still don't trust me. So the actual reason you're considering moving here is to keep your eye on me. Isn't that right? That's why we had to have this lunch today – so you could check out Randall. So that you could check up on me. That's the *only* reason you're moving down here. The rest of it is all window dressing. How could you do this to me?"

"Erika," her mother said slowly and ominously.

"No, I'm serious. It just happens to be convenient that dad has provided you with an excuse." She glared angrily at her mother. "You're treating me like a little girl."

Ashby realized this conversation was probably not going to get better with time. He folded his napkin placed it on the table. "Mrs. Nolan, it's been a pleasure meeting you but I have to go. There are committee deliberations and a committee staff meeting beginning soon. Would you excuse me and Erika for just a moment?"

He led her to a small alcove off the main dining room and drew close to get her attention.

"I'm so sorry you had to see that," Erika began, her look angry, her eyes flashing like polished sabers. "My mother is so judgmental and controlling it's embarrassing. Can you believe it? – the way she grilled you and then declared she's moving here to spy on me. On us. How irrational!"

"You've got this all wrong, Erika."

"What?! How can you say that? You saw what she's like."

Ashby grabbed her by both arms. "You ought to be real glad you have parents who care enough to risk your petty, childish little outbursts to keep you out of harm's way. This is a brutal town populated by mostly brutal people – people who are out for power and self-gratification at the expense of the inexperienced or the innocent, like you. I know a lot of people like that. For all your parents know I could be one of them. You ought to be thanking your mother, not giving her a lot of grief. Now, I'm going to go up front, take care of the bill, and go back to my office. If we still have a date tonight, give me a call. If you're the kind of person I think and hope you are, I expect you'll be spending a fair amount of time this afternoon apologizing to your mother.

"Erika, good day – and perhaps… goodbye."

Chapter 13

Colonel Leighton Timmons stood at the large window in the ready room above the hangar looking out onto Kelly Field now bathed in the hot September sun of south Texas. On his left stood the Airfield Commander, Lieutenant Colonel Dan Raye and next to him Major Carl Broussard, the chief of training for fighter transition located at Moffett Field in Sunnyvale, the West Coast Army Air Corps Training Center. They were watching the AT-6 trainer make its last of three touch and go landings on the north-south runway.

"So far so good," Colonel Timmons remarked to Broussard. "Most cadets don't try to do crosswind landings in the T-6 – not on purpose anyhow."

"Nolan's not your average student, sir," Lieutenant Crippen offered. He was Mitch Nolan's instructor for this last phase of flight school and was still unsure and a little unnerved by the attention being paid to his student.

Colonel Timmons looked away from the window and glanced at the flight instructor briefly and then returned his gaze outside. "He's above average overall, according to his records. And he's excelled in instrument flying and, of course gunnery – that's why we're all here. But strangely he's not the top graduating pilot. Why is that?"

"It happens," the base commander replied. "Students who are really good at the controls don't always do so well in the classroom. Nolan is one of them. We know he's helped a lot of his classmates through the class work for instrument flying for example, but didn't do so well on the written test himself. But when it came to the instrument checkride, he was the top man in the class. The only class work he seemed to really excel at were those classes based on aircraft mechanics – systems and the like. On the rest he coasted."

Major Broussard was only half listening; his full attention was on the approach and landing of Nolan's AT-6. He'd already made two impressive three-point landings. The big North American trainer had a reputation for being difficult to land in a crosswind – so difficult most students would say that any landing you could walk away from was a good one. The major wondered if the lieutenant at the controls wasn't just showing off for the brass.

The small crowd of officers watched the final approach and landing, and followed the aircraft as it turned off the runway, down the taxiway and across the ramp to the base of the hangar in which they now stood. After shutdown, the student pilot got out of the cockpit, completed a quick post-flight inspection then walked across the tarmac and into the hangar. A few minutes later he entered the student briefing room where Crippen introduced him to the other officers seated around one of the many small rectangular metal tables used by flight instructors with their students.

"So, Lieutenant Nolan," Colonel Timmons began when they all sat down, "explain this to me." A sheet of paper with the letterhead **Gulf Coast Army Air Corps Center (GCAACTC)** was pushed across the table; it was a report dated a week earlier about Advanced Flight School Class 41-5 performance in Gunnery Training at Kelly Army Air Field.

"I'm not sure I understand, sir."

"You know what that is of course," Colonel Timmons replied.

"Yes sir. It says it's the report of our class in gunnery training: air-to-ground and air-to-air gunnery. The training squadron commander, Lieutenant Bigsby, said we set some kind of record. We were told our scores were the highest seen here at Kelly Field in some time."

"Actually they were the highest scores ever recorded in aerial gunnery in any of the three training centers. By far. Yours was the first class in which no pilots washed out because of gunnery training performance. Well over half your class qualified as 'expert.' That's never been done before either – the next highest class had just under a third. Tell me how you did that?"

"Sir, class 41-5 has spent a lot of time and effort on the flight line mastering the T-6, and that effort showed up not only in gunnery but in instrument training as well. We're a pretty highly motivated crew and have been all the way through flight school starting back on the first day of Basic at Randolph."

"That's bull." Colonel Timmons leaned back and crossed his arms over his chest, looking closely at Mitch Nolan and then at Major Broussard before responding. "Your name is at the top of that list, lieutenant. Your score is the first thing that grabbed my attention when I saw this report cross my desk a week ago. How did you do it? And don't give me any cock and bull story about being part of a highly motivated class or being lucky that day or any other BS like that. Nobody has ever come close to the score you turned in. Major Broussard here set the old record at 44.3 percent six years ago. You more than doubled that. I want to know how you and five other of your classmates beat my top gunnery instructor's record. How did you do it?"

Mitch saw that Broussard was smiling knowingly at him. At last the major said, "You cheated, didn't you?"

"I wouldn't call it cheating." He took a deep breath and looked at Colonel Timmons. "Sir, we like to think what we did was improve on gunnery training practices."

"All right, son, tell me how you did it."

Mitch took a deep breath and contemplated. *Do I really want to do this*? he asked himself. *What's that line in the old Cadet Prayer? – have no fear when truth and right are in jeopardy.* Finally, he rose from the chair, walked to the chalkboard and drew a side view of the air to ground gunnery range – it looked like an elongated right triangle.

"Qualifying 'expert' requires hitting the target with 30% of rounds fired. The range looks like this from the side. Entering the range and heading down this long shallow angle, the procedure is to begin firing at the 6' x 6' target one thousand yards out, and cease firing at a distance of three hundred yards."

"That's been the Air Corps standard training procedure for well over a decade," Colonel Timmons acknowledged.

"With all due respect, sir, that practice produces low scores and poor aerial gunnery proficiency in pilots. And let me show you why," he added quickly, drawing a top view of an airplane going towards a target. "It's a simple trigonometry problem. The line from the centerline of the aircraft to the target creates a very small angle of allowable error before the pilot completely misses the target."

He drew a long thin right triangle on both sides of the centerline and a small arc in the angle closest to the aircraft. "When we looked at this we knew from our own experience that no one could keep the T6 perfectly on this line to the center of the target. We assumed conservatively that we could keep it within 1° either side of the centerline. Actually, that's very optimistic; but assuming that, and beginning to fire at 1000 yards, the simple trigonometry is that the gunner would be fifty-two and a half feet to the right or left of the target. Fifty-two and a half feet wide at one thousand yards – almost twenty yards off at a thousand, which is where the Army says to begin shooting."

Mitch glanced around the room and thought he saw disbelief in their faces.

"At three hundred yards – where the training procedure says to cease-fire – the gunner would be almost sixteen feet wide of the target with the same deflection of one degree. That's why aerial gunnery scores have always been so low. Getting three rounds out of every ten into a 6' x 6' target the way the Army teaches it now becomes just a matter of pure luck rather than piloting or gunnery skills. We looked at all that and tweaked the procedure – we didn't cheat, we just changed it a little bit."

The colonel looked hard at the diagrams and numbers on the board, glanced at the other officers in the briefing room and said, "Continue Nolan."

"Basically what we did was to start firing at the point where the current procedure said to cease-fire in order to give ourselves a fighting chance at hitting the target."

"What you did was dangerous, lieutenant," Colonel Timmons finally said. "You violated established, long-standing safety procedures."

"Sir, we had no accidents and experienced no damaged aircraft or range facilities while significantly improving our scores. Same thing with air-to-air. Getting closer was safer – certainly for the ship towing the target sleeve. I've hunted a lot, colonel. I always found my chances of precisely placing a round on target was a lot higher at a hundred yards than it was at five hundred or a thousand. Closer is better. That's even more true in aerial gunnery."

Colonel Timmons remained quiet and took in the simple diagrams on the chalkboard. Finally, he turned to Major Broussard. "I want you to check this out, major. Lieutenant Nolan can demonstrate tomorrow morning out on the range and I'd like you to fly the course his way as well. We'll see for ourselves just how that all works out."

*   *   *

The two AT-6 trainers climbed away from Kelly Field in formation headed west, Nolan leading. He should have felt nervous being on the hot seat with the commander of pilot training for the Air Corps, but he wasn't. He was in his element, and the thought of failing this little test in front of the brass was the furthest thing from his mind.

It was a typically hot, clear September morning in Texas. Off their right wing they could see San Antonio clearly and as they made a wide turn headed toward the gunnery range north and east of the city, Mitch thought the visibility was probably seventy miles. Minutes later he made the initial radio call to the air-to-ground gunnery range.

"Range six-six-able, this is Baker flight of two inbound, ten minutes out,"

Baker flight of two, this is Range six-six-able. Range is clear all traffic. Wind three-one-two degrees at eight. Baker Two hold north two miles at one five hundred feet, right traffic. Baker One is cleared onto the range, three passes, left traffic, call base and final. Over.

Mitch looked five miles to his front and saw the simple layout of the air-to-ground range below. *"This is Baker One, roger six-six-able."* He looked over and saw Major Broussard bank left and climb away to the north of the range. *"Range six-six-able control, Baker One reporting control point Thunderbird."*

He flew the normal traffic pattern while looking down past his left wing at the range and the new white target sheet with a bright red circle in the middle. He'd loved the gunnery practice and check ride, and was sorry to see it over.

There hadn't been a minute of the entire last nine months he hadn't enjoyed – after the three weeks of ground school he'd had to repeat. He now felt he was finally getting into the real fun and guts of being a military pilot. He'd put in for fighter transition and gotten it easily as the number two ranked man in the class. In another three weeks he'd be reporting in to Moffett for fighter transition, a rated Air Corps pilot finally. Lucky Lindquist and Marvelous Marv had stayed in touch and were now only a week away from assignment to a front line squadron. They'd both requested and gotten slots in the 1st Pursuit Group. Word had it they were being re-organized into the 82nd Fighter Group and stationed at Muroc up in the high desert. They would be transitioning into a new twin engine fighter called the Lightning built by Lockheed. Everything he'd heard about the ship made it sound like exactly the plane he wanted to fly. He hoped they still had some slots left in the 82nd when he finished his fighter transition.

"Range control, Baker One entering left downwind."

He'd liked most everything about the AT-6 that everyone was starting to call the *Texan*. It flew and felt like a fighter without all the high powered performance expected in the new generation of fighters like the Lightning; still, this was a big piece of iron.

He enjoyed aerobatics in the plane. The *Texan* loved the big smooth barrel rolls and chandelles as well as lazy eights. It could be flown so smoothly if one minded rudder control that it was possible to place a plastic glass of water on top of the panel and do a tight three-sixty turn without spilling a drop – Crippen had shown him that. Later while practicing solo, he'd tried it himself and then perfected the practice with a lazy eight and even a barrel roll. But the plane could also be handled roughly when necessary. He'd learned from experience that accelerated stalls could be a thrill if he wasn't mindful of trim. In the midst of playing around with accelerated stalls one afternoon he'd discovered a way to almost stop dead in the air and completely reverse course by stalling the plane and yanking it quickly out of trim. But he'd decided never to try it without at least ten thousand feet of altitude, discovering his chicken quotient was nearly as high as his talent quotient.

"Range control, this is Baker One turning base," Mitch called and rolled the trainer into a tight but smooth turn.

"Range Control, this is Baker One, Base to final. The gun is hot."

That sounded funny – as it always did – when he said it over the radio. They'd mounted a single .30 caliber machine gun on top of the fuselage with ammo storage for a thousand rounds. But it was a trainer after all. The P-38 carried four fifty caliber guns and a twenty millimeter canon all in the nose. *Now that's real firepower,* he thought, switching the gun on and lining up on the target now less than a mile away. *Airspeed one-forty, altitude twelve hundred, coming up on the approach path, Nolan, in three-two-one... nose down, crosshairs on the red ball. Thousand yard marker... Now!*

The airplane felt particularly solid this morning and the glide slope angle felt perfect. *Five hundred yards – halfway there, son. Little gust from the right. Tap the rudder. Dead on. Four hundred yards...Three hundred coming up... NOW!* The red circle on the white canvas loomed large now as he gently squeezed the trigger and saw rounds tear into the target and kick up dirt behind. There was no sensation of recoil or buffeting from the machine gun, only a slight hint of burnt powder smell in the cockpit. He saw a few puffs of dust just to the right of the square target and touched the left rudder pedal gently. Suddenly the target seemed to fill the windscreen and he let off the trigger just as he pulled the stick abruptly into his stomach for an instant as the white square disappeared beneath him. He centered the stick in the next instant and then immediately applied aft pressure to start a steady climb.

Good run, he told himself and started a shallow left turn at five hundred feet. By the time he reached twelve hundred feet and turned left he was setting up for his next run.

The next two runs were equally satisfying and he departed the pattern to the south after calling the range control who immediately cleared Baker Two into the range. Mitch circled to the east giving the range a wide berth as Major Broussard entered for his three runs. Watching him from a couple of miles to the north, Mitch could tell he was scoring well on each of his runs and when it was over the other trainer pulled into formation on his wing.

Baker One, let's turn north and climb to ten thousand, the major said over the radio. *Follow me.* They continued climbing for another ten minutes until Broussard called again. *How much experience do you have dogfighting, Baker One?*

Mitch looked out toward the other aircraft and could see the Major's face clearly. "*Kelly Field SOP prohibits dogfighting for Flight Training Cadets.*"

That's not what I asked, Major Broussard replied quickly. When he got no further answer, he finally said: *You head west for a full minute and I'll head east. At the end of sixty seconds all restrictions are off. Consider this an introduction to fighter transition. I'm curious if you can fly as well as Lieutenant Crippen seems to think you can. One minute, and then we'll see what you're made of.*

Mitch immediately turned west in response, flying straight and level and watching the sweep second hand on the panel clock. At the minute mark he banked hard left in a tight 180 degree turn and scanned the sky.

Broussard was nowhere to be found.

He cruised on for a minute weaving back and forth, checking completely around, above and below. Still no sighting of the other AT-6. *The sun!* He started to turn in the direction of the sun and suddenly saw Broussard diving on him from above and to his right. His immediate reaction was to turn into the attack head on and climb at the attacker. The rate of closure had to be over three hundred miles per hour as the other aircraft hurtled past him barely avoiding a collision. Mitch did a hammerhead stall and tried to follow the attacker.

But Broussard had anticipated the maneuver and turned inside him and maneuvered with more speed and momentum drawing Nolan into a turning duel that he was losing with each turn. Mitch turned away diving, but Broussard stayed in trail, easily staying with him. The major inched closer, followed him through a roll to the left and one to the right. Mitch realized he was being outturned, and if they'd both been armed Broussard would be very close to getting his guns to and through him to finish him off. This was becoming embarrassing.

He pulled a tight right turn and then reversed to the left; Broussard remained tight on him and was only seconds away from shooting him down. Mitch decided to try something he'd only done twice before, each time scaring himself. But he thought he could make it work. A quick glance at the altimeter showed they were about ten thousand.

Suddenly, he turned hard right pointing the right wing at the ground and immediately pulled the stick hard into his stomach and stomped hard on the right rudder peddle. His head hit the top of the canopy hard and he saw the world beneath him spin as the nose pointed straight down. He threw the stick full forward for an instant and then neutralized it. His vision blurred and it appeared he was looking down through a long dark tunnel that was growing more narrow and closing in on him.

And then everything went black…

Major Broussard was having just about as much fun as he could think of boxing Nolan's ears in the dogfight. The kid was good. But not good enough. The rolls and tight turns were not going to get him loose from an experienced dogfighter latched to his tail. He'd learn that over time and with a lot more practice. He was about to call Nolan and tell him he'd been dusted when the AT-6 in front of him suddenly disappeared.

For the briefest fraction of a second Broussard thought he saw Nolan's aircraft abruptly tumble out of control and then glimpsed the trainer from directly above rushing past him. He let out an involuntary shout of fear and turned hard left. He righted the airplane, and continued searching the sky.

Nolan had simply vanished.

Mitch regained consciousness and saw he was still pointed straight down and wasn't flying but falling like a rock through nine thousand feet. The controls were sluggish to the point of being unresponsive and the airspeed was well below stall speed… but it was increasing. In another thousand feet with airspeed and control response growing, he was back in control of the aircraft. He saw the sun glint off the major's trainer a couple thousand feet above him and two miles away. He was flying back and forth searching, and in a few minutes Mitch had come up on him from behind, sliding into a formation position off his right wing and slightly behind. A few seconds later the major looked over and saw him; immediately he turned hard left and Nolan followed. Over the next five minutes Broussard twisted and turned and dived through everything he could think of to shake the other aircraft off his wing. Finally he pulled level, set his airspeed at cruise, and waggled his wings in surrender.

Nolan smiled. *"I'll see you back at the briefing room, Baker two,"* he called on the air-to-air frequency, and then peeled off headed for Kelly Field.

*   *   *   *

They stood in formation on the concrete taxiway, twenty-six newly graduated pilots facing the open hangar, with their freshly acquired pilot's wings shining in the hot noonday sun of late September. The harsh, dry heat of central Texas smothered them like a heavy wool blanket while they listened to Brigadier General Harlan Kerr come to the end of his overly long graduation address to USAAC flight school class 41-5. Although Mitch Nolan had positively enjoyed every single moment of his flight school experience, this final event of a formal graduation ceremony found him in a rare disgruntled mood.

He had expected upon graduation to continue on to California for transitioning into fighters before assignment to one of the Pursuit Groups. But somewhere in the labyrinths of Air Corps assignments in Washington something had gone horribly wrong. Now he was going to California but not for transition into the type of aircraft he had been pointing toward his entire flight school experience. What awaited him was a sour disappointment.

Major Carl Broussard watched the formation break up when General Kerr dismissed them at last; his eyes followed Lieutenant Nolan who had turned and walked away from the revelry going on around him.

"He's really PO'd," Broussard said to the colonel standing next to him.

"He'll get over it," Colonel Timmons said, offhandedly.

"I hope you're right, colonel. I guess we'll see in another month when he reports in to Moffett. Big disappointments sometimes break the best officers. Hope we did the right thing."

"Don't second-guess yourself, Broussard. I know some people in Washington who knew his old man back when, and they say he was one tough old bird. If he's anything like his father, he'll shake this off and come back for more. Just keep feeding him that old saw about this being for the good of the service. And keep reminding yourself that in the not too distant future we're going to need a lot more instructor pilots like him. Frankly, one good instructor pilot will give us a hundred fold return, maybe more."

"Unless he up and quits on us."

"You don't really think that's going to happen do you, major?"

Broussard took a deep breath and looked at Timmons. "I hope not, sir. I really would hate to lose him. Right now, from what I've seen, he's already at least as good as anyone I have."

The major had been utterly unprepared for what he'd seen and experienced that first day on the aerial gunnery range. He'd done almost twice as good as he'd ever scored on the best day in his life following the practices and examples of the new lieutenant - over 80% hits on a 6'x6' target. He'd realized immediately they needed to change Air Corps practices and approach to gunnery – and, he'd wanted Nolan and five others on his instructor roster at Moffett as soon as they graduated. In the next few years he expected to be facing a huge influx of pilots and sending them off in better, faster planes than he'd cut his own teeth on.

"We need instructors like this Nolan," Colonel Timmons was saying, "and others like him. A lot of 'em. Sure, he'll balk at missing out on operational assignments – most of the good ones do. He'd probably have made a good combat pilot. But, mark my word, one of these days he'll thank us."

Chapter 14

"That now makes three sets of orders we've each received in the last month alone."

Lucky Lindquist removed the cap from a cone top can of Rainier Old Stock Ale and passed it to Mitch Nolan who lounged on the seat adjacent to the sailboat's wheel. "Meanwhile, they put us up in a hotel in San Francisco on call until noon each day in case they need us to ferry a plane somewhere. We charge all our meals to the room and we spend most days sightseeing around the Bay. Marv's old man told us about a buddy of his from Yale – a guy named Stanaway who owns a rail car shop, three foundries, a bunch of ships for transporting scrap metal to Japan and this little fifty-two footer. We got nothing to complain about – at all."

Mitch still found it hard to believe the incredible story Crosley and Lindquist had been feeding him from the time they'd left the dock in South San Francisco. They'd gotten in touch the day before, nine weeks after he'd reported in to Moffett Field. They were amazed to hear he was an instructor and unable to join them on what sounded like world's greatest boondoggle.

His two classmates had graduated from the fighter transition course three months before he'd finished flight school at Kelley Field. Since then, according to them, they'd been assigned to four different fighter squadrons in three states plus the Philippines. Every time they got ready to move, something had happened and their orders were rescinded, rewritten and they were sent back to the hotel in San Francisco to cool their heels and await further instructions. And they weren't the only ones.

The fledgling Army Air Corps at the moment seemed in total disarray; his two buddies had logged more time in the borrowed sailboat than at the controls of an Army fighter.

For them, the time since graduation from West Point had been a long party. Flight school had been interesting, the transition into the current inventory of fighters a little challenging, and the marching and counter-marching to orders out of Washington annoying but worth the privilege of living in luxury and touring California.

"I wouldn't want to switch with you guys," Mitch declared, holding up his can to indicate his needing a refill. "Things have a way of evening out over time."

"That might be true, Mitch," Crosley said, placing his hands on the wheel and looking up at the Golden Gate Bridge as they passed by Alcatraz headed for the ocean. The traffic on the span was light at mid-morning. "Sixty degree weather in the first week of December doesn't seem fair, I guess. Maybe we should have to pay some dues. But –"

"Hey you two! Look at that behind us – six formations of three headed our way," Lindquist said, pointing aft of the boat. "I didn't think those squid pilots on Alameda got out of bed before noon on Sunday mornings. Must be something important to get the Navy up and moving this early."

*   *   *

In Washington, D.C. White House Press Secretary Steve Early was still at home in his pajamas at 2:20 PM when he got the press services on the telephone and announced the Japanese attack on Pearl Harbor fifty-five minutes after it started.

*   *   *

Nineteen year old Donald Blaxton, was walking past the Fifth Regiment Armory in Baltimore where a youngster standing on the street corner beside a large stack of newspapers was waving a special edition of the *Baltimore Sun.* "Extra! – read all about it here! Extra! Extra! Japs bomb Pearl Harbor!" Blaxton had the same sinking feeling about the world ending that he'd experienced when he'd heard the Germans invaded Russia. He looked up at the armory and it suddenly struck him there was going to be a war, and, he knew he and others his age were going to have to be part of it. He trudged on dogged by two questions: could he talk his older sister Dorothy into signing papers allowing him to enlist? and – where in the world was Pearl Harbor?

*   *   *

Omar Bradley and his wife Kitty enjoyed their time together working in the garden at Camp Benning, especially on Sunday afternoons. They were outside weeding their flower bed when a car passed by, stopped suddenly and rolled back in reverse. The driver – Harold "Pink" Bull, a friend and instructor on post – rolled down the window and yelled out, "Did you hear about Pearl Harbor?!"

*   *   *

Chaplin Howard Forgy stood next to a gun crew on the deck of the USS New Orleans at Pearl Harbor; he was sweat soaked and soiled from exertion. As the Japanese planes roared overhead, he apologized to the men around him for not holding church services that morning but encouraged them to 'praise the Lord and pass the ammunition.'

* * *

President Franklin Roosevelt was informed by his closest aide – his son – of the news about the attack on Pearl Harbor. "Phone Bill Donovan," he said immediately.

* * *

At West Point, New York, Major Cole Alford was sitting in the living room of his quarters reading the latest installment of Prince Valiant in *PUCK*, the Comic Weekly when the telephone rang. It was Colonel Fauser telling him, "The damned Japs just bombed Pearl Harbor. Get hold to Judd Haggerty and the both of you git over here as soon as you can. We got to figure us a way out of this damned Yankee rock pile and back into the real Army."

* * *

Water swirled into the USS California where Machinist's Mate Robert Scott in the forward air compressor station was trying to feed air to 5 inch guns. The others ran, yelling to Scott to get out in a hurry. He shouted back, "This is my station – I'll stay here and give them air as long as the guns are going." They let him have his way and shut the watertight door.

* * *

Brigadier General Harrison Reeves heard the announcement over the radio as he sat in his study reading one of J.B. Bury's histories of the Roman Empire. He smiled, thinking to himself that now he would quickly get his second star and his third not long after. He reasoned if the War went on long enough even a fourth was well within his reach. He put away Bury's history and retrieved one on Alexander's conquests, thinking it a more fitting study now.

* * *

At the Polo Grounds, Wild Bill Donovan grumbled to his friends he was not at all satisfied with the performance of the New York football Giants who were losing 7-0. The public address system cut through the crowd noise: *"Colonel Donovan, Colonel William Donovan come to the box office at once, there is an important phone message."* Over the phone FDR's son told Donovan to make his way to LaGuardia airport where an Air Corps plane was waiting to bring him and Vice-President Wallace to D.C.

*   *   *

Henry Smythe-Browne got a call from his old school chum 'Jack' Colville, Churchill's personal secretary. "The Japanese have attacked Pearl Harbor. Churchill has been in contact with President Roosevelt but they have very few details. I can tell you this: the prime minister went to bed with a smile on his face. We're not alone anymore. Sleep well, Henry."

*   *   *

William Howard Payne was awakened by the knocking at his door, feeling like a vise had been clamped to his sinuses and was being inexorably tightened by some fiendish malevolent spirit. He'd had this latest bout of sinusitis for five days and was ready to accede to his daughter's pestering about taking the codeine prescribed by the doctor. Before he could drag himself out of bed, his daughter Michelle entered with a glass of water and two pills.

"You have to take these and get a hot shower," she insisted. "There's been an attack on Pearl Harbor and the president has called a cabinet meeting. He's asking that you attend also."

"So, the damned Oriental demons have finally done it. The fat's really in the fire now."

"Megan, Erika and Randall are already in transit to your office. They'll have an information packet ready for you by the time we get there. There won't be much."

"How bad is it?"

"Nobody really seems to know. It'll take days or weeks – or more – to sort through everything. But it sounds really bad."

The tremor in her voice alarmed him. His daughter had a reputation on Capitol Hill as one of the most calm and level headed people in Washington. "You're afraid."

"I am. There might be a ground attack following the air attack. They might have ships off the coast of California. They could attack elsewhere. Like I said, it sounds really bad. Fear the worst and hope for the best. Now, take these pills and off to the shower you go."

185

*   *   *

In the Philippines, General Jonathan "Skinny" Wainwright jiggled his phone to contact his aide and told him, "The cat has jumped!"

*   *   *

Dr. John Devereux and his three assistants at the Honolulu blood bank were swamped by blood donor volunteers and ran out of containers. He used sterilized Coke bottles. His best volunteer at cleaning bottles and tubes was a local prostitute.

*   *   *

Jim Laubach – just shy of his sixteenth birthday – and his best friend were watching the Sunday afternoon matinee in Wooster, Ohio when the lights went on in the movie house and the manager walked on stage to announce the bombing of Pearl Harbor by the Japanese. "This means there will be a war," the man declared. Walking home the two boys decided to go into the military. Jim wanted to be a Marine – he liked the look of their Dress Blue uniform; his friend wanted to be a tank driver in the Army. Eventually they both got their wish.

*   *   *

Glenn Nolan sat in the parlor alone at his parents' Washington home, a small row house in Georgetown, listening to the sketchy reports about the Japanese attack in Hawaii coming through the big Motorola console. His stomach was tied in a knot. Nausea, tight and sickening, swept over him – a feeling of solid dread. At least they hadn't attacked the Philippines; he had more than a dozen friends whose families were still assigned there.

*   *   *

A newly promoted brigadier general stationed at Fort Sam Houston was awakened from a fitful mid-day nap by the ringing telephone in his quarters. "When? All right, I understand. I'll be there as soon as I can."

Dwight Eisenhower kissed his wife Mamie goodbye and told her he had to go down to headquarters. He left without telling her the reason why or when he'd be back.

*   *   *

In Boston, twelve year old John Galvin was at his Aunt Florence's in Fenway getting ready to go home to Wakefield with his family. His aunt turned on the radio for some music; as she rotated the tuning dial they heard an announcer say, "…disaster at Pearl Harbor." As they paused to listen to the weak reception on the small plastic radio on top of the refrigerator, the enormity of the catastrophe to the American base in Hawaii began to come through. Shortly after, on the way home in the car, Galvin's father became more and more enraged until he suddenly banged on the steering wheel and said, "We'll destroy them in thirty days!"

*   *   *

Dave Nolan looked up at the stop light from inside the Chrysler wondering if the traffic signal wasn't malfunctioning. Denise was fiddling with the car radio but all she seemed able to get was static. It had been that way since they'd left the parking lot outside Griffith Stadium after watching the Redskins beat Philadelphia 20-14. At last she gave up, switched the radio off, and leaned back on the big bench seat. A car pulled up on the right and the driver gazed at them with a strange, faraway look in his eyes.

It was nearly half past five and already dark.

"Did you notice that?" she asked when the light turned green. "Everybody seems to be acting really strange – like that man in the car. I'd swear everybody has turned to some kind of vacant faced zombie."

"No, haven't noticed," he replied, thinking she was always saying outrageous things like that since she'd moved to Washington. He sniffed twice, then covered a sneeze. *Going to the game and sitting through hours of damp chill was a mistake*, he thought to himself. He felt sapped – from the weather, the cold he sensed coming on, the fatigue that was catching up on him because of all the travel he'd done in the last six months. The absence of leaves on the trees and approaching winter seemed to dull the color of nature, serving to deepen his sour mood.

"And what was going on with all those announcements in the last quarter of the game?" Denise asked. "It sounded like a roll call of everybody in attendance above the rank of corporal junior grade to go pick up a phone call."

"Who knows?" But he had noticed it also. It had given him the old sinking feeling that something serious was happening – something ominous.

It was a dismal drive back to their rental house through the misty night and dark streets; he was strangely irritated – at himself, at the weather, at her for what seemed like a constant running acrimony on the fringes of her relationship with Erika. She was even upset with Glenn because he wasn't measuring up to her expectations in school.

Dave felt there was a lot of pressure on him now from a host of government bureaucrats and cabinet level staff functionaries who seemed to expect him to tell them how to do their jobs and to shoulder their responsibilities. And, although he still enjoyed the confidence of Edgar Barrett, some of the Board directors were questioning the amount of time he was spending away from the core of the enterprise's businesses. The Christmas season was just around the corner, yet he was anything but in a holiday mood as they pulled to a stop.

Glenn was sitting in front of the large console radio when they entered the house. He glanced at them with the saddest and most disconcerted look Dave had ever seen on his young face. "What do you think it means, Dad?"

"Depends on what you mean by 'it', Glenn," Dave replied, removing his hat and placing his coat on a hangar in the hallway closet.

"Pearl Harbor. Haven't you heard? It's been all over the radio for the past three hours."

"What about Pearl Harbor?"

"They attacked – the Japanese did. It happened early morning – about eight a.m. Honolulu time. And all the reports say, it's still going on, one wave of bombers after another. They say it's a war."

Denise gasped. "Oh, no. No!"

"Are you sure, son?" he asked, knowing in his gut it had to be true. He'd run through the scenario of a surprise Japanese attack with Eisenhower in the Philippines back in early '36 when he'd been a major in command of one of the battalions of the regiment stationed in Manila. He'd seen the utter unpreparedness of the garrison there still in "spit-shine" mode rather than being combat ready. The defense plan had been a farce – just like the amphibious doctrine that had almost gotten him killed the first time they tried it in Lingayen Gulf. He hoped for the sake of the troops they had straightened out both plans in the years since he'd left. He sat down next to Glenn and listened; it was all about Hawaii, not the Philippines... yet.

Georgie Patton had predicted a surprise attack on Pearl when he was stationed there in the '30s. He'd seen the Japanese expanding in the Pacific and observed, "the Japanese have been fighting the Chinese, the Koreans, and the Russians since '04 and never once declared war. The bastards won't declare war when they come for us, either."

Sunday morning at Pearl. Smart move, he thought. He'd stopped in Hawaii on his way back to the States from Manila years earlier and seen the Navy's lazy, idyllic tempo of early Sunday morning. The Air Corps was just as indolent, if not worse. Nolan felt his stomach tighten and he stared at the console, listening and worrying. He pictured Ford Island and the surrounding deep draft waters and the facilities on shore. *Did the Japanese target the port fuel depot?* – it stored every drop of fuel for all the ships in the Pacific and it was irreplaceable. If they got that, and it would be easy to blow it to kingdom come with only a handful of bombs, it would be years before they could rebuild it and supply even a small Navy. *Did they destroy the Navy shipyards?* If so, the Navy would have to go an added six thousand miles round trip to repair their vessels – the turnaround time would kill any sustainable offensive naval battle plan.

He was shaking with rage inwardly at the thought of what this potentially meant.

The Japanese could take and hold Hawaii, the Philippines, Guam, and other island chains with their now superior Navy, and offer peace terms favorable to them while consolidating their gains and making the South Pacific their own lake – the same way the Romans used the Med at the time of Christ. *Brilliant*, he thought, *brilliant and diabolical*. If the Japs landed…

He and Denise had friends on Oahu, at Schofield: Bert Caldwell, a classmate at the Academy; Sam O'Hare from the Company Commanders' course at Benning in '26. *They and their families could be dead or dying now*, he thought, now inwardly churning. He could see faces from his battalion – men he'd known well in Manila not long ago.

"Did they say anything about a follow on land attack?" Dave finally asked. Glenn shook his head no. "What about the Philippines? Guam? Midway? The Canal Zone? Alaska? What about California?" Each question received a negative response.

"California?" Denise gasped. "That's where Mitch is – near San Francisco. They've got that big Navy base across the Bay, the city itself, the Air Corps base. Targets galore! They might even invade the West Coast!"

"It's a very distant possibility. I doubt they'll try that."

"Why?" she demanded. "Is there some kind of house rule against it? Some kind of silly rule of war that is irrevocable – like declaring war before one attacks an enemy? Their envoys are still here, still negotiating a treaty to avoid a military clash. They don't seem very reluctant to lie and play dirty, do they?"

"I guess not."

"Did Mitch call?" Denise asked shrilly. Glenn again shook his head negatively without looking away from the radio. She turned toward the kitchen. "Then, I'm going to call him!"

"You won't get through," Dave said, stoically. "You can bet the telephone lines into and out of every military facility in the country are jam packed, and right now we probably couldn't get a long distance operator in this town if our life depended on it."

"That doesn't mean we shouldn't try! He could be in danger!"

"And what could we do for him? What could we possibly tell him to do from three thousand miles away that would help him? No, we're better off to stay calm and collected until we find out what's really going on. It'll probably be days until we can get a line to the West Coast. And the military will have priority for a long time to come."

"Dave, we've got to do something!" she exclaimed, beginning to sound panicky. "We can't just sit here and –"

"I'm going to join up," Glenn said quietly, as if talking to himself.

"You're going to – no! Don't you dare say such a thing!" Denise's eyes went wide. "Put that out of your mind this instant!"

"I've been sitting here most of the afternoon, thinking." He looked at his father. "You always said war is a young man's game, didn't you? I'm a young man."

"You're just a boy!" Denise exclaimed, shocked at what she was hearing; she looked at Dave for support.

"Glenn, look," Dave began slowly. "This is not the time to be making life altering decisions. This is a time to find out the facts, what's really going on and which way the winds are really blowing, all right? None of us have the facts – none of us even knows what's really going on. My guess is that even the president and his closest advisors just a few miles from here are just as much in the dark as we are. Nobody, even the president, will be making really big decisions today or tonight, and maybe not even tomorrow. I know some of his closest aides, and I know how they think, and how they make decisions. They won't go off in any direction half cocked. You shouldn't either. When the time comes, we'll talk about, all right?"

"No we *won't* talk about it!" Denise said adamantly. "We already have one son in the military, that's enough." She was frightened, unsure, her mind swirling in a vat of naked fear and resentment – at the Army for letting this all happen, and at him for not sharing her anxiety.

"Denise," Dave said in a low, controlled voice. "Like I said, when the time comes we'll talk. That means all of us. You, me, *and* Glenn. Right now is not the time to be setting things in concrete; we don't have the information to do that."

Denise glared hard at him, fuming at his stubborn, indomitable calm. *It just isn't fair*, she thought. After all those years of scrimping and scraping by in the Army, after his finally getting a decent job and a home of their own – now this! Another war. She knew him – he'd be in the thick of it somehow, somewhere. He'd already gotten himself mired hip deep into the latest shenanigans dreamed up by that damned Irishman, Bill Donovan. And now she had two sons, one already in the service and her baby talking about it. She couldn't do anything about Mitch, but she certainly could about Glenn.

"And I'm telling you –"

The phone rang, interrupting her. Dave walked into the kitchen, picked up the receiver and said, "This is Dave Nolan."

"Dave, this is Ike. I'm calling from Fort Sam Houston. General Hollings gave me your phone number. I'm sure you've heard about what happened at Pearl by now. I've been called to Washington, and I'll be there before the week is out. I've been tapped for a pretty important assignment. I need to talk to you about it."

He was momentarily speechless. It had been over three years since he had talked to his old comrade although Eisenhower had written him a dozen letters in that time. It was good to hear from his longtime friend, but it also unnerved him. Again his stomach knotted.

"I'm not interested, Ike."

"You don't even know what I want to talk to you about, Dave."

"And the answer is still no."

There was a long silence on the phone and finally Eisenhower said, *"I'll call you when I firm up my travel arrangements. Say hello to Denise for Mamie and me."*

*   *   *

The late afternoon wind was chilly as Marv Crosley navigated the narrow channel and they motored into the yacht club in South San Francisco. The sun was only a few degrees above the horizon and gave the sky a yellowish-gold cast.

"So, Mitch," Linquist began as he emptied another can of Rainier Ale, "did you get back with the base commander's daughter at Randolf when they let you back into flight school?"

"Of course," he replied easily, feeling lethargic and carefree. He remembered the young girl fondly – half child, half woman; fun, but not the culmination and quintessence of female grace and beauty. Not like Smythe-Browne's daughter. He thought of Aynslee often it seemed – was it because she was unattainable? Thinking about her now, after hours of sailing and drinking, seemed part of the faintly baffling tranquility of the day; a glorious, fragile instant of pleasure that tugged at his heart.

The docks were strangely empty as they pulled into the slip – Mitch had expected at that hour they'd be full of boat owners eking out the final moments of pleasure the weekend offered – sailors stowing sails and battening down hatches, the owners of large motorized pleasure boats sitting around on back decks or inside at their lounges, drinking cocktails and eating *h'ors deurves*. The absence of people made it eerily quiet. There were lights on in the clubhouse, and after tying up the boat and securing all the lines and gear, they went inside.

A large crowd of mostly older people had drawn up in a semi-circle along one side of the club's bar and lounge facing a sideboard on which sat an oversized wooden table radio that looked like a high-shouldered tombstone. It was brightly polished and had a circular dial indicating four different radio bands. A man sat directly in front of the radio turning the tuning knob now and then to sharpen the warbling tone or find another news station.

"What's going on?" Marv asked when they bumped into Jonathan Stanaway, his father's friend who'd loaned them the sailboat. He was a big, balding man with a ruddy complexion and a strong jaw that jutted out when he grinned or laughed, which was often according to Marvelous Marv. But at the moment he wasn't grinning, and his face looked like iron beaten and tempered in a forge. "I didn't think *Fibber McGee and Molly* came on Sunday evenings," Crosley offered, smiling and looking around.

Stanaway stared back slack-jawed. "What do you mean? Don't you know? The Japs bombed Pearl Harbor this morning. Those squinty-eyed little yellow monkeys attacked without warning. It's on all the stations, almost non-stop now. The same thing over and over. It sounds like it was a complete surprise. There's now some reports the Navy sighted Japanese warships and submarines not very far off the coast."

"Of California?" Lindquist asked.

"Of course off California," Stanaway answered, openmouthed and dumbfounded. "What's wrong with you boys? Are you as worthless and irresponsible as the rest of the damned military?! Why in the world did you let this happen?!"

A number of scared faces turned toward them briefly at the sound of the outburst. Mitch felt as if he'd taken a punch to the solar plexus and his neck seemed to have broken out in prickly heat. His face felt warm and flushed. He suddenly felt inordinately guilty – not because of what Stanaway had said, or because of any look that the crowd in the bar had given him.

"Where in hell were all the admirals and generals and all the rest of the officers?" Stanaway demanded loudly. "What were they doing while this was going on? – playing polo?"

"No, sir," Mitch heard himself say though it seemed to come from somewhere outside of himself. "Cricket is reserved for Tuesdays; polo limited to all day Friday. Boozing it up and sleeping late is normally scheduled for Saturday. Sundays are set aside as a general malingering day in both the Navy and the Army."

Stanaway's face grew choleric and red. "Are you some kind of smart ass?"

"No, sir. The fact is we're all at fault."

"Somebody's at fault, that's for damned sure! But the Army and Navy, and all those liars in Washington will cover it up. They let those little yellow monkeys sneak in and blow up most of our Navy, for crying out loud – and they got away with it! If something this outrageously incompetent happened at my plant over in Oakland there'd be hell to pay and heads would roll. I can guarantee you that."

"Don't worry Mr. Stanaway, heads *will* roll over this," Mitch said quietly, holding back what he really wanted to say and listening to the garbled sound coming from the radio. "We all need to be careful when it comes to pointing fingers. Including you."

The man looked hard at Marv who lifted his hands in an open armed gesture of surrender as he shrugged and raised his eyebrows. Then Stanaway turned his attention back to Mitch.

"I don't know who you are or how you came to know Marvin, but I can tell you this – you're no longer welcome on my boat," the man said, angrily.

Mitch took a step closer, to within inches, and looked up into the taller man's eyes until the older man looked away; then he turned and left quickly, got into his car and drove like a madman back to Moffett Field. When he got there he saw all the planes were being fueled and armed with a full load of ammunition. Looking around the ramp at the sad array of obsolete fighters that now formed the Army Air Corps, he shook his head thinking: *I really hope the Japs don't show up tonight, or any other night as long as I'm here.*

An hour later he was patrolling above the coast, peering into the dark void of the Pacific.

*   *   *

Edward R. Murrow had been invited to dinner with the President that evening. Soon after the announcements about Pearl Harbor began, his wife phoned the White House and asked if they were still expected. Eleanor Roosevelt said, *"We all have to eat. Come anyway."*

Later that night, in the Oval Study upstairs in the White House, FDR pounded the study desk as he described to Murrow how the U.S. planes were destroyed on Oahu.

"On the ground, by God!... on the ground!"

Brian Utermahlen

.

⁓ ADORIMINI ⁓

Brian Utermahlen

Chapter 15

Dave Nolan knocked once on the office door and entered.

"My name is Nolan – Dave Nolan," he said to the secretary when she looked up from her typing. "I have an appointment with General Marshall at 1400, and I'm a little early. Hope you won't mind my waiting here – or if there's another office with a phone, I could use the time to catch up on some calls. Local calls," he added smiling at her.

"Let me check with the general, Mr. Nolan. He said he wanted to see you as soon as you arrived. It'll just take a moment." She lifted the phone and punched a button, and a few seconds later announced Dave's arrival. "Yes, sir, I'll send him right in."

When he entered the Army Chief of Staff's office, he saw he'd interrupted something between Marshall and a one star general sitting with his back to the door. Marshall waved him over and indicated a leather chair next to the general who turned and gave him a disapproving look before his face changed and he produced an utterly charming smile.

"David. *Camerado.* So good to see you again after – how long now? Four years at least." Harrison Reeves beamed at him, thrust out his hand and slapped his old classmate on the shoulder. "You look like you're doing very well with Barrett Enterprises."

"It pays the rent, Harrison."

Reeves turned toward General Marshall and said, "David and I were classmates at the Point, and served together at a number of different posts thereafter. Of all of our classmates, he was the one we least expected to retire somewhat early. How many years ago was that, David? Three years perhaps?"

"Just about, Harrison."

"General Reeves," Marshall said, "please leave those numbers with Colonel Scott, and I'll have him get back to you after he has a chance to review them."

"Certainly, sir." Turning to Dave, Harrison Reeves said, "It would be wonderful catching up with you again if you have some time later this week. Perhaps you and Denise could stop by the house for dinner." He reached into his pocket, extracted a calling card and handed it to Dave. "Bring Erika and young Randall Ashby as well if they can make it. I understand they're both doing very good work with my father-in-law."

"I'll see what we can do, Harrison," Dave said noncommittally. "I find the older I get the less control I have over the females in my life. I'll give you a call."

"Thank you, General Reeves. I'll have Colonel Scott get back to you as soon as he can," General Marshall interrupted. Harrison took the hint, excused himself and closed the door as he left the office. "You seem to be very much in demand, Mr. Nolan. I'm going to call you Dave, if that's all right with you. I keep running into people in these halls and elsewhere who seem to want a piece of your time."

"Between the Corps of Engineers and the War Resources Board, I have a pretty full schedule whenever I'm in Washington. The amount of construction the Army has bid out in the last year is keeping all of us in the industry hopping."

Marshall leaned back in his chair and intertwined his fingers in front of himself. "Yes, I know all about your work at Barrett Enterprises, and from Mr. Stettinius your consulting assistance to the administration. You're a well known commodity."

"I guess I am, sir. My job is to be the face of the construction and manufacturing arms of Mr. Edgar Barrett's corporation, and we have a lot of work we're doing for the Army."

"So I've learned. It seems the Air Corps has you paving half of Texas and major swaths of Louisiana and Arizona with concrete runways. I see where your company did a major expansion of Benning this year and you're also on the short list for similar work in several other jobs across the Bible Belt. But far more than that – I'm curious why it is my theater commanders in both the Pacific and the Mediterranean have your name on their lips. Why is it, Dave, that both Eisenhower and Doug MacArthur have asked for you – specifically, by name?"

Marshall had taken him by surprise, and Dave said as much. "I'm shocked, sir. That's the first I've heard of it. Just after Pearl Harbor, Ike floated an idea with me to come back into the service and work with him while he was developing some part of an overall strategy for the conduct of the war."

"Well, he's asked for you again. I had my people look into your background and into your career – or should I say careers. You've made something of a name for yourself in Barrett Enterprises these last few years. "

"Edgar Barrett is the visionary and driving force behind the corporation. I was simply in the right place at the right time."

"Not always," Marshall corrected him. "Your service record indicates some high spots and some strikingly low spots. During the last war, you showed yourself to be an exceptional soldier. After that your performance was sometimes good and sometimes not so good. True?"

Dave smiled. "The truth is what it is, sir,"

"Obviously right now we need people like the Dave Nolan who served with distinction in the Rainbow Division." Marshall leaned forward resting his elbows on the desktop and tapping his fingertips together. "When both my theater commanders ask for the same man by name, it gets my attention. After reviewing your record at the Academy, both as a student and later as special assistant to the superintendent, I'm inclined to listen to them. Throw into the mix the diplomatic work you did for William Donovan and the current Administration..."

"I'm flattered. Surprised and flattered. I don't know what I'd have to offer, really. I'm sure you're aware I retired after almost twenty-three years at the rank of major. Even if the Army offered to promote me to lieutenant colonel, I'm getting a little long in the tooth to run a battalion, not that I couldn't do it. I commanded two during the war and one in the Philippines."

Marshall pursed his lips and squinted at him. "What Ike and MacArthur are doing now is creating a team of commanders around them that will win us the wars in Europe and in the Pacific. What you saw MacArthur do at West Point after the first war is exactly what he's doing now, and precisely what Ike is doing in the Med. Commanders at their level are very careful about the people selected for their staffs and particularly about the commanders at the Corps and Division level. How much do you know about our current military situation?"

"Only what I read in the newspapers, general. It could be more encouraging."

"The truth is we're not doing very well right now. A year after Pearl Harbor MacArthur sits in Australia while the Japanese control all of Southeast Asia, including much of China, and essentially the Pacific west of Hawaii. Germany and Italy sit astride most of Europe and North Africa plus a large chunk of Russia and have made the Mediterranean a Nazi lake. Ike is fighting the Afrika Korps with untested troops and commanders. The only good news is that the British managed to hold onto their own little island, and the Navy seems to have won a battle at Midway. Frankly, the outcome of this war is very much in doubt. That's why you and I are having this conversation right now. Both Ike and MacArthur are looking around and they don't like what they see. What they need and what they're trying to get to lead these untried untested troops is a cadre of senior leaders they know and trust. That's why you're sitting across this desk from me right now.

"How interested are you in putting on the uniform and going to war again?"

*   *   *   *

"Moffett tower, triple nickel seven, flight of three P-39's – Hayward inbound for landing," Mitch Nolan said into the radio mic as he looked down past his right wing at the eastern edge of the toll bridge crossing the southern portion of San Francisco Bay.

"Roger, triple nickel seven, this is Moffet tower. Enter right downwind runway three-two. Wind three-zero-zero at one-two. Call Pabrico. Palo Alto pattern is active – left traffic. Remain well clear."

"Roger, triple nickel seven." Mitch began a slow left turn and headed towards the siding factory building in Alameda. "All right, two and three, fall into line astern with a five second interval. Let's see if you can do an engine out landing to three-two," he said over the training frequency. "Chop the throttle when abeam the end of the runway."

He knew Walrath and Fortner would fudge on the landings – they'd have their gear down and flaps at 30° before entering the landing. They wouldn't get the benefit of the practice by anticipating the engine out. When he failed them both on the evaluation, again, Broussard would once more be unhappy. *Tough*, he thought, as he looked out his right wing.

"Moffett tower this is triple nickel seven, reporting Pabrico."

Mitch entered the traffic pattern twelve hundred feet above the airfield, slowed to approach speed, and pulled the throttle back to idle as the end of the runway lined up with his right wing. Immediately he pushed the nose down and turned hard right as his left hand slapped the landing gear lever down then immediately moved the flap lever to landing position. The world in front of him spun to the left as the Bell Airacobra fell from the sky in a tight turn. He glanced quickly at the airspeed, saw he was ten miles per hour above stall, slowed his rate of turn and had his nose aligned with the centerline of the runway at hundred feet above the ground. After landing, the aircraft taxied to the hangar on the east side of the field and parked following the directions of the ground guides.

Later in the debriefing room he ran through with his two students the shortcomings he had witnessed in the two-hour evaluation session. He gave them the bad news that they had failed the check ride, and detailed what each had to do in order to pass the re-evaluation.

Lieutenant Colonel Broussard was clearly unhappy later when he looked over the reports and finally into the eyes of Mitch Nolan.

"Lieutenant, your record's still intact, I see," Broussard said sarcasticallly. "You haven't passed a single student on a check ride in the last ten months. You're beginning – no, let me rephrase that – you're continuing to be a real pain in the ass. What's your problem?"

"Actually sir, the problem isn't me, it's the trainees we're getting. I know there's a need to push through more pilots to fill all the new Fighter Groups the Air Corps is creating, but I can't in all good conscience pass students that don't meet standards."

"You mean that don't meet *your* standards."

"No sir, I mean that don't meet minimal standards. We don't do these guys any favor by passing them through when they're not ready to go to a front-line unit and fly against German or Italian or Jap pilots with years of experience."

"In your opinion."

"In reality, sir. Look, colonel, if you think I was too tough on Walrath and Fortner, you do the re-evaluation and see for yourself. If I'm out of line, you should get rid of me."

"Part of your plan, Nolan?" Broussard sat back in his swivel chair and for a long minute looked at Mitch with a frown on his face. Finally, he opened a desk drawer, extracted a file folder and dropped it on the desk. "Your requests for transfer – approaching two dozen now. It's all very transparent."

"I meant it to be, sir. I believe I've done the duty you assigned me while I was still in flight school a year ago. I came out here, improved the aerial gunnery training, and despite what you might think, I helped improve the air to air combat training. Mission accomplished. It's time for me to move on."

"And if Training Command disagrees?"

"My three year military obligation is up in six months – June 14 of next year."

"You'd quit the service at a time like this? What happened to Duty-Honor-Country, Nolan? You'd walk away from that kind of responsibility?"

"No. I'd go fly for Chennault's AVG, or maybe the American Eagle squadron in the RAF if the Air Corps refuses to let me fly in combat."

Broussard remained silent as he looked at Nolan and then turned in his chair to look out over the airfield from his second floor office above the main hangar. He knew it would eventually come down to this with the lieutenant. At last he turned around.

"Nolan, despite the fact that you're a royal pain in the butt, you've done some good work here for me and I'm inclined to cut you some slack. I think you're smart enough to know that going to the AVG or the American Eagle squadron is a non-starter. If you tried something like that the powers that be would keep it from happening and would forever ruin not only your career, but any opportunity of ever flying so much as a mail run. Frankly, I'd hate to see that happen. So, I'm gonna offer you something – a compromise that hopefully will make both of us happy and keep both of us out of trouble. To be honest, Training Command in general and I in particular don't want to lose you. But I can understand your wanting to get into the action. So, here's what I've come up with…

"I'm going to let you check out in the P-38. That includes picking one up off the production line in Burbank and delivering it to North Africa. Once you've accomplished that, you'll return here and establish a new phase of training in which you'll become the commander of the unit that transitions pilots into that aircraft. I want you to take some time and think about it, and when you're ready we can discuss the particulars."

Mitch thought for a few seconds and replied, "I don't need to think about it. I'll do it, colonel. The only thing I ask is that I be allowed to start sooner rather than later."

"No more requests for transfers?"

Mitch contemplated, breathing a heavy, resigned sigh. "No, sir."

"All right, lieutenant, we have a deal," Broussard said, opening the file folder and taking out two sheets which he passed across his desk. "Orders from Western Training Command."

Mitch looked at the typed sheets, taking in the particulars, including the signature of the commanding general of USAAC Training Command. The orders were effective 22 December, less than two weeks away.

"You pick up the aircraft at Lockheed in Burbank, and proceed to Miami to rendezvous with five other Lightnings and a B-26. From there to Caracas Venezuela, Belem Brazil, Natal Brazil, Ascension Island, Abidjan along the Ivory Coast, and Atar in West Africa. Then on to Casablanca, and finally Tafaraoui. Ten thousand miles one way. You ought to know the Lightning pretty well by the end of the trip. Any questions?"

To Mitch the names of places ran together in a cacophonous jumble of strange sounds, less than half of which he'd even heard before. Ten thousand miles? The cruise speed of a B-26 couldn't be much over two hundred he reasoned. Fifty hours? It sounded like a heck of a long time. "How many days enroute?" he asked, not finding that in the order or any of the coordinating instructions.

"We don't know," Colonel Broussard admitted. "Nobody's ever done it before. The 14th Fighter Group flew their Lightnings across the North Atlantic at the end of last summer but nobody has ever flown the Southern route which is a lot longer and more treacherous when you consider there's a lot of time over both the Atlantic and the North African desert. If everything went perfectly, the weather cooperated and you could stand being strapped to a fighter seat six or seven hours every day, it'd be ten days. Nine long days and one short one once you leave the States. My guess is probably more like two weeks. It's a long and boring slog, Nolan."

"This is a guinea pig flight."

"I guess you could look at that way. The Air Corps has to find out if it's humanly possible. You seem to like that kind of thing. Any other questions?"

"Yes, sir, just one for now," Mitch Nolan said, wondering if he'd been rewarded or played by Broussard. "Where the hell is Tafaraoui?"

*　*　*　*

Dave called Edgar Barrett after leaving Marshall's office and found him in. He recounted their conversation in as much detail as he thought prudent over a public phone line, but the message was short and simple as was the obvious question. "What do you think, Ed?"

There was a long pause from his father-in law.

"Dave, I've always trusted your instincts and your judgment – I see no reason to stop now. We currently have a lot on our platter, but it's all being managed according to plan. You told me when we started into the construction business in a major way your goal was to set up a self-perpetuating business model and management team. The Board and I give you high marks for achieving that, the reason for the bonus at the fall meeting and the additional stock options in your Christmas stocking. If you decide to leave you'll be missed, certainly, but your departure would create opportunities for advancement in our management team, not cripple or hinder it. We put no barriers in your way. Actually, General Stanley warned us at the last Board meeting this was likely, so it won't be much of a surprise to them."

There was a long pause on the line, and for an instant he thought maybe the connection had been broken. "Dave, there's an article coming out in the *Wall Street Journal* next week about our corporation and the miracle of our transformation over the last three years. Everyone here knows to whom all the credit goes. You created a lot of jobs, good paying jobs for families that needed them, and it made many of our investors wealthy. You'll never get the credit you actually deserve. You want my blessing? – you have it, along with those of the people in Barrett Enterprises. And Dave, if you do finally decide to re-enlist so to speak, I plan on continuing your salary while you're gone."

"You don't have to do that, Ed. I'd be reinstated at a fairly high rank."

He heard the chuckle on the other end. "Dave, I know what the military pays its officers. Even the top generals don't come anywhere close to what you earned, even in your first year."

"That's very generous of you."

"I see it as another investment – like the one I tried to make that first summer you worked for me thirty years ago. Hurry up, win this war and get back. I'm not sure everyone outside our little company will react as benevolently, if you know what I mean. Good luck, son."

"Ed, I appreciate your understanding." He reckoned his father-in-law was all right with his tentative decision and that the major hurdle had been overcome.

But he had reckoned without Denise...

"You told him what?!" she exclaimed before he could finish his explanation of Marshall's request or even begin telling of her father's response.

"I told him I'd consider it and get back to him."

"Even somebody as dense as a four star general can figure that out!" She glared at him, a hard stare, her mouth working; then she shook her head rapidly as if shuddering. "Did you ask for this? Did you volunteer?" Her voice faltered. "You never grew out of it, did you? – you're the same misguided Galahad in khaki who walked down that road and out of my life at Allery."

"Denise, please –"

"Don't *Denise* me!" She walked over to the small bar in the dining room and slowly, meticulously made an Old Fashioned with her back to him. She tasted it and added a little more bourbon before turning around and giving him another long, hard stare.

"I didn't volunteer – they asked for me," he said after a moment.

"They?! Who is *they*?"

"Ike... Ike and MacArthur both."

"MacArthur?! That brass-buttoned sycophant! I thought even you would have been able to see through him by now. He's out at the far end of the supply line for beans and bullets and replacements now, isn't he? – tucking tail and sneaking out of Corregidor, leaving poor 'Skinny' Wainwright behind to take the fall and rot in a sweltering Japanese prisoner camp."

"He was ordered out by the president," Dave replied in a low voice.

"You wouldn't have left the troops to fend for themselves."

"I don't know."

"I know you – you wouldn't have." She started, her eyes suddenly wide as if having just received a revelation, and quickly she said, "But this isn't the same, Dave. What you're doing now with the corporation is having more of an impact than you ever had in uniform. That's what you told Bill Donovan more than once before, isn't it?"

"Things have changed."

"Changed?! Of course they've changed!" She laughed harshly at him, an indrawn gasp of derision. "When my father installed you as the chief operating officer, he was running a small metals company with three plants and a tiny side business making auto parts. He's now head of a nationwide construction company and a metals company quadruple the size it was. They're even starting to assemble tanks at the New York plant. He never dreamed of profits like this – not even in the 20's. He's being consulted by the government movers and shakers and written up in the *Journal* and every business magazine from coast to coast. What happens to that if you go off tilting at windmills with the Army again?"

"I talked to your father and he understands." Dave took a deep breath, and looked back at her sadly.

"I knew this would happen," Denise muttered aloud, shaking her head angrily and turning away. There was a long, silent pause and suddenly she banged the Old Fashioned glass down, spilling some of the drink; she suddenly whirled around, hands on her hips, and faced him. "I knew this was going to happen. Just as surely as I knew you'd go back to your beloved damned Rainbow Division when we were at Allery. I hate how history repeats itself."

"I haven't given General Marshall a final answer."

"After all these years, Dave, please… please don't lie like that to me."

"I'm not lying."

"You are! You agreed, didn't you?! You went into Marshall's office and as good as told him you were in. And you did it without as much as a thought for me, or the children. Look me in the eye and tell me that you didn't leave Marshall with the impression you were going to accept his offer and go back into the Army."

"There's a war on. We're not doing very well, and it's a long road back."

She took a swallow of her drink. "I've heard this song before – every verse and chorus… something about how irreducibly responsible you feel about the men in the field under the burden of their backpacks and inferior officers. How only you can lead them out of –"

"That's enough!" he said, raising his voice for the first time. "I never said that!"

"You didn't have to. You've always thought you were the only one who could possibly right all the wrongs, reverse all the setbacks, lead all the desperate underlings to safety. How little things change. How easy it is for the Donovans and MacArthurs and now the Marshalls to stroke your ego and pull your little strings." She paused and lowered her hands in resignation; her eyes were red, filled with tears and she said softly, "Good grief, Dave, are you going to let all those hidebound military martinets yank you around again? In yet another war to end all wars to save mankind from itself forever?"

"Yes, hopefully it's the end of war."

"Why can't you let the professional Army take care of it?"

"The careerists can't. There aren't enough of them. When Germany invaded Poland, our Army was less than 200,000 troops. It's more today, and growing, but our forces are essentially citizen-soldiers – draftees. Back then we had less than ten understrength and unequipped divisions, but we need over a hundred to win in both the Atlantic and Pacific, and four or five times as many support and service troops. The Army needs leaders who can manage large, complex organizations and think strategically."

"And that has to be you?! Are you actually going to go vagabonding around all those stinking miserable countries while the sensible world at home goes on making something of itself… without you, again?"

He moved toward Denise, seized her gently by the shoulders and was rocking her tenderly while looking deeply into her eyes. "This isn't going to be a lark, or a vacation," he was saying tightly. "I'm as qualified as anyone to do the job – more than most, actually. I can't turn my back on this."

"Bill Donovan tried to get you to work for him more than once over the years, didn't he?" Dave nodded, tight-lipped. "And he tried his best to convince you it was your duty?"

"Yes. But he was wrong on that back then. This is different."

"He once tried to convince you it was because you should honor a commitment to defend the Constitution. He was wrong on that, too, I assume – you always live up to your promises."

"I try."

She stared at him a minute longer, stepped away from him and shook her head violently. "Oh, Dave! I just don't see it. I don't get it. Why?!"

"Denise, listen –"

"No!"

"Listen to me."

"No!... No! – I just don't see it the way you do! I really don't, Dave. You've always been the very soul of honor. Everybody said it – at the Academy, in the Philippines, and every hole in the wall Army post in between. Why not now? Now that we've finally put down roots and made something of our lives – something meaningful! Why have you changed?"

"I haven't changed."

"Really?! Really, Dave?! You always kept your promises before. Why are you breaking the promise you made to me years ago to get out and stay out of the Army?!"

"Denise –" He moved to take her in his arms, but she broke away from him and ran out of the dining room, down the hallway. He heard her footsteps on the stairway, moving quickly up the steps to the second floor. When she slammed the bedroom door, the sound resonated through the house like the report of big artillery echoing through mountains.

Chapter 16

North Africa, The Western Desert
23 Jan 1943

The desert, flat and desolate – mind-numbingly boundless – slid beneath them so slowly it appeared they were standing still although the airspeed indicator remained steady at 205. It seemed to Mitch Nolan this had been the longest flight in aviation history. And it still wasn't over. Casablanca lay four hundred miles ahead – the next to last stop on this endless journey.

So far he had read the Lightning's operating manual completely through twice, written two letters on blank pages inside the manual to his mother, and one to his father since leaving Natal in Brazil. He'd also written letters to Kate Stroud reminiscing about their time in Bermuda, to two other girls he'd dated his senior year at West Point, and to a girl from Santa Clara he'd met while at Moffett. Until the ferry flight of seven had started the overwater legs – to and from Ascension Island – he'd tried to stay awake, alert even, by navigating along with the B-26, but had given up and begun letter writing. It was simple enough – the P-38 was stable and easily trimmed to fly in very loose formation off the bomber allowing him time to pen his letters while only occasionally having to look up to make sure he was still in formation.

"*Wake up call little buddies.*" The scratchy static of the radio call from the B-26 shook him alert – he had been daydreaming, and when he looked at his watch, he realized they'd been in the air five hours since leaving Atar. "*Two hours until dinner at Rick's Café Americain. Last one tied down and post-flighted buys drinks and dinner.*"

That had to be Strickland, the navigator, who had been the only one of the pilots and crew who'd seen the new Bogart movie in the States before leaving. He talked incessantly about it although everybody largely ignored him. Mitch looked around the sky and saw the other five P-38s strung out loosely on either side of the bomber in Vee formation – *formation? Not quite! More like a loose gaggle heading in the same general direction,* he thought. But this was a ferry flight, not the graduation flyby at Advanced back in flight school.

Glancing out over the right engine, he could see the bomber's navigator watching him through binoculars. Strickland was kind of an odd duck, he'd decided, but they'd hit it off over drinks at Happy Hour in the officers' club at Palm Beach when they stumbled across the realization their fathers had served together in the Big War – the same company even, in the old Rainbow Division. Peculiar or not, he'd at least found Ascension Island, one of his big worries from the outset of this ferry trip. He'd asked Mitch in Natal when they briefed the first over water leg how in the world he could be expected to find that one tiny little island in the middle of the Atlantic.

"No problem," Mitch had said nonchalantly, remembering Lindquist's casual answer to a similar question enroute to Bermuda. "It's the only island out there."

He ran through his cockpit scan again, still amazed at all the toggle switches and instruments and gauges of the big fighter. The airplane seemed to handle okay straight and level and all things considered it was a fairly comfortable but chilly ride. Still, he was a little disappointed in the Lightning – the controls were heavy and it was too big to be a fighter. He doubted it could handle well enough in a dogfight to keep from being shot down much less knock one of the smaller, more nimble Messerschmidts or Focke Wulfs out of the sky.

Well, you won't have to worry about that, he thought, gloomily. *Drop off this plane, catch a B-26 or Gooney Bird to Gibraltar and then a ride to England followed by a long North Atlantic winter cruise back home. So much for getting into the War.*

This had not been as much fun as he'd hoped, and the Air Corps had told him this was as close as he was likely to get to the War. He stretched and settled back in the seat. *Less than two hours now to Casablanca. Two hours...that'll be forty-five all told in this bird.*

It now seemed a geologic age since his first hour in the Lightning…

Kelly Field in San Antonio was about the mid-point of his cross-country from Burbank to Miami, and by the time he reached there, he'd had another four hours flying time in this new machine tacked on to the half hour orientation flight.

The scrawny little crew chief at the Lockheed factory in Burbank had shown him where all the switches were, had helped him start the engines, do the run-ups, and then sat on the wing with the cockpit open as Mitch taxied around the field getting the feel of the throttles and props and the brakes. In a little while, the sergeant had clambered down the back side of the wing and waved him toward the runway. The first takeoff was everything he'd expected – the heart pounding exhilaration from the sense of having a runaway horse under him, even though he'd been instructing students for almost a year. But this was *some big machine.* He made two quick trips around the pattern, got in a couple of touch-and-go landings, then went on a twenty minute tour up the California coast raising and lowering the gear, the flaps, testing the mixture settings and pitch in the blades. *Two engines is a lot different from what I've been flying lately,* he'd thought then. And later, just south of Phoenix, he'd shut down the engines one at a time to see how it flew on single engine. Halfway across New Mexico, he decided to wring it out and see what it would really do.

He started slow with a few chandelles and a couple of lazy-8's, then an aileron roll to the left and two to the right. His first attempt at an eight point roll felt mushy, but he excused his sloppiness with a reminder he only had a couple of hours at the controls. Still, he was unhappy with himself. Full stalls were gentle enough and the ship broke clean and straight ahead. Hammerhead stalls were pretty docile, he decided, and then he put it through a couple of inside loops and some accelerated stalls in both directions.

A half hour went by quickly and he realized he'd lost sight of both Las Cruces to the north and Ciudad Juarez inside Mexico to the south. A water tower ten or fifteen miles away beckoned – they all had the town's name painted on them; the best navigation aid around. From twenty thousand feet, he put it in as steep a dive as he could, until it felt like he had the nose completely tucked under, beyond vertical; in an instant, he was hanging by the safety harness pointed straight down... and immediately the aircraft began to shake, just a little at first but then more powerfully as the airspeed indicator wound up quickly past 375.

Soon the machine was shuddering so violently he couldn't read the instruments and the airplane felt like it was shaking itself into a thousand pieces. Chopping power to idle only marginally improved it, and he pulled with all his strength on the column until he was sure he'd yank the steering yoke off or bend it beyond repair. The ground was rushing up at him at a dizzying speed and he was seized with panic as he had the sense of absolute certainty he'd never pull out before auguring the machine into the ground. *Think! THINK!!* He was yelling out loud through clenched teeth... and then – a moment of crystalline clarity, a wholly unbelievable calm washed over him that made the world slow almost to a halt.

He saw his hand move to the trim wheel and crank in full up trim; the nose seemed to come up ever so slightly and the control column began to move backward just enough. He wasn't sure how long it was before the shuddering stopped enough for him to read the airspeed; it was beginning to work its way back toward 425. The vertical speed indicator came off the peg, and the horizon came down toward the Lightning's nose. At seven thousand feet, he was just beginning to fly the plane instead of the plane flying him; at four thousand the shuddering had nearly stopped; at three thousand he had the nose nearly level with the horizon but he was still going too fast. At fifteen hundred, he started to climb, still going well over three hundred.

Wild excitement seized his gut as he pushed the throttles full forward. The plane climbed skyward with air rushing past the cockpit in a deep-throated roar, and the big Allison engines thundered on his wings...

"Casablanca tower, Cyclops ferry flight of seven 20 miles south for landing," he heard the B-26 pilot transmit over the radio.

"Negative, flight of seven," came the immediate response. *"The field is closed to all traffic. Proceed to Rabat, over."*

Mitch had no immediate idea where Rabat was in relation to their position and wondered if they had enough fuel after nearly seven hours of flying to try to find it. He pulled out an old French map of North Africa and began searching. Almost immediately the radio came to life with the southern drawl of the bomber pilot.

"Casablanca tower this is Cyclops ferry flight of seven declaring an emergency."

"This is Casablanca tower. Please state the nature of your emergency, over."

Mitch looked outside the cockpit and smiled – the prop on the left engine of the Marauder was feathered. *Pretty quick thinking*, he thought, impressed at the swift creativity of the B-26 crew. *Gotta remember that, Nolan – could be useful some day.*

"Casablanca tower, this is Cyclops flight. Declaring a failure on the left engine of our navigation aircraft...reporting low on fuel, requesting immediate straight in landing."

From off his left wing he saw a flight of four aircraft approaching from the west and a few thousand feet above. Mitch watched as they closed in and soon identified them as P-38's.

"Tower, Jack Rabbit patrol, confirming friendly flight of seven, twenty south, Marauder with one feathered and six little friends tagging along."

"Roger... Ferry flight of seven, Casablanca tower, cleared straight in to land runway 33. Winds three-one-zero at one-five. Flight leader report to the tower immediately upon landing."

It was two hours after noon when they finally completed their post-flight inspections and the aircraft were refueled. Immediately upon parking near the base of the tower the B-26 crew chief jumped out, opened the engine cowlings, and began work. Eventually, as it turned out, two of the P-38s actually did have engine problems requiring maintenance. The airfield at Casablanca was under the tight security of American infantry troops and military police – clearly something important was going on.

The ferry flight officers procured some military transportation and soon motored into the center of the city to find a place to eat and locate lodging for a couple of days before the last leg of their journey. The narrow streets were clogged with Arab merchants as Mitch and the other pilots drove past the large white-sided Anfa Hotel overlooking the beach. They found it surrounded with barbed wire and armed guards – both British and American. They continued three more blocks to register at a little out of the way hotel packed with British and American reporters. After registering and having a late lunch with the ferry flight crews, Mitch walked back toward the Anfa, curious about the obvious and excessive security.

Arriving at the military checkpoint outside the hotel, he surveyed the front of the huge building and several minutes later caught sight of an attractive young girl exiting through the tall main doors of the resort lodge. He watched her descend the short flight of stairs and walk through the MP guard station, thinking she was one of the prettiest women he'd ever seen. Her long blond hair cascaded over her shoulders in smooth waves, curled on the ends. Though not very tall, her slim figure and classic features made her look like a fashion model. Her face suddenly brightened into a smile as she ran toward and threw her arms around an American wearing a floppy service cap and a chrome-tanned A-2 flight jacket over khakis.

Damn, Nolan! he thought, *if you didn't have bad luck, you'd have no luck at all.*

Still, he watched her closely as she gave the lieutenant a peck on the cheek. The girl saw him and showed a quick frown before looking back to the pilot who still had his arms around her slim waist. She chatted away for another minute, tossed her head and laughed gaily before glancing at Mitch again. Her eyes flashed a warning and her expression showed disapproval; she said something to the lieutenant and nodded in Mitch's direction. The young aviator turned slowly, his face betraying irritation. He gasped and produced a face-cracking smile.

"Nolan!" the lieutenant sang out.

"Lindquist?... is that you, Lucky?"

"Holy smokes, man, what are you doing this far from Moffett? I thought you were there for the duration?" Lindquist took the girl's hand and walked over to Mitch and punched him on the upper arm. "Wait 'til Marv hears this."

"He's here, too?"

"Not here, here. Not in Casablanca. He's back with the squadron at Telerghma." Lindquist turned to the blond girl. "This is the guy I told you about that almost killed me and my friend in a sailboat on the way to Bermuda."

Mitch looked at the girl who now appeared puzzled. She wore a small military name tag above the right breast pocket of her dress – Aida González. "Are you going to introduce me?" Mitch asked at last.

"Sure – this is Aida. Aida, an old friend of mine – Mitch Nolan." Lindquist pronounced her name '*aye-ee-da*' with his abstruse variety of a Spanish accent. "Her father is the Portuguese ambassador to Egypt and she's the hostess for the big shindig going on inside. Most of the time she's an interpreter for the British Embassy in Cairo." Lowering his voice and leaning toward Mitch, Lucky said, "She speaks six languages, and fortunately for me one of them is English, and in my own *Baltimoron* dialect."

Mitch took the hand she offered and tried his best not to gawk – up close the girl was even more attractive than he'd first thought at a distance. "It's a great pleasure to meet you. Looks like you're throwing quite a party. Do you do this often?"

"My first time. I'm only responsible for the meals and administrative chores such as typing and translation services. I also coordinate between the hotel services and the personal staffs of the three countries represented. I'm not alone – a friend from the Cairo embassy is co-hosting; she's an interpreter also and we each have four assistants."

"Sounds like a big responsibility. What's going on? Why all the troops and barbed wire?"

"Actually, Mitch, nobody's supposed to know," Lindquist interrupted, "… at least until it's all over and everybody's back home safe and sound. My question is: why are you here?"

"I'm ferrying a P-38 to your group at Tafaraoui, along with five others and a B-26. We just got here two, three hours ago and they told us we couldn't land because the field was closed. Does the party inside this hotel have anything to do with that?"

"That was you?! I was in the flight that intercepted you guys inbound. I've been here for over two weeks now. Our flight of four along with two from the 14th Fighter Group and a heavy squadron of RAF Spitfires is providing round-the-clock aerial coverage."

"This *is* some kind of big deal, isn't it?"

"The biggest," Lindquist said. "And that's all you're going to hear from me."

Aida checked her watch quickly, looked at Nolan's friend and said, "I must be going back. Makara and I have some work to do before supper. It should only take us two, or maybe three hours. I could meet you at *La Sqala* around six."

"Six is perfect," Lucky said. "Why don't you bring Makara? We'll make it a foursome."

"You really don't have to do that, Aida," Mitch insisted. "I don't want to impose. Please don't let my friend put you in an awkward position on my account."

She looked at him and shrugged. "Perhaps she might want to come. It's been a terribly long day for both of us – we haven't had a chance to do anything since before the sun came up but work and snack on some cheese. Who knows? She might enjoy a good seafood dinner at the expense of two wealthy American pilots."

"There you go, Nolan."

"All right, but please don't go out of your way." They watched her turn and go back through the MP checkpoint and up the stairs, stopping to turn and wave. Mitch looked at Lindquist. "I wish you hadn't done that, Lucky. I know how that works – the really gorgeous ones usually travel with a girl that doesn't present a lot of competition."

"Trust me, Mitch. I've never steered you wrong before, have I?" Lindquist guided him down the street away from the hotel. "Let's go have a couple of beers before heading over to *La Sqala*, and let me tell you why you won't be going to *Gooey* Tafaraoui. To begin with, there ain't nobody there no more. We all moved out to a little patch of paradise called Telerghma where we sleep in a little dugout holes with a shelter half for a roof and six inches of straw for a mattress. Trust me, it's a place you don't want to get assigned permanently."

*   *   *

The headwaiter at *La Sqala* seated them in a back corner of the dining room where they had an unobstructed view of the restaurant. It was a little nicer than the bar Lindquist had taken them to where they spent the better part of an hour drinking and catching up on what each of them had been doing in the last six months.

"You know, don't you, that Marv and I finally got assigned to the 82nd Fighter Group in late spring last year," Lindquist told him as they waited for their beer. "They were at Muroc a few hours south of San Francisco in the high desert."

"I tried everything I knew to get transferred there," Mitch replied.

"Be glad you didn't, friend. There were no living quarters except a few old wooden barracks in disrepair. The sand and wind were miserable, and there were no trees – just sagebrush, jackrabbits, and rattlesnakes. It was 120° in the shade, but there wasn't any shade. The parking ramp and runway were so hot you could fry eggs on them. The sandstorms were so bad the only thing we could do was wear gas masks and wait for them to be over. The only good thing was being assigned the new P-38F, and later the G-model."

Lindquist told him about the Group's relocation to England on the *Queen Elizabeth*, waiting for a couple of months to receive their aircraft from the States and the long flight from southern England to North Africa six weeks ago, which cost them several pilots and aircraft. They had begun combat operations against the Luftwaffe on Christmas day 1942.

"It's not been a picnic, Mitch. I always thought the Air Corps lived in nice quarters, got three good hot meals every day, visited officers clubs every evening. Not so. We've had to live on C-ration stew three meals a day without bread or crackers since I got to North Africa. And, I always thought it was the infantry that slept outside in the mud and rain. We don't have fuel trucks, mess halls, heaters, or tents to sleep in. I've never been more miserable. When they asked who wanted to go TDY to Casablanca, I would've run over anybody who got in my way to be the first in line. Tafaraoui was a big open dry lake bed which turned to ooze when it rained – and it's rained just about every day I've been in Africa. We moved to Telerghma two days before I came here." Lindquist caught the attention of a waiter and ordered drinks.

"How do you refuel your aircraft without fuel trucks?" Mitch asked.

"By hand. They send in fuel by C-47 Gooney Birds in five gallon cans. Pilots have to fuel their own aircraft because all our ground crews – crew chiefs, fuel handlers, mechanics and armorers – haven't arrived yet. We use the empty fuel cans to line the sides of the holes we sleep in so the walls don't crumble in on us."

Mitch let out a low whistle. "That *is* rough."

"Yeah, but it's worth it. We get to fly the G-model Lightning."

"How about operations against the Luftwaffe?"

"Tough. They're good – really good – and they like to mix it up."

"Casualties?"

"Heavier than we expected." He took a sip of the drink, suddenly glanced at his watch and then pointed a finger toward the door. "How about that? Our dates are on time." He looked quickly at Nolan, sighed deeply, and said, "Hate to say it, but you were right, Mitch. The really gorgeous ones always travel with a *plain Jane*."

Her name was Makara Foulkes,

She was taller than Aida, and her long perfectly black hair framed a remarkably beautiful face with high cheekbones and expressive eyes. He was riveted, unable to do anything except concentrate on her physical beauty, content simply to watch as she moved across the room with effortless grace. Their eyes met and she smiled radiantly, a haunting and sensuous smile.

During the course of dinner he learned she was the daughter of an English diplomat and an Egyptian mother. Like Aida, she was conversant in multiple languages – five to be exact, and working on a sixth: Italian. She'd been born in Egypt but educated in England through grammar school, and later in France for middle school. Her high school years were spent in Turkey and she'd attended the Free University of Amsterdam graduating with a degree in Foreign Relations. She'd spent a year in Cairo as a correspondent for the BBC before her language skills landed her a position in the British embassy there.

He was captivated by everything about her: the faint but unmistakable British accent and precise articulation; the quick smile and pleasant, melodic laugh; her self-confidence and intellectual curiosity. She seemed interested in, but not terribly impressed by, his being a fighter pilot or his having just flown across the Atlantic.

It was strange having her explain the Arabic menu and then to have her order for them. In answer to his questions she explained she spoke *Cairene*, the language of Egypt's capitol and the *lingua franca* of the Arab states in general. She could communicate in all the countries of the Muslim world – *the Ummah* – North Africa, Arabia and the ancient Persian states. For the first time ever he felt overmatched by a young woman. It was unsettling, but he so enjoyed her company he was willing to overlook the vaguely humbling experience.

In time he noticed both girls checking their watches and realized they'd been there almost two hours. It dawned on him they were eager to leave and he felt mildly disappointed. Had he done something wrong? Were they bored? *What's going on here? – this kind of thing doesn't happen to me!* he said to himself.

Makara whispered something to Aida and the two girls excused themselves with a promise to return quickly which they did soon after Mitch and Lucky had settled the bill. As they left the restaurant and strolled down the narrow back streets, the dark-haired girl slipped her arm under his and briefly leaned her head against his shoulder. Looking quickly up into his eyes, she said, "Thank you for a wonderful dinner."

"I can't remember a time when I ever enjoyed an evening more," he replied, trying to think of something to prolong his time with her. *Should I ask her out for tomorrow, or try to get her phone number?* "Dinner was over way too soon."

"I was thinking the same thing." They walked on a little further in silence until she asked, "Would you like to go to a movie show, Mitch Nolan?"

"Right now I'd do anything as long as I could do it with you," he responded immediately, his pulsed quickening.

"Aida and I thought we might smuggle you and your friend into the Hotel Anfa for a movie. Our party inside is showing that new American picture titled after our little city here. It just came out in America. The one with Bogart."

"You can do that? This won't get you in trouble, I hope."

"We're the ones hosting and making all the arrangements for our guests. Aida and I are the daughters of diplomats – we have a certain immunity. You and your friend however... If you get caught, I will send you a cake with a file in it." She laughed aloud and tossed her head while squeezing his arm. As they walked, she kissed his cheek and whispered seductively into his ear. "You are not afraid of a little danger, are you?"

"Not as long as it involves a beautiful, exotic Egyptian woman."

She stopped and turned toward him, gazing into his eyes, measuring him. "You're very quick with a word, Mitch Nolan, and perhaps too confident."

"Usually, but not tonight." *She is really beautiful, and exotic,* he thought. "I've been off balance and tongue-tied since you walked through the door at *La Sqala*. And to tell the truth, around you I'm not frightened, but I *am* a little nervous."

Makara turned her head and looked at him furtively out of the corner of her eye, then smiled and took his arm again. "You should be."

Getting through the first checkpoint on the outer ring of barbed wire around the Anfa was no problem – the two girls were well known by the young MPs who gave their access credentials and the two pilots' military ID cards only a cursory look. Inside, at the hotel's main entrance, was altogether more difficult.

Two senior sergeants – one American and one British – manned desks on either side of the long hallway effectively blocking entrance into the hotel while four armed infantrymen stood behind them: two Brits with Sten guns, and two Americans armed with Thompson submachine guns. An RAF officer was rationalizing to the British sergeant that he must be let in. He he had an official document for General Sir John Dill and orders to deliver it directly into the hands of no one but the general. The sergeant was explaining to him with equal calm and insistence why that was not possible. Mitch quickly realized that he and Lucky had no chance of getting in to see *Casablanca*.

"I'm sorry, Miss González," the American sergeant said after looking through pages listing persons cleared for access, "but your guests are not on our approved list."

"An oversight when my staff retyped the list this afternoon. I'll have it corrected before the end of the movie," she said, tilting her head and coyly smiling at him. "You know Makara and me. And we can vouch for Lieutenants Nolan and Lindquist."

"Unfortunately, Aida, we both know that's just not the way it's done – even for you two."

"Perhaps I should just go talk to General Marshall about them."

"You could." The sergeant looked up at her and smiled, a phony smile as if he knew she was trying to bluff him. "If he comes out here and tells me I have to let these two officers in I'd be glad to. But, other than that –"

Mitch touched her elbow and motioned with a nod toward the big front door.

"It was a nice thought, and a game try, but I don't think you're going to sneak us past him and his four troops," he said in a low voice. "Did you say General George Marshall? What is he doing here?"

"He's part of the American delegation," Aida replied.

"I heard that Brit officer use the name of Sir John Dill. He's here, too? Is that what's going on? Some kind of joint military conference?"

"I'm not actually sure. It's something like that."

"And it's been going on for ten days now," Lindquist added. "But it's all hush-hush; nobody's supposed to know about it."

"Good luck keeping that secret. The little hotel down the street where I'm staying is chock full of reporters and photographers. They won't be quiet."

"They will," Makara insisted. "They've been sworn to secrecy, and promised access."

Mitch was sure she was wrong but at the moment had no desire to chance what he thought was the beginning of an interesting relationship. His mind searched for a way to prolong the evening and ensuring he could see her again – tomorrow or the day after. He was just about to ask how he could get in touch with her the next morning when a familiar British voice behind him caught his attention.

"I say, squadron leader, the message for Sir John Dill is safe with me. I shall ensure he has it and gives its contents proper attention immediately."

Mitch turned and looked over his shoulder.

"Brigadier Smythe-Browne. Good to see you again, sir," he said nonchalantly.

"Young Nolan?!" Utter surprise registered on the British general's face. "Good *heavens,* man, what on *earth* are you doing here?"

"Trying to get in to see a movie, sir. Actually, I'm ferrying an aircraft to one of our forward squadrons and happen to be overnighting in a hotel a few blocks down the street."

"Ladies," he said, straightening his posture and nodding quickly and precisely at Makara and Aida. "I take it you know these two chaps."

"Yes, of course," Aida said simply. "We just had dinner and we were hoping to view the motion picture in the auditorium."

The idea seemed to catch Smythe-Browne completely by surprise as he cleared his throat and looked flummoxed. "Well, I… I suppose that is possible." Regaining his composure, he looked at Lindquist and asked, "What is your reason for being here lieutenant…?"

"Lindquist, sir. I'm flying cover, in one of the P-38s."

"I see."

"These two Americans were kind enough to buy us dinner and we had hoped to return the favor," Makara said quickly. "Unfortunately their names are not on the access list. But, both Aida and I vouch for them. Since you know Lieutenant Nolan, and both these officers are providing a service for your conference, perhaps you can grant them access."

Smythe-Browne debated. "Of course," he said at last, and then spoke quietly to each of the two sergeants before waving the four of them through. He led them down the hall and asked they wait outside the ballroom while he delivered the package he'd just received.

"What was that all about Nolan?" Lindquist asked.

"That guy is Brigadier Henry Smythe-Browne. He and my dad go back a long ways, to the last war when they were both in the same ward in some hospital in France. My mother was his nurse back then."

"How does he know you?"

"I spent a few days at his house a couple of years ago when I passed through London. It's a long story, Lucky." He was about to tell Lindquist more when the ballroom door opened and Smythe-Browne returned.

"Mr. Prime Minister, this is the young man whose name came up this afternoon just before tea – Mitchell Nolan. Of course you know Miss Gonzalez and Miss Foulkes."

Churchill, his shoulders hunched and a long cigar stuck in his mouth, squinted at him. He removed the cigar and offered his hand as he looked Nolan over. "Nolan? I remember a Nolan from nearly three years ago now. Came over with William Donovan during the Blitz."

"Yes, sir. This is his son – the young man who was the American end of the ferry operation with Bennett two years ago. Lord Beaverbrook spoke highly of him at the time."

Recognition crept into Churchill's face and he smiled ruefully. "Ah yes. You're the one who saved Max's lordship and his cabinet post by arriving in Ireland with a half dozen Hudsons at the last hour of the final day," the prime minister said in a deep and gravelly voice. "He tried to get you and Bennett a knighthood for it more than once. But he never prevailed."

"He shouldn't have," Mitch said. "Every pilot in Fighter Command deserved it more."

"Right you are, lieutenant. More than either of us will ever fully appreciate." Churchill looked at him fiercely from beneath bushy eyebrows for scant seconds and then mellowed. "How is your father? I hear good things about him from the president and from General Marshall. George briefed us this afternoon on the progress of your mobilization – I see where your father is forming a new division, one of many, at your Camp Benning."

"I haven't corresponded with him since Christmas, sir," Mitch responded, astonished. This casual disclosure was a bombshell, and he could only begin to imagine the heated conversation between his parents over his father's decision. "I'm unaware of what exactly he's doing. The last time we talked by phone he was still a businessman."

"And doing rather well, according to General Marshall who told Smythe-Browne here it took *all* the considerable persuasive powers of Generals Eisenhower and Bradley, and himself, to prevail upon him. I've witnessed for myself he's not easily dissuaded of his opinions."

"Your mother as well," Smythe-Browne offered.

"We've had that conversation before, haven't we sir?" He was still shocked and confused by the revelation; he didn't know what to say or how to react. Finally managed to say, "And how is your daughter sir, Corporal Glendenbrook?"

"Quite well, thank you. She never did ride that horse you trained for her; she sold it at auction months ago. I tried to persuade her otherwise, but she has a mind of her own."

Churchill cleared his throat – a signal. "Henry, we should be returning to our seats. I savor every minute with the president... and the picture show is beginning any moment. I'll tell the president of our little visit, Lieutenant Nolan. So good to meet you all. Thank you for your attention to our every need here ladies – the success of our deliberations is a direct result of your pampering our fragile male egos. And to you young men, my sincere thanks for your service to this great and crucial endeavor of ours, now and in the coming years."

The prime minister shook each of their hands, excused himself and returned inside.

"Ladies and gentlemen, enjoy your evening," Smythe-Browne said in his courtly manner, then leaned toward Nolan and whispered, "I would like a word with you before you leave – if not tonight, then tomorrow."

Mitch nodded and watched Smythe-Browne disappear inside.

"What in the world was that all about?" Lindquist asked, obviously astonished. "Those aren't the kind of people that folks like you and me chit-chat with all the time."

"I'm as surprised as you are. I told you about Smythe-Browne, but I had no idea Churchill had ever met my father or knew him well enough to describe his stubbornness."

"And a knighthood?! Sir Mitchell? That's rich. Wait til Marv hears this!"

"Back off, Lucky. I never bought a suit of armor – only got measured for one."

Lindquist's mouth opened; his lips began to move, but he calmed and finally said, "That's good… that's really rich, Nolan."

Makara was looking at him with a new awareness. "You know Churchill and Roosevelt?"

"No, but apparently my father does, and he never mentioned it to me. Let's go find a seat before they change their minds."

Aida and Lucky went through the door together, but Makara held back, grabbed his arm and signaled with a finger on her lips for him to follow her quietly. They went around the corner into a small vestibule where she produced a key from her purse and unlocked a door leading to a flight of stairs. They quietly went up the dark stairway and entered a small, empty balcony fitted with a dozen upholstered theater seats overlooking the large ballroom. The lights had already dimmed and the opening credits were running by the time they sat down.

He put his arm around her shoulders and she snuggled against him.

"You are a very intriguing man, Sir Mitch," she whispered in his ear.

"And you are a very mysterious woman," he whispered back. "If you drop the '*Sir Mitch*' I won't call you Lady Foulkes. Do we have a deal?"

She answered with the elegance of silence and moved closer. Seconds later, she pulled his face down to hers and gave him a lingering kiss that stole his breath away, as did every one after it. When the final credits rolled, he realized he hadn't a clue about the plot line.

Chapter 17

Final leg – *811 miles as the crow flies*, Mitch Nolan thought, stretching his back, then his shoulders and finally his legs as best he could. The cockpit was cold, and he could feel ice forming against his cheeks inside the oxygen mask. *Would a crow fly this straight a line at this altitude requiring oxygen?... and with the worst heater of any aircraft in the whole damned inventory?* Thank goodness it was a short leg – four hours and six minutes with a ground speed of 197 according his calculations on the E6-B 'whiz wheel' he'd been issued in flight school.

Four hours this leg, made it what?... almost forty-nine hours he'd have in the Lightning? *Nolan, you're an old hand in this bird now. A real pilot can fly anything – as long as it has at least one engine and a pair of wings.* He smiled to himself remembering the first time Pug Johnston told him that, the day he'd soloed in the Philippines.

A hundred miles from Casablanca they passed directly over the small town of Khemisett which told him the wind was more out of the north than forecast, and they were drifting south of the line of flight to Telerghma. He pulled out the flight computer and worked the calculations again – anything to keep his mind occupied... and off of her.

He'd spent a week in the most famous ocean front city in Morocco, maybe the world. By the end of the first day he thought he'd never been happier and more excited in his life; by the end of the last day, he'd never been more depressed or discouraged. From beginning to end, throughout the entire emotional roller-coaster ride she had taken him on, she had played him. *Why?* he asked. Echo answered.

Makara – the most exhilarating and stimulating woman he had ever known.

After that first night with her in the balcony of the main ball room, he was certain they had shared an evening that was the start of something exceptional. The next day she had seemingly disappeared. She didn't answer her phone or return his calls when he left messages with the switchboard. The day after, they had lunch together on the veranda of the Anfa and dinner again at *La Sqala*. That night they walked the beach together in the chill of the evening beneath an almost full moon and kissed lingeringly among the rocks of ancient ruins guarding the city's small port. She'd hinted at their spending the night together in her room.

The next day she had seemingly vanished without a word.

He tried to find her in the hotel, stripped now of its barbed wire and military security; all had evaporated as if it never existed. He learned the RAF was flying the Cairo contingent out and tried to intercept her at the airfield, arriving too late.

She was gone.

In the days that followed, he pored over the operator's manual and spent long hours working on his Lightning, blocking any thoughts of her from his mind. The weather turned bad, so he busied himself with maintenance – changing the oil on both engines, removing and checking the plugs to see if he'd fouled them with the settings he'd used during the crossing to improve fuel consumption and increase his range.

He studied the map and determined that an hour west of Telerghma they'd be just about within range of the German fighters. Mitch decided he wasn't going there without a way to defend himself, and removed his personal clothing from the ammunition trays and ejection chutes. He requisitioned as much .50 caliber machine gun ammunition and 20mm cannon shells from the American ammo dump on the airfield as they could spare, but it was less than half what the ammo trays would hold. He convinced an armorer to show him how to properly load and charge the nose-mounted weapons. The same evening, after dark, he convinced another armorer to help zero the weapons and teach him how to do it himself.

By the time the weather broke on the last day of January and they set off from Casablanca, he knew much more about the Lockheed airplane, and he'd forgotten the girl.

Almost.

*   *   *

Nolan nosed the big Lockheed over and saw the tiny dots just a few miles ahead and several thousand feet below.

"*Redfish three, this is Cyclops... don't even think about it.*" The warning in the southern drawl of the captain piloting the bomber was unmistakable.

They were all single engine aircraft – 109s and 190s he thought – a dozen or more, crisscrossing the wide flat area that looked like an airfield bordered on the south by a low line of hills. Parked in a haphazard array were a couple dozen twin-tailed Lightnings, some in revetments, plus a few C-47 Gooney Birds, two of which were on fire. He looked around the sky, saw no other planes – German or American – and nosed his aircraft into a steep dive.

"Redfish three, this is Cyclops... you know the rules. Get back up here... What do you think you're doing?"

Nolan thought through a quick pre-fire checklist he'd read in the Dash One operators manual, nervous now as he flipped the arm switch for the nose guns and looked through the crosshairs of the sight projected on the windscreen. *I'll be doggoned... it worked.*

"Back up in formation, three. Nothing you can do by yourself." The flight leader's voice had hardened, as if this was the final word.

Nolan pressed the firing button and saw a line of tracers arch out in front. *Okay, guns work... I should be zeroed. Still gotta get close, son.* The fingers of his left hand tapped the throttles levers nervously.

"Redfish three, this is lead... I say again, get back in formation... back... in... formation."

Nolan debated… and decided to ignore the flight leader. He felt the shoulder straps and seat belt tighten against him just as the big plane started to shudder. For an instant, his heart leaped, and then settled as he remembered the same onset of instability on the long, lonely stretch through New Mexico.

"...Nolan!... that's an order..."

In his peripheral vision, he saw the altimeter winding down, the big hand almost a blur; the world around him had slowed again, and it seemed almost silent in the cockpit now as he hurtled downward, the Lightning beginning to shake violently. He'd learned after that incident near Las Cruces how far he could push it, had practiced several times on the remainder of the trip until he knew exactly how far he could push the Lockheed. Then he'd read the Dash One after he'd landed… *Idiot! – should have done that before*, he'd chastised himself at the time. He leveled at four thousand feet just north of the airfield, saw below his right wing a flight of four Messerschmidts lining up for strafing run.

He put the Lightning into a hammerhead stall pulling the nose straight up and chopping the throttles back almost to the stops and kicked in full right rudder. The right wing came down, pointing at the ground; the Lightening fell quickly until he leveled the wings and pushed the throttles full forward. He turned in behind the flight of Messerschmidts, surprised no one had noticed his big airplane. *Target fixation*, he thought… *bad thing to slip up on… gotta keep a scan going, even on a strafing run.* He looked around the sky. *Why no top cover?*

When he rolled out, he was directly behind the Me-109 on the far right of the echelon, had him centered in the crosshairs of the gunsight. His heart beat furiously... *a kill already!*

And then a stream of tracers crossed not more than five yards in front of his windscreen.

Suddenly the sky around him filled with tracers and airplanes. Two of the Germans in front of him pulled up sharply, went almost vertical and disappeared; the aircraft he had sighted in on started to pull up, more slowly. Nolan pulled back on the yoke and pressed the firing button. He saw his tracers go by the German's left wing. Still pulling back on the controls, he kicked in a little right pedal and fired again from less than a fifty yards and saw the cockpit of his target fly off, shattered in the midst of a fireball as the plane instantly flipped on its back headed nose down, trailing thick black smoke.

Tracers were coming in from two different directions, passing just beneath him. A plane with a yellow nose spinner and a large black cross behind its cockpit suddenly filled his windscreen crossing ninety degrees from right to left. He pulled the nose up quickly but the German was gone before he could take the shot. He turned hard left, pulled the yoke back into his stomach and felt the shudder of the onset of a stall. Pushing the yoke forward and leveling the wings, he saw the ground coming up, pushed on the throttles and found that for some reason he'd retarded them. *How did that happen?* The airframe surged forward, nose pointed downward; his head swiveled looking around for other aircraft, and then off to his left he saw two 109s quartering away from him. Turning toward them, he fired a short burst, saw a thin cloud of gray smoke start to trail from the lead aircraft as he and his wing man both turned east. He turned with them, closing from above when a line of tracers went over his canopy, so close he cringed and ducked involuntarily.

Breaking hard right he started to climb, looked over his shoulder and saw the German turn sharply to follow him, then he banked hard left and abruptly dove for the ground – dirt and tiny bits of paper floated in the cockpit. The German overshot him and continued in his tight left turn. Nolan glanced over his left shoulder to get a look at the -109 as P-38s in revetments suddenly flashed by a hundred feet beneath him. Two more Messerschmitts were headed east away from the field a half mile ahead of him and slightly above. He pushed the throttles to the firewall and took up an intercept angle, watching the -109 off his left tail boom turning toward him now three or four miles off. *This is chaos*, he thought, amazed.

He was coaxing and cajoling the Lightning toward the two Messerschmidts. The -109 behind him seemed to be gaining ever so slightly every time he looked. *One shot, Nolan, that's all you'll get... six hundred yards... five hundred... scan... nothing above... right... left rear quarter... where is that damned German behind me?... three-fifty... three hundred...just a little closer...now or never...low house station six on the skeet field, son... nothing to it... you can do this... just a little bit further out, that's all... just...*

He pressed the firing button... *no sensation of recoil... nothing at all...how odd... just...* tracers floated away from him, curving down and to the right, passing behind the lead aircraft's tail. He started to kick in some left pedal, pressed the button and... he was out of ammunition.

NO! he yelled at the top of his lungs. He was still swearing when the trailing aircraft in front of him caught fire and nosed over, headed toward the ground in a smooth, ever steeper curve. He watched, mesmerized, until it hit the ground in a great fireball.

Suddenly, he realized he'd forgotten what was behind him, and in desperation, he pulled back hard on the column and twisted in his seat so he could see where the German was, all the while cringing as he waited for the bullets to rip through his own cockpit. *Nothing*. He looked around frantically. *Still nothing*. Not a single plane in the sky except the B-26 and the other five Lightnings at about ten thousand feet, fifteen miles southwest of the field above the hills, turning north. On the ground, there were two fires emitting tall pillars of black smoke, one to the east of the airfield about four miles and one just on the northwest corner. He pulled into a climbing left turn looking above and through a 360 degree arc.

The Germans had vanished.

Now there was a lot of activity beneath him; trucks were moving toward the burning Gooney Birds and a red cross ambulance headed toward one of the P-38 revetments; people were running around. A green light was flashing at him from a small wooden structure on the south side of the hardpack dirt runway. The tower, he decided, and looked at his fuel gauges. Surprise!... plenty of fuel. *Got time before I have to get this thing down.* He turned east toward where he'd seen a half dozen Messerschmitts heading, climbed to five thousand and flew a figure 8 pattern looking for any other aircraft. Out to the west, the B-26 had begun an extended approach for landing, followed by the fighters in a long descending trail formation.

Nolan circled to the north of the field until the last aircraft was on short final then entered the pattern. *Flaps – thirty; gear – down; carb heat – on; props...* he ran through the pre-landing checklist glued to the instrument panel. His breathing returned to normal, and he took his left hand off the throttles long enough to unfasten the oxygen mask. At fifty feet above the runway he started his flare, at ten feet he chopped the throttles and continued to slowly pull the nose up as the aircraft settled and finally touched down on the hard, rocky soil of North Africa.

Welcome to Africa goats and pigs, he thought as he slowed and turned off the hard-pack. *Wasn't that the opening line to a Kipling story?...Only the place was Crete, not Telerghma.*

A jeep was headed toward him as he turned toward the tower after rolling out, following behind the line of just arrived aircraft toward where a truck was leading the B-26 to parking. A small crowd gathered at the base of the wooden tower on the east side of the field near the revetments. As he swung the twin tailed Lightning around following the ground guide's hand signals, he saw a dull OD green truck turn toward him followed by two jeeps and a gaggle of men on foot. Across the dirt runway a mile or more north in front of him, the remains of a German fighter still burned furiously, the black smoke cloud drifting west on a light breeze.

As Nolan shut down the engines someone clambered up onto the wing and knocked on the window, motioning for him to roll it down and release the canopy. That done, Nolan shook the sergeant's hand, released the safety harness, grabbed the airplane's log book and pulled himself up out of the seat. One of the jeeps came to a stop behind the plane; Mitch slid down wing and dropped to the ground as a young major unwound himself from behind the wheel of one of the dilapidated vehicles.

"Major Harley Vaughn," the officer said, approaching Nolan and offering his hand. "I'm the commander of the 96th Squadron."

"Lieutenant Mitch Nolan."

The major was tall and thin, almost too thin; his eyes were darkly circled and bloodshot, and his skin was pallid. Up close he looked like an old man. Turning to a captain standing nearby, Vaughn said, "Art, take these ferry pilots up to group headquarters and sign them in. They can come back for personal gear later. Make sure they have the aircraft log books with them. See what you can do about getting all this equipment assigned to the 96th."

"Sure thing, Harley," the captain said and started to walk back down the line of newly arrived planes. Mitch started to follow but only got a few steps.

"You! Come with me," Major Vaughn said to him and motioned with his head. "I want you to see something."

They walked a hundred yards south of the makeshift control tower, a sad-looking square plywood structure with a tin roof sitting atop a frame of rough-hewn four by fours. A lone tent sat in the open with a half dozen holes covered with shelter halves in a circle around it. "Welcome to the home of the Slugging Desert Jackrabbits," Vaughn said, pulling back the flap of the small tent. "This is headquarters, operations, and where the commander hangs his hat."

Inside it was fairly dark although two sides of the tent had been rolled three-quarters the way up and tied. Along the left side was a table on which sat a scarred OD field telephone, a small black Remington typewriter and a large open journal; a sergeant sat shivering in front of a radio on the field desk. The floor was made of wooden planks from ammo crates nailed to pallets – the place was rancid and smelled heavily of wet, rotted canvas.

Mounted on a low tripod against the wall opposite the table was a large blackboard chart with names down the left side – some had been erased and three had been crossed through.

"Our group, the 82nd, moved here to Telerghma on New Year's day. The 96th arrived with thirty-six pilots, thirty-four P-38s and a B-26 for maintenance and supply runs. Three weeks ago we were ordered to give up half our airplanes to the other P-38 Group – the 14th. They're in worse shape than we are. They got here in November, a month before us, and they're still living in foxholes. The 14th is on the brink of becoming combat ineffective and being pulled out of the line. They will be next month if current loss rates continue and replacements aren't forthcoming. Your Lightnings are the first replacements we've seen. My pilots were doing their own maintenance until ground crews got here two days ago. I'm hoping my exec is eloquent enough to get your ferried ships assigned to the 96th. We're told there are some that recently arrived in England but need to be reassembled, test flown and pilots found to bring them here.

"In the first twenty-nine days of January, I lost six aircraft and five pilots in action plus another three to illness." Vaughn paused, biting his lower lip and catching his breath before continuing. "This morning, I lost three more of each. As of tomorrow this squadron on an average day will only be able to muster nine combat ready Lightnings for missions, less than a third of what we should, according to Air Corps Doctrine and Plans in Washington. The other two squadrons – the 95th and 97th – are only marginally better. The fact that the Luftwaffe can come in here and shoot up our Group airfield in the daytime tells you they're confident we're on the ropes. They're right – we are."

Mitch was stunned. The situation the major and his group were facing was far worse than Lindquist had let on in Casablanca. "Why are you telling me all this, sir?"

"This is my recruiting pitch, lieutenant. Right now is a time when one person and one plane can make a difference. From what I just saw, I think you're that kind of person."

"I don't have a lot of time in the P-38, major."

"I don't care. The way you handled that Lightning and your marksmanship was as good as any I've seen over here so far, and better than most. What were you doing when they assigned you to this ferry mission?"

"Instructing at Moffett – dogfighting and gunnery in Bell P-39's."

"What do you think of the Airacobra?"

"Not much, sir. To tell the truth, I was a little leery of the P-38's performance against the 109s and the 190s. I'm not sure I am anymore."

The squadron leader looked at him, and nodded his head knowingly. "I thought the same thing until I got a chance to fly the -G model in combat. It's a real war machine – it'll carry as heavy a bomb load as that B-26, and flown properly it's a good match for the -109 and pretty even with a -190 if the pilot's smart enough to fight his fight instead of the German's."

"The bird I'm flying made me a believer this afternoon, sir."

"Well, what about it, Nolan? I know your orders say to drop the plane off here and hurry your butt back to America. Orders can be canceled or amended. I'm sure you're a good instructor, and they've told you by being one you'll multiply the positive impact you can have on the overall war effort. There's some truth to that when you're saying it from behind a desk in California. From where I sit in this cold little tent in North Africa, that's bullshit. Stay here, learn the lessons, help the squadron and this group get back on its feet. When your tour is over then go back home and teach the newcomers what you've learned."

Mitch could hardly believe what he was hearing.

Hoping for the best, he had sold his share of the car he co-owned with one of the other flight instructors at Moffett before leaving. He'd closed out his meager savings account, but had left the BOQ room in his name while boxing up his few personal belongings and storing them with a friend. His uniforms had been stuffed into a B-4 bag, and other items had been put in a duffel bag and both shipped to Miami for storage on the navigation aircraft for the ferry flight. For all intents and purposes, his worldly possessions were with him.

"Sir, you've convinced me," Mitch said after a short while. "I'm your guy. I don't have my 201 file or my shot record. I hope that not having my records won't be a problem."

"My exec will figure it out," Vaughn replied wearily. "For now, get your personal stuff out of the aircraft, and take it to that ragged looking tent back behind the tower. For now that's officers' country and all my pilots live there. It's not much, but it's better than what they had three weeks ago, and better than what the ground crews still have to endure."

"When can I start flying, sir?"

"Maybe as soon as tomorrow. I want you to meet the other pilots, have our operations officer give you a rundown on the missions and intel officer to brief you on what we're facing. You'll have to sign in at Group. After that we'll get you into the rotation and we'll shoehorn in an area orientation flight as part of your first mission, all right?"

"Fine with me, major."

"Good. Get as decent a night's sleep as you can tonight because once you're in the mix you're going to find it's a lot more tiring than what you might think now. The cold North African desert in the winter takes a lot out of you. We don't have any of the equipment we packaged and shipped over here – tents, heaters, cots, blankets. Nor do we have most of the tools and equipment our crew chiefs and mechanics need. I've got my supply officer out scouring all along the north coast where our troops and the Brits came ashore in November. Maybe he can scare up some of the amenities of home. But I wouldn't hold my breath."

Mitch turned to leave, but stopped and turned to the squadron commander. "The chow hall, sir. Where is it?"

Vaughn laughed mirthlessly. "In the evenings and mornings we meet down by the tower and heat up c-rations in a large tub of water. The first sergeant makes coffee. Bring your own mess kit and canteen cup. You're on your own for lunch."

"Sounds like a plan, sir."

"No it doesn't, Nolan. Sounds like a fouled up supply system. But we're working on it."

"One other thing, sir. I'd really like to have the aircraft I ferried over assigned to me. I've gotten sort of attached to it. Is that possible?"

"Possible, but not likely. I wish we could, and we will when we get some more ships in, but right now we all fly whatever we can put up," Vaughn responded wearily. "A few pilots have their own assigned aircraft, but it's the guys who have proven themselves over time or in combat. Not having your own assigned aircraft isn't a deal breaker, is it Nolan?"

It was a disappointment but not reason enough not to stay, and he said as much. "I told you I'd stay. I'm not backing out, sir. I'll do whatever you need me to do."

Harley Vaughn held Nolan's gaze for several seconds and finally said, "You know, I'm going to reconsider, lieutenant. I'd say you *did* prove yourself this afternoon and the evidence is those two burning piles of Luftwaffe rubble you can probably still see from our flight line. Those two kills tie you with my top pilot, a guy named Dixie Sloan. I think giving you that airplane just might provide some incentive to him and others."

Nolan left the tent and walked back down to the flight line where two pilots in heavy fleece lined leather bomber jackets sat on the left wing of his P-38. They watched him closely as he approached. Another pilot, a baby faced youngster, stood leaning against the tail.

"I think you boys need to come down off my airplane," Nolan said.

The two on the wing looked at one another. "I used to think Dixie Sloan was the cockiest s.o.b. I ever met until this guy Nolan showed up. What do you think, Marv?"

"I'm right there with you, Lucky."

Nolan smiled with them when his two friends from the Academy broke up laughing and slid off the trailing edge of the wing onto the ground. Lindquist grabbed him around the neck and Crosley playfully punched him in the stomach.

"Cocky, eh? You two really think so? And who is this guy Sloan."

"That'd be me," the baby faced lieutenant said as he pushed away from the P-38. "Ah come down ta see what the fuss these two boys was makin' is all about – sumthin' 'bout how some shiny new hotshot jest up and tied my record. That be you, son?"

"Mitch Nolan," he said extending his hand. "I'm new here, and Major Vaughn just signed me up for the 96th squadron. Apparently he's going to credit me those two -109s."

"Well, we gonna haf ta see fer ourselves what comes of tomorra, Nolan. Anybody kin git lucky – even blind squirrels find acorns now 'n agin."

For an instant, Mitch was certain Sloan was putting him on, but the look on his face said he was dead serious. He frowned at Nolan, then at Lindquist and Crosley before straightening himself and walking away toward the tower.

"I think he was serious," Mitch finally said.

"He was serious all right," Lucky replied with a smirk on his face. "Damn Nolan, you haven't been here an hour and already you've made yourself an enemy."

Marv Crosley laughed out loud. "You make one hell of an entrance, Mitch."

*   *   *   *   *

Berlin – January 30, 1943

It was dark outside the windows of Admiral Wilhelm Canaris' high-ceilinged downtown office when someone knocked on the large door and his two most trusted assistants entered. One carried a large folder with the *Abwehr Eagle Crest* stamped on the front above the German Intelligence agency's motto: *Licht von der Schwarzung* – Light from the Blackening.

"Something has come to our attention through *Amtsgruppe Ausland*, but it also may be planted by the SD as a test of your loyalty to der Fuhrer and the OKW," Hans Oster, Canaris' second-in-command said, opening the folder and placing it in front of the head of German Intelligence. "We cannot be certain of its authenticity – it is possible it is a ruse engineered by Kaltenbrunner who was named Chief of the *Sicherheitsdienst* by Himmler just this morning."

Canaris, a very precise and deliberate man, slowly placed his pen at the top right corner of his desk blotter, and took the folder in hand, looking carefully at the face in the portrait photograph. He gazed at the face for many seconds, and then looked up at Oster and Colonel Erwin von Lahousen, his Section II Chief.

"I know this man," Canaris said. "His name is Nolan – he is an American business man, and from time to time a close working associate of William Donovan."

"According to this report, he is now a general in the American army forming a new division at their major infantry training facility in Georgia. It is designated the 12th Division," von Lahousen offered. "Beyond that we know he is apparently a close confidant of a number of the senior commanders in their Army – Eisenhower, Patton, Bradley, MacArthur."

Canaris continued to look at the face. "Do we know anything else about this division? Is it mechanized or strictly infantry? Are there any special qualifications required for its members such as airborne, mountain or ski qualifications? Extreme cold weather? Amphibious assault? Jungle training? Is this truly a combat division or a cover for a political arm of the American military or civilian government?"

"So far we know almost nothing, except the table of organization includes many names of officers associated with him in the past. We have no other information, save his military history file which is the second tab," Oster replied. "Section One discovered the first clues in a report from I-H West concerning Anglo-American military activities."

"What is your analysis of this meager information thus far?" Canaris asked, looking at each of them in turn.

"There is concurrence among I-H West and Section III – Counter-Intelligence Division that this information is likely valid as the Americans continue mobilization," Oster replied. "Further, there is agreement amongst the majority of analysts in the *Foreign Intelligence Group* that this officer and his division may well provide us early warning of their strategic intent and tactical planning."

"How?" Canaris wanted to know.

"We believe the Americans have assembled their top military strategists and field commanders under Eisenhower. Their war in the Pacific is essentially a naval conflict with the majority of island ground fighting likely done by their Marines who are skilled in amphibious operations. The American Army under MacArthur will be relegated to follow on, except where the battlefield necessitates or provides adequate and suitable terrain for large Army engagements. Wherever the group under Eisenhower is assembled will indicate to us the priority and likely near future intentions of the British and Americans opposing us."

"My section also included your own observations about this officer behind the third tab," von Lahousen added.

"And you think I would forget my own report to Herr Reichsmarschall Hermann Göring? Are you spying on me also Erwin, like that weasel Reinhold Heydrich used to do? I did not appreciate it in him and won't stand for it from you."

"Only attempting to stay a small half step ahead of you," the Section Chief replied obsequiously, "as you yourself stayed ahead of the former *SS-Obergruppenführer.*"

"You are wise to do so."

"As were you concerning Heydrich, Admiral."

"So why do your analysts think my observations are of any value?"

"As you observed years ago, this Nolan shows up, but only briefly, in the strangest places under the oddest circumstances. He was in Russia as a young major doing the bidding of William Donovan. Afterward, he was assigned to their foremost officer training school as MacArthur's chief assistant and while there worked with Eisenhower and Patton developing their armored forces doctrine. He also was posted to Berlin at the arm of Charles Lindbergh. He is a close friend of one of Britain's senior military staffers, General Smythe-Browne. We believe he may have been with Donovan in Great Britain in mid-1940. Otherwise, he is a man in the shadows as if they are intentionally keeping him out of sight until needed for something important. I would not argue with the brilliant deductions of the Chief of the *Abwehr*, sir."

"You don't have to stroke my ego, Erwin. I'm not *der Fuhrer.*" Canaris thought for a while as his gaze traveled back to the face in the picture.

Maybe this officer was someone to watch for the reasons his two top assistants had noted. Maybe not. But one thing was for certain – it was a test, likely by Kaltenbrunner, to see if he could find something to pin on the Abwehr so the SD could usurp all the nation's intelligence power and consolidate it.

"Anything else?" Canaris asked.

"Yes, we have the complete report on the meeting in Casablanca between Roosevelt and Churchill almost finished – it should be on your desk within the hour. It will be another week before a public announcement of the meeting from the two leaders, but we believe we have most of the important details. We had three spies on the scene, one of which had access inside the meeting compound."

Canaris shook his head, pleased, closing the Nolan folder and passing it back to Oster.

"Hans, ensure information on this officer is placed unobtrusively into tomorrow's intelligence summary to the OKW. Maybe someone in the High Command will have some ideas of his own for us. And have one of our analysts assume the responsibility for keeping track of General Nolan. I'm curious about his activities once this division is formed.

"He may be able to teach us something some day."

Chapter 18

"Every officer in this division will be issued the M-1 Rifle and the 1911 semi-automatic pistol, and will qualify as expert in both, by order of the Commanding General."

Colonel Pat O'Grady stared at the small group of officers in the 67th Infantry Regiment seated in bleachers gazing down on him and the pistol range at his back. "Every officer will complete the Division's Professional Infantryman course and those with the highest scores will be retained as company grade officers. Those officers will then train all non-commissioned officers and the men of their companies. Again, by the order of the Commanding General. Any questions about the basic requirements to become an officer in this Division?"

There was a long silence.

"If I were in your place, I'd have a lot of questions – so I'm going to tell you what the answers are to questions you should have after the toughest week you've ever experienced – so far. Question number 1 – what is this outfit… this 12th Division? Answer: the 12th Division is a brand new infantry division formed thirty-nine days ago on the afternoon of December 24th as the Commanding General's Christmas present to the United States Army. This division has no history, no heroes, and no excuses. The unit history will be written by the officers and men of the division – the ones who survive the next four months of training. The heroes of the division are to your right and left and will also be found in abundance among the enlisted men out on ranges scattered across this hell hole called Camp Benning. Excuses? – there are none. There is no excuse for failure, and no substitute for victory. You will become an officer in the 12th Div by virtue of merit proven in every aspect of soldiering.

"Officers in this division fight, lead, and train. Your first assignment is to become the best infantry soldier in the United States Army; your second is to train those under your command to be at least as good. Only then will you be allowed to lead."

Damn O'Grady, you are good! the forty-five year old colonel thought. *I got this group's attention. Wish I'd been this spellbinding that afternoon in Cirey with those replacements.*

"You are what's left of the forty-two officers initially assigned to the 1st Battalion of the 67th Regiment after one week of physical training. Each of the other three battalions in my regiment have experienced similar attrition rates. Aside from the battalion commander, each battalion requires twenty-nine officers - whether or not you are one of those depends entirely on you. This week brings another hurdle you must overcome – qualification as expert with the 1911 semi-automatic .45 caliber pistol. I'm now going to turn you over to CSM Considine who will instruct you in this phase of weapons qualification. Sergeant Major."

Colonel O'Grady walked to the side of the bleachers as the senior noncommissioned officer came forward and began his introduction to the pistol qualification. O'Grady saw the two general officers standing out of sight next to the bleachers; he approached them and saluted. "Good morning, sirs."

"Morning, colonel," General Fauser said, saluting casually.

"You were laying it on kinda thick there weren't you, Pat?" Dave Nolan asked.

"No sir. That was only the first layer – I try to put the fear of the Almighty and the division in all troops under my command. Just like you always did, sir."

"I might have to stick around just to hear that. You've improved your delivery and diction since the last time we served together. I guess these boys are the beneficiaries of the diatribes you were always delivering to the Pirates down at Camp Whalen."

"Perfect practice makes perfect, sir." O'Grady noticed both generals were wearing a new patch on the left sleeve of their fatigues – a black-bordered red shield on which was embroidered a bright yellow spotted leopard with four wings on its back appearing to be leaping with fangs and claws bared. "Is that the new division patch, sir?"

"Just got these in last night. General Fauser and I kinda like the way they turned out."

"We oughta – we're the ones what thought it up," Fauser added, frowning as if Nolan had uttered one of the stupidest things he'd ever heard. "Decided we needed us some warrior, a little Bible and a whole lot o' color."

"Looks good sir. Does the division have a nickname and motto yet?"

"A motto? – *Semper Fortis* – Always Brave. We might add a scroll beneath the shield that says that. We're going to let the nickname reveal itself – let the Japs or the Germans name the 12th after they've had a skirmish or two with us. Always better to let your enemies describe you in combat. It'll reveal something about them as well as us."

The three officers stood out of sight behind the stands as the firing began minutes later and continued for the next ten minutes. The sergeant major finally glanced at O'Grady who nodded quickly and then looked at Nolan and Fauser. "Are the two of you ready?" he asked, and strode to the firing line after the instructor called a cease-fire and ordered the junior officers back to their seats in the bleachers.

"That may not be the worst exhibition of shooting I've ever seen but it comes close," O'Grady began. "When the 2nd Battalion was here, I heard a lot of griping and complaining about what a lousy pistol the 1911 is – how it's all sloppy, the sights aren't any good and the handgrip is uncomfortable; how the thing rattles when you shake it. You might be tempted to say the same." O'Grady turned and looked downrange. "I want to see the shooters on lanes eight and eleven."

Two second lieutenants slowly made their way out of the bleachers and approached the short colonel who told them to retrieve their targets.

"It looks like Lieutenant Kelly here managed to hit the target four times and even put two of those inside the circle – the six ring," O'Grady said as if impressed. "Lieutenant Maxwell did marginally better; six hits on target and half of those inside the target circle. How many shots overall did you two officers each shoot to get that many hits?"

"Three magazines," Maxwell replied, looking embarrassed, "six rounds in each."

"Eighteen rounds down range from each of you – and you, Lieutenant Kelly got four hits; Lieutenant Maxwell got six. My math says that's less than fifty percent – way less. I'm guessing that every one of you sitting up there right now is thinking to yourself that this pistol is basically worthless – at best, nearly impossible to hit a target just twelve paces away. Maybe if the pistols were worked on by a good armorer they might shoot better. Truth is, they probably would. But that's not the pistol you're going into combat with. The pistol you're going to take with you into combat is loose and it rattles and in the hands of an average officer it really isn't worth very much. It's made with large tolerances so that when you drag it through the mud or the sand of North Africa or the surf of some Pacific Beach, it'll fire when you really need it. That's why you're going to have to work at being a good shot with this pistol. It can be done. I'm going to let two of our division officers prove it."

O'Grady had the lieutenants put up two new targets on each of their stands downrange and then move them back an additional five paces away from the firing line. He then motioned for Nolan and Andy Fauser to come out from behind the bleachers and approach the firing line.

"These two elderly gents are now going to show you just how good a weapon the 1911 really is – using Kelly's and Maxwell's pistols. They'll each have thirty seconds to shoot two magazines each loaded with six rounds. Let's see how they do."

Fauser and Nolan loaded the first magazine into their pistols, waited for the command to fire and then shot both magazines – the first with the right hand and the second left-handed. O'Grady sent the two lieutenants down range to retrieve the four targets.

"What we have here as you can see," O'Grady began, "is proof that the 1911, .45 caliber semiautomatic pistol is a pretty darned accurate sidearm. Both shooters put all twelve rounds on target in less than thirty seconds. One of them somehow missed by a hair on one of their shots and put a round through the nine ring. Even so, not too shabby. You men have a ways to go to become experts with the pistol, but it's obvious that it can be done. Let me introduce my two demonstrators.

"This is General Nolan, the commanding general of the 12th. Next to him, General Fauser, the assistant division commander. Both of them were infantry troop leaders in the 42nd Division in the Great War. Both of them were on a rifle and pistol team captained by then lieutenant now general, Omar Bradley, who was once the post and infantry school commander here at Benning. Both are also qualified expert with the M-1 rifle. General Nolan, anything you'd like to add?"

Dave Nolan stepped forward and gazed across the bleachers at the officers who sat in the chill of the January morning.

"I want you to know the United States Army is about to saddle you with the most daunting responsibility with which a man can ever be burdened. That responsibility is to lead infantry soldiers into combat. There is no greater privilege or duty. The most important person in this war is the individual American fighting man. He's the one who'll win this conflict for us as sure as he won the last one. He's more important and his role more decisive than anyone else in the chain of command. If you don't believe that now, you will soon. Believe me.

"I demand excellence and more than 100% effort. Know your weapons, know your tactics, but above all know your people. Our training week will be seven days long until we're ready. The only breaks will be Sunday morning for church, Tuesday and Thursday afternoons for team sports. Everybody will work hard and play hard. By this time next week, I expect every one of you to be qualified experts with the M-1 and the 1911. Once everyone in the division is qualified with his individual weapons, we move to crew served weapons. Then we will practice small unit tactics and patrolling, followed by platoon and company operations. After exercising battalions and regiments, we'll go on a series of maneuvers against other combat divisions, and we'll whip them like government mules, as General Fauser likes to say. We don't have much time to accomplish all that needs to be accomplished – four months max. You will be ready… or, you won't be here. That's a promise."

Nolan looked at the young faces. *Kids*, he thought. *Just kids. Did I ever look that young? Did my troops in the old Irish 69th look like that? Probably.* He looked at a red-headed youngster in the third row and thought: *that's Ed Higgins.*

"From this moment on, every time a soldier in the 12th Division renders a salute to a superior he'll say, *Semper Fortis.* The superior will respond, *Semper Valida.* It's what we're about in the 12th Division. It's Latin. *Semper Fortis* – always brave; *Semper Valida* – always strong. It's not just a motto. It's a rifle soldier's way of life.

"In the 12th Infantry Division we're all riflemen – all sixteen thousand of us."

*　　*　　*　　*

Mitch Nolan watched the squadron takeoff in sections of two for the early morning mission to cover a B-26 squadron's bombing run on German navy convoys north of Bizerte. When he could no longer hear the sound of engines, he went back to helping his crew chief and another mechanic work on his plane. He'd decided to name the aircraft *Mitch's Mistress*. He looked at the nose of the P-38 and visualized an exotic looking dark-haired beauty in something revealing – a *Vargas girl*. Maybe Makara. He wondered again why she'd left Casablanca so suddenly, without a word.

He'd listened in on the mission briefing held out in the open by flashlight at the base of the ramshackle tower. It was all pretty much seat of the pants – surprisingly so, even though he'd expected it would be a lot less formal than his experience at Moffett. Five leads, five wingmen. Rendezvous with the bombers over Bone at eighteen thousand. Keep the enemy off the bombers during their runs on German ships and release the bombers once back over the coast on the way home. Debrief at the CO tent twenty minutes after landing. He wished he'd been able to go with them but had to admit it made sense to give the new aircraft a close inspection before releasing it to duty.

And there was something important to fix – rerunning wiring from the harness through the control yoke and giving the aircraft the ability to fire the cannon and the .50 caliber machine guns simultaneously utilizing a single firing button. He'd landed the day before with 20mm cannon ammo still in the boxes because in the excitement he'd not thought about the other firing control for the cannon. Best to shoot everything at the same time, he decided. He was inside the cockpit pulling wire through the firewall from the gun platform in the nose of the ship when the assistant mechanic climbed up on the wing with three spark plugs in hand.

"Hey, lieutenant. Did you say you replaced these plugs a couple days ago?"

Mitch looked up and then at the plugs the mechanic was holding. "No, just pulled 'em to check for fouling. They looked fine so I put them back in. Did I screw up something?"

Phil Kupcinsky, his crew chief stepped off the ladder, leaned against the wing and took a look at the plugs. "You sure you didn't change those plugs, lieutenant? They look brand new. How many hours you put on this bird?"

"Right about fifty, all told. It was new off the line at Lockheed, so it couldn't have more than seventy-five or eighty total."

Sergeant K and the other mechanic – a corporal named Haskell, who wore his baseball cap set back on his head with the bill at an odd angle – looked at the plugs again. "When you landed you had an hour more fuel left than the other planes in your formation. That's a lot for a short flight. What was it? – eight hundred miles? What were you using for settings, LT?"

"The same as I used on every other leg. I fly the lowest rpm I can to stay in formation, about 1600. I boost the manifold pressure and increase the prop pitch so they take a bigger bite out of the air even though they're moving at a lower rpm."

Kupcinsky frowned at him. "Listen lieutenant, when you do that you're doing serious damage to the engine. Valves get burned, cylinder heads overheat and the spark plugs foul a lot faster. You did that most of the way over – the whole fifty hours?"

"Every bit of it, except for some aerobatics over New Mexico and Georgia, and that dust-up with the Luftwaffe yesterday when we arrived. I read it in a book by Lindbergh – he said that's how he got all the way to Paris in '27 without running out of gas. It's an old mail pilot's trick. If what I did is such a problem, why are the spark plugs in such good shape?"

"Look, lieutenant, you do the flyin' and leave me do the mechanicin', all right? We're going to have to pull the engine covers and check every valve and cylinder head," Sergeant K said to Haskell, clearly miffed. "Who knows what the pistons are going to be like. We'll never get a couple of replacement engines. Damn! I was hopin' to get my own ship again and looks like this bird is probably goin' to end up bein' a hangar queen, a parts bucket for the squadron." He cursed under his breath as he went back to the ladder and climbed down to the ground then headed off to the maintenance tent.

"I'll give you guys a hand pulling those covers," Mitch said to Haskell. "But I tell you this, those engines aren't damaged. I'd bet my flying career on it."

Haskell smiled half-heartedly. "You already done that, sir. If this bird has two damaged engines, you prob'ly won't be flying. We're about out o' planes that's still airworthy."

"We'll see."

"That we will, lieutenant."

Fifteen minutes into the job of removing covers and inspecting the engines, they heard the distinctive sound of a P-38 headed towards the airfield.

"Lieutenant Wolfe again," Haskell said to Kupcinsky. "Third mission in a row he's aborted. What do you want to bet they don't find nothing wrong this time either."

Nolan wondered.

Marv and Lucky had told him the previous night that Ted Wolfe was either real unlucky or one of those guys who aborted for no reason just to keep out of combat. It had happened before in this and other squadrons in the group. But his two friends thought they knew him well enough to think he wasn't a shirker or one of those guys who just wasn't cut out to be a fighter pilot under the stress of combat.

Mitch watched the P-38 land and taxi over to the revetment next to his and stop the engines; he rolled down the windows and swung the top canopy piece back. Wolfe climbed down and stood in front of the plane looking at it disgustedly with his hands on his hips. Mitch walked over, wiping his hands on a shop rag. "What's the problem, Ted?"

"The damned coolant overheat light keeps coming on after takeoff as we start the climb to cruise altitude and I open the coolant flaps." He shook his head disgustedly. "I know what people are beginning to say, but I'm telling you I'm not aborting because I'm afraid to go on the damned missions."

Nolan pondered. "How many aborted missions is that so far?"

The lieutenant turned and scowled at him. "Three. Three in the last five days. But I'm telling you I'm not dropping out because I want to; it's a mechanical problem with the airplane, not a mental problem with the guy in the seat."

"Is this the plane you been flying since you got here to Telerghma?"

"Most missions, but not every single one. Sometimes the requirements and the rotation of the schedule put me in another airplane but not usually."

"But you've been flying it for the last three missions and that's when the problem started?" Wolfe nodded. "How about the ones before that? Any problems then?"

"Four missions ago I had a different aircraft because the mission before that I took a few rounds in the right side – in the engine and wing and the right tail boom."

Nolan walked around to that side of airplane and saw where there had been some metal work done on the engine cover and a small section of the tail boom aft of the turbo-supercharger. He looked closer and saw tool marks on the coolant flaps which were wide open.

"What does the maintenance officer or the test pilot say when they take it up to check it out?" Mitch asked after a while to the pilot and Sergeant Kupcinsky, as they he looked into the wheel well.

"We don't have a maintenance officer," Wolfe replied with a sarcastic laugh, "and we're all our own test pilots."

"Tell you what – let me take it for a trip around the pattern and while I'm gone get a set of jacks – we'll jack up this airplane, check the wheel wells and see what's up." Mitch grabbed his own helmet, gloves and goggles and climbed into the cockpit of Wolfe's P-38.

He taxied out to the runway, took off and was back twenty minutes later.

"The coolant high temp warning light came on for me, too, just like lieutenant Wolfe said. Let's put somebody in the cockpit and jack this thing up," Mitch said opening up the small green loose leaf log book that recorded all the flights and all the maintenance done. "I see here on the day repairs were made to this bird there was more than one person making entries in the logbook. That tells me there were several people all working at the same time on this ship. Is that right Sergeant K?"

"Yeah. That was back about the time that all the ground crews showed up and people were pitching in wherever they were needed and wherever they could. Had a lot of work to catch up on. I had six or eight mechanics swarming this machine. Why?"

"We'll see in a few minutes," Mitch replied. "Once we get this bird up, we'll raise and lower the landing gear a few times and watch what happens."

A half hour later they had the Lightning up and sitting on jack stands so the landing gear could be raised and lowered without touching the ground.

"Jackson, battery on and raise the landing gear," Mitch called out. As the gear retracted and the cover panels closed over them, the coolant flaps also closed. "There's what's happening. When the gear is raised and the wheel covers close, something inside that wheel well is closing the coolant flaps in a way that the switch inside can't open them. There's no air coming in to provide cooling and that causes the high temp light to go on. Now all we have to do is find out what's binding and causing those flaps to close."

They cycled the gear down and up two more times with the same result, and then searched around with flashlights directed up inside the well until the crew chief found a bolt sticking out a fraction of an inch too far.

"That's it. I'd bet a stripe on it," Kupcinsky said, shaking his head. He cut off about a quarter inch of the bolt and filed it smooth. He had Jackson raise and lower the gear two more times and the coolant flaps worked perfectly. "When we gang-jobbed this thing back a couple weeks ago, somebody just happened to pick up an off size bolt and put it in by mistake. That's some good diagnosing there, lieutenant."

"Just lucky," Mitch replied easily, but he was pleased with himself, and hoped he was as right about the engine situation on his own Lightning.

"Nolan, I owe you," Wolfe said earnestly. "I know some of these guys were thinking I was aborting for no good reason, and my morale was pretty low because of it. I wish I could buy you a drink but we'd have to go an awful long way to find a place in this Muslim country where they'd sell you one."

"You don't owe me anything, Ted."

"Yeah, I do. And I won't forget it."

Two hours later, the mission that had departed earlier returned, made a low pass over the field and fell into a long gaggle for landing; the flight was one aircraft short. The remainder taxied to their dirt revetments and turned facing what served as the runway.

To the north a dot in the sky gradually grew in size until it became a twin-tailed P-38; the distinctive sounds of its props swelled until the Lightning flashed by a hundred feet in the air over the field from west to east and did two climbing aileron rolls before slowing and entering the traffic pattern for landing. It touched down, turned toward the revetments and minutes later stopped a hundred yards from *Mitch's Mistress*. Dixie Sloan emerged from the plane's cockpit and sauntered toward where Nolan stood talking with Lucky and Marv as the maintenance crew worked on the engines.

"What'd you do there, Nolan? Mess up your aeroplane already?" the Virginian asked in his lilting southern accent. He flashed a smile and raised two fingers in the form of a 'V' as he walked away headed toward the CO tent. "Best get a move on, boy. You're two down already and the day's not half done."

"Dixie got a -109 and a Dornier DO 217 bomber today," Lucky said in response to Mitch's question. "He took some ribbing last night about you coming in here and catching up to his score on your first day. He's probably going up to Ops to post the scores himself to make sure everybody sees it at debriefing. Cocky little s.o.b. – had to wait and make sure everyone was down to make his pass over the field."

Mitch smiled as he watched the young southerner walk past the tower. Harley Vaughn had predicted something like this would happen. It told him the major was probably a pretty good judge of people, and savvy about what went on among the troops in the squadron. He decided he'd been pretty lucky to wind up in the 96th Squadron – until later that night when Vaughn called him in for counseling.

"Sir, that's really not something I'm interested in doing," Mitch told the major anxiously, as they sat under the dim light of a lantern in the commander's small, musty tent.

"Interested or not, that's your new assignment. I heard from sergeants Hayworth and Kupcinsky this evening after dinner and they're two of my best crew chiefs. Ted Wolfe independently confirmed Sergeant K's story, and I find my aviation maintenance people talking about you. You're the right guy, and you *will* be the squadron maintenance officer."

"Sir, I came here to shoot down Germans, not bend wrenches."

"Look Nolan, I know you're a West Pointer which tells me you figured out by now how to obey orders. And this is an order, not a suggestion or a topic for discussion. You're the squadron maintenance officer – end of discussion." Vaughn watched Nolan's face carefully and finally said, "You'll get plenty of operational flying, don't worry about that. As short as I am on planes and pilots and as long on missions as we are, you'll be in the cockpit plenty. Maybe more than you want."

Mitch doubted that and said so.

Harley Vaughn smiled. "I'm going to remind you of this conversation the first time you come to me asking for a break from flying duties. You think it won't happen. You're wrong. But here's what I want from you: I want you to keep an eye on the overall activities of the crew chiefs and maintenance section sergeant. Don't tell them what to do – by and large they know what to do. You make sure work gets prioritized properly. But I also want you to spot check the work. There's an old military adage that goes: nothing gets done that the commander doesn't check. Frankly, I can't check the maintenance work – what I heard today says you can. You got some credibility already with two of my top crew chiefs and my maintenance section chief. I overheard Kupcinsky telling some of his peers about how you showed him a thing or two today. None of my other pilots have that."

"But, sir –"

"This is an additional duty, not a primary one. You're also our test pilot, and I want you to train one or two more. Find out from Group how to do it and get yourself on orders. There are some perks, lieutenant. Our squadron B-26 is your second airplane. You schedule it through Ops – fly it yourself when and where you want or have to. You have top priority for picking up parts and supply runs but it's also used for rest and relaxation jaunts for everyone in the squadron. A jeep and trailer goes with the job, too. You're totally in charge of that vehicle. Hopefully that takes a little of the sting out of the assignment. If it doesn't… well, tough. Like I said, it's an order."

Vaughn leaned back on his small camp stool and laced his fingers behind his head.

"You're officially in the 96th Fighter Squadron now, Nolan," the major said. "Group published the orders this afternoon. Just to make sure we understand each other, I'm the commander and everybody in the squadron does what I tell them to do… even hotshots like you and your new best buddy, Dixie Sloan."

Chapter 19

The bleak North African desert, blanketed in early morning haze, fell away as six P-38's climbed in two three-ship Vee formations away from Telerghma heading east. Their mission that morning was to strafe ships unloading German troops and supplies in the harbor at Tunis.

In the number two slot of the first flight of three, Mitch was tucked in tight at a forty-five degree angle off the right side of Dixie Sloan's airplane while Lucky was similarly positioned on the other side. Nolan had trimmed *Mitch's Mistress* so all he had to do to stay close in the formation was slightly adjust the throttles in his left hand. His right hand loosely held the big round wheel of the Lightning and his eyes were constantly moving – lead ship; up; straight ahead; down; right front; right; right rear; inside glance at instruments; back at Sloan; do it again. Now and then he'd glance out the left rear to ensure their backs were covered by the second flight two hundred yards behind.

Hunched in the cold cockpit Mitch was nervous, and irritated.

It was his first combat mission – that made him nervous. The irritation had been provided by the mission leader, Dixie Sloan, who had made it known throughout the squadron he thought Nolan's two scores days earlier had been plain luck – a fluke.

Most of the pilots had earned a nickname over the weeks since arriving in Algeria. Ed Waters was "Duck Butt", because of the way his parachute hung low and made him waddle when he walked. There was "Black Mac" McNulty; "Slick" Monaghan; "Bulldog" Barker; the "Five Musketeers" of former sergeant pilots; and the "Un-Holy Four" designated by the group chaplain. Everyone knew Lindquist as "Lucky." Dixie Sloan had decided he'd call Nolan "Fluke" and by his third day in the squadron the name had stuck.

Sloan's plan had been briefed by flashlight in the darkness at the foot of the tower – an east departure, climbing left turn northward to three thousand until crossing over the coastal town of Bone. There the flight would descend and turn east flying at wave top altitude just off the shoreline following the coast until reaching Bizerte. At Bizerte they would turn southeast toward Tunis where they would make a single pass over the harbor strafing ships, troops, trucks – anything that presented itself. On the way out, they would turn west toward Telerghma and continue to climb until clear of the German lines, now indicated by Intelligence as currently static sixty miles west of Tunis running through the Kasserine Pass.

Simple.

Soon they could see the blue waters of the Mediterranean and not long after they began a descending right turn passing over Bone. Mitch saw the small town where British commandos had come ashore and the nearby airfield where British paratroopers had landed back in mid-November. It all looked very peaceful now – most of the buildings showed little damage and the airport's runway appeared serviceable. Parked among some of the buildings nearby were lorries with British markings and soldiers standing alongside, many of whom looked up and waved or pointed.

The next twenty minutes were the most exhilarating of his young life.

At less than a hundred feet altitude and almost three hundred miles an hour the shoreline out his right side was a fear-provoking blur. He concentrated on staying exactly in position on Sloan, knowing at this altitude and airspeed he couldn't divide his attention even for an instant. His heart was beating faster than he could remember, until he realized some minutes later he was getting used to the visual stimulus from outside the cockpit and was enjoying it – immensely. A quarter hour later Sloan climbed while entering a wide right turn. Bizerte passed to their left as the flight leveled and headed southeast toward the port city of Tunis.

Suddenly Sloan's aircraft rose to four hundred feet and immediately entered a shallow dive headed for a pier a mile and a half ahead where ships swarmed with men unloading cargo. Nolan moved right and lined up on a row of tanker trucks just inland and with his right thumb pressed the firing button on the yoke. Tracers spewed out just short of the line and then ran through two of the tankers setting them on fire. *Heavy truck filled with troops.* He loosed another burst. *A huge fireball left front – fuel storage tank?* The ground below him packed with vehicles and soldiers passed by too quickly, in a phantasmagoria of color and implausible shapes. He saw rounds pass through trucks laden with boxes, sending the vehicles wildly skewing – shaking and tipping over. Sloan's aircraft appeared in his peripheral vision oscillating up and down – *or is that my ship?* Soldiers were running in every direction seeking cover. Some were firing at him he thought, though it was all happening so fast he couldn't tell.

Before he could catch his breath they passed over the center of the city.

The flight was just leaving the target area turning toward the west and initiating a climb when Lucky called out a dozen Messerschmidts coming from behind – eight o'clock high – and closing rapidly. Instantly Sloan turned hard right directly in front of Nolan only yards away, filling the windscreen; Mitch immediately pulled the control yoke into his stomach, chopped the throttles and kicked in left rudder to avoid a collision.

Sloan and Lindquist were separated from him, diving for the deck and running for home. Nolan pushed throttles to the firewall, turned left back into the -109s to knock them off Lucky's tail. He fired a long lead shot at two streaking across in front of him. Suddenly two Me-109s were on his tail and he was on the tail of a third one in a long twisting and turning daisy chain. The one he was following attempted to reverse direction from a left to a right turn. Nolan kicked right rudder and led the aircraft as if it were a quartering skeet shot. He quickly closed in to less than 50 yards, fired a short burst and watched the German aircraft explode on the spot in a great fire ball.

Mitch did a quick half roll and pulled the yoke all the way back into his stomach pointing the nose of the P-38 straight down. He then rolled right, and leveled 200 feet above the deck.

He looked over his right shoulder and saw two Messerschmidts had followed him down – one was directly behind him by maybe 500 yards and closing, the other trailed 100 yards behind his leader and a little higher. *Stupid! The -109 dives better than the Lightning – you know that!* Off his right wing, to the north, another section of two -109s flew parallel to Nolan's ground track about a half mile away. To the south about a mile away flew another element of Messerschmitts. *Boxed in – not many options now, Nolan.*

Red tracers flew past his Lightning, ten feet high and a half dozen yards left. The air was rough at this altitude and he guessed that was why they hadn't knocked him out of the sky yet. For the first time since his solo in the Philippines, he was scared inside a cockpit.

You haven't been here that darn long," he thought. *You're too new to become a statistic. If we were higher I could bail out of this crate.*

Instantly an idea formed.

He chopped power on the right engine, kicked in full right rudder and aileron, and spun a flat turn. When he came out of it a second later, the nose of the big Lightning was pointed almost 90° off his original heading – he'd lost 100 feet of altitude and was flying almost sideways. Out of the corner of his eye he saw the closest Messerschmidt on his tail flash by behind him and his wing man fifty feet directly over the P-38 cockpit a fraction of a second later. Instantly he shoved the throttles full forward, centered the rudder and pulled the nose up just above the horizon. The Lightning shuddered as its props clawed for air. Within a few seconds, his *Mistress* was gaining altitude and airspeed.

He was climbing slowly but directly at the two Germans who had been a mile off to his right just seconds before. He aimed in front of the first Messerschmidt and let loose a short burst. Almost immediately the aircraft began to trail a dark cloud as it dove for the deck, his wing man right behind him.

Nolan watched the wounded German ship as he continued his shallow climb, gradually picking up airspeed. He looked back over his left shoulder and saw neither of the aircraft that had been following him initially; the only sign of any other Germans was a faint and dissipating trail of slate gray smoke now bending toward the south. He was alone – sweating profusely despite the cold, but alive.

The whole fight had taken no more than two minutes.

He felt lucky, but then realized he had no idea where he was.

Somewhere over Tunis; maybe Algeria, he thought. *Find Bone, take a heading of 225 to the railroad track running north-south through Constantine; then twenty-three miles heading 195 to Telerghma. Ought to be able to see the field from there at 20,000 feet. Hope that's right.*

He continued north to the coast, then due west to Bone, recognizable to him now. A half hour later he was following the railroad track south through the town of Constantine. Within a few minutes he saw the Group airfield at Telerghma and headed for it careful to keep his head swiveling as he let down to pattern altitude. Two miles north, he saw the flashing green light from the tower and entered the traffic pattern, landed and taxied to his parking spot.

"Thought we mighta lost you, lieutenant," Kupcinsky said, kneeling on the left wing as Nolan finished shutting down and made an entry into the log book.

"Almost did," Mitch replied, standing up and stepping out of the cockpit onto the wing.

"How about that... you did make it back, Flukey," Dixie Sloan said, standing near the *Mistress's* horizontal stabilizer. "You missed the de-briefing. Anything you wanta report?"

"Yeah, I do," Nolan replied, then descended the small steps welded to the trailing edge of the Lightning's wing. "I got back no thanks to you."

Sloan smiled, a look made more innocent by his babyface features. "I told you to stay on my wing, Fluke. But you didn't listen. You'd a-come back with the rest of us if you had. Sometimes when you're outnumbered and otherwise disadvantaged by airspeed or altitude, a wise man knows it's time to jest cut 'n run to fight another day. Ah don't hold it against you 'cause you're the new boy here. But next time..."

Mitch glared at the Virginian's smirking face. "Well, I did get a -109 kill and damaged another after you left me in the middle of all those Messerschmidts back there west of Tunis."

"Really, now. Anybody see, it?"

"I guess not. Everybody else had already headed to the barn."

"Too bad. Claims have to be verified, ya know. We need some kind o' evvy-dense, ya hear what ah'm sayin'?"

"It'll be on the gun camera."

"Don't think so," Dixie replied seriously, frowning and sadly shaking his head. "Ya see, there's problems with that. First, we ain't got us no way to process that film around here, not at group anyway. This is kind of a rough cobb sorta operation we got goin' on here in Africa. And the few times we got film back we couldn't tell nuthin' 'cause the camera's mounted right underneath four .50 cal. guns and a big ol' cannon. Camera shakes so hard it's all a blur." Sloan grew even more serious, rubbing his chin and cocking his head. "Guess you just gonna hafta fergit about them two unconfirmed scores. Fixin' that dang camera setup... I'd say that's a job for the maintenance officer to work on. That'd be you, wouldn't it, Fluke?"

*　　*　　*　　*

Harley Vaughn declared, "Nolan, I'm putting you in charge of this mission."

"You want me to go steal supplies from the Brits?" Mitch asked, incredulous.

"We're not stealing. There are crates there labeled *'82nd FTR GRP'* and a few others with American unit designations," a captain named Hodgson said. He was the 82nd Group supply officer and had found the equipment two days earlier. "Don't know how the Brits got it or why they brought it ashore but a bunch of the stuff in one of the warehouses is ours – at least the stuff marked *82nd Fighter Group.*"

"How much is there?" Mitch asked.

"Probably a good four loads in deuce and a half trucks," Hodgson replied frowning as he thought through the logistics.

"Where are we going to get four or five trucks that size we can spare for a week? It's almost two hundred miles from here over Algerian roads – at least two days each way plus loading time in Bone. All told five days. If it rains, add another day each way – maybe more. Can any of the squadrons give up a truck for that long? How about manpower" We'd have to take at least three men per squadron for that time period. Can you afford to lose crew chiefs or maintenance men for that long?"

"Maybe, maybe not," Vaughn said, sounding uncertain. "You Pointers are all logicians, aren't you, Nolan? You can figure this out."

"I don't like it, sir."

"I didn't tell you to like it – just told you to do it. You said when you first joined up you'd do anything I needed done. Well, I need this done. Group wants it and it's now our job. That settles it. You have all the time you want as long as it's done by the end of next week."

He spent the afternoon at Group Headquarters with the operations and supply sections. What he learned from Sergeant Ragland in supply about vehicle availability for his mission was discouraging and what he saw on the maps he was given by the Ops sergeant was worse. The maps they had for him were two decades old French cartography with Foreign Legion markings showing few roads and only the major towns – barely good enough for the simplest aviation use and wholly inadequate for his purposes of leading a convoy of trucks and troops two hundred miles. He could imagine getting lost, wandering around in the Algerian wilderness, straying into Tunisia and running across German lines. He remembered his father's disparaging comments about French maps from years earlier during their hiking trips through the Philippine mountain jungles and thought now the ol' man was probably too generous.

The aircraft situation was just as bad.

The 82nd had once had three C-47's; two of them had burned less than a week earlier the afternoon the *Cyclops* ferry flight had arrived from Casablanca. Now only one remained – the *Squawkin' Hawk* – belonging to Group Headquarters. He decided if he was going to get in and get out of Bone quickly and safely, he needed a minimum of five aircraft – five cargo ships. Gooney Birds not bombers. Neither Ragland in Supply nor Major Steinburg in Operations held out any hope for that many being assigned to a supplies run like this. Almost all the C-47's in North Africa were committed to hauling aviation supplies and fuel in five gallon jerry cans – two dozen Gooney Bird flights came in to Telerghma every day.

He went to sleep that night tired from his first mission, glad to be alive but worried about this job the commander had given him. His sleep was restless in the close-packed tent, lying under a musty smelling blanket on a pile of straw covered with a shelter half. For the first time he questioned whether it had been a good idea agreeing to stay on. This was nothing like he'd imagined while complaining to Broussard at Moffett. *It is what it is, Nolan* he thought, still worried and still irritated at Sloan, now for more than one reason; he was sure the list would grow. The next morning he awoke with a plan.

Roscoe Curry was a maintenance tech sergeant who had a reputation in the squadron for getting things done regardless of difficulty – exactly what Nolan needed. Nolan laid out the outline of his plan to Curry over coffee in the maintenance tent early in the morning. Within an hour, the two of them had pre-flighted and taken off in the squadron B-26 headed to Bone.

It was a risky mission, Nolan realized, for a lot of reasons.

He'd never flown the B-26 before, but had time in the twin-engined Lockheed Hudson and the P-38. Minimal risk, he decided and halfway to Bone determined it was no big deal. Detailing Lucky and "Little Ricky" Zubarik as test pilots without Group orders and assigning them P-38s for test rides between Telerghma and Bone might be a different story. But he'd decided to chance it thinking that Vaughn wouldn't be happy to lose his B-26 because there was no fighter coverage on a flight that close to German airspace. The three aircraft landed at Bone mid morning.

The old, partially destroyed warehouse where the 82nd Fighter Group supplies were located sat not far from the runway, close enough for an aircraft to park and be loaded fairly easily. Nolan showed the British sergeant who was guarding the warehouse a set of orders with the group code number; he and Sergeant Curry looked around inside the warehouse which was subdivided into a half dozen smaller areas surrounded by chain-link fence and padlocked. They found the area where the 82nd Group supplies were and decided there was enough there to require no more than two C-47s for transport. But, to load out the entire warehouse would take at least five, and there was a lot of equipment in there the squadrons in the group could use.

An hour after landing, the three aircraft were again airborne headed back to Telergma.

"Here's what I'm thinking," Mitch Nolan said to Sergeant Curry, Lucky and Ricky Zubarik shortly after noon as they sat around a small field table eating cold C-rations and drinking lukewarm coffee. "We're going to load out everything that's in that warehouse and bring it back here. I saw all kinds of stuff in there that we can use – tents, cook stoves, heaters, cots. There was a complete welding machine with oxygen bottles in one of those spaces. Think we can find a use for that Sergeant Curry?" The maintenance tech nodded. "We have to get in and get out quickly, but I think it can be done."

"How?" Lucky wanted to know, frowning at him. "We've got one Gooney Bird in the 82nd and it's an hour flight to, and an hour flight from, and probably an hour on the ground as well at each end. Four hours per turnaround with one C-47 – and you said it was going to take probably five loads, five trips. That's twenty hours, even without refueling. Not real swift, Mitch. The Brits will be all over you."

"Done that way, they would be. We have to load at Bone in under an hour. And, if we had three or four Gooney birds…"

"Where are you going to get four?" Zubarik asked. "We've tried to get the transport squadrons to loan us a bird from time to time since we've been here, but they just won't do it."

"Not a problem," Mitch said easily. "We'll just steal a couple of them. Well, not really steal because that would be a violation of an officer's honor code. But we can borrow them."

"Borrow them?" Zubarik repeated. "How you gonna do that Nolan?"

"I'm going to put Lucky and Marvelous Marv in charge of that. Those two stole the sacred Reveille cannon at West Point three years ago. They'll figure this out." Before Lindquist could object, Mitch continued. "14th Group has a C-47 and our group commander thinks the group commander there owes him a big favor for the 82nd turning over half of our Lightnings to them a month ago. The colonel is pretty sure he can call in that favor. And it's really not much – the loan of their C-47, with crew, for one lousy little morning. We'll get it.

"I don't have all the details and the timing worked out just yet but I will before supper. Basically what we're going to do is this: first, I take the B-26 in and land at first light with Sergeant Curry and eight men from the maintenance section, followed immediately by the *Squawkin' Hawk* and the 14th Group C-47. We cut the lock off of each of the six stalls inside the warehouse while our men load out all of the 82nd Group supplies into the first C-47. That's probably one full load. If it's not we throw on some more stuff; if it's more than one load, we put on what we can and start loading the second Gooney bird. By the time the 14th's bird is loaded Lucky is landing with our first borrowed C-47 and soon after that Marv with the second one. That way, at least for the initial four loads we always have two birds on the ground – one loading and one waiting. As soon as one bird is loaded and taxies out of the way, we start on the next one. The unloading at Telergma should go faster than the loading at Bone because there's more people and there's no need to properly stack and distribute weight. Unloading should take less than half the time of loading. We just have to keep that daisy chain going between the two locations. But the way I see it, we should be able to load that whole warehouse out in six loads max and somewhere around four hours – five tops. If we start loading at zero seven hundred, we should be finished more than an hour before noon."

"When are you planning to do this, lieutenant?" Sergeant Curry asked.

"The sooner the better. Tomorrow morning if we can set up the loan of the 14th Group Gooney bird and schedule the arrival of the first C-47 loaded with Jerry cans before zero seven hundred. We give that Brit sergeant on guard too much time to think about what happened this morning and we might find a bigger welcoming party. We'll meet again here at seventeen hundred and by then we'll know for sure if we can get everything in place to go tomorrow."

After the others had gone, Lindquist looked at him. "This is really crazy, Mitch."

"No more than the Reveille cannon, or that spur-of-the-moment trip to Bermuda. With your luck going for us, this thing is a dead solid cinch. Trust me. You'll be telling this yarn to all our classmates at reunions for years to come and laughing like the lunatic you are."

He slapped Lucky on the shoulder and went out of the tent headed for Group Operations.

*   *   *   *

Mitch lowered the gear of the B-26 as he turned into the traffic pattern. Looking out the left window and down at the Telerghma airfield he saw a C-47 take off and just beyond it, near the base of the tower, another Gooney bird being unloaded. Men were loading boxes and pieces of equipment onto trucks and into trailers – even into Doc Mounce's Red Cross ambulance. People and supplies seemed to be moving in all directions. As he flared the bomber on final approach and let the airplane settle onto the hard pack runway he suddenly felt utterly exhausted. It wasn't yet noon, but he'd been up for almost nine hours. The first person to greet him as he climbed down from the B-26 was Dixie Sloan.

"Fluke, it looks like you stomped on the hornet's nest, son. Major Vaughn and the other squadron leaders are here along with the group commander and most of his staff. Seems you got some explaining to do."

Standing in the group at the base of the makeshift tower, Harley Vaughn looked at him and nodded. Mitch had no idea what that gesture meant. He didn't know the group commander, had never met him and only heard of his reputation. Lieutenant Colonel William Covington, was a 36-year-old West Pointer who had previously commanded the 1st Group's 27th Pursuit Squadron. He had become the 82nd's first real commanding officer in June the previous year when the unit was formed at Muroc and he had a reputation for being fair, hard, and demanding. The look on his face confirmed the hard and demanding only.

Major Vaughn waved him over to the command group and the staff. "Colonel Covington, this is Lieutenant Nolan."

Covington gave him a penetrating stare and finally asked, "This was your operation?"

"Yes, sir. The mission was assigned by Major Vaughn, but the conduct of the operation was my responsibility."

The group commander looked him up and down as if inspecting guard mount. "You're willing to be held accountable?"

"That's correct sir."

"Mission accomplished, lieutenant?"

"I believe so, sir. I can't say with absolute certainty but first appearances are that we got all we went after. I'll know for certain once we inventory and debrief."

"I don't think either will be necessary, lieutenant. My supply officer already looked at the first planeload and confirmed it was all the equipment belonging to us he had seen while in Bone. The next five planeloads are apparently a bonus; however, I received an interesting call from the British commander responsible for the security and defense of the airfield at Bone."

Mitch tried to read Covington's face and found it impossible.

"The British officer – a Major Hawkens – was inquiring whether or not all of our aircraft and personnel had returned safely to Telerghma. He advised me that shortly after our last aircraft departed, a fleet of four German bombers escorted by -109s attacked the airfield and its buildings. It seems the warehouse where you found our supplies and two other buildings nearby were hit, caught fire and burned to the ground. I'd say you were lucky on two counts."

Mitch thought he saw the slightest indication of a smile working its way into the colonel's features. "Yes, sir, I'd have to agree with you."

"I was certain you would. It seems your quick response to a mission order saved our equipment for us. You're to be commended for that. In the process it appears you've also found a few items which will make life within our group a little more comfortable. Captain Hodgson tells me we now have enough tentage that noncommissioned officers will have a roof over their heads, enough cots that we can get our pilots up off the ground, and enough kitchen equipment to set up a mess hall to feed at least one hot meal a day to all hands. I haven't seen them, but I hear we now have enough generators to run lights in the squadrons and my headquarters. All very commendable. On the other hand... I also received a call from the 60th Troop Transport commander an hour ago. Those are the fine folks flying Gooney birds who keep us supplied with aviation gas."

Mitch could see the smirking faces of Marv and Lucky over the commander's shoulder.

"He says that your little operation here stole two of his airplanes this morning and pressed them into service moving this equipment. Colonel Martin was not nearly as worried about your well-being as Major Hawkens. In fact, I think he wants a piece of your hind parts, Nolan. He plans to be here first thing tomorrow morning to collect. Does that bother you?"

"No, sir, because we didn't steal his planes, we just borrowed them and diverted them for a couple of hours in a good cause."

Covington grinned a little at this. "I don't think he's going to buy that, lieutenant. Hell, I *want* to believe it and I don't buy it. You know what quibbling is, I'm sure."

"I still think it was a good cause, sir."

"Actually, so do I. That's why I'm doing you the favor of getting you and your co-conspirators out of the way for a few days. I'm going to give you and Lindquist and Crosley a three-day pass to Constantine, so you're out of sight until Colonel Martin cools down."

Mitch hesitated, contemplating. The colonel seemed to be in a good mood. *It's worth a try.* "Sir, if it's all the same, I'd rather the pass was for Cairo. Lieutenant Lindquist and I met a couple of girls in Casablanca who work there for the British Embassy and –"

"Don't push your luck, lieutenant."

Mitch sighed. "Sir, actually the people who really deserve three-day passes are Sergeant Curry and his eight-man detail who did all the heavy lifting today. I'd rather you give passes to them and let me and Lieutenants Lindquist and Crosley take our medicine."

Covington paused and chewed on his lower lip for a moment. "I'm going to let you all go. I don't condone stealing, even if it was from the British. But the Germans bombing that warehouse to the ground could, in a pinch, be viewed as extenuating circumstances. You got away with it this time, lieutenant. Don't let it happen again."

The group commander turned and walked away; his staff followed and slowly the group broke up. Harley Vaughn came up, slapped him on the shoulder, told him he'd done a good job.

When all the equipment was off-loaded and everyone else had gone, Dixie Sloan sidled up to him as he talked with Lindquist and Crosley.

"Well, how about that? Another lucky fluke. You done screwed up when you tripped and fell in the manure pile, but somehow you come up with a rose between your teeth."

"Some of us are just blessed that way, Dixie," Nolan replied. "Some folks got it and some folks don't."

"I have to give it to you, Flukey, it was a smart move to borrow them two Gooney birds like you did. Tell you the truth, I wouldn't have minded being a part of that little sideshow myself, you know?"

"Have you ever flown a C-47, Dixie?"

"No. These two oddballs never had either. You shoulda picked me, because a real pilot can fly anything that has wings."

"No offense, but you see Dixie, that's exactly why I chose Lucky and Marv. After flying your wing on the Tunis mission, I decided I didn't need someone like you along. You're right, I needed real pilots, and you just didn't measure up." Mitch smiled broadly at the Virginian, and winked at Lucky. "I have to go conduct a debriefing and then get ready to go on leave. Have yourself a good afternoon there, Lieutenant Sloan."

Chapter 20

Stay with the bombers! Stay with the bombers!

Mitch decided Major Harley Vaughn was a carnival barker in a previous life and had been reincarnated as a broken record. He'd also realized his perceptions from Moffett about the war in Europe – at least the Mediterranean Theatre, the MTO – had been wholly romanticized. He'd been in the 96th ten days, flown three missions and realized that while flying fighters was in his blood, there was no future in it in Africa.

Rumors abounded about the Luftwaffe fighter pilots they faced. Many American pilots and some of the aircrewmen were convinced an elite German fighter unit was based at Gabes – a small town about forty miles south of Tunis. This unit was often referred to as *"Goerings's yellow-nose squadron"*, and everyone who had been flying out of Telerghma had reported tangling with -109s sporting distinctive white or yellow noses. Mitch wasn't so sure about the Germans and their master race. He guessed anyone flying Messerschmidts in the MTO against both the Brits and the Americans was probably a pretty seasoned pilot who had been in action almost continuously since the beginning of the war in Europe. Compared to the pilots of the 82nd Group, who had less than two months combat experience, every German was elite.

His major complaint so far was that while escorting bombers over land targets they often had to watch in frustration as whole formations of German fighters took off right before their eyes and climbed above them to attack with the advantage of altitude and airspeed. He, and others, had argued that if they had more latitude in pursuing the enemy they could neutralize most of the advantages enjoyed by the Axis pilots. But the usual bomber escort assignment for the P-38 pilots was close cover. *Stay with the bombers!* was a phrase he had come to know by heart and hear in his dreams in less than a week.

On his second mission, two pilots from the 97th squadron were lost escorting B-26s to the Borj Toual German airfield along the Bay of Tunis, south of the capitol city. His third mission took them to the Cagliari/Elmas airfield complex in Sardinia. It was their first raid on a European target, and was made in retaliation for an attack by aircraft from those bases on an Allied convoy just a few days before. It was the first time Mitch had escorted B-17 bombers.

On the way back they were suddenly attacked by a large number of -109s not long after picking up bombers coming off the target. It turned into a wild and frightening three-ring circus, the kind of thing he had read about from accounts described by World War I pilots.

The P-38s broke formation and there were individual dogfights everywhere he looked. He spotted a -109 off to his left with a P-38 on its tail and another -109 on the tail of the P-38. He pulled in behind the second -109; before firing he cleared his own tail to make sure he wasn't the target of some other German. He had to climb a few feet to get a clear shot at the German without hitting the Lightning. Closing to within fifty yards and taking up a slight diving attitude, he lined up on the left wing root of the German fighter and let go with four .50 caliber machine guns and a 20 mm cannon. The Messerschmitt came apart, disintegrating before his eyes in a great cloud of black smoke and fire. Flying through the smoke and debris, he pulled a hard right turn and scanned the sky trying to locate any other German fighters, wondering how many Lightnings were left. All at once, the fight was all over. The only planes he could see were friendlies; nothing but P-38s.

That night he learned JT Duncan from their squadron hadn't made it back and was presumed KIA. Soren Anton had brought his badly damaged P-38 back, but he was seriously wounded; Doc Mounce determined his flying career over.

The 96th was now down to ten aircraft, two of them needing major repairs. Things looked desperate for the squadron, Mitch thought as he looked down at the formation of ten B-26s two thousand feet below. He and Dixie continued to scissor back and forth, covering and clearing each other's tail as they provided top cover for the bombers.

All eight of their flyable airplanes were up for this mission – covering the bombers in search of convoys from Sardinia headed for Bizerte or Tunis with desperately needed supplies for the *Afrika Korps*. Off to the right of the formation he could see a section of two P-38s flown by Lucky and Marvelous Marv. Ted Wolfe, the flight leader, and 'Duck Butt' Waters covered the left side of the formation, while a half mile to the rear, Ricky Kubarik and 'Bulldog' Barker spread out to cover the rear of the flight.

Nolan felt they were operating on a shoestring.

A half hour after leaving the coast behind, the bomber flight lead called "Tallyho" on a convoy headed due south toward the Tunis Gulf. The B-26s began spreading out and losing altitude; Mitch looked up, saw black dots against the azure blue sky, and called out over the radio: "Two dozen bandits, 11 o'clock high, eight miles."

"Stay with the bombers!"

Mitch couldn't tell who made the call – probably Ted Wolfe. Looking up at the enemy convoy cover above him, he thought he could make out a combination of -109s and Italian fighters – Macchi MC 202s. A half dozen of the black dots detached themselves from the flight above them and started down. Mitch and Dixie turned left and started to climb directly at the diving enemy fighters who immediately retreated.

Good so far, Mitch thought to himself. *But this won't last.*

A minute later, another half dozen enemy fighters entered into a steep dive. Again Mitch and Dixie turned and aimed their guns up at the descending fighters, but this time the enemy continued down – not directly at the fighters but off to their left about two miles. Mitch started to turn back towards the bombers to take up his original position but Sloan continued to turn into them, pulling away from the bombers.

"Stay with the bombers! Stay with the bombers!" This time Mitch could definitely tell it was Ted Wolfe's voice over the radio. As he looked up at the German covering flight he saw two -109s detach themselves headed down toward Sloan.

"Red One this is Red Two – back to the bombers," Mitch said over the radio.

"Stay with me wing man," came the immediate reply from Sloan.

Nolan debated. The cardinal rule of combat flying was: *never leave your wing man.* Sloan had left the bombers to go chase after another fighter kill – a stupid and selfish act and contrary to all the tactics of flying a cover mission. But Mitch knew he couldn't leave him alone, not with two aircraft approaching from his six o'clock. He immediately pushed the throttles full forward and turned to follow Dixie, switching his guns back on.

The two Italian fighters were suddenly upon them.

Mitch fired a short burst of tracers across in front of them as he turned. One immediately pulled up and turned right; the other was a little slower but followed his leader. The maneuver allowed Mitch to pull behind Sloan by going nearly inverted, pulling through the dive and coming out just off his right wing. The half-dozen -109s continued down and swept beneath the B-26s coming out on the other side of the formation in a climbing left turn. Sloan fired a short burst and missed, turned hard right and got on the tail of another aircraft.

There were radio calls now on the mission frequency – bomber pilots calling out the locations of enemy fighters. Mitch followed Sloan through a series of turns and climbs as the Virginian picked out and shot at fleeting targets of opportunity. He could see in his peripheral vision a section of two -109s turning and heading toward them for a head-on pass; the closure rate was breathtaking. He targeted the plane on the right and let loose a long burst while seeing the Messerschmidt's tracers float toward him and pass over his canopy. He fired another burst and saw rounds hit home; the Messerschmidt rolled, it's right wing knifing through the air at him like the dorsal fin of a predator shark. He gasped and braced for a collision.

The Messerschmidt's wing hit the nose of his P-38, and he felt it scrape down the length of the underside of his aircraft. There was a sudden jolt which for an instant seemed to stop the Lightning in midair. Then he was thrown about in the cockpit, his head hitting the right window and then the top of the canopy as the world in front of his windscreen swirled. He was falling away, out of control, the nose of his aircraft swinging wildly to the left. When he pushed hard on the right rudder there was no response, and the control yoke seemed similarly disconnected from the rest of the airplane. By playing with the throttles, he managed to gain a little control; the right engine started smoking badly and he shut it down.

I hope the life raft works!

He scanned the airspace, saw enemy fighters in every quadrant and realized he'd be easy pickings. In an instant he decided to jump before any of them had a chance to make a pass raking him and his disabled P-38 with their guns and canon. He looked quickly at the rear view mirror Sergeant Kupcinsky had installed for him – the horizontal stabilizer was completely severed at the root of the right tail boom.

Can't believe this thing is staying together – should have torn itself apart by now.

"Red flight, Red two bailing out. See ya after the war," he called out on the radio.

Damn!... that sounded goofy as hell – Hollywood B movie crap. 'See ya after the war'...

He released the canopy, rolled down the left window, unfastened his safety belt, and took off his oxygen mask in quick succession, all in preparation for leaving the Lightning. He pulled off his gloves to make it easier to grab the ripcord of his parachute and surveyed the sky around his badly damaged Lightning once again.

Hope those stories of Sloan's are wrong about the Krauts shooting guys in parachutes. Little bastard said that just to rattle me...

He was making only about a hundred and twenty miles per hour losing about four hundred feet every five minutes while keeping the plane level and headed straight south by pushing on the left rudder pedal with both feet.

Altitude. Need altitude. Think, Nolan. Get some altitude! Can't jump from this low.

He discovered that by doing something he'd been told never to do - turning ever so gently into the dead engine - he could gain almost three hundred feet every time he made a complete 360° turn. He continued this maneuver pointing generally in the direction of Telerghma. He wanted to climb to at least 10,000 feet before he bailed out. His good engine was running extremely hot and when it started detonating he pulled the throttle back to cool it. But then he started to lose altitude and realized he had little hope of ever getting back.

Don't think I can belly land this thing. Gotta keep both feet on the left rudder pedal – right rudder cable must be severed... my hands and feet are nearly frozen.

He could neither send nor receive on the radio and decided that it too was frozen. Finally he came over the coast near German-held Bizerte at 8,000 feet and it seemed as if everyone in the Afrika Korps down below started opening up with 88 millimeter flak. With the canopy gone he could hear rounds go past him and heard them when they burst, often much too close for comfort. The air became so turbulent it almost turned the ship over. To escape the antiaircraft guns he turned into a cloud bank but at about 150 miles per hour the horizontal stabilizer started vibrating so badly he was afraid it would completely rip off. When he slowed and came out of the clouds he was hidden from the antiaircraft gunners by a lower cloud layer.

After banging on the radio with the butt end of his hunting knife three or four times it lit up and he managed to call for a DF steer. Getting a reply he decided it was worth taking a chance to get back to the base.

Forty miles northeast of Telerghma, where he could just make out Constantine, his good engine quit... *gotta be due to overheating...* He called in his position and started to descend, again weighing the possibility of jumping. Passing through 6000 feet the engine caught again apparently having cooled off. He radioed the homing station and told them the engine was running and that he intended to try making it back to base. Ten minutes later, he went over the field at about 3000 feet.

No choice now son, you're going to have to try to land this thing. Good luck with that... put your cotton-pickin' seatbelt on – you can't belly this thing in when you're unbuckled!

He circled south and east of the makeshift runway on a wide right downwind for landing gradually descending and turning slowly onto a base leg. Continuing the wide turn he lined up with the runway heading about 7 miles out slowly reducing power and airspeed.

That's too much Nolan, gotta slow that rate of descent or you're going to end up breaking your back. A little power... not too much. Keep this landing attitude...

At the slower airspeed he was having a hard time keeping the nose of the aircraft up, certain it had to be because the horizontal stabilizer was hanging on at an awkward angle. He thought about lowering the flaps, but decided against it because of damage.

You're going to be long, don't worry about it. Better smooth than long or short or whatever. Ambulance rolling... Lots of people milling around over there... Eyes up on the horizon – don't look left or right. Things going by real fast now ... nose up just a little. 20 feet. 15. Ease the power back. Don't let it fall out from under you! Chop the throttle... nose up a little more. A little more. Just a little –

The sound was like thousands of fingernails screeching across thousands of chalkboards, and the force of the deceleration threw him hard against the seatbelt restraints. The nose of the Lightning started to move right and he forced all of his strength through his legs onto the left rudder pedal. Somehow he managed to straighten the nose of the aircraft. It was the roughest ride he'd ever experienced, worse than riding a big Harley Davidson with no suspension or coil springs across the potholes of Hell. Somewhere in the midst of the rough ride he'd turned off the fuel switches and stiff armed the control yoke forward. He had no idea how fast he was going or how far he had traversed across the field, but abruptly and unexpectedly the aircraft nose dipped violently forward and he found himself hanging almost face down from his safety harness for a brief instant. The tail assembly collapsed downward hitting the ground with a loud metallic crash that raised a huge dust cloud.

Without knowing how, he found himself sliding down the back of the left wing to the ground. Hopping over the left tail boom just aft of the turbo supercharger, he ran several yards, stopped and turned around to look at the wreck.

From out of nowhere, ground crewmen with fire extinguishers surrounded him, pushing him away from the flames and spraying the wrecked plane. An ambulance with medics pulled up followed by a crowd of pilots from the squadron.

"Mitch!" Marv said loudly, grabbing one of his arms and pulling him further away from the wreckage. "We'd given you up for sure after that radio call –"

" – and seeing you fall away almost straight down streaming white coolant and chunks of the *Mistress*," Lucky yelled above the noise. "How'd you get that thing back?!"

His two friends guided him to the ambulance where Doc Mounce checked him over.

Dixie Sloan ambled over, looked Nolan up and down quickly, then sidled up to the airplane and did a slow walk around stopping now and then, taking in all the damage and shaking his head sadly. He knelt by the right vertical stabilizer, looking at the gaping holes and the entirety of the horizontal stabilizer now lying on the ground. Finally he walked up to Nolan, stopped and looked him over once again.

"Well, ain't we got us a fine mess here," Sloan said in his drawl, shaking his head. "Nolan, looks like you done gone and wrecked that nice new airplane you just flew all the way over from California. Now, we're short on airplanes again because of you. You been here for less than two weeks, flown a couple of short, simple little missions – and got nothing on the scoreboard to show for it but this pile of junk you left in the middle of our runway. Hell, son, you didn't even let that corporal – what's-his-name?... Haskell? – even finish up paintin' that girl on the nose of this airplane you was flyin'. Don't know what to tell you 'cept maybe that you're just gonna have to go back to the Lockheed factory there in Burbank, USA and get you another one. And the next time you gonna have to do a better job of taking care of the airplane that your Uncle Sam gave you. And that's all I got to say 'bout that."

*   *   *

"Nolan, that was a wreck that should never have flown," Major Harley Vaughn said, pouring coffee from a small percolator into a canteen cup and passing it over.

"Just got lucky, sir. If the field had been another two or three miles further or a quarter mile shorter, I'd never have made it."

Vaughn was quiet for a while, sipping the coffee and staring at the chalkboard. Finally he said, "Wolfe didn't make it back today. His crew chief is really taking it hard."

Mitch felt despair knife through him; Wolfe had gone out of his way making him feel welcome and a part of the squadron. "He was a good man – good pilot and flight lead, too."

"Worst part of this job, Nolan; writing those letters – wondering if I could have done something to keep it from happening. I should have been up there leading rather than him."

Mitch understood the guilt the major was feeling. Vaughn was wrong of course, but telling him that probably wouldn't help. The major flew and led most missions – that was probably as it should be, Mitch thought, but he couldn't do them all, it was impossible. Wolfe was gone. He hated to hear of another loss, but it had happened in the squadron on every mission he'd flown.

"I had a full strength squadron when we left England to come here, but in the seven weeks we've been in North Africa, I've lost half the pilots I trained at Muroc," the commander said. "It's the same across the whole Group. You're the only replacement pilot the 82nd has seen since we got to Tafaraoui. And we haven't gotten a single new aircraft other than the ones you were with the day you got here. After today, the majority of them are gone, too."

Vaughn sipped his coffee and poured some more into each of their canteen cups.

"Got another job for you, Nolan."

"Sir, I'm not –"

"We're critically short of aircraft and Colonel Covington is tired of waiting," the major interrupted. "He wants each squadron to go get replacements in England. We're told they're arriving but they don't have pilots to ferry them here. You're to take seven pilots with you and bring back that many planes. The colonel was impressed with your inventive approach in Bone and wants you to be the first to finagle some birds for us. He thinks you can figure out a way around Army red tape for others in the group to follow. You leave for Gibraltar in the morning on a C-47. Pick up your orders at group, select seven pilots and brief them tonight. Be back here in a week – or less. The colonel doesn't expect they'll likely give up the planes to a bunch of rowdy lieutenants so make sure you wear these." Vaughn slid a pair of captain's bars across the top of field desk. "Don't worry – you're not impersonating a real officer. Pick up your promotion orders at Group. You earned the railroad tracks, Nolan.

"Just don't screw up on your first mission wearing them."

Chapter 21

"What was the observation you made about Gauguin and his sunsets that first dinner we had at Denise's quarters in McKinley?" Nita Haggerty asked. She wrinkled her brow while looking at Elise Fauser, who stood at the French doors of the Reeves' kitchen overlooking the rolling hills behind the big house.

"Don't *you* start in on that! Good grief, it was seven or eight years ago," Elise complained. "All right, I admit it, he never painted a sunset. There! Now can we stop? Isn't there a statute of limitations on dumb comments?"

Michelle looked at Muggs Alford and winked then went back to pouring wine.

"Was it really that long ago?" Nita asked no one in particular and then wistfully continued. "I miss those days in Manila before the war, when the boys were company grade and life was easy. I'll never forget those shopping trips to the markets – especially that first time, and the dinner afterward. What was that awful stuff the woman at the roadside stand tried to sell us to keep us young forever? Was it Kalamansi?"

"No, that's what we used to make the drinks," Denise said, handing glasses of wine to Muggs and Elise. "I seem to remember we were all a little unsteady by the end of the evening because everyone wanted more of it in that spiked punch we made."

"It was Durian fruit, Nita," Kate Hanley said, "the stuff that smelled like rotten cabbage marinated in turpentine or asphalt. Michelle said she'd just as soon grow old than to eat or bathe in the stuff. None of us disagreed."

Michelle sipped her wine and listened contentedly as the reminiscing continued among her friends while she tossed a salad. The get together had been her idea; the purpose to relive one of the more pleasant times in her life. Harrison was out of town and she'd decided on the spur of the moment to try to pull her closest friends together. Reliving those memories reminded her how lucky she'd been to share those times in the Philippines with them. It was the first time she'd lived on post and was able to participate in all the social life it offered.

Her favorite memory was that initial trip to the Filipino markets and dinner at Denise's which followed – it was the first time she'd felt a part of the group. Harrison, she realized, had intentionally made her a recluse since their marriage. The Philippines had been a turning point. She had always been close to Elise, her old college roommate, but virtually none of the others, until assigned to Camp McKinley. Two seminal incidents from her days in the islands stood out – the night she put her foot down and stopped letting Harrison walk all over her, and the moonlit evening spent on the veranda at the Officers Club with Dave Nolan.

She'd gotten to know Muggs and her outrageousness effrontery, Nita's brashness, Kate Hanley's quiet confidence and common sense concerning everything from raising kids to excelling at cards, Denise's iron will and independence. Three of them – Elise, Nita and Muggs loved military life – while Kate was ambivalent. Denise had always bridled at the many hardships and lack of opportunity for her children, and now sounded a muted note of betrayal at Dave's leaving a high visibility and lucrative civilian career to go back into the Army. She tried to put a happy face on her situation, but Michelle knew she was not pleased.

"Judd says this new division is the best outfit he's ever been in," Nita Haggerty was saying as she set the large oval kitchen table. "He tells me it's the best of all possible worlds considering some of the assignments he could have drawn – and Dave hand-picked him to take a regiment!"

"Take that with a large grain of salt. Kosher salt," Muggs replied, shaking her head and grimacing. "Cole said the same thing. But he's said that about every unit he's been in with Dave. He's not a reliable witness and Judd isn't either, not since Dave somehow got us out of Manila. Our spouses think Dave and Andy are forever cleaning up the Army and making it a better place to live and work. Ha!"

"Andy's pretty happy."

"He would be, Elise," Michelle offered. "With Cole to order around like a Plebe and Dave to harass the way he did when they were cadets at the Point. He's likely in Razorback heaven. And Doc Hanley – the perfect audience to laugh at all his inane stories."

Denise listened to the light banter of the wives, reminded of the times at Benning when they would all sit out on the back stoop after their husbands got home from playing baseball. Missing now was the noise of kids in the back yard under the big elm, and the sense she'd had that everything was finally going to work out for them just because he said it would. She'd lost that simple trust in him. Listening to Muggs and Nita and Elise chatting happily about their husbands again down at Benning grated on her now.

Of course Harrison wasn't down there, Denise knew. He'd always been able to avoid the messiness of Army life. While Cole and Andy and the rest of them more often than not found themselves out on maneuvers or sweating through training along with the poor grunts, Reeves had managed to stay above all that; the starched and spit-shined staff officer, always at the right hand of power but never having to deal with the nasty side of commanding. One way or another he was able to maintain his distance and remain unsullied by the harshness of pushing troops or having to worry himself with the personal problems of the enlisted men. While Dave, Andy, Cole and Judd had lived and crawled on the ruggedness of terra firma, Harrison resided unfazed among the gods on the Army's Mount Olympus – the general staff in Washington. There was a time when she thought less of him for it, but not anymore. Not now.

As she looked around the room she realized, as she had at West Point when MacArthur was superintendent after the War, these were her true friends. Good girls – all of them. They all had skimped and saved during those long lean years, helped one another out with food and hand-me-down clothing and watching each other's kids; worried together – about their men's careers and the lack of post activities and opportunities for their children. Except for Michelle, she thought, they had all paid with hard won coin, and because of it, there was a solid, somber dignity about each one and their little group born of hardship shared.

Their conversation continued on through the various courses Michelle had prepared – all of it excellent, and Denise wondered where she'd learned how to cook – not just this well but at all. Harrison was rarely home and she infrequently cooked for him; she'd had neither a mother to teach her or children to be her taste testers. Everything Michelle touched and everything she did turned out perfectly. She remained an accomplished equestrienne, moved in important political circles in Washington, and maintained this large estate house in picture-perfect order. She found herself at once envious of Michelle and also sorry for her, remembering the evening in Manila when Harrison had been so overbearing and contemptuous of his wife that she had felt compelled to step in to rescue her. Being married to a prig like Harrison, despite his money and position, had to be difficult. But then, so was being married to a man who thought more about the Army than he did about his own wife. Suddenly she was sure she'd never in her life felt so utterly depleted.

"Denise, you've hardly said two words all evening," Elise Fauser said, interrupting her thoughts while taking the dessert dish in front of her.

"A lot on my mind, I guess."

Elise looked around and then leaned close, almost whispering. "Are you all right?"

"Never better."

"Andy's... wondering. He and Dave share a small room in one of the barracks out in Sand Hill where the troops are quartered. Dave hasn't said anything, but Andy doesn't think he's seen a letter from you arrive since he's been there. Is that possible?"

Denise glared at her briefly and looked away. "Tell Andy that's none of his business."

"I was just –"

"For your information, things might be a little strained right now. All right? We're just like everyone else. Sometimes Dave and I have our disagreements, like all married couples." Denise took a deep breath. "I apologize. I was just sitting here feeling a little sorry for myself. Honestly, I wish he had stayed out; we had a little fight over it. Did he put Andy up to this?"

"No. You know how close they've always been. Maybe as much now as when they roomed together as cadets."

"The Gold Dust Twins. Joined at the hip."

Elise smiled. "That's them. Gold Dust Twins with Jeb Stuart mentalities. I'm not sure Andy would appreciate it. Dave might, but not my Butternuts. He really is stuck back around Antietam or Chancellorsville, I'm afraid. Still, he's all mine – for better and worse."

In a way, she envied Elise Fauser. Her life with Andy had always been so uncomplicated.

Her father had been a career officer and an instructor at West Point once upon a time; she'd always planned on marrying into the military, and settled on the Arkansas Razorback early in his second year at the Academy. From that point on the deal was sealed, consummated by the brief wedding ceremony in the Cadet Chapel the day after his graduation. While Andy was always flirting on the edges of insubordination, Elise had ensured he followed all the Army's many protocols for social behavior. She made sure he had the proper number and style of calling cards; that the expected calls on senior officers were made at the appropriate times and Andy's cards were properly deposited in the small silver plates inside the entrance to their quarters. Andy's disdain for military social etiquette was outmatched only by his wife's ability to intervene and ensure he followed martial protocols, whether he wanted to or not. The Army officer's wife was a role she'd always played perfectly.

The rest of the evening passed quickly as their conversation drifted across the years and over events at one post or another where their paths had crossed: the Academy, Benning, Meade, Huachuca, Lewis, McKinley, Leavenworth. For widely disparate reasons they had all decided to stay in and around Washington for the time being. They were fascinated with Denise's trip to Germany just before the war and prodded her to tell them about it. Had Dave requested the assignment? Had she met Der Fuhrer, or Goering or other high-ranking Nazis while there? What were the people like? Did they get to any of the Bavarian resorts like Garmisch-Partenkirchen, or bring back wood carvings from Oberammergau?

When the evening finally drew to a close, Denise stayed behind to help finish cleaning up but more importantly to talk with Michelle about Erika.

"She's been a godsend for the Senator – and for me," Michelle told her as they stacked dishes and put away flatware in the kitchen. "What she does now in summarizing legislation and putting together position papers is what I used to try to do before she came. She's not only doing a better job than I ever did, she's freeing me up to do coordinating work with other senators' offices working on things my father has been after me to do for a while."

"I know she enjoys it."

"That's not the half of it. She absolutely revels in it and she has the confidence of her convictions. She's well read, her positions are grounded in the Constitution and the Federalist Papers, and she knows how to make a sound argument. She challenges people – everybody, especially my father and young Ashby. I think it's safe to say he almost worships her."

"She does seem to guide him around by the nose."

"Most of the time, but not always. I think he gets tired of it sometimes, but then he realizes what a terrific catch she is and settles back into letting her have her own way. It's really amusing to watch from the sidelines. But he also genuinely appreciates her abilities for making and interpreting legislation. My father, too. He thinks we don't pay her enough, but I told him how you feel about us overpaying your children." Michelle looked at her, cocking her head. "Do you remember giving me grief at McKinley because you thought I was paying Mitch too much for taking care of my horses at the post stable?"

"Because you were."

"I wasn't, but I couldn't convince you. I see where Erika gets her stubbornness. I know you'll say it's from Dave, but it's not entirely. You can be pretty hardheaded yourself."

"It's bad manners to insult your guests."

"You're not a guest, Denise. You're family like the rest of the girls here tonight. And I can say anything I want to the family."

They put away the last of the dishes and sat down at the kitchen table for one final glass of wine. It was dark outside now. Denise reached over and patted Michelle's hand.

"I really do appreciate how you've taken Erika under your wing and watched out for her. It's one less thing for me to worry about. If I hadn't put Glenn into that Gonzoga High School I'd probably go back to Long Island now. But he's doing so well at school – for the first time he seems interested in getting an education and bringing home decent grades. I don't want to put a damper on that."

"And he seems to have struck up a friendship with Ashby," Michelle added.

"He's hoping for somebody to take him fishing on the Chesapeake when summer comes. You know, I really ought to give him a phone call. It's getting late. May I use your phone?"

"We haven't put one in the kitchen yet so use the one in Harrison's study."

Denise walked down the hallway, found the study and made the call to her youngest; when she hung up the phone and turned to leave she was startled to find Harrison Reeves standing in the doorway leaning against the frame and looking amused.

"Harrison, I thought you were on another trip."

"Cut short by two days," he replied, straightening and entering the study. "I didn't want to interrupt Michelle's little hen party so I came in by the side entrance. Thought I'd come to the study and catch up on some correspondence only to find it occupied. I hope I didn't intrude."

"No, not at all. I was just finishing. That was Glenn."

"How is he doing at the new school?" Harrison asked in a tone suggesting he really didn't care but felt the need to make small talk.

"I think he likes it."

"He should, what with the tuition those people charge. I expect it's a financial strain even on a brigadier general's salary. How is David, by the way? I haven't had a chance to catch up with him since he's gone to take over command of his division. I trust he's doing well."

"Apparently he is."

"Have you talked with him lately?"

"Not for a while. Apparently he's very busy."

Reeves drew down his face in a worried frown. "Do I detect a note of disapproval? I tried to warn him off, you should know."

"I didn't know, Harrison. What exactly do you mean by 'warn him off'?"

Reeves crossed the room, opened the humidor on the corner of his desk and extracted a large cigar. "I advised him, for his own sake – and for yours – that he decline the commission and assignment he was being offered. I did it as a friend; a longtime friend of you both. From a number of the comments you made when we were all in Manila, I perceived you were likely much happier up in Long Island, away from the Army, with Dave working for your father. I hope you don't think I was trying to meddle. What I did ran counter to all the responsibilities I have for Army personnel worldwide, but I was willing to risk it for a friend. Was I out of line, Denise? Tell me, please. Did I misread your thoughts and intents?"

She looked at him warily, wondering how much was true and how much was artfully crafted illusion. Had he really advised Dave against going back into the service? Possibly, but she really didn't know. And, why was he telling her if he had?

"Not totally, Harrison, on either score," she said at last. "The truth is I didn't want him to go back to the Army. But Dave has a mind of his own."

"As well we all know," he replied airily. "One doesn't dissuade my old classmate once he has his mind made up, does one?"

"Certainly not," she replied with a hard edged tone. "If I've learned anything in my life since I met him, it's that."

"I wish there was something I could do, Denise," he said, solicitously, clipping the end of the cigar and reaching for his lighter. "If there is ever anything I can do for you – and I mean anything – I'm completely at your service. I hope you'll take me up on that."

"You know, Harrison, I just might. Thank you for the offer. And now, before you light that stinking thing, I'm going to leave."

"A good cigar is one of my few vices so I won't apologize. I've always found it's the best way to relax at the end of a long hard day, and this last trip was filled with them. When next you talk to Dave, please give him my regards."

After Denise left he walked across the study, closed the two large doors and returned to the desk. He sat down in the large swivel chair, pulled a bottle of single malt scotch from the lower right-hand drawer and poured himself a drink before picking up the phone and dialing the U.S. Capitol switchboard. He asked for Congressman Callahan, a former classmate from many years ago in prep school at Gilman in Baltimore, and waited.

"Harrison, how good to hear from you," the congressman said when he came on the line a minute later.

"Trevor, I knew I'd catch you at the office even at this hour. Still the patriot and overachiever, I see."

"I've taken up residence here for the time being since Margaret and I separated."

"I'd heard of the separation. I was sorry to hear of it, old chum," Harrison lied. He didn't give a tinker's damn about the marital woes of his former classmate from private school days or where he slept either. "I hope you're bearing up."

Reeves knew well how the congressman was doing. He was one of about two dozen high school classmates in Washington whose situations he kept up with and from time to time used to his advantage. Most were now successful lawyers or government officials who had come to owe him favors over the years, and Harrison Reeves kept excellent records. Congressman Trevor D. Callahan, Democrat, 4th Congressional District, Maryland was one of those.

Callahan was a fourth term Congressman from a very Catholic and very liberal district in the Old Line State. He had been helped financially in each of his four political campaigns by the *C.S. and Abigail Reeves Foundation* established by the estate of Corbin Sinclair Reeves, Harrison's grandfather and the man responsible for both his and his father's inheritance. Callahan came from old Boston money, much of which had vanished on Black Tuesday in the Crash of '29. He had wandered aimlessly in the financial world until finally stumbling on the idea of running for national office. Someway he had gained the confidence of Trenton Reeves, Harrison's father and the senior U.S. Senator from the state of Maryland who guided the young first timer through the labyrinths of the state Democratic political machine and eventually into the U.S. Capitol. He had become well-known and well-liked among his colleagues in the House of Representatives; he was personable, handsome, well spoken and could always be counted upon to vote with the party faithful. His lack of intellectual depth and frequent minor embarrassments over personal behavior were easily overlooked by Democratic leaders in Congress and the Roosevelt Administration.

"Of course I'm bearing up, Harrison," Callahan said. "But you didn't call up just to check on my mental state, now did you?"

"As a matter of fact, I did. When I heard you and Margaret had separated I wanted to do something for you but had no idea what that could be. From our days at Gilman I knew you to be a man of intense physical urges and wondered how I might ease the stress you're under."

"Are you offering to hire me a prostitute, Harrison?" When Callahan laughed it came over the telephone wire as a haunting cackle.

"Of course not, Trevor. That would be highly out of character for both of us. But, I do know a certain woman – a friend of Michelle's – suffering under similar circumstances of separation as you. She's extremely attractive, and also very lonely. I'm only suggesting you two may well have something in common about which to converse. Perhaps comfort one another."

There was a long pause on the other end of the telephone. "All right, I might be interested. You say she's attractive?"

"As well as highly intelligent. And she comes from a good family background – I know how important proper breeding is to you Bostonians."

"Marylander, Harrison. 4th District – remember?"

"How could I forget?"

"When do I meet this woman? Are you going to provide us an introduction?"

"Not a formal one, but I shall arrange the circumstances and let you know."

"Good enough. Thanks Harrison. I owe you another one."

Reeves rang off promising to get in touch again soon. He then slowly lit his cigar, poured more scotch and held the glass up to the light to toast himself and his old friend, Dave Nolan.

"*Salud, Camerado.*"

Chapter 22

Painted a deep British racing green, it was a striking thing to behold.

Behind a pile of assorted odds and ends – three crates of old newspapers, a sleigh, a farm wagon, and an old chest of drawers split down one side – sat the little sports car up on blocks. Over it was stretched a canvas cover thick with dust and splattered unceremoniously with pigeon droppings. But the car itself appeared to be in excellent condition and needed only a wipe with a damp cloth to make it shine. The odometer read just under 8500 kilometers.

"It's a shame to let a roadster like that sit under a tarp in this dusty old barn," Lindquist observed reverently, as if they'd stumbled across some holy artifact being meanly treated by unbelievers. "Something that beautiful shouldn't be on blocks, and I can hear it begging us to set it free. Think you can get it running, Mitch?"

"The real question is: should I? The last time I was here I thought I heard a horse telling me it wanted to be ridden. What I really heard was a quality dressing down from a sharp tongued English girl and my head being handed to me. I'm not suffering through that again. Maybe we ought to just cover it back up and go on about our business."

"But Mitch, something that gorgeous shouldn't be left to rust in some old barn."

The eight pilots from the 82nd Fighter Group had arrived at the airfield in Southampton a few minutes before six that morning after an eight hour trip from Gibraltar in a C-47. It was the most miserable flight any of them had ever suffered through; sleep came in brief fits and starts during the long, dark night over the Atlantic as they shivered from the cold and worried over the chance encounter with German aircraft. By the time they landed in England, they were totally exhausted and were taken to barracks on the airfield where they slept until midday.

They learned their orders would allow them to pick up all eight planes which were being reassembled in makeshift hangars and flown out at the rate of nine or ten a day. They were placed in the queue and told their planes would be ready in four or five days. Mitch gave his pilots three day passes for London and promised dishonorable discharges for those not present or unable to fly at noon on day four. After making arrangements to pick up the aircraft and for staging at RAF-St. Eval in Cornwall, he and Lucky Lindquist commandeered a jeep and drove to General Smythe-Browne's estate outside London. They arrived just before dinner.

The large old house sat aloofly on the top of a small rise, well off the main road, guarded by stately old trees much as Mitch remembered – it had been almost three years.

"We'll cover the roadster back up and head in for drinks with the general before dinner," Mitch was saying. "Compliment his wife about her cooking, no matter what. Got that?"

"Tell me more about this sharp-tongued girl."

"She's a hand grenade with the pin already pulled. Even you don't have enough luck to escape unscathed if you cross her. You can take that to the bank."

As they walked across the broad back field toward the estate house, a staff car turned onto the long narrow entrance road drawing a thin ochre trail of dust until slowing and pulling into the circular drive in front of the house. General Smythe-Browne exited the back seat and noticing Mitch walking toward him waved and waited as the car departed.

"So good to see you again young man," he offered, extending his hand to Mitch. "And you also. Lindquist, isn't it? You had an attractive young blond woman on your arm when we met in Casablanca. She was one of the hostesses of our little conference. Aida was her name if my aged memory serves."

"Yes, sir. Right on all counts," Lindquist replied, shaking the general's hand.

Smythe-Browne turned to Mitch. "I wish I'd known you were coming. We would have re-hired the cook and slaughtered the fatted calf."

"It came up suddenly, sir. We're here for only a few days to pick up some replacement aircraft before returning to Africa."

"So, you managed to stay for the fight in Tunisia! Quite good. That's where the real battle will be. We'll have a drink before dinner and you can tell me all about how you managed it," the general said enthusiastically, slapping Mitch on the back before leading them into the house and down the hall to his study. After pouring them each an Irish whiskey, he asked, "Have you heard from your father lately?"

"Two weeks before I left – a brief letter well over a month old telling me he'd gone back into the Army and was in Benning. Not much else. I'm sure my mother isn't happy about it."

"I should not like to be in your father's shoes in that case." The British general stuffed tobacco in a worn Meerschaum pipe and lit it. "And how do you lads fare?"

"Things for us are not going all that well; the loss rates in our fighter group and our sister group are unsustainable," Mitch replied.

"As they are also among your ground units. This struggle between the Afrika Korps and your General Fredendall's II Corps appears on the surface to be a disheartening American loss, however we believe it presages significant improvements in American command structures."

"How so?"

Smythe-Browne smiled paternally. "I wish I could tell you but that's obviously strategic information. But I can tell you that your father is being flown to England, thereafter to North Africa to meet with General Eisenhower. All of us here see that as a positive development, a good omen – one of several in the past few months despite the slow progress in North Africa due to the winter rains."

"Good omen, sir?"

"Ah, quite likely. Among other things, it appears to us now that Hitler has a possibly fatal strategic blind spot. He appears psychologically incapable of giving up ground once it has been won. Quite remarkable. The Germans have shown themselves ready to run the risk and pay the price to hold the Tunisian tip. In Africa, many of us see the same master hand that planned the attack on Stalingrad, which has brought upon the German armies the greatest disaster they've ever suffered in all their military history. "

"From where I sit, general, that sounds awfully rosy," Mitch offered skeptically.

"Perhaps. Perhaps not. In any event," Smythe-Browne continued, "Tell me how you got yourself assigned to the air corps in Africa."

For the next twenty minutes Mitch and Lucky explained how their fighter group had come to Algeria and what operations had been since. Later, over dinner, the two American pilots met an intriguing and entertaining young British lady.

Cateline Glendenbrook.

She'd soon be five years old, she declared in response to Lucky's question. From her table conversation it was clear she was intelligent well beyond her age and supremely self-confident. Smythe-Browne's wife told them the girl could spell her own name, write complete sentences, and read at a second grade level. Mitch could see the resemblance to Aynslee – the very slight cleft of her chin, the aristocratic tilt of her head, and the look in her eyes that both challenged and closely observed him at the same time. It came as no surprise when she asked him to read her a good night story as if it was more an order than a request.

"Leftenant Lindquist and I were just about to send out a recce to see if something untoward had happened to you," Smythe-Browne said when he finally returned to the general's library for an after dinner brandy. "I take it you were held captive by my granddaughter."

Mitch chuckled as he reached for the snifter being offered. "You might say that. On the other hand I could honestly say it's the first really adult conversation I've had since I left the States. That's one very sharp little girl." He took a sip of the brandy and continued after sitting down in the high-backed library chair. "She asked me to tell her a Bible story – specifically, a New Testament story. I tried the parable of the Good Samaritan, which it turns out she knows better than I do. I started to ad lib it as best I could but she kept interrupting and telling me that

I was getting it all wrong. She finally went over, pulled a Bible out of her bookcase, opened it, and pointed out where to start reading. She followed along to make sure I was reading it right."

"That's Cateline. Takes after her mother. Aynslee was the same way at her age."

"Yes, I could see the similarities," Mitch said contemplatively. "I'll be more careful around both of them from now on."

"General," Lindquist said after a brief moment. "Mitch was showing me around the place this afternoon and we ran across a green roadster in your barn."

"Of course, the MG, in the carriage house. I put it up on blocks two years ago when petrol became harder to come by and when it simply stopped running. I suppose someday I should get a mechanic to look at it, but for the time being I'd rather forgotten. Yes, it was a fun little auto – a '38 model TA roadster."

"Well, sir, Mitch seems to think he can get it running. Would you mind if we tinkered with it and maybe got it back on the road for you?"

"Have at it young man. Be my guest."

Early the next morning after breakfast the two pilots returned to the carriage house.

The MG was a classic little roadster, with a flat, square hood hinged down the center. Running boards flowed into sleek fenders fore and aft that gave the racy little machine a handsome line. For the first half-hour, while Lindquist located a bicycle pump and put air into the tires, Mitch sat on the dirt floor leaning against the wall reading through the owner's guide. He found a toolkit behind the driver's seat and adjusted the carburetors, cleaned and gapped spark plugs, cleaned fuel lines, and checked all the liquid reservoirs. He sent Lucky into a nearby town for a 5 gallon can of gas, Castrol engine oil and brake fluid. By mid afternoon they had it running.

Mrs. Smythe-Browne had come out onto the back porch to watch as they pulled the car out of the carriage house.

"If you're going to take the MG for a ride," the general's wife told them, "you're going to have to take Cateline with you."

"Sure, no problem," Mitch replied, waving the little girl over. "She can sit on Lucky's lap. Cateline jumped into the car's left seat and grabbed on to the handgip. Mitch guided the roadster around the house onto the lane leading to the front gate. Halfway there a British staff car turned onto the lane from the narrow road and started toward the house, pulling aside and stopping. A young woman in a deep blue WAAF uniform got out of the car and stood with her hands on her hips by the side of the road as the MG roared toward her.

"That WAAF doesn't look real happy, Mitch. I think she's trying to get us to stop."

"Smile and wave back, Lucky, but no matter what we're not going to stop. Hang on tight to our little passenger."

He could see out of the corner of his eye that Aynslee was monumentally displeased, glaring and waving frantically for them to stop. He wondered if she could see him smiling as they went by dragging a cloud of dust in their wake. When they came to the hard surfaced road and turned south, Mitch glanced back at the lane and saw she was standing there watching them with her hands still on her hips. *This is not going to be a lot of fun when we get back,* he thought. But he put it out of his mind for the next hour as they toured the countryside.

It was half past four and growing dark when they finally returned to Smythe-Browne's estate and parked the MG inside the carriage house.

"That's almost as fun as flying a P-38," Lucky said, as he uncoiled from the driver's seat. "That limey southpaw way of driving really takes some getting used to, doesn't it? I need to get one of these and take it home after the war."

"Can we do this again tomorrow, Mr. Mitch?" the little girl asked.

"Well, we'll just have to see, Cateline. I guess it's okay if –"

"It most certainly *is not* okay! You run along to the house right now, young lady."

Mitch turned around and looked into the furious eyes of Aynslee Glendenbrook.

"Hello, Aynslee," Mitch said airily. "It's good to see you again. Let me introduce – "

"You have some nerve!" she hissed at him, her eyes wide and infuriated. "If it's possible, you have poorer manners, greater indecorum, and even less civility than the last time you were here Leftenant Nolan."

"That's *Captain* Nolan now, Corporal Glendenbrook," he replied, smiling genially at her. "In the American Air Corps, enlisted personnel show respect to officers."

"In the British RAF officers are respected because they're worthy of it."

"You're saying I'm not?"

"I'm saying you have some nerve coming here and once again rudely taking property that is not yours and having your way as if you owned it. First my horse, and now this?! How dare you drive around in my husband's automobile. How dare you take my daughter for a ride without asking my permission. How dare you!"

"How dare I?... Your father said –"

"My father doesn't own this car, nor does he have any say over how I raise my daughter – what I let her do, where I let her go, and with whom I let her associate. Let me be very clear, *Captain* Nolan, as it appears I was not unambiguous enough the last time you were here. You are not to use my personal property. You are not to do anything with my daughter or take her anywhere without my express approval. I won't have it! Do you understand that very simple English?" She suddenly turned toward Lucky Lindquist and asked, "Who might you be?"

"Lieutenant Lindquist. Roy Lindquist. I'm a friend of Mitch's – we went to school together and now we're in the same fighter squadron."

"You look intelligent enough. Do you realize a man is known by the friends he chooses?"

Lindquist looked at Nolan quickly, his face a mixture of discomfort and amusement. "I'm proud to call Mitch my friend."

Aynslee glared at him and finally said, "Perhaps, then, I was wrong about your intellect."

"Now, look Aynslee," Mitch began, trying unsuccessfully to keep from smiling.

"Oh, so you find this amusing?"

"No, not really. I'm very sorry about the car," Mitch replied. *You're too pretty to be mad at me*, he thought to himself. "We really did think it belonged to your father. Didn't we, Lucky? Sure, we wanted to take it for a spin, but we also thought fixing it up would be a nice gesture and a way of saying 'thank you' to your dad for allowing us to spend a few days here."

Her eyes became scornfully expressive. "Oh? So now you're moving in?! How cheeky of you," she said nastily, placing her hands on her hips and thrusting out her chin.

He was suddenly angry and was sure it showed on his face as he turned to Lindquist and said, "Lucky, would you excuse us, please? I have a few things to say to Mrs. Glendenbrook that probably shouldn't be said in polite company." Lucky gave him a sideways glance, nodded quickly and walked outside looking back over his shoulder at them.

"You know something, sweetheart?" Mitch began when he was alone with the general's daughter. "I'm tired of apologizing to you for things that don't really require an apology. Instead of being thankful for a kind deed, you get mad at me and insult my friend. What's wrong with you lady? You're acting like a spoiled little rich brat who needs a good spanking."

"How dare you!"

"How dare I?! I'm not even warmed up yet."

"You arrogant simpleton. Just so typical of all you bloody Yanks – overpaid, oversexed, and unfortunately for us, over here. Did I mention overbearing? I should have!"

"Is that what you think? I'll tell you what, darling, when it comes to being haughty, condescending, pompous, pretentious – all that crap – you Brits are centuries… no, *millennia* ahead of us. And you, darlin', seem to be way ahead of the average Brit."

When she slapped his face, the act as well as the sound seemed to astonish her more than him; she gasped audibly and recoiled, her hand briefly covering her mouth. Mitch grabbed both her arms above the elbows and roughly drew her close, his lips a thin hard line, his eyes staring into hers. She struggled against him, but he held tight.

"Let me go you lout," she demanded through clenched teeth, again trying to pull away. "You will never be a gentleman."

"And you're an unpleasant, self-centered little brat who'll never grow up to be a lady."

Suddenly he released her, scowled and strode angrily from the carriage house.

*   *   *   *   *

"I tell you, Marv, that girl's really got him tied in knots," Lindquist said to his classmate as they walked through the fog-shrouded dark toward the airfield operations at RAF Station - St. Eval after pre-flighting their aircraft. "His mind is all messed up, and I think he's not in any shape to lead this flight back to Algeria."

"Come on Lucky. We've both seen him like this before; he's not going to let any girl mess up his mind and keep him from getting done what needs to be done. I saw the same thing you described happen with a gal from Albany halfway through baseball season our junior year. Never saw him play better – before or after."

"This isn't some game Marv, it's about getting all eight of us back to North Africa in one piece. I'm telling you, that English girl really got to him. Why else would he start a fight with that RAF pilot at Southampton, and then challenge him to a dogfight over the field for everybody to see? He hadn't even test flown that P-38. Marv, I'm telling you he's not right."

They had packed up and left General Smythe-Browne's country estate that night in the dark, immediately following the brief confrontation between Mitch and Aynslee Glendenbrook in the carriage house. The wild Jeep ride through the shadowy countryside of southern England had left Lucky wondering what had gotten into his classmate. By the time they arrived at Southampton, Lindquist was certain Nolan had lost his mind. Two days later, at noon, they picked up all their Lightnings and Mitch, as their aviation maintenance officer, checked the aircraft, declaring them flight-worthy. They left Southampton the next morning headed for St. Eval, near Lands End where they would spend the night before taking off on a twelve hundred mile over water flight.

The following morning, fog shrouded the airfield and heavy dew settled on their P-38s' windshields making it nearly impossible to see out.

"We crank at 0600 - everybody crank on me," Mitch said, beginning the briefing in the small shack beneath the RAF tower. "If the field is still closed due to fog, I'll monitor the tower and crank the moment it's open. The B-26, callsign *Fisherman*, flown by Captain "Squeak" Barnett, is our navigation aircraft. He's done this before so he knows the way to Gibraltar. The A-20 will fly tail end Charlie, but Perrone you keep your head on a swivel back there, too. Maintain three-minute separation between two flights of four. First flight is Red; second flight is White, and chalk assignments are the same as they were coming here from Southampton. Everybody make sure you get a copy. Both flight leads – me and "Marvelous" Marv – are responsible for their own navigation in case we get separated."

Marv Crosley looked at a briefing form provided by British airfield control. "Here's some good news. RAF Operations here on the field indicates we'll have good weather all the way, unlimited visibility, no Germans en route, and tailwinds."

"Well, we all know what that means," Lindquist said loudly. "Now we're sure to have crap weather, low viz., stiff headwinds and the whole damned Luftwaffe on our tail."

"Thanks for that bit of encouragement, Lucky," Mitch replied when the murmuring from his pilots subsided. "En route – very loose finger 4 formation, max altitude at or below 200 feet to keep the German radar from spotting us. Cruise speed – 170. Engine settings – 1600 RPM and just enough manifold pressure to stay in formation. Keep away from jockeying the throttles and we'll all have plenty enough gas to make it to Gibraltar with a decent safety margin. All aircraft are loaded with just a hundred rounds of .50 cal. and twenty-five 20mm. cannon. Sorry, it's all they'll give us for a ferry flight, so that means we avoid rather than engage enemy aircraft. Radio silence the whole way until we're in the pattern at Gibraltar – unless enemy aircraft are sighted. At that point, Lucky and I will release drop tanks and cover the flight while everybody else continues. If it's more than the two of us can handle, we'll figure that out when it happens. No overflight of Portugal or Spain at any time – they're officially still neutral but you never know. Be especially careful of that when we get to Gibraltar. Flight time is seven and a half hours – eight with headwinds thirty or less. Pretty simple. Time is now zero five one zero. The chow hall has been open for ten minutes. Get a good breakfast. Questions?"

"A comment, actually," Lindquist said, standing up and starting to pass out flashlights to all the pilots. "These are courtesy of our fine friends in the RAF – for those of us who can't hold it for seven or eight hours."

"Where did you get those?" Mitch asked.

"You don't want to know. But as someone who made this flight before – a couple of days before last Christmas, I can assure you this thing will come in real handy. We're all sitting on an inflatable rubber dinghy for this over water flight, right? That puts the relief tube cup six or seven inches too far away, and that's a real problem when you have to hold it for seven or eight hours. These flashlight barrels are ol' Lucky's urinal extenders. Once you remove both ends and the batteries, they're just about the right length."

"And how did you learn this?"

"The hard way. You know that smell that's still in Ricky's airplane back at Telerghma? He didn't have one of these back about four months ago the last time we flew from this very field to North Africa. Providentially, I did. One guy, identity to remain secret, used a towel he'd wrapped some personal belongings in as a – "

"Lucky, I want to thank you for telling us all that right before breakfast."

"Trust me, Mitch, and the rest of you guys, too. You'll be real glad I gave you this thing long before we reach the coast of Spain."

Forty minutes later, all the pilots were in their cockpits watching the flight leader and looking around the fog shrouded airfield. Just as the tower gave Mitch the light signal indicating the field was now open for flight operations, a jeep rolled up to the front of his P-38 and stopped. A tall, strapping Brit sergeant armed with a Sten gun got out and climbed up on the wing next to the American mechanic.

"An important note for you, sir," the British enlisted man said, handing over a small white envelope with *Mitch* written on it in flowing feminine script.

"What's this and why is it so important?" Mitch asked, looking quickly at his watch and seeing he was already two minutes late starting his engines.

"Haven't a clue, sir. But the corporal over there could probably tell you." Mitch looked beyond the man's shoulder and saw through the fog Aynslee Glendenbrook in her deep blue uniform standing beneath St. Eval's tower. "She says she's hoping for a reply, captain."

Mitch started to open the envelope but glanced at his watch, knowing all the eyes in his flight were on him. Quickly, he put the letter in the side pocket of his flight jacket.

"Tell her I didn't have time to read it. Tell her... tell her I'll probably get around to it sometime in the next few weeks. Right now, I've got a mission to fly."

Mitch motioned for the sergeant to climb down, and then set the throttle of the left engine to start position. He stole a quick glance at her just as the prop began turning.

Chapter 23

"I've never heard of – what did you call it? A Ponzi scheme? What in the world is that?" Denise asked her daughter after the waiter deftly left the check at Ashby's elbow and departed.

The four of them – Denise, Erika, Randall and Michelle – were holding down their usual luncheon table set aside for them by the *maître d* on every first Thursday at *Kavanagh's* restaurant. It was a routine Denise had begun several months earlier on Erika's birthday.

"A Ponzi scheme is a fraudulent investment scam that promises to pay investors from their own money or funds provided by subsequent investors," Erika replied between sips of coffee. "It doesn't include the idea of profit being earned by an individual or organization running a business to pay dividends or returns. It's based on the idea that whoever is running the plan can get more and more investors to invest more and more money to keep the whole thing afloat, so it's destined to certain and eventual collapse."

Denise wasn't sure that she understood all her daughter was saying and cast a questioning glance at Ashby.

"Erika seems to think that the whole idea of Social Security is somehow a big fraud," the young lawyer said.

"Well it is! It's grand larceny on a national scale being run by our government!"

Ashby took a deep breath and smiled paternally at her. "That's a little bit exaggerated, don't you think Erika?"

"Not in the least. Didn't you even read the position paper I gave to the Senator about it?"

"Of course I did."

"Then why don't you agree with me?"

"I'm not saying you don't have some good points, but… it was just a little heavy on the hyperbole, don't you think? Calling the administration and the Congress a criminal conspiracy probably isn't going to garner a lot of support for your position."

"Did you really say that Erika?" Denise asked, obviously surprised.

"Know no fear when truth and right are in jeopardy – isn't that what dad always says?"

"Your father says a lot of things – he has a pithy statement or a homespun homily for just about everything. Isn't there something treasonous about calling the government criminal?"

"Denise, have you heard from Dave lately?" Michelle interjected, hoping to steer the conversation away from what was becoming something of a heated debate between Erika, her mother and young Randall Ashby. She had read Erika's position paper to her father and thought it had much good substance and a lot of sound thinking woven throughout her argument, but the young lawyer was right about the language overshadowing its substance.

"He writes now and then," Denise replied offhandedly and quickly changed the subject. "I'm thinking about going back to New York for Easter – there's always a very nice spring cotillion in Oyster Bay. I haven't been for years – since I was in high school."

"You're going to a big social affair like that out on the Island by yourself? Without dad?" Erika asked, surprised.

Denise smiled halfheartedly. "Well, he went off to his war without me, didn't he?"

Ashby saw the look come over Erika's face and quickly said to her and Michelle, "We're running a little bit late. If we're going to complete pulling that package together for the Senator before his hearing this afternoon, we had best get cracking. I'll take care of the check while you two get the car and meet me out front."

They said their goodbyes at the table. A few minutes later, after finishing the last of her coffee, Denise left the restaurant and turned left toward the Capitol building. A half block away, she was just about to unlock the driver's side door when she heard a voice from behind.

"Excuse me, but I don't think you're going to get very far with that flat tire."

Denise was startled, and looked up in the direction of the voice. He was handsome, and middle-aged; his voice was pleasant, his smile reassuring.

"May I give you a lift, or a hand with that? I'm sorry if I frightened you, but with the price of rubber and the short supply of replacement car tires I thought I should warn you."

"Yes, of course. Thank you – very thoughtful of you," she said absently, frowning and looking irritably at the passenger side flat. "I guess I'll have to call a tow truck."

"Maybe not," the well-dressed man said. "You wouldn't happen to be from nearby in Maryland would you?"

"No. Why do you ask?" Denise said, wondering about the odd question.

"I was hoping that maybe you were a constituent, and that by helping you out I might convince you to cast your vote for me in the fall election. Trevor Callahan, U.S. Representative from the 4th District in Maryland. I don't expect it to be a close contest, but one never knows."

"So you're saying you won't help me because I can't vote for you," Denise said amiably.

"No, not exactly."

"What exactly *are* you saying then?"

"Actually, I'm not saying another thing – I'm asking a question before I get myself in trouble. Can you open the trunk for me while I get out your spare tire and jack?"

"I can't ask you to do that," Denise told him. "You'll ruin your suit."

"Better to ruin one's suit than to alienate a potential voter. Politicians credo. Are you going to open that trunk or not?"

They chatted as Callahan proceeded to change the tire. It seemed he, too, was fond of *Kavanagh's* and frequently ate lunch there when time allowed; he recommended several entrées she had not yet tried as well as some of the best Rhine wines from the restaurant's rapidly dwindling wine cellar. He seemed genuinely pleased to hear her daughter was working for a fellow Democrat, telling her with intentionally exaggerated seriousness, "Don't ever vote for a Republican – only we Democrats really care about people. You'd never find one of my so-called 'colleagues' from across the aisle stopping to help you like this."

"I thought you were doing this in hopes of buying my vote?" Denise said, smiling at him.

The congressman looked at her out of the corner of his eye. "I guess I should admit I'm not really doing this out of the goodness of my heart. It's because my Democrat friends would force me to change parties and become one of those nasty old Republicans if I didn't."

Denise laughed out loud and said, "My father is very involved in the Republican party."

"Let me just say, if you're still living at home you should escape immediately," he replied with an exaggerated seriousness. "Let me suggest this: I'll have my staff assistant get it fixed and drop it by your house. I'll have the tire repaired and you either move to my district and vote for me, or find a Republican voter in my district and put in a good word for me." Callahan stood up and waved down the street. "My assistant. I should have had him do the heavy lifting here.. Do we have a deal?"

"I think I got the best of it, Trevor. But yes."

He reached into his coat pocket and retrieved a business card. "Here, write your address on the back of my card and I'll have my assistant drop off your repaired tire this evening, if you're going to be home. Please don't think me forward, but do you mind giving me your phone number so he can call ahead of time to ensure you'll be there."

"Thank you very much. And people say there are no gentlemen in D.C."

"Actually, there are darn few of us left," he replied conspiratorially, causing her to laugh.

Moments later, after Denise drove away, Callahan's assistant pulled into the vacant parking spot and placed the flat tire into the trunk of the Congressman's car.

"Andrew, put the valve stem back in and pump the tire back up after you drop me off. Not a word of this to anyone; do I make myself clear?" The congressman smiled to himself as he got into the passenger seat and his assistant drove him back to the Capitol building.

Harrison was right, he said to himself – *she is… very attractive*.

*   *   *   *   *

The Scilly Isles off Lands End slipped beneath them as the eight P-38s and two bombers settled into loose formation after taking off individually on instruments.

They had departed from RAF Station St. Eval with a thousand foot ceiling and three miles visibility, barely enough for visual flying; but, within a half hour the horizontal visibility increased even as the ceiling lowered to five hundred feet above the Atlantic. They settled down for the long grind on the deck at two hundred feet altitude, went into their long-range cruise settings, and listened to radio silence.

Mitch looked around the formation and down at the sea. The waves indicated the wind was out of the northwest which would add a tailwind component and shorten the flight. He guessed the wind at fifteen knots and thought it would pick up a little as the day wore on. After doing another quick scan of the cockpit instruments, he pulled out his E6B and calculated their airspeed on their current heading and how far they would travel each hour. This he recorded in the small green notebook he placed in the breast pocket of his flight suit, and did another quick scan of the instruments.

With the ferry flight from Burbank across the Atlantic to Telergma only weeks behind him, he hadn't looked forward to this long haul from England to North Africa. By the end of his earlier ferry mission, he was totally exhausted and determined not to try that again. But, this was a short flight by comparison – if sitting on a compressed rubber dinghy for seven and a half hours could be considered short. Only two hours into their flight his seat was getting sore and his legs were showing signs of wanting to go to sleep. He stretched his back and arms, rubbed his calf muscles, and stomped his feet to keep his circulation going.

Mitch kept himself alert by recalculating their airspeed and time enroute every half hour. In between he made notes to himself about each aircraft they'd picked up and the maintenance gigs requiring attention as soon as they landed back at Telergma, before putting them up for combat missions. None of the aircraft in the flight had even had their guns bore-sighted – that worried him. In the event they did meet up with any Germans it would require good luck and even shorter range shooting. But, he consoled himself – it was a big ocean and an even bigger sky. The chances were very slim of running across German fighters this far out at the edge of the Bay of Biscay, and even slimmer that German radar could pick them up while they continued wave hopping.

At midmorning, he snacked on a handful of stale crackers and sipped tomato juice from a canteen which left a harsh metallic after-taste; he hoped the in-flight sandwich the St. Eval mess hall had fixed them would be better. When Mitch looked out the window toward

Lindquist's plane he saw his friend lighting up a cigarette and for the briefest instant wished he had one, not so much because he liked the taste – he'd tried it a couple of times and hated it – but it would give him something to occupy himself for the next four hours.

There was something besides his maintenance notes and the navigation exercise every half hour – Aynslee Glendenbrook's letter. As curious as he was, he really didn't want to read it. He reached into the side pocket of his flight jacket and pulled out the small envelope the Brit sergeant had handed him at St. Eval. He placed it on top of the radio console between his legs and left it there for the next hour, telling himself he really wasn't interested in anything Aynslee Glendenbrook might have to say about anything. She was short-tempered, mean-spirited and married. *Poor bastard. Better him than me*, he thought.

Reluctantly, he opened the envelope and extracted the card.

Dear Mitch,

My behaviour toward you now on two occasions has been unquestionably horrid. I owe you an apology, and I do hope you will accept it.

I shall not make excuses for the inexcusable but will only say your attempts at kindness in hindsight now seem utterly genuine and honourably intentioned.

My reactions, on the other hand, were ill-mannered and appallingly boorish. Please forgive me.

I do look forward with sincere anticipation to a future time when you do me the favour of making amends and delivering this expression of regret in person.

Hoping you accept my heartfelt apology,
Aynslee

What is with this girl, he thought and quickly stuffed the small card back in his flight jacket. For the first time in his young life he was completely stumped. A few minutes later he pulled the card out again, read it slowly and mulled it over before jamming it back in the flight jacket. He remembered the first time he'd seen her and their brief, pleasant conversation at the entrance to her father's estate. How enormously different she had been after that. *And why am I even worried about it?* he asked himself.

"What's going on with her?" he said aloud, the first of many questions he asked himself over the next half hour.

He had more questions than answers and while he knew the best and honorable course was to steer completely clear of her, there was something magnetic about her. *She's off-limits. She's married, Nolan. Though the old school's Honor Code didn't address it, that would be frowned upon. The ol' man wouldn't think much of it either – he knows the girl and her father. Nope, give them all a wide berth – a real wide berth, son.* Mitch unscrewed the cap from his canteen and took another sip of the foul-tasting contents as he double checked his radio was on channel D and the volume was turned full up. Then, against his will, he thought of Aynslee.

"A-20 on fire!"

Perrone's radio call snapped him out of his reverie. Nolan spilled some of his tomato juice in a mad scramble to charge his guns, firewall the rpm and throttle until detonation set in, and began a sharp left turn toward the A-20 at the rear of the flight. Lucky had anticipated and was already easing into a left turn to stay on his wing. Just as they completed the turn, Mitch saw the A-20 hit the water on fire.

Beaufighters? Mitch wondered, but quickly realized the four twin-engined aircraft trailing their ferry flight were actually Ju-88s. Immediately three of them pulled up and entered the cloud base while the fourth one continued on probably planning on working his way up the flight, knocking them off one by one from back to front. Suddenly the lone Junkers fighter bomber also pulled up into the low overcast as Nolan and Lindquist closed head on from two miles out. Mitch jettisoned his drop tanks, pulled back on the yoke and climbed into the cloud with his wing man in tight formation; both of them broke out above the overcast in a matter of seconds almost dead astern of an -88 and closing rapidly.

Lindquist jettisoned his drop tanks, entered a shallow left turn and closed to within 100 yards before firing one short burst exploding the German's right engine. Pieces flew off the wing and he leveled just on top of the overcast. The two P-38s throttled back, flying formation with the crippled German aircraft for another minute until he descended and reentered the overcast. They followed him down through the clouds breaking out a few hundred feet above the sea and watched the fighter bomber hit the water nose down and come apart.

Climbing back up into the overcast they broke out on top but the rest of the German element was gone. Mitch turned back to his course to intercept the *Fisherman* flight, came back to long-range cruise settings and gave Lucky the thumbs up OK sign. Lindquist, on the other hand, was madly signaling that things *were not* okay with him. After exchanging many hand signals, Mitch concluded Lucky's props had run away – inability to throttle back would mean higher fuel consumption, and without the extra fuel from his drop tanks his chances of making Gibraltar were slim to none.

"*Fishermen,* this is Red one," Mitch announced over the air, breaking radio silence. "Enemy aircraft no longer a factor. Everybody tighten up on *Fisherman lead.* Red two has an engine problem. I'll be sticking with him. Out."

Nolan and Lindquist again descended through the overcast, leveled at two hundred feet, and altered course eastward to pick up the coast of Portugal in the event Lindquist ran out of fuel. For the next hour they flew on in silence ten miles off the beach until Lindquist called.

"Red one, this is Red two. Not gonna make it. Will find an airfield and hope the folks are as neutral as they claim. Be seeing you later. Sayonara."

Mitch watched in silence as his classmate waggled his wings and slowly turned left headed inland toward a hopefully welcoming Portugal. He wanted to say something, but couldn't find the words, and reconciled himself to watching the Lightning pulling away from him and disappearing into the haze soon after crossing the coastline.

The next few hours seemed to last an eternity.

Mitch settled back alone in the big sky over the Atlantic and busied himself with trying to pick up where he had left off in his personal navigation. He decided the best course was to continue flying within sight of land, hugging the coast until it turned decidedly east and follow it to "The Rock." That decision made, he sat back to remember all the good times he and Lucky had had over the years at West Point.

He was one of the true characters in the school's long and storied history. They had been together since the first day of Beast Barracks – July 1, 1936…

After that long and bewildering summer, they had both been assigned to the 2nd Regiment's Company D. It was during the first half of plebe year that Lindquist earned the nickname Lucky and his reputation was cemented for an ability to dodge disasters which claimed many of their classmates. The years that followed served only to enhance his standing as the luckiest cadet in the class of '40, and maybe the most fortunate since the time of Thayer.

The memories flowed back in his mind's eye now in pleasant visual kaleidoscopes, running together and tumbling over one another like currents in a swift moving stream, the images like rocks roiling the water. He saw mental pictures of games on the dusty skin field just north of the field house down by the Hudson, hops at Cullum Hall after football games, triumphs and disappointments on Doubleday Field, pranks in the barracks of Central Area after taps. The trip to Bermuda with him and Marv was their most recent memorable episode…

The loss of pilots in the squadron had not bothered him as much as he'd expected. Yet nothing had prepared him for seeing Lindquist slowly disappear into the haze over the Portuguese coast as he had. Mitch found it impossible to think he'd never again see Lucky or hear his laugh again.

Three hours later, he touched down on the British field at Gibraltar and rejoined the *Fisherman* flight for the final leg to Telerghma the following day.

When they returned to the squadron that next afternoon everybody wanted to hear about their trip. Harley Vaughn had sent one of the guys on a liquor run to Cairo – an attempt to raise everyone's spirits as they had lost two more pilots while the ferry flight crews were gone. Over drinks, they told their tales of the British women they'd met in London who'd warmed them following the long, cold Gooney Bird flight from North Africa.

Nobody pressed Nolan for details about Lucky – and for that he was grateful.

Chapter 24

"So, everybody in II Corps from the deputy commander on down is still in utter shock," Omar Bradley said to Dave Nolan as they drank coffee in the corps headquarters located at Djebel Kouif. The old empty, unheated French schoolhouse – long ago stripped of furnishings and plumbing by Arab looters – sat in the middle of a small Algerian town twenty-five miles' northwest of the Kasserine Pass, a two mile wide gap in the Grand Dorsal chain of the Atlas Mountains in west central Tunisia. "George is about as different from Lloyd Fredendall as any commander could be. He's already turned the Corps around. Just in time, I think."

"He's the one I'd have picked. How'd he do it?"

"Rather than waiting for the word to filter down through the ranks, George looked for a 'something' to instantly notify every G.I. there was a new commander. He found what he was looking for in the corps headquarters mess hall hours and in his own personal interpretation of the Army's uniform regulations."

Nolan smiled. "I remember the first time I met him he jumped on me for being out of uniform. He called me slovenly and my battalion undisciplined. It was a novel introduction."

"In this situation," Bradley said, "George knew before his arrival that both the corps headquarters and the units assigned to it were riddled with sloppy discipline. In his mind, the symbol of that perversion was the popular and omnipresent, wool beanie cap. He immediately banned it. He replaced it with the steel helmet and required every soldier regardless of rank and organization to always wear it. In addition, every soldier is now required to wear leggings and neckties, even front-line combat soldiers. And the fines for not doing so are stiff."

"How stiff?" Nolan asked.

"Fifty dollars for officers and twenty-five for enlisted men. The word spread like wildfire and every officer and man in II Corps was fighting mad when the new rules came out – only they were mad at Patton more than the Germans. They still are, pretty much."

Dave smiled again. "That's the way I felt the first time I met him."

"The most irate were the officers here at Corps headquarters. George ordered breakfast served before dawn rather than at midmorning."

"You mean the staff can't sleep in until noon?" Dave asked, raising his eyebrows in mock surprise. "No wonder they hate him!" He took a sip of coffee and asked, "Was Kasserine as bad as I've heard?"

"I don't know what was sent back to Washington, but yes, it was bad. Real bad. That's why Ike replaced Fredendall with Patton last week."

The battle at Kasserine Pass was the first large-scale meeting of American and German forces in the war and from all accounts had been a debacle. The relatively untested and poorly-led American troops suffered heavy casualties and were pushed back over fifty miles from their positions west of Faid Pass in the initial days of the battle. Reinforced by British reserves, the Americans finally held the exits through mountain passes in western Tunisia, but the effect on American morale and British confidence in their ally had been devastating.

"Patton's assignment I understand, but why am I here?" Nolan asked, trying to shake off the exhaustion of a nearly non-stop twenty-five hours of flying from Georgia, through Newfoundland, England and finally on to North Africa. "I've still got a division to train for the next four or five months."

"Actually, Dave, that's going to be cut short. We need the 12th here now."

"Brad, we're not ready yet. The division was formed just three months ago."

"I know, but we don't have the luxury of time. Washington says you're the only division-sized unit back in the states currently far enough along to help make a difference over here. Ike knows you, your assistant division commander and two of your three regimental commanders; he's familiar with what each of you is capable of."

"Nobody can form and train a division into combat effectiveness this fast, Brad."

"Ike thinks you can. You know the old saw – a unit mirrors its commander. That's why he asked for you months ago and why he bent Marshall's ear more recently. We need the 12th to shore up II Corps in the short term. The corps now consists of the 1st, the 9th, and the 34th Infantry Divisions, along with the 1st Armored Division. And the 9th and the 34th each have a regiment detailed elsewhere. We're shorthanded to begin with and each of our division-sized elements are now understrength. We also need you for the next operation after North Africa."

Their conversation was interrupted by the shrieking of sirens outside and the sound of a procession of half tracks and armored scout cars wheeling into the dingy square opposite the school. Bradley and Nolan stepped outside in time to see the lead car come to a stop. George Patton was standing up in the front seat of the armored car like an ancient Roman charioteer, holding on to the windshield and scowling into the wind. His jaw strained against the web strap of the polished two-starred steel helmet. At last he jumped down from the armored car, walked up to Dave Nolan and glared at him from inches away.

"What the hell is this, Brad?! Did Ike send me another damned spy?" Patton asked unhappily. "Am I going to have both you and this half-assed has-been battalion commander from a long ago war looking over my shoulder and reporting back to him?"

"Dave is here to get read-in on operations before his division arrives."

Without taking his eyes off Nolan, Patton said, "Tell him he's out of uniform."

Dave smiled, knowing that Patton was deliberately trying to shock him, just as he had set out to jolt II Corps upon assuming command. It was clear the pre-Kasserine days under Lloyd Fredendall had ended, and a new era under Patton had begun.

"Dave's not the only one out of uniform," Bradley was saying as he handed over an envelope. "President Roosevelt decided to promote you to lieutenant general and recommended it to the senate. But remember, it's not effective until they vote approval."

"The hell you say Brad," Patton replied, his face lighting up as he opened the envelope and read the note from Eisenhower. He turned to his aide, nodded and said, "Chuck, time to unfurl the new banner."

They followed Patton inside the school to his office where Major Codman went to a closet and retrieved a red flag with three gold stars embroidered across the middle. After replacing the two star flag behind Patton's desk, the aide reached into a desk drawer and pulled out a pair of three-star insignia handing one to Bradley and the other to Nolan.

"You know, Brad, I think if George were promoted to full admiral in the Tibetan Navy one of his aides would have the appropriate insignia of rank on hand," Nolan said while pinning the three stars on Patton's left collar. Hugh Gaffey, Patton's hand picked Chief of Staff took a picture of the impromptu ceremony and then handed the camera over to Colonel Monk Dickson so he could join the ceremony and have more pictures taken.

"I want those negatives, Hugh," Patton said when it was over. "I won't have photographs circulating around II Corps of me standing next to Nolan while he's not wearing a tie and a steel pot – unless he's got $50 on him so you can take a picture of him handing it to me."

Patton produced a bottle of whiskey and poured each of them a shot before toasting himself and his promotion. A little while later, he talked privately with Bradley and Nolan.

"How long before your division gets here, Nolan?" Patton asked, sitting heavily in his large leather swivel chair.

"Three weeks at the earliest if we started loading out today. More likely five or six."

"Then you're going to miss all the fun that's left in North Africa. If it takes you a month, you and your division will miss being in on the action when I push that magnificent bastard Rommel into the Bay of Tunis."

Patton had not changed at all since they'd first met one hot and muggy afternoon during the Ste. Mihiel Salient operation during the Great War. The contradictions in Patton's character continued to bewilder him. While he was profane, he was also reverent. While he strutted imperiously, he knelt humbly and quietly before God. He believed that profanity was the most convincing medium of communicating with his troops – or anybody else, as Dave had learned on French battlefields and stateside posts soon after. Yet, he commissioned prayers be written by the unit chaplain. It seemed Patton had never learned to command himself.

"Brad," Patton was saying, "This morning I talked with Bedell Smith and told him to clear it with Ike to make you my new deputy commander. He said he would. I'm expecting Ike will concur and then you can stop being a spy in my cabinet. It's all right that you were Ike's legman when Fredendall was here, but now I'm calling the tune and paying the piper. Clear?"

"If Ike okays it."

"He will. And you Nolan? What the hell are you going to do?"

"Find an M-1, commandeer one of your armored cars and a driver, and get a look at the lay of the land – spend some time with Terry Allen in the Big Red One and Manton Eddy in the 9th. I want to find out what they're doing and how they're doing it."

"Don't get in the way of my commanders."

"You don't have to worry about that, George."

"You've always worried me, Nolan. And get a damned tie!"

*   *   *

Mitch Nolan looked around the clear noonday sky 10,000 feet above the Mediterranean. The twenty-nine P-38s he could see patrolling the box around sixteen B-25s accounted for nearly all the flightworthy aircraft of the 96th and 97th Squadrons.

Below his right wing he could make out the tiny volcanic island of Pantelleria in the Strait of Sicily. The intelligence briefing from Group said the underground hangars dug out of the volcanic rock were capable of housing as many as eighty fighter planes. As the Afrika Korps was getting squeezed tighter and tighter into the northern tip of Tunisia, it was rumored a number of the German fighters had relocated to the island. Since the island was only 30 miles from northeast Tunis and 60 miles from the south coast of Sicily, it made a perfect place from which the Germans could mount fighter sweeps over the North African battlefields as well as protect their convoys of troops and supplies.

This day the mission of the B-25s from the 321st Bomber Group, was to locate and sink as many German supply boats and troop transports as possible.

As they continued to the north and west of Pantelleria, Mitch continued his scan of the sky, every now and then looking out his left side thinking that's where Lucky Lindquist should be flying his wing. It had been almost two weeks since he saw Lindquist's plane disappear into the haze over Portugal. Neither Harley Vaughn's liquor nor pep talks from Marv Crosley and others had raised his spirits. Losing Lucky had been the worst moment of his entire time in the Mediterranean area, and no matter what he did or how hard he tried, it seemed impossible to shake his melancholy.

"Tally-ho... two convoys at eleven o'clock, twenty miles," came the call over the radio from the B-25 mission leader. *"Element one will take the far convoy further to the west, element two take the near."*

The first eight B-25s began a slow turn to the left while the remainder broke right and headed down covered closely by the 97th fighter squadron aircraft. A minute later the first eight bombers began a steep descent toward the nine small ships now directly ahead of them. Out of the corner of his eye, Mitch could see six audacious – or were they suicidal? – He115 floatplanes rising to attack the bombers being guarded by Lightnings of the 96th. Turning the tables on them, the White flight of Dixie Sloan, Bill Rawson, Crosley and Perrone turned head on into the floatplanes who tucked tail, dove to the surface and headed towards Tunisia with the four P-38s in hot pursuit.

The first eight B-25s made runs in elements of two bombers dropping their bomb loads, setting three of the freighters burning furiously while another, trailing a large black cloud, was left nearly dead in the water. But the bombers had taken almost a half-hour to complete their mission giving enemy fighters time to intervene. As the last two bombers came off their final run and started a climbing turn back towards North Africa, Mitch looked around the sky and thought there had to be at least four dozen German fighters descending on them.

For what seemed an eternity the dozen 96th squadron pilots fended off a mixed enemy force of Me 109s, FW 190s, Me 110s, JU 88s, and at least one unidentified Italian aircraft. The fight quickly degenerated into a melee of individual dogfights from the surface to 20,000 feet.

Hawes shot down a JU 88; Harley Vaughn downed another not long after. Immediately after the fight began, Linc Jones lost power in one engine and dove for the surface headed home. Mitch saw Claude Kinsley and his wingman, Ed Anderson zoom by in a forty-five degree dive on the tail of a two seat Italian fighter, both of them firing away.

From his right front, tracers looking like exploding golf balls rushed straight at him but missed high. He turned into the Focke Wulf firing at him and it immediately rolled onto its back and went beneath him. A P-38 flashed directly in front of him with a -109 on its tail; he got off a short burst and the Messerschmidt broke away. He saw another Messerschmidt off to his left on fire and spinning out of control toward the sea. Twisting and turning aircraft were everywhere he looked in all quadrants, and he wondered, *how in the world am I ever going to survive this?*

But then, like most of the action he'd seen so far, a sky that had been filled with enemy and friendly aircraft was suddenly empty.

Way off to the southwest he could see the bombers closing up in formation and not far away twin tailed Lockheeds were grouping up and covering them. Before long they were all crossing the North African coast near Bone; twenty minutes later the bombers broke off and the P-38s headed for Telerghma.

At the debriefing they learned everybody had survived the ordeal. Linc Jones and Jackson had made it back to Telerghma on single engines. Nikodem had landed at Bone low on fuel and Frank Duncan had crash landed there with severe damage to both engines. Several of the Lightnings had been holed but that was only minor damage. They had downed two JU 88s, eight Me 109s, damaged another and chalked up two 'probables'. Kinsley was given credit for one Italian fighter after winning a coin toss with his wing man since both had hit the plane just as it caught fire and came apart. It was Kinsley's fifth victory making him the third 'ace' in the squadron along with Harley Vaughn and Dixie Sloan.

All in all, it had been their best day yet.

But to Mitch Nolan it made little difference. He was glad everyone had gotten back alive and that the damage had been less than anyone would have thought possible considering the odds they'd gone up against. Still, he could not shake the disappointment of not having Lucky flying his wing.

The pilots in the squadron each received a shot of 'mission liquor' from Harley Vaughn, trooped back to their tent, dropped flying gear on their cots and made their way to the 82nd Group mess hall. What they found shocked all of them.

At one of the large squadron tables, behind a row of bottles sat Lindquist sipping wine and casually smoking a cigarette.

"Heard you fellas had yourself a pretty good day today. Hope you saved some Krauts for me," Lucky said nonchalantly.

"Lindquist! What are you doin' here, boy?" Sloan asked, caustically. "Nolan here tol' us all you was either MIA or POW. We had us a good cry, divied up what little you had in your footlocker that was worth havin' and took your name off the scoreboard."

"You're just a little early on all that, Dixie." They crowded around him as he poured wine for each of them and answered their questions. "Had a runaway prop just off the coast of Spain after we chased those JU 88s away from the ferry flight. There was no way I was going to make it to Gibraltar, especially after I dropped my tanks, so I just headed into Portugal and found an airstrip near a nice little town. The folks there seemed friendly enough but the police hauled me off to jail for four nights. On the fifth day this high ranking officer and his entourage showed up in no small convoy. I've never seen a uniform like the one he was wearing. All white. Huge epaulets. A chest full of medals. And a hat with so much gold braid on it he must have been Chief of Staff of the *world*."

Lindquist took a long swig from one of the wine bottles and continued.

"He was fascinated with my P-38. Every morning he'd show up and have me explain everything while he sat in the pilot seat. After a few days he declared that he wanted to learn how to fly it. I told him that was impossible because the plane was broken. But that didn't satisfy him – he just ordered me to fix it. Well, hell, I'm no mechanic like Mitch Nolan but he insisted. So I monkeyed around for a few hours and couldn't figure out at all what happened or how to fix it. I got real frustrated and took a rubber mallet and pounded the hell out of the prop hub once I took the spinner off. And guess what? It worked. When I tried the engine again it ran fine. Surprised me! Since I didn't have any gas I told that ten star general there was still no way I was going to be able to teach him how to fly.

"Early next evening a tank wagon shows up with aviation fuel, so I filled it up. Right away the colonel or general, or whatever he was, insisted on flying. I convinced him that was only going to get him killed, but I did let him sit on my lap and we taxied it up and down the runway once. Then I told him I could demonstrate how to fly it, give him and the people in the town a little airshow, and then he could try it himself. Next morning I cranked it up, waved to the crowd that showed for an air show and took off due west. I turned left at the ocean and followed the coast until I found Gibraltar about three hours later. And here I am."

"It's a wonder you didn't crash land into a pot of gold at the end of a rainbow," Marv Crosley said, shaking his head. "Never seen a body with your luck."

"Luck? I don't know," Lindquist said wistfully, looking conflicted. "Didn't want to leave, but had to because of my highly developed sense of responsibility. A lot of pretty gals in that town fighting over bringing me my food when I was in jail, but I was willing to sacrifice my love life for you guys because that airplane was needed for the good of the service."

Nolan picked up a full bottle and tried to pour it over his wingman's head but was stopped by Sloan and Ricky Zubarik before he wasted some really excellent wine.

*   *   *   *

The dull green wing of the C-47 dipped, dipped again and the plane's airframe gave a long mournful groan like aged oak timbers. *Maybe that's why they call these flying machines ships*, Dave Nolan reflected, looking out of the window at the dull monochromatic landscape of Algeria. It was the most desolate place he'd ever seen.

Soon he could hear the squealing of electric motors and the grinding of gears as the trailing edge flaps dropped into place; next came the bumps and thumping of the landing gear lowering and locking into place. Presently the pitch of the engines dropped in preparation for landing and he could feel the onset of the always unsettling sensation of his stomach floating. As efficient and time-saving as it was, he was sure he'd not ever come to the time or place in his life when he found flying pleasurable – useful, of course; enjoyable, probably never.

When the Gooney Bird stopped and the large cargo door was opened, Colonel Covington and three of his staff were waiting to greet him.

"Welcome to the 82nd Fighter Group, general. My staff and I are prepared to brief you on recent operations and future plans. We're at your disposal, sir."

Dave returned Covington's salute and led him aside. "Colonel, I'm just passing through. I'm not here to get a briefing or interrupt your business. Just want to say a quick hello to my son and I'll be on my way. His name is Mitch Nolan and if you'll point me in his direction I'll get out of your hair and you can go back to more important matters than squiring me around."

"Of course, general. His squadron is headquartered a half mile that direction," the group commander said pointing west down the flight line. "You should be able to locate him there. His squadron isn't scheduled for a mission today, although anything can happen at any moment. You can use my Jeep, sir."

"That I'll let you do for me. Won't need a driver, and you'll have it back in an hour."

He drove down the flight line passing a long line of empty revetments until he came to a sign picturing an angry jackrabbit wearing boxing gloves leaping over a cactus plant. Under the circular insignia was written '*The Slugging Desert Jackrabbits – 96th Fighter Squadron*'. A little further on he came to a P-38 where two mechanics were installing a plexiglas cover over something on the right side wing. He stopped and got the attention of the older enlisted man.

"Sergeant, I'm looking for one of your pilots – Lieutenant Nolan. Know where he is? Or, can you point me to where I might find your commander or operations officer?"

The mechanic turned around, did a double take when he saw the stars on Dave's helmet. "Sir, that'd be *Captain* Nolan, and this is his airplane. He's in the cockpit right now helping us run some wiring for this new gun camera layout."

"How about telling him his old dad would like a word with him?"

"Yes, sir." The sergeant scrambled up onto the left wing, said something into the cockpit, and then helped Mitch out from an awkward position inside.

"Welcome to Telerghma, general," Mitch said as he stood on the wing wiping his hands on a shop rag and looking down on his father. "This isn't the end of the world, but you can see it from here. Are you lost or just trying to get as far away from my mother as you can?"

"A little of both, I reckon," Dave replied, smiling. "Get down here and buy your old man a cup of coffee and I'll tell you about it. I've only got an hour before I leave."

They motored to the group mess hall and took a table in a quiet corner after drawing hot coffee from a British kettle. Inside the tent it was dark and the damp canvas of the tent smelled overpoweringly musty; it was a stench Dave associated with an Army on the battlefield, even more strongly than the odor of cordite.

"Have you written your mother lately?" Dave asked as they sat down at the long table. "She worries about you."

"I know. And I have – twice. The censors don't let much get through so there's not a lot left to tell her."

"Sure there is – send her a letter every couple of days describing one of the misfits in your squadron, leaving out the names of course. Don't tell me you don't have any either. Every outfit does. Just getting a page in her son's handwriting – even if it doesn't say anything – will cheer her up. Trust me."

"I thought keeping her cheered up was your duty," Mitch said, grinning and hiding his face behind the tin cup.

Dave laughed and replied, "I could use a hand now and then."

"Yeah, when Brigadier Smythe-Browne told me you were in Georgia forming a division I thought you'd soon be calling for reinforcements. Is that why you're here?"

"They sent me over to get the lay of the land and some face-to-face time with the other division commanders here. It's been a full week and I've learned much."

"Like what?"

"It seems pretty evident the Germans can't win here in North Africa, but they can still prolong the fighting and inflict heavy casualties – they sure did that to us at Kasserine Pass. We Americans weren't ready. That's already raised reservations in Algiers at the joint forces headquarters about the competency of American commanders and command structures."

"That's why you're here?" Mitch asked.

"That's the proximate cause. The Army has some real questions about the adequacy of our training and the worthiness of U.S. weapons. I got to roam the battlefield and learn first hand some things that'll be helpful in the combat training of my division back in the states. I also saw some successes and failures in leadership."

He'd seen two distinctly different styles of leadership. Manton Eddy in the 9th Division was both aggressive and charismatic, not entirely unlike Patton – inspiring but somewhat aloof and distant; a stern but fair disciplinarian. Terry Allen, in the Big Red One, and Teddy Roosevelt, Jr. in the 34th both looked upon strict discipline as an undesirable crutch used by less able commanders. Roosevelt especially tried to command by personal charm and a cheery bullfrog voice. Long ago, in the fields of France, Nolan had decided leadership was a combination of both. What he saw in the three different divisions and what he heard from the troops on the front line now confirmed it.

"I also got to observe both good and bad staff work in all the divisions. Now, after a week I see some things we can improve on in. I never was much good at staff work."

"I remember you didn't much like staff officers."

"Like I said, I learned a lot. Fortunately, we have an excellent staff – and I'm not saying that just because it's my outfit. I'll put my primary staff up against anybody's in II Corps. Most importantly, I managed to locate and bring on board the best supply guy I've ever known – Shelby Dickerson, the supply officer from my old battalion in Manila. After a week, I'm much better informed and more confident about the division than I was before I came. I hated the trip over, but it was worth every minute."

"So, what happens with you now?" Mitch asked as he refilled their coffee mugs.

"A visit with Eisenhower at Algiers and then one long and very uncomfortable ride back to Georgia starting tomorrow morning. I think they've already alerted my division to get packed and ready to ship out. I wish we had more time to train, but the war doesn't work on my personal schedule, I'm afraid."

"Will you have time to stop in to see Brigadier Smythe-Browne on the way home?"

"Probably not. Why?"

"Just wondering," Mitch replied nonchalantly. "Thought you might, that's all."

Dave looked carefully at his son and finally said, "She's pretty enough but headstrong like your mother. With all the women in the world and your plentiful supply of Nolan charm… you need to forget about Aynslee."

"I wasn't thinking about her."

"Really? The Vargas girl you painted on the nose of your airplane is a surprisingly good likeness of her. I can't vouch for the negligee she's wearing… I'm hoping you can't either, son. A word of warning – steer well clear of married women. And for cryin' out loud, don't send a picture of that nose art to your mother."

"I didn't do the painting – I'm not that good. Just gave a general idea to a machinist in the maintenance section. The picture came from his imagination – the name came from my crew chief. First day here he told me to treat *his* airplane like a favorite mistress and the name just stuck. This one's number two – I wrecked the one I ferried over."

"And how does one treat a favorite mistress?"

Mitch grinned mischievously and tilted his head as he squinted back at his father. "Dad, is this that little 'birds and bees' talk we never had back at Lewis when I turned thirteen?... What do you want to know?" He laughed cheerily and then looked at his watch. "This could take a while. You said you only had an hour. Tell you what – I'll fly you to Algiers in the squadron's B-25. It's a little faster than the Gooney Bird and more comfortable if I put you in the right seat. You can even get some stick time. I've been wanting to check it out anyway. We just got it in to replace the B-26 the squadron used to have."

"Have you flown it before?" Dave asked, a little hesitant.

"I've read a lot of the operating manual."

"That's not what I asked. My question is: are you sure you can fly it?"

Dave thought he saw in his son some of that same complacent self-confidence he'd seen in Lindbergh when they'd toured the Luftwaffe bases and German airplane manufacturing facilities years earlier. He wasn't sure he liked it any more now than he did then.

"Dad, I flew a Hudson across the North Atlantic in the winter and a P-38 across the Southern Atlantic a few months back. I fly a twin-engined bird almost every day, half of that against the Luftwaffe. I think I can handle a simple little two hundred mile VIP ferry run. And if it turns out I can't, we'll each be wearing a parachute." He grinned at his father.

"I know you're familiar with that piece of gear. Mom told me all about the time you and Colonel Fauser learned to use one."

Chapter 25

"The cherry blossoms are utterly gorgeous," Denise observed wistfully. "Still, it seems unpatriotic to enjoy them while we're at war with the country that gave them to us."

Trevor Callahan nodded and replied, "But they were given three decades ago. It was a different Japan then, and we're a very different America now. The whole world has changed. I hope against hope our Navy in the Pacific and the Marines on Guadalcanal convinced the Japs to cease their expansionism and return to the home islands."

"You don't really think that'll happen, do you?"

"I guess not. I'm afraid the war against their empire will last a long time – several years. The Pacific is so vast and taking back all the territory and every island they've conquered in the last decade will take at least that long to wrest it all from their control."

She immediately thought of Glenn and Mitch, and cringed at the thought of their going off to island jungles in the Far East to fight. "I hope you're wrong, Trevor."

"So do I." He patted her hand softly. "Enough war talk. Let's just enjoy the scenery."

They had dined at a small, elegant restaurant a ten minute walk from the Tidal Basin – a quiet, even romantic little place. The *maître d* had chosen for them a quiet private alcove in a small dining room of the old renovated Federal house so they could enjoy a quiet conversation. Now, as they walked beneath the brilliant pink and white blossoms of ornamental cherry trees, Denise felt a certain guilty pleasure.

The congressman had surprised her weeks earlier by delivering her repaired tire in person. He had been pleasant, visibly uneasy and quick to leave after replacing the tire in the trunk of her car. Several days later he called and apologized for his earlier abruptness, chatted nervously for a few moments and rang off. Two days later a small box of chocolates arrived by messenger with a hand-written note inviting her to the Cherry Blossom festival; he was a congressional sponsor and a member of the festival's steering committee. A small, full color brochure was tucked beneath the box's ribbon.

Lunch was a delightful surprise and their conversation centered around the many facts and details of the festival with which he'd become familiar over the years.

"Tokyo's original gift of three thousand trees was made by Dr. Jokichi Takamine, a world-famous chemist," he said as they walked. "I'm biased, but I think the Washington cherry blossoms are a national treasure, every bit as much as the Golden Gate, Mount Rushmore, or the Statue of Liberty." She found the idea as strangely interesting as the congressman himself.

"I'm really glad you came today," Callahan said as they strolled through West Potomac Park near the Tidal Basin. "I like showing these things off to an appreciative audience. In the midst of the hustle and bustle of industrial commerce, and now the war, I think we give little thought and altogether miss the real treasures we have in this country. Teddy Roosevelt preserved our land with national forests and wildlife preserves. I like to think that I'm playing a small but important role in preserving the beautiful natural resources of the cherry blossoms for future generations. Does that come across as harebrained?"

"I think it's commendable."

"I wish there were more like you. As I look around the country and rub shoulders with colleagues in Congress I find most people are singularly focused on industrial manufacturing. Most care only about the acquisition and industrial development of our natural resources without any consideration for the long term costs and diminution of the planet." The congressman stopped and took a deep breath. "Sorry, Denise, I sometimes get too wound up."

"You sound a lot like my son, Glenn," she replied, patting his arm and looking up into his eyes as they continued slowly along the walkway at the edge of the water. "He says much the same thing about the fish in Long Island Sound and the ducks along the Chesapeake."

Callahan paused for a while and looked out across the Tidal Basin toward the Potomac before looking directly at Denise.

"I have to tell you," he said hesitantly, after taking a deep breath. "I didn't ask you here just to talk about cherry blossoms or preserving nature. I pride myself in being able to read people both quickly and accurately, and the day we met I saw something intriguing in you during our brief conversation. I had to see if my first impression was right or not. I'm still not sure. If I asked you to take a job on my campaign staff, would you consider it?"

Denise felt her breath catch in her throat and she gasped audibly. "You thought I'd be interested in politics?"

"I know it's a surprise and I'm sorry if I embarrassed you," Callahan said quickly. "But my gut instinct tells me you'd be perfect for the job."

"Oh, you run on instinct do you, congressman?"

"Yes indeed. Denise, you're extremely personable. It comes across instantly and very naturally, even in an unpleasant circumstance such as the one under which you and I met. You were incredibly poised."

"What is the job? And why do you think I'd be suited for it?"

"I don't have an official title as yet, but basically I see it as the executive event director for my re-election campaign."

She frowned at him and looked unsure. "Event director? Sounds like an overblown title for secretary. That's not me. I think your normally reliable gut just failed you."

"Please hear me out." They sat on a park bench facing the water and he turned to her, his demeanor animated. "I have to run a continuous re-election campaign because every two years I go before the voters. Last year I was almost beaten by a very inexperienced opponent with not much of a campaign strategy. The reason? I didn't have a plan for executive level events – fundraisers, social affairs, even town hall-like rallies focused on rubbing shoulders with people. My chief of staff does an excellent job of getting me before crowds to listen to my stump speech, but I also need a more well-rounded approach in my district to meet and greet people. That's what I need help with. I need somebody with a knack for instantly connecting with people. You're that kind of person. I knew it within seconds of meeting you. And today you confirmed it. Denise, you're a unique person – one who listens with her heart, not just her ears. How rare! And it's why I'm hoping you'll come on board and help me to do that. "

"Shouldn't you have some idea of my politics before you ask me to be on your campaign staff? What if I'm a diehard Republican? My father is."

"None of us is perfect. Everybody has faults," he said as he smiled charmingly at her, taking her hand and patting it. "If that's one of yours, we can work on it together. We both love cherry blossoms and nature in general. See, we have things in common. We could start there." He tilted his head and looked at her in mock seriousness. "You're not really a dyed in the wool Republican, are you? You're too nice for that."

"Actually I'm unaffiliated." She paused, reflecting. "I appreciate the offer – I think. But it goes against everything I told my daughter about not getting involved in politics."

"I know what most people think about politicians. Mark Twain got laughs and fame by railing against the congress, mostly with hyperbole. We're not a home grown criminal class as he claimed. I do this because I want to make a difference. A positive difference. Plato once said, 'If the decent are not willing to rule, they are punished by being ruled by worse men'. I'm a decent man trying to make this a better country. Help me, won't you?"

"Tell me more."

"The position I have in mind would involve your learning everything about my district – the people who live there and what makes them tick. It's an interesting district: almost 50-50 working-class Catholics and upper class businesspeople – doctors and lawyers, industrialists – and a smattering of academics from Johns Hopkins University and the University of Baltimore. Fascinating people, but a real challenge for a politician trying to represent them all. I need you to find out how to best connect with these people on a personal level. Help me talk to them in language they understand, and become one of them regardless of which group I happen to be with in any given instance. Help me keep from drinking expensive sherry when I'm with a group who drinks National Bohemian Beer and vice versa; making sure I don't miss important events for any one of the groups I represent."

"In other words, helping you be a social gadfly."

"No it's more than that. Much more," he replied, looking distressed. "I'm not trying to be something I'm not. I'm trying to better know the people I represent, who need to be helped by their government in Washington to improve their lives. I grew up in Boston in a working class neighborhood. My father was a home plaster installer in Fenway whenever he could find work. He scrimped and saved to give me a good education and a head start on a more prosperous lifestyle than he knew. What I need is help connecting with all of my constituents the right way. Will you help me?"

Denise contemplated. Since coming to Washington she had often found herself at loose ends with nothing to do. Still, something about this didn't feel right.

"There's another thing you should know," he was saying, interrupting her thoughts. "I have to be absolutely transparent with you even though it might put you off. I hope it won't. It's personal, but you need to know because I don't want you to get the wrong idea about me, or about this job." He gave her a pained look and sighed deeply. "In previous campaigns, except for last year, this was my wife's job. She was good at it and we made a very effective team. She no longer does it because we're separated and have been for almost two years."

"I'm sorry," Denise said quietly.

He blinked rapidly and turned his face away. "We're Catholic so divorce is absolutely out of the question. I'm still passionately in love with her and keep hoping and trying for a reconciliation, but… I don't need to go into that and burden you, so I won't. You'd find it out sooner or later anyway so it's better to tell you now. It happened. I wish there was something I could've done about it so I wouldn't be asking you to take her place in those kind of public events. Obviously, having an attractive articulate woman at my side at those times is certainly not a hindrance." He glanced back at her and abruptly stood, looking adrift. "There I've gone and ruined a perfectly enjoyable afternoon with my rambling and inarticulate chatter. I'll take you back to your place and we can both mark the whole thing off as an unfortunate waste of an otherwise pleasant day. I'm sorry, I shouldn't have…"

She smiled reassuringly at him. "I didn't say no, did I? I'd like to hear more."

He looked at her appreciatively. "That's wonderful! Come by the campaign office tomorrow afternoon and I'll show you around. You could talk to my chief of staff and —"

"And then maybe you could take me to dinner at the restaurant in Georgetown you were telling me about."

"Are you warming to the idea?"

"Maybe. Each journey begins with a single step."

"I'll set up the tour for three in the afternoon and make reservations for six-thirty." Callahan took both her hands in his and looked deeply into her eyes. "You won't regret this," he said, as they began to stroll back toward where he'd parked.

That was easy enough, he thought. *This is working out better than expected..*

*　　*　　*　　*　　*

"I don't know Mrs. Reeves," the investment counselor said to her. "Your husband has always left those decisions to me in the past – based, of course, on general guidelines he and his father laid down for me some time ago, along with principles we jointly agree upon at the beginning of each calendar year. That's a significant amount of money to be moving into an investment area in which he's never before shown much interest."

"Harrison and I have talked about it for years," Michelle said, smiling beguilingly at the sixty year old senior vice president of the investment firm. "The last time was just a couple of months ago. We agreed if the property came available at a reasonable price we'd move on it."

"But I really think –"

"Remember when Harrison's father bought land on the Eastern Shore?"

"Of course, Mrs. Reeves. The acreage just north of St. Michaels."

"Yes. The waterfront acreage fronting on lower Eastern Bay. Do you remember how that worked out, Mr. Spaulding?"

The older man grimaced and shook his head. "His father made a few improvements and marketed it as a future resort and business conference center. He sold it two years after purchase at a handsome profit."

"Do you remember the exact numbers?" Michelle asked, offhandedly.

The investment executive looked pained. "He bought three properties at a total cost of a hundred and fifty-six thousand, and sold them as a package for over seven hundred thousand."

"And that's what Harrison and I are doing on Long Island."

"But Mrs. Reeves –"

"Long Island right now is just a vast meadowland, but in a few years the population there will explode. Everyone knows that, but few have the resources to capitalize on it. Now is the time to invest in real estate, and Harrison sees we have a prime opportunity."

"I should really contact your husband, Mrs. Reeves."

"You have a notarized copy of the Power of Attorney he gave me."

"Yes, but –"

"He and I had that drawn up for just such an eventuality. The offer from the owners of the five contiguous properties expires in seventy-two hours. Our attorney has negotiated them to the price point my husband and I set as the threshold. I'm going to strike while the iron is hot as he and I agreed before he went off to Australia to confer with General MacArthur."

"As the Reeves' financial advisor, I can't in all good conscience make this transaction."

Michelle's face changed abruptly; gone was the pretty smile and pleasant demeanor.

"I too am a Reeves, Mr. Spaulding, and don't you forget that," she said, her nostrils flaring as she glowered at the executive. "Harrison and I have been married a quarter century, some years longer than your association with our family. I can assure you, your services will not be needed if you persist in trying to thwart the financial planning my husband and I have done on this. Now, sir, sell our holdings in Bell Telephone and transfer the cash to the bank account I provided you. If you don't, I shall be forced to call my father-in-law, the Senator."

The older man breathed deeply and shrugged, slowly shaking his head in resignation. He picked up his phone, spoke a few words and minutes later a young office boy entered and placed a form on his desk. Spaulding quickly scratched out a few words, checked two boxes and affixed his signature before handing it back to the clerk. "Bell stocks in the amount of $120,000 will be sold this afternoon and the money transferred within thirty-six hours."

"I hope for all our sakes it is. Thank you for your time." Michelle rose, left the office and walked outside to a car waiting at the curb.

"You look like the cat that ate the canary," Randall Ashby observed, starting the car and pulling out into traffic after Michelle got in. "I assume all went well."

"Very well, thank you. The power of attorney and the cover letter typed on the law firm's stationary did the trick. How did you manage it?"

"You don't really want to know, and I don't really want to tell you."

"Something illegal, Randall?"

"Not currently so far as I know."

"But how –"

"One of the lawyers at your husband's law firm is an old friend. I helped him pass Contracts Law in school. Politics and law both run on the same fuel – favors and accommodations. A senior partner on retainer with your family would naturally pass on a simple task like writing a power of attorney to a junior lawyer like my friend. Nobody pays a firm's partner $200 an hour to fill out simple forms. Beyond that, you don't want to know."

"You're sure I haven't done anything illegal or improper?" Michelle asked.

"Nothing illegal according to law currently on the books. Improper? That's a question of morality and conscience. Only you can answer that."

And I can, Michelle thought to herself. After twenty-five years of being spliced to Harrison Reeves, there was little she could do or imagine doing to him which seemed immoral or unconscionable.

Their drive back to the Capitol office building went by quickly in mid-afternoon traffic. Ashby parked his car on the street; not many minutes later the two of them entered Senator Payne's office and found a distraught Megan who looked at them in relief while sounds of an argument filtered through the transom.

"Erika and her mother," the secretary said, rolling her eyes and nodding her head toward the door. "I'm glad the Senator isn't here."

They heard Erika say in a loud voice, "How could you?! After all the grief you gave me about coming here to Washington to work in the congress?"

"Everything all right in here?" Michelle asked, opening the door while looking at Denise and then at her daughter.

"As a matter of fact…" Denise replied, exasperated, turning her head while still facing her daughter who stood defiantly less than a foot away with both hands on her hips.

"She's going to work for some congressman from Maryland she barely knows – not work actually. She's going to be his surrogate wife! Have you talked this over with dad or –"

"I'm not going to be his surrogate wife! I swear, Erika, you take every word, every thought to the worst possible extreme," Denise interrupted. Michelle could see she was furious, her breast rising and falling, her body tensed like some embattled warrior. She'd never seen Denise this angry though her temper had never been a secret in their crowd all those years at Benning or Lewis, and especially in Manila. Michelle remembered their confrontation back then when Mitch had been appointed to West Point. Denise had blamed her as much as Dave for what she saw as a clandestine pact between the two of them leaving her out of a say in her oldest son's future. "And as for talking this over with your father – he's on a boat somewhere with his precious division halfway to who knows where."

Michelle glanced at Randall Ashby and nodded in Erika's direction.

"You and I have a meeting with the clerk of the Senator's committee," the lawyer said quickly as he moved across the room and took Erika's arm. "If we leave now we won't be late."

Michelle motioned to Denise to have a seat and then followed Ashby and Erika into the outer waiting room, closing the door behind her. "Erika, look at me and listen to what I'm about to tell you. Screaming arguments between you and your mother, or you and anybody else are strictly forbidden in this office."

"But she –"

"You're not listening to me," Michelle interrupted. "There will be no more of that in this office at any time. I know you two argue a lot. But it won't happen in here. It's unprofessional and unacceptable. One more time and you're no longer employed by this office. I don't care who starts it or what it's about, if this ever happens again your days on Capitol Hill are over. When it gets around that you were fired by the easiest going old senator in all of Washington, you'll never work in this town again," she said in a hard flat voice, while anger held her as if suspended. "Are we clear on this, Erika?"

"Yes, but I –"

"You're *still* not listening to me. This is not up for discussion; there is no mitigation for your behavior and no excuse for it ever happening again. Now you go somewhere with Randall and think about what I just said." Michelle turned and went into her father's office closing the door behind her. Sitting down behind the senator's desk, she opened the lower right drawer and extracted a bottle of bourbon along with two short glasses, both of which she filled halfway. "Talk to me – and tell me how I can help."

The glass was something a man would drink from – short and broad-mouthed; probably unwashed since the last time it was used. Denise fixed her gaze on it and finally took a good-sized sip which burned fire down her throat. "This isn't your problem, Michelle."

"It most certainly is. Everything about what just happened – what keeps on happening in this office makes it my problem if for no other reason than it reflects very poorly on the senior senator from Pennsylvania. Even more than that, Erika is a remarkably competent young staff analyst who we need right now. And you and I are friends, Denise. I owe you – for including me in your crowd of wives on Luzon and for inviting me into the bridge group there. You'll never know how much it meant to me."

"But you returned the favor. Many times over."

"That's what friends do. Please let me help you now with Erika."

There was a long silence between them. Denise took another sip of the bourbon and said, "She's upset because she sees me doing the same thing I so adamantly opposed in her."

"Are you?"

"All I wanted to do was grease the skids and get her to think about it, hoping she'd give me a reasoned response. I haven't said yes or no to anything yet. I just wanted to tell her."

"Tell her what?"

"That I *might* go to work on Congressman Callahan's re-election campaign. That's all."

Michelle's skin instantly felt like prickly heat. "Trevor Callahan from Maryland?" Michelle looked at her in amazement, unable to speak.

Callahan?! This was not good news – Michelle was certain.

She'd met the man on a half dozen occasions over the years and each time had come away with an uneasy feeling bordering on foreboding. He was, she decided, the worst kind of political chameleon – an unethical operative rather than a public servant like her father; a man with his finger in the wind rather than his roots in the soil of conviction and principle. She didn't trust him. And there was an even bigger demerit in his character.

He was a close friend of her husband.

"Denise, let's get out of here and go to my house for drinks and dinner. I'll call Elise and get her to join us. All right? She does this really good jambalaya that can sit and cook while we talk over cocktails. Say around six?"

Michelle called her oldest and dearest friend after Denise had left.

"For right now we need to listen closely and find out exactly what's happening," Michelle told her friend after relating the news she'd just learned. "She doesn't know how dangerous a piece of ground she's on. This Callahan can't be trusted – I'm certain of it. Isn't it interesting that within days of the boys' division sailing from Jacksonville, this man accidently bumped into her? It's all too contrived. Too convenient. I'm going to do some checking around while you round up what we need for dinner. I'll see you at my place at five. If you get there before me, let yourself in. We need to talk before she arrives."

Michelle rang off, found a name in her address book and immediately dialed.

"*Phelan Investigations.*"

"Mr. Phelan, Michelle Reeves. I have another job for you – someone else I need to have you research and report on – a congressman this time. I'll be at your office in twenty minutes."

Chapter 26

"Junkers – two o'clock high, ten miles."

The radio call from Claude Kinsey leading Red flight two miles off to his right came just seconds after Mitch spotted the planes – five JU-52s silhouetted against the azure blue sky above them. There had been a growing number of the tri-motor transports filling the airways between Tunis and Sicily in the past week. They were easy targets when unescorted by German fighters and he'd downed two during a similar mission over Cape Bon a few days earlier. That had officially made him an ace along with Kinsey, Harley Vaughn, Ricky Zubarik and the ever-vocal Dixie Sloan who led the Group with seven kills and claimed two additional probables. Sloan also claimed a real pilot wouldn't count an easy target like the lumbering transports – 'like shootin' chickens out behind the hen house… no sport to it.'

Mitch watched as Red flight dropped their belly tanks and began a steep climb from their 5000 foot cruising altitude. He kept an eye on Duck Butt Waters who was leading White flight and continued scanning the sky above the German transports.

"Bandits, 10 o'clock high White flight!" Mitch called out over the mission frequency, and immediately he saw Waters jettison his external tanks as he began a climb directly into the sun while turning head-on into the attacking Luftwaffe and Italian fighters.

"Drop tanks." He heard the flight lead call over the radio and almost immediately they were in the middle of a swarm of Me109s, 110s, Focke Wulfs, and Italian Macchi MC202s.

Mitch concentrated on staying in his wing man position as Waters knifed through the melee, firing on targets as they would briefly appear and then disappear from in front of him. He was climbing almost straight up, firing wildly at the underside of a Focke Wulf when Waters disappeared from his sight. He stood the Lightning on its wing and saw his flight leader headed straight down. He instantly nosed over when he saw an Me-109 latch onto Waters' tail and begin firing. Mitch closed to within a hundred yards of the German fighter and fired a short burst. He saw hits register along the left wing and the enemy plane immediately disengaged, trailing gray smoke. Mitch continued down keeping Waters in sight and quickly realized the props on the Lightning in front of him weren't turning.

"Duck Butt! Main fuel – main fuel…*main fuel*!" he yelled into the radio. He held his breath as the Mediterranean rushed up at them. He turned hard, pointed his wing down at Waters' aircraft and watched helplessly, overwhelmed with a desire to keep his feet dry.

Suddenly both the props on the Lightning below him came to life in a blur surrounding the nacelles of the Allison engines. Waters leveled and began to climb; Nolan turned to intercept him and swung into position to his right rear as the two planes climbed back toward the swirling dogfight a few thousand feet above.

The Junkers transports off to the south were twisting and skidding in a futile effort to avoid Kinsey's flight. Meanwhile Waters's White Flight tried to keep the German and Italian fighter cover occupied and out of the way. One by one in quick succession the outclassed German transports fell from the sky in horrendous balls of fire or long glides trailing gray and black smoke. And then Kinsey turned his flight of eight toward the looping, tangled dogfight that raged from twenty thousand feet down to sea level.

Mitch saw Waters swing in behind a Focke Wulf who was on the tail of one of the P-38s. Out of the corner of his eye, Nolan spotted a -109 well to their left lining up for a long lead shot. He pulled up and turned toward their attacker, firing a long range burst across his nose that caused the German to roll inverted and pull through headed straight down. Immediately he found Duck Butt and tucked back into his wingman slot. Three times in the next minutes he took long deflection shots to keep German fighters off his leader. Finally the Germans broke contact and headed back towards Sicily. Mitch counted twelve ships as the P-38s formed into one large gaggle headed home; two of the original 96th Lightnings were missing.

He realized he was soaking wet with perspiration.

This was always the worst part of any mission when they tangled with German fighters – when the adrenaline finally stopped coursing through his veins; when he had time to catch his breath and contemplate. It was the phase of combat flying when he was always dogged with doubt and second-guessed himself, even after he'd seen the primary targets of the mission shot down and was certain they'd gotten the better of the Luftwaffe fighter cover. Always the nagging uncertainty – had he done all he could? *Why me – why am I one of those returning?* It lasted only until his pulse returned to normal and his breathing slowed. There was never any lingering remorse or guilt or sorrow, and he wondered why.

Soon they were over the coast west of Bone heading toward Telerghma.

"*All right, you Jackrabbits, good day*," came the call over the radio a half hour later from Lynn in the lead aircraft. "Time for a little show. Here's the drill. Dress right dress on me – everybody on line to the right, wing tip to wing tip. Over the field at 300 AGL. On my count, at three second intervals pull the nose up, do a left aileron roll and continue around to enter the pattern on a left downwind for landing."

Less than twenty minutes later, all the squadron aircraft from the mission were down and the ground crews were shaking the pilots' hands, congratulating them on the flyby and hearing reports about an unusually successful mission all around. Mitch climbed down the back wing from his P-38 and looked worriedly up and down the flight line.

"Sergeant K," he said to his crew chief. "B-8 and B-14 are missing. Any idea why?"

"Yeah, captain. An hour after your flight took off this morning, a call came down from Group for a mission supporting II Corps near Fondouk. B-8 and -14 were the only ships we had so Ops sent them."

"Both those planes were restricted," he said, growing irritated. He'd test flown both and grounded them the previous afternoon. "Who approved sending them?"

"Major Vaughn."

Mitch cursed under his breath and muttered to himself. *Damn him! What the hell does he think I was doing? Both those planes were grounded with safety gigs needing to be worked off.* "Who were the pilots?"

"Lindquist and Crosley. They knew there were still some open write-ups, but agreed to go anyhow. Lucky really wanted to blow up those Panzer tanks for one of the infantry outfits."

"He did, did he?"

Duck Butt Waters waddled over with the parachute banging against the back of his thighs. "Hey, Nolan. Thanks."

"For what?"

"For telling me to turn on my main fuel. Geez! Am I stupid or what?! I was flying on aux tanks and when you called out the bogies I just dropped 'em and headed into the fight. Forgot to change over to mains."

"You know better than that."

"Sure I do. But as soon as the engines stopped that Kraut jumped my butt and I couldn't force myself to flip the switches – all I could think about was bein' shot down and gettin' wet. When you got him off my ass and yelled about the main fuel I finally got my act together. Hell, Nolan, you can have my mission liquor for the duration. Thanks."

"Yeah, well, you do the same for me some day," Mitch replied, still angry – at Vaughn for sending out two birds he'd specifically grounded, and at Lucky and Marv for taking the mission. He was still simmering a half hour later when he entered the commander's tent.

Harley Vaughn looked up from writing at his desk.

"Mitch. Really good work today. Great mission! It feels like a turning point of some kind. Latest tally is we knocked down ten and damaged another five of their fighter escort. The 95th got two more, and the 97th got seven and three probables. This is the best day the Group has had since we got here. Colonel Covington is even going to overlook your flyby."

"We lost two – Kinsey and Lee Lawrence. Waters thinks he might have seen Claude's parachute, but he can't be sure. And I wouldn't be one bit surprised if Lindquist and Crosley don't make it back either." Mitch saw the look on his squadron commander's face. "I grounded B-8 and -14 for damned good reasons. That's my responsibility as your maintenance officer. If you have that little faith in my judgment you need to find yourself another guy. If it happens again, I guarantee you'll have to."

"Now just a minute, captain," Vaughn replied stiffly. "I'm the commander and –"

"No, major, you wait a minute. I didn't volunteer for this job and I'm not even qualified by Army regulation to be in the slot. But as long as I'm assigned to it –"

"Sit down, Mitch," the commander interrupted. "Let's just take a step back from the edge here and take a deep breath. You need to think for a minute – and so do I – before one of us says something we both end up regretting."

"If it's all the same, I'll stand, sir."

"You can if you want. But I'd prefer you sit down with me," Vaughn said calmly. After a long hesitation and a deep breath, Mitch pulled up a camp stool and sat. "I assume you just came from the debriefing at Group."

"Yes, sir."

Vaughn paused, then opened a desk drawer and retrieved a bottle of Irish Whiskey. "Mission liquor. Had your shot yet?"

"I'll pass, sir," he replied tersely.

The squadron commander ignored the reply and poured liquor into two tin mess hall cups, pushed one toward Mitch and said, "Marv and Lucky weren't ordered to go – they volunteered because of what it was. Sergeant Kupcinsky told them the ships were grounded."

"You could have stopped them."

"I've sent men out in aircraft much less airworthy – many times." Vaughn took a long pull on his drink and looked back at Nolan. "Remember the day you showed up? It was the very same day all the crew chiefs and mechanics of the 82nd Group finally got here from England. Up 'til then we'd been flying almost a month without inspections or maintenance work done by mechanics. I know a lot less than you do about aircraft maintenance, but a lot more than any of the other pilots in the squadron. And I can tell you there wasn't a day that went by when I didn't allow pilots to fly planes we all knew were well below standards."

Vaughn paused, lit a cigarette, and continued.

"None of my pilots had any idea what they were looking at when they opened the engine cowlings on pre-flight. If there wasn't oil flowing all over the place or wires unattached then the plane was ready to fly; sometimes they were like that and we flew them anyway. All the ships had multiple pages of gripes and half the radios didn't work. Gave me a lot of sleepless nights but we mostly survived. War is hell," Vaughn said, taking a quick sip of his whiskey. "Looking back on it I'm absolutely certain I sent pilots out in airplanes that were literally deathtraps. I'm equally certain some of the guys didn't come back solely because of my decision. We all flew planes we knew were on the ragged edge – at best. We did it because there wasn't any other choice. When you survive something like that time after time maybe it warps your perspective on what's mission essential and what's not."

"We're not in that mode anymore, major," Mitch said when Harley Vaughn paused to take another sip of his drink.

"Thanks to you and the maintenance section and the crew chiefs, that's true. And don't think it goes unnoticed or unappreciated. I'm not trying to blow smoke up your kilt, Nolan. You've done a hell of a job. But we're still in a war, and we still fly against the best damned air force the world has ever known. Between us and the Brits, I think we have the Afrika Korps on their heels – we've got them bottled up in a shrinking area in Tunisia. We've seen some good days recently, and today was that in spades. Still, this isn't a time to declare victory and start celebrating. It's a time to put on all the pressure we can. Someday, hopefully sooner than later, we'll get into the mode of doing everything by the book. But right now that's just not possible. Lucky and Marv knew that. I'm guessing you know it, too."

Mitch realized what Vaughn was doing in going slowly and purposefully through the squadron's history in combat. He was relaxing the tension between them and getting him to think. They were silent for awhile and then Mitch downed his whiskey in one swallow.

"I've been looking over the flight time logs in Operations," Vaughn was saying. "I found you haven't had a stand down from flying since you got back from the ferry flight to England."

Mitch frowned. "I haven't been flying any more missions than anybody else. I always get at least a day or two between missions just like everybody else."

"True, but… this might surprise you – it did me. You're high time pilot in the 96th. In fact, it appears you're high man in the whole Group since we first began flying missions back in December."

"How? I fly the same rotation as all the other guys, but got here more than a month later."

"Well, you've been averaging almost four hours flying time every day – I checked. It's your flying test flights most days between missions. You've got Doc Mounce worried. He's come to me twice in the last week. He says you've busted every Air Corps crew rest requirement by more than just a little bit. Doc is pretty adamant about your getting away for at least a week."

"I had time off when we went to England."

"Doc factored that in. You're still overdue for a stand down – a week's worth of rest somewhere. I went to Agadir last month and got in some sailing and swimming in the Atlantic.

I highly recommend it. You'd like Agadir. Great little hotel – lots of pretty French girls. Lindquist and Crosley are due also. Didn't you guys once sail to Bermuda together?"

"It's a long story, major."

Vaughn smiled, relaxed now. "I can believe it. Tell you what – I'll get Group to cut orders for you three to go there for rest and utter relaxation. You wouldn't argue with that?"

"No, sir. Guess not."

"Good. Then it's a done deal. Get away with your buddies and enjoy yourselves."

"Sounds good to me, sir."

But it didn't sound as good when the sun went down five hours later and neither Lindquist nor Marvelous Marv had returned. It sounded worse three days later when one of the bomber crews from the 381st reported two crashed P-38s with 96th Squadron markings and no signs of survivors in the southern Algerian desert two hundred miles from Telerghma.

*   *   *   *   *

"Gentlemen, the corps commander," Colonel Alford said loudly, and all the regimental and battalion commanders came to attention as Omar Bradley entered the large tent.

"At ease and seats please," Bradley said almost apologetically as if embarrassed at the ceremonial entrance. "It's good to see you men again. I'm glad the 12th made it in time for the final week of fighting to help us finish off the Afrika Korps. You'll be interested to know that all told, we bagged about 275,000 Axis prisoners. While your time in the line was limited, your contribution was not. Severing the Bizerte-Tunis road as quickly as you did and marrying up with the British 4th Tank Battalion at Protville cut off the escape of essentially all the remaining Italian forces and a good part of the Germans. General Nolan tells me your division has been blooded but not bloodied, and that's a good thing." Bradley glanced around the room and said, "From all the reports and from what little I've been able to witness, the 12th is a good fighting outfit. I'm here to say thanks and tell you some things about your next mission."

From the side of the room Dave Nolan looked around at the officers of his new and still untested division. It amazed and delighted him to be the commander of this many men.

They had debarked at Bone, where the British 6th Commando Battalion had come ashore in mid-November. Bradley had immediately placed the 12th in the American II Corps line between the 34th and 9th divisions and given them the mission of seizing the town of Mateur from the German 334 Division. The arrival of fresh troops had surprised the battered Germans and the new Americans' aggressiveness immediately gained the upper hand and sustained the momentum of a weeklong offensive push. The operation soon became a rout with the German Fifth Panzer Army unable to stop and catch its breath or establish a defensive position. Dave was especially pleased with the leadership displayed by his three regimental commanders – Cole Alford, Judd Haggerty and Pat O'Grady. They had led from the front and set the example of rifleman first. O'Grady even had an M-1 thumb to prove it. Going into the line immediately upon arrival had paid dividends and confirmed his observation of the 42nd Division in the First War that spending additional months in rear area training after arrival was counter-productive to unit cohesion and morale.

"General Patton and I were invited by General Eisenhower to the victory parade in Tunis," Bradley was saying. "It was clear from our reception by the population, especially the impassive Arabs and chastened Italians, this parade signified the end of an era of French impotence. And it was equally obvious from the jubilant French of the city they were celebrating the rebirth of a Fighting France. As welcome and heartening as our victory in North Africa obviously is, there is still a lot of tough slogging ahead in the Mediterranean. General Patton is at this moment hunkered down with his staff planning the next major step against the Axis." Bradley paused briefly as if choosing his next words carefully.

"I can only tell you your next mission is certainly weeks, not days, from this moment. I charge all you leaders to put the time to good use. I also charge you to maintain discipline and control among the ranks. Already we've had instances of looting and theft and conduct unbecoming the soldiers of a free country." Bradley paused and looked sternly around the room at each of the officers. "I expect better of our soldiers and I expect *much* better of our officers. You will not disappoint me."

Omar Bradley had already begun to establish a reputation as a "soldier's general." He was not as flamboyant as Patton, nor as politically astute as Eisenhower, but he had a common touch which resonated with the rifle toting G.I.s under his command. He was known as affable, approachable, and a good listener. But Dave Nolan knew from experience he was also a superior strategist and – like Patton – a no nonsense disciplinarian with high standards and low tolerances for poor performance or behavior.

"I expect you officers of the 12th not only to maintain discipline within the ranks but also to train your soldiers. It would not be giving away any secrets to alert you to the need of training your commands for amphibious landings under fire. I can't tell you where that will be or exactly when it will be, but I can guarantee you will be transported by ship and you will have to fight your way ashore. Your division will be among the first to land. You will be using, for the first time, new beaching craft which allow landing of large forces directly on the beaches without intermediate transfer to small landing craft. Use the time wisely between now and the upcoming D-Day to plan your logistics and train your soldiers on the use of these new craft. The upcoming battle will be one unlike any our Army has ever fought – it will be a combined arms operation distinct from any in our military history. Not only will we be fighting alongside and coordinating with our British allies, we'll be combining the assets of armor, infantry, and parachute infantry for the first time. There is much to learn and much to do in the next few weeks. I expect your best effort, but even more, I expect success." Bradley paused, looked around slowly and said, "That is all."

The II Corps commander abruptly turned and left.

Outside, Dave and Andy Fauser caught up to Bradley walking toward his jeep.

"Holy smokes, Brad. That was a quick exit stage left," Andy Fauser said.

"The first thing a general officer should learn is when to shut up and leave. I think you have a long ways to go on that front, Butternuts." When Fauser hesitated, Bradley continued. "I see you're still hot on my heels, Andrew. Eighteen months ago you replaced me as commander of the Infantry School at Benning and now you show up here. Are you following me? Be forewarned, you're not going to get this job of mine any time soon."

"Wouldn't want it if offered, Brad," Fauser replied quickly. "Got a better one already. Besides, in the 12th we don't get all duded up like your folks in headquarters."

"I care more about how you fight than how you look. You and your boss still as good on the rifle range as you were back at the Point?"

"I can still part the hair on a flea at two hundred yards, but Davie's slowin' down a mite."

Bradley laughed out loud, his face lighting up. "You haven't changed, have you?"

"No need to. Only reason to change is to make somethin' easier or better."

"And you, Dave?"

"Imperfect as always, but I'm working on it," Nolan replied.

"Well, imperfect is not a word that I'd associate with you. I might have before you went into the line 10 days ago, but the performance of the 12th was exceptional. You still have my operations G-3 wondering how you were able to move so fast against pretty stiff opposition. How *did* you manage that?"

"Something we war gamed and then practiced in the field back in Georgia. We called it 'Rolling Thunder'. Basically, it's the squad tactic of fire and movement but on a larger scale using regiments instead of six man elements."

Bradley pondered for a moment. "Tell me about it."

"When a regiment encounters stiff resistance, it lays down a base of fire using organic weapons, artillery and hopefully someday air to ground support from the Air Corps. The reserve regiment immediately moves to and through the forward regiment and continues the attack. They go as far and fast as they can until they too encounter significant resistance; they lay down the base of fire, establish a new front line, and the next regiment moves through them and continues the momentum of the attack. We field-tested it back in the States and thought we could make it work in combat. We did a postmortem after the fighting and our analysis said that it worked as planned. Interrogation of German commanders we captured confirmed it."

Bradley thought for a while and liked what he heard. "You have it written down anywhere? I might want you to brief it for George and Ike and other division commanders."

"Our documentation is pretty sketchy right now. We're making it up as we go along." But Nolan was pleased to see the Corps commander's response. "Where to next, Brad?"

"Sicily. I don't want that to be common knowledge, but division commanders need to know. You don't look particularly surprised or happy about it."

"This wasn't Ike's idea, I assume."

"No, it was agreed to by Churchill and President Roosevelt at Casablanca. Alexander will be commanding. Why the long face?"

"I was hoping for something different this time around. In the last war the Brits looked down on us as junior partners, and it sounds like nothing's changed."

"To tell the truth, with only a few exceptions, we still have a long way to go. Our allies still have the most experience – and the most successes to date."

"Sad thing is, they don't have much imagination," Dave replied. "I can probably tell you right now how they plan to go after Sicily – unfortunately, so can the Germans. We'll land on the southern beaches and from there it'll be a bloody, head-on slugging match on an island offering precious little room for maneuver. As soon as Alexander finds he's lost the four-to-one numerical advantage their doctrine requires for offensive operations, he'll stop and wait for reinforcements. It'll be Flanders fields all over."

Bradley frowned at him. "You'd do it differently?"

"Actually, I wouldn't do it at all."

"Now you've got me scratching my head. What do you mean you wouldn't do it at all?"

"I'd bypass the whole place. There's nothing making Sicily strategically important enough for us to commit all our ground forces in the Med. What does Guzzoni have? A handful of undermanned coastal divisions. The only real fighting force on the island is the Herman Goering division. The value of Sicily lies in the airfields the Luftwaffe and the Italian Air Force operate out of. But they can be neutralized by air power. As soon as it looks to Guzzoni like there's an invasion on the southern shores he'll blockade the coastal roads and start moving his troops back toward Messina and the Straits. The Italians will be more interested in escaping back to the mainland than in resisting. The mountainous terrain will be more of a deterrent than Italian ground forces. Still, they'll be able to inflict a lot of casualties on us."

"Your solution?"

"I'd make a couple of naval feints in the south around Gela and Syracuse – maybe even land a few companies of American Rangers and British commandos. I'd mine the hell out of the Messina Straits to eliminate their only escape route, and cover it with the British and American Navy plus our Air Corps. But I'd make my major landing on the toe of the Italian Boot to Guzzoni's rear. I'm guessing we'll have fourteen or fifteen divisions to put into this operation, and that's more than enough to occupy and defend the narrow peninsula on Italy's mainland. With nowhere to go and his sole escape route rendered useless, Guzzoni either starves or surrenders. And, we effectively neutralize for good the one really first-rate unit on the island – the Hermann Goering Division. That way we wouldn't have to fight them later on the mainland."

"You've spent time thinking about this."

"I have."

"Pretty bold plan, general."

"L'audace. Toujours l'audace."

Bradley smiled broadly and looked sideways at him. "You sound like George."

"I speak better French and my voice is a lot lower."

"He asked for you to work with his staff on the planning for Sicily. I'm going to suggest to Ike he keep you and George apart somehow and both of you away from the British so we don't irreparably damage this fragile relationship we have going." Bradley climbed into his jeep and looked with satisfaction at Fauser and Nolan. "It's good to have both of you back on my team. You've done a whale of a good job with the division. Keep it up… but Andy, don't set up another still – I frowned on it twenty years ago and still do. Dave, keep him in line. I'm counting on you. And in your next letter, tell Denise I said hello… from Kitty and me both."

Dave nodded and then Bradley's jeep was moving off toward El Alia.

"… *in your next letter…*" He realized he hadn't written a letter to her since the evening before they sailed from Jacksonville. And he hadn't received one from her in two months.

"General Nolan?"

Dave turned toward the voice coming from behind his right shoulder and gazed at a young man standing in a casual slouch. He wore fatigues, an issue field jacket without insignia of any kind and a wool cap – the kind Patton had outlawed months earlier. A canvas messenger bag hung over his shoulder; one hand was in his pocket, a cigarette dangled from between his lips, and it appeared he hadn't shaved in several days. He looked to be in his late twenties.

"Don't reckon he's one of ours, Davey," Andy Fauser said, nonchalantly. "Musta fell off the mud flap of Brad's jeep. What outfit you from, boy?"

"U.P."

"You pee on what, son?"

"United Press Associates. I'm a reporter assigned to cover the war."

Fauser and Nolan looked at one another. Andy shrugged his shoulders, turned to the young reporter. "Well, you missed it. We finished off the Afrika Korps and the Eye-talians a week ago. You might try catchin' a plane to the South Pacific. I hear there's shootin' still goin' on over there in some o' them islands. You'll like the Marines. They're real interestin' folks. And MacArthur can give you a two hour quote for any question you can think up."

"Actually, I was sent here by General Eisenhower. He suggested I spend time with the 12th Division – talk with General Nolan and somebody named Butternuts."

"I'm Nolan," Dave said cautiously. He didn't like the idea of having a reporter hanging around. There was too much to do in the next few weeks that needed his undivided attention. "Grab yourself a cup of coffee at the mess hall and I'll meet with you in an hour or two."

"Actually, general, I'm working on a deadline and if it's all the same to you –"

"Neither I nor the German Army care much for or work according to your deadline. What did you say your name was?"

"Kilroy. Eamonn Kilroy."

"Like that cartoon character on the side every railroad car in the States?" Andy asked. He looked sideways at Dave and sadly shook his head. "How long have you been a reporter?"

"Two years."

"How long?"

"Nineteen months, plus a few days."

"Let me tell you something, Eamonn," Dave said, looking hard at him. "Absolute honesty is real high on the priority list of the chain of command. You'll get that from me and the men of this division. Let that be the last time you ever shade the truth with me. Clear?"

"Yes, sir," Kilroy replied, straightening and looking a little shaken. "It won't happen again, sir."

"You're right about that. Now, get some coffee and wait for me." After he'd gone, Dave turned to Fauser. "Get on the horn to Ike and find out what in the world's going on. Don't talk to Beedle or any of the staff, but to Ike himself. I can't believe he sent us a cub reporter to babysit. And tell him I want copies of all of this Kilroy's dispatches in the last year. We need to know what we're dealing with here… and why."

*   *   *   *   *

With the fall of Tunis and the disappearance of the Luftwaffe from the skies over North Africa, the 82nd Group suspended flight operations and breathed a collective sigh of relief.

Except for Mitch Nolan.

Doc Mounce and Harley Vaughn had pressed him to take time off, but he'd deftly dodged their suggestion. Half the Lightnings needed repairs and test flights; some new aircraft had been received, and the B-26 couldn't be spared at the moment. Instead of standing down he was flying more than ever. It showed in his attitude; his tent mates gave him a wide berth.

It was the second day of the Group stand down when he landed from a test flight and got the news from his crew chief he had visitors in the mess tent.

"I don't have time for visitors. Who are they?"

"A couple of pilots you probably won't mind talking to."

"Zubarik and Sloan? They got back? I was hoping they were locked up somewhere."

"No, not our AWOL lieutenants."

"Replacements from Casablanca?" A week earlier, replacement pilots had started flooding in – five dozen for the Group all told. With winter receding, replacement aircraft had been coming in as well, increasing the workload on the squadron's maintenance section.

Sergeant K shook his head. "They told me not to ruin the surprise. I'm sworn to secrecy."

"I don't have time for games, Kup. Tell me."

"No, sir, can't do that."

Mitch completed entries in the aircraft log book and headed for the mess hall. When he heard the familiar voices inside, he threw back the tent flap and entered. "Where the hell have you two malingerers been? Do you have any idea where you left my airplanes?"

"Who wants to know?" Lindquist replied, looking up from pouring whiskey from a bottle into his canteen cup. "You know Marv, the boy sounds a little overwrought, doesn't he?"

"I was expecting a more cordial welcome," Crosley replied, looking disappointed.

"I'll give you cordial!" Mitch replied and grabbed them each by the collar. "Where have you two been for the last week? You look like fat ticks."

They wrestled in the tent and knocked over some chairs and one of the trestle tables. Finally, winded and laughing, they sat down and Lucky poured Mitch a drink.

"Okay, so tell me," Mitch said, still amazed, and relieved, at seeing them again, "where in the world have you guys been for the last week. The 381st found your birds in the desert."

"Well, it's a long story," Crosley said with a Cheshire cat grin. "You tell him, Lucky."

"O.K. Before we took off, the major told us French intelligence had reports of an armored column near Mateur, and that we should fly to a place just south of Bizerte and turn south to find a formation of German tanks. When we got to Bizerte we headed south lookin' all over the place for those damn Nazi tanks. We never did see 'em," Lucky said, pouring some whiskey into a cup for Nolan and handing it over. "There we were the both of us all dressed up, ready to dance and nowhere to go – we each had two five hundred pound bombs and ammo."

"So, he suggests we go strafe Fondouk just for the fun of it," Marv Crosley said, rolling his eyes, "Probably the most fortified piece of German-held ground in all of Tunisia. Another typical 'Lucky Lindy' boondoggle. What followed was one pass with guns blazing through *the most* heavily garrisoned and defended piece of real estate in the whole German line. It was like going down a bowling alley with a million golf balls coming at you."

"It was wild!" Lucky said his face lighting up. "Even with all those tracers coming at us I swear I dropped those two bombs dead center on some kind of command post."

"And I got hit numerous times and was having trouble staying in the air," Marv Crosley added, looking less than amused.

"Worse than that," Lucky said, "we got jumped by a *schwarme* of 190s who chased us… musta been a hundred miles south. By the time they got tired of it or ran out of gas, we are plain lost," Lindquist said, taking another sip of whiskey. "We turned west thinking that we'd eventually find Telerghma. Turns out, that didn't work all that well."

"*Didn't work?!?* Ha! That's not even close," Crosley interrupted. "It got dark, my bird is all shot up and out of gas so I started looking for a place to land. Lucky said he would find a spot to put his plane down and then I could follow. The plan was to fly out the next morning – both of us in his P-38. He went in low and slow but when the nose gear hit, it collapsed so it was as useless as he is. By that time I was out of options. Lucky radioed to me to come in wheels up which I did and that completely wrecked my airplane. By now it was dark, and I spent a lot of time just trying to find Mr. Lucky here – and when I did, he was sound asleep."

"No use two of us running around lost at night in the desert," Lindquist said simply.

Marv Crosley shook his head again. "Well, we spent a frigid night together, taking turns on watch, and as the sun started to rise, we heard bleating sheep and camels and saw shadowy figures moving around. Both of us had our .45s out because we didn't know if these people were friendly. Turns out they were."

"They greeted us by placing an egg at our feet," Lindquist explained. "And by the time it was all over each one of us had a big pile of eggs. Seems that's some kind of A-rab greeting – kind of like a friendly hello. We spent a couple of days with those folks… just goofin' off."

"You two are aces at that," Nolan said sardonically. "Double aces."

Lindquist shrugged noncommittally and continued. "Next afternoon – day three I think – here comes this majestic horseman appearing over the sand dunes wearing flowing white robes and riding a big white stallion. No doubt in our minds he was the man in charge."

"Yeah, so Lucky here starts calling him 'the Sheik of Araby'. We were lucky he didn't speak any English. But neither did we speak whatever it was that he was talking either, so Lucky tries some of his West Point French on him, and I'll be go-to-war he understood that."

"So, my friend the Sheik proceeds to take us to his master tent – a great big old thing with fine Berber carpet laid out all over the place inside," Lindquist explained. "We all take off our shoes and we sit cross-legged while they treat us with something that looked like large pancakes along with an egg mixture seasoned and mixed with olive oil. Best thing either of us have had since we came to North Africa. Sure beats C-rations or that slop from the Group mess. After dinner we sat outside under the stars drinking some kind of drink that had a nice little kick to it until we fell asleep. Next morning we woke up covered with blankets and pretty soon they're serving us breakfast. Then they trotted out a couple of donkeys and a guide."

Crosley gave him a forlorn look. "It was terrible. Forty… fifty miles and two awful sore butts later we end up at – of all places – Tafaraoui, home of that Gooney bird squadron that we stole the two C-47s from back when we raided Bone."

"And before you can say '*aw damn*' we ran into one of the crews we stole those C-47s from," Lindquist added as if it was the most unbelievable assertion in Western history. "That's when I was really glad we had been kind hearted souls that day and left behind two cots and a couple of those real nice British comforters in that plane as payment for the use of their bird. Those boys gave us a nice tent to sleep in, this bottle of Irish Whiskey and a ride back home early this morning."

"That's some story… if it's true," Mitch said when they were done. "You ruined two of my airplanes in exchange for breakfast and a burro ride?"

"*Your* airplanes?!" Lindquist asked, looking incredulous.

"My planes – I'm the one who keeps them in the air."

Crosley and Lindquist looked at one another, and finally Lucky said, "Do you and I know this asshole? Should we tell him where he can find *his* airplanes?" Then he broke up laughing and pounded the table with an open palm. "I tell you Mitch – if it hadn't happened to me I don't think I'd believe it either. It was the doggonedist thing I ever heard or dreamed of in all my unnatural life."

"So you two spent the last week lying about in some tent, eating Arab delicacies and – sure you don't want to add some French girls to your story? This sounds like a Hope and Crosby *Road to Somewhere* movie."

"C'mon Mitch. It's a true survival saga, Jack London and all, without the woods – living through a crash in the desert and managing to find our way back home across the shifting Sahara sands. It's the stuff of great adventure novels and movies."

"Lucky, every time you survive one of your own landings it's some kind of amazing adventure. Never seen anybody like you – Houdini in a flight suit. Every time you get dumped in the middle of the manure pile you come up with a rose between your teeth."

"No, that's what Dixie always says about you."

"And what's even more amazing now – you two boneheads are on Group orders with me for seven days of rest, relaxation and sailing at Agadir."

"You're kidding," Crosley said, his face creased with a wide smile.

"Not going to Agadir," Lucky declared, shaking his head slowly. "Don't know anybody there and not real keen on sailing with land lubber Nolan."

"You got a better idea?" Crosley asked.

"Yup – a much better idea. Even ol' Nolan the grouser will like this one – *gare-on-tee*."

Chapter 27

al-Qāhira

Mysterious and ancient Cairo – seething with immensity; the thousand year old city, largest in the Arab world and African continent. First given life by the Romans as a small fortress three centuries after Christ, fought over by dynasties and caliphates, occupied by Muslims and allied with Crusaders; once a primary stop at the crossroads of the spice trade. Now teeming with archeologists and soldiers of the British Empire – and at least three U.S. Army Air Corps pilots.

"State your business, Yank," the Sten gun-armed soldier at the entrance to the British embassy inquired of Mitch Nolan in an unfriendly tone.

"We're here to see two embassy interpreters – Aida Gonzales and Makara Foulkes."

"I asked your business, not who you'd like to meet." He looked Nolan over, then inspected Lindquist and Crosley who were standing a few steps away. "I know 'em both and they aren't neither one the type to go hangin' round with the likes of you and your mates."

Mitch smiled at the guard. *I wonder if I'd get in trouble for yanking this Limey outside and shoving that gun down his throat. It might be worth it if I didn't want to see that girl.*

"Tell you what, private" Lindquist offered amiably, "give Miss Gonzales a call and tell her Lucky from Casablanca is here to pay up on the promise he made back in January, and we'll see what happens."

They had driven the six miles from Telerghma to Bertaux airfield in the early morning darkness and finagled a flight to Cairo on a B-25 from the 310th Bombardment Group – an easily coaxed favor when it was learned they were P-38 pilots from the 82nd. The bomber crew assured them they'd have a return flight waiting five days later and offered some suggestions of things to do and places to stay in and around the city. Nolan told them he and Lucky wouldn't have a hard time keeping busy. Crosley wanted to see the pyramids, then sail the Nile to its headwaters so he'd have something to boast about to his father and friends in Annapolis. It was mid-afternoon by the time they checked into a hotel and arrived outside the British embassy.

"What is it with this guy?" Nolan wondered out loud after the soldier disappeared inside.

"Jealousy. And a dose of envy with equal parts inadequacy and helplessness," Lindquist opined. "Think about it. Here's a fella who's probably ogling our two gals every day, hoping to make some time. Our Brit here is guarding a building at least fifteen hundred miles from the nearest action; no glory in that. And up shows two handsome, dashing fighter pilots full of piss and vinegar planning to steal those two pretty gals right out from under his long English nose. Change places with him and you'd have your bowels in an uproar, too."

"Got it all figured out, don't you?"

"Yup. Right down to where I'm going to spend the night. And, it's not with you in that dusty, airless hotel room either."

"You two don't need my help to screw up relations with our allies," Crosley said. "Before it gets too dark I'm going to find out where I can get a boat for the next four days. Sure you don't want to come along?"

"Nope. Ol' Lucky has better things to do than watch the shoreline go by four or five days in a row. Sailing with you or spending time with a blond beauty from Portugal? That's not even a contest, Marv. Only if clouds of locusts or an infestation of fleas and frogs overran this place, might I want to get out of here and join you."

Crosley soon drifted away leaving his two friends at the embassy gate; their wait seemed interminable until Aida finally appeared.

"Lucky!" she sang out and threw her arms around his neck, kissing both his cheeks. "And you too, Sir Mitch."

"I was hoping you'd forgotten."

"How could I? A knight of the realm. The ambassador will want to meet with you." Her pretty face lit up – she was obviously enjoying the moment.

Looking past her he said, "Actually, the only person I really care to see is Makara. She does still work here, doesn't she?"

Aida's face underwent a quick little quiver of distress. "She is so busy these days. There are so many Italian ex-patriots looking for asylum she hardly has time for a bite of cheese or a drink. But I will tell her you are here. Perhaps she can break away even if just for a minute." She kissed Lucky quickly on the lips and ran back inside, returning several minutes later.

"I am so sorry. She sends her regrets, but the people – they are many and so demanding. You know the Italians. She says perhaps tomorrow if you will still be here. And she asked me to give you this." Aida put her hand on his chest and gave him a peck on the cheek. He felt a slight tug and knew she'd slipped something into his breast pocket; she kissed him again and whispered quietly into his ear. "Her address... but I was not the one who gave it to you."

Lucky stepped in and took her arm. "How about your schedule? Do we have time for a drink and dinner?"

"But of course!" the blond girl said happily and put her head on his shoulder. "I am so sorry Mitch. Perhaps things will change for the better tomorrow."

"Maybe so," he replied. As his friend and Aida walked down the crowded street, he pulled the small scrap of paper out and looked at it, then at his watch. *How in the world am I going to locate this place? Find a cab. There must be cabs here.*

A half hour later he was seated at a table outside an open café diagonally across a small square from a three story apartment building whose address Aida had given him. It was six o'clock when a black Mercedes pulled up and Makara got out. She leaned over and said something to a person in the back seat he couldn't see. Watching her made the breath catch in his throat as it had that first night in Casablanca. She hurried inside as the car pulled away.

He entered the building, found her second floor apartment and knocked. The door opened suddenly and he found himself staring at the most exotic, expressive face he'd ever known.

Startled, she gasped and her eyes looked panicked.

"Hello, Makara," he finally said. His pulse quickened and the skin on the back of his neck tingled. "You're more beautiful than I remembered."

"Oh, Mitch," she said softly, looking fleetingly past him. Quickly she pulled him into the apartment, closing the door and pressing his back against the wall as she covered his mouth with hers. "Why did you? I didn't want to see you – but I wanted to be with you even more. Why do you do this to me?" she pleaded, kissing his face and neck while running her fingers through his hair. "We can't, we shouldn't… oh, Mitch."

"I had to find you," he whispered between her kisses. "I traveled more than a thousand miles today just to see you, and it was worth every minute in that cramped old bomber."

"I'm so glad you did. I've wanted to be with you… so much… for so long now." She pressed against him and held his face between her hands, kissing him over and over. Stepping back she looked at him intensely, gasping, her chest rising and falling. Suddenly she took his hand, led him into her bedroom and pushed him backward onto the large the double bed.

She knelt over him, her long black hair cascading down over his face.

*   *   *   *

She called the drink *Araq*, a cloudy liquid heavy with anise and not terribly appealing – at first. But it was growing on him. It also carried a 120 proof rating according to Makara.

They were seated at an outdoor table on top of an old three story building not far from her apartment. A surprisingly cool and refreshing evening breeze blew softly across the porch from which they could see the Nile, now bathed in the day's final rays of sun. Mitch wondered if one of the small sailboats on the river might be carrying his buddy Marvelous Marv.

"I'm entirely in your hands," Mitch said to her as he looked over the spread of small bowls on the table between them. "I'm clueless as to what I'm eating. What did you call this?"

"*Mezze*. It is all called *mezze* when served together; it is the combination of many dishes from all over the Mediterranean and beyond. Tonight we are having falafel from Syria, artichoke salad and kalamata olives with Greek feta cheese drizzled with olive oil. *Kibbeh* from Turkey. The grilled meat on the skewer is *souvlakia* – bite sized pieces of lamb."

"Which is the *kibbeh*?"

"This. It is a cereal called burguhl mixed with chopped meat and spices. And we also have *pastirma* which is seasoned beef that is air dried."

"That stuff in the red bowl looks like eggplant. Finally, something I recognize."

He had always thought of life as a intersection of aptitude and chance – something his father would have disputed. Arrival that day over Telerghma at the precise time and place of the Luftwaffe attack on the Group airfield in hindsight had been timed so precisely it seemed unquestionably providential. Now, as he gazed across the table at this mysterious and strikingly beautiful woman, everything that had happened to him the last six months seemed unreal. Just weeks before Christmas he'd been stuck at Moffett in a tedious dead end assignment from which there seemed no chance of escape. Without warning, an incident inconsequential in the grand schemes and decisions of the Air Corps had put him in the cockpit of an airplane destined for North Africa. Now, a half year later and half a world away, his life was wholly changed and his course patently different from anything he'd ever dreamed.

"I only have five days," he told her. "And I want to spend every minute with you."

Sipping her *Araq*, she smiled coyly at him over the rim of the glass. "This may not be possible. I have so much work to do now. But I will speak to the ambassador."

The words and tone hugely disappointed him; her insouciance seemed a casual dismissal of his desire to be with her, and it took the wind out of his sails. She had done this to him months earlier at Casablanca in the days after the big conference – arousing him with eager attention one day, then casually ignoring him the next. No girl had ever done this to him before and he found it vexing beyond words. He was quietly angry but then she gave him an alluring smile and a passionate kiss; his testiness vanished like morning mist.

"Aida tells me you are, like Lucky, a product of your military academy. A baseball player. A game like cricket, is it not?"

Mitch chuckled. "Distant relatives. In baseball the fielders wear the gloves, not the batter; catchers wear shin guards instead of the hitter. In cricket, unlike baseball, you can get a home run on a foul ball."

"You don't think much of the game, do you?" she observed offhandedly, her attention on skewering a piece of the lamb. "Do you Americans hold your British ally in similar disregard? I hear there is much disagreement among your top generals."

"Differences of opinion over a pastime is one thing, the conduct of the war is another. I'm sure our goal of defeating the Axis is the same. But there will always be differences on how to go about it between the generals. They all have big egos and big egos always clash."

"You know this because you associate with generals as a matter of course," Makara said skeptically, looking at him out of the corner her eye. "But then, you did know General Smythe-Browne that night in the Anfa Hotel. How is that?"

"He's a long time friend of my father's. And, it turns out my father's a general now, too."

"Really? You're not just saying this to impress me? It seems rather convenient."

"No, really, he got out of the service a few years ago and went to work for my grandfather about the time I went to West Point. He did pretty well, too. But now he's back in the Army."

"Doing what?"

Mitch laughed. "He told me I couldn't tell anyone. But he's doing what he really loves, and what my mother really hates. But I want to talk about us – about you and me, not them. What can we do tomorrow?"

"I'm not sure I have any time tomorrow," she said quietly looking apologetically at him with sorrowful eyes.

"Makara, please. This opportunity may not come again for a long, long time."

"I hope I don't have to disappoint you," she was saying. "But I have this terrible burden. I cannot escape the sound of suffering this present war causes. Perhaps someday as an old woman I will take comfort in pottering around and accept suffering with indifference. But not now – I cannot."

"I can't imagine you as an old woman."

Her eyes suddenly sparkled; she laughed merrily. "Honestly, neither can I. Sorry. I was rambling. Do you think people in their prime are honor bound to act on their convictions?"

"When you put it in terms of honor, then I have to agree – it's my old school motto."

"Is that why you do what you do? Or is there something else driving you?" She looked at him quizzically. "And what is it exactly you do? I don't really know."

"I'm a fighter pilot."

"You kill Germans."

"I shoot down German airplanes and sink German ships; and, I keep them from doing that to our bombers and navy vessels."

"But isn't that basically killing Germans?"

"I've never spent time thinking of it that way. When I shoot down a German plane I take a piece of equipment out of their inventory – a machine that will no longer be able to kill my friends or American soldiers on the ground."

"So, you and your mates have removed yourself a step or two from the ugly business, the unpleasant reality that is war."

He thought for a minute. "Not totally. It's true I don't much think about it when I shoot down an enemy plane – usually there's not time to dwell on it the instant it happens. I'm more affected when we lose one of ours because I know the pilots." Even as he spoke, he knew it wasn't wholly true. The sense of loss was fleeting and something rarely dwelt on. Now, she made him wonder. Maybe he wasn't as close to the squadron's pilots as he thought.

"I've heard some RAF officers talk of chivalry amongst the fighter pilots on both sides. Is it true? Are you present day knights of the air with a shared code of honorable conduct?"

He chuckled and shrugged. "Hadn't heard that. Sounds like something made up on a movie studio back lot. Aerial combat is called a dogfight for good reason. I found it's more like a knife fight than a duel. There are stories going around about German pilots shooting our guys hanging in parachutes. I haven't seen it, but there's enough talk to tell me there's something to it. We don't do it so far as I know. I doubt the Brits would either because to them it would be bad form; to me it's just plain indecent."

"You would never do it then?"

"Absolutely not."

She gave him a heart stopping smile and patted the back of his hand. "There is a decent side to you isn't there?"

"You say that like you're surprised."

"Should I be?"

"Why do you answer questions with questions?"

"Why shouldn't I?"

"See. There you go again." He squeezed her hand and looked into her deep, dark eyes. "I should be the one asking questions. I want to know everything about the girl I'm falling in – no, the girl I've already fallen in love with."

Makara looked away and took a deep breath. "Don't say that, Mitch Nolan. It's too soon. You can't possibly know."

"But I do know. I know it to an absolute certainty."

"You can't. You're infatuated with me, that's all – as I am with you. But we really don't know each other."

"That's why you have to break free from the embassy to spend the next five days with me so we can get to really know one another."

"I can't. Aida told you about the flood of work since the end of fighting in Africa. And I told you I just cannot stand idle in the midst of the noise of suffering that continues to cross my desk." She looked away and spoke very softly. "I must do something about it while I'm able."

Her words surprised him and sent a spontaneous chill down the back of his neck. "You say that as if your time is short, as if there's some deadline approaching."

"I'm not getting any younger," she said plaintively.

"You're not going to be old anytime soon."

Her eyes misted and she sighed deeply. "None of us is promised tomorrow."

The words shocked him; he blinked as if she'd slapped him. "What on earth does that mean? Are you in some kind of trouble or –"

"No, no. I just feel this terrible sense of urgency about the needs of all these people who are now flooding our embassy. I hear their stories; I see the fear in their eyes and hear it in their voices." Tears formed in her eyes and one ran down her cheek. She removed a tissue from her purse and wiped it away. "I'm sorry. It's just that sometimes I feel overwhelmed. Please, excuse me. I must go to the ladies' powder room and compose myself. I won't be long."

Mitch stood to help with her chair as she rose and walked back into the rooftop café. He saw her pause and quickly say something to a waiter who nodded and moved out of sight. Many minutes later she returned and told him she had to leave.

"So soon? I'll walk you home," Mitch declared, strangely worried now and leaving cash on the table amidst the dishes and bowls of their mostly untouched dinner. "I'm sorry if I said something to upset you. Tell me and I'll make it right."

"No, it wasn't you. It's me. The whole world seems terribly out of balance and I haven't handled the pressures of the last two weeks very well."

"How can I help? Maybe we should just sit down and relax and finish our dinner."

"Mitch, I must go home. What I need now more than anything is sleep. You can help by letting me go back to my apartment."

"All right. But please, call on me for anything you need – any hour of the day or night. Here's where I'm staying," he told her, writing his hotel's name on the back of a card from his wallet and handing it over. "Call me. Anytime day or night. I mean that."

They left the café and walked the four blocks back to her apartment building. By the time they arrived it was dark. Over her objection, he insisted on walking her to her door.

"Maybe you really are a knight of the air, Mitch Nolan," she said after unlocking her door and turning to him. Suddenly she threw her arms around his neck and gave him a deep, lingering kiss. "I shouldn't say this, but I'm afraid I too am falling in love. How can it be when we have only known one another for a few short days? I want to invite you in to spend the night with me. I can't – it would be wrong. So wrong for both of us."

"Makara, I meant it when –"

She placed a finger on his lips to silence him as she looked unblinking into his eyes.

"Tomorrow," she whispered, and kissed him again.

*   *   *   *   *

"I've never worked this hard for an interview in my life," Eamonn Kilroy said, pulling a spiral-bound pad and a couple of pencils from his messenger bag as he sat at a table across from the 12th Division commander.

Dave Nolan gave him a sideways smile and nodded his head. "You'll appreciate it more."

Andy had learned that sending the young reporter to the 12th Division had indeed been Ike's idea. Eisenhower wanted to place reporters in units where they could see, experience, and understand the lot of the average G.I. He'd chosen the 12th for a variety of reasons, chief among them his long-standing relationship with its commander dating back to West Point, their postwar work together with Patton at Meade, and their years under MacArthur in Manila.

Ike trusted Dave Nolan.

"So Eamonn, what did you learn in your week with Colonel O'Grady's regiment?"

"I learned to be damned glad I'm not a rifleman in your division. Specifically – how long a twenty mile forced march is, how hard the ground is to sleep on, and what a lousy shot I am with the M1," the reporter replied ticking off each item on the fingers of his left hand. "Your regimental commander almost killed me. He's the toughest SOB I ever met."

Nolan's eyes lit up and he chuckled. "That's exactly what all the replacements said about him when he was a lieutenant in my company in France. Back then I think it was true."

"You did that on purpose."

"Of course. I wanted you to know what a combat soldier goes through when you write about them. You're going to witness some of the most incredible acts of bravery you can imagine. You're also going to see a lot of fear, and maybe even some cowardice. Put all of that in context. So far, you haven't experienced anything approaching the crucible of combat. But I promise you, you will if you stay with us because I'm going to make sure you do."

"You're going to place me in a rifle squad? In combat?"

"From time to time, yes."

Kilroy pondered this for several seconds. "You had other reasons for getting me out of your headquarters these past several days."

"I was checking up on you through a friend in London. I wanted to know your background and your previous work. I know you bluffed your way into journalism by convincing a Hearst News executive you could speak Egyptian – which was a lie. In 1939 you replaced a woman named Nancy Wake who had done the same thing and probably told you how to fake it. I know you left Hearst and went to UP the following year because they offered you an extra seven dollars a week. I read many of the stories you filed with UP-London from the time you left Hearst and signed up with them. Anything else I should know about?"

"The Egyptian hieroglyphics thing was a ruse not a lie."

"A distinction without a difference. Like I told you before, I expect absolute honesty. That goes both ways. If you ask me a question, you'll get an honest direct answer. It may not be what you want or like, but it'll be absolute truth. You'll have to earn my trust and the trust of my commanders. Don't expect complete transparency until you do and that will take time – much is still at risk in this war."

"All right, general. I can live with those ground rules. Can we begin?"

"Fire away."

Kilroy opened the notepad and made an annotation. "Where to next for your division?"

"I know but I won't tell you." A shadow of consternation crossed over the reporter's face and Nolan saw him hesitate. "It's not easy, I know. But what do either of us have to gain by my answering that question right now? You can't go public with the information because it's a military secret; I gain nothing other than to show you what I just said about your having to earn trust wasn't true. It was a wasted question. Got another?"

Kilroy bridled over the thinly veiled rebuke but continued. "General Bradley said you'd be going into battle next by amphibious landing on a beach somewhere. How does the division conduct amphibious operations? And what kind of new equipment was Bradley alluding to?"

"That's planning and operation detail I don't want to get into right now."

Kilroy took a deep breath. "If you can't or won't tell me about operational matters, what's left to write about? Back home they want to know what's going on over here."

"At the moment, there's nothing operational going on in my division. We're training, conditioning and re-equipping the troops. You've seen and experienced some of that. We're planning the next operation based on guidance slowly seeping down the chain of command. But we're not doing any operations. If you want to write about operations, you should go visit the Air Corps. They're busy bombing the islands between us and the enemy where the Luftwaffe has forward operating bases. Those are the operations currently being conducted."

"You're saying there's nothing going on?"

"Didn't say that at all. Operations aren't the most important thing in any event. The most important thing I say grace over is the people under my command. You want something to write about that folks back home are eager to hear, tell the story of the soldier who is four or five thousand miles from home, hiking twenty miles and sleeping on the ground and cleaning his weapon and missing his wife or girlfriend. That's the really important story. And that story touches millions of people. They may not know the name or recognize the face, but they want to hear the story because they know someone, somewhere living through it. It's the individual soldier that's important above all else. He's the one who's going to win the war in the final analysis. Write about him. When the operations begin you'll have more than enough of that."

Kilroy mulled it over and decided he wasn't going to get the story he wanted – the story London was badgering him to produce. Maybe he could hold them off for a while. For a moment he wondered if he should go back to Eisenhower and request a different division because Nolan was uncooperative; obstinate even.

"But here's what I will do," Nolan said, breaking into his thoughts. "You stay in my hip pocket. Where I go, you go. Briefings I get, meetings I have, visits I go on – you'll be there. You'll see everything I see, hear everything I hear – except for secret material for the eyes of the commander only, and operational planning for the upcoming campaign. You can talk to anybody in the division you want to. Is that fair enough?"

"I can work with that."

"Good."

"I still have some questions for you."

"All right, Eamonn, go ahead."

"Colonel O'Grady. I want to know the story behind him. I'd like to start there. I didn't get a lot of time with him, but he struck me as a pretty complex Irishman. Maybe more than most of us. You mentioned he was one of your platoon leaders in the last war."

"He was. I'll tell you everything about him in more detail than you bargained for – what he's done, how he thinks, and why I picked him to run that regiment. He was one of the true heroes of the last war and he'll be one of the heroes of this one, too. We need some more coffee because this is going to take a while. Trust me."

Kilroy sensed he'd passed some milestone with the general; he wondered what it was.

* * * * *

It had been the worst week of his life.

The RAF airfield in Cairo was blanketed with an early morning pea soup mist. Mitch Nolan sat on a bench outside flight operations in the pre-dawn darkness shrouded in his own personal fog. He no longer knew what to make of Makara Foulkes, the woman he was certain he loved – at least he'd thought so at the beginning of his short leave. His mind was a muddle of conflicting thoughts and emotions and he found himself unable now to distinguish truth from fiction about her.

He had visited the embassy early in the morning after their shortened dinner to find she'd not shown up for work. Nor had Aida Gonzalez, but the Portuguese blond had called in to take the day off. No one had heard from Makara – she had simply vanished.

He looked for her four days and nights before deciding it was a fool's errand.

"Coffee, Mitch?" Lindquist asked, offering a tin cup before sitting down next to him. "You need to come inside, son. It's too wet to sit out here in the dark."

"I've been in the dark all week, Lucky. What's going on? What does Aida say?"

"She's about as clueless as you are."

"I thought they were friends."

"They are. Pretty close ones too but she says there's a real private side to Makara where no one is allowed. Aida thinks it has something to do with her family. Her mother is a Muslim you know, and her being married to a Brit makes things real complicated in this part of the world." Lindquist took a sip of his coffee and let out a deep sigh. "She also told me the story about the Italian ex-pats wasn't entirely true. It was something Makara made up on the spur of the moment to keep from seeing you that first day. She was dealing with some of them but the workload wasn't anything like what she wanted you to think. Sorry pal."

"Not your fault," Mitch replied, staring across the field into the fog. He thought back to the evening at the hotel in Casablanca. He'd never encountered a girl like her. She had been affectionate beyond his wildest dreams in the ballroom's dark balcony – her passion had left him breathless for the entire length of the movie as she swung him hammock like between the extremes of fiery kisses and sentimental whispers. He hated to admit it but she had played him for a fool; it had all been an act. Why?

To his left, a hundred yards away beyond a hangar, a car edged slowly around the corner. It's twin beams diffused the light all around as it crept slowly toward him until it came to a stop a few yards away; the driver killed the lights and the engine sat ticking as it cooled. A man in uniform got out of the passenger side and opened the back door wide allowing a tall dark-haired woman to exit. She walked slowly toward him in the dark.

"Hello Mitch," Makara Foulkes said softly. "I couldn't let you leave Cairo without saying goodbye. I owe you an explanation."

"Damn right you do," he said angrily, but inwardly he was elated. "More than one."

She glanced quickly at Lucky then back to him. "Walk with me."

She slipped her arm underneath his and silently led him away from the operations shack further into the darkness. Makara stopped beneath the wing of a Lancaster bomber and turned to face him. "This has been very hard, these past few days. I could not allow you to be with me. It was too dangerous, but I couldn't tell you."

"Danger?! From what?"

"From whom – my mother's family. For some time they have planned to kill me."

"You can't be serious," Mitch said, standing close so he could look into her eyes.

"But I am," Makara said emphatically. "Do you see the man standing by the car. He is a Cairo policeman and he's been my bodyguard for over two months now. He was in the café with us that first night. You might remember him – he was one of the waiters, and he followed us to my apartment that night. I tried to talk you out of walking me home but you were so insistent."

"Is that why you wouldn't invite me in?"

"I had my reasons," she said stiffly as if not wanting to talk about it. "One was it would be too dangerous for both of us since I have been marked for death. It is really because of my mother for shunning an arranged marriage and wedding an English aristocrat 'infidel'. They call it an *honor killing*."

He had never before heard of anything called an *honor killing* and was confused. "What does your mother's marriage have to do with you – with us?"

"My mother left Egypt with my British father before the sentence could be carried out and she has never returned. I have. I carry not only the stigma of being the daughter of a *Kafir* but am myself viewed as an arrogant *Kufrul-Kibr*, a practitioner of unbelief. My strict muslim family thinks I do it out of pride, like the devils. I dress in western clothes which many of them see as too revealing and decadent. I work for a western government which is viewed as an oppressor of Islam. My aunts and uncles think I comport myself openly as an unbeliever."

"Are you a muslim?"

"In their eyes – and my own – I was born into Islam."

"That's not an answer to my question."

"Are you a Christian, Mitch Nolan? You were born of Christian parents, I assume, in a Christian nation. Does that then make you a Christian? In a sense, perhaps. But is it not more complicated? My being born of a Muslim mother and Christian father makes it more so for me. My being here only adds to the complication and potential danger – for both of us."

"Then leave."

"You weren't really listening to me at dinner in the café. I told you about my personal duty, my being honor bound to use my abilities while I still have them. I have to help relieve the suffering I see and hear all around me because of this war."

He was suddenly furious. "Don't talk to me about honor. You lied to me. I know that was a false story about your being overworked because of the number of Italians seeking asylum."

"I did it only to protect you. That is not a lie. I couldn't spend time with you for your own good." She paused for a long moment, breathing deeply. "I've been falling in love with you since our first night and couldn't bear the thought of being the cause of something dreadful happening to you."

"I don't know if I believe that either," he said caustically, but felt his heart bending toward her. He was certain he'd never been in the presence of a more lovely and exciting woman in his entire life. "You gave me the runaround off and on for days in Casablanca, too. One day you're all over me and the next you break a date without so much as a note or phone call. That's not how a person in love acts."

She looked away, contemplating. "I thought back then you were a married man. In the darkness of the balcony, I felt the ring on your left hand and thought it was a wedding band. The next time I saw you, you weren't wearing it and I assumed you took it off so I wouldn't see it." He started to reply but she cut him off. "I know now I was wrong. A month after returning to Cairo, I met an American who was also a graduate of your Military Academy and noticed he too had a ring on his left hand. He told me of the school tradition about the wearing of class rings and I realized I'd been wrong about you. I'm sorry for the way I treated you back then. There were days I wanted to be with you so much I was willing to overlook your being married, and other days my British propriety won out and I avoided you."

"You could have written."

"To you? I had no idea where you were or what you were doing. When we met you were ferrying an airplane to your Air Corps in Africa and expected to return back to America. Where? I didn't know. If I had known how to get in touch with you I would have. Believe me."

"You can write me now."

"And I will." She placed her hands on the sides of his face and pulled him to her, kissing him deeply. "I love you, Mitch Nolan. Stay here with me for a few days. The Cairo police arrested two of my uncles yesterday. I still have many uncles and cousins in Egypt, but for now I am safe. We can explore the city together by day and the river front by night. I will show you Memphis and Saladin's Citadel, Al-Gawhara Palace and the pyramids." She kissed him again, lingeringly, and then whispered into his ear. "I want us to be lovers."

His heart beat rapidly – it all sounded so perfect. But it was beyond his reach – this time.

"I can't," he moaned softly. "My travel orders end midnight tonight. After that I'm AWOL. And I can't afford that."

Dixie Sloan and Ricky Zubarik had gone on leave and managed by some means to get back to the States to see their wives. Colonel Covington had covered for them when the MPs came around because they were both aces and he thought this was not the time in the war to court-martial heroes. But it was clear no one else would get preferential treatment. The next man to go AWOL would get the book thrown at him. Nolan didn't want to be that person.

"Tell me you love me and you'll write me often," Makara whispered softly into his ear.

"I do love you, and I'll write every day."

Down the flight line, past the operations shack, an engine of a B-25 sitting on the ramp coughed to life.

"That's my plane. The fog is lifting enough for them to get airborne, I guess." He held her close and gave her a final drawn-out kiss. "I love you Makara, more than I can say."

He heard Lindquist call his name and reluctantly turned and walked toward the Mitchell bomber. Looking back through the wisps of fog, he saw her wave.

He waved back and climbed aboard the bomber.

Chapter 28

"A toast and hearty thanks to the 'Mad Bombers of Messina' for providing this fantastic Sicilian vino for the 96th squadron going away party," Major Buddy Strozer said, holding up his tin cup. "To Lucky Lindquist, Paul Cochran, Mitch Nolan and Marv Crosley – thank you!" There was a chorus of catcalls and several repetitions of: *Mad Bombers*! *Mad Bombers*! "Special thanks to Mitch Nolan, the *fer-tile* mind behind the creation of the 165 gallon 'Silver Carafe' which transported our nectar of the vine – a vessel strangely similar to the drop tank which mysteriously disappeared from the Group maintenance inventory earlier this week."

The battle of Sicily still raged on the small triangular island no bigger than New Jersey, and missions in support of the campaign were being flown daily from Telerghma. Tomorrow was a stand down day for the 96th after eight long days of non-stop missions; the new squadron commander had called a going away party in the Group mess for those who had completed their fifty mission tour – or would within the week. It included nearly all the surviving pilots from the original contingent who had arrived in North Africa a little over six months earlier.

Obtaining a supply of Italian wine had been an idea hatched by Lindquist one night in the pilots' tent after their second mission to Sicily when he'd noticed countless vineyards over the western third of the island. Lucky had learned the best wine was in the Trapani region along the coast north of Marsala, and west of Palermo. When the 82nd Airborne took Castellammare and the 2nd Armored Division captured Palermo, they decided on a plan. Four days later Lindquist, Crosley and Nolan volunteered for a bombing mission over the Messina Straights. Cochran just happened to be assigned but liked the wine raid as fitting for his final mission. Their four aircraft were each loaded with two 1000 pound bombs, except for Nolan's, which had a single bomb and a special 165 gallon drop tank he'd nicknamed the 'Silver Carafe.'

After the dive bombing run on Messina's docks they skirted north of Sicily over water and put down halfway between Trapani and Palermo on the abandoned Italian airfield now occupied by a company of paratroopers from the 82nd Airborne. Over the next two hours the troopers helped move and transfer four full barrels from the vineyard's cellar into the 'Carafe'.

"Colonel Covington told me when I took over from him I'd better keep my eye on you," Colonel Weltman said to him when the toasts were over and the serious drinking began. "He was right. My compliments on the wine. Best I've had in a long while. I'm disposed to overlook this little escapade once. And because you'll be moving on after your next mission, I expect there won't be a next time."

"Not for me, sir."

"I doubt there will be for anyone," the Group commander observed, smiling and giving an appreciative look at the wine in his cup. "I've ordered Major Strozer to press the 'Carafe' back into the aviation service for which it was originally intended. I doubt there are many maintenance officers around with the savvy or the guts to create another."

"I wouldn't know, sir."

Weltman took another sip of his wine, looked around the room and casually said, "Some interesting information is filtering over from the States you might be interested in. It's caused the Air Corps chain over here – me and Colonel Keith in particular – to do some thinking."

"Always good to know the leadership in the theatre is exercising the ol' brain, sir."

"I'll overlook the thinly veiled sarcasm, captain," the Group commander casually replied, taking another sip from his cup. "Take a walk outside with me so I can clear my head. I want to discuss something with you." Mitch followed the colonel outside until they were alone under a clear, star-peppered sky, away from the party. "You probably heard there's an improved model of the Lightning coming into the inventory in a few weeks. We knew it was in the works. From everything we've learned, it's significantly upgraded over the G-models we've been flying."

A new model. This is good, Mitch thought, still a little fuzzy-headed. *About damned time.* He wondered how many iterations the Germans had gone through over the years since the introduction of the -109 and the Focke Wulf 190.

"Exactly how this is going to work is a little muddled, I'm afraid. The government bought about six hundred –H models. It's a half assed improvement over what we're flying now and they'll go directly to operational units. We'll probably get some – how many, I don't know. It's basically a fine-tuned –G model with a little better radio. Not a big deal."

"How did that happen, colonel?"

Weltman shrugged. "Who knows. It's Washington; enough said. Even so, the first of the new –J models will start showing up in a trickle at about the same time. Our Group will be the first to get one or two. Improvements are significant. First, bigger engines – 1425 horsepower. Also, a new core-type intercooler that gives it a sizeable increase in rated power. It'll be housed between the oil coolers instead of the leading edge of the wings," the Group commander said.

Mitch thought about that revelation for a brief instant and pictured the arrangement and what it meant. "That leaves a void in each of the wings."

"Very good, Nolan. You *do* know your airplane. Each void will be filled with a fifty-five gallon fuel tank. That means even longer range. In addition, it has hydraulically-boosted ailerons, a first for a fighter. So, it'll have a significantly improved rate of roll and reduced control forces required from the pilot. It'll be more powerful and a lot smoother. Lockheed thinks they've alleviated – maybe solved – the compressibility problem in a dive by adding sets of electrically-actuated dive recovery flaps just outboard of the engines. Lockheed's engineers are predicting a dive speed of almost 600 miles per hour."

Mitch let out a low whistle. "They do all that and the P-38 will so far out perform the -109 and the -190 the war will be over by Christmas."

"Maybe not that quick, but it'll give our side more of a chance. You want to fly one?" Colonel Weltman asked casually, as if the question was an afterthought.

"Right now, sir?"

"In the next week or two. I can arrange it for you."

Suddenly, Mitch's mind cleared. "What's the catch, Colonel?"

Weltman chuckled and took another sip of wine. "There's no catch, Nolan. The first of these J-models will start arriving in North Africa soon. We're planning to bring them in at Casablanca and start a transition school there. First, we'll qualify pilots currently in operational squadrons of my group and the 14th. Then we'll focus on replacement pilots coming from the States. Other than the training school in Morocco, all the new models will be coming to front line units that need them. For now, flight schools back home are way down on the list."

Mitch mulled over the new Group commander's revelations. If Lockheed had done what he said, the new Lightning would be a game changer. "Why are you telling me this, sir?"

"I'm recruiting you on behalf of myself and Colonel Keith. We both want a cadre of experienced combat pilots as instructors. You should be flattered your name was first on our list. Shouldn't be a surprise to you. You have seven kills, four probables and five damaged on your scorecard. You were a fighter transition instructor at Moffett for a year and you know your maintenance. Son, you're a 'three headed monster'. That's a compliment by the way."

Mitch thought about it. He knew a lot of the guys returning home were being placed in instructor assignments around the country teaching primary, intermediate or advanced. As much as he had loved the Stearman and the AT-6, he had no desire to go back to teaching fledgling pilots. Lucky and Marv had talked about transferring out to the Pacific where the long range twin-engine P-38 was in its element and the armament of the Lightning made the Jap Zero an easy kill. But there was no guarantee an inter-theatre transfer would go through, and there was nothing drawing him to the Pacific Rim.

In the Med, he had something worth sticking around for – a *someone* actually.

336

Makara had written as she'd promised; not as much as he'd hoped, but her letters were filled with reassurance of her love and her longing to see him again soon. He saved and read them each night until a new one arrived. Lindquist had been receiving letters from Aida, and she confirmed the impression Mitch was getting about his blossoming romance with the strikingly beautiful interpreter. He worried for her safety but none of the correspondence indicated any apprehension over her family.

"How soon would you need me, sir?"

"A month ago. But I'll settle for the day after tomorrow when you fly your 50th mission."

This was disappointing and he said so. "I have some leave coming, sir, and I'd really like to take time off to visit Cairo. I have a girl there and we have a history of false starts and missed opportunities."

"Sorry Nolan, but there's no time. Right now this operation is a blank sheet of paper. It's nothing but an idea in the minds of Lieutenant Colonel Keith and me. The 14th is just getting back on their feet after being decimated a few months back and they can't help much. It's up to us – actually, it's up to you. You're the foundation we build on, the one to breathe life into this thing. After developing and organizing it, you'd be the one running the school in Casablanca."

"Does that mean that I'd be a desk jockey, colonel?"

"Not at all!" Weltman said, as if it was the furthest thing from his mind. "That's the last thing we want. In essence, you'd be your own squadron commander, only you'd be reporting directly to my boss, the general. You have to recruit the instructor pilots, develop a course of instruction, and set up all the logistics. And you've got just seven weeks to accomplish it all."

Mitch's mind was swirling as he contemplated all the facets of such an operation. But he was beginning to warm to the idea. "That's a lot to do, colonel."

"You're right. As far as I can tell you're about a month behind already."

At least a month, Mitch thought. First he'd have to get himself well-versed in the mechanics of the aircraft and its new systems. Then he'd need to develop his own proficiency well enough to teach a cadre of instructors – pilots he'd have to start recruiting right away. There were maintenance people to find, fuel handlers, armorers… he wished he'd paid more attention to how Harley Vaughn had run the squadron before he rotated back to the States.

"It's a lot of work setting up something like that, and you'd be basically on your own. After it's in place and running smoothly you can catch your breath. It'll be a great challenge, and, it'd be a real nice feather in your career cap. You do this job well and you can probably write your own ticket for the remainder of the war, and maybe beyond. What do you say?"

"I think I could do it, colonel." His father liked to say success was opportunity meeting preparation. This was just the kind of thing he liked: a new challenge, something nobody else had done before. It reminded him of the ferry mission with Donald Bennett a few years back.

"I'm not here just to drink this wine or evaluate whether or not you're capable. To me the question is not *can you?* – I already know you've got the ability. The real question is: *will you?* What do you say, Nolan? Are you going to step up or not?"

Without hesitation Mitch said, "I'm your man, sir."

Weltman smiled broadly and shook Mitch's hand. "That was simple, wasn't it, Nolan? Now, I'm going to get a refill on this excellent wine you *Mad Bombers* commandeered and then I'm going back to Group operations to phone my boss. By this time tomorrow, you'll be on orders for Casablanca to arrive there before the end of the week. On the orders you'll notice something else comes with the job.

"Congratulations, Major Nolan."

*   *   *   *   *

"I doubt he's here to pat us on the back, Eamonn," Dave Nolan said to the reporter.

The driver, PFC Ronnie Krueger, pulled the division commander's Jeep to a stop beside concertina wire haphazardly strewn around the two large tents sitting under a stand of trees alongside Sicily's north coast road. Krueger had been wounded while knocking out a German machine gun position during the landing near the Irminio River two weeks earlier. Doc Hanley had patched him up and taken a liking to the youngster from Kentucky; two days later when Nolan's driver was killed, the division surgeon suggested Krueger take his place.

The general unwound from the passenger seat of the scarred, dirty vehicle, grabbed his M-1 from the rifle holder and slung the weapon over his shoulder. Dave looked at the overly large WC-57 command car with its prominent Seventh Army and red three-star plates and said to the reporter, "The only thing worse than getting shot and hit is getting a visit from the Seventh Army commander… but only marginally. Ron, pick up C-rations for us and wait for me. If I don't return in a half hour, you find General Fauser and tell him it's his division." Nolan shook the dust from inside his scarred old helmet, placed it on his head and mumbled to himself. "Let's get this over with."

When Nolan entered his command and operations tent, he saw Bradley and Patton standing in front of the large intel map on the far side. Cowering in the corner were some of his primary staff. Beyond them, trying to look busy, were three section sergeants and a couple of radio operators. Nolan caught their attention and nodded toward the tent's entrance for them to leave. Bradley turned and looked at him, rolling his eyes; Patton let his gaze fall on the reporter, then glanced at Nolan again.

"General Nolan!" Patton roared, glaring at him. He crisply slapped the map with his riding crop making a sound like the report of a high powered rifle. "I haven't seen any damn movement from your division for the last two hours. What the hell's wrong?"

"To begin with, the map's an hour behind, general. Second regiment just seized the high ground south of Cefalu and tanks from the 753rd Tank regiment along with my third regiment are again moving."

"What the hell took you so long?"

"The Germans had two well-protected 88 millimeter guns on the high ground dominating a narrow defile. We had to take them out or risk losing a bunch of tanks and the recon company of Colonel Haggerty's regiment. The Krauts weren't real accommodating about letting us destroy them, but Colonel Alford got through and took them out."

"Damn it, Nolan! I'm not asking for excuses – I'm looking for progress! If you can't deliver I'll find somebody who can and put him in your place! Am I making myself clear?"

"I'm well aware I serve at the pleasure of those above me in the chain of command," Dave replied flatly. "You can relieve me at any time. That's your call."

"Dave, nobody's talking about relieving you as division commander," Bradley interjected, gesturing with an open palm and almost imperceptibly shaking his head in warning.

Patton continued to fume and glare at him. "Why the hell aren't you in uniform?"

Nolan frowned for a brief instant and finally said, "Because I refuse to make myself a sniper's target. I never wear a shiny black helmet with silver stars." It was a good excuse and a better reason; plus it was true… mostly. But, not wholly. He wore an old issue steel pot without rank to remind the Seventh Army commander he wouldn't be bullied, as he'd refused to allow a lieutenant colonel named Patton to browbeat him the first day of the Ste. Mihiel operation twenty-five years earlier. Dave viewed himself as an old soldier who followed orders – but he refused to be intimidated – by anybody, including George Patton.

"Did you say Alford? Is he that son-of-a-bitch who pointed a rifle at me at Ste. Mihiel years ago? He is, isn't he?"

"He was a superb platoon leader at the time, one of the finest in the AEF. And he's an exceptional regimental commander now. He wouldn't be in the position if he weren't. If you're thinking he's not as audacious as you'd like, your issue is with me, not him."

"My problem, Nolan, is that I needed you in San Stefano by now!" Patton growled, jutting out his jaw and stomping his foot for emphasis. "How the hell am I going to beat Montgomery to Messina with this slow down of yours on the north coast road? If I come back tomorrow and this operations tent of yours isn't pitched in San Stefano's town square, we *will* talk. Clear enough?"

"Abundantly so, general."

"Good. Now get your ass down to that next town!"

"We're working on it, sir. It would be a great help if your headquarters could rustle up the close air support my G-3 requested to help soften the enemy's fortified positions on the high ground. We also need Corps artillery to give us priority of fire."

Patton looked hard at him. "The army takes ground, general, not the Air Corps. I'll see you tomorrow afternoon in San Stefano," Patton declared and stomped outside.

Omar Bradley shook his head slowly and walked over to Dave Nolan. "Mr. Kilroy, would you excuse me and General Nolan for a moment? We have some catching up to do."

"I gave Eamonn my promise he'd get to sit in with me on all my briefings and meetings so long as they weren't about top-secret issues or future campaigns," Nolan interjected. "I don't mind his hearing anything you want to say to me, Brad. He's earned a little consideration – I sent him with O'Grady's regiment when they were attached to the 2nd Armored to take Palermo. Plus, I've got him bunking with Butternuts. He's okay."

Bradley glanced tentatively at the reporter and then back at Nolan. "Some advice, Dave – and a request. Don't tweak George like that. One of these days you're going to catch him in a bad mood and he *will* relieve you whether you deserve it or not. Between now and then, I'm the one who catches all the flak for you, and it's getting a little old."

"That's your job, Brad. You catch flak for me; I catch flak for Haggerty, O'Grady, Alford and Fauser."

"Just don't make it a full-time job for me. Fair enough? By the way, the 12th is doing a hell of a job. Privately, George is pretty well pleased with the way things are going. It's just that he really wants to beat Monty to Messina."

"So do I. But I don't want to kill all my guys doing it. And I know you don't want me to do that either. Nor does Ike."

Bradley looked over his glasses at him, and finally shrugged. "True. But you listen to me when it comes to tweaking George's nose."

"Hear you loud and clear, Brad. I'll watch my step. That's a promise."

"I'm going to hold you to it." Bradley smiled and patted him on the shoulder, took a last brief glimpse at Eamonn Kilroy and left the command tent. When he was gone the reporter sat down and pulled out his notebook.

"Looks like you dodged a bullet, general."

"Not really. Patton is Patton. He scares hell out of almost everyone. He's one of those guys who's always all over you if you work for him. He pushes, he prods, he intimidates. If he can get you to back down, then he doesn't have any respect for you. The challenge for me is to push back hard enough to let him know I won't be intimidated without being insubordinate. In my position, I have to let him give me orders without allowing him to browbeat me."

"How do you know this?" Kilroy asked, puzzled but interested in this little insight into the colorful character.

"Figured it out the first time we crossed paths – back during the last war when I was a young major and he was heading up the tank corps of the AEF."

"He mentioned something about Colonel Alford. What was that about?"

"It was during the first day of the first major offensive the American Expeditionary Force undertook; it was called the Ste. Mihiel Salient operation," Dave began, remembering clearly the hot and humid day in September 1918. It was the day he'd been shot in the shoulder. Suddenly, he felt overwhelmingly melancholy, thinking about Denise and the hospital in Allery – and that time in their life. *I miss her*, he thought.

"To make a long story practically endless," Dave continued, "George tried to subordinate my battalion to him personally that day. I refused to let him. After our first episode of head-butting, we got along famously for the rest of the day, and for three or four days afterward. A few years later, he and I and Eisenhower did some work together at Camp Meade, Maryland. Same thing. He tried to run over me and I wouldn't let him. After a few rounds of that we got along well and actually accomplished something, I think."

"What was that business about Colonel Alford pointing a gun at him?"

Nolan smiled, cocking his head and looking at his watch. "Maybe you'd best hear that from Alford himself. I know he remembers the day – probably in excruciating detail. When I see him I'll warn him to brush up on his story."

"I'll ask him about it." Kilroy paused, thinking and tapping the tips of his fingers together. "Are you going to make it to San Stefano tomorrow?"

Dave gave him a long, enigmatic look. "Good question. The answer is this: If it's humanly possible, we'll be there."

"You're not hedging are you, general?"

Nolan chuckled silently and his eyes lit up. "Not in the least. We both heard what General Patton said. He gave me a mission and he expects me to accomplish it. Is it a stretch? Of course it is. But, in a contingent universe anything is possible. So we're gonna give it a run – our best shot. And I'll tell you this, it can be done and we can do it."

Kilroy was confused and it showed on his face. "All due respect, general, that's not what I heard you tell Generals Patton and Bradley. Sounded to me like you said it wasn't possible."

"You weren't listening closely. I'd never tell a superior that I couldn't meet an objective. When my boss gives me an order, it's my job to figure out *how*, not *whether*. If Patton really wants San Stefano – and I believe he does – I can do it… as long as he gives me what I need to get it done. That's where the issue really lies."

Eamonn Kilroy pondered, wondering exactly where Nolan was taking him.

"I learned long ago that no mission is impossible. Changing a woman's mind or the physical laws of the universe comes close, though. But in a military context, all a commander needs to accomplish a military objective is a proper plan."

"You're telling me every military plan will work."

"No, I said a *proper* plan. A proper military plan in its simplest form is an achievable objective married to adequate resourcing. Americans have a tendency to overreach on objectives and underdo on resourcing. The Brits – like Alexander and Montgomery – do just the opposite."

"You're saying the Americans are daring and the British are timid," Kilroy offered.

Dave Nolan thought about it briefly and said, "Timid? Not what I'd say publicly. I'm saying they're more... restrained."

"How so, general?" Kilroy asked, scratching some notes.

"You want the thumnbnail sketch answer or the tedious military one?"

The reporter smiled broadly. "Give me the long answer. If you get boring, I'll just fall asleep on you."

"Your poison, Eamonn," Nolan replied, and began. "Historically, military doctrine calls for a three to one superiority in equipment and manpower to undertake offensive operations. It rarely gets that good. When Rommel attacked Montgomery's Eighth Army at El Alamein, the Afrika Korps was beaten badly. They were out of fuel and ammunition but Monty waited a whole month before attacking so he could build up a huge four to one advantage. The Brits were way too cautious. They've done the same thing here on Sicily. They came ashore, ran into resistance and stopped to build up supplies. Despite giving them the best roads and shortest route to Messina, we've taken twice the real estate and in the end will be the first into the city."

"You're not painting a very pretty picture of our British allies," Kilroy observed, aware he'd just heard something potentially incendiary from an American general. He'd watched Nolan closely for a month and a half, had some interesting yet superficial conversations but the general had always been reticent in his comments. Something had changed.

"I'm simply revisiting recent history," Nolan replied. He sat back and gazed at the tent ceiling, deep in thought. "The Brits field a good army and they have a lot of good leaders; so do we. But I've learned there's a pretty significant difference in philosophy between us. It'll be interesting to see how that plays out over time. Both sides still have a lot to learn about one another. If we can marry the best of both we'll win this war. If we can't..."

Kilroy's senses were fully alerted. Nolan seemed to indicate a serious problem within the alliance. "Are you saying relations between us and the Brits aren't all that good? Is it because of this difference in philosophy?"

"Relations are not as good as they could be. We're both new at working together. In North Africa we each ran our own separate operations until the very end. In a joint operation like this the differences between us and the Brits get magnified beginning with our approach to command relationships. As a general rule, in our Army, commanders issue orders which are followed by their subordinates, period; end of discussion. In the British military, when a senior commander issues an order to a subordinate, the order is viewed as the beginning of a conversation, not a directive to be immediately obeyed. That's a huge difference that sets up the real possibility of serious misunderstanding between commanders and command structures."

Kilroy scribbled some more notes and said, "I've heard you use the term 'achievable objective'. Frankly, that comes across as hedging."

"It's not," the general replied directly. "An objective that's not properly defined really isn't an objective, it's a wish. An objective is a goal with attributes: first, is that it's achievable; second, it's measurable. And finally, it has a time restriction. Take the objective I was given to secure San Stefano tomorrow. Is that achievable? Of course. Is it measurable? Of course it is. Does it have a time limit – yes, by the end of the day tomorrow. Therefore, it's an objective."

"Does that mean the 12th will be in San Stefano this time tomorrow?"

"Maybe."

"Still sounds like you're hedging your bets, general."

"Let me show you something," Dave Nolan replied, with a passion reminiscent of professors Kilroy remembered from his undergraduate days at Princeton. "Suppose I give you the mission of capturing and holding San Stefano by the end of the day tomorrow. That's an objective because it meets the criteria I just outlined for you, but it's not really an achievable objective until you're given the resources you need to complete the mission – troops, artillery support, air support, maybe naval guns. That's what I asked Patton for just now. If General Patton really wants San Stefano by tomorrow, he'll give me the resources to do it and I'll do the job because properly resourced the objective is achievable."

"He didn't sound like he plans to give you what you asked for in the way of air support."

"He didn't say no, did he? In fact, I'm sure he agrees with me on my need and I'm also sure he'll raise hell with Alexander and Eisenhower to get it for me. If he gets the close air support and Bradley gives this division priority with Corps artillery we'll most likely be sitting in the San Stefano's town square some time tomorrow listening to another demand from him. If not, I'm still going to work like hell to get there because if I don't, he's going to chew me out."

"Even if you get what you requested it's still a tough job to make all that work together."

"The solution to most military problems is very simple. It's the execution that's a bitch. Getting all the 'stuff' together can be a challenge, sure, but making it work together, that's where a commander earns his spurs. That's my job, and the job of every troop leader in the division from me down through the squad sergeants." Nolan sat back and looked at the reporter. "I see you're still awake."

The division command post staff began filtering back in and Nolan spent a few minutes with each section receiving brief updates on intelligence, recent operations reports received and supply. Andy Fauser entered the tent minutes later and joined in the short briefings.

"We got us a couple of problems brewin', Davey," Fauser began when the section briefings were over. He brushed dust from his fatigues and scrubbed his close-cropped hair with his knuckles. Ammo for artillery battalions is slow comin' and so's 37mm. anti-tank rounds. Both Judd and Cole are gettin' antsy about arty support – they could use a little hand-holdin'. Big news is we might lose Doc Hanley, leavin' us shy o' leadership and a sharp scalpel in the med battalion."

"Lose Doc? Why?"

"Seventh Army is settin' up another big evac hospital in Nicosia and they want him to run the dang thing," Andy replied, taking out a cigarette and tapping it against his thumbnail.

Nolan walked to the wall map and found the town; latest intelligence showed it was still in enemy territory. "Have we taken that place yet?"

"1st Division got there an hour ago."

"And Seventh Army is already setting up a hospital?"

"Kinda. It's in the works. But they already decided they want Doc to run the thing. Georgie wants it up 'n runnin' as soon as the town's cleared. Makes sense in a way. It'd be forty miles closer to the front than the one in Barrafranca."

"Why don't they just move that one forward?"

"Too many wounded there already. Hell, Davey, I don't claim to unnerstan' all that damn gibberish them med folks talk. Doc says it makes sense, even though he don't want to leave the division. I told him we'd get him back to the 12th as soon as we take this little rock, but for now I guess we lost him. Doc McElroy can handle it until then. Best we can do," Andy said, shrugging and lighting his cigarette.

Dave took a deep breath feeling an annoying frustration wash over him. This was Patton's doing – had to be. The old tanker's penchant for making snap decisions was understandable in the tactical context but he almost never considered the practical and often far-reaching negative consequences of his ideas and orders. Nolan was glad he had Andy to take care of the myriad logistical headaches Patton was always bestowing on the division. His old roommate had a gift and aptitude for it, leaving him to command the battle waged by the regiments and supporting division artillery while Andy took care of the quartermaster, medical, signal, ordnance and the division staff. They worked together now much as they had in Manila when he commanded a battalion under MacArthur.

"I have to get back out to Alford's position. I told G-3 to work up a plan for taking San Stefano tomorrow and be ready to brief it tonight at 1800."

Fauser got a pained look on his face. "Tomorrow? Davey, that's twenty mile o' bad road and us not real well fixed for artillery support."

Dave left the tent after speaking briefly with Kilroy who passed on going with him to the front in order to work on a column. Fauser got a cup of coffee and ambled over to the reporter.

"You oughta be out wanderin' 'round with the commander," Fauser said as he sat down on the bench seat. "Whatcha workin' on there, boy?"

"A past due submission," Kilroy replied, hoping Fauser wouldn't become a distraction as he made some notes about his brief conversation with Nolan. After a short while, he looked at the assistant division commander. "I just had a strange conversation with General Nolan."

"Hell, son, don't go complainin' to this ol' Razorback," Fauser said, slowly sipping from his tin cup. "He's been doin' that to me goin' on three decades. Go see the division chaplain."

"I'm serious."

"So am I," Fauser replied with practiced indifference as he finished his coffee.

"He got sort of philosophical with me."

"Oh, you brung to the surface *professor* Nolan. Davey can get kinda preachy sometimes. What sermon did he give you?"

"He talked about military plans and also about British leadership."

"Really? I'm not too flummoxed with him goin' on about field orders and objectives and coordinatin' the instructions and the like. He can be a real stickler on how orders get wrote up and transmitted. So he also said somethin' about our friends the Brits."

"He said they were too restrained; too cautious."

Fauser laughed out loud. "That all? You caught him in one of *his* restrained moments. Did he tell you about this difference in philosophy betwixt us and them?" Fauser lit another cigarette off the one he was smoking. "He's beginnin' to trust you, Irishman. Good sign for you. Now you're gonna start really learnin' what this whole thing is about."

"Really? It's hard for me to tell. He's a pretty complex person."

Fauser looked disapprovingly at him. "You ain't even close, boy. Davey Nolan is one of the simplest men in this whole damned Army. He's a soldier from muzzle to butt plate. Loves every soldier and everything about soldiering. That's why he's back in the Army after leavin' us a half dozen years ago. Everything he's doin' now and the way he does it is rooted in two beliefs he's had since I first met him – there ain't no bad soldiers, and there ain't no good wars.

"Remember that boy and you'll unnerstan' most things he does and some things he says."

Chapter 29

The young nurse with long blond hair gathered at the base of her neck navigated down the middle of the tent in the narrow aisle described by closely spaced cots. All eyes in the ward of the evacuation hospital followed her, including those of the young-looking colonel with his leg in a cast and the two star general sitting on a camp stool at his side.

"Half the soldiers in here have proposed to her," Cole Alford said, leaning to the side to get a better view. "And the other half – including me – will pretty soon. Haven't heard a grumpy word since she showed up two days ago."

"I can imagine," Dave Nolan replied. He watched the female lieutenant stop at the foot of a bed halfway down the tent's length and make a notation on a patient's chart. Even in the baggy dull green fatigues she was attractive. He felt a quick tug at his heart when she laughed at something one of the patients said; her profile, the sweet smile and the way she related to the patients reminded him of so much of Denise.

"She charmed the socks off Andy when he came by yesterday, and she's got a sense of humor," Cole was saying. "She played right along with Butternuts and Doc when they tried to convince me Hanley was going to amputate this leg."

Lucian Truscott's Third Division had relieved the 12th four days earlier, after Alford's regiment had taken San Stefano the last day of July. Without close air support or naval gunfire, the fight through the narrow valleys under the German guns above the road had been slow and costly. Nolan had agonized over the casualty reports each night and continued to press Bradley about the lack of Corps artillery support, once getting into a heated argument with him. But the division had finally broken through and even Patton had grudgingly admitted to him in private that German resistance was more difficult and determined than anyone had expected. Now it was *The Rock of the Marne's* turn in the barrel as Nolan's division had been pulled back a few miles behind the line for some well-earned rest. Truscott had been given the mission to go farther and faster than Nolan by executing an end run of amphibious operations originating from San Stefano and landing on beaches twenty to fifty miles behind the German main line of resistance. Lucian had initially balked at the idea but Patton was adamant; the Third Division commander had sought Dave out as a sounding board to discuss details of his plan.

"Had to spend a couple of days with General Truscott," Nolan said in a conspiratorial low tone. "He's drawn the assignment of executing amphibious landings along the coast road to bypass the kind of problems we encountered."

"I'm glad we didn't draw that duty," Alford said, still watching the young blond nurse as she made a notation on another chart. "That's gonna be some tough sledding. Lucky for us the omniscient Georgie Patton doesn't know you, me, Andy and Judd wrote the book on amphibious landings for MacArthur when we were in Manila."

"Just doing our duty, Cole." Dave remembered with dazzling clarity the abortive first attempt under Colonel Rybicki's doctrine at landing on the shores of Lingayen Gulf just south of Bauang – a pleasant little town with its series of watchtowers erected centuries earlier to provide early warning of invading Moro pirates.

"Man, that was a great time, wasn't it? You running the battalion and all of us company commanders working for you again like we did in the big war. Andy and Doc Hanley swapping outrageous stories at officers' calls; Denise creating her bridge clubs and Saturday night dances for the enlisted men. Best assignment me and Muggs ever had."

"That was all long ago and far away, Cole," Nolan said absently.

It had been one of the truly satisfying times in his career. The islands had confronted him with all the gaiety, peculiarity and expectant passion for life he had so missed at his previous assignment at Camp Lewis and other meager Army outposts. He remembered the first sighting of Manila he had enjoyed with Mitch and Glenn while standing on the bow of the old steamer as the sun rose beyond the city. It had been the first of many magical moments his family would share in his all too brief assignment. He remembered Denise's exuberant response to the Filipinos and their intriguing marketplaces. His daughter became a woman there, and his sons had forged their own personalities in the jungles where they loved to hike, and along the beaches where they fished the surf.

He'd enjoyed a sense of accomplishment unlike any that he had experienced since his time in the Rainbow Division under Donovan. But the real joy had been the people – Andy, Cole, Judd and a dozen more whose paths had crossed his prior to Manila. And there was Ike. They'd known one another at the Academy as cadets and had worked side-by-side at Meade, but both their personal and professional relationship had flourished under the harsh realities of MacArthur's administration and the dire predictions of another war, this time in the Far East.

"– except for having to put up with MacArthur, and Rybicki… and that asshole Harrison Reeves," Alford was saying, interrupting his momentary contemplation. "You ever run into him after you left the Philippines?"

"A couple of times," Dave replied.

"One would be too many for me."

Doc Hanley entered the tent and looked around, said something to a soldier just inside the tent's entrance and then guffawed at the patient's response.

"Doc sure fills up this place when he laughs," Alford observed.

"Always had a way of doing that," Dave agreed and watched as his old friend steered through the tent with an encouraging word, a comment, a story to tell for each of the men in the mobile ward. "Never imagined he'd stay in after his commitment was done. I was the most surprised guy in that whole officers' club when I saw him there my first day in the islands. Always thought he'd go back to Baltimore and become head of Johns Hopkins Hospital."

"Not Doc. He's in this for the big money and the chow – same as you and me."

Hanley approached the cot where Alford lay. The doctor wore reading glasses perched on the end of his nose and a stethoscope draped around his neck and down the front of his long white lab coat. His hands were thrust deep into the pockets and he looked apprehensive. The doctor was a tall man and heavyset; through the years Dave had found it amusing that this huge bear of a man had married a diminutive girl a good foot and a half shorter and much less than half his weight. Kate Hanley had always been one of his favorite people. She was one of Denise's closest friends and Dave's preferred bridge partner.

"*Semper Fortis*," Hanley said as he approached Alford's bed.

"*Semper Valida*, Nolan responded. "Glad to see you haven't forgotten your roots, Doc."

"Forget? How could I?" Doc Hanley replied sounding tired. "Half my current patients are from the 12th Division. Wish it weren't so, Dave. I liked it a lot better when I was treating these boys for runny bowels and stuffy noses instead of chest wounds and crushed appendages."

"And I liked it better when you were my division surgeon. McElroy is doing a sturdy job, but he's no Doc Hanley. Say the word and I'll lean on Patton to let me have you back."

Hanley looked around and then moved closer, whispering. "To tell the truth, I'm not real happy with my new boss," the surgeon said with a surprisingly fierce scorn and a quick, dark glance. "I've only been here three days, but he keeps pressing me to push the wounded out the door and back to their units almost as fast as we can patch them up."

Dave was amazed at Hanley's tone. Along with Andy Fauser, Doc had always been the most jovial, easy-going one in their crowd. And he'd maintained that affability through the operations in Tunisia, the landings in Sicily and the long trek from the landing beaches to the north shore. Working directly for Patton had brought about a surprisingly swift change in him.

"Send me," Alford volunteered, touching his chest with a quick little movement of his thumb. "I'm ready to go back."

"You won't be for a while, Cole," the doctor said brusquely, thrusting his hands deeper into the pockets of his coat. "And when you do, you'll be riding a desk or the passenger seat of a jeep instead of leading marches."

Alford's eyes went blank for an instant and Dave noticed he was perspiring a little, and his skin seemed paler. "Not funny, Doc."

"Didn't mean it to be."

"Looks like that pretty little nurse is moving your way, Colonel Alford," Dave observed as he looked around trying to think of a good reason to get Hanley off somewhere away from the ward. "If you're going to propose to that girl, I don't want to be a witness to it. I'll need some plausible deniability when Muggs corners me and asks me to explain what happened. Doc, can you give me a list of all my troops you've got recovering here?"

"Like every other outfit in the Army we do a morning report each day."

"Great. Walk me back to your orderly room and let me steal a copy from you." He glanced quickly at Alford. "Cole, I'll stop back before I leave. Like I said, I'm denying anything that happens between you and the young lady." He rose and patted his old friend on the shoulder, then followed Hanley outside and down rows of tents to one marked as the medical headquarters. Before going inside, Nolan took him by the arm. "What's going on, Doc?"

"What's going on? I'll tell you what's going on – running this hospital. This is a damned nightmare, Dave," Hanley burst out, his voice raised an octave in an uncharacteristic rant; he looked away and took several deep breaths. "I'm short of surgeons, nurses, equipment and supplies. The only thing we're not short of is wounded and demands from the Seventh Army commander. Andy was here yesterday morning and told me there were fifty thousand men on this island, not including Italians and Germans, that would like to shoot that three star bastard – now I know why. He showed up yesterday afternoon in that big wagon of his with bells ringing and sirens wailing and lights flashing to announce his presence. While we were in surgery! *In surgery!* Count me among the fifty thousand."

"Patton takes a little getting used to."

"Wrong, Dave. He takes a whole lot of getting used to. I told his driver if he ever came in here with all that obscene pandemonium blasting again I'd take his tonsils out through his rectum – without ether… Don't laugh. It's not funny."

"I'm sure it's not," Nolan observed respectfully. This was so unlike the happy, gregarious doctor he'd met at West Point that night almost a quarter century earlier when he'd taken Denise to the post hospital in labor. Over the years they'd served together around the globe and become the closest of friends.

"This isn't what I'd expected," Hanley was saying softly but he looked baffled, frightened and strangely angry – an anger like a headlong, reckless fury surfacing for the first time. "I didn't think it would be like this – not at all."

"I know it can be difficult working for Patton, but –"

"No, Dave," the doctor interrupted, his face ashen and his eyes beginning to tear. "It's not just working directly for him. It's the war and the casualties – the whole bloody mess of it all. It's not the Army I knew, or thought I knew, at West Point and Walter Reed – or in the Philippines when I was your battalion surgeon. Even the operations in Tunisia, or the first few weeks here on Sicily. All of that made sense, but not this. I'm not making people well here, I'm doing butcher shop surgery to keep people alive and little more. I don't have the equipment or the staff, or the time to do things the way they should be done. This isn't medicine! And most of them are just kids who should be at home going to movies or roller skating; attending picnics on Sunday afternoon or taking a girl for a cherry phosphate at the local soda fountain."

"It's the terribly unfortunate reality of war, Doc. It's a young man's game."

"It's not a game," the surgeon observed, forcing a half smile but his voice was shrill.

"I know," Nolan replied uneasily. *Nobody knows that better than I do*, he thought, remembering the fresh faced boys from the last war who quickly became the aged older brothers of their former selves before his eyes. Suddenly he saw the face of Ed Higgins as he lay there on the floor of the bombed out little house in that trivial little town only days before the Armistice.

"You know?! That's easy enough for you and Patton to say. You can smash up all the fine china and crockery but I have to put it all back together."

"That's not how it really is," Dave replied quietly, but Hanley's thoughts had moved on.

"It's not just the brutality visited on their bodies that's so bad, it's the atrocity visited on their minds. That's the real violence," the surgeon lamented, looking vacantly skyward and shaking his head, "and it's something I can't do a single thing about. It either didn't exist back in the division, or I didn't notice it, but I see it so clearly now in these past few days. "

Nolan wondered if Andy had seen this side of their friend the previous day and decided this was something that needed some down time and serious deliberation. "When I come back tomorrow, we'll take a ride up in the hills. Maybe Butternuts can come, too. There's a nice little town not far from here that looks out over a pristine valley. We'll have some wine and lunch and shoot the breeze like we used to do back on Luzon. Remember that modest little settlement south of Manila along the coast? What was the name of that place? Anyhow, I need to visit my troops while the sun still shines. How many boys from the 12th on your list?"

Too many for one day's visiting it turned out. After a quick glance at the carbon copy of the hospital's morning report he started down the first row of tents and visited briefly with a dozen and a half of his soldiers in the first two hours. It was almost lunch time as he was leaving a tent when he bumped into Patton.

"Glad to see you're here, General Nolan. I give it as my fixed opinion that it does a man good to spend time with the fine young soldiers we have in the Seventh Army. The way the wounded are bearing up is the best antidote to the immediate weariness and long term fatigue that comes with command. I'm so damned proud of these lads it brings a tear to my eye."

"I couldn't agree with you more, George." Dave looked at Patton for a moment; the worried frown told Nolan the Seventh Army commander had something serious on his mind.

Patton took his arm and led him away from the entrance to the tent. "Tell me, Dave, have you seen any signs of malingering in your division?"

Nolan frowned and looked at him skeptically. "No. Why do you ask?"

"General Huebner made an off-hand comment twice in the last few days indicating he was seeing some signs of shirking in his division. Can't let that kind of thing go on unaddressed. The only thing worse is outright mutiny."

Nolan wondered. He didn't know Clarence Huebner very well – Bradley had just installed him as commander of the Big Red One after relieving Terry Allen. Everybody viewed Brad as the easy-going, genial and likable general – which he usually was. What people didn't know was that Bradley was even harder on his direct subordinates than Patton. George had yet to relieve anyone in Seventh Army, despite many loud and public threats to do so. Being harangued by Patton worried him little; however, Bradley… that was a different matter.

"George, neither I nor any of my direct subordinates so far as I know, have encountered anything like that. But I agree, you can't let that kind of thing go on. I wonder if it's not just an isolated case here and there, or simply a lack of leadership, at some level anyway. Is anybody else reporting morale problems like that?"

"No, not directly. I know that we've been pushing pretty hard and for good reason. Lucian pushed back on the amphibious end runs until he realized the operations are actually saving lives. The sooner we push those Nazi bastards off this island the quicker we stop taking casualties and filling up these field hospitals."

"Can't argue with that, general."

"Hell, Nolan, I think you've argued with me about almost everything since the first day we met. You're the most disagreeable man I've ever had under my command," Patton declared loudly, slapping his leather gloves in his palm and then moving away, entering a nearby tent.

Dave Nolan shrugged, looked at his watch and decided to postpone lunch.

The next tent held two men from Pat O'Grady's regiment – both were in the same squad and had been wounded by the same '88' shell the morning the division captured San Stefano. When he entered, one soldier recognized him immediately.

"General Nolan. Sir, what in the world are you doing here?" the soldier asked, his eyes filled with surprise as he raised himself up on his elbows.

"Came to see you and bring a purple heart to decorate your bunk." He looked down at the printed sheet to find the name of the other soldier from the division in the tent. "Looking for two guys actually. Farrier and Pritchard."

"That'd be us," one of them said pointing to himself and the bed next to him. "I'm Farrier, and that's Pritchard. B Company, 1st of the 34th Infantry."

"You boys were wounded at San Stefano, I see."

"Yes, sir," Pritchard replied, still amazed he was talking to his commanding general.

"That was a good piece of work you fellas in B Company pulled off that day. You got me off the hook with General Patton by taking that town as quickly as you did. I'm grateful. He was all over my butt up until then." Nolan reached into his worn canvas messenger bag and retrieved two boxes. Opening them, he removed the Purple Heart medals and pinned one to each of the soldier's pillows, then rendered a salute to each of them in turn. He sensed everyone in the ward was watching – a ring of faces measuring him. It strangely unnerved him now. "I want you to know how grateful all of us in the 12th are for your efforts. I'm grateful for your service. You guys need anything from the division? Gotten any mail?"

"We're doin' jest fine, sir," Farrier replied in a lilting twang reminding him of Andy and a few hundred other southerners he'd served with over the years. Most of the soldiers in his division came from below the Mason-Dixon Line. What was it about the South that caused their young men to volunteer and serve in the Army as a first choice?

"I want you to know you're getting the best medical attention imaginable. Doctor Hanley, who runs this place, was my choice to run the division's med company until General Patton found out how good he was and stole him from me. He delivered my son and my daughter years ago – that's how much I trust him. You have any problems, you talk to Doc Hanley, and I guarantee he'll fix it. If he doesn't, you let me know. You hear?"

"Yes, sir," Farrier replied with a grin that lit up his face. "It's passable fine to have folks in high places lookin' after you. Ain't that so, Billy-boy?"

Before Pritchard replied a loud commotion from outside filtered through the canvas tent.

Patton's voice – loud, high pitched, and unmistakably angry – pierced the relative quiet of the sprawling 15th Evac Hospital. The Seventh Army commander was yelling at the top of his lungs, startling everyone in the tent where Nolan stood. *What in the world?* Nolan excused himself and quickly left the tent.

The noise seemed to be coming from nearby. He quickly covered the distance and found the commotion was coming from the tent where he'd earlier been with Alford. He entered.

Looming over a soldier who was sitting on the edge of a cot with his head in his hands stood George Patton. His face was crimson and he was bellowing at the top of his voice.

"What do you mean your nerves won't take it?!"

The young soldier refused to look up. "I just can't take it any more – the shelling and being shot at all the time."

"You can't take it?!" Patton swore loudly, turned away briefly, pointing and staring hard at the blond nurse and two doctors who stood halfway down the tent cowering. "I won't have a sniveling quitter like this boy stinking up a sacred place where brave men are recovering from *real* wounds! You send this gutless little bastard back to his unit immediately! Do you hear me?! Don't admit this son-of-a-bitch!!"

"But, general," one of the doctors said, "Doctor Hanley specifically said to –"

"I don't give a healthy damn what Hanley said or thinks!" Patton turned and stood like a great brooding shadow over the boy, finally bending over and leaning closer to his face. "You're going back to the front my friend. You stinking little bastard, get up and get out of here. *NOW*! You will not dishonor these fine men with your presence any longer!"

The soldier finally looked up at the general, his young face deformed in haunted anguish; tears danced along his lower lids. "General. My nerves… can't take any more."

"Can't take it?!" Patton thundered. "You're nothing but a damned coward."

Dave Nolan took a step forward and began to reach for Patton's arm, and then everything settled into a slow motion kaleidoscopic frieze of faces and voices that sounded hollow – distant and distorted. It was like the instant the German bullet entered his shoulder in the wheat field years earlier on a hot September afternoon.

He saw Patton draw his hand back in agonizing deliberateness and then swing it forward slapping the soldier with the leather gloves. Behind him the doctors began to react – their mouths dropped open and their eyes grew wide; the nurse covered her mouth with a hand in instinctive dismay. The general slapped the youngster with his gloves twice more in rapid succession. The soldier covered up awaiting another slap as Patton drew back his hand again, pausing as he caught sight of Nolan. "This is what I was talking about! I'll not have shirkers and gutless malingers in my command. And I don't tolerate commanders who allow it!"

"General, a word outside with you please," Dave said.

"As soon as the staff here sends this little bastard back to his unit!" Patton grabbed the soldier by his collar and dragged him to the tent entrance and pushed him outside, giving him a kick in the seat of his pants. The general turned to the patients and said, "I'm sorry you had to suffer through the indignity of being in the presence of that coward."

Nolan stepped forward and said in a low voice, "George, we need to talk. It won't do –"

Doc Hanley burst into the tent, his expression agitated, demanding to know what was going on and why all the noise. One of the doctors spoke briefly to him in a low tone and then Hanley came over and stood directly in front of Patton only inches from his nose. "You don't run this hospital, general. I do. I make the triage decisions."

"Then you're not doing a very good job of it, doctor. How dare you allow that coward to stink up this hospital."

"And how dare you physically assault a patient under the care of my facility."

"If you can't do your job, doctor, I'll fire you and find someone who can!"

Dave Nolan stepped between. "We're going to take this outside –away from these men trying to recover," he said in a low, calm voice looking back and forth between them. "These boys need peace and quiet and the model of officers who can discuss things in a reasoned rational manner. I'll meet you two outside the orderly room."

"General Nolan, you are way out of bounds," Patton said, his eyes still angry and glaring at Nolan with fierce intensity.

"George, I'm trying to help you now," Nolan responded, remaining calm and continuing to talk in a low voice. "But you've *got* to help me, too."

Nolan turned to Hanley. "Doc, you need to back off from this right now, calm down and listen to me."

"What he did is unconscionable. Don't ask me to forget what I saw simply for the 'good of the service.' That never sailed for you before."

"I just want this handled the right way – for everyone's sake, including them, too," Dave added, nodding in the direction of the patients whose eyes remained glued on them. "You know me well enough to give me a chance to set this right."

Hanley took a long, deep breath. "For you I'll do it. But this has to be dealt with."

"It will be. I promise. The right way." He looked into his old friend's eyes and saw the tension visibly diminish. "Doc, don't put yourself in the position of having to walk away from what the good Lord placed you on this planet to do. These guys in here need you. We all do. Now, for all our sakes, take a stroll and think about that for a while. I'll see you later."

The surgeon held his gaze momentarily, but finally nodded and left the tent.

Dave turned to Patton. "General, I would appreciate your coming outside with me."

"Damn you, Nolan."

"We'll all be damned if you don't let me help you with this."

Patton fumed and restated his order to send the young soldier back to his unit, picked up his riding crop and glistening black helmet liner festooned with three stars, and left the tent.

Nolan glanced around and saw everyone looking anxiously at him. It was always the same – that haunting, expectant look he'd seen on the faces of troops hundreds of times in two wars over the span of three decades. He'd seen it the first time one cold and rainy afternoon in the trenches of the Salient du Fey when he first led men into battle. When would it end?

He motioned toward the young nurse.

"Jean, isn't it?" he asked when she approached. "I need your help. Very quietly, very matter of fact. Would you please get a written statement, in their own words, from each person here who witnessed our little outburst? Staff and patients. It has to be legible and signed, too."

"Yes, sir, I can do that," she replied in a silky voice tinged with nervousness.

"I see some of these guys may not be able to write it out by themselves. Could you and some of the other nurses give them a hand?"

"Of course. We help them write letters home all the time," she responded, treating him to a heart melting smile. "How long do they have to be?"

"Length isn't an issue. It can be as long or as short as they want. What I need from them is a factual statement of exactly what they heard and saw. Emphasis on factual."

"By when?"

"I'll be back here tomorrow afternoon. You ought to be able to do it in twenty-four hours, don't you think?" He looked closely at her pretty face and was instantly homesick. "I really appreciate what you do here for these soldiers. My wife was a nurse in the last war, so I know firsthand how difficult your task is. Thank you from all of us."

She smiled again and tilted her head. "That's very kind of you, general. I'll pass that along to the other nurses."

He went over and sat down next to Alford's bunk.

"Well, Dave, wasn't that interesting? I hope they throw the book at that son-of-a-bitch. You know, most of the troops on this island don't think much of all that grandstanding of his – all that Minever Cheevy crap about being a warrior in some ancient epic battles, not to mention driving around the place like some circus barker in a firetruck."

"We all have our own styles, I guess."

"That's not style – it's BS. Always thought he was dangerous and way off the bubble from the time I first met him. I should have shot him at Ste. Mihiel when I had the chance."

Nolan's face went hot as he glared angrily at his long time friend.

"Cole, I'm going to pretend I never heard that. And I'm going to allow you to pretend you never said it. But I promise you this – if you ever say that again, you'll be up on charges."

Nolan abruptly stood, turned on his heel and left the tent.

Three weeks later, in the middle of preparing the division for the Salerno landing on the coast of mainland Italy, he was summoned to Armed Forces Headquarters in North Africa.

*   *   *   *   *

The C-47 skirted north of the cliffs and beach of Cape Bon and flew down the middle of the Gulf of Tunis to a military airfield near the ruins of the city of Carthage where it landed and left its solitary passenger, Major General Dave Nolan. He was met by a staff car and driven through the ancient ruins to a colony of villas high on a hill overlooking the sea. Here sat homes of North Africa's rich European colonists. Eisenhower had decided to commandeer them as his forward headquarters for a plethora of sound military reasons: rich appurtenances, majestic views of the sea, and most importantly – indoor plumbing.

Dave Nolan entered Eisenhower's villa and checked in with Bedell Smith, Ike's chief of staff who was uncharacteristically tense, tired and worried. With nothing scheduled for him by AFHQ and being advised Ike wasn't expected back until late afternoon, he decided to test drive the large sunken marble tub in his suite and took his first warm bath since arriving in the Med. Later, he found a well-stocked bar on the first floor, 'requisitioned' a bottle of 12 year old bourbon, and sat on the broad patio outside his bedroom nursing a bourbon on the rocks and again reading letters he'd received just before leaving Sicily.

Senator Payne had sent him yet another of his masterfully crafted letters laced with a blend of quiet Pennsylvania Quaker simplicity and his own manifestly extroverted brand of optimism and gregariousness. His correspondence, as always, hinted at more than his words themselves conveyed. He was everywhere optimistic about the war. "The Russians after retaking Stalingrad have now launched a promising summer offensive beyond Kursk pushing Kluge back almost to the Pripet Marshes and recovering tens of thousands of square miles in just the last month. The Marines, having staved off countless Jap attempts to take back Guadalcanal are beginning to move up the Solomons Chain. And you know better than I the remarkable success in North Africa and Sicily." Dave wasn't as sure.

The Russians still fought on Russian soil and from what he could tell the from the map, the Solomons were very tiny little dots in the Coral Sea far, far from Japan. Recovering a few of them in the last year said victory in the Pacific war was still very much in doubt and an awfully long way from over. He wondered how many of his men from the old battalion at McKinley had survived the Nipponese onslaught against the Philippines. Not many he guessed, and he speculated it would be many years before MacArthur fulfilled his promise to return.

There was a mildly chaotic letter from Erika, interesting and filled with information yet challenging to follow. It was uncharacteristically disorganized as she jumped back and forth between topics, flooded her narrative with run-on sentences, and never seemed to get to her conclusion before she was off in mid-thought on another subject or tangent. It was clear from this and the previous letter she was in love with two things: her job, and the young lawyer she had introduced him to more than a year earlier. He smiled as he reread the letter and when he closed his eyes he could see her face and her expressive mannerisms.

The last letter was from Denise – one of the few she had written. It was clear she was frightened. Glenn had declared his intention to enlist in the Army and skip his senior year of high school, against her wishes. While Denise knew he was under age, she was still worried that somehow he would manage to work around her will and her direct command that he put out of his mind any thought he had of going into the service. She insisted he do something to stop their son from making the mistake of his life. Dave doubted there was anything he could do in his current situation, an excuse she anticipated and chastised him for in the letter. He felt sorry for her, and more than that, he felt overwhelming guilt for putting her in this situation.

He was sitting on the porch off his bedroom, looking out across the deep blue Gulf and nursing his second drink while writing responses to the latest letters when Eisenhower joined him, poured himself a bourbon and lit a cigarette.

"I want Bedell's job," Nolan said when Eisenhower sat down.

"Sorry, he's really good at it – and, as much as I like you, Dave, you wouldn't be."

"All right, then I'll be his assistant. Or his driver… I'll be his shoe shine boy if I can keep this little bedroom."

Eisenhower blew a large cloud of smoke that immediately dissipated in the cool onshore breeze. "You're not qualified for any of those either. You had the worst spit shine in my squad during Beast Barracks – maybe in the entire Corps of Cadets during our time on the Hudson."

"You always were a hard-ass back then."

"And you were always frivolous as a plebe."

"And also as a first classman, but you were long gone by then."

"I should have worked harder at running you off."

They were quiet for a while as Eisenhower chain-smoked and looked out across the quiet waters of the Gulf. Finally Nolan asked, "So, why am I here getting the VIP treatment?"

"Wanted to talk to you about a few things. Incorrigible people keep the old brain nimble. We've had some memorable conversations and arguments over the years – in the Philippines, at Meade when you and I and George got our heads handed to us by the Infantry Board for publishing those articles they didn't like. Ever wonder what those old retreads would think after what we did in Tunis and Sicily?"

"Not really. I wouldn't get any pleasure out of gloating about our being right all along."

"Liar." Eisenhower sipped slowly at his bourbon. "You and I have a long history with George. I'm sure you remember the day you saved our bacon at Meade. I know I do."

While he was at West Point as MacArthur's assistant after the first war, Ike convinced him to come to Meade to work on tank doctrine with him and Patton. One day after a heavy rain they were working on pulling a stuck tank from a mud hole using a single length of cable. Dave had called a halt to the operation and insisted Patton and Eisenhower move away. After heated words between Nolan and Patton, they moved everyone back. Suddenly the cable snapped and cut through the woods neatly severing a six inch tree trunk less than a foot from where Ike and George were standing.

"You sent that packet of witness statements to help me, and him, again," Ike said and turned to look at him. "So, I'm interested in what you think."

"Bad news doesn't get better with age. I wanted you to know exactly what happened so you wouldn't be blind-sided by some bright spark reporter or a letter from a U.S. Senator. Or a wire from Marshall. It's going to come out some day and land on your doorstep. You needed to know. I suspect you already did by the time my package arrived."

"After you gave Brad a heads up, naturally he passed it on to me. Was it really as bad as I think it was?"

Dave nodded. "In a way, probably worse. Not because of what happened but because of how George has rationalized it to himself. I had a talk with him the same day it happened and he didn't think what he did was wrong in the least. Even today, he'd probably still tell you Private Kuhl was yellow and should have been shot for cowardice, that he'd actually helped restore the man's self-confidence by what he did. Ike, I don't think you want to be standing up in public trying to justify that kind of thinking."

"You're right. I'm sure you've given this some serious thought."

"I bet you have, too." Nolan dropped a few ice cubes into his glass. "Otherwise you wouldn't have given the Salerno landing to Mark Clark."

"It was time to give Seventh Army a rest. A fresh commander and fresh troops – that all makes sense when you realize this is going to be a long war."

"Then why is the 12th Division transferred to Fifth Army and placed in the first wave?"

"Two reasons. Yours was the only division any of us trusted to go in at the Sele River and make it to Ponte Alla Scafa by the end of day one to sever the north-south rail line. And, Clark asked for you." Eisenhower was silent for awhile and finally said, "I've already been approached on the QT by several reporters."

"About the slapping incident?" Nolan found this disturbing; it raised the old worrisome specter of security breaches he'd harbored from the moment Ike had sent Eamonn Kilroy to him. He'd become gradually more open with the reporter over time and had even told him 'off the record' details of the incident at the 15th Evac Hospital. Now he was second guessing the wisdom of his transparency. "Was Kilroy one of them?"

"No he wasn't."

"That's a relief. What was the gist of the conversation with reporters?"

"They offered to keep silent if I fired Patton and sent him home." Eisenhower frowned and lit another cigarette off the one he was smoking. "Of course I'm not going to do that. But I'm interested – what would you do in my place?

Dave had expected this from the moment he got the message Ike wanted to see him at AFHQ. "George is an exceptional combat leader and retaining him is essential to winning the difficult battles ahead of us. If I were you, I'd immediately give a heads up to George Marshall and Henry Stimson to get the Chief of Staff of the Army and the Secretary of War on my side. I'd make them understand our military history is replete with exceptional field commanders who had strong and difficult personalities – Grant, Sherman, Custer, Pershing, Wild Bill Donovan. I would let Marshall and Stimson deal with the likely outcries from the American press and from Congress."

"In essence, you'd convince them to give him a pass on this."

"No. Not a pass. George needs to be taught a lesson by you. The really tough part is that he needs to be taught some humility without breaking his spirit. I'd put him on the shelf for a while, until he can't stand it anymore. It looks like that's something you've already done. Only when he's willing to listen – and make amends – would I consider bringing him back."

"How does anybody teach George Patton humility?" Eisenhower wanted to know as he looked at Nolan with raised eyebrows and poured himself more bourbon.

"I have an idea. It worked once for me and I think it might work for you."

Eisenhower put out his cigarette and indicated for him to continue.

"I once had a guy who was a harder case than George. I don't think you've met Colonel O'Grady, one of my regimental commanders, but the first time I met him, he led a mutiny against me. My first morning on the job as a company commander in the Irish 69th he refused an order of mine to participate in a forced march, and he led five others into doing the same." As he spoke of it, Dave closed his eyes and remembered back to that morning in formation. It had been a classic experience – one he had always thought he'd write up some day when he published his anthology of military leadership. "Like George, he was easily *the* best soldier in the unit. Before it was over, I had busted him, taken money out of his paycheck, and told him he was being transferred to another regiment in the Rainbow Division. None of that really solved the problem and it left the outfit the poorer for not having his services. I ended up keeping him – with strict conditions. Later, I gave him a field commission and he became probably the best officer I've ever had reporting to me."

"You think I can do the same thing with George? Alright, what's the magic formula?"

"Make George apologize."

"Apologize?! To whom?"

"Everybody he offended: the soldier he slapped, all the soldiers in that ward tent, all the medical staff at the hospital, and every single solitary person in the Seventh Army. Everybody. Make him do it unit by unit – that should keep him occupied for a while. And make sure it's a sincere apology. Make him write it out for you and deliver it just as he's written it."

Eisenhower looked at him with hooded eyes, not quite sure he agreed with Nolan's medicine. "You think he'd do that?"

"To get back into command? Damn right he will. You give him a personal reprimand. Not an official reprimand that would go in his records – that would leave him open later for who knows what. When you reprimand him, it says you're serious about this. When you make him apologize, it sends a clear message that what he did is unacceptable and everybody knows it. Then, you take him out of the rotation for command and tell him he'll stay out until he proves himself worthy. It worked for me with O'Grady. When he got back his stripe and later got a commission, I couldn't ask for a more loyal subordinate. He still is."

"I've never heard of such a thing," Eisenhower said, contemplating. "Never in all my time in the Army or in any of the leadership books I've read."

"I hadn't either," Dave admitted, remembering again the conversation with Francis Duffy in the chow line one night that had been the inspiration for his dealings with O'Grady. "I got the idea from the regimental chaplain. He was a wise old man. Not so old back then, I guess."

"I'll take it under advisement, Nolan. I think you might just have earned this little two day rest and relaxation trip."

"One caveat, though. If you do decide to go ahead and do that, you can never tell George I was the one who gave you the idea. He'll crucify me if he finds out. I'm serious, Ike," Nolan said when his old friend laughed heartily.

"I'll do my best." Eisenhower became reflective, turning away and gazing out across the blue waters below. "I appreciate your counsel, Dave. Always have. You've done well with the division, and we expect you'll continue to in this next phase." They relaxed silently and watched the fishing boats coming back into the docks at the end of their work day, followed by clouds of gulls skimming the surface squawking and screeching as they rose to circle the vessels. Finally, Eisenhower broke the silence.

"Tell me – why'd you come here instead of going to the Pacific with MacArthur? I know he asked for you."

"So did you."

"That's not an answer."

Nolan chuckled. "After working directly for him twice during the '30's you have to have me spell it out for you?" When Ike didn't respond, Nolan continued, "I did my time in hell.

Besides, he's twenty years older than me – I'm just a stripling by comparison and he's always been more comfortable surrounded by men his own age. I'd have been a field grade coffee runner or shoeshine boy in the Pacific. I wasn't going to risk upsetting Denise for that. If I was going to jeopardize my marriage to do my duty, it was going to be for something worthwhile."

"So, how is she? I wish I could have gotten to know her better when we were all in the islands together."

"She's upset with the men in her family – all of us. Me, Mitch, Glenn. Even her father for not stopping at least one of us from running off and leaving her alone."

Eisenhower looked surprised. "I knew Mitch was in the Air Corps. Did I ever tell you we crossed paths in Casablanca one day during the Conference? But Glenn? That's a real surprise. He was so young – and quiet – when I knew him in Manila. Was he drafted?"

"Volunteered," Dave replied. "Surprised me as much as anyone. Neither his mother nor I saw that coming."

Eisenhower nodded and remained quiet, smoking and looking out over the Gulf. "Do you remember Jakie Devers?" he finally said.

"Sure do. A classmate of Patton's – came back to West Point as an instructor when I was a plebe and coached the baseball team while we were there. He was a good man – good coach and outstanding mentor to all of us on the team, too. I remember he really liked Brad."

"Marshall picked him out of the ranks a couple of years ago when he was an aging bird colonel and promoted him to major general… pretty much like he did you."

"At your request in my case."

"I asked for you, sure. In times of war, the old slow promotions go by the board and leaders get put in their proper positions in spite of time in grade regulations. I like to think that was the case with me, too." Ike chuckled self-consciously as if he'd just told an off color joke he realized was out of place but still got a laugh. "Jakie is tasked with accumulating troops and equipment for a cross channel invasion of the continent. But he's also acting as the watchdog for the U.S. Joint Chiefs of Staff on combined invasion planning with the British. A month from now, I'm going to send Brad to London to take on the responsibility of coordinating planning with the British. He's been tasked by Marshall to round out the First Army staff and also to form an Army Group staff."

"Big job," Nolan observed, taking a sip of his drink and wondering why Eisenhower was telling him this, and wondering even more why Ike wouldn't look at him.

"President Roosevelt and Prime Minister Churchill decided to put me in charge of planning and executing the invasion of France. Marshall would have been a better choice in my opinion, but he's really an irreplaceable man as Chairman of the Joint Chiefs. I'm going to be leaving the Med and going to London after the first of the year."

"Congratulations," Nolan said earnestly. "They couldn't have picked a better guy for the job. I mean that."

"I know you mean it, Dave… and I appreciate it."

"The only thing you lack is the ability to accurately predict the future."

Eisenhower frowned, bemused. "What makes you say that?"

"Your own words. Back in Manila a few years ago you told some people that one day you'd be working for me, and now we see how far off that was."

Eisenhower's face lit up and he smiled broadly. "I must have had too much of Butternuts' high octane home brew. He's not still doing that is he?"

"Not since a JU-88 blew up his still on Sicily."

"Really? He still has a drinking problem I take it. You really ought to help him with that. It's not good for a general in the field to have an alcohol problem."

"I give him some leeway. I like to think it's just a serious affection and not something that hinders his leadership and ability to get the job done. I seem to remember Lincoln had the same problem with Grant."

"Fauser is no Grant."

"I'm no Lincoln either." Ike frowned again, looked away and remained silent for a few minutes. At last Nolan asked, "Why are we having this conversation, Ike? Is there something I should know?"

"We have plans for you. After you take the 12th ashore and the Salerno operation stabilizes so we can start the push up the Italian boot to Rome, we're going to move you."

"Ike, I want to stay with my boys."

"Look Dave, I know you're really happy in the 12th and you've done an outstanding job of training the unit back home and leading them in combat. I also know you well enough to be confident you've developed your subordinates so they can carry on without you."

"Despite what I said about wanting Bedell's job, I'm really not staff material."

"You're a commander, I know that. But you have other talents we need right now and will even more in the future. You know top level people in the British Army and you showed even before we entered the war that you can work with them. I know how good you are at amphibious landings. I need you to concentrate on that and smoothing over the relations with our British friends. Tempers are already growing short on both sides in London. We need to head that off and at the same time speed up the planning overall. That's why I'm sending Brad there in a month or so.

"I want you – no, I need you – to go with him."

Chapter 30

"Yes, ma'am, I'll have to check General Reeves' schedule," Valerie Ebert said into the phone and jotted the name on a pad next to her blotter. "If you'll leave me your phone number, I'll get back to you as soon as possible. I don't have access to his calendar right now, but if you've known him that long, I'm sure he'll be back to you very quickly. Is it possible to contact you in the evening as well at this number?" When she rang off the secretary rose, knocked on the polished door to the office adjacent to the entrance foyer and entered.

"She said she was an old friend, but since I couldn't recall her ever contacting you before, I decided to take her number and give an indefinite time for a reply. I hope I handled it correctly, general."

"My dear, persuading you to stay on after General Kruger's departure remains the most astute decision of my time in Washington," Harrison Reeves replied with a paternal smile and an appreciative glance at the sweater outfit she wore. "Of course you handled it wisely. I honestly can't remember when I ever had a moment's doubt about any of your actions."

Valerie Ebert smiled back at him. Her relationship with General Reeves had begun a half dozen years earlier and flourished since in mutually beneficial rapport.

She had been assigned as his secretary when he was a junior section chief and had quickly realized his talent for cultivating people as allies and information sources. He had a knack for the office politics inherent in Army Headquarters and swiftly ingratiated himself to superiors while exploiting his subordinates. Although guardedly appreciative at being promoted to the post of General Kruger's secretary, she soon recognized Reeves' influence in her transfer and repaid him with timely inside information from the Army Chief of Personnel's office. Later, when Kruger found himself in trouble over his handling of the Lindbergh incident, someone quietly sabotaged the general. The new Chief of Personnel, Harrison Reeves, rewarded her with a position level upgrade; Valerie responded with increased loyalty. She thought they were made for each other and assumed the general felt the same way.

"What exactly did she say she wanted?" Reeves asked, indicating for her to take a seat.

"She was hoping to discuss a personal matter and was certain you could help her. She made that very clear – as if she was calling in a favor."

Reeves leaned back in his chair tapping his fingertips together and gazing up at the ceiling. "Calling in a favor? I owe that woman and her family nothing."

"She said that she needed to talk to you about her son – something about his enlistment."

The general nodded. "That's all she said? Nothing else?"

"She was cryptic. It was clear she didn't want to tell me her problem or how you could help her. Like I said, she indicated it was personal and I assumed private."

Harrison Reeves contemplated and reasoned Denise Nolan must be talking about Glenn, her youngest. He knew only that the boy was entering his senior year at Gonzaga high school. That would make him seventeen and too young to enlist, even with parental permission which he was certain she'd never give. But she had mentioned 'his enlistment.' As the wife of a career Army officer for more than two decades, she would know exactly what that meant.

"Valerie, have General Lenox stop by before lunch. I'd like to talk with him before I return this woman's call." He looked at her and produced a warm smile. "And also tell Captain Jenkinson to stop by this afternoon. I have a mission for him to accomplish before I leave for home." Valerie Ebert recognized this as his casual way of dismissing her and stood to leave. "One other thing. You're coming up on your tenth anniversary of civil service. Of course there'll be an office recognition with cake and coffee but I'd like to show my personal appreciation by offering dinner for you and a few friends at the restaurant of your choice."

"Thank you, general."

"No Valerie, thank you. I can't begin to tell you how much I appreciate your contribution to the efficient operation of the Personnel Directorate. Millions of men – young and old alike – benefit greatly from what you do. None more than I."

"You're too kind."

"No, I'm not. And I apologize sincerely for not saying more frequently how much you're appreciated." He sighed deeply, appearing distracted. "Well, I shall be on the phone for a while. I'll call the Nolan woman later this afternoon or early tomorrow morning after I've had a chance to talk with Lenox. If she calls again, set up a tentative appointment for her late next week." When his secretary left the office, Reeves picked up the phone and dialed a number on Capitol Hill; when it was answered he said, "This is General Reeves at Army Headquarters. Please put me through to the congressman."

"I'm sorry, but the congressman is in conference and –"

"I don't think you heard me… Mildred, isn't it? This is General Harrison Reeves and I wish to speak to Congressman Callahan immediately. I'm sure if you tell your boss, he'll be grateful you interrupted, even if he is actually in conference as you say."

A moment later, Trevor Callahan came on the line.

"Harrison! So glad you called, old chum. How goes the war?" the Maryland congressman said convivially.

Reeves was strangely irritated at Callahan's cavalier familiarity but shook it off. "I have a similar question for you. How are things with you and your new hire? The Nolan woman."

There was a pregnant pause. "Why do you ask?" Callahan guardedly probed.

"We just received a phone call from her requesting an audience with me to talk about her son's enlistment status. Do you know anything about it?"

"Of course. It's her primary worry right now," the Congressman replied sounding relieved, a change of tone not lost on the general. "Apparently, he failed to come back from Annapolis this past weekend. Yesterday afternoon she found a note from him saying he had enlisted and was enroute to basic training somewhere – destination unknown."

"Tell me more. What was the boy doing in Annapolis and why did it take three whole days before she found the note?"

Reeves heard Callahan chuckle quietly on the other end of the line. "Because she was with me in Ocean City."

"And...?"

"It's not what you're thinking, Harrison, as much as I might wish it was otherwise. The state caucus had an informal planning and strategy session over the weekend, and of course I had to take Denise along. She's become quite indispensable, if you know what I mean."

"I'm not sure I do, Trevor."

This time a raucous belly laugh came through the line. "No, not that. Not yet anyway. I'm being very slow and careful with her. She's a very independent, strong-willed woman. But she's becoming more comfortable in her new political role."

"How soon before it becomes a personal role?"

"I don't know what you're talking about, Harrison. Certainly you'd have to agree gentlemen don't discuss such things."

"You're not a gentleman – certainly not in the original British sense of the word – you never will be and we both know it. What else can you tell me about her situation?"

"She's a woman with a lot to deal with right now in addition to worrying over her youngest son running off to join the Army – I assume it's the Army. She admits to having become something of a worrier. She's never been comfortable with her oldest son flying fighter airplanes although apparently he's no longer in the front lines of the air war. I don't know what that means exactly except that he's evidently in some kind of instructor role somewhere. The relationship with her daughter apparently continues to be confrontational, as you probably know through your wife. She never mentions her husband, at least not to me. But she has indicated to one of the other women on my payroll some feelings of desertion. I sense she feels abandoned by him and that's probably why she's so protective of her youngest."

Reeves pondered this momentarily. Finally, he asked, "Is she aware yet you and I know one another?"

"I don't believe she knows. I certainly haven't told her."

"Good. Let's leave it that way – at least for the time being. Thank you Trevor, I wish you well. I'll be in touch… Wait. Annapolis. What was he doing there? Any significance to that?"

"I'm not sure," Callahan replied slowly trying to recall something Denise had said. "I think he spends a lot of time there with friends of a friend. He's a fisherman – likes the Bay."

"All right. Don't know if that helps or not. Keep in touch, Trevor." Reeves rang off. A half hour later, Valerie knocked and ushered General Lenox into the Chief's office.

"Raymond, something has come up – a personal matter – and I need your help. You're the only one I can trust to develop some information for me discreetly and confidentially."

Brigadier General Ray Lenox owed his present position and the capstone of his career to Harrison Reeves and they both knew this although neither spoke of it. Lenox had been an aged lieutenant colonel without a future and barely holding on to a Reserve commission. He would have been retired five years earlier had it not been for Reeves who inexplicably tapped him to replace one of the five heads of section. He was promoted to full bird colonel which breathed life into his essentially dormant career. Two years later he had been installed in the new position of Assistant to the Chief and made a brigadier general.

Worry creased Reeves' face as he looked at his second in command. "A very old and dear friend of mine has a problem and asked for my assistance. I'm inclined to help. Her youngest son may have enlisted in the past week despite his being underage. I'd like you to canvass the recruiting stations in Washington and nearby Maryland and Virginia to see if in fact the young man did manage to sign up despite his age."

Lenox had his small green pocket notebook out scribbling comments. "Name? Age? Address? Any description, sir?"

"His name is Glenn Nolan and he would be seventeen by now. I suspect he passed himself off as eighteen. The last time I saw him he was a pudgy little ten or eleven year old so I don't have a description. He apparently spent a lot of time in Annapolis. I don't know if that means anything. He might have given something nautical-related as an occupation to a recruiter." Reeves pulled a dark leather-bound address book from a side drawer and flipped through the pages then wrote on a pad at his elbow."Here's his home address in D.C. His mother's name is Denise Barrett Nolan. His father's name is David and he has a brother, Mitchell, in the Air Corps and a sister, Erika. All of this is strictly confidential; you are the only one to know any of this. Raymond, I'd like you to make this your top priority."

"Yes, sir. I'll get right on it."

Reeves leaned back in his oversized chair appearing deep in thought. "One other thing, Raymond, if you'll think along with me for a moment. I've been reflecting on the directorate's future and I've given serious thought to staffing and my own replacement when I move on."

Lenox looked back at him in surprise. "You're leaving us, sir?"

"Eventually. General Marshall has been dropping some hints lately, and I think we both know I'm overdue a change of assignment. I really like this job, but in all honestly I hunger for a command. Sooner or later we'll invade the continent and I should be there when we do."

Reeves liked his job, but he'd hit the top rung of the administrative ladder in Washington. Although still the senior man in his graduating class by date of rank, a number of others had received their second star and he was no longer unique among the class of '16. He hungered for a third star and the only way to the next rung was by commanding. With the invasion of northern Europe imminent, he thought he'd press Marshall for a Corps. He wouldn't take anything in the Pacific – he'd never liked MacArthur when they were in Manila years earlier. The Marines were getting all the glory and it looked like the war there would go on for the next decade. Besides, the Pacific command was populated with old men in the mold of MacArthur himself. Europe on the other hand was staffed with a bunch of younger men – like Eisenhower, Bradley, Truscott, and half the damned class of '15. That's where the rank was for youthful men like himself. First, he'd have to have a reasonable succession plan. Lenox was the answer. Though not terribly bright, he was loyal.

"When it's time for me to leave, I want to be able to assure General Marshall that Personnel is in good hands. I plan to recommend you to take over. Would you be interested?"

"Definitely, sir. I'm honored you would consider me."

"You've definitely earned it," Reeves said, smiling. *And you'll continue to earn it by doing everything, including this Nolan thing exactly the way I tell you*, he thought.

"I appreciate your confidence, General Reeves."

"Not a word of this now, Raymond. I haven't greased the skids yet with the Boss, but I will when the time is right. We'll talk more later."

Brigadier General Raymond T. Lenox abruptly stood to attention, saluted crisply and exited the room.

Before departing for home that afternoon, Lenox had completed his mission and Reeves knew everything about the fraudulent enlistment of Glenn Nolan. He had caught a break by following the Annapolis lead first and learned the boy enlisted at the recruiting station in the Maryland capitol. Valerie Ebert arranged a meeting with his mother for the next morning.

*   *   *

"Thank you, Harrison, for seeing me so quickly," Denise said apprehensively as she was ushered into the richly appointed office.

"My pleasure," Reeves replied coming around his large wooden desk and embracing her. He stepped back and looked admiringly at her from arms' length. "It's been a long time. You're lovelier than ever. Please have a seat and tell me what I can do for you. Tea? I have some Matte Leão. It's Brazilian and quite good. Oriental tea is hard to come by these days."

She allowed him to pour her a cup from expensive sterling service that was as pretentious as the rest of the office; it appeared he'd hired a New York decorator to fix the place to his liking. All the other offices in the building presented the cheap drab green paint scheme and steel furniture décor of every other military office around the world. This was so like Harrison. The old aversion to him reawakened – she'd never trusted Michelle's husband in all the years since they'd met at that Founder's Day dance at West Point right after the war. Their other encounters since had only served to cement her feelings toward him. Even now, as he sat across the huge desk staring at her with eyes as pale as Greek agate and a mirthless smile on his face, she felt that same old suspicion and antipathy toward him welling up. But she forced it from her mind, knowing he was the only one on the planet right now who could help her.

"I'm in a terrible quandary, Harrison, and I desperately need your help."

"My secretary's note said something about your son. Which one?" he asked blithely, enjoying her pitiful plea and the worry written across her face.

"It's Glenn. I found this when I got home from a trip two nights ago." She slid the note across the desk and watched him pick it up and read it. "It's not dated, so I don't know exactly when he wrote it."

"When do you think he wrote it?"

"Sometime between last Friday morning and Wednesday night when I got home."

Reeves' screwed his face into a frown and stared again at the letter. "What kind of help can I provide you?"

"I want you to find him and invalidate this enlistment of his. He's just a child!"

"All right, I might be able to help. But I'll need more information. This says he's enlisted and gone off for training. Any idea in which of the services he enlisted?"

"I assumed the Army, of course. He's an Army brat. Or was. And he worships his father and older brother."

"But he could have enlisted in the Navy or the Marine Corps. Even the Merchant Marine. It doesn't say here." Reeves looked pensive and jotted a note. "Did he have any friends who talked about volunteering for any of the services? I find a lot of these boys today go into a service because they get talked into it by their buddies. If Glenn had a friend at school he was really close to who was gung ho about the Navy or Marines, he might have joined up with him. Is that possible?"

"I don't know," Denise admitted, her stomach knotting as the thought dawned on her that she had no idea what had actually prompted Glenn to do this. *I should have paid more attention when he first started talking this drivel instead of insisting he just stop. None of this would have happened if I'd paid more attention... or if his father had been home. Damn you Dave Nolan for running off and leaving me to deal with this!*

"I can investigate that. I and my counterparts in the other services share information quite freely on many things. We all owe each other multiple hundreds of favors. I'm sure they'll help. It would be helpful to put together a profile on Glenn – who his close friends are, what they like to do together, what hobbies he has. I know from our time in Manila that Mitch loved flying. Did Glenn share that? If so, maybe he enlisted in the Army to get to the Air Corps. Did he like to sail? Maybe that would push him in the direction of the Navy. It would be helpful if you could compile a biographical sketch including a description. He had to take a physical and we might be able to locate him that way."

"But you'll find him and put an end to this, won't you?" Denise pleaded, realizing this was probably a much more difficult task than she'd originally apprehended.

"I shall do all I can. But you should be realistic. At the moment what we don't know about Glenn's enlistment far outstrips what we do know. That doesn't make it impossible, just more time consuming. Here's what we don't know... we don't know where he enlisted or what service he enlisted in; nor when he enlisted and left. We don't know if he used his real name or not. We don't know what age he claimed or what documents he used to verify his age."

"You make it sound impossible," Denise blurted out, unable to control the sinking feeling engulfing her now.

"No, it's not impossible, just very difficult. We have hundreds of new volunteers every day in just the local area alone. If Glenn enlisted within a hundred mile radius of here, he was one of a thousand or so since last Friday. It's one needle in a haystack of needles. That's why you need to help me narrow it down as best you can." He took a deep breath and stubbed out his cigarette in an ash tray made from a brass artillery casing. "When we do locate him, there's another problem with which we must deal. If he lied on his enlistment application... I shouldn't say 'if' because he had to lie to get past the recruiter. Providing false information on an enlistment document is a federal offense. The last time I looked it was a felony."

"A felony?!"

"I'm afraid so. That means some prison time. And a felony is something that follows one for his entire life.

"Oh, no!" Her eyes went wide in shock. "A criminal record? For the rest of his life?! He's just a child!"

"I don't think it has to come to that," Reeves opined, giving her a comforting look. "I'll do everything I can to keep it from happening, Denise. I promise."

"Would you?" She was on the verge of tears and looked at him, pleading with her eyes.

"Of course I will." He came around the desk, helped her to her feet and gave her another hug. "I have two exceptionally gifted officers on my staff who solve deeper mysteries than this every day, I assure you. I'm putting them on the trail of young Glenn today. We will find him, Denise. And we'll make this go away. I give you my word on it – my solemn word of honor."

She felt utterly distressed and tears trickled slowly down her cheek. For reasons wholly foreign, she leaned toward him and kissed his cheek.

*   *   *   *

"I'm not sure I understand, sir," General Lenox said, confused.

"Very simple Raymond," Harrison Reeves explained. "I want you to work with Colonel Scoskie to assign this Nolan to jump school after Basic Training and then ultimately to the 82nd Airborne Division. That's very simple. The reasons are complex and private between me and the family. So, just do it and be done with it. All I require is that you show the leadership expected of my replacement."

Lenox remained perplexed. The airborne was a volunteer specialty and this boy had just arrived at Benning to begin Basic Training. Nothing in his enlistment file indicated a desire or aptitude to become a paratrooper. His physical indicated he was unremarkably average in stature; if anything, he was underweight and not well muscled. The medical interviewer recorded Glenn Nolan as quiet and reserved, not particularly aggressive, not particularly passive – in a word: average. Lenox found this wholly unlike what he knew of the airborne and doubted the youngster would have been accepted even if he had volunteered. The casualties for the 82nd were higher than expected in both the Sicily and Salerno operation. His conscience bothered him; the kid was underage in the first place. This didn't add up.

"General Lenox, something amiss?" Reeves asked, looking up from his desk and seemingly surprised to find his assistant still standing in front of him.

"Sir, I was just thinking –"

"Raymond, there's a time for thinking and a time for acting. With an assignment given you, this is a time to act. Work out the details with Scoskie and let me know when you've gotten it wrapped up so I can call the family and let them know. That will be all."

Reeves looked up when the door shut behind Lenox.

"I must tell that man every little detail and lead him by the hand," Harrison mumbled under his breath, frustrated as usual with his slow-witted assistant. *Carrot and stick*, he thought. Looking at his watch, he saw it was past quitting time. He reached into the bottom desk drawer retrieving his bottle of single malt and a Bolivar Cuban, 52 ring; he clipped it and lit the cigar before pouring himself two fingers of the Scotch. As he smoked and drank, the words of his favorite Whitman poem from *Leaves of Grass* came to mind and heartened him.

As I lay with my head in your lap, Camerado,
The confession I made I resume—what I said to you in the open air I resume.
I know I am restless, and make others so;
I know my words are weapons, full of danger, full of death;
Indeed I am myself the real soldier;
It is not he, there, with his bayonet, and not the red-striped artilleryman;

Reeves looked up the phone number and dialed.

"Denise, Harrison here. I know this has been a long three weeks for you. I wish for all the world and your sake it weren't so, but I have little I can report. My investigators are telling me Glenn has masterfully covered his trail. And my Judge Advocate counsel had similar bad news concerning the potential legal difficulties surrounding his fraudulent enlistment.

"But be assured, I will not rest until I have run this to ground and returned your son to you. My word on it, Denise…"

Chapter 31

Lindquist frowned deeply.

He looked worriedly around the flight line as he ambled toward his friends Crosley and Mitch Nolan who stood together outside the wooden shack that served as Operations for the Casablanca Training School – *Classy C*. He'd just landed with four aircraft in his flight having been recalled to the field before finishing their dive bombing training.

"There's an ugly rumor floating around we're going somewhere tonight within spitting distance of the front lines in Italy," Lucky said, rolling his eyes and shaking his head in disbelief at the chaos going on around him. Aircraft were being fueled and armed, equipment was being loaded into C-47s, maintenance tents were being struck and folded. "Mitch, you gotta stop that chinwag before folks start believing it."

"Look around you, Lucky. Whatta ya think is goin' on?" Marv Crosley said looking unhappily back and forth between Nolan and Lindquist. "We're going, I'm afraid."

"I say we find the looney tunes s.o.b. who said that, gift wrap him and give him to the Krauts as an early Christmas present." Lindquist looked at Crosley who shrugged and nodded at Nolan. "You're not serious, Mitch. A fifteen hundred mile formation flight in bad weather? – a good part of that at night?! That's a death wish. Besides, I got a leave coming up and I plan to be in Cairo before the end of the week making sweet music with a pretty little Portagee blond." Lucky laughed aloud, but quickly grew stone-faced. "You cancelled all leaves, didn't you?"

"The Luftwaffe did," Mitch said as he spread the map out on the hood of a jeep and looked at it with his two friends. "The Group has ordered the school here closed and all of us to Bari, Italy as soon as we can get there."

"Is it too much to ask why?" Lindquist asked.

"Big problem on the Italian mainland," Crosley replied. "Last night the Germans hit the port of Bari. They sank twenty seven out of thirty cargo and transport ships in the harbor."

"How many bombers?"

"Somewhere between a hundred and two hundred JU-88s. Air Corps intelligence says it's impossible to tell right now exactly where they came from. They think about half came from northern Italy and the other half from the east across the Adriatic. It was a well-timed and well-executed combined operation. That harbor was important and now it's a mess."

"How many of them did we get?" Lucky asked the operations officer.

"Not a one. The German bomber force obtained complete surprise and was able to bomb the harbor accurately. There's no Air Corps or RAF fighters assigned to the defense of Bari; everything is committed to close air support of ground troops or escorting bombers to Austria, Yugoslavia, or southern Germany. And they're in way over their heads on those missions."

"I'm really not liking the sound of any of this."

"Neither am I. But we've been ordered there and we're going. Here's what we're going to do," Mitch said, his mind weighing alternatives, guessing at distances and flight times. "Marv, plan for four flights of six. I want all the old hands flying; split the best of the new guys among the flights and send the rest on transports with the gear. Lucky, you lead the first flight – Red flight; Jeffers leads second flight – White; Wilcox Blue flight, and Marv bring up the rear in Green flight. I'll fly weather ship and leave here at 1030 hours. Flights depart at half hour intervals. We'll have to refuel once at Bone. Let's keep this nice and simple, okay?"

Crosley nodded and drew lines on the map. "Route of flight is five direct legs – first is direct to Oran, second to Algiers, then to Bone for refueling. Alternates if Bone is socked in are Youks les Bains and Grombalia. From Bone direct to Gerbini airfield on the east coast of Sicily, then direct to Bari. I'll work up the headings and distances for each of the legs, plus frequencies for each field we'll be using for navigation and landing or alternate. I'll make sure each flight lead has maps and a mission sheet with all that info on it. We'll use our training frequency, but maintain radio silence except for you in the weather ship and flight leads."

Mitch nodded agreement. Marvelous Marv had shown himself to be an exceptional operations officer over the last three months during the set up and running of the flight school. While Lucky was the better pilot of the two, Marv had proven to be the better planner and administrator – together they made an excellent team. "Once we're airborne, I'll give weather updates at least every half hour and at navigation points along our route. Flight leaders make the decision concerning whether or not to continue on after the first check point." Mitch continued staring at the map. "What do you think?"

"All depends on the weather," Marv Crosley replied, shaking his head while looking less than confident. "I wish you hadn't promised we'd have all these aircraft there tonight."

"I told the colonel the port would be covered. What I promised was a presence."

Crosley furrowed his brow, looking at Lucky, then back at Nolan. "You're going to try to make it by yourself regardless of weather? Mitch, your ego is making promises your body and that airplane can't live up to."

"My job is to observe and report weather all the way to Bari. I plan to do just that."

"Or die trying?" Lucky asked.

Mitch replied with a shrug and walked back to his *Mistress*, hounded by worry.

*   *   *   *

Glenn Nolan was the first man into the C-47, pressed hard against the bulkhead behind which sat two pilots in front of the myriad gauges and levers and toggle switches.

I should have figured out some way to get into the Air Corps like Mitch did, he thought, watching the rest of his twelve man 'stick' waddle toward him and sit down on bench seats along both sides of the cargo plane. Then he took a deep breath and calmed himself. *You're about to do something your hot shot brother has never done. In a half hour, you'll have bragging rights over both him and the ol' man.* He was pleased – until the thought returned which had dogged him all night.

I hope I didn't screw up packing this parachute.

It was the first day of "D" week at Camp Benning's Airborne School and despite the worry gnawing at him over his ability to pack a chute on the last day of "C" week, his morale was sky high. Now, he looked forward to making the five jumps, and even more to the long furlough at the completion of the training – he could see the light at the end of the tunnel. He and the others sitting in the plane with him had so far survived the most challenging and difficult training the Army had ever conceived.

Assignment to the Airborne Course had come as a complete surprise during the last week of basic training when, along with the rest of his barracks, he learned of his first assignment. He knew the parachute course was voluntary and was certain he hadn't volunteered – the recruiter in Annapolis had told him with sincere, direct clarity: never volunteer. Glenn had decided to withdraw at the earliest opportunity the first day of paratrooper training but never got around to it because of his basic training bunkmate Howie Norbert from San Leandro, California, and because of a braggadocios young 2nd lieutenant.

On Monday morning of the first day of "A" stage, Glenn Nolan had assembled with the rest of his class at the 5 AM reporting time on the orders. Before he could find an officer to explain he'd not volunteered and was opting out of the training, a cadre of twenty sergeants ran them all through two obstacle courses, each a mile long, followed by group calisthenics for a half-hour. Then before breakfast a stocky, muscular lieutenant had them at attention in formation inside a large hangar-like building.

"People call me Flash Gordon," the young officer began in his deep parade ground voice, "and you'll learn I'm the meanest, toughest son of a bitch this side of anywhere you've ever been. Meeting up with me is the worst disaster in your entire sorry life so far. You're going to hate my guts, but I don't give a rat's ass because you guys don't amount to a piece of barnyard dung to me. Every one of you get down on your stomachs and give me ten push-ups."

Glenn rolled his eyes, convinced now his career in the Airborne with all its sophomoric depredations and foul language was at an end. But he did the pushups.

When done, the lieutenant continued, striding back and forth in front of them. "To make sure you sorry pieces of crap listen and pay attention, I'm gonna holler: *JAB!* from time to time, and when I do I want to hear one unified loud *thud* as you punch your chest. Heaven help anyone I catch with a late *thud*. These sergeants are my personal disciples and are in charge of your training and riding your sorry asses to be sure you learn everything there is to know about being a paratrooper. On a scale of 1 to 10 on toughness, they all rank a solid 11. They each have one goal in life and that is to make you as miserable as all hell while you're learning to be a jumper... *JAB!*"

One hundred forty fists hit their chests in unison.

Flash Gordon had Glenn's attention.

"If any of you sorry little wimps think I'm kiddin' and you don't want to put up with this shit any longer, just step forward now and you can save the government a slew of money by not wasting our time training a bunch of gutless cowards."

"Go ahead, Nolan," Howie Norbert said loud enough to be heard by those around him in ranks. "Be the first spineless wonder to step forward and quit."

"You can go to hell, Norbert. I'll whip your ass again if you don't shut up."

"You and who's army?"

They had gotten into a fight days before graduation when Glenn had told a couple of the guys in his squad about his intention to opt out of airborne training. Norbert, who was a little bit heavier but a couple of inches shorter than Glenn, had scoffed and questioned his courage. They had taken it out behind the barracks and with the whole platoon looking on, had fought until someone had ended it by dousing both of them with a fire hose.

"You! You there in the second rank!" Flash Gordon yelled out, pointing at Glenn. "You don't talk in my formation. Get down and give me ten, and they had best be damn good push-ups. Or maybe you just want to quit. Is that what you want skinny boy?!"

"No, sir!"

"You sure?! Give me ten more on top of that. And instead of breakfast with everybody else you're gonna run around that training field outside until I tell you to stop." It had not been the way he'd planned it, but some jerk from California and a barely literate farm boy butter bar lieutenant who'd graduated from OCS weren't going to make him quit.

He'd often questioned the decision over the first three weeks.

Flash Gordon had promised he'd make them forget how to walk and set out to make them run everywhere they went. The first week was nine or ten hours a day of physical training that included everything from obstacle courses to rope climbing, tumbling to pull-ups, and push-ups – thousands of them it seemed – and five-mile runs. Near the end of the week they began sessions of hand-to-hand combat in the sawdust pits with the goal of learning to kill silently with a knife, a bayonet or bare hands. It was an all-out effort to thin the ranks. And it worked. By the end of "A" week, one in four entrants had quit or been eliminated.

During the next two weeks, in addition to continued physical training, they spent endless hours practicing parachute landing falls from ever-increasing heights, exiting aircraft from a mockup called the 34 foot tower, and duplicating the parachuting experience from 250 foot towers on the training field. As time wore on, Glenn found himself increasingly enjoying the experience; he was stronger, more agile, and more confident in his physical abilities than ever before. By the time they were to make their first actual jump, he wondered why he'd ever considered walking away from this fun and games.

The loud sound of rushing noise from the aircraft slipstream grabbed his attention and he saw the red light had come on in the back of the plane.

"Stand up!" the jump master near the rear of the Gooney Bird yelled above the noise while gesturing with his hands. "Hook up!" The jumpers hooked the metal snap at the end of their ripcords over the cable running through the cabin at eye level and tugged once or twice to make sure of a good connection. "Check equipment!" Each of them checked the front latches and the reserve chute and the back of the parachute in front of them. Norbert turned around to check the back of Nolan's parachute. *He's scared!* Glenn thought, seeing the Californian's eyes big and round. *Good! I hope you piss your pants you little jerk!* "Sound off for equipment check!" The routine and the calls added a sense of drama and increased the tension he felt.

"Stand in the door!" The first jumper shuffled forward and turned looking straight ahead outside with his hands pushing against the fuselage of the plane. He was an officer, Glenn knew although nobody wore rank or any other insignia on the coverall jump suits; everybody was equal in training except it seemed the sergeant cadre especially enjoyed dropping the officers for extra pushups. He was thinking it was better to be a private when suddenly the bright green light next to the cargo door went on.

"Go!" the jump master yelled and slapped the first jumper hard on the butt.

People were disappearing out the door; those still inside were stomping their feet as they shuffled to the rear and the cavernous hole in the plane all the time chanting *Go! Go! Go!* Glenn was pushing Norbert as hard as he could and suddenly –

Norbert disappeared ahead of him and unexpectedly he was staring at the empty sky; he gasped, feeling himself plummeting facedown with his elbows clasped tightly to his sides as he yelled, *one one thousand! Two one thousand! Three one –*

Abruptly, the chute opened and he was swinging pleasantly in the breeze. It was amazingly quiet, and wildly exhilarating – the most pleasurable sensation he could imagine. Looking up he saw the full round canopy over him and then reached up to grab the risers. After stabilizing the chute, he looked around and saw off to his left and below the parachutes of those who had jumped ahead of him, like stair steps to the ground. Directly beneath him he saw the fully blossomed canopy of Norbert's chute and realized it was stealing air from his own canopy causing him to fall through the sky more quickly than he should. His feet touched the top of the chute and he sank up to his knees in the silk. *What do I do now?* Before he realized it, he was running off the edge of the canopy and pulling his risers to separate from Norbert.

He heard someone yelling and whooping. He could see for miles and miles which excited him, but he didn't want to chance looking straight down between his legs.

"Hey, Nolan. Is this hot stuff or what?!" Norbert yelled, and then someone else nearby let out a catcall.

When he looked down, he realized he was only a couple hundred feet above the ground and ran through the quick pre-landing checklist they'd drilled into him. Feet together; legs bent; hands up high on the risers; slow the drift. *Stay relaxed*, he reminded himself. *You're going backwards Nolan – reach the right hand over the left shoulder and pull that riser to do a one-eighty degree turn; headed the right way now. Look straight ahead at the horizon.* He was close to the tree line and for a while the treetops seemed stationary, until suddenly they rushed upward quickly and before he could think, he hit the ground and rolled. Without knowing how, he was on his feet, collapsing the parachute and gathering it in.

The most incredible feeling of euphoria came over him; he felt like he could whip ten men his size; or more. *This is really living!* Glenn said to himself, utterly ecstatic. It was like some kind of overwhelming drug, and the feeling stayed with him the rest of the day.

*   *   *   *   *

This is how people kill themselves in airplanes, Mitch Nolan thought to himself, hunched over and peering forward into the darkness.

He'd been in the air now almost seven hours, not counting the hour with Lucky's training mission early that morning. With only a break at Bone four hours into the long flight, he was weary – he hadn't been this tired since the ferry flight across the North Atlantic with Bennett. The weather had been real iffy and he wouldn't have taken off if he hadn't promised the group commander so unequivocally. He cursed himself now, a hundred miles south of Bari by his best estimate as he followed a rail line running along Italy's Adriatic coast. He'd reduced airspeed to 160 mph as night fell and the visibility further deteriorated. If it got any worse, he planned to beat a retreat south and hopefully find Lecce on the heel of Italy's boot where the 82nd Group had been located for a little while a month earlier.

Lucky and his flight had arrived at Bone before he took off across the wide Tyrrhenian Sea three hours earlier and Mitch had told him the best thing to do was to keep the formations there until morning and take another look at the weather before going on. Ceilings as well as visibility were coming down as the afternoon wore on and he guessed the forecasts wouldn't get any better. He'd learned to be skeptical of weather forecasters in the Mediterranean with winter again coming on. Although he continued broadcasting weather observations in the blind at least every half hour there had been no responses from the other flights and he hoped it was because the old hands had decided to remain overnight at one of the North African bases still active. He was sure they were smart enough to figure that out.

Smarter than me, Nolan thought as he continued to squint into the darkness.

His mind wandered and he was constantly talking to himself out loud to stay alert. Even at this speed, trouble could overcome him in a heartbeat.

He'd hoped to take some leave after three months of setting up and running the school. One of the inducements he had used early on to recruit instructors for *Classy C* was the promise they would get an uncharged seven-day leave within the first six weeks of their assignment. To some that made the difference, and everyone in his cadre had taken a leave so far except him. He had planned on getting to Cairo within the next week to ten days, but that seemed out of the question now. In a brief moment of self-pity, he wondered if he should simply forget about Makara and move on.

"Dammit! You've got to knock this off and start paying attention, Nolan!" he yelled aloud to jolt himself back to some measure of vigilance. "Didn't I tell you this is just how people kill themselves in airplanes?!"

Something bright white went off in his field of vision over the right engine, making his heart jump into his throat and chasing away his fatigue. *What was that?* he wondered. *A bomb? A flare? Landing light? Maybe a lighthouse – I should be right over the shoreline... sure looks like it down there.* He made a shallow turn pointing his nose toward where the light had erupted. *Maybe –*

He banked hard left away from the light source. "Maybe an antiaircraft gun! After last night they're probably as skittish as anyone on this side of the planet. Just my luck to get shot down by some nervous Greek or Turkish or British merchant seamen. You're not thinking real clearly, son."

Mitch could make out some lights on the ground which he thought just might be the port at Bari on the other side of the railroad, and he was just barely able to distinguish the outlines of a city on the west side of the tracks. *I'll be damned – that's Bari.* He flicked on his flashlight and glanced at the map. *All right, the airfield is just twelve or thirteen miles north northwest of my location. If I fly this heading keeping a mile west of the tracks, I should see it directly ahead. There it is! That's it. No tower beacon, no runway lights, but that sure looks like a couple of intersecting runways.* He stole a glance at the altimeter which indicated just over 500 feet. *Let's see, the airport is supposed to be 177 feet above sea level. That means I'm about 300 feet above ground level. Not much wiggle room here.*

He made a shallow turn and lined up on what appeared to be a runway. As he got closer he saw through a haze three buildings off to one side. Squinting, he thought he could make out the form of a tower on top of one of them. *Nolan, you've got to get this thing dirty and slowed down to landing speed.* His hands flew over the controls in the cockpit lowering flaps, retarding the throttles, setting the mixture and props. When he lowered the gear and the landing lights came on there was an immediate wall of white in front of him. *Ground fog! Not this!* As he descended lower the fog slowly dissipated; he saw a runway in front of him and in the next few seconds he felt the main gear touch down. He taxied very slowly toward the buildings, found himself on a ramp and swung the nose of the P-38 toward the middle of the field.

He was completely alone.

Mitch made a radio call in the blind with a previously agreed upon code word indicating he had arrived at Bari. Glancing at the gauges, he saw he had close to three hours of fuel left.

"Enough fuel and ammo to run off a handful of JU-88s. Well, colonel. The 82nd Fighter Group is here as promised. If any Luftwaffe bombers are stupid enough to come by on a night like this, I just might be stupid enough to go up and take a shot at 'em… But probably not." He shut down the engines, opened the canopy and climbed down the back of the wing to the ground to stretch out the kinks in his back and legs. Looking up he saw no stars; his watch told him he had at least nine or ten hours before sunup. "Nolan, this ranks right up there with the dumbest thing you've ever done."

A quick tour around the outside of the buildings showed him the effects of the American bombing campaign the previous two months. He guessed it would take a week or more for the engineers to make the field ready for round the clock operations. Finally, he climbed back inside the cockpit and pulled the canopy down to ward off the chill.

Soon, he found himself fighting sleep while thinking about Makara.

He closed his eyes and saw her as he remembered from the first night in the restaurant in Casablanca almost a year earlier. Everything about her still captivated him – the sensual smile and pleasantly melodic laugh, the hauntingly suggestive grace with which she moved and her remarkably beautiful face. She was the most beautiful, erotic woman he'd ever met, and his sense that she still remained just barely outside his reach made him want her even more.

The mystery surrounding her had from the start intrigued and beguiled him. His inability to draw her out and get beyond small talk when they were together was as maddening as it was perplexing. Her correspondence was another story altogether.

She sent him long and intimate love letters. It was as if he'd met and dated one woman who was shy and withdrawn while exchanging letters with another, wholly different personality. The woman he corresponded with was the one he'd kissed on a moonlit beach, the one with whom he'd spent an intimate evening in the Anfa Hotel balcony. But it was another woman entirely who had avoided him most of the following week and seemed distant, even scared of him, in Cairo.

He saw her in his mind's eye walking toward him from across the restaurant, long perfectly black hair framing an exotic face with high cheekbones and expressive eyes. He was again riveted, unable to stop staring or to do anything other than admire her physical beauty. Their eyes met and she smiled radiantly, speaking to him in her faint but unmistakable British accent with its precise articulation and aristocratic inflections.

So, you're Mitch Nolan, the famous American aeronaut – the one who flew with Bennett across the North Atlantic in the middle of winter... how daring... how foolish of you Mitch Nolan and how lucky... lucky... lucky Mitch Nolan... lucky Mitch... Mitch it's lucky... Mitch... Mitch!... Makara's face grew dim and she floated away from him, engulfed in mist ... *Mitch! Mitch!...*

"Mitch, come on, listen up! It's Lucky! Wake up pardner and open the canopy!"

He looked through the side window at Lindquist's face, distorted and barely recognizable. It was still dark and Mitch rubbed his eyes, aware of the pain in the side of his neck; in his back and legs. His watch indicated it was a few minutes after midnight. He flipped back the canopy and rolled down the left window; standing on the seat, he looked around while stretching and rubbing the kink in his neck. "What the hell are you doing here?"

Lucky laughed out loud. "It's just real damned good to see you, too, commander! My flight is still at Bone, getting a good night's sleep like most sane people on a night like this. So is Marv's Green flight. White flight planned to stay at Youks les Bains and Blue flight was landing at Gromalia last I heard on the radio. Weather over the whole western Med is terrible. This is worse weather than my first ferry flight from England a year ago. Nolan, you have ships spread out over half of North Africa."

"But you got through."

"Me and Marv both. He was landing at Bone just as Red flight was about to crank. After talking about it, we decided to turn over our flights to DeAngelis and Bartelme and have them wait until the weather broke. After he refueled the two of us took off to try and catch you. We could hear your calls but guessed you couldn't hear us. We were almost at Lecce when you called arrival at Bari so we got fuel and headed here as fast as we could following the railroad tracks up the coast. We couldn't get above two hundred and fifty feet the whole way up. I swear we flew between buildings in Brindisi and Torre a Mare."

Looking quickly around the ramp Mitch saw only one other P-38. "So, where's Marv?"

"Boring holes in the sky over the port, looking for Kraut bombers."

"I can't believe you knuckleheads did this."

Lindquist shrugged. "We said the same thing about you when we ran into one another at Bone. Couldn't let you have all the fun by yourself when the Krauts showed up again. Besides, he and I have firsthand experience with the trouble you can get yourself into when on your own in bad weather without adult supervision. Didn't feel right leaving you by yourself."

Mitch was silent for a while. "I owe you, Lucky – both of you guys."

"Damn right you do. Since you already got some snoozin', you can relieve Marv while he and I grab some sleep. I'll relieve you in a couple of hours." Lindquist helped him out of the cockpit and threw the parachute down to the ground. "One other thing, pal – in the next couple of weeks you're going to get me on Cairo leave orders to go see that blond gal."

Chapter 32

After the British debacle at Dunkirk, Winston Churchill made a gallant, defiant vow to carry on the struggle "*... until in God's good time, the New World, with all its power and might, steps forth to the rescue and the liberation of the Old.*"

He waited two years for the opening act in that play, until the Americans first entered the fight in North Africa with the three-pronged Operation Torch. It was an optimistic, even romantic moment for both Chamberlain and Roosevelt and their countries. But to the American soldiers and their leaders, despite a Patton or a Truscott or a Dave Nolan here and there, the operation had failed to live up to the rhetorical flourishes of the British Empire's leader.

The underlying technical challenges of desert warfare interested professional soldiers, but most American generals and privates regarded Torch and the whole effort in North Africa as a dirty job they had to get over and behind them. Eisenhower feared the decision for Torch might go down as one of the great mistakes in American military history, as did his direct superior, George Marshall. Still, given their orders and the desires of the senior partner in the alliance – Great Britain – Eisenhower, his staff and his commanders methodically set about the business of defeating Germany, first in Africa, then in Sicily and finally on the Italian mainland.

Initially, Churchill viewed the war in the Mediterranean as crucial, even primary to defeating the Nazis by attacking them through the "soft underbelly of Europe." But nearing the end of 1943, as American troop strength neared one million on his island, there was a change of heart in London and the primary focus shifted toward the cross channel invasion of Europe for which the American military planners had been lobbying since just days after Pearl Harbor. So complete was this shift in British perspective that by the time Dave Nolan arrived at America's First Army headquarters in Bristol, much of the skeleton, muscle, and command responsibilities of the invasion had already been decided by Great Britain's military staff.

OVERLORD was the code name coined by Churchill for the cross-channel assault.

Prior to General David A. Nolan's arrival, General Sir Frederick Morgan as the Chief of Staff to the Supreme Allied Commander (COSSAC), was given the assignment to develop the plan for the invasion and the first months' battles on the continent. By the beginning of 1944, the British were well satisfied with their work. American planners were livid.

It was into the middle of this conflict between staffs and planners of the Allies that Dave Nolan arrived on English soil and got sucked into the vortex of the intramural squabble.

"What do you think of Sir Frederick's plan for Overlord?" Omar Bradley asked Nolan as they sat in his office inside the red brick building at 20 Grosvenor Square in downtown London which served as the U.S. 1st Army Group headquarters. The offices were located a brisk ten minute walk from the Dorchester Hotel, a classy West End structure near Hyde Park where Bradley had decided to make his home for the time being.

"In what role?" Nolan asked. "As a soldier, or some kind of military politician?"

"Let's say as an old friend, the guy who taught me to hit a curve and a drop ball," Bradley replied. "After that briefing, I already know what Jakie Devers thinks. What I'm interested in is your take on things."

Devers had been abundantly vocal in his displeasure over the British plan for the invasion. As he'd just explained in Bradley's first briefing since arriving from America, the British outline was somewhat sketchy tactically, but very clear strategically concerning the leadership roles of each country. One American division was to land on the right of the Normandy coast and two British divisions on the left – exact locations yet undetermined. All three were to be under the command of the British Army. Once the Americans put more divisions on the continent, the American First Army would assume command in their sector. At that point a British Army Group would take command of both the British and American armies and would direct the ground campaign. In other words, the British would exercise airtight tactical control of both the channel crossing and the first few months ashore – at least.

"Brad, it's exactly the way it felt dealing with the British and the French in the last war. America is still a junior partner at best. The British military has been thinking for a long time about how they could cross the channel, engage the Wehrmacht and defeat them on the fields of France and eventually inside Germany. Before Pearl Harbor they looked to us as a source of matériel. Now, they look to us as a source of matériel *and* manpower. They don't want, and don't think they need any of our help in determining strategy or tactics or providing military leadership. It's just like it was in 1918 – other than the number of American troops and the lethality of weapons, nothing's changed except we're all a quarter century older. Jakie was more of a diplomat that I would've been. For the sake of the good old alliance, he filed down some of the rough edges that both he and I see in our little love fest with the Brits."

Bradley frowned and looked sideways at him. "Are you sure you're not being a little too sensitive, Dave?"

"Brad, the last couple of weeks I've done exactly what you asked me to do. I've gotten acquainted with all the senior British staff, including Sir Frederick Morgan. I already know General Smythe-Browne, a longtime friend who's been very accommodating in introducing me to the senior Brits. You and Ike both know I'm a pretty good judge of people. Let me put it this way: in the last war the British looked upon us as 'those *trivial* colonists' but now they look on us as just 'those *damned* colonists.' We've gone from being dismissed to being a nuisance. There's a lot of veiled criticism about how we performed in North Africa, especially at Kasserine Pass. I'm not trying to start an argument here, I'm just telling you how it is."

Bradley listened closely, sensing Nolan was right. Their long history since before the Great War convinced him that Nolan was a reliable evaluator of people and absolutely honest. It was why he'd readily agreed with Ike they had to find a way to use him in Overlord. "Have you met Field Marshall Montgomery?"

"Just once."

"Your impression of him?"

Nolan sighed deeply. "I used to think Douglas MacArthur was the most arrogant and egotistical person I had ever met – until I was introduced to Montgomery. Immediately, he had to tell me how the planning for Overlord was all bolloxed up until he got here and straightened it out. But I will say, of all the senior British military leaders, he's their best field commander."

"Better than Alexander?"

Dave knew Bradley had developed a unique personal relationship with General Alexander from their work together in North Africa and Sicily. "He's out of the picture. Since Brooke replaced Sir John Dill, Alexander's stock has gone down in the British Army. Monty's running the British Army Group, and although I don't much like him as a person, he's earned the respect not only of the prime minister but of his troops as well. Aside from all of the legend the British public is being fed, and the fact that he looks like a frumpy little old man in ill-fitting corduroy, Montgomery really is a tough, hard-nosed commander. He's George Patton with a British accent and a bigger ego, if you can fathom that."

"Can this war accommodate two Pattons in the same theatre?"

"Are you telling me Ike's ready to bring George on board for Overlord?"

"Maybe, but you didn't hear it from me. You talk about Monty as if you're a fan."

"Not really. The ego gets in the way for me. You should know that better than I do – you worked with him before. He's a guy who always has to be center stage and will be writing his memoirs for the next several decades recounting how he won the war single-handed. Still, I have to admit there are some things about the guy I really like."

"Go on," Bradley said, leaning back in his chair and clasping his hands behind his head.

"Montgomery seems to be thoroughly disliked by his contemporaries and for the typical reasons: spiteful jealousy and personal rivalry. I think it's because he's honest, which combined with his rasping personality, creates detractors by the boxcar load. That indicates to me Monty wasn't picked for high command because he was pleasant or a gentleman. He's not scared to ruffle feathers or to be unpopular among his peers when he's convinced he's right. That's gutsy. Especially in the British Army that for decades has been marked by their aristocratic 'good old boy system'. Something about that makes me like the little guy – some… arrogance and unbridled ego aside. He'll demand to be in the lead and the spotlight all the time. My problem with him is that he's too cautious and he has to plan everything down to the last paper clip."

Bradley nodded appreciatively. "Actually, that's a pretty good read on Monty from my experience. All right, what other little gems do you have for me before we head out to General Smythe-Browne's for dinner?"

"Don't be surprised if some time during the evening Henry subtly recommends you help convince Ike to take on Leigh-Mallory as his second-in-command at SHAEF. I suggest you listen closely but don't commit to helping him one way or the other. There's a reason for all this maneuvering on his part."

In his new role as Churchill's liaison to the Washington-based Joint Chiefs of Staff commission, Henry spent a lot of time lobbying several issues, including most importantly the staffing and responsibilities of the Supreme Headquarters - Allied Expeditionary Forces (SHAEF). At Smythe-Browne's insistence, Dave had reluctantly agreed to dining at Henry's country estate and bringing Bradley along. "It looks to me like the Brits are trying to set up a way of actually running the show even though Ike is nominally the commander."

"You're kidding," Bradley said, scoffing at the idea. "Sounds like hyperbole to me."

"You know I don't exaggerate or embellish." Nolan replied with a hard edge to his voice. "I don't dabble in conspiracy theories or play politics. If you think I'm giving you bad information, you can send me back to the 12th in Italy or have me transferred back to the States. I told Ike back in Africa I didn't want this job."

"Whoa, hold on, Dave," Bradley said, holding up his hand in front of his chest to calm his old friend. "Don't go off half-cocked. Tell me why you say that."

"Smythe-Browne is going to propose two men as potential second-in-command to Ike: Trafford Leigh-Mallory and Arthur Tedder. Leigh-Mallory is a politician; he's gotten close to Air Chief Marshall Portal since the Battle of Britain. Tedder's not political and would be a better choice for lots of reasons. But from what I hear, many if not most, of the senior British staff prefer Leigh-Mallory."

"I know Arthur Tedder from our joint planning for Sicily," Bradley said, remembering the man's determined but quiet nature in the months of detailed British planning sessions under Alexander. "He was their Air Officer Commander in Chief. I remember he lived up to his reputation for excellence in both aerial operations and administration."

"That's a good take on him. He gets a lot of praise from the British Imperial General Staff for turning the RAF in Africa into a highly effective combat force. He also gets credit, along with Keith Park, for the RAF being key to defeating Rommel at El Alamein. That takes some of the spotlight off Monty, which apparently has caused some friction between them. He's not one to seek after glory or personal prestige; he's genuinely a team player in the mold of our buddy Eisenhower. I think they'd work together well. On the other hand, Leigh-Mallory is more like Monty, but with an unreliable twist. I don't trust him, and Ike shouldn't either."

"You know him well enough to say that?"

"I don't know him personally. Met him twice in the last month and once during the Battle of Britain when I was here on a fact-finding mission with Bill Donovan. But I know what happened to the two men most responsible for the defense of England during the blitz and that tells me all I need to know about Sir Trafford Leigh-Mallory."

Nolan paused for a few seconds weighing his words before continuing. This Brit had all the characteristics he hated in the military men he'd known over the years who were willing to say or do anything necessary to advance themselves regardless of consequences to others. For a brief instant his mind darted away and he saw the face of Harrison Reeves.

"The two people most responsible for winning the Battle of Britain were Keith Park who commanded RAF 11 Group in southeast England defending London, and Sir Hugh Dowding, the head of Fighter Command," Nolan continued. "Leigh-Mallory commanded 12 Group, located north and east of London. On more than one occasion I had the opportunity to personally observe the actions of Park and Dowding in the heat of the German Blitz. I can guarantee their leadership saved this little island. Leigh-Mallory thought he wasn't getting as much of the limelight as he should and quarreled with both Park and Dowding over tactics. I saw firsthand what was going on in the defense of Britain and I assure you Dowding and Park were right and Leigh-Mallory was dead wrong. Maybe over a beer some night I'll tell you all the details if you're interested.

"The other thing you should know is that Leigh-Mallory has a history of failed operations and failed tactics even before the Battle of Britain. He made false claims about his successes, and worked energetically in political circles to bring about the removal of Park from 11 Group and Dowding as the head of Fighter Command. He still reports to Air Chief Marshal Portal, and Portal is maneuvering to take overall command all U.S. and British air forces, and do it outside SHAEF and therefore beyond of Ike's control. Think about what that would mean.

Political jealousies and cliquism are rife in the RAF right now. Leigh-Mallory, as second-in-command and beholden to Portal, would bring that mess into the joint command. That kind of thinking has no place in SHAEF. Tedder is a guy we can work with; Leigh-Mallory is a guy we should avoid at all costs – in my opinion. And I'm damned sure going to tell Ike that."

Bradley remained silent for a moment, gazing at Dave Nolan, digesting this bit of military intelligence "What else? Surely there's some good news about the Alliance."

Dave uncrossed his legs and leaned forward, his elbows on knees and hands clasped. "I want to know when I can get out of here and go back to soldiering. I'm a fish out of water, Brad, and you know it. I was serious when I told you to send me back to the 12ᵗʰ Division, or give me a division here to command… or a battalion or something. I can't take much more of these constant briefings and cocktail parties and playing nice with Henry Smythe-Browne and the British staff. This is not me. I hate it and I'm not good at politicking. Every day I get pushed and shoved and politically manipulated."

Bradley chuckled, looking genuinely amused. "Ike knew you'd react like this. But he also knew you were the perfect guy to do the job. Don't worry. You'll get back in the saddle soon enough. When the time comes, you'll be back with the troops – count on it. But for now, you're more valuable helping us work our way through this alliance than you are leading hikes through the English countryside. The next thing we need you to do is take apart the amphibious plan of Sir Fredrick's staff piece by piece and put it back together so it works the way it should. Double the size of the American landing force and add a Canadian division."

"That exceeds the amount of landing craft on hand by a factor of three and the planners are already complaining about the lack of lift because of what's going on in Italy and the proposed invasion of Southern France."

"I'm sure you can work it out."

"Brad, this is staff logistics work. I hate that, too."

"It won't be for long. A few months at the most," Bradley replied with a grin and hand wave. "We have something in mind for you. I swear you'll be happy with how this works out. Keep your head down and your eye on the front bead, soldier, and this too shall pass."

*   *   *   *   *

Berlin – Mid December, 1943

It was overcast and growing dark outside the windows of Admiral Canaris' office.

An authoritative single rap on the ceiling height door was immediately followed by his two most trusted assistants entering and marching briskly across the room. One carried two large folders, each with the *Abwehr Eagle Crest* stamped on the front.

Hans Oster, Canaris' second-in-command of German Worldwide Intelligence, opened the folders and placed them in front of his superior. "*Amtsgruppe Ausland,* has uncovered what we believe is a significant development in the American forces in England."

Canaris slowly placed his pen at the corner of his desk blotter, and took the first folder in hand, looking carefully at the portrait photograph. He gazed at the face for many seconds, and then looked up at Oster and Colonel Erwin von Lahousen, his Section II Chief.

"General George Smith Patton, Jr.," Canaris said. "The significance, Hans?"

"According to this report, he is now in England."

Canaris continued to look at the face. "Do we know why this might be significant?"

"So far very little," Oster replied. "He has been in Egypt for some months purportedly as punishment because of some minor incident involving a soldier in his command during the Sicilian fighting. Supposedly he physically assaulted an enlisted man in one of their hospitals. We assume it was a diversion, a fabrication to throw us off. Why would they relegate to obscurity their most effective general for such a minor incident?"

"What is your analysis of this thus far?" Canaris asked, looking at each of them in turn.

"We believe the Americans have assembled their top military strategists and commanders in a group in England under Eisenhower. All along, we have believed wherever the group under Eisenhower is assembled, there will be the priority and likely intentions of the British and Americans opposing us. There is more."

"Proceed."

"We have reports of Generals Bradley and Nolan also converging in England. As you must remember, you told us to keep an eye on this Nolan. You were correct, Admiral. Nolan shows up under the oddest circumstances in the strangest places. It is not by chance he is in England along with Eisenhower, Bradley and Patton. Our spies in England continue to operate unimpeded and report Patton is in the process of forming the American 14th Army with Nolan as his foremost battle commander."

"What makes you so sure, Hans?" Canaris demanded.

"It appears, sir, Nolan was relieved of his division command in Italy and moved to England to establish the XXXI Corps at Bury St. Edmonds. This new Army under Patton is located across from the Pas de Calais. It is currently composed of the 11th and 48th Infantry Divisions plus the 25th Armored Division. We know from the fighting in North Africa and Sicily this Nolan is an accomplished commander of combined infantry and armored units, as is Patton. Our research shows they developed this tactic together with Eisenhower soon after the last war."

Canaris shook his head, pleased, closing the folders and passing them back to Oster. "Keeping track of Generals Nolan and Patton seems to have paid dividends for us. I'm most curious about Nolan's activities once this Corps of his is fully formed and functioning."

Hans Oster clicked his heels together and bowed perfunctorily. "We have intercepted already radio traffic between Patton's and Nolan's headquarters and between various units. A confirming development. Colonel James Gavin of the American 82nd Airborne Divison was promoted to general and sent from Italy to London, England three weeks ago. Not long after, on 18 November, the rest of the division left Italy aboard ships. We have now confirmed the ships dropped anchor in Belfast Ireland. We know only of their 505th Parachute Infantry Regiment location which is in Cookstown. All this is surely the beginning of final arrangements for a cross-channel invasion."

Canaris sighed deeply, deep in thought while looking at the pictures of Patton and Nolan. "We need more, Hans."

"We believe Gavin to now be the assistant commander of the 82nd Airborne Division and suspect he is coordinating parachute infantry plans for the invasion. In a serendipitous incident at a charity event in one of the English towns, one of our spies overheard General Nolan say to General Gavin he would rendezvous with him soon in Calais."

"Our man was close enough to hear him say that?"

"As apparently were others in the crowd. A strangely unguarded remark."

Canaris nodded, satisfied. "My compliments to you and your spies. Nolan's imprudent comment and Patton's location verifies what we've always assumed. It is most beneficial to know where the main thrust of their invasion will be. You must continue to monitor events in England and keep me apprised. I shall inform the Fuhrer and General Rommel of what you have discovered."

*   *   *   *   *

Glenn Nolan stood nervously in front of the door to the house in Georgetown.

It was two weeks before Christmas; a covering of snow lay on the ground and many doors were decorated with wreaths. People he'd met on the long walk from the bus stop had been in holiday spirits – smiling, laughing and greeting strangers. It seemed out of place to him with a war raging across the globe and it served only to heighten his anxiety.

This is going to be thorny, he thought taking a deep breath and reaching for the brass door knocker. He'd gotten a three week leave en route to his first assignment after the Airborne course and despite a gnawing apprehension, he'd decided to finally deal directly with the uncomfortable task of facing his mother after three and a half months of silence. Now, standing in the cold December air, he wondered at the wisdom of coming to see her unannounced. Nervously, he reached for the door knocker again, hoping she wasn't home so he wouldn't have to face her just now. *What was it dad always drilled into us kids growing up? – Bad news doesn't get better with age. Deal with it now*. He was about to reach for the brass knocker a third and final time when the door was violently flung open.

Denise Nolan glared at him.

Her face was a mask of rage, her complexion clearly reddened despite makeup and her eyes narrowed making the scowl on her face frightening. Her mouth was a tight thin line; she glowered, looking daggers at him until her whole expression slowly softened and her appearance transformed from fury to bewilderment and finally to unbounded joy.

"Glenn? Oh my! Is that really you?! I can't –"

He was suddenly smothered in the tightest hug he could remember, engulfed in the smell of perfume and the soft silk-like touch of his mother's hair. She held him at arms length's shaking her head in amazement, repeating his name over and over again. Tears streamed down her face, and she nervously bit her lip.

"Erika! Come in here. You're not going to believe this," Denise exclaimed, turning her face away and dabbing at her eyes with a tissue she'd pulled from her sweater sleeve."

"What is it now?!" Erika retorted angrily as she came into the hall and looked at the scene. She, too, was at first angry, as their mother had been – recovering quickly she ran to him and threw her arms around his neck as her eyes also filled with tears. "You crazy little mutton head. Why didn't you wire us you were coming?!"

He looked back and forth at them. Finally, shrugging nonchalantly, he said softly, "I was afraid if I warned you, you might move away before I got here."

His mother and sister fussed over him, helped him remove his wool Army overcoat and hat and hang them on the coat rack next to the front door. After a brief recounting of his last three months which went much better than he'd imagined it could, Erika went upstairs with him to his old room while their mother busied herself in the kitchen with dinner.

"Glenn, this is the greatest Christmas present ever!" she trilled happily while he took off his uniform jacket and undid his tie. "I can't believe you just appeared like this out the clear blue without so much as a phone call. You showed up at just the right time."

"You and Mom been fighting again?" he asked his sister as he opened the duffle bag and dumped its contents on the bed.

"What in the world makes you ask that?" Erika asked, looking aghast.

He smiled at her knowingly. "I saw the looks on both your faces when I showed up. Maybe I should thank you for creating a diversion to cover my entrance. Always thought you'd be worth something some day."

She frowned at him and then laughed aloud. "I ought to box your ears, little brother."

"Careful. I'm taller than you and I'm not the same guy who left here a few months ago."

Erika sat back on the bed and looked at him for awhile. "No, I guess you're not. You're not that shy, scraggly haired kid brother I used to know. You're more like dad. Mom's father always used to call you 'little Dave', and he was right. You look more like him now. I don't know, you even walk and move like him a little."

"Where is he now, do you know?" Glenn asked as he opened the chest of drawers and began filling it with his clothes.

"In England. That's all I know."

"Last I heard he was in Italy. The ol' man does get around, doesn't he? Is he still in the doghouse?" When Erika looked away, he said, "I'll take that as a 'yes'. Is that what you and mom were arguing about?"

"More or less," she replied without looking at him, remaining silent for a lingering moment. "Actually, more than that. I think she might be... well, I think she might be *involved* with that congressman she's been working for. What I mean is –"

"I know what it means, Erika!" he snapped at her. "That's a pretty serious allegation you're making against our mother. I can't imagine her doing something like that. Do you know for certain she is?"

"Not for certain. I hope she's not, but she's been spending more and more time with him, going to dinners in the evenings and so-called weekend planning sessions – just the two of them. It just doesn't look right. I think Michelle – Mrs. Reeves – has the same misgivings. I trust her. She responded the same way you did at first when –"

"You've told this to other people?!"

"Only to her. She and her father have been good friends of the family from the time I can first remember as a kid. She's always helped us – Mitch with a job in the Philippines and then an appointment to West Point; you with getting that motorbike. She taught me how to ride and got me this job in her father's office. She and mom have been friends for a long time and now she sees some of the same things I do. She's worried about it, too, because she knows this guy and doesn't trust him either; he's got a reputation. He's cheated before."

Glenn shook his head, hardly able to imagine something like this happening in his family. "All right," he said at last, "I'll go talk to him."

"I'm not asking you to do that."

"And I'm not asking your permission," he replied.

"You can't just go confront him. For crying out loud, the man is a congressman."

"And I'm an paratrooper."

"Glenn…" She paused and looked into his troubled, determined eyes. "What's happened to you? What became of the sweet, quiet boy who liked nothing more that fishing and sleeping late and just lazing around?"

"This war happened. When it's over, that boy may well return. Right now it sounds like our family just might have a problem on its hands. When I ask myself: *What would dad do if he were here?* the answer I hear is telling me to find out what's happening, figure out what needs fixing, and then go fix it."

Erika met his unwavering stare, looking now at her brother in a way she never had before. At last she said, "I don't know why I told you all that. Yes, mom and I were arguing about it when you came in, but when I saw you, my first thought was that I couldn't ruin this Christmas for you – for us, all of us. I didn't want to tell you, but I did. I've been wishing Mitch was here, because he'd know what to do. I never dreamed you would. But I was wrong. You've grown up – you really are like dad, and I'm so glad you came home for Christmas."

Glenn pulled a small box from his duffle bag and handed it to her. "I didn't have enough money to buy any presents so I thought I'd give mom this picture. Think she'll like it?"

Erika looked at the framed photo of Glenn and Mitch standing in a boat holding a large fish between them. "When and where was this taken?"

"About two years ago, right after Mitch got out of flight school and came home on leave. We rode the train up to New York and went fishing on the Sound for a few days. Just he and I. That's the last time I saw him. I put him on some big stripers out by the lighthouse and an old man happened by and took this picture. I was thinking about becoming a hunting and fishing guide back then – guess that's on hold for awhile."

"She'll absolutely love it. What a great gift. You're such a sweet guy, Glenn."

He hugged her as he whispered into her ear, "Love you, sis."

"Love you too, muttonhead."

Chapter 33

"I'm Major Nolan, your new squadron leader."

Mitch looked around *Hangmen's Hangout*, the 49ᵗʰ Fighter Squadron's makeshift Officers' Club. "I almost didn't make it here to Triolo today because after the tower cleared us to land my wingman and I were nearly run over on short final by a flight of four. In the last year, the Air Corps lost more pilots in this theatre due to accidents than from enemy action. Today, my wingman and I plus four aircraft of the 49ᵗʰ almost became part of that inglorious statistic. I want to see lieutenants Leeman, Steininger, Van Horn, and Hayes up here after I'm done. We need to talk … Be seated."

Well, that got their attention, Mitch thought as he turned his head and winked at Lucky.

It was New Years' Eve and he'd been in Italy for two weeks – eight days not counting his trip to Cairo to see that elusive exotic girl he'd met a year earlier in Casablanca...

During his first week at Bari, combat engineers with earth moving equipment had shown up and begun repairing runways and buildings, installing generators and running electrical wire. All the floor to ceiling hangar doors had been replaced and numerous Italian planes strewn about had been bulldozed to the north side of the field out of the way. A construction battalion descended on the former Italian airbase and began renovating office buildings and barracks. By the third day they had running water and a mess tent had been set up in the shade of a hangar. Things began to look up though the Mediterranean winter weather had not cooperated.

It had taken four days for all the aircraft from the Casablanca school to straggle in and another two days to get aircraft maintenance up and functioning. The helter-skelter nature of operations still prevailed, with round the clock flights to cover the mostly destroyed Bari harbor. The Germans had not returned – either because they thought they'd done all the damage possible or their intelligence had picked up on the squadron-sized element now dedicated to guarding the port. Still, Mitch kept a flight of four on patrol around the clock and another sitting strip alert. That routine lasted nearly a week until the new Wing commander and a skeleton headquarters staff showed up eight days before Christmas to commandeer the planes and pilots under Mitch's control.

He and Lucky were the last pilots assigned out to operational squadrons; Lucky had pitched a fit with Wing operations about his assignment to their intelligence section, and the personnel officer had no idea what to do with Mitch. "When you figure it out, let me know," Nolan had told him. "In the meantime, I'm going on leave to Cairo and I'm taking Captains Lindquist and Crosley with me. We'll be back before the New Year." His two classmates had been pleasantly surprised when he told them, "I haven't had a leave or a day off in three months, and Lucky wants to see that blond girl in the Brit Embassy. My dad always said it's harder to ask for permission than forgiveness so I'm taking the B-26 and heading to Egypt with our enlisted men. Come if you want."

En route, the mechanics declared they wanted to visit the Acropolis. The British had put all facilities in Greece off limits to American air traffic, so upon entering the Greek airspace Mitch shut down an engine, declared an emergency and landed in Athens. Five hours later, when they finished their tour, the crew managed to 'fix' the engine problem. They continued on to Egypt leaving behind an irate RAF airfield commander.

To Mitch, the side excursion to Athens turned out to be the only highlight of the trip.

Over a late dinner at a rooftop restaurant that first night, Aida told them Makara no longer worked at the British embassy. One day, late in the previous month, she had simply disappeared. Initially, some of her friends had gone to her apartment and when they found it empty reported it back to their section chief. Embassy life continued normally. Three more days passed without any contact from her. The Ambassador launched an investigation, and finding nothing turned the case over to the military a week later. On the first day of December military intelligence, MI-6, took over and soon interrogations were being conducted with nearly all the embassy staff. By then rumors were running rampant.

Conjecture relating to her whereabouts soon gave way to rumors concerning her identity.

Speculations ran the gamut. Some said she had been the victim of a Muslim honor killing executed by her family. Others said she was a German spy on the verge of being discovered and had fled the country. Another story had it she was an agent of the British Special Operations Executive, SOE, and had been secreted to London in preparation for assisting the Maquis inside France against the Nazis. There was no separating truth from fiction concerning her, assuming *anyone* had somehow stumbled onto what the truth really was.

Where are you Makara? he'd asked himself over and over again.

The week that followed served only to deepen his disappointment. By the time they returned to Bari, he'd decided to transfer to the Pacific to shake off the nagging frustration of his mystifying relationship with Makara. Equally vexing were his less than honorable thoughts and feelings for the married daughter of his father's friend, Smythe-Browne. *Best leave all this behind*, he'd decided.

The Air Corps had other ideas.

There had been a 'situation' arise in the 14th Group and the 49th Fighter Squadron needed a new commander. Mitch Nolan fit the bill and was unassigned at the moment. Over his protest, the Wing commander issued the orders and sent him. But after sleeping on it overnight, he began to warm to the idea. He realized taking command of a fighter squadron was something he'd wanted from the moment he first touched down at Telerghma. *I guess the apple doesn't fall far from the old tree*, he'd thought. The ol' man had always told him the best assignment he ever had was commanding soldiers and now he understood his father's relentless pursuit of troop commands all those years…

"I talked to Colonel Taylor at 14th Group an hour ago and he's very high on this squadron," Mitch was saying. "I hope I can say the same in the next weeks and months. I don't know you and you don't know me, but that's all going to change in short order. I asked the colonel to up the tempo of our mission scheduling so I can see the unit in action and get to know all of you better." He looked around the room and saw some familiar faces. "Some of you I know already – Hitchens, you came through the *Classy C* school in Casablanca when we first opened up three months ago, didn't you? And Farquar. You and Jennings there came through just a few weeks ago."

Two others – Daniels and O'Toole – spoke up as having been through the course.

"Captain Lindquist over there against the wall was our senior flight instructor at the Casablanca school. Those of you who came through learned a lot from him about the J-model and how good it is in the dive bomb role with the dive flaps installed. He's here as my right hand man, utility infielder, or whatever I care to call him. Basically, he's my squadron IP and check-pilot – every new pilot we get in will be cleared by him before going on missions."

Mitch looked around the room at the young faces, some attentive. Most of the pilots looked him over with that time worn indifferent look of men who had witnessed and survived death in the skies. Kids. All of them, except for a handful. He'd had a brief conversation with the Operations officer and learned, among other things, there were a half dozen pilots who had joined the squadron within the last week. Because of bad weather, some of the new arrivals hadn't yet been checked out or given an orientation flight of the area.

"I don't know what happened with the previous commander, and don't much care," Mitch said, deciding it served no purpose to ignore the obvious reason for his being there. "I'm not him, but there are some things you should know about me.

"I spent a year as an instructor at Moffett before the war started. Flew the North Atlantic in the winter of '40 and ferried one of the first P-38s across the southern Atlantic route to Africa a year ago. I have fifty missions with the 96th Squadron of the 82nd Fighter Group over Sicily and North Africa in G-models. I have over a hundred hours in this new J-model and I'm convinced it can outperform any German plane in the air… if a good pilot is at the controls."

"For my money, leaders fly, lead and train, in that order. I have three goals as a squadron commander: First, to knock out every German plane, locomotive and weapon we encounter. Second, to make sure every bomber we escort makes it back. Finally, to see that every pilot in this squadron survives fifty missions and goes home. I expect each of you to be the best pilot in the Air Corps. The maintenance in this squadron will be second to none. I work hard and play hard. You will, too. That's about it. Any questions?"

Silence ensued until a captain in the back of the room spoke up.

"Captain Gilkey, sir. Intelligence officer. If you were in the 96th Fighter Squadron in Africa, did you fly with Dixie Sloan?"

"I did. Both Lucky… Captain Lindquist, and I did."

"Was he as good as they say?"

"Depends on who *they*" is. Even though he's back home, Sloan is still the top ace in the Med with twelve kills. Anyone who ever flew with him would tell you he was an excellent fighter pilot. Dixie will tell you he was the best who ever lived. He had some problems, but shyness was never one of them. Yes, he was exceptional." He asked again for questions and when there were none he said, "Reminder, I want to see Hayes, Leeman, Steininger, Van Horn. Also, I want to see Blaxton and Weatherford as well. After chow I need to meet with the operations officer, intelligence officer and section leaders as a group in Operations. Tomorrow being New Years' and the weather over southern Europe forecast to be even worse than it's been the last two weeks, there won't be any missions scheduled. Happy New Year."

Lucky sidled up to him as the meeting broke up. "Surprised me, amigo. You actually sounded like a squadron commander. Where'd that come from?"

"The Fred McMurray character in *Men with Wings*," Mitch said sarcastically. "Lucky, I want you to talk to those four who almost caused us a mid-air over the field today. Read 'em the riot act and let them know that crap doesn't cut it. We could have lost a half dozen planes and pilots because of it and that's stupid. You let them know just how stupid."

Lucky looked at him suspiciously. "Me? Chew them out? That's what commanders, do."

"No, that's what you do from now on. I can't begin this command that way. If I chew those four out right now, I'll set a bad tone before I even get started here." Lindquist wasn't following and said so. "This is a tight spot for me. Brand new commander; everybody knows these guys almost caused a mid-air. If I chew them out without imposing some kind of punishment, it looks like I'm all bark and no bite. On the other hand, if my very first action as a commander is to impose punishment, I'll be pushing a rope uphill for the rest of my time here because I'll always be the 'bad guy' in their eyes. They won't be following me, and that means I won't be leading them."

Lindquist frowned at him. "As your best friend Dixie would say, don't you think you're overcookin' your grits on this, Nolan?"

"I don't think so. These guys need to know that when they screw up and are called on it by the commander bad things will always follow – there's no talking their way out of it. Hopefully that keeps them from going over the line. This was a serious incident today. If I talk to them without imposing some penalty that doesn't help me, them or the unit."

Lindquist thought about it for a brief while. He wasn't sure he agreed with Nolan's logic, but Mitch had earned a favor for getting him out of the staff assignment at the new headquarters, and for sticking his neck out so he could see Aida.

"All right, I'll talk to them – one pilot to another," Lucky said at last.

"One pilot to another. That's what I need. Thanks."

"I'm not real happy about a near mid-air myself. I'll let 'em know they got off lucky this time, but that it'll be the last time they do."

Lucky was about to say something about now being owed a favor but Nolan had already turned away to introduce himself to two kids dressed as second lieutenants in flight suits. Four pilots were standing by the near wall, talking and watching Nolan suspiciously. Lucky walked over to them and introduced himself.

"Who was leading the flight today we almost ran in to?"

One of the pilots pointed a thumb at his chest. "That was me. Frank Steininger."

"Tell me what happened."

"We were up on squadron ops frequency instead of tower freq. That's pretty common. Usually we just look for the green light from the tower instead of calling for clearance. Weren't expecting any other aircraft." The lieutenant shrugged. "Just didn't see you, that's all."

"Any of you guys ever been involved in a mid-air?" Lucky asked, looking at their faces one by one. "Me neither, but Nolan has. A -109 collided head on with him and severed his horizontal stabilizer at the boom root one day over the Med nine months ago. Took him three hours and a lot of sweat to get it back to our base. He really doesn't like mid-airs. And he can tell you about every one that's happened in this theatre and how it shouldn't have been. Most of them happen in the pattern and he won't stand for it happening in his unit. He's a fanatic about safety. You guys just stuck a sharp stick in his eye and he won't forget it, so you need to work at getting on his good side."

"We didn't mean to do it," one of the other pilots said.

"Ever met anybody who meant to get into an accident? Me neither. Here's the drill. You four need to become the most safety conscious Lightning drivers in the squadron. I mean be real obvious about it, too. You tell the rest of the guys what I just told you. You heard Nolan say he plans to get everybody here back home in one piece? He means it. Clear enough?" They all nodded. "Good. One more question – are there any good looking Eye-talian gals in any of these towns close by?"

*　　*

"Baltimore, Maryland, for the last year before signing up." the young-looking lieutenant said in response to Mitch's question. He swallowed hard making his prominent adams apple bob up and down and looked a little nervous at being grilled by the commander. "I grew up just outside a little farm town in Carroll County and left there after high school."

"So you went to the big city seeking your fame and fortune, eh?" Mitch offered to pour the young lieutenant a shot of bourbon but the new pilot declined.

"Haven't earned any mission liquor yet, sir," Donny Blaxton said.

"This is my bourbon. Brought it all the way from Cairo. You've got more time in the squadron than I do, and I'm having a shot. Sure you don't want one? Captain Lindquist will tell you I'm pretty much a tightwad so my buying drinks doesn't happen all that often."

"No thanks, sir. I'll pass for now."

"Up to you… so, you were saying you went to Baltimore after high school."

Blaxton had arrived in the Group the evening before along with a dozen other new pilots. He and his friend Rob Weatherford had been assigned to the 49th Squadron, pretty much by chance the way he'd explained it. Back in the States, they had been in the same training squadron through Basic, Intermediate and Advance flight training as well fighter transition. They had both gotten married to their high school sweethearts just before P-38 transition training in California. When shipped overseas, they traveled on the same ship to North Africa, the same C-47 to Foggia and the same 2 ½ ton truck from there to Triolo. They would have been in the same four man tent except none of the pilot's tents had more than one vacant cot. Neither one of them had a good reason for volunteering for flight training except they both thought it would be more fun than carrying a rifle.

"I went to Baltimore a week after graduation for a job. Not for fame or fortune – just for money to live on. At the time I didn't have a cent to my name, except three or four dollars my older sister lent me. Everything I owned I was wearing."

"That's all you had when you left home?! Your parents didn't help you?"

Blaxton took a deep breath and looked away from his squadron commander. "My dad died in the spring of my senior year, and my mom passed when I was nine. My older sister was the only family I had and she was married with a daughter of her own. Times were tough. Always had been. It was the Depression and all." Blaxton looked back at him, troubled. "It's not much of a story, sir. Are you sure you want to hear all this? I don't have any complaints. The Army's been real good to me."

"I'd like to hear it, if you don't mind. A commander should know his people – that's what my ol' man taught me. I need to know as much as I can about everybody in the 49th, not just you, but you're the first. Tell me what you like most about the Army, other than flying."

"The chow, sir. I'm really liking that rule about taking all you want and eating all take."

"Never heard *that* before," Mitch replied, shaking his head. "I'm not sure I want to know why. So, do you have any other family?"

"None that could help me much. My aunt Edna let me use a room at her place to take care of my dad the last half of my senior year. I mostly slept in a recliner chair and Dad was in the bed. He died in May just before graduation. They say it was because of the cancer, but he was an alcoholic and never could hold a job most of the time when I was growing up. I think that's probably what got him. He left me a car worth about fifty dollars. But that's another story. I found a job working construction at Camp Meade but I had to join a union to work there. Turned out the union got my first two week's salary and left me with nothing, so I quit them and got a job as a mail clerk with the telephone company. By the time the Japs bombed Pearl Harbor, I'd been promoted to pole climber running telephone wires. Still couldn't afford to get married, but I had a nice little apartment downtown. Took me a year to get my sister to sign the papers for me to enlist. Getting into the Air Corps is the best thing that ever happened to me, sir, and I'll work hard to be the best pilot I can for you."

Mitch wondered if everyone in this new wave of pilots came from this same sort of background, and suspected they did. The guys he'd flown with in Africa were a different breed; most of them were former sergeants, and most had a few years of service in the "old Army". They had stood in the gap early on, holding the Germans off, flying old machines or outclassed versions of the newer models until the Blaxtons and Weatherfords got off the farms or out of the factory to get trained in vast numbers. The Dixie Sloans and Ricky Zubaricks had been the American finger in the dyke until the new breed arrived in numbers and equipment sufficient to turn the tide. So far, despite all the hoopla to the contrary, he sensed the Germans were still winning the air war; the number of fighters and bombers being lost week in and week out told him it was probably a stalemate at best.

But he sensed that was about to change in the new year. Blaxton and those like him were going to be the agents of that change, and he guessed they had no idea of it.

"How'd you do in flight school, Blaxton? Top man in your class?"

The lieutenant gave him a sideways grin. "Not at the top. But not at the bottom either. Somewhere in the middle, I guess. Maybe a little better… better than I expected going in. There were plenty of college boys and I didn't think I had much of a chance keeping up with them. My high school class was less than thirty and the school probably wasn't as good as the ones in the big city, but I surprised myself. It turned out I could keep up with those boys. I even helped some of them in ground school and later on with navigation. Not bad for a fella who used to throw .22 bullets into the stove now and then for entertainment in elementary school."

Mitch smiled and nodded knowingly. "I did the same down in Texas when I was a kid. Seems like it turned out okay. You got into fighters, anyhow, and that means you were high enough in the class to have a choice. How many hours flying time do you have, Blaxton?"

"A little over two hundred, sir."

"How many in the P-38?"

"A half dozen in G-models, another twenty-five in the P-322."

Mitch nodded. Not much, he thought, although some of the replacements they'd gotten in North Africa in mid-summer had less, and none of them had flown the stripped down Lightning – the 322. He'd never flown one himself but heard it was actually faster and more fun than the line aircraft with all their war gear. "Tomorrow, you and I are going flying. We need to learn the area, and I want to see how well you handle the J-model."

The young lieutenant's face lit up. "I'm all for that, major."

"Glad to hear it."

*   *   *   *

"I just about had him in my sights – almost ready to tell him he was toast. Suddenly Weatherford says: '*Where'd he go?!*' cause he flat disappeared."

It was New Year's day and the Group was celebrating its arrival with a special meal and spirits. Some of the older hands who had been in North Africa enjoyed the marginally better living conditions in the Foggia airfield complex and could even see some progress in the war.

"What do you mean he disappeared, Blaxton? Did he fly into a cloud or something?" Steininger asked reaching across the picnic style mess hall table for the bread and butter.

"No. One second he was there and the next he was gone. G--O--N--E… *gone*. That kind of disappeared. In a second, maybe less."

400

Steininger looked around at the other pilots and at Gilkey who sat across from Blaxton as he recounted the afternoon flight he and Weatherford had taken with Nolan and Lindquist. "You don't make a P-38 just disappear, rookie."

"Well, he did. Isn't that right, Rob?" Weatherford nodded agreement. "I caught a real quick glimpse of the nose and wings of his plane just beginning to turn like he was in a flat spin. Just a fraction of a second and then nothing but air. Next thing he was on our tails. Both he and Lindquist. He told me how he did it when we debriefed. Captain Lindquist said they all used to do it in the 96th Squadron. They called it the Nolan Roll."

Gilkey listened attentively to everything the new arrival was saying, taking notes and asking questions so frequently it was almost becoming annoying. He sipped at his coffee and reached for the butter while continuing to watch and listen to Blaxton.

"Wait a minute, Gilkey," Steininger said, reaching across the table and grabbing his hand. "That's the pilot's butter. It's not for ground pounders."

The intelligence officer recoiled and looked stricken. "I'm sorry. I wasn't aware."

"All right, I guess," Steininger said, solicitously. "Just don't let it happen again. Can't have the pilots missing out on their butter because the ground crew gets a little ahead of themselves." Steininger gave a quick glance around the table looking pleased with himself. "Anyhow, Blaxton, so that's what you did most of the afternoon – played a little follow the leader grab-ass with the new commander? I call that apple-polishing, or boot licking. Did he make you polish his brass when it was all over?"

Blaxton was becoming a little irritated, but figured this harassment was part of the drill for newcomers. Why they were doing it to their intelligence officer mystified him. Maybe Steininger was just a jerk. "No, that's not all we did this afternoon. We downed an Me-109."

Steininger and a few others quickly looked at him and frowned. "On an orientation flight?" Leeman asked, looking surprised. He was from a small town in Texas and had one semester under his belt at A&M in Bryan/College Station when Pearl Harbor was attacked. He'd enlisted immediately, finished flight school and was near the end of his fifty mission tour. "You shot down a German?"

"Not really," Blaxton replied. "He kinda surrendered."

"What do you mean – '*kinda surrendered*.' How does a German pilot *kinda* surrender?"

"Well," Blaxton began, "we first went out over the Adriatic and flew the coast south toward Bari to get some landmarks fixed. Then we followed the coast north past the front lines into northern Italy for I guess a hundred miles or so, up to Pescara, and turned inland. We'd gone maybe thirty miles when Lucky spotted a lone -109 underneath us headed toward Rome, so we broke into two elements and dived on him. The major and I got on his eight o'clock; Lucky and Rob got on his four o'clock, and then Nolan closed in to signal him to follow us.

The German turned away and Lindquist sprayed some tracers in front of him – he turned left and the major and I shot, not to knock him down, just to scare him. That went on for another minute or two back and forth until the Kraut finally waggled his wings. I thought maybe he really would come back to Foggia with us. Next thing he goes into a steep climb, rolls over on his back and falls out of the cockpit; he opened his chute at about four thousand and drifts down waving at us."

Gilkey looked perplexed. "I never got a report."

Blaxton shrugged and reached into his flight suit for a cigarette. "Lucky wanted to claim a kill, but the major said no. They argued for a while until Nolan said he'd have to produce the gun camera footage before it was legal and no one in the flight would vouch for him. On the way back we low-leveled over the Adriatic – Lucky and the Major were so low they drew a wake. It was like they were dragging their tails through the water. Rob and I stayed a little higher but even there it was kinda scary being that close to the water at three hundred miles an hour. I'd say the two of them know how to fly."

"An understatement," Weatherford offered sipping on his coffee. "Nolan buzzed an Italian fishing boat and tipped it over. A little later, Lindquist did it to another one. I didn't think I could get low enough. We tried a DF steer from a hundred miles off shore to see how it works just in case we ever had to use one. Then we did some one on one and two on one dogfighting south of Foggia. That's when Nolan showed us that roll thing he does. I'm going to have to practice before I ever think of using it. It was a lot packed into four hours."

"So where's the new commander now?" Steininger asked, looking around the mess hall. "He's going to miss the best meal we've had in four months if he doesn't get here soon."

"He said he was going to spend some time in Maintenance," Blaxton answered, looking around for an ash tray and finally giving up and tapping the ashes onto the dirt floor. "Nolan said he'd show me how to zero my guns tonight if I was interested. He thinks most pilots know too little about the maintenance and mechanics of their aircraft."

"Don't need to know a lot about it," Steininger said sarcastically. "That's why they have emergency procedures. Ain't that right, Van?"

"If you say so, Lyle."

Lindquist came into the small mess tent, scooped some food into his mess kit and grabbed a cup of coffee before sitting down with them. "The chow here stinks," he said picking a piece of turkey up with his fork and sniffing it. "Makes me long for some canned C-Ration stew. How you boys doin'?" Without looking up he pushed the food around with his fork.

"Where's the new C.O.?" Van Horn asked.

"Down on the flight line with the maintenance sergeant. What's his name?"

"Mac. Mac McGruder. He's been with us as long as I've been here. I'm pretty sure he came over with the first contingent that showed up in North Africa. What are they doing?"

"Checking the yoke wiring on each of the aircraft to see how the weapons firing and release buttons are set up," Lindquist responded dropping his fork disgustedly and sipping on his coffee. "Not much standardization there as far as he can tell. Probably going to make some changes. All the ships we had in Casablanca were wired the same way once we got to work on them. Makes sense."

Van Horn and Steininger looked at one another, unhappy.

"Maybe it makes sense to you, but it doesn't to me," Steininger said, lighting a cigarette and tossing the match on the floor. "It's always been the practice around here that old hands could wire up the buttons on their yoke whatever way suited them best. Van, let's you and me see what's up down there and have a little talk with the CO."

Lindquist looked at them with a grin. "Good luck boys," he told Van Horn and Steininger as they left. When they were gone, he turned to Blaxton and Weatherford who sat across the table from Gilkey. "I could've warned those two but they strike me as the kind who need to learn by experience. Hard teacher, experience with Mitch Nolan when he's in charge, and those boys won't soon forget it, especially since they're wrong."

Blaxton stole a quick glance at Weatherford and then at the intel officer. "What do you mean?" he asked Lucky.

"What I mean is this: you don't always fly your assigned plane when you're in a line squadron. So if your aircraft is rigged a certain way and the plane you're flying is different – and most of us have had that happen – you could be in a world of trouble." Lindquist smirked at them. "Ol' Mitch has experience with that back in Africa. He had lots of little rules and SOPs back then. Still does. And those boys are about to find out. You don't move ScrapIron Nolan too easily, if at all," Lindquist said, and chortled.

"ScrapIron?" Gilkey asked.

"Yeah, that's what his teammates on the baseball team called him."

"Odd name."

"He can be an odd duck. Our second year at the trade school, Navy game – Nolan was a catcher and he blocked the plate when one of the squids tried to score from second. Mitch stopped him dead two feet from the plate just as he caught the ball; he took the ball out of his mitt and clunked him on the head with it. Knocked the kid out cold. It's not a long story but I have others. Don't have time to tell 'em though. Got to get down to the flight line and help those two boys get back home after they get their heads handed to 'em."

Chapter 34

Nolan cursed silently to himself as he scanned the sky ahead, above, below and then around a semi-circular arc from due north to south.

Ice was forming constantly inside his oxygen mask forcing him to break the seal every few minutes to let the frigid wet buildup fall out onto his lap. The Lightning was a lot of things, but warm wasn't one of them – especially in the wintertime at the altitude necessary to cover the bombers. He adjusted the hard rubber mask resting uncomfortably over the bridge of his nose as he tried to moisten his parched lips. He checked the position of his flight and then glanced back inside the cockpit. Time for a little housekeeping – a continuous preoccupation with tuning the machine's performance that kept him alert on long missions. Lower the rpm to 1600, boost the manifold pressure, increase pitch and the props. Save a little gas until the Luftwaffe showed up and then shove everything to the firewall and to hell with fuel economy.

He could see Lutze's Red flight crisscrossing two thousand feet above the large box-like formations of B-24 Liberators, flying just below contrail level. To the left of the bombers, White flight was strung out from the front to the back of the formation weaving left and right so as not to out run the bombers. Blue flight followed on behind the large box formation. A squadron of Mustangs – not more than twelve or thirteen – covered the right side. Having the P-51s along bothered him. He would rather have had another squadron of P-38s; he knew them and they were more reliable than any of the Mustang squadrons he'd worked with. The P-51 was a hot airplane, and the guys flying them knew it. They were much more likely than P-38 squadrons to break away from the heavies and chase German fighters; his experience with them over the last five weeks since taking command had not been good.

He had a full complement of his own squadron, plus his three best flight leads were running the mission. They'd mixed it up with the Luftwaffe on a half dozen occasions over the last month and the Hangmen had stood up well. It was nice for a change to sit half way back in Carhart's flight and worry about nothing but how well his wingman would stand up under fire. But Weatherford had shown himself to be a fast learner. So had his buddy Blaxton, now flying Lucky's wing. All in all, this new wave of pilots seemed about as good as the initial contingent in North Africa plus there were a lot more of them. And, they had a better airplane to fly. Absently, he wondered why Gilkey had given the kid from Maryland the nickname *Girk*.

Still, he cursed the ice in his oxygen mask. And he was less than happy with the bombers.

As usual, they had shown up late at the rendezvous point over the small island halfway out in the Adriatic. He wondered why the B-17s could always be on time, at the right altitude and flying in tight formation which made them an easier assignment to cover. They were everything the Liberators weren't and he wondered if someday he could get a chance to fly the B-24 and see if it might be a lot more difficult to fly. He was considering all that when a radio call crackled in his earphones.

"Bogies, one o'clock high. Tighten up. Stay with the heavies."

The calm, authoritative voice sounded like Lutze's.

Red flight made a shallow climbing turn toward the Germans ten thousand feet above. The Messerschmidts turned and headed east, away from the bombers. Red flight eased back and resumed their crisscrossing pattern. Fifteen minutes later, another flight of Germans, this time only a half dozen appeared at the same position and altitude. Again Red flight turned slowly into them. Suddenly, all the Mustangs jettisoned their drop tanks and started climbing rapidly toward the -109s.

"Stay with the heavies," one of the flight leads said over the radio, but the Mustangs continued up and then maneuvered to pursue when the Germans turned tail and dove away.

Damn! Nolan said to himself. *They did it again! Colonel Taylor and I are going to have another talk about the Mustangs, and this time the Wing Commander is going to hear about it.*

Twenty-five miles South of Trieste the bombers began a slow left turn due west, headed directly toward Venice and beyond that to the town of Padua which was the initial point to begin the bomb run on the rail yards in Verona. The escort would leave the bomber formation at that point and pick them up on the west side of Verona as the Liberators came off the target. Neither the American nor the German fighters would chance flying through all the flak and other ground-to-air fire.

From twenty miles away Mitch watched the bombers as they released their bombs, glad that he wasn't in one of the big hulking B-24s being hammered by the exploding balls of flak thrown at them by the German 88s on the ground. Worse, Luftwaffe fighters in large numbers were waiting for them on the far side of the target and fell on the bombers and their escorts with a vengeance.

A pandemonium of radio calls filled the frequency as the bomber crews reported sightings. One second the skies had been clear and he had been wrapped in that curious isolation of noisy neutral background – an odd silence that seemed thick, heavy. In an instant the airspace transformed into a crazy swirling aquarium of darting forms. It looked like the

Luftwaffe had sent every machine they could fly to scramble formations and knock down all the lumbering Liberators.

White flight headed straight into the oncoming German fighters as the P-38s gained altitude and dropped their external tanks while separating to give themselves maneuver room. In less than minute the sky turned into a furball of twisting, turning, diving fighter aircraft. Chaos, quick and violent. His stomach muscles tensed and tightened.

The air was crisscrossed with strings of tracers as he fired at a green and yellow fighter that filled his windscreen crossing in front of him in a shallow dive, growing larger as he closed the distance between them. Strangely he could make out all the markings – the red and white stripes of the crest painted a few feet back of the propeller, the vertical chevrons behind the cockpit just in front of the black cross outlined in white. Puffs of incandescent smoke erupted from around the engine and then the German's clear canopy flew off and rushed past Nolan's right wing as he crossed only a few yards over the crippled enemy fighter. He glanced back and saw the plane in a steep dive dragging a spiral of black smoke.

The streamlined form of a -109 hurtled down off his left wing closely tailed by a twin-engine Lightning. The German threw the plane into a desperate turn and began trailing a white wisp, then suddenly belched a thick cloud of dark smoke and bright yellow flame before exploding. A ball of fire dropped from the dark cloud of debris – probably the engine – and one of the wings began tumbling end over end toward earth.

A Messerschmitt flashed by in front of him firing on a Lightning whose left engine was on fire and trailing smoke. Mitch turned hard right, fired too quickly and missed the target but got on its tail as it dove toward the ground. Again he fired at the -109 but couldn't tell him how many rounds had gone home as both planes in front of him gyrated wildly.

Tracers arched over his canopy from directly behind; he looked into the rearview mirror he'd had Kupcinsky install on the *Mistress* back in Casablanca and saw the Focke Wulf 190 coming from behind. He quickly jogged left, then right, and rolled inverted headed straight down with the enemy fighter following closely on his tail. The Lightning began to shudder as the airspeed indicator passed 400 mph. The ground was coming up quickly and he could see the -190 was catching up to him as he continued firing. Suddenly Mitch deployed his dive flaps, pulled back hard on the yoke, and chopped the throttles; the effect was like stomping on brakes. A quick glance into the mirror showed the -190 following him in the pullout from the dive, but the sleek German fighter was going too fast. The Focke Wulf quickly overtook him and flashed by a scant few feet above the Lightning's cockpit. Mitch raised the *Mistress's* nose, pressed the firing button and from less than fifty feet, raked the underside of the German plane which flipped on its back and plowed into the ground in a great fireball.

Nolan added power and realized he was breathing rapidly, that his flight suit and gloves were soaked with sweat. *The old G Model could never do that*, he thought as he climbed toward the melee thousands of feet above him, all the while looking around for a wily German waiting to pounce on the low, slow Lightning clawing for altitude.

He scanned the sky and saw Weatherford straining to catch up to him.

Lucky Lindquist was heading directly for a FW190. He fired and saw rounds exploding around the -190's spinner just before the German's engine caught fire. The enemy aircraft flipped over and hurtled past him a few yards beneath his P-38. An Me-109 flashed across his field of vision from right to left but before he could get off a shot it disappeared into the melee.

Tracers floated over his canopy from behind and he instinctively hunched his shoulders, lowering himself in the seat. He tucked the nose of the Lightning, made a hard left turn and hoped that Blaxton could keep up with him. Immediately he saw a -109 on the tail of a P-38. He squeezed off a short burst, saw smoke erupt from the German's engine and pulled back hard on the control yoke to avoid a P-38 diving from left to right on the tail of another -109.

He was twisting and turning to avoid collisions; now and then a fleeting target would present itself and he would fire a quick burst hoping to at least do some damage. In an instant, he realized he was alone in the sky and the fight was some distance away and above him. He looked around and was surprised to see Blaxton was still on his wing and that they were both very close to the ground. Machine guns in sandbagged emplacements were shooting at them as they streaked by below treetop level, hopped over a tree line, and strafed a German gun crew on the other side.

Ground fire was hitting his right engine and he saw a large hump on the top of the cowling, then a red glow coming from a hole in the middle of the hump. Instantly the engine erupted in flame and his windshield cracked from a shot that came from out of nowhere; he felt a sting on his head and a warm trickle down the side of his face.

Lucky's hands did a war dance over the controls, shutting down the damaged engine, turning off the fuel and feathering the prop without conscious awareness of doing it. Coolant flowed from the engine, across the wing, trailing behind him; now his other engine was running rough. He saw an open field not far ahead. *Got to get this thing down quick if you want any control over the landing. Forget about everything else; concentrate on putting the damn plane down!* he said to himself. *Two quick turns and a sideslip and you're in position – over some trees and down!*

He had let Litton, one of the new pilots fly his airplane. Litton was a feather merchant – five foot six and barely a hundred and twenty pounds. Lucky had switched and now flew

McMonegal's ship because the Boston Irishman was on leave and Litton couldn't reach the controls of the six-foot-six pilot's specially modified Lightning. The thought flashed through his mind this was not the time to be having an emergency in an aircraft reconfigured with its seat well back and lowered down so it fit a much larger pilot.

He slid over the last tree line by a few feet, hit the ground hard and felt his forehead slam into the gun sight. His last conscious thought was that the plane was bouncing across a field like a Harley riding over the potholes of hell and his face was being pummeled, oozing blood.

Then all went black.

Mitch Nolan saw the P-38 on the deck not far from a German airfield west of Verona streaming coolant and flames from its right engine. Tracers from several machine gun positions on the ground converged on the crippled aircraft. He stopped his climb, dove for the ground and strafed two of the gun emplacements. Pulling up, he saw the wounded Lightning hop over a tree line and skid sideways across a rectangular field. He recognized the wing man's aircraft. It was Blaxton – and he realized the crippled aircraft as Lucky's.

Immediately he felt sick to his stomach.

Twice he circled low over the field looking for any signs of life. At last he saw the canopy open and watched Lucky struggle out onto the wing and place the demolition canister just above a fuel tank. He saw Lindquist pull the ring before sliding off the back of the wing and heading for the nearest tree line. He could see several trucks laden with infantry troops headed for the crash site from the nearby airfield. Making a quick strafing run on the trucks he pulled up and saw a P-38 two miles from the field with his landing gear and flaps full down.

It was Blaxton.

That's impossible. You can't land the P-38 on a soft unimproved field– the long skinny gear won't handle it. Don't you know that, Blaxton?! Nolan wanted to yell at him, and finally keyed his radio saying, "Blue six, you can't put your aircraft down on that field."

"*Gotta try,*" came the immediate response.

"Abort. That's an order." Silence answered. "I say again – abort… Abort!"

Mitch could see Lucky now running across the field, stopping and gazing at the P-38 just clearing the obstacles at the end of the field approaching along the long axis of the furrows. Blaxton made a perfect short field landing, stopped immediately and opened the canopy of his ship. Lindquist turned and began running toward the P-38 now two hundred yards away. German trucks were stopping at the far end of the field and disgorging their cargo of infantry troops who began firing at Blaxton's P-38 and Lindquist as he ran toward it. A few miles west, a half dozen Me-109s ducked in and out of some low clouds, lining up to come down and strafe the stranded pilot and Blaxton's aircraft.

"White four, you strafe that tree line where the Germans are and I'll take care of the Kraut aircraft," Mitch said quickly over the radio as he turned in the direction of the German fighters. The *schwarme* headed directly toward him as he maneuvered to block their attack. He fired a burst at the lead ship and saw its engine erupt in flames. He kicked right rudder hard for another burst at another target and saw smoke coming from the second aircraft. Turning left he fired two more short bursts. The German attack disintegrated and the remaining enemy aircraft turned tail. As he pulled into a climbing turn he looked over his shoulder and saw the first German aircraft he'd hit crash in a ball of flame, nose down into the field no more than fifty yards away from Blaxton.

Mitch circled back and followed Weatherford on a strafing run of the tree line where the German infantry were. As they lined up for a another run, he saw Lucky clamber on wing of the P-38 with Blaxton's help and watched as they jumped into the cockpit. Almost immediately the plane was moving slowly and the canopy was being lowered. From where he sat, Mitch was certain they weren't going make it, but ever so slowly they gained speed and managed to clear the farthest tree line without mushing in. He tried three times to raise them over the radio without success and finally he and Weatherford provided cover while Blaxton stayed on the deck until they got to the coast.

Three hours later they arrived back at Triolo.

*   *   *   *

Nolan taxied *Mitch's Mistress* across the perforated steel plate ramp toward where the rest of the squadron was shutting down. Obviously word had gotten out about what happened. When both Lucky and Blaxton emerged from the same cockpit, a crowd of crew chiefs and maintenance technicians gathered around the revetment pressing in on the two pilots. Mitch rolled down the side windows and pushed back the canopy after making entries in the aircraft log book. As he started to get out, a hand reached down into the cockpit offering assistance.

"I want to thank you for helping to save my valuable carcass," Lucky said cheerfully, flashing a wide grin.

Mitch stood on the wing of his plane and looked at Lindquist's face and the blood-soaked bandage around his forehead. "You should see Doc Maislen about that knock on your head. I hope not too many of your brains fell out."

"As a matter of fact… That was some kinda flying Blaxton did today, don't you think?"

"If by '*some kinda flying*' you mean stupid, I agree."

"Well, Mitch, I think Blaxton's just too new to realize that what he did couldn't be done. So, he just went ahead and did it. We had a long talk about it on the way back."

"You did, eh? Did he tell you I directly ordered him not to land. Twice?"

Lucky grew silent and looked troubled. "He told me. Don't think it registered at the time with him. We've hammered into the new guys about staying with the bombers and sticking to your wingman. He was caught between two competing orders and just picked one. From where I stand, he did the right thing. We wouldn't be having this little *tête-à-tête* if he hadn't."

"I know you believe that. It's why you came up on my plane to try to convince me to overlook what he did. I can't do that."

"No, Mitch. I'm trying to keep you from making a damned fool out of yourself over nothing." Lindquist gave him a hard stare. "What in the hell has happened to you? Sometimes I don't think I even know who you are since you became squadron commander. I think it's gone to your damned head, and it's not pretty, friend. And another thing – turns out you're not all that good a commander anyhow. One minute you're being a hard ass, and the next you're tipping over Eye-talian boats. You're sending mixed messages, pal, and it's confusing to all of us. Back in flight school you were the only one in the class who buzzed the tower and in Telerghma you stole a couple of Gooney Birds to haul supplies you stole from the Brits. Now you've got all these damned little rules that everybody has to follow to the letter like you're some South American dictator. And the next thing you're up there playing grab ass with the Mustangs. You're the one who got the entire 14th Group called on the carpet by the wing commander for messing with them and causing that one guy to have to bail out before he crashed." Lucky was poking Mitch in the chest with his finger for emphasis as he spoke and his volume increased almost to a shout. "How about that for disobeying a direct order not to play with the Mustangs? What would happen to you if that ever got out?"

"Lucky, if you poke me one more time with that finger," Mitch said in a slow, ominous cadence, "I'm going to toss you off this wing twelve feet to the ground so you land on your head. And that *will* cause what's left of your brains to fall out. I've got to go see Colonel Taylor. For now, you tell the flight leads to hold everybody here on the flight line after debriefing. I want to talk to everyone in the squadron when I get back. That means every officer and every enlisted man. You and I will finish this later."

Mitch climbed down and walked off in the direction of group headquarters.

A half-hour later he and the group commander along with Captain Travers, the group adjutant, arrived at the 49th Squadron flight line. The first sergeant called them into formation facing Colonel Taylor.

"Lieutenant Blaxton. Front and center," Mitch said loudly.

Captain Travers handed a small box to the Group commander and began. "Attention to orders. Headquarters Fifteenth Air Force, Foggia, Italy. Dated 4 February, 1944. Award of the Silver Star for gallantry in action against an enemy of the United States on 4 February 1944 to 2nd Lieutenant S. Donnie Blaxton, 49th Fighter Squadron, 14th Fighter Group, 306th Bombardment Wing… Lieutenant Blaxton distinguished himself while on a mission to Verona, Italy escorting bombers of the…"

Mitch watched Blaxton's expression closely. He'd never seen anyone exhibit as much bewilderment and angst.

"… exhibited great courage when his wingman was struck by enemy ground fire and crash landed in an open field. Disregarding the heavy fire from enemy ground units as well as enemy fighters, and at great personal risk, Lieutenant Blaxton landed his Lockheed P-38 Lightning, rescued his downed and badly wounded wingman. He then took off, still under enemy attack, and flew his single seat aircraft three hours back to his home base in Triolo, Italy. During the return flight, he rendered medical assistance to the wounded officer. Lieutenant Blaxton's daring rescue of a downed airman is in the best tradition of the U.S. Army, and brings great credit to himself, his squadron and the entire Army Air Force. Signed – Nathan F. Twining, General, 15th Air Force, Commanding."

Colonel Taylor stepped forward and pinned the red, white and blue ribboned medal on Blaxton's dirty, sweat-stained flight suit, shaking his hand.

Mitch stepped forward and shook the lieutenant's hand next. He leaned close and whispered. "That was an incredibly brave thing you did today, Blaxton. Not very smart, but real brave. You get my drift?" The lieutenant nodded giving him a startled, wide-eyed look. Dave then turned to the Group commander. "Sir, I need a few minutes with my men, but I would like to continue our earlier conversation when I'm done, if you have the time." Colonel Taylor agreed and left with his adjutant.

When they were out of earshot, Mitch stood the squadron at ease. "It was a good day and a bad day. The bad news is that we lost a bomber. Just one, and considering what they threw at us most people would think that's good. It's not – especially if you happened to be on that ship. We had a lot of our aircraft shot up, some pretty bad. But the good news is all the pilots got back even if Lindquist left his airplane in a field up north. And to top it off one of our own was awarded a decoration that's rarely given to aviators. Congratulations, Girk.

"The best news is that our supply sergeant – Sergeant Velarde – has found a reliable, legal and military funded source of spirits on his latest scrounging trip. This translates into a changed policy concerning 'mission liquor' in the 49th. Effective this evening, all enlisted as well as officer members of the squadron will receive one shot of liquor after each mission flown. But tonight and tonight only all hands get a double hard liquor ration of two shots in honor of Blaxton's award. Let's not abuse this and let's not talk too freely about it around the rest of the Group. *Comprende?* Still got some time before supper so let's get these ships inspected and started on repairs if you haven't already."

They wandered away from formation in good spirits – it had been an exceptional day, and one to be proud of, but shaded with sobering reality. *We were lucky*, he thought to himself and then recalled a night in the Philippines on the shore of Lingayen Gulf with Glenn and his father. Andy Fauser and his son, Zach had been with them on the three day fishing trip. The subject of luck had come up after dinner as they talked about their catch that day around the fire on the beach beneath the South Pacific sky. His father told them about a conversation he'd had during the Great War with a chaplain named Francis Duffy, an old time Augustinian Catholic who convinced him there was no such thing as luck. Mitch remembered well what his father had told them that night. Luck was really good planning, hard work, sober reflection and Providence meeting opportunity. He'd tested it over the years and for the most part agreed.

All the little standard operating procedures he'd instituted since taking over the 49th were a case in point. Each was based on his experience since coming to North Africa – sober reflection about the causes of accidents or malfunctions on the aircraft or simple operating policies he'd seen which could have avoided the deaths of friends. In the last month, they'd not had an accident, small or large. That couldn't be said of the other P-38 squadrons in either the 14th or 82nd Groups. He knew some of the pilots griped about his ways; someone had even called him a 'ring-knocking martinet'. He didn't like the grumblings but the gripes were decreasing, or at least they seemed to be. The ol' man had told him it always happened when you assumed responsibility for people and tried to do the right thing for the unit and for the individuals' own good. The trick was to put the welfare of people first and to let the grumbling roll off your back.

As he walked back to his aircraft deep in thought, he heard Lindquist call him.

"Okay ScrapIron, how'd you do it?" Lucky asked as he came alongside.

"Do what?"

"Get Blaxton that medal so fast. Awards take weeks and months… and he gets a medal pinned on him in a half hour after landing – signed by General Twining. That guy is so high up the chain of command he's on oxygen twenty-four hours a day. So, how did you do it? My other question is why did you let me run off at the mouth and make a fool of myself?"

"Which one do you want answered first?" Lindquist shrugged and nodded. "I knew commanders up the line have some discretion to give out what they call 'impact awards' for some action they deem exceptional and worthy of immediate recognition. I don't have any discretion but Colonel Taylor does. I've talked to him about it before. He gave me sort of an idea of what he could and would do. I thought Blaxton's action was worthy and also fit the colonel's template, so I radioed back to Group on the way home. As it turned out, the colonel agreed. Preparation meeting opportunity. Simple as that."

"And you let me make a damned fool of myself knowing he was getting the award?"

"It's a role you play real well, friend."

"You're a son-of-a-bitch, you know that?"

"Is that an apology?"

"I don't know. It could be. I'll think about it. We've been through a lot and been friends for a long time. You know I didn't mean none of what I said to you before."

"Tell you what – you give me your mission liquor tonight, and we'll call it even."

"My double shot? After what I went through today? Good luck with that."

"I don't believe in luck."

"Doesn't mean you don't have any," Lindquist said, pointing up at the nose of Nolan's aircraft where his crew chief's helper was filling in two new small black swastikas with black paint. "Two today gives you ten. Two more and you're tied with Dixie Sloan – and you still have thirty-some missions to go this time around. Three more makes you top ace in the Med. That takes a lot of luck."

"Like I said, I don't believe in being lucky… or unlucky."

Mitch released the small stair step at the back of his P-38's gondola and climbed up onto the wing of his *Mistress*, leaving his friend staring after him.

Chapter 35

"You're not serious are you?"

"Dead serious, commander. Serious enough to tell you I want to fly lead on the mission."

"What did you say is the name of this … *undertaking* on behalf of the OSS?"

"Operation Cracker Jacks, major."

"Cracker Jacks? At first blush, B.W., it sounds just nuts to me," Janowski said looking around the table in Hangman's Hideout at the other five officers. "What did they hit you over the head with when they moved you up to headquarters?"

Carhart had been transferred to Wing headquarters operations the last week of February over his pleas to stay with the 49th. With help from Marvelous Marv Crosley and approval from Mitch, B.W. had negotiated an agreement from his new boss at headquarters allowing him to continue flying missions from time to time with the Hangmen. He and Lutze were still the best two flight leads around and that was why Mitch had agreed now to listen to Carhart's proposal.

"If you want to blame somebody for being a little touched in the head, look to Wild Bill Donovan himself. I was told this comes straight from him."

"So let me get this straight, B.W.," Lieutenant Janowski said. "The idea is that we're going to fly from here to Vienna and bomb a German post office train and then drop thousands of phony letters on top of it while it's supposedly burning. Do I have that right?"

"Johnny Jazz, you were always a man quick on the uptake when things were made simple," Carhart responded to Nolan's operations officer.

John J. Janowski, like all the pilots in squadron, had been given a nickname by the other flyers doubling as a radio callsign on the squadron frequency. He'd been born in New Jersey and grew up in New Orleans where he'd picked up both a thick Cajun accent and the ability to play a mean trumpet. In flight school his talent was quickly recognized and he was pressed into service as the reveille bugler. Those who had been in his training squadron all commented it wasn't half bad getting up to Johnny Jazz's Dixieland rendition of the Army's wake-up call.

"And the purpose of this is to accomplish what?" Lucky asked, frowning and leaning over to get a closer look at the map.

"Propaganda, and demoralizing the German people," Carhart replied. "The idea is to get the letters we drop mixed in with actual letters from the German front lines – from soldiers in southern Russia and northern Greece and northern Italy who are writing home. The way it was explained to me, we airdrop these special canisters of false but properly addressed mail in the vicinity of the bombed mail train. When they go to recovering the mail during clean-up of the wreck, the postal service will hopefully confuse the false mail for the real thing and deliver it to the various addresses throughout Germany. They tell me the OSS has lists of real addresses in German cities. The letters contain information about how Germany is losing the war and how the troop morale is down, the war is lost and how they just want to get home. The postage stamps used on the envelopes are forgeries printed by the OSS in different values of genuine German stamps. The mail also includes copies of *Das Neue Deutschland*, the Allies' German language propaganda news sheet."

"Copies of what?" Lucky asked.

"*Das Neue Deutschland.* Pretty good German accent for a farm boy from Hattiesburg, don't you think, commander?" Carhart glanced at Nolan.

"And you've got this whole mission planned out so it'll work," Johnny Jazz said, looking and sounding skeptical.

"I'm ready to listen," Mitch said to the group. "Somebody must think it's a good idea if it hasn't yet been killed by any of the levels of command it had to get through to get all way down here to us. Lay it out, B.W."

"Actually the plan is pretty simple. And the execution shouldn't be all that hard for ace pilots like you guys – and me."

"We don't need all the commentary, just get on with it," Don Lutze said. "Sometimes I think you could talk a hungry dog off a bone."

B.W. laughed out loud. "All right, here it is. Every Tuesday and Friday there's a mail train made up in Vienna, Austria. It leaves the central rail station at exactly 0745 headed to Prague and then on to Berlin. You boys know how the Germans are about their trains being on time. That's how Hitler came to power right? – makin' the trains run on schedule. The mail train passes through a little town called Floridsdorf on the north side of the Donau River at exactly 0802." B.W. tapped the map. "That's when we hit it."

"Why so close to Vienna?" Janowski asked, tapping a finger on the map. "Isn't that an airbase about twenty or twenty-five miles away? Looks like they ought to be able to get to our ambush spot pretty quick."

"Yes it does. But all our Intel and experience from missions flown to Czechoslovakia, Hungary and southern Germany shows bases this far inland alerted but not scrambled when their radar picks up our bombers. Every time they see a big swarm of targets over the Adriatic headed north, they wait and intercept us close to their bases because their fighters are range-limited. But, if we go in below the radar – especially at that early hour –we can get in and out before they're alerted, much less airborne."

"That's a lot of 'ifs' in your plan, B.W.," Janowski said. "And we haven't even got to specifics yet."

Nolan waved his hand. "Let's hear this out. That's a good call, B.W. Continue."

"We attack the train just outside Floridsdorf at 0803. That's getting kinda precise, but it's only a four hundred and sixty-eight mile flight – timing should be easy for old pros, right?"

"That's straight line distance," Lucky observed. "We'd have to detour around larger towns and cities like Zagreb; probably have to fly some valleys to stay under the radar. Looks more like five hundred plus miles to me."

Carhart gave him a sideways smile. "You're right. Flight planning on this has to be a lot more precise than just about anything we've done before. I've marked out three initial points on the map because there are three flight elements, each with a different job." Carhart rolled out a schematic of the train. "So basically, the concept is this," B.W. concluded. "Red flight stops the train and engages the anti-aircraft cars with guns and five hundred pound bombs. White flight strafes any troops on the train and drops the letter canisters. Blue flight finishes the job with high explosives and incendiaries to scatter all of the letters – our phony ones and the real German ones. We rendezvous about thirty miles south of Vienna over the big lake and head home. Real simple."

"The devil's in the details," Nolan said, looking at the schematic. "Run through it again."

B.W. opened a map and circled the place where they were to conduct the raid. "Where we ambush the train, the track runs almost exactly north – south. Element one, Red flight, makes a pass from north to south directly over the train firing on the locomotive and every car in the line. That includes the engine, the antiaircraft cars, and all the postal cars. Element two, White flight, makes their pass immediately after that from east to west firing on all the cars and dropping the canisters of phony letters. There's about four thousand of them from what I'm told. Coming in from the east puts the rising sun at their back and adds to the difficulty of the anti-aircraft gunners picking them up. Element three, Blue flight, makes a bombing run with thousand pounders and incendiaries from south to north trying to hit all of the postal cars after White flight drops the letters."

There was a long silence in the room as everyone turned and looked at Mitch Nolan.

"I think it'll work if we rehearse a few times and practice some night formation flying," the squadron leader finally said. "We'll put up eighteen ships. Johnny Jazz and I will work out more details with you. It's not your normal mission, but what the heck, why not? It'll be a story to tell folks some day. Lucky should lead Red Flight – he's our best locomotive buster."

"And best dive bomber and best all round pilot," Lindquist added.

"I'll lead the mission and navigate," Carhart said quickly. "Red flight will guide off me. I want Lutze to lead Blue flight, and I want you, commander, to lead White flight and drop the phony letter canisters."

Nolan looked at him and frowned. "You want me to be the '*Bullshit Bomber*', do you?"

"Seems appropriate," Lucky said nonchalantly.

*   *   *   *   *

It was dark as Mitch passed by the Hangmen's Hideout and the noise from inside spiked followed by an outburst of laughter. It was the end of another long day; he was tired from an extended briefing at Group and hadn't planned to go in, but curiosity prevailed over his fatigue. Since Operation Cracker Jacks, Colonel Taylor had piled on the missions.

The Great Mail Train Caper, as it had been renamed by Lindquist, had been successful beyond anyone's expectations. Carhart's planning and navigation had gotten them on station almost to the second after flying formation in the dark for almost two hours followed by another hour of fence hopping throught the mountains. Lindquist had had his section load their aircraft with a special ammunition configuration designed to burst locomotive boilers. The normal load for each of the .50 calibers called for one tracer and one armor piercing projectile for every four rounds of lead jacketed bullets; Lucky had decided all rounds except the tracer be armor piercing. Later, he credited this idea with blowing the locomotive off the tracks and derailing all but two of the other cars on their initial run. After that the rest of the plan became easy. Both Lucky and B.W. were awarded a Distinguished Flying Cross by General Twining, and the squadron was recommended for a Unit Citation that was still pending somewhere in the chain of command between Triolo and Washington.

As Mitch walked into the squadron club, he heard swing music playing on a radio recently procured by Parcells, the acknowledged *Scrounge Officer*. So far he'd managed to find a way to locally barter for bacon, bread, fresh fish and cigarettes. Blaxton and Weatherford were playing ping-pong, and Frank Mullinax was holding court nearby, surrounded by all the newly arrived pilots and several of the old timers.

Mullinax was one of the original members of the 49th and had flown the Atlantic from the States to North Africa in late '42. A few days after Christmas, on his second mission of the day while flying in the place of a pilot who had become sick, he'd been shot down and captured by the Germans near Tunis. He was taken to Italy and soon after escaped with another prisoner by jumping from a moving train as it slowed while climbing an incline. For several months, he and his partner lived in a cave, kept alive by some Italians in a nearby town. When General Clark's Army invaded the Italian mainland, Mullinax found his way to friendly lines and was repatriated. Now, a year later, the Air Corps had sent him back to the Group to tell his story to others and teach them what he knew about surviving captivity. To everybody in the squadron, he'd become something of a folk legend.

A lieutenant named Sparks was standing just inside the door arguing with Lucky as Mitch entered.

"We need you to referee a bet, major," Sparks said.

"What kind of bet?"

Lindquist quickly interrupted. "We were listening to that '*Home Sweet Home Hour*' with Axis Sally out of Berlin, and Sparky here thinks there's three or four different women playing her. I say they're all the same gal. Tell him I'm right."

Mitch looked back and forth between them, and sadly shook his head. "Arguing about this is the only thing the two of you can find to entertain yourselves?"

"It's worth a pack of cigarettes to me, major," Sparky replied.

"I didn't know you smoked."

"I don't, but a pack of cigarettes is worth three eggs and I know where I can find some for breakfast tomorrow – even at this late hour. So, which one of us is right? "

"Turns out neither one of you are. It's actually two gals – one is an Italian girl with a sexy voice and the other is an American turncoat. I guess that means Lucky's cigarettes are mine, so I'll be the one having eggs for breakfast."

"You're making that up," Lindquist declared suspiciously.

"You don't know that for certain, and I'm sticking to it. And you, Lucky, need to get your three friends ready for an early mission tomorrow. Johnny Jazz just posted it over in Ops. Group sent down word there's a bridge outside Trento in the foothills of the Alps that needs to be dropped in the river. The Germans are bringing reinforcements over it headed south, probably for Anzio. We need to stop that."

Anzio was in a tenuous position. Winston Churchill had said, "We had hoped to land a wildcat that would tear out the bowels of the Bosche. Instead we have stranded a vast whale with its tail flopping about in the water!" Since the third week in January, 14th Fighter Group had conducted strafing missions on the roads leading to the beach. They destroyed a number of vehicles, but the low-level work subjected them to intense small arms fire. From where he sat, Mitch thought the Nazis could easily destroy the forces inside the small perimeter. German reinforcements in any size at this point in the battle just might turn the tide against the Allies.

"I'll take that mission, major," Sparky quickly said. He was nearing the end of his tour and had become a 'mission hog', trying to get as many operational flights as he could so he could get back home early. Sparks was constantly coming up with ideas for missions he could fly, or volunteering to take the place of others. He'd even flown an extra aircraft in smaller formations in case one of the aircraft developed mechanical problems and had to return to base.

"Don't need you, Sparky," Lucky told him. "Me, Weatherford, Blaxton and Trembley have it covered, thank you very much – or *merci beaucoup* as Trembley says."

"How about I just go along anyway? You never know what might happen."

Lindquist frowned, deep in thought. "I might be persuaded if someone crossed my palm with a pack of cigarettes."

"Nobody's bribing anybody over missions in the squadron," Mitch told them. "This time, I'm with Sparky. If the Germans really are moving armored columns over that bridge, they could have fighter cover, and probably have anti-aircraft deployed. A couple of extra ships watching out for the dive bombers isn't a bad idea. He and I will fly as your cover during the mission. And Lucky, this time no going back to take pictures after the strike. You hear me?"

The two of them had taken the B-25 down to Bari a few weeks earlier to pay a visit to Marv. It had been a good break and a welcome relief to enjoy a good Italian meal in the city with friends. Lindquist had purchased a small camera at the small PX established by Wing headquarters. Shortly after, on another bombing sortie, he'd lingered behind to take pictures. Mitch had warned him not to do it again because it was too dangerous, but Lindquist had laughed and shrugged it off.

"What's that, Mitch, rule number twenty-three? Damn! If this war goes on another six months you'll have more rules than the whole rest of Army regulations."

"Rule number twenty-four... the Lindquist law of holes. When you get yourself into one, stop digging. Sparky and I will make sure you don't get jumped in the middle of the dive bombing run. Period, end of discussion. Now, why don't you boys get yourself some sleep."

Halfway through the next morning Mitch wished he had taken his own advice.

The target below them was barely distinguishable from 22,000 feet through an early morning haze as Mitch and Sparky circled above the flight of four P-38 Lightnings lining up for their bombing run. He had a headache and his eyes itched; there was a pain at the base of his neck. He could have used a few more hours of sleep.

"*Red flight, commence on my mark...* Nolan's thoughts were interrupted by the flight leader's radio call. "... *three-thousand, two-thousand, one-thousand. Mark!*"

The first aircraft turned hard left and continued through the turn until he was inverted and the nose of the aircraft pointed straight down. At three second intervals the others in the flight followed and soon all four Lightnings were lined up one behind the other in a perfect trail headed straight down at the bridge. Others might try a shallow dive angle lined up with the long axis of the target, but not Lucky – this mission more than any other was what he lived for and he'd found three others in the squadron who loved it almost as much.

"Sparky, stay high and I'll follow them down," Mitch said into the radio as he rolled left and followed on the last aircraft's tail.

Within seconds the P-38 began to shudder as the airspeed wound up through 300 mph, 350, 400. 425… The altimeter was winding down just as quickly. He could see each of the four planes in front of him, giving him the sensation he was not going straight down but actually had tucked the nose beyond vertical. "*When you think you've gone beyond vertical, go a little further and you'll be just about right,*" Lucky had said the first time Mitch went on a bombing run with him over the docks at Tunis months earlier. Back then everybody thought Lindquist was crazy – and he was, Nolan decided. But he'd never known his friend to miss a target.

He deployed the dive flaps and sensed the shuddering had diminished some, even though he felt he was hanging face down, held in the aircraft solely by the seat belt and shoulder harness. The instrument panel was completely blurred but he could make out that the vertical speed indicator was pegged and the airspeed indicator was inching past 500. *Good grief! Five hundred miles an hour and still gaining airspeed!* He saw Lucky's lead aircraft nose up just a little, his bombs drifting away. Then it happened with two and three, and then four just ahead of him – all of them seemingly rushing upward past the top of his canopy as he hurtled earthward. He pulled back on the yoke, and unlike that time over Texas on his first cross country, the plane responded under control. Over his shoulder, Mitch saw the center of the bridge collapse in the river, shrouded in a cloud of gray smoke.

"Mission complete, Red leader," Mitch called over the radio. "Bridge destroyed. Let's head back to the barn." Sparky joined up on his wing, climbing with him to ten thousand feet. A moment later Red flight came alongside.

But something was wrong – Blaxton was leading and there were only three aircraft.

"Red leader, say your position," Nolan called out quickly on the radio.

"*A few miles behind at five thousand. Gonna get some pictures of that bridge for Gilkey.*"

"Negative Lucky, no pictures this time."

"*Sorry there ScrapIron, you're breaking up.*"

"Lucky, back in formation. That's an order!"

"*Say again…*"

Mitch was furious. "Red flight form up on Sparky and head home. I'm going back to get him." Immediately he shoved the throttles full forward and started a climbing turn back toward Trento. He called Lucky twice more without an answer, and swore under his breath, knowing he was being ignored. A minute later, Mitch located him about ten miles away at less than five thousand feet and descending toward the bridge.

"Lucky, I know you can hear me. Don't go back to a site you've just bombed. I saw several 88 anti-aircraft guns on the ground. You're a sitting duck! Turn around!" As if on cue, a dozen or more angry black puffs of flak sprung up on both sides of Lucky's P-38. "Lucky, get out of there! Get out of there now!" Nolan dove at the two gun emplacements he could see next to the bridge as Lindquist's plane turned hard left and immediately ran into a sky full of flak.

"Lucky!"

It appeared Lindquist's P-38 abruptly stopped in mid-air and immediately snapped into a spin. Black smoke came from his left engine which suddenly erupted in a yellow tongue of flame licking at the cockpit and the tail boom. The aircraft spiraled down trailing a long, dark plume of smoke and fire.

"Lucky, get out of there. Get out! Get out!"

Mitch watched, horrified, as the plane quickly lost altitude and agonizing seconds later crashed in a horrendous ball of flame onto a hillside less than a mile from the destroyed bridge.

He was torn with rage and thought about attacking the two German 88 guns, cursing them out loud, but he knew he was an easy target now. And even if he managed to knock out one or both of the German gun batteries, he couldn't bring his friend back.

"Why, damn it, WHY Lucky!" he yelled and beat his fist on the side window.

He turned south toward Triolo alone in the skies above Italy. He remembered his father's words from a time long ago at West Point during his senior year when he'd been elevated to command of a cadet company – *everything that happens or fails to happen in any unit is the responsibility of the commander.*

For the first time since graduation he felt utterly demoralized.

A friend with whom he'd attended classes, gone on leaves with during his cadet years, and spent most of his time with since graduation was gone… and he'd watched it happen. He'd known personally many pilots who'd met the same fate in the last year, but none of their losses came close to affecting him like this.

As he droned through the clear sky a still, small voice hounded him.

This is your fault… your responsibility, commander.

Chapter 36

"Congressman Callahan on the phone, returning your call."

Harrison Reeves looked up from the documents and scowled at the new mahoghany Executone intercom on his desk. The thing could be nuisance, but it was usually better than having his new secretary open the door and interrupt, plus it was a conversation piece he enjoyed showing off now and then. No one else in the War Department had one – not even General Marshall. That reminded him he'd have to jog the boss's memory about his desire for a field command in the upcoming invasion of the Continent. It was time to once again be thrust into the middle of the rattle and clatter of musketry – at an appropriate three-star level, of course. Reeves debated briefly about taking the call. He was busy and Callahan probably just wanted to touch base and keep the Washington 'good old boy' network greased. Deciding the congressman from Maryland might be useful to him at the moment, Reeves took the call.

"Trevor, to what do I owe the pleasure of this call?" the general said genially, leaning back in his leather swivel chair. "Perhaps you called with a 'thank you' for my recommending the company of one Denise Nolan. Is this an announcement of a conquest?"

There was a chuckle on the line before Callahan replied, "Not yet. Besides, a gentleman never divulges such things anyway."

"No one every accused you of being a gentleman, old friend."

"Nor you, Harrison. But that's not why I called. I have a bit of information you might find useful… and, I have a request for you to consider. First the information. Just yesterday I dined with your father's collegue, the junior senator from Maryland."

"Steven Trombley. Of course, I know him well."

"Trombley's on the military appropriations committee chaired by your father-in-law. Senator Payne has been quietly delaying the Democratic caucus' approval of your promotion to a third star."

"Honestly, I'm not surprised," Reeves lied, angry but keeping an even, measured tone. "My father-in-law has always been a stickler for military propriety and he knows my current position in the War Department is a two-star billet. I find myself in something of a career box canyon, as it were. As much as I think I'm making a major contribution, I can't really expect a promotion in my current position. In fact, and this is just between us, I've mentioned the desire to return to a field assignment – not for glory or promotion mind you, but to open up a slot for deserving junior officers. Beside, it's time to get back into the fray myself. This is a time of national distress and I've been away from the battlefield far too long."

"I understand completely, Harrison. But, according to Senator Trombley, Payne has also thrown cold water on any advancement. I just thought you should know."

"Thanks, old chum, but alas that's old news. My father-in-law and I have a very open and frank relationship." Yet even as he said it, warning sirens were going off in his head. This would bear looking into. *Michelle...damn her. She's behind this*, he decided instantly. She'd essentially abandoned him in the last several months, having moved into her father's house in Georgetown for the supposed reason of being closer to work. *How abysmally transparent*, Reeves thought. She was poisoning the Senator's mind about him – he was certain it.

"Very well," Callahan was saying. There was a long pause. "On another matter. Your father, Harrison. I don't know when you last saw him, but his health is declining. Some of his friends in the Maryland Democratic organization are anxious about him."

"As am I," Reeves responded, quickly understanding where the congressman was heading. "I've been thinking for some months it might be wise for him to retire and take care of himself. He is, after all, pushing eighty. I appreciate your concern, Trevor."

"I just wanted you to know, I'm ready and willing to help in any way I can. His support of my first run for office years ago set me on the right path and I am indebted to him, and to you for the introduction and continued encouragement."

Reeves knew exactly what Callahan was driving at and decided to play along just for the fun of it. "It's important in politics as well as the military to plan for contingencies. My father has lived a long and well-spent life, something no one can possibly argue. But it's obvious his days are numbered. It's sad, but it's part of life. He will be greatly missed." *But not by me*, the general thought.

Harrison and his father had never seen eye to eye. He'd never been able to please the man; even his athletic achievements at the Gilman School in Baltimore and his academic honors as the number two man in scholarship had failed to impress the senior Reeves. Senator Trenton G. Reeves was dying, and it was sad. Sad for his son who hoped to some day exceed the accomplishments of his father while the old man was still alive and lucid enough to know he'd been surpassed. A U.S. Senator was a somebody, but a cabinet officer, especially one tasked with re-shaping the world after a global conflict, was altogether more consequential. That's what he wanted to throw in his father's face. He needed the old man alive and clear-headed for it to be the most meaningful. "Perhaps my father might entertain stepping down and looking after his own health if he knew someone close to him would carry on his legacy."

"Perhaps, so," Callahan said tentatively.

"Someone in the family would certainly qualify, but I have no interest at all in politics and I'd not be good at it. Frankly, I'd be out of my element with all the… shall I say, less than honorable ways of the political realm. No offense, Trevor."

"None taken."

"You've been almost like a son to him. Would you consider stepping in behind him?"

"If you and he and the Maryland Democratic committee thought it wise and appropriate, considering the circumstances."

Reeves almost laughed aloud. This moment had been the whole reason Callahan had called. Trenton Reeves was dying and already the vultures were circling. He would have been appalled at the situation if it hadn't been about his father. "I could speak to the committee chairman and the governor on your behalf, if you'd like. They were both classmates at Gilman when I was there and might still remember me."

"Really?! That would be a great help. I wasn't aware you knew them both."

Again, Reeves stifled an amused chuckle. *Of course you knew, Trevor. I told you so myself two years ago at one of my father's boring Christmas parties – before you got drunk.* "Consider it done. Now, Trevor, you must excuse me. I'm working on an assignment for the boss, and he won't be happy should I fail to produce. The exigencies of global conflict…"

"I understand completely. Harrison, my prayers are with your family."

"Thank you. And mine with you and your success with your one particular *friendship*."

Reeves hung up and went back to his work but his thoughts still dwelt on the phone call. He didn't particularly like Callahan but the man was useful from time to time. Maybe if he did become one of the senators from the Old Line State he'd be helpful again some day.

Later that afternoon, as Reeves dropped a stack of correspondence into his briefcase and prepared to leave, his office door suddenly opened.

Why didn't Vivienne ring over the intercom first? he wondered, irritated at the intrusion. *She's just not going to work out, and it's such a simple thing.* He'd had a string of bad luck with secretarial assistants over the last several months since getting Valerie Ebert a Top Secret clearance, another promotion and relocating her in War Plans. That move had worked fine; he now had enough advance intel on worldwide operations to get ahead of the game, position himself and his recommendations to garner the most favorable reactions from Marshall.

"Vivienne! You know very well –" Reeves abruptly stopped, stood to his feet and produced his most charming smile. "William, I'm surprised. Delightedly so, however. Always a pleasure to see my favorite senator and father-in-law. Please, have a seat, and join me in a cigar," he said amiably coming from behind the desk. "To what do I owe this honor?"

"Sit down," Senator Payne said evenly. "I'll take you up on the cigar, and on two fingers of that single malt scotch you keep on hand."

"Of course." Reeves poured each of them two fingers of scotch and opened his humidor, sliding it gently across the top of his polished Andiroba desk.

"No, Harrison. I don't want one of your everyday cigars. Surely you can spare one of those fine Bolivar Cubans for me. You've got a box of *Belicosos Finos, 52 Ring* hidden in here somewhere. I was disappointed when you didn't offer me one the last time I was here."

Reeves responded with an exaggerated belly laugh as he reached into a desk drawer. "As I remember, that was some months ago. I'm not sure I had any back then. But I'm surprised you know about both the cigars and the scotch. I always thought they were the best kept secrets in the entire War Department. How did you learn this?"

"I have my ways. I know a lot that'll surprise you." Senator Payne unwrapped the cigar, clipped the end and then removed a thick expandable folder from his brief case. He briefly held Reeves's gaze and then dropped the file with a solid thud on the desk between them.

"And what is this, William?" Reeves asked, a little apprehensive about the look on his father-in-law's face and the tone of his voice.

"This is a little dossier I've been building for over a year. It's the story of your life and your career," the senator said, pausing to slowly light his cigar. "Let me tell you what it contains, and what it means to you."

"William? Are you quite all right? This is so unlike –"

"Shut up, Harrison! Just sit there and keep your mouth closed. I'll do all the talking and you'll do all the listening. The instant you stop listening is the moment a copy lands on George Marshall's desk. You don't want that. And I'll tell you how to keep it from happening."

Harrison Reeves had never seen the senator like this and a swift dread swept over him. He realized a sudden sea change had come over their relationship. For the first time in his adult life, he felt a tinge of panic.

"I've learned – and it's now documented in that file in front of you – that from the first moment I met you at your father's Christmas party a few weeks after the end of the last war, you have never spoken a single word of truth to me."

"William, I don't know what's come over you, but I assure –"

"Shut the hell up, Harrison! And I warn you, if I have to say that again, a copy of that file will in fact immediately be in the hands of the Chairman of the Joint Chiefs and any hope you might've had of any kind of a future – in anything – will be shot down in flames. I can't be more clear than that, and I won't say it again. Now sit back… keep your mouth shut… and listen to everything I'm about to tell you."

Reeves glared fiercely at the congressman trying to intimidate him by the sheer force of his will, but he was inwardly terror-stricken.

"I respect your father. He and I have worked side-by-side for decades on important legislation. We've not always agreed, but we've shared a mutual esteem. I'm sad to say, you inherited none of your father's integrity. None whatsoever. That night of the Christmas party when you showed me the letter concerning the death of your classmate Dave Nolan, you lied intentionally to me and to my daughter. You knew full well he wasn't dead because you were the one who forged his death certificate. This file contains a sworn affidavit from the man who was your commanding officer at the time, and it's attested to by three witnesses. Falsifying government documents is a crime. Fortunately for you the statute of limitations has run out on it. But that won't help your reputation and it will totally ruin your military career when and if it becomes public knowledge. You alone can keep that from happening.

"Prior to that, you filed false charges against Nolan accusing him of mistreating German prisoners of war. That went nowhere because it was untrue and a court of military inquiry dismissed the charges. There are two affidavits in that dossier sworn to and attested by witnesses to the truth of what I just said. A few years back, you guided this personnel office you now head up through a sad excuse of a hearing and trumped up charges on Dave Nolan over that Lindbergh affair. It led to his demotion and ultimate resignation from a career he'd spent a quarter century building. At the same time you managed to get one of your peers and your direct superior discredited and canned. You ended up taking over and it got you to where you are today. Does the name Barton Scarborough mean anything to you? He was another of your classmates you stepped on to get ahead. Of course, duplicity isn't a crime but it sure isn't something you want on your résumé in or out of the military. You've left a trail of people strewn in your wake over the years who don't much like you and would be so glad to see you fall, they'd dance on your grave. Turns out I happen to be one of them. I always wondered why your father was so reticent to talk to or spend time with you. Now I know.

"I know you've been lobbying General Marshall for a new assignment – commanding a corps under Eisenhower. I know that a corps is the largest maneuver element in the U.S. Army and it's the pinnacle for a troop commander. General Marshall has taken up your case with Ike, and I also know Eisenhower isn't too keen on the idea. He knows you, and doesn't much care for the way you do business. You never did quite grasp the concept of treating people well on your way up. Eisenhower is planning to give the corps that you would like to someone a whale of a lot more qualified than you in every way.

"Lest you think I'm just a mean-spirited old man, let me tell you this: while that's a part of it, the main reason concerns what you've done to my daughter. You lied to us that night of your father's party so you could marry her even though she was engaged to young Nolan. To my everlasting shame, I allowed myself to be fooled and ended up ruining her life. All these years I never knew how poorly you treated her; how you battered her emotionally and physically from the day you two married. She never told me anything about it, but she was smart enough to record in pictures what you did to her. I have corroborating evidence of that also. If I know one thing about George Catlett Marshall, I know that he abhors people like you. If this dossier gets to him, you'll be drummed out of the military in a way that will follow you forever. And a lot of people who know you will stand on the sidelines and cheer."

The senator finished his scotch and slammed the glass down on Reeves' expensive desk.

"I also have proof of your marital infidelity. While the rest of this sordid past of yours has outlasted the statutes of limitation, your adultery doesn't. And it's still a court-martial offense in the Army according to the most recent re-write of the Uniform Code of Military Justice. The Army won't refuse a sitting U.S. Senator a full prosecution on the matter.

"So, Reeves, there's only one way out of this mess you've created for yourself. This is what you're going to do. First, you're going to advise General Marshall you're no longer interested in commanding a corps in Europe or anywhere else. You're going to tell him the stress of this position and the worry over your father's failing health has so affected you that you're seeking psychological counseling and will be resigning from the Army so as not to hinder the war effort. Inside the dossier is a psychological evaluation from a reputable civilian doctor and confirmed by a psychologist at Walter Reed – all you need to do is affix your signature on the last page. The next thing you're going to do is grant my daughter a divorce." Senator Payne reached inside his briefcase, withdrew a legal document with a blue cover, and tossed it unceremoniously toward Reeves. The general quickly scanned the first page.

"That's a divorce settlement prepared by my lawyer. It's already been reviewed with Judge Bronfman who has jurisdiction since you both live in Maryland. He'll sign off on it as soon as the two of you agree to the proposed settlement and sign the document. Notice that Michelle has already signed. Notice also, to keep you from contesting it, she has agreed to request nothing in the settlement except her personal items – clothing, one automobile, and cash from the Union Trust bank account in Baltimore amounting to less than two thousand dollars. She makes no claim on any other property held jointly, including your house, bank accounts and real estate. Nor does she make claim on any trusts or other Reeves family accounts which you stand to inherit now or in the future. She and I just want you the hell out of her life. There is also a restraining order signed by Judge Watts requiring you not contact her in any way or approach within one hundred feet her. That's effective now and is enforceable."

"This is character assassination," Reeves finally managed.

"Maybe. But you're the assassin. And it's an airtight case that can be made in any court in the land according to the rules of evidence formulated by Judge Story and Simon Greenleaf. Read that dossier and look at the pictures of you and your girlfriends. You'll see what I mean."

"You son of a bitch."

"Been called worse. Worked side by side with many. But you take the cake, son. You be at the law offices of Hayes, O'Meara and Connelly in Baltimore tomorrow at nine a.m. along with your lawyer to sign those divorce papers. Don't be late."

"You crazy old man. No one can possibly review all these documents with a lawyer on such short notice."

Senator William Howard Payne smiled for the first time as he stood and looked at his pocket watch and then back at the general. "You can. You've got eighteen whole hours. You be there and you be prepared to sign divorce papers in front of witnesses. There won't be any discussion or argument going on, just signing. I'll be in conference with General Marshall for an hour beginning at 8:30 a.m. If I don't receive a phone call from my lawyer by the end of our meeting, my last agenda item with him will be this dossier, a copy of which will also be delivered anonymously to the editor in chief of the Washington Post."

Reeves' face grew red and a thick purple vein in his neck welled up and began to throb. "I don't think you know who you're dealing with old man."

"We'll see. And if you and I can't come to an agreement, then we'll have to ask General Marshall his opinion," the senator said, moving to the door. "See, just before stopping by here, I was with him for an hour discussing funding for additional troops and equipment but just didn't have enough time to finish up. That's the reason for our resuming early tomorrow morning. He's still in his office and is apparently working late. It'll give you the opportunity to tell him about your planned resignation. You have a nice day now."

The senator left the office and walked down the long corridors of the War Department, nodding now and then to acknowledge greetings from the many people who recognized him. He walked outside to a car parked halfway down the block with its engine running; the wisp of white smoke from the tailpipe dissipated quickly in the crisp March breeze.

"Told you it wouldn't be all that long," Payne said to his daughter. "I think I'm ready to go home, change into pajamas and a robe and have a cigar and a scotch."

"You smell like both already, senator. Don't keep me in suspense. How did it go?"

"It's safe to say, by this time tomorrow you'll be a single woman again. It's what you wanted, isn't it? It's certainly what I hoped for all along. When I left he looked like somebody poleaxed him and if I'd had one, I would have. He's got until tomorrow morning at nine to make up his mind and give you a divorce. I'd be shocked if he didn't."

"Are you going to tell me how you did it?"

The old man took a deep breath blew it out noisily. "Someday, maybe. Suffice it to say, he made it easy to make a case against him. The fact you didn't want anything of his in the settlement will make it easier. Men like him like to beat up women in divorce decisions. He probably thinks he's accomplished that already, so that'll help him make the right choice. We could have squeezed him, you know."

Michelle smiled at her father. "No need to, senator. I'm just fine. My father taught me not to steal, but he never told me not to go after what was *rightfully* mine."

*　　*　　*　　*　　*

Dave Nolan stormed into the commanding general's office at the 1ˢᵗ U.S. Army Group Headquarters located inside a red brick building at 20 Grosvenor Square in downtown London. Nolan placed his hands on General Omar Bradley's desk and leaned forward, glaring.

"Brad, you better find a new job for me," he said, very slowly and deliberately. "If you send me back to St. Paul's school again to negotiate with Leigh-Mallory, one of us won't walk out of there alive. I swear it."

"You'd commit a homicide against a member of Ike's Joint Staff?"

"And beat the rap in any American court."

Bradley gave him a sheepish grin. "Did you scare him?"

"You bet I did…and his ancestors back to a great uncle several generations removed who lived in a cave and wore a loin cloth. He was tut-tutting all over himself, trying to convince me to calm down and go see a psychiatrist. I told you about him months ago." Nolan took a deep breath and stood up straight. "I might not kill him, but I'll darned sure disable him."

"Glad to hear you say that, Dave. I thought it was just me he was giving a hard time."

"I'm telling you, Brad, Ike made a big mistake letting himself be talked into taking on Leigh-Mallory as Commander-in-Chief of the Allied Expeditionary Air Forces."

"Ike had no choice. It was decided before he was named the Supreme Allied Commander for ground forces."

"This guy Leigh-Mallory now has it in his head he's going to withhold our own C-47s from us because he doesn't like the drop zones for the American airborne divisions."

"I know. I tried nicely to talk him out of it but got nowhere. That's why I sent you in my place this time. If you managed to scare him, then I'd call your mission a success. We're chipping away at it." Bradley now gave him a broad smile. "Next time you should carry that beat up .45 of yours… maybe jack a round in the chamber at the start of the meeting."

"There won't be a next time, Brad."

The door opened behind him and Dave Nolan turned to see Eisenhower enter the office.

"Next time for what?" Eisenhower asked, looking at the cracked panes in the door.

"There won't be a next time for me to talk with Sir Trafford Leigh-Mallory."

"Yes, I heard about that from Smythe-Browne. The British are a little concerned about you, Dave. Too much pressure, they think."

"They're probably right, Ike. I'm at the breaking point. I could snap at any moment."

"We need to find you another job," Ike said, frowning and looking thoughtful. He lit a cigarette and blew a cloud of smoke toward the ceiling. Eisenhower pulled a folded sheet from inside his uniform blouse and handed it over. "Maybe something like this."

Nolan unfolded the single sheet of paper, read it through twice and looked up at Ike. "I don't know what to say. Thanks, I guess. I'm at a loss."

"That doesn't happen often."

"No, it doesn't. A corps command?" He looked at Bradley. "What does a guy say? Did you know about this?"

"I knew it was in the works. Four divisions – three infantry and one armored. You have a lot of work to do in the next two months. You won't be on the initial assault – that'll be Gerow's V Corps. But you'll be somewhere fairly close behind. Corps command is as good as it gets for a rifle toter. That's the good news. The bad news is that you'll be under Third Army… Patton, again."

"I can handle him. After Leigh-Mallory anything looks easy."

"That's another thing," Bradley was saying. "You're still working for me to finish the planning work you began back before Christmas. But we have someone coming on board who can carry on as your deputy commander when you're away. I think you'll be pleased. He takes a little getting used to – maybe a lot getting used to, but you have the interpersonal skills to handle just about anybody – maybe not Sir Trafford Leigh-Mallory all the time, but…"

"So who is this *enfant terrible* you're saddling me with? Do I know him?"

"He's a guy Mark Clark relieved just a week ago," Bradley said, looking troubled.

Dave thought for a few seconds and came up with no clues. "Staff guy?"

"No, a division commander – 12th Division," Bradley replied, smiling now. "Butternuts wore out his welcome in Italy and Clark was going to send him back to the States. Ike and I learned of it and decided we knew a place where he could be put to use and a guy who could rehabilitate him. You up for it?"

"Is this what passes as a reward I get for putting up with the Brits all these months?"

"Nope. There's more. Andy's bringing two guys named Alford and O'Grady with him – they made Clark's excremental list, too. They spoke up and supported Andy in a heated debate concerning the strategy in the Italian campaign. They were shown the door, too. Haggerty was Andy's deputy commander and assumed command of the division when the smoke settled."

"The troops will be glad. Judd was an excellent regimental commander – a real fighter and leader. I'm still not sure having Andy looking over my shoulder is any kind of reward."

"Maybe this will help you feel better about it," Bradley commented as he opened his desk drawer and then slid a three star insignia toward Dave. "Don't let that go to your head. We're all dime store generals over here – none of us are any more than permanent lieutenant colonels running around with stars on our collar. There won't be any fanfare over the promotion and the assignment. For now, you're officially still in command of that phony baloney corps in Essex as far as the world is concerned, and will be until Overlord goes ashore."

"You think that ruse is really working, Brad?"

"I know it is. You ever heard of a German agent named *Garbo*?" Dave shook his head no and Bradley continued. "He's the head of the spy ring Canaris sent to England some years ago. The Brits turned him and all his agents, plus a few more they've sent over. *Garbo* and his clan have convinced the Germans your rubber blow up tanks and trucks are the real thing staging for an attack on Calais. Having George set up in that area in command of a phony army HQ pretty much cements that. So, no public announcement of your new XXX Corps."

"Does that mean I don't have to put up with Andy officially either?"

Bradley chuckled aloud and said, "That's for you and Butternuts to work out. Frankly, I had enough refereeing between you two back when we were all on the same rifle team."

Dave picked up and fingered the three stars. *Lieutenant General.* He was now in territory well beyond his wildest dreams conjured up in that little airless bedroom of the tiny house on High Street overlooking the Susquehanna.

Chapter 37

The southern coast of France came into view in the early minutes of morning nautical twilight as Mitch Nolan and the four planes behind him approached from the southeast flying fifty feet above the Mediterranean Sea. They were on a photo recon mission escorting one of the droop-snoot P-38 aerial photography planes based at Bari.

They had been aloft for two and a half hours, having taken off in the dark at four thirty so as to arrive at Cannes just as the sun was coming up.

Mitch had Johnny Jazz assign him the mission to photograph potential allied landing beaches and inland approaches along the coast of southern France defended by the Vichy. He'd chosen Blaxton, Weatherford, and Trembley to fly with him. It was his fifth mission in the last seven days, a pace he'd been flying since the loss of Lucky Lindquist. With Sparky's rotation home, Mitch was now the squadron 'mission hog' and this photo mission was his forty-first in the two and a half months since he'd taken command. Both the squadron and group flight surgeons had warned him he wasn't getting proper rest, but he ignored them. Keeping busy was the only way he could keep himself from thinking about the loss of his best friend.

Their flight path had taken them over Corsica which they would photograph in the daylight on the return flight. They had flown under radio silence and below radar level the entire trip; now as they neared the coast and light conditions improved they descended to wave top level to avoid detection. At Cannes, they climbed to twenty-five hundred feet to allow the photo aircraft the best field of view. They flew from there southwestward along the coast, past St. Tropaz, Toulon, and finally to a point thirty miles west of Marseilles.

As they made a sweeping right turn in the direction of Avignon, Blaxton called out a flight of four enemy fighters coming from the west.

"Red flight, this is red lead," Mitch called over the radio as he dropped his auxiliary tanks and started a climb toward the enemy. "I'll provide cover while you escort our package back to base. Red two is now the flight lead. You know the way home. I'll see you tonight at the Hideout." He flicked on the gunsight and saw the pipper light up immediately.

"Red one, red three here; I'll stick with you as your wingman."

"Negative red three. I say again, return the package back to base."

Blaxton's voice came over the radio. *"But red one, there's four of them. I can help to –"*

"Damn you red three! Doesn't anybody follow orders in this outfit any more?! I said take the package home. That's an order! I can handle this by myself. OUT!"

But he wasn't as confident as he wanted to make it sound. The Germans had altitude and numbers on him, but he had the sun at his back and hoped the Krauts flying in this part of France were young and inexperienced – at least more inexperienced than those in the north, where the allied air action was a lot more frequent and concentrated.

The flight of four -109s split into two flights of two and he headed straight for the pair on the left who started firing at him wildly and way too far away. Briefly, their reaction calmed and reassured him as he held his fire and continued climbing. When he finally did fire, his first burst connected and the target immediately belched smoke and dove away; he swung the nose left and fired again. The second plane was closer now and immediately caught fire and exploded. Mitch quickly turned hard right to locate the other flight of enemy planes.

One scratched. One wounded. Odds better, he thought. *Where are you two?*

He located a single -109 above and to his left. As he continued to climb, twisting and turning his head to locate the fourth aircraft, a stream of tracers went over his cockpit from below and to his right. He immediately turned hard right into the attack and dove, sighted his attacker and set up an intercept. A few seconds later he was on the German's tail and following him through a series of turns and rolls; at last the enemy made the mistake of turning against his single engine's torque, and Mitch led him with long burst. The rounds walked through the engine and canopy, which flew off as the plane tumbled wing over wing on fire toward the ground. He saw no parachute open.

All right, Nolan. One scratched, two down. Even better odds now. Where is the other s.o.b.? One more is all, son. For an instant his thoughts were arrested. *Two down?! That's twelve and thirteen! How 'bout them apples, Dixie Sloan? Finally outdid you. At last!*

He could feel the bullets hitting the left boom near the air cooler. He turned hard to his right, then immediately reversed, swiveling his head in all directions. *Where are you?*

The left window shattered in a storm of plexiglass. His right engine was smoking and his leg felt like it was on fire. Smoke filled the cockpit as his head slammed forward.

Pain erupted in his forehead; everything went deep red and ended in black.

*   *   *

He was tumbling slowly, out of control, freefalling through eight thousand feet without any memory of how he'd gotten out of the crippled Lightning, only that the canopy had disintegrated and separated from the plane in a roar of rushing wind. He'd not even had a chance to get on the wing and dive between the twin tail booms like they taught him when he'd picked up that first P-38 in California.

The tumbling slowed and he stabilized on his back looking up at the pale blue sky; it felt like he was floating though he knew he had to be at or close to terminal velocity. Wisps of cloud rushed by and when he turned his head the French countryside filled the horizon. For a brief instant he could see Marseille and the blue water of the Med way off in the distance. Beneath him the ground was rushing upward but he resisted the impulse to pull the ripcord handle clutched tightly in his fist.

The Krauts shoot at guys hanging from parachutes. Damn them – strafing parachutes. Got to get below the clouds and as close to the ground as I can before I open the chute.

Out of the corner of his eye he could see forests and fields and the rubber dinghy he had been sitting on during the flight across the Mediterranean in case he went down; it was still attached to his parachute harness and flapping in the air. He fumbled for the clip and finally released the now useless life raft as he fell through a cloud that buffeted him and restricted his vision so he couldn't even see his boots. He panicked, started to pull the thin metal handle in his fist, but forced himself to wait counting *one-one thousand, two-one thousand, three –* Suddenly he was clear of the cloud and saw the ground closing in at a terrible velocity.

Now!

He yanked hard on ripcord. There was a terrific jolt and then the parachute blossomed over him, braking his fall and setting him oscillating wildly beneath the light green silk canopy. The countryside below him looked serene and peaceful – a patchwork quilt of plowed fields and dark green forests, pastures and hills.

What's that black smoke? ... that's The Mistress burning! And now every Kraut in France can see me up here. I'm easy target practice for anyone on the ground. Can't this thing go any faster?! Work the risers toward that pine forest to the north.

Trees moved slowly upward toward him, quickly accelerated and suddenly swiped at his face and hands. He reached out, grabbed the top of a tall, thin pine tree and held on as it bent over while the silk parachute spilled its air and floated down to cover him. Mitch's feet hit hard on the ground and he rolled with the fall and quickly got to his feet, stepping out from under the green silk. Hurriedly he got out of the harness, grabbed the top of the chute and pulled it straight, then rolled it up and wound the shroud lines tightly around it so he could carry the load like a knapsack and use it for shelter if necessary. He pulled the hunting knife from the sheath strapped to his calf, cut the harness away and quickly covered it with brush.

There was blood on the front of his flight suit, on his leather flight jacket and his ripped and torn flying gloves. Blood also dripped from a cut on his forehead; his left calf burned with a searing pain and he guessed he had taken a piece of shrapnel there and probably elsewhere. But he had no time to dwell on this as nearby shouts in German and heavy vehicle engine noise drifted toward him.

So this is what it feels like to be in German held territory and on the run.

The woods were dark and still as he ran as fast as he could away from the sound of the voices. He ran until he could no longer hear the voices or the sound of engines when he paused to listen; then he ran another twenty minutes for good measure and stopped in the most dense area of brush he could find. Twice in that first hour he'd had to find cover under thick trees when slow, low flying Storch observation aircraft flew over at treetop altitude. Finally, winded and worn down, he stopped and took inventory of his injuries and situation.

Under a thick heavy pine, Mitch treated his wounds. His hands and legs had multiple shrapnel punctures – there was a deep cut in his forehead that still dripped blood. He guessed that happened when he'd fallen out of the cockpit as the plane flipped over on its back and headed toward the ground. He sprinkled sulfa powder on the gash in his leg and wrapped it with a bandage from his survival kit, and did the same with the head wound.

Just two days earlier he'd been on a strafing mission two hours north of Foggia with a flight of four and bagged his third locomotive, then shot down his eleventh confirmed kill – an ME-110 that was coming into a German landing field. He'd crossed the enemy airfield at over 300 mph and fifty feet of altitude with tracers from the German anti-aircraft guns flying past his cockpit barely ten feet over his head. When he suddenly pulled up, the red stream was only five feet below him. Amazingly, when he returned, the ground crew couldn't find a single hole in the aircraft. He'd awarded himself an extra shot of mission liquor at the Hangmen's Hangout for his exploits. *Now, some lucky German who made an even luckier deflection shot is drinking his own mission liquor in a Kraut squadron somewhere celebrating shooting me down.*

He realized he was in shock from the ordeal – after several minutes could feel the cold seeping into his body and settling in his joints. He pulled the silk escape map from his flight jacket and looked at it trying to think through his next move and formulate a longer range plan. He looked at his watch; it was two hours before noon.

Step one – get more distance between me and the place I landed; change directions now and every twenty minutes. Stay under the cover of the forest until dark. Two - figure out exactly where you are, somehow. Step three – get something to eat; it's been eight hours since breakfast. Fourth – some sleep, I guess. Maybe sleep before you eat... I don't know. Making this up as I go along and I already went beyond Nolan's Law of Threes. What would the ol' man do if he were here? Laugh his ass off at me for getting shot down in the first place. Am I hallucinating? Got to get moving. I can do this – I know I can live off the land. Got my hunting knife, pocket knife, .45 caliber pistol. I will not become a POW! No way. You're not a pilot any more, Nolan. Your sole occupation now is to evade capture and escape across the Pyrenees to Spain and then to Portugal and then... I'll figure that out when I get there.

He had been moving generally southwest since he'd landed so he turned ninety degrees and headed southeast, moving slowly now to keep the noise down, stopping every five minutes to listen. Twenty minutes later he turned back southwest, and twenty minutes after that headed due west. He took his first rest break two hours later when he came to the edge of a small clearing through the center of which ran a rutted dirt road. Off to the west he could hear the sound of wood being chopped. After observing the clearing for a quarter hour, the chopping sounds stopped and he skirted to the east, hoping to find a farm he could raid after dark for some potatoes or radishes or turnips – maybe even a ham from a smoke house.

He was getting really hungry now and ate a stale, dried out chocolate bar from the survival kit. It tasted bland and had a consistency reminiscent of hardwood shavings. Twice more he had to dive for cover when search planes came over – still looking for him he assumed. Later in the afternoon, as darkness crept into the woods, it got colder and started to drizzle. Huddled under the parachute, despondent and utterly exhausted, he finally dozed off.

*   *   *   *   *

When Dave Nolan returned to his office at Grosvenor Square after the latest briefing on the invasion beaches, Fauser was waiting for him with his feet up on the desk and a full bottle of bourbon plus two glasses.

"To what do I owe this nocturnal visit, Butternuts?"

"Was lookin' for a drinkin' buddy since ah'm lonely an' betwixt assignments."

Nolan threw his notepad into a drawer and locked the desk. "Not tonight, Andy."

"Son, you done taken this Pennsylvany Quaker thing a mite too far. I remember the time when you was a real man – a night when you almost got drunk with me and those Alabama boys in that Rainbow regiment of the ol' Anal Enema First."

"A different war and long, long ago, Reb."

"Ya think?"

"I know."

"Well, have a drink with me anyway."

"Not tonight. I've got too much to do before the sun comes up. And we have a busy day ahead of us. You and I have to pull together a Corps staff. We've got to meet the division commanders, get reacquainted with George… did you know he spent the last six months holed up in some castle in Palermo? I'll bet he's a real case of pent up nerves. Hate to think about what he's going to be like to deal with again."

Fauser poured two fingers of bourbon into each glass and pushed one toward his old friend. "Drink up, son."

"Andy, I told you I don't have the time or inclination."

"On brave old Army team," Fauser said loudly, knocking back the shot of bourbon and shuddering. "Davey, you're fallin' behind already. "

Dave sipped at the drink and then finished it quickly in one gulp. He placed the glass on the desk top and then reached for a pencil and pad of paper. "Thanks for the drink, but I've got work to do," he said while Andy poured more bourbon for them both and raised his glass.

"Alabama!" Fauser said with gusto and downed his drink.

"I already told you, Andy – not tonight."

"Drink with me son. This is your ol' room mate and pardner. More than anything in the world right now I need you to drink with me."

Nolan looked at his old friend and wondered. "All right… Alabama." He raised the glass and drank it in a single gulp that tasted like fire. "Doesn't have the mule's kick of that Alabama joyjuice you used to brew out in the woods behind Camp Mills."

"See, that weren't so bad now, was it?" Fauser asked as he poured more liquor in both glasses, raised his own and then said, "Arizona! – last state in the ol' Union."

"Andy –"

"Drink up son. Yessir, tonight we're jest liable to do the whole danged Yankee union. How 'bout that, blue-belly?"

"Andy? What the hell is it with you?"

"Arizona!" Fauser raised his glass and drank it down.

"Listen Fauser. You tell me exactly what's going on. This is strange even for you."

"You gotta drink to Arizona first. No lie, amigo."

Nolan took the drink and glared hard at his best friend. "Andy, I'm serious."

"So am I, my friend. Ah'm more than a little sorry you don't seem inclined to –"

Nolan grabbed the bottle as Andy poured another round for them both. "You're acting mighty peculiar even for you, Butternuts. You tell me what the hell's going on before I have you sent to the headquarters surgeon."

Fauser grew serious, looked away for a brief instant and then gazed deeply into Dave Nolan's eyes. "A wire just come in from Nat Twining down at Fifteenth Air Force. It's about Mitch… He was shot down over south France."

The room went out of focus, seeming to turn on more than one axis, tumbling like a wobbly, run down gyro.

"Oh, no. Poor Denise." He blinked back tears and was suddenly frantic to get in touch with her. "Did anyone contact Denise. This will crush her, I know it will. When did this come in? When did it happen?"

"It was on a mission he was leading yesterday morning. Details are real sketchy. Ike just got a message meant for you a few hours ago while you was away at the briefing. I'm sorry, pardner. Wouldn't have you to hear this for all the world."

"Better it came from you, I guess. He's all right… I know he is. Don't know what to do."

"Don't need you to do nothing. I got SHAEF commo working on a link for you back to the States so's you can talk to her. Ike says he's tryin' to get hold to Mamie to have her get in touch with some of our war widows in D.C. to go see her."

"Nice of him to do that." He took a deep breath, and poured himself another drink. "Didn't ever think about how I'd handle something like this. My own kid."

"Don't want to go makin' light of things, Davey, but the way I look at it, Mitch has a lot goin' for him in this. If anybody can find a way to evade and escape them Nazis, it's your boy. He's a Nolan and he's probably the best outdoorsman of the lot of you. I give him a near perfect chance of getting' away. And the luck you Nolans have, the boy probably parachuted direct into the second floor of some fancy French bordello in Marseilles and is right this minute learnin' all about that Frenchy round the world kinda lovin' that most men can only dream of."

"I don't think I want his mother to hear all of that."

"Well, some folks can't stand the pure quill truth, I reckon. But I tell you this – in this here sityation, I put my money on your boy," Andy said, not wanting to think the unthinkable.

Nolan poured them both a drink. "Thanks, Andy. I think he'll be all right, too. I'm more worried about his mother than I am about him."

*   *   *   *

Denise sat on the couch in the small living room of her Georgetown rental staring at the floor, wiping her eyes with a tissue. It was dark and she was alone now. Elise and Michelle and Kate Hanlon had come earlier. Muggs Alford had stopped by later and fixed them all dinner.

The news about Mitch had come as a shock to all of them.

It felt like the whole world had unexpectedly opened and swallowed her. Nothing made much sense or held any meaning. All she could think about was her little baby – his whole life growing up in the far flung places Dave had taken them for a quarter century. She remembered him kicking his legs in the little crib Dave had made for him when they were at West Point, and the skinned knees and elbows from exploring the wilds of south Texas with the Mexican kids outside Camp Whalen. His first fish caught from the Chattahoochie River at Benning, the salmon he'd caught and the elk he'd shot; the baseball trophy he'd won in high school – all of it came back to her.

After Erika and her friends departed, she turned off the lights and sat in the darkness for a long time. Dave's mother, whom she'd only barely known had once told her, 'It takes a lifetime to raise a boy to become a man, and only a second to lose one.' She'd often wondered about the strange comment – until now.

There was a knock on the door.

For a moment she wanted to ignore it, be alone, wallow in her grief. As much as she loved and appreciated her friends – and they were her very dearest friends – none of them had ever suffered what she was suffering now. *It's a poor comforter who never needed comforting.* Where had she heard that she wondered?

At last she went to the front entrance and opened the door.

"Denise, I just now heard," Trevor Callahan said, looking more stricken than she herself felt as he stood beneath the poor illumination of the porch light, holding a large bouquet in his hands. "I felt I had to come ask if there is anything, anything at all I can do. Words are so very inadequate at times like these."

She opened the door wide for him to come in.

Without warning, he hugged her tight and stroked her long blond hair. She found herself melting toward him, crying, throwing her arms around him, craving the closeness and comfort of an embrace.

"I'm so glad you came," she whispered in his ear. "I needed to be hugged tonight. More than anything in the world."

She pulled him close and kissed his cheek, and began once again to cry.

Chapter 38

Crawling on hands and knees through the wet undergrowth, Mitch came to the edge of a rutted dirt road that ran alongside an open pasture before turning north into the dark woods. He paralleled the road until he saw an old man shouldering a heavy chopping ax; he stayed concealed for a half hour watching the woodcutter work.

All right, Nolan. It's now or never. You have to make contact somehow, some time. Is this guy friend or foe? Who knows? And you never will unless you take the chance. All right, here's the plan. Rush him. Get that ax away from him so he can't use it as a weapon... and do it without making a lot of noise.

He'd spent the last three days hiding in the woods and moving generally south toward the Pyrenees all the while wondering how he'd get over them. He had stolen turnips and potatoes from farm houses in the dark of night. On the second night he'd broken into a smoke house and taken a whole ham – a small ham, he'd rationalized. It was stealing, but it was also survival. He rationalized the theft and moved on.

The old man's back was to him as Mitch stood and covered the twenty yards of the small clearing. As the woodcutter swung the big ax over his shoulder for another chopping cut at a tree, Nolan grabbed it and pushed the old man away when he turned. The Frenchman stared at him and the big .45 automatic with eyes as big as silver dollars, not crying out but muttering incomprehensibly in rapid fire French.

"*Je suis American,*" Mitch began, pointing toward his leather flight jacket and flying suit, and unable to dredge up another word of French he started talking to the man like Johnny Weismuller playing Tarzan. "Need help. Find Underground. Find Maquis. Not Deutsche. Not German. Me American."

The old man still looked scared, anxious and prattled back at him in rapid, excited French saying something that sounded like – as best he could tell – a willingness to help. His face seemed friendly as he smiled and nodded when Nolan again said, "*Je suis American.*" The Frenchman put a finger to his lips and replied, "Shhhh... Boche." He looked around the quiet forest, grinned and again said, "Shhhh... Boche." After signaling to Nolan to hide in the deep cover, he went off down the narrow path leading away from the open pasture.

Well, Nolan, that seems to have gone pretty well, Mitch thought, not at all certain it had. *Is he a friendly local or a Vichy stool pigeon? How do you tell? Can I trust this guy? Should I take off or wait here for him to come back?* His stomach grumbled reminding him it had been more than a day since he'd had anything decent to eat. He decided to wait and burrowed into the wet ground several yards into the forest. It was almost noon before he heard the returning footsteps coming down the trail.

It's more than one person. But how many more? Can't tell. It's been three hours since that old man took off. Why so long? Maybe it took that long to recall all the German patrols so they can surround this area? I won't get very far if that's what happened. Move further back under cover and see if you can slip through the cordon. Damn, Nolan!... Idiot!

"American... I am a friend, and I am here to help you. Come out, please." It was the voice of a woman – an elderly woman.

Mitch slowly got to his feet, pistol in hand and pointed in the direction of the voice. Slowly he moved forward, aiming the .45 at the back of the old man and the woman he had brought back with him. The woman heard the noise behind her and turned slowly, looking at the worried expression of the American pilot. Her face lit up and she snickered aloud at him.

"You're just a child!" she said, laughing. "Have the Americans already run out of grown men to send over to fight the Nazis?!"

*   *   *

The small tool bin where they hid him was in a dark corner of the barn's loft.

The old woman's name was Margot and she spoke nearly perfect English as she asked him his name and background and other questions trying to determine if he was truly American or one of the German infiltrators speaking English and disguised as an *Ami* pilot to fool the Resistance. Her husband, the woodcutter, was called Gérard. They gave him an old flannel shirt, bib overalls worn at the knees and frayed at the bottom of one leg, and a crumpled hat with a brim wide enough to partially hide his face. The boots were too large, but comfortable enough if he wore two pair of socks. While he ate a piece of ham and a chunk of cheese, Gérard buried his flight suit and boots somewhere deep in the woods and then led him through the densest undergrowth to the back of their farm.

"Our people will help you," Margot told him inside the barn. "But you must do exactly as we tell you. Exactly. Do you understand? If you are caught, you will suffer the same as us – they will torture you and when they are satisfied you have nothing more to reveal, they will stand you up against the barn and shoot you in the back of the head along with us and everyone who has helped you. The Vichy police and the Germans are very active looking for you right now – the first week is the most dangerous time for you – and for us. You must trust us completely. Do you?"

"Yes!" he said, hoping he'd convinced her.

"*Allons*," Gérard said finally, and led the way up the ladder to the hayloft and to a long, flat tool bin that looked like an old wooden coffin. He indicated for Mitch to get inside, and put a finger to his lips as he had at their first encounter in the woods, then closed the cover and locked it from the outside. There was no light and almost no room inside the short structure – he could only sit up, and that just barely with his head touching the lid and his back against a wall. At first he was afraid to move for fear of making noise. He could hear the sound of hay being pitched against the sides and top of the little tool bin with a nagging fear that this was all an elaborate ruse to keep him a docile prisoner until the Germans came to get him.

He spent the next few hours with his mind swinging hammock-like between worry of being duped and wonderment at being alive and apparently safe.

Awaking from an exhausted sleep, he heard the sounds of a large vehicle outside and harsh, guttural German – orders being shouted and the sound of hobnail boots inside the barn. The clatter of farm implements being tossed around and crashing noises as if the soldiers were wrecking the place sifted up to him in his dark little cell. Someone climbed the ladder and then walked around searching – now and then he could hear a noise he imagined was the sound of a pole or the bayonet on the end of a rifle thrusting down into the hay. He held his breath and listened to his pulse thundering in his ears. The search went on for what seemed an eternity and finally he heard the soldier's boots on the wooden ladder, descending.

It seemed like hours until the truck's engine started and moved away with gears clashing, the sound growing more and more faint until he could no longer hear it.

It was quiet and pitch black outside when they let him out of the tool bin and led him quickly to the house. He was taken to the kitchen of the farmhouse where a young girl fixed him some kind of vegetable soup, cheese and slices of bread. It was the first real meal he'd had in almost a week and he wolfed it down, savoring the glass of wine Margot poured and later refilled after he'd finished eating. They took him back to the barn and again locked him into the bin until close to midnight when he heard a car pull up outside.

Minutes later, Gérard unlocked the tool bin and led him back to the house where an older man sat in the kitchen, nervously clutching a small black leather bag and eying him tensely.

442

He was the village doctor and immediately began examining the American under the dim light of a kerosene lantern. It took an hour to remove the shrapnel from his hands and legs, and sew closed the long tear in his left calf. The cut on his forehead was cleaned, closed with a half dozen stitches and covered with a new bandage. After giving instructions to Margot, the doctor looked at him and gave him a short, finger wagging speech in French and left.

"What did he say?" Mitch asked when the last sound of the doctor's car faded away.

"He said these wounds are the least of your problems... and if you are caught, he was never here." She poured him a little more of the wine. "You will stay with us until you are healed and we can make arrangements to pass you along."

He sipped at the wine and then looked up. "I'm grateful for what you're doing, and I'm sorry to put you in danger for helping me."

Margot smiled at him. " We do this not just for you, but for France. There are many like us. People we can trust already know about you. Everyone in town knows our family – that we have two sons and a daughter still living with us and curious children in the village have heard a whispered tale for some time that we have another who is rarely seen; a strange child – a crazy one we don't let go into town because he eats little boys and girls. They stay far away from here and will not bother us or you. You are not our first 'crazy son' and I imagine you will not be our last. "

It was a pretty little farm with a large house that sat on the edge of the woods alongside what looked like a farm to market road, not a major thoroughfare but fairly well-traveled by hay wagons and carts and an occasional camion. Still, he ate breakfast before the sun was up and supper after last light, and made no other moves without asking permission or being told. Mitch spent the next week in the tiny loft cell which he'd cleared of the rakes and shovels and other miscellaneous implements so he could stretch out while sleeping. After a few days he was allowed to spend some time outside when word circulated that the Germans had seemingly given up or lost interest in finding the downed pilot. The number of search patrols had dramatically decreased. Still, he found it impossible to sleep for more than a half hour at a time without waking up and listening for the sound of German voices and vehicles.

On the ninth day just as dawn was breaking, he was finishing breakfast in Margot's kitchen when Gérard entered and excitedly spoke to his wife while gesturing wildly toward the road. Margot led him upstairs to an empty bedroom in the attic and warned him to stay there until she or Gérard personally came to get him. Then she left and padlocked the door from the outside. He went to the dormer window and looked out from back in the shadows where he had a view of the front lawn and the road.

Soon a woman rode up on a bicycle with a small suitcase strapped to the luggage carrier over the rear tire. She wore a plain red scarf that covered most of her dark hair; a shawl was wrapped around her neck flowing over the white peasant's blouse. Her full skirt looked worn and faded. The woman exchanged pleasantries with Margot for a few minutes, allowed one of her sons to remove the small piece of luggage and the other to move the bicycle in the direction of the barn. He was puzzled, wondering why Margot's family had been so nervous earlier. When everyone outside had moved beyond his field of vision, he sat down looking around at the boxes and trunks and assorted odds and ends filling the attic. He took off his boots and silently placed them on the plank floor and lay down on the soft bed, amazed at how comfortable it felt compared to the coffin-shaped tool bin with a couple of inches of hay inside. In a matter of minutes he was sound asleep.

He was startled awake from a wildly disjointed dream by a metallic sound coming from the direction of the door; in the back of his mind, Mitch realized he'd been asleep for a good long while. As he raised himself up on an elbow, the door slowly opened revealing an extremely attractive dark haired woman who looked strangely familiar. He found it impossible to take his eyes off her as she stood mostly in the shadows from the late afternoon light coming through the dormer window.

"Mrs. Reeves?" he asked, still half asleep. *No, that's not possible, Nolan. Get a grip.* As he quickly shook off his drowsiness, he thought she was much younger than Margot, and perhaps just a few years older than himself. "Who are you?" he asked at last.

"You may call me Michelle, Major Nolan," she replied in a soft voice with an entrancing accent. "*Eet ees* better for us both that you do not know my real name. I have come to meet the son of the man I took to my bed long ago in another place in a different war, when he was your age. We will drink the final bottle of his favorite wine and I prepare for you a special dinner – the one I cook for him our last night together."

*   *   *

Margot had prepared a bath for him outside behind the barn, his second in the week he'd spent with them, and she'd laid out fresh clothes – a white linen shirt, dark trousers and an even darker coat. He'd shaved using a straight razor provided by Gérard. When he finished dressing, Margot looked him over, smoothing out the coat and straightening the collar of his shirt the way his mother had done years ago in Manila before he went out on his first date. "There," she said, looking him over carefully. "You look presentable as a Frenchman should."

"Who is she?" Mitch asked, embarrassed at the pampering by the old woman.

"A special guest this night."

"I could tell that." Margot, Gérard and their two sons had been effusively courteous and subservient to the dark-haired woman. "What makes her so special?"

"Since the White Mouse has gone, this woman, she is the most famous of the Maquis."

"The White Mouse?"

"Yes, that is what the Germans called her. I did not know her real name, only her reputation. While she was still here in France, she was much hated and much feared by the Germans – they are the ones who gave her that name because she was so good at escaping from the traps they set for her. She was the first to organize the Resistance in this part of southern France and she recruited this woman who now cooks you dinner in my kitchen. They say the White Mouse is now in England but will return some day when the English and you Americans come back to France with DeGaulle to defeat the Germans. She helped many like you to escape from the Germans over the Pyrenees, disrupted their communications and planned and executed a successful raid on a Gestapo garrison and an arms factory in central France. For that the Gestapo placed a large bounty on her head. That she evaded capture and death so many times added to her mystique, but she was finally forced to flee."

"So, you knew her?"

"No," Margot replied, still inspecting him and smoothing the wrinkles in the dark jacket. "We only knew her by reputation. We know only a few of the others so that we cannot do much harm to the movement if we are caught and tortured. But the fame of our White Mouse was wide-spread, as is the reputation of this woman about whom there are also many stories. That she would come so far to see you says you must be very important."

"How far?"

"I do not know exactly. It is said she lives somewhere in the mountains around Grenoble – that is two hundred kilometers from here."

"She told me her name is Michelle."

"None of us use our real names, for the sake of protection – both yours and ours. You do not know exactly where you are now, nor do you know our real names so that you cannot later reveal them if caught. It protects us both, you see."

"But, this woman…"

"Ah, yes. Well, her name is surely not Michelle. The Gestapo calls her *dritte Falken* – the third falcon. We call her by our ancient French *Tiercelet*, which means the same thing. The falcon is the swiftest living creature and the most deadly of hunters – especially the male. Falcons lay just three eggs when they mate and only one of them, the third egg, is a male. That is why the Boche call her the third falcon, because she is the deadliest and most vicious killer of the Germans according to all the stories – a beautiful and feminine woman but when the fighting starts she is like ten men. She was an ambulance driver at the beginning of the German invasion and that is where she met the White Mouse who later recruited her into the Maquis. It is told that she has deeply hated the Boche since the last war when they killed her husband and later an American officer she fell in love with. She has not married since, and she now seeks her revenge. That is the legend; who knows how much is true. Perhaps we shall find out after this war is over and we have defeated the Germans with your help."

Mitch pondered what he'd learned, not sure he believed it all. Hadn't someone – either Aeschylus, or more recently Senator Hiram Johnson – once said the first casualty of war was Truth? *Got to look that up when I get back stateside*, he thought. But for now he was more intrigued by the woman *Tiercelet* and by the cryptic comment she'd made about his father.

When he entered the kitchen, she was sitting alone at the rough wooden table, calmly sipping wine from a glass held in both hands. She looked up at him and smiled.

"I see the family resemblance, *un peu*," she said, looking him over and then holding his gaze. "You are shorter, perhaps, but more handsome – like a leading man in the movies rather than some *bockskin* cowboy like your father." She rose and walked to him then ran her finger along the line of the wound on his forehead. "When this heals it will leave a long thin scar. Your father has one like it along the line of his jaw, here to here, *n'est-ce pas*?"

"You're right. Very faint, but it's there, especially visible when he tans. You really did know him."

"*Certainment*. But I want you to know so you are *com-for-ta-ble* with me that our dinner can be pleasant between us. The wine also should make you relax with me. It is my father's special vintage and one of the last two bottles left. I drink it with your father the last night we are together and I hope to drink the last bottle with him again at the end of the war when we kill all the Boche."

He felt self-conscious and ill at ease in her presence. "I don't know how to say this, but this is very awkward for me. I don't even really know what to call you or –"

"I tell you to call me Michelle."

"But that's not your real name."

"It may be; or not. Tomorrow I will be gone and it matters then not at all. Tonight we talk, enjoy together a meal and some wine. In war such moments are rare and we should simply take pleasure, *n'est-ce pas*." Her accent was like music and he found himself entranced by her voice and her loveliness.

"This is very good wine," Mitch observed sipping from the glass she offered him.

"But of course. It complements the *friande* I fix for you." She smiled at him and he was again struck by her resemblance to Michelle Reeves. "You are the first man I cook for in many years, and your father was the last man ever to taste my *friande*. I learn to make it from my *grand-père*... how do you say it? – my grandfather, who was to me one of the great chefs of all France. I hope you too like it as much as your father once told me he does."

The first bite of the meaty dish wrapped in a flaky crust told him why his father liked it, if in fact he had really said that many years ago. The whole idea of his straight-laced father spending a similar evening with this mysterious woman still seemed strange, and more than a little far-fetched; he wondered what this whole unexpected occasion was really all about. As he continued eating he asked, "So, how did you meet my father?"

"It was the spring of 1918, when one morning he comes into our little bakery. He was drinking our coffee when I see him from our back room; when I come out with some fresh pastries, I see him watch me. He tries to make conversation with me by asking for a pastry but his French it was not so good, so I play a little game with him. He is tall, with broad shoulders and a little shy with me. He is handsome and I fall in love right away."

"Just like that?"

"I am French," the woman said with a smile, her eyebrows expressively raised and with a slight shrug of her shoulders as if that should explain everything. "I offer the pastry for free but he insists on paying. I insist he does not pay, so we compromise on sharing it and he buys me a coffee for the sake of allied unity, so he says, but I know he wants just to talk to me. So we talk. My *grand-père*, he is not so happy about the attentions of this soldier, but I am a young girl in love and he understands when I allow the Ami officer to take me to lunch."

"1918? The spring – he would have been my age. Twenty-four," Mitch Nolan mused.

"And I am seventeen. He thinks I am so young, but I am married and widowed already by my Etienne. We eat and then we walk around my city so I can show off my tall, handsome Ami officer while he thinks I take him on a – what do you call it? – a sight-seeing tour?" She wiped her mouth with a napkin, rose and walked around the table, then leaned down and kissed him on the lips. Stepping back, she watched him for several seconds. "You are not like your father. When I kiss him like that he blushes – you do not."

"Is that supposed to indicate something?"

"It does to me, my Ami pilot," she replied with a peculiar, furtive smile. She sat down across from him, put her elbows on the table and rested her chin on her clasped hands, looking at him with an enigmatic gaze. "It tells me you are a man who is not yet settled on any one woman. When I know him, your father is already a one woman man who takes his commitment very serious."

"That's my ol' man – real serious about commitments. He married my mother within a month after returning from the war."

"I see. And your mother's name is –?"

"Denise… Denise Barrett back then."

"A very pretty name – so very much French," the woman said pensively, without visible expression, thinking: *I wonder whatever happened to his Michelle.* "One afternoon a few days later, he again comes to our bakery with his company cook and a wagon full of butter and flour and sugar and he asks us to make croissants for his men because of some silly promise he makes to them. It is too much ingredients for a thousand croissants – ten thousand even – but he insists. It is a gift from God that keeps us from closing the bakery. So, your father does not know it but he saves our little bakery and I am even more in love with him. I insist he let me fix him dinner that night and I prepare for him a *friande* like this which he likes very much and we talk and drink my father's best wines into the night."

"What did your father say when he found out you raided his liquor locker?"

"It is impossible. He cannot say anything. He and my mother died shortly before the war in a ski accident from an avalanche in Switzerland while they were on holiday." As she said it, a tear formed along her lower eyelid. "I will never forget the kindness in your father's gift to us and… other things."

They ate the rest of the dinner in awkward silence, until the woman cleaned away the plates and refilled their glasses. "Now, when you see your father, you tell him you have also eaten a *friande* made by the same bakery girl. I would love to see the look on his face when you say it to him."

"So, did you ever see him again after that?"

"*Mais oui, monsieur.* The next morning, very early, my *grand-père* takes me to the place outside our city where your father's soldiers are on the front line against the Boche. We bake them breakfast. When I see your father, I run up and kiss him and call him *Capitan Croissant* – he is very *un-com-for-ta-ble* and his men are very entertained. And I am happy at his blushing, but he is not so much." The woman calling herself Michelle was obviously amused and enjoying the memory. "He tries to cover his discomfort by ordering me and my *grand-père* to leave because it is too dangerous. I say we will not go and we argue, your father and I, for the first and only time. But, in the end the Boche settled our difference. They attack with artillery and tanks – your father throws me and *grand-père* onto our wagon and whips the horse. The last time I see him is over my shoulder as shells explode around him and his men." The woman sighed and looked away. "Your father is a very brave soldier – he stops the German tanks and their infantry at the edge of my city, and the Boche never in the rest of the war threaten us again. He is a hero to us that day, and even to this day in our city."

"So that's it? You never saw or heard from him again?"

"I am afraid, never again. I think of him often after that, and when I do it makes me sad sometimes, but I am glad he found our tiny bakery. Perhaps one day, as I say, we will drink the last bottle of this my father's special wine."

Mitch looked at this beautiful woman across the table from him and wondered what else had passed between her and his father. Surely there was more.

"You wonder why when I wake you this afternoon I say that I take him to my bed. Wishful thinking I am afraid. I see you on the bed and you remind me of him. I wished us to be lovers, but he has that iron will about his promises. That night I entice him as far as my bedroom down the hall from the kitchen. I want much for him to make love to me, but in the end he will not, and to this day I am – how do you say it? – heart-broken... such is love."

*　　*　　*

The light coming in through the dormer window woke him and he realized he was alone in the bed and wondered if he'd dreamed the whole thing – the dinner, the wine, the conversation... the beautiful, dangerous French partisan...

After dinner, she had led him to the attic bedroom and they'd talked while finishing the excellent bottle of wine. He had dozed off when she left the attic, and some time later he'd awakened – or had it been a dream? – to find her standing at the foot of the bed wearing a nightgown and watching him. She had slowly removed the silk garment and let it drop to the floor, then...

"Monsieur," Margot said, standing just inside the attic door. "Wake up! Wake up! It is late and *petit-déjeuner* is ready."

"The woman?" Mitch asked.

"*Tiercelet* left on her bicycle two hours before the dawn. You must come to breakfast quickly if you are to get something to eat. Another young boy arrived an hour ago with our doctor and he is eating both his breakfast and yours. It seems I am right about you Americans running out of men to send us to fight the Boche – I think he is younger even than you."

It turned out he was – by three years. His name was Yeager, a P-51 pilot downed three weeks earlier in Normandy somewhere close to Roquefort; he'd traveled over three hundred miles south and had been handed off to different groups several times in the process. He was a square-jawed young guy from West Virginia who talked with an accent that puzzled Margot.

"Nice little farm," Yeager said between big bites of toast and cheese. "Makes me homesick for my mountains and my girl. Wish I had a picture of Glennis to show you. Prettiest girl in the world." Yeager was eager to talk – about anything. He'd not learned much if any French and now that he'd found another American he gushed forth with three weeks of pent up conversation. His story paralleled Mitch's except that he'd been moving south across France for a couple of weeks now under the care of the Resistance, usually at night and almost always unaware of his location.

"That first place they hid me was something like this – sat on a nice little road. After almost a week, I got restless and a little bored, fed up with this little shed they hid me in; got careless, I guess. Found a shady little sycamore out front of the farmhouse, by the side of the road and went out and sat under it one morning. Next thing I know there's a squad of German soldiers marching in formation around the corner and bearin' down on me. Couldn't get up and run, so I just sat there like I'd been doin' it all my life. They marched right by me, not ten feet away. The farmer's name was Gabriel and he sees all this, and nearly dies. When the Germans were gone, he cussed me out in French, I think, and made a slicing motion across his throat. The next night he led me away from his place and dropped me off with a tough looking band of fellas heavily armed and wearing black berets. Figgered ol' Gabriel had enough of me and handed me off as quick as he could."

After breakfast they went out behind the barn into the woods and sat by a small stream.

"What's it like traveling with the Maquis?" Mitch asked.

"Never boring. They're pretty well armed with British Sten guns and Enfields, Spanish Llama 380s, German semi-auto pistols they've picked up here and there. They move at night mostly and sleep by day, sometimes in the pine forests, and sometimes in barns in remote farms – places like this. They know these mountain forests like I know my woods back home."

"Any close calls?"

"Every day is a close call. I should say every night is – that's when they blow up bridges, sabotage railroad tracks, hit ammo trains and convoys, set ambushes. The Maquisards stay busy. And when you travel with them, you do too. They're always on the move – until today I don't think I've spent more than a couple of hours in any one place since I left up north. Never had any idea where I was. The Maquis are wired into every little village in France and they do know where and how things happen. It's tricky – because every village has its double agents or Vichy collaborators, but their numbers get pruned from time to time. The band that dropped me off here said a couple of double agents in the village down the road were eliminated an hour or so before we arrived. Right at sunrise."

"*Tiercelet...*" Mitch mused out loud.

"What?"

"Just thinking out loud. So, you were flying a Mustang when they shot you down?"

"Yup. Great plane – made for dogfighting. I really loved that machine – had 'Glamorous Glen' painted on her nose. Man, it's amazing how fast your luck can change."

"I remember thinking the same thing when my parachute finally opened – there I was, almost finished my second tour with forty-two missions behind me, and that had to happen. My own fault. Taking too many chances trying for number twelve so I could rotate out to the Pacific with a reasonable reputation and maybe give Bong and McGuire some competition. And the worst part is that I did get number twelve… and thirteen – but the flight was already gone and now the gun cameras are too."

The old hands had branded him a "mission hog" – unusual behavior for a squadron commander. He'd been trying too hard this last month, flying lead in all the small section-sized missions where he'd be more likely to see some action instead of sticking tightly to the box formations of the bombers. He took a lot of pride in their discipline, and while it brought back the bomber crews, it didn't help his score. He'd hoped to pass Dixie Sloan's tally, but knew that was never going to happen now, not officially.

"You've been here a long time, Nolan. Someone like you would be in for a nice cushy job back in the States managing one of the flight schools."

"Not in my blood. I'm a pilot, not a desk jockey. Once you've flown a fighter in combat, you can't go back to anything like that. The day they force me behind a desk is the day I resign." He smiled thinking of that conversation at Moffett with Broussard. "A couple of years ago they tried to keep me in California as a transition instructor. I told my CO I was going to resign. When he said I couldn't in time of war, I told him I would probably flunk my next flight physical in that case, and end up in China flying P-40's for Chenault. We compromised on letting me ferry a new P-38 from the Lockheed plant in California to North Africa. Somehow I never made it back to Texas. Been in the Med since."

Yeager smiled at the story, nodding. "I like that attitude. When we get back, you can be my wingman."

"When we get back, I'll be your squadron leader and tell you if you can fly at all!"

They laughed together and Mitch thought how much the cocky young West Virginian was like him when he'd shown up at Telerghma. But he also saw the differences – Yeager was a lot like his dad. He was committed to this gal, Glennis, in a way that Nolan found hard to comprehend. Chuck sent almost all of his monthly check to this girl he intended to marry but hadn't yet proposed to, and Mitch found that strange. But all Yeager's talk about going back to England and flying over Europe shooting down German Messerschmidts and Focke-Wulf 190s was so much idle chatter. The rules were iron-clad – nobody shot down over the continent and managing to escape back to England with the help of the Resistance was allowed to fly again over Europe. The reasons were obvious, and Nolan thought they were probably as inviolate as the laws of thermodynamics.

That night, well after dark, Gérard awakened them and led the two Americans through the dark pine forest on footpaths little more than game trails. A few hours before sunrise, he halted and had them remain in place while he went ahead. Nolan and Yeager waited most of the day, until he returned mid-afternoon with a group of about twenty heavily armed men wearing black berets and bandoliers of ammunition strapped across their chests like Mexican banditos in the movies. The leader of the group was named Christophe; he looked several years older than either of the American pilots and spoke English almost as well Margot.

"Which of you is Yeager?" the leader of the group asked. Chuck replied with a casual salute. "I hear you are good with explosives."

"When I was a kid I used to help my dad shoot gas wells with plastique. I know my way around fuses and sears and I like blowing up anything that belongs to the Nazis."

Christophe nodded, looking satisfied, and then turned to Mitch. "What do you bring to my group besides another mouth to feed?"

"I know weapons and I'm a good shot," Nolan replied.

"That is true of all my men. You have no other skills to earn your passage across the Pyrenees into Spain?"

"I can live off the land, any land. I've hunted animals as large as elk and as small as doves. I can harvest any kind of animal, field dress and cook any kind of game."

The Maquis leader looked him up and down for awhile and finally shook his head. He turned and said something in French to his men that made their eyes light up and brought a smile to their faces. Turning his attention back to the two Americans he said, "I tell my men we have a matched pair of Americans – one a bomber, the other a butcher. You will both earn your keep between now and the time when the snow melts in the mountains. *Allons.* We have many miles to go before nightfall."

The four hour march through the forest ended just after sundown.

"You two will stay here with our cook and three of my men. We return tomorrow morning. Until then, no fire, no movement or sound," Christophe warned in a voice indicating he was used to having orders obeyed. "There is a farm not far from here; do not bother it."

The rest of the band moved silently into the night; it became deathly quiet and cold under a heavy overcast. Well past midnight, Mitch awoke from a fitful sleep and heard the far off sound of engines. A multi-engine aircraft miles away was flying very low then circling briefly before departing a minute or two later. The luminous hands on his watch indicated it was just after one in the morning. He listened for many minutes and heard nothing more; a short while later he dozed off.

Yeager roused him from a disturbed sleep. "They're back. Time to move again."

Though Nolan couldn't see to count the Maquisards the band seemed much smaller. An hour later they arrived at a small farmhouse and entered a barn dimly lit by kerosene lanterns; two large cylindrical canisters sat on the dirt floor surrounded by Christophe's band. When his men opened the first one, Mitch saw it contained many Mark2 model Sten guns along with cases of 9mm ammunition and extra magazines. There were also several Enfield rifles, many boxes of .303 ammunition, and a dozen Llama pistols with two boxes of cartridges each. A number of fuse packages rounded out the contents along with a map marking German locations across Vichy France indicating possible targets. The second dark canister contained cases of one pound blocks of composition B explosive and bundles of counterfeit French franc notes.

The weapons and explosives were divided among the Maquisards. Yeager was given a knapsack containing fuse packages and Nolan was given another filled with 9mm ammunition for the Sten guns. The explosive cases were placed on a small wagon and a half dozen of the men disappeared into the darkness with it. The rest of the band set off again through the forest, stopped briefly a half hour later to bury the canisters and the parachutes, and then pressed on until they arrived at another small farm just as the eastern sky started getting lighter.

"We stay here in the barn until dark," Christophe told the Americans. "Then we hide the guns and some ammunition under haystacks and in root cellars for bands in the area."

They spent the daylight hours asleep inside the barn after posting sentries in three locations around the perimeter of the farm; the farmer and his family went about their business paying no attention to this rough looking crowd that had taken over their farm. Around noon, two of Christophe's men rode off on bicycles, returning three hours later, each with a sack tied over his shoulder. The farmer was given a few packs of cigarettes and the rest were divided among the band. Meat and cheese were distributed and a bag of medical supplies was given to a man they called Marcel.

"We live off the villages," Christophe told Mitch when everyone had gotten his share of the booty and most had gone back to sleep. "The woods and the farmers hide us but the towns provide much of our food and other needs. The towns are dangerous because they are crawling with Germans, collaborators and Vichy police, but it is a necessity and the merchants never question our forged documents or our phony ration stamps. I have lost a few men in these villages over the years but never lack for volunteers to go. There are other benefits in towns that make it worthwhile to my men, especially the younger ones."

"How long have you been doing this?" Mitch asked.

"Since the Vichy government began the *Service du Travail Obligatoire*, the STO. I didn't want to be transported to Germany as slave labor in their war factories so I escaped to the mountains and joined others. Over time we became more and more organized, were given a name by our enemies and became the Maquis – the "Bush", and more Maquisards joined in the resistance. Leaders emerged in the bands and over groups of bands; most fight the Germans in obscurity but over time some became famous."

"Like the White Mouse and *Tiercelet*?"

"I suppose all of France has heard of them. And there are a handful of others."

"This *Tiercelet*, what can you tell me about her?"

Christophe shook his head and gave him a sardonic smile. "I have never met her, nor anyone who has. I can only tell you the stories which seem more designed to strike fear in the hearts of Nazis and collaborators than anything else. If you asked every man in my band about her, you would get a different story from each one. Some say she is young, others say well advanced in years; one story is that she is a high priced courtesan in one of the larger cities and another that she is a plain – even ugly – woman who cleans public houses or works in a small market. I have heard she has killed dozens of German officers. Who is to know? The last thing to die in war is a legend. Perhaps she is none of these, and perhaps she is all, but in different people. That is not my worry. But if you ask me about the White Mouse – I knew her well, even before the war, and fought by her side after she became our leader in this part of France."

"I've heard of her also," Mitch replied. "You knew her before the war?"

"She married a man that I did business with, and she was more than a legend – she was young and beautiful; some would say she looked the part of a sultry glamour girl from the movies. She was from New Zealand by way of England before the war. She married my friend whose tastes, like hers, ran to caviar and champagne midmorning and love in the afternoon. They were living near Marseilles when the war ignited. She began hiding downed Allied pilots in her home and leading them over the Pyrenees to Spain. She helped organize thousands of Maquisards into coordinated resistance, developed the contacts and arranged arms drops like ours last night. She became such a threat to the Germans they placed a huge price on her head, and our contacts in London begged her to make her way to England through Gibraltar. It took several tries before we were able to get her to Spain in the back of a coal truck. Her husband, my friend, promised to follow after settling family business but was shot by the Nazis not long after she left. We miss her, but are glad she is where she is – for her sake and ours. She is safe and we are now better supplied than ever, and we are sure it is because of her. You are right, she is a legend, and one that will not die. Someday I may tell you more about her, but now is a time to sleep, not talk."

The following day, after traveling most of the night, Yeager showed him how to set the fuses for different delay times – two, four, six or eight hours. When Christophe became convinced that the West Virginian knew what he was doing, he put Yeager in charge of all the explosives, cutting the cords of plastique and attaching them to the fuses.

A few days later two Maquisards entered the camp in the deep woods with a calf in tow that they had "borrowed" from a local farmer they thought was a collaborator. Yeager and two others held the animal while Nolan slit its throat then he and Yeager field dressed the calf as if it were a deer or small cow elk. Mitch butchered the animal the way he'd learned from his father on elk hunts in the Canadian Rockies when the family was at Camp Lewis. The whole episode seemed to amuse the Maquisards. Dinner that evening was a welcomed improvement, consisting of a large kettle of beans and cuts of beef grilled over the fire, eaten under the trees with a long board serving as communal table. Afterward the Frenchmen asked the two Americans questions translated by Christophe. They wanted to know about the American airplanes and had some laughs when Yeager and Nolan got into an argument about which was the best plane for shooting down German fighters.

The following week the band took the Americans along on nighttime missions to set charges to blow up a railroad trestle and a couple of small bridges. The next week, they were allowed to go along to set charges on a bridge over which German trucks often traveled when delivering ammunition to their garrison in Toulouse. Then, on a very wet afternoon in late March, Christophe approached and said, "It is time for you to leave us and each other. Nolan, you will go with Paul-Henri; Yeager, you go with Marcel. Don't worry, just stay close to my men and follow their lead." With that the Maquis leader turned and walked away.

Nolan and Yeager exchanged wary glances, sensing this was dangerous and wondered why they had to be separated. But the two Frenchmen took off through the woods in different directions and they had no choice but to run to catch up. When Nolan looked back over his shoulder, Yeager and Marcel were out of sight.

Mitch followed his Maquis guide throught the dense woods for an hour until they came across an idling van parked on the side of a logging road. As he approached, the back door opened and a young Frenchman motioned for him to come aboard. Marcel pushed him in, the door closed and the vehicle sped off.

Inside the van it was pitch black as they rumbled and jolted down back roads for a half hour before the ride smoothed out. For the next few hours the journey alternated back and forth between lurching down unimproved roads and smooth going on good hard surfaces. The Frenchman spoke no English and the ride passed in silence and utter darkness. As time wore on, Nolan's anxiety grew until the van noticeably slowed and began turning frequently as if navigating through city streets. Suddenly they lurched to a stop and the van sat idling for a few minutes until he heard the approach of another vehicle.

Without warning, the door was flung open and another Frenchman stood there motioning for him to follow. It was early evening, dark and drizzling rain, as he was led across the street toward another van parked against a high stone wall with its engine running. He hopped into the back of the truck when its door opened and then the vehicle took off almost before the door could be closed and latched. There were three or four other men inside sitting on benches and he heard mumbled curses when the van took a tight corner at high speed throwing them against the side of the vehicle. Soon they were gaining speed and being whipsawed back and forth in the back of the van. Mitch dwelt on the notion this was the beginning of the end of his long journey through France.

His guess was that the snows hadn't melted this early in the spring. *How high are the Pyrenees*? he wondered. *Twelve or thirteen thousand feet in places*? It would be hard going on foot, even if there wasn't any snow. He recalled that first elk hunt with his father – they had camped close to ten thousand feet in the Canadian Rockies, and hunted even higher. He remembered how hard it had been to climb and hunt in the thin air and the headaches he'd had before his body was conditioned to it. The second year he'd worked hard at getting in shape the entire summer before the hunt and handled it better.

In a little while the driver slowed and the gears of the van began clashing as they started up a steep incline. A flashlight came on, held by a Frenchman who spoke excellent English as he handed out hand drawn maps of the mountains and their path through them to Spain. He knelt between the passengers and spread out his own map.

"We're just outside Lourdes in the foothills of the mountains," he began. "When we stop, there will be a small cabin directly in front of the van about five hundred meters through the woods. That's your starting point. Stay there and rest until daylight. Get some sleep. It is cold, but no fires and no talking. The area is patrolled. You can split up into two teams or stay together, your choice. Do not try going it alone – very few ever make it that way. It will take you four or five days to cross into Spain and the most dangerous part will be when you get to the border; the Germans patrol that heavily because there are all sorts of people crossing over the frontier – smugglers, refugees, military escaping like you. They will not take any prisoners. And be careful in the northern part of Spain – the Spaniards there have a way of turning in captured Americans to the Gestapo for rewards. The Germans will torture you to get everything they can learn about us, and then they will shoot you."

There was a pile of knapsacks in the front of the van which the Frenchman handed out. "It is not much – cheese, bread and chocolate to eat, a small tin cup, four pair of woolen socks, a small rubber poncho and a compass – but it will get you across if you are determined. Good luck. *Vive la France*."

A short time later the van stopped. It was dark and wet in the woods and well past midnight as the group of downed fliers found their way to the tiny cabin. They spent what remained of the night inside the woodsman's shed shivering in the dark, getting little sleep. At first light they set out as a group headed up the steep slope. By noon, Mitch and Ken, a B-17 radio operator who'd been shot down near Soissons, reached the timber line and stopped to wait for the others. After forty minutes, their fellow escapees were still nowhere to be seen.

"Kenny, we're going to have to move on," Mitch said, picking up his backpack and shouldering it. "Even if they catch up in the next hour, we'll be a half day behind already by the time they rest and eat. At that rate we'd run out of food days before we hit Spain."

The radio operator hesitated and a look of anguish spread across his face. "Let's give 'em another half hour. These guys were part of my crew and we've been through a lot together. Besides, we'll have a better chance with numbers, with all of us together."

Nolan debated. He understood the boy's anguish and even admired his loyalty, but this was survival and they would be slowed and hampered to the level of the weakest member. If they were this far behind at the beginning, what would they be two days from now, having traveled through snow with little to eat and not much real rest, hampered by thin air and freezing cold? "I'll give them another twenty minutes, but after that we have to get moving."

A half hour later the rest of the crew still had not arrived and Kenny decided he had to go back to find them against Mitch's warning that to turn back now meant never getting out. They wished each other luck and left in opposite directions.

After reaching the timber line the climb grew harder and soon he found himself knee deep in wet snow. At first he rested every hour, and then every half hour; by dusk he was stopping every fifteen minutes to catch his breath in the rarefied air. Elk hunting in the Rockies had been arduous, but this was physically demanding in a way he'd never known. His body was more unprepared than he'd realized after weeks of fretful sleep and infrequent exercise. Late that afternoon he crossed over his first ridgeline and started down, an exercise even more demanding than the ascent. Nightfall came upon him swiftly in the wet woods and he found an outcropping of rock to give himself some protection from the freezing wind. Wrapping himself with the poncho, he tried to get some sleep. It came in fits and starts. Finally, he gave up and started out again before sunrise, crossing a small flat valley just as the eastern sky began to grow lighter.

The climb up the next hill became an endless agony and he began to question if anybody ever made it through or if they all simply became buzzard bait. His mind grew as numb as his feet and as weary as his legs, and by the end of the second day he began to wonder how many days he'd been on this endless trek. That night, on a mattress of dry needles under the boughs of a pine, he collapsed into a deep sleep filled with nightmares. Again he awoke off and on but at four in the morning he was awakened by a freshening wind and couldn't get back to sleep. Deciding to warm himself through exertion, he started up a steep slope headed generally south. Within an hour he was so exhausted physically and so numbed mentally he began to think he was irretrievably lost and stopped to eat a small bite of cheese.

Late in the afternoon he approached the top of another mountain shrouded in low hanging clouds that restricted visibility to less than a hundred feet. He realized he'd been staggering like a drunk and even catnapping on his feet, dreaming about his time in the Philippines back before the war – recalling the warm days on the beach fishing with his father and Colonel Fauser and Zack. He was leaning against an outcropping of rock trying to catch his breath in the thin cold air when a machine gun opened up with a long angry burst, less than a hundred yards away.

Instantly he was wide awake, his heart pounding and his legs no longer feeling like waterlogged appendages attached at his hips. He found a crevice for cover and waited, his senses alive and on alert. Random rifle firing continued for several minutes and soon he heard German voices shouting and moving away. He waited an hour before moving cautiously in the direction where he'd first heard the firing. He moved slowly, pointing the big .45 Colt semi-auto, wondering if his frozen finger could actually pull the trigger.

And then he found the woodsman's cabin.

The front door had been shot to splinters as had the windows on one side. In a tree out front hung a pair of woolen socks; inside there was only a small table and two shattered chairs. And blood. Fresh blood and plenty of it. His mind raced and he quickly figured the blood was probably American or British and the Germans had caught one or more men resting in the cabin and shot up the place. The lone back window had been shattered outward and in the snow beneath it there was more blood and many footprints. A trail of blood went westward thirty yards until it reached a steep decline that looked like a log slide headed downhill into the fog, similar to the flumes he'd seen the loggers in the northwest build.

Mitch debated. Should he try to find the wounded escapees and join them or press on alone? For no real reason, he decided on the former and set off down the steep hill.

He paralleled the snow-covered log flume for almost a mile until it ended in a deep creek. By the time he got there light was fading quickly. He found a place not far from the end of the log slide where there was more blood and then footprints headed south and drag marks; two men – one walking, one being pulled like a heavy sled in the snow. He decided to track them as soon as it got light enough the next morning. He found a big pine and snuggled underneath it, wrapped in the poncho. Strangely buoyed by the idea there were other escapees not very far up ahead and because he was exhausted from the climbing and coming down from the burst of adrenaline that had sustained him all that afternoon, he fell sound asleep.

Very early in the morning Mitch filled his lone canteen from the stream and ate a bite of candy before starting off. The trail was fairly easy to follow in the deep snow, but when it crossed an ice field he lost it for almost an hour before acquiring it again. Whoever was up ahead knew the woods and how to shake off a tracker. But Mitch had hunted and stalked some of the wariest animals in North America and he'd learned from the best – his father at Lewis and Colonel Fauser in the Philippines. Still, by the end of the day he'd not caught up to the men he was following.

Late the following afternoon he was crossing yet another of the seemingly endless ridgelines, barely able to put one foot in front of the other; he was hungry and daydreaming about Thanksgiving turkey and Christmas goose. When he checked his compass, Mitch realized the trail he was following had turned back toward France. It made no sense, but his mind wasn't able to decipher what it meant and he stopped for awhile trying to put it together. He looked at the tracks in the snow, decided they were very recent and gazed around. Something about these tracks was wrong. Very wrong. But he couldn't force himself to figure it out. He heart was beating rapidly as he reached inside his jacket for the pistol.

"Don't do that, *kamerade... nicht... nein*."

Nolan turned and saw the square-jawed face behind the barrel of the pistol.

"Yeager? Is that you? Point that thing somewhere else, will ya?"

"Nolan? Damn. That was you following us? All by yourself? How'd you get here?"

"I wish I could say something real funny right now but I'm too damned tired and worn out. I'll tell you later. Right now I just need to sit down and catch my breath."

"Follow me. I'm camped pretty close to here. We can sit and talk a spell if you're up to it. Got a fella with me in real bad shape. He's alive, but barely." Mitch followed Yeager a hundred yards until he ducked under a pine tree and sat down next to a figure wrapped in a poncho. The man's breathing was shallow but regular.

"Who is he?" Nolan asked.

"His name is Pat. We never got past first names. He's a B-24 navigator. We paired up that first day in the mountains and a couple days back he got shot up in a shack on top of a ridge line. Guess the German patrol saw his socks hanging out front in the tree to dry out."

"I heard the shooting and located the shack. Saw the socks."

"Turned out that wasn't real bright. The bastards caught us asleep and just opened fire. I grabbed my knapsack and jumped through the window. Pat got hit but made it out. I dragged him away and found a log flume and pushed him down it and jumped in myself. We went ass over teacups down the thing for who knows how long until it dumped us into a stream. Good thing it was deep. Pat's leg below the knee was hangin' on by a single tendon so I cut it off and used my shirt to wrap the stump. He's been out just about every minute since."

"You've been dragging him for two days?" Mitch asked, incredulous.

"Draggin' and pushin' both. Couldn't let him die out here all alone. I wanted to get out from under that big hundred and eighty pound load but as long as he was still breathin' I couldn't leave him. Figgered he'd probably do the same for me. He woke for a few minutes just a couple of times – long enough for me to feed him some chocolate. Walked through the night because parts of me was still wet and I knew I'd freeze if I didn't. The only thing that kept me goin' was thinkin' about my girl back in Oroville."

Mitch was astonished, knowing how many times he'd felt like giving up over the past – what? – four days? "You're a hell of a man, Chuck Yeager. Most guys would have let go of him a long time ago. When we get back, I *will* be your wing man."

"As far as I can tell, gettin' back is still up in the air. Seems to me this ridge, maybe the next one, is the one markin' the border with Spain so we still have at least another day to go. Haven't eaten since that little dunk in the stream ruined what was left of my bread and cheese. I'm so hungry I could eat the south end of a northbound horse."

"Lucky for you, I have enough left for both of us." Mitch took out his remaining half loaf of bread, the small chunk of cheese and his last candy bar. He cut each in half and split it with Yeager. "You get some sleep. Take my poncho and wrap up while I dig us a fire pit so we can get warm and you can dry out. We'll be like new men when the sun comes up."

He found a large flat rock and used it for a shovel to dig out a two foot by three foot pit about eighteen inches deep under the pine tree. He found enough kindling to start a fire and plenty of deadfall to keep it going; an hour after sundown he started the fire using Vantrease's Zippo lighter he'd won in a card game at Telerghma. *Maybe this thing's a lucky charm after all.* He'd made it four days through the mountains by himself, hadn't been wounded or injured and had found Yeager. The fire dwindled after an hour and warmed by it, Nolan fell asleep on the carpet of pine needles for almost five hours until the West Virginian stirred and woke him. Nolan restarted the fire and they placed the poncho over the trench to keep the warmth in and the smoke contained; they sat with their feet in the pit, waiting for the sun to rise.

"How much farther do you think we have to go?" Mitch asked the West Virginian as they sat side by side warming themselves.

"Another day – day and a half maybe, if my map is correct. Yesterday I had a good look around from a high spot on this ridge line. There's one more big mountain ahead, I think. We'll be in Spain late this afternoon or tomorrow morning is my guess."

"I was told that the Spaniards in the north have a nasty way of turning American fliers into the Gestapo for rewards."

"Heard the same thing," Yeager agreed. "I'm thinkin' a wise man wouldn't stop until he got to Madrid, or until his money ran out." Pat moaned and stirred for a moment. "You know, I'm thinkin' he's the lucky one in this. He's unconscious and every muscle I got is sore like I got the world's worst whuppin' with more to come. Yesterday when you caught up I was thinkin' it was time to stop and either sleep or die. To tell the truth, at the time it didn't make much difference to me which one it was after a whole night of crawlin' through the snow and haulin' ol' Pat up the side of this mountain."

After eating a breakfast consisting of a bite of cheese and a bite of bread, they set off down the side of the ridge to the small valley before what they hoped would be the last mountain between them and freedom. They made a stretcher using one of the ponchos and put "the bomber guy" – as Yeager referred to him – on it and pulled it over the snow. By mid day, they reached the bottom of the valley and started up the next mountain; every muscle in their bodies pounded and complained. When nightfall came, they decided not to rest because they were afraid of falling asleep and letting go of the navigator. But it turned out, they both succumbed to sleepwalking and Nolan was certain that the time between dusk and dawn had flown by in a matter of seconds. One minute the dark vault of the mountain night had swooped in over them and the next instant the red dawn was splayed across the surface of a mountaintop sheet of ice. He looked into the distance and through the morning haze and saw the land flattening out into rolling hills. A thin sliver of a road ran from left to right in front of them.

Spain.

Yeager walked over to the edge of an outcropping of rock and looked down the steep slope in front of them. Then he went over to a stand of dwarf pines and cut down two long pine boughs, throwing one of them at Nolan. "Here you go. Our transportation down this ice slide." He walked over to the edge of the long sloping run and pushed Pat and his poncho over the edge and watched them slide a couple of hundred yards downhill before stopping in the snow. Yeager then put the pine bough between his bent legs as if riding a broom handle. "Used to do this back home on roller skates using a broom for a brake. If I bust my ass, you might want to try something different."

Nolan watched as Yeager navigated the steep slope, staying upright until he hit the soft snow. He got to his feet and waved an arm uphill, then turned and pushed Pat again, this time sending him another twenty or thirty yards. Finally, Mitch summoned the courage to try it, put his weight against the bough and launched himself over the edge. With his heart pounding he plummeted down the slope. He hit soft snow near Yeager and went face first into a drift and slowly got to his feet.

"First time in five days I found something to laugh about," Yeager told him as Mitch wiped the snow off his face and removed some from inside his jacket. "Your eyes were big as supper plates all the way, Nolan. Damned if you didn't look like a raccoon riding his tail."

"I'm surprised we didn't both break our necks trying a stupid stunt like that."

"Tell me that wasn't a hell of a ride! Made the whole trip worthwhile, didn't it?!"

They crunched through the glazed snow field and continued to push Pat down the hill until the snow ran out. From there they carried him for the last half mile to the road.

Yeager checked the navigator's pulse again and shook his head. "This here is one tough bomber guy," he said, sitting on the trunk of a downed tree next to the road. "I think we done about all we can for him. He'll be better off if we leave him by the side of the road and let some good Samaritan passerby take care of him – get him to a hospital or something."

Nolan agreed and they placed him in a conspicuous spot on the side of the road after making him as comfortable as they could. Together they walked twenty miles south until early afternoon when they reached a small town. They turned themselves in to the local police who decided to place them in their jail until some officials from Madrid could come and tell them what to do with two Americans just recently escaped from France.

"I'm not staying in some filthy stinking cell my first night of freedom," Yeager declared angrily when the policeman locked the door and left. "I want a bath and a shave and a nice soft bed to sleep in. And I got just the ticket out of here, Nolan. They didn't search me and I still have my survival kit."

Yeager's kit contained a small steel hacksaw blade and the American steel made quick work of the Spanish brass bars on the window of their cell. Within an hour they were through the window and had located a small boarding house near the edge of town.

Nolan soaked in a tub of hot water for an hour, almost immediately falling asleep with his head pillowed on the enamel rim. When he awoke, he was given a hot meal of chicken and pork with flatbread and some kind of spicy beans. After his second helping of each and a third glass of wine, he fell into bed and slept soundly for two solid days until awakened by loud, recurrent knocking.

He was still half asleep when the door flew open and a mustachioed Spanish officer wearing a khaki uniform with gold braid epaulets came in and stood over him at the foot of the bed. Looking past the officer, he saw Yeager standing outside in the hallway between two glaring soldiers, each tightly grasping him by an arm. To get his attention, the officer banged on the steel bedpost twice with a policeman's baton.

"You and your friend entered our country illegally. You will come with me at once," the officer said ominously. "Such things we do not take lightly."

Chapter 39

Dwight Eisenhower, always the diplomat, had populated his direct staff and commanders with a preponderance of British officers; Brad and Bedell Smith were the only Americans. Montgomery was the invasion's ground commander, Admiral Sir Bertram Ramsay was the Naval commander in chief, and Air Chief Marshall Sir Trafford Leigh-Mallory commanded all air assets for the assault on the Normandy coast. Air Chief Marshall Sir Arthur William Tedder was Ike's deputy commander.

Dave Nolan stood in the back of the large room and watched the photographer once again re-position Eisenhower's Allied Headquarters primary staff for a different portrait perspective. As he stood next to Henry Smythe-Browne, he wished he was elsewhere. Preferably home.

The first letter from Denise after Mitch's disappearance had not been encouraging, and the few short notes since then were troubling. Even though the other wives in the D.C. area had grown closer to her and to one another, she complained of being alone and out of touch. Her state of mind worried him. Erika's letters on the other hand were upbeat and full of news about her job, Senator Payne, Michelle (and her surprise divorce), and this young lawyer she was still smitten with – Randall B. Ashby, Esquire. The name sounded to him like some character out of *Gone with the Wind*. *Protect my little girl from lawyers involved in politics,* he'd thought each time she'd mentioned the young man.

Tempering his desire to go home was Glenn's situation in the 82nd Airborne.

He'd visited his youngest son twice now – the first time in early March, the week before Mitch went missing, and then again the first week in May. The boy had changed greatly. He was the 505th regimental boxing champ in his weight class, an event resulting from a fight he'd gotten into early in his assignment while the division was still up north after transferring from Italy. The whole affair seemed entirely out of character for Glenn, the most mild-mannered and easy-going of any in his brood. As always, he'd made friends easily and quickly; now his closest buddy was a veteran of two combat jumps into Sicily and Salerno. He too, was small and slight, but four years older and ages more mature in the ways of the world and the Army. Earl Wright was from Kennett Square, Pennsylvania and had twice made it up the ladder to buck sergeant, but each time fell back for 'military indiscretions' – insubordination.

"I should warn you, David," Smythe-Browne whispered conspiratorially. "Leigh-Mallory has again changed his mind on the airborne drops behind the American beaches. I inform you only out of courtesy. I find myself wholly in agreement with him."

Dave remained silent, bristling at the comment but saying nothing. *Damn these Brits. Every one of them… including you, Henry.* The conference after this portrait fiasco now had all the earmarks of a donnybrook instead of tidying up a few small details. Even Ike could be unhappy with this development.

Twenty minutes later after excusing the photographer and adjourning to the map room, SHAEF staff reconvened for what most hoped would be a quick and final briefing before Operation Overlord; D-Day.

Not long after the dismal and disappointing weather report from both the American and British meteorology teams, Montgomery turned his portion of the briefing over to Omar Bradley. The American general began detailing what had been agreed upon during the final airborne planning session at St. Paul's school. As he came to the portion of the plan for Utah Beach, Leigh-Mallory spoke up.

"General Bradley, I cannot agree with or approve your plan. After reconsideration, I propose that we altogether spike the airborne plan for Utah." Bradley paused, and both he and Eisenhower glanced quickly at Dave Nolan.

"I know there was some disagreement initially," Eisenhower said testily, looking back and forth between Bradley and Nolan. "I'd been led to believe that was all worked out days ago. Was I misinformed?"

"No, sir," Brad replied, now staring harshly at the British Air Chief. "I also thought we had reached agreement."

"After once again reviewing General Bradley's plan, I must register my strong objection. After rigorous examination and much deliberation, I see clearly that the courses to be flown by troop carrier aircraft present greater risks than perhaps his planners realized. It is much too hazardous an undertaking for the aircrews. Losses will surely be excessive; far more than I am willing to accept, General Bradley. I cannot go along with you on this."

"Very well, sir," Bradley replied, in a surprisingly unemotional voice. "If you refuse to support me, then I have to ask the supreme commander to eliminate the assault at Utah Beach. I won't send men to land on that beach without ensuring we've got the exits behind it secured."

Good response Brad, Dave Nolan thought. *Throw it back in his face and make him tell Ike why he won't support the invasion the way it should be done.*

"Your selection of drop zone locations, General Bradley, are untenable not only for the aircrews flying the mission but for the paratroopers themselves. Should you follow the course you propose, I suggest your parachute infantry losses will exceed fifty percent and eighty percent among the gliders. I know of no commander willing to accept that level of loss, do you?" Leigh-Mallory responded haughtily. "Who would possibly send men into the face of such impossible odds?"

"I would!" Dave Nolan said from the side of the room, suddenly attracting everyone's attention. He knew he was out of order but stood up and continued. "For two reasons. First, the airdrops are essential if we are to secure the road networks and approaches to Utah Beach so that seaborne infantry doesn't have to wade across the expanse of a flat killing zone. Secondly, your estimates of aircraft losses are incorrect – they're based on inaccurate and basically nonexistent intelligence, as you know. We went through that before, not too many weeks ago." He was about to sit down when he stopped and paused to look at Ike and Bradley. "And another thing. That eighty percent number you tossed out is just a guess. None of us know for certain. Would I send airborne troops according to General Bradley's plan? I would, and I will. I have a son who is a private in the 82nd Airborne. Right now, according to plan, he will be jumping from one of the first Gooney Birds to enter the airspace over France. You could say I have a lot riding on the feasibility and accuracy of General Bradley's plan."

Leigh-Mallory stared back at him from across the table. "You cannot convince me, General Nolan. Let me make this clear – if you go forward with this airborne operation you'll do it in spite of my opposition." The Air Chief Marshall squared himself in his chair and addressed Montgomery. "If General Bradley insists upon going ahead he will have to accept full responsibility for the operation."

"That's perfectly fine with me," Bradley responded. "I'm entirely agreeable and in the habit of accepting responsibility for any and all of my operations."

Montgomery quietly rapped his knuckles on the tabletop. "Gentlemen, this is not at all necessary. I am the ground commander for the invasion, and I shall take full responsibility, including the Utah Beach airborne plan which will go forward as outlined by General Bradley."

"Very well," Eisenhower said. "I'm glad that's finally settled. Now, let's continue."

Dave Nolan heard little of the remainder of the discussion. He was still angry at Leigh-Mallory's duplicity when the meeting broke up and he quickly exited the briefing room and walked outside to his car.

A half-hour later he was sitting behind his desk at the headquarters looking over operational reports from the divisions in his newly created XXX Corps, still angry at Leigh-Mallory's high-handed grandstanding. *Time to put that behind you*, he counseled himself. *Don't let the bastard get you down. You've got a Corps to pull together and run. Let Ike and Brad and Bedell Smith play touchy-feely with the Brits; surely they'll let me get out of this stupid planning job now.*

He was reading a message from Patton when Andy walked into his office with a bottle of bourbon and three glasses.

"Andy, for crying out loud, not again. It's not even lunchtime yet. There are some expectations of officers in your position. Put that stuff into a filing cabinet or somewhere at least until supper."

Fauser smiled and leaned against the doorframe. "I got me more good news than a fella is authorized to be issued in this man's Army and I don't give a damn what time it is because ah'm gonna celebrate. You can sit there all pucker face if you want but I'm guessing when I'm done telling you my news you'll be wantin' to pour us each another drink or three. Who's your favorite classmate of ours?"

"What?"

"Yup, me too. I'm talkin' about Harrison *A- for asshole* Reeves." Fauser drained his glass and poured himself another drink.

"Is this going somewhere Andy?"

"Drink up, son, you're fallin' behind as usual. Seems as how Michelle not only divorced his sorry carcass but managed to walk away with a fair piece of change from his estate without him even knowin' it. Good for her. You'd drink to that wouldn't you?"

Dave wasn't sure. He'd never understood what she'd seen in Reeves, or why she'd married him. Thinking about her now made him feel guilty. "Not so sure that's something that concerns me one way or the other."

Fauser leaned toward him and said. "Boy, you never was a very good liar. Another piece of good news: Harry Reeves is no longer Major General Reeves, he's *Mister* Harrison Reeves in Silver Spring, Maryland and U.S. Army ree-tired. Tell me that ain't good news."

"I never was one much for *schadenfreude*, Butternuts," Dave replied.

"Damn, friend you got some hard bark on you if that don't make you smile. After all he done to you over the years?"

"This really isn't going anywhere after all, is it?"

Fauser lit a cigarette, looking reflective. "I come upon this young Air Corps fly-boy brass – handsome kid with one of them big ol' black-faced chronometers with a dozen dials that does everything but fix breakfast and press your britches... Got somethin' to show you. Look what I run into roamin' around the building." Andy reached around the door and pulled Mitch into the office. "Lookit that boy, Davey. Suntanned brown as a hog in mud, and fat as a tick to boot. I swear I didn't recognize him when he showed up here and I been knowin' him all his life. Look at this here," Fauser said, tapping the silver oak leaf on Mitch's collar. "Barely two years out of diapers and a lieutenant colonel already. You and I been in the wrong branch all along."

Dave was instantly on his feet and grabbing his son in a tight embrace. "When...?"

"Got to London late last night. They put us up in a hotel somewhere downtown."

Dave heard little of Andy's prattling as he held his son at arm's length and looked him over. "Fauser's right, you look like you've been on a two month luxury cruise."

"The first month was anything but pleasant. But the last five or six weeks made up for it."

Fauser handed them each a glass. "Let's us toast Mitch's return, then I'll get out of here and leave you alone while I set up a commo link for you two to call home." After the toast Andy left and closed the door.

"Your mother is going to be beside herself to hear your voice. Tell, me what happened – the whole tale."

Mitch related his story, as he had for Army intelligence the day before after arriving back in England from Spain. When he got to the part about meeting the dark-haired mystery woman at Margot's house he stopped and asked, "Who is she?"

"Nicole Bouvier. I met her during the last war in the city of Rheims. Her family owned a bakery I happened into one day. I traded a pistol I'd captured for flour and other stuff that I gave to her grandfather so he'd make croissants for my company." He hadn't thought about her for a long time, and thinking of her now was a pleasant ache in his heart. "I'm glad to hear she survived. I only knew her for three or four days and the last time I saw her, she and her grandfather were trying to outrun a German barrage in an old wagon with an even older horse. She was real young – probably sixteen, seventeen. Always wondered what became of her. I'm surprised she remembered me."

Mitch finished his story of the escape over the Pyrenees with Yeager.

"After we made it to Spain we were eventually taken to Alma de Aragon where they put us up in a resort hotel on the beach, all paid for by Uncle Sam while the Consul bargained for our release. We had nothing to do but sun ourselves on the beach, loaf, eat, flirt with the chambermaids. I got real good at that."

"I'm sure you did. How did they finally get you out of there?"

"Apparently there was a lot of posturing back and forth. It took awhile but the Spaniards agreed to trade us for gasoline. I found out I'm worth about twenty-five thousand gallons of Texaco. Next time I get shot down, I'm bailing out over the Iberian peninsula."

Dave laughed easily and realized they'd spent the better part of an hour talking and drinking Andy's bourbon. "Tell you what, tonight after dinner we'll call your mother if Andy can arrange it, and then tomorrow we'll go out to the 82nd Airborne to see Glenn. He's a boxing champion in his regiment."

"Glenn? My muttonhead little brother is a boxer?"

"I'd be careful, Mitch. He's not the same guy you remember. He's grown and toughened up – and he always did have faster hands than you did in the ring."

"I'll be on the alert. But, I'd like to go do that later – in a day or two. I have someone else I need to see first."

"Aynslee?"

"Just to say hello and return something that belongs to her. That's all."

"Let me tell you something you should know before you visit out there."

*   *   *   *

Aynslee Glendenbrook opened the door to her parent's house on the second knock and instantly recognized the youngish pilot in uniform who stood there looking uncomfortable.

"Duncan, what brings you by?" she said, trying to sound friendly and calm. The nervous look on the RAF officer's face and the brown cardboard box held beneath his arm made the question both awkward and unnecessary.

"It's about Muck's kit, Ayns – it came in to Hornchurch today. The major rang up Fighter Command and learned you were off duty and had me to bring his belongings by. I'm sorry it took the RAF so long. Waitin' almost a year, well, there ought to be somebody court-martialed and run up –"

"It's all right, Dunc. I got it all out last fall when Major Howsham and the chaplain came by. I'm over the worst of it," she said, smiling bravely. "Is that all there is?"

"Yes, just the one box is all. Personal belongings. His wallet and some money, uniform identification tags, pictures, a set of keys. The squadron pitched in some photographs of him his friends had took. There's an inventory sheet inside. He had a metal personal box and that was left locked and untouched as they found it, looks like. There was also a stack of letters from you tied in a ribbon he kept in a footlocker next to his cot. His mates said he talked about you all the time."

"Not much to show for five years of marriage and six years in the RAF is it, Dunc?"

The pilot momentarily glanced away, embarrassed. "Guess not, luv. But it's the full monty for a chap in a place like that – none of 'em carried much to a place like North Africa. I heard it was awful desolate and more primitive than we can imagine. They say not to expect to get any of his uniforms back. They're still short of necessities down there in the Med. His squadron mates would likely go through his issue gear and divide up what was needed among the other pilots."

"I understand."

"But the squadron did include his medals and copies of the citations. You can be proud of those – he was quite highly decorated."

"Of course. Always the bold adventurer Malcolm was." She took the box from the young captain, noticing he still relied heavily on the cane – a souvenir of the Battle of Britain when his leg was badly damaged. "I'd invite you in, Duncan, but surely that's improper etiquette for a grieving widow home alone. Perhaps some other time."

"Yes, of course." The pilot replaced the service cap on his head, and touched the bill with his finger in salute. "You're bearing up well, Ayns. Muck would o' been proud of you. We're all sorry about him. All the lads are. He was a good pilot and a man's man. Sorry for your loss. If there's anything –"

"I'm well and doing fine, Dunc. Thanks for stopping by." Aynslee smiled gamely at him, nodded and closed the door. She walked down the hall and placed the box on the large desk beneath a window that looked out behind the house toward the stable and another out building. Reaching inside the box she withdrew the typed inventory list of its contents entitled: *Personal Effects of Major Malcolm Hyde Glendenbrook, RAF, No. 72 Squadron, Souk el Arba, Tunisia.* In addition to what their friend Duncan had told her, there was a calendar and an address book.

I wonder if he was that careless – or callous, she said to herself and began to thumb through the expensive leather bound address book with his initials on the front. In the letter M section there were three entries in her husband's expressive, undisciplined handwriting. Two were names she recognized; the third entry was simply three letters: RSM.

It was not the first time she'd seen those initials, and seeing them now didn't shock her as it had initially. She knew the address as a small flat in Chelsea and she also now knew the name of the person renting it: Rose Shannon McMartin. She wondered how the woman was paying the rent now that Malcolm no longer could. There was a time when discovering those initials or that name would have greatly upset her. No longer.

After rummaging through her father's center desk drawer and finding a cigar lighter, she took the box outside to a metal container on the far side of their small barn. She retrieved a hammer from inside the barn and broke the hasp on the metal personal box. Inside was one of their wedding pictures, a picture of Malcolm with their daughter, along with his university ring and wedding band.

She crumpled some newspaper and stuffed it into the burn can. Then she took the items in the cardboard box and unceremoniously dropped them into the can – the decorations, citations, wallet, address book, letters, pictures – the whole lot, including the cardboard box. Then she lit the contents with the cigar lighter; soon the flames engulfed everything and were leaping upward. Satisfied, she turned and went back inside.

"Aynslee, dear, whatever are you doing?" her mother asked when she entered the kitchen and placed a bag of vegetables on the counter. "What was so important you had to go traipsing around outside in the barn before changing into work clothes and wellies?"

"Finishing some old business, mother," she replied.

"Old business? Why the necessity of fire?"

"Flames have a way of purging things in need of it."

"Oh, dear, that's certainly cryptic. Does it have anything to do with young Duncan? I saw him driving away as I was coming back from the store."

"He brought a box of things belonging to Malcolm sent back by his squadron."

"And you burned them?!"

"Every last thing."

Her mother busied herself making a pot of tea, poured two cups and sat down at the kitchen table motioning for her to take a seat. "I know you're upset, but is burning up all that once belonged to him really the answer?"

"It will just have to do until something better comes along. But I do believe a ritualistic purging is good for my frame of mind."

"You don't seem much happier for it. Is that also why you sold the horse?" her mother asked tilting her head and eyeing her daughter over the top of her teacup.

"I was angry at Malcolm when I did that. I was also angry at that Yank who thought it perfectly appropriate to waltz in here and have his way with my possessions without so much as tipping his hat or asking my permission."

"I wish you wouldn't say that. I'm surprised you would in deference to his father. The young man did have permission, more or less. Your father also said the young man was very contrite and apologetic when you confronted him."

"The *young man* was neither so far as I could tell – he was a typically pushy Yank." She stopped and took a deep breath. "Perhaps you're right. In hindsight, I guess he wasn't such a unpleasant soul – it's just we got into the argy-bargy right off and never got out of it. It is sad he's gone. I didn't know him that well, but his father is a good sort."

"Your father and I were rather fond of him, as we are of his mother and his father." Maud Smythe-Browne looked away and blinked back a tear. "I do hope his mother is well. I can't imagine what she'd going through hearing her eldest was lost. How is his father bearing up?"

"He doesn't talk about it. He's thrown himself into his work, I imagine to keep himself occupied. Seems rather resigned to the reality of it all." But there was more to it than just keeping busy. The news that his son had been lost on a mission over southern France had hit his father hard. "I imagine it takes a while to deal with the loss of a loved one."

A loud double rap on the front door knocker echoed through the high-ceilinged hallway and filtered in to the kitchen.

"I'm not expecting anyone," Maud Smythe-Browne said. "Are you, my dear? Would you see who it is while I clean up here?"

Aynslee nodded and hurried down the long hall. When she opened the front door her eyes went wide and she gasped, covering her mouth with a hand. For what seemed an eternity, she simply stared at the American officer standing just inside the alcove who was presenting her with a small, worn card.

"Hi. I'm Mitch Nolan and this note says you have something you want to say to me. I came by to find out what it is."

*　　*　　*　　*

It was mid-morning when he parked the bicycle next to the woodshed at the side of a cottage on the edge of the small town. Up ahead he could see the old wooden steeple of a church with its five bells of differing sizes. He walked up the village lane past several quaint cottages, the comfortably manicured grounds of the manor house, and an old rectory, all the while thinking he must have stepped back in time three or four hundred years. Not too far along, on the left-hand side of the lane was a gate and a path leading to the village church.

It was there at the old wooden gate in the ancient stone wall that he found Aynslee hard at work.

She looked somehow different to him; it wasn't the kerchief tying her hair back, or the old worn clothes or the gloves or the high top leather boots. There was something about her now alive and approachable and altogether exhilarating. He felt a swift tug behind his heart and realized he had never before experienced that sensation in quite the same way around any of the girls he'd known.

The ancient stone wall where she worked was almost completely covered with grass, dirt, ivy, weeds and thorny brambles. Aynslee was wielding a small, curved sickle against the overgrowth and saw him coming up the path when she paused to catch her breath.

"I wasn't sure you would come," Aynslee said, smiling at him and wiping her arm across her forehead. A smudge of dirt adorned her cheek.

"Oh ye of little faith, even here on the grounds of the village church. I told you I would."

"I've learned not to take as gospel anything that a fighter pilot says."

"I'm not just any fighter pilot."

"So you've told me. Grab a hoe or a shovel and make yourself useful. Help me to unearth what I think is a treasure beneath all of this overgrowth. I used to ride my bicycle through this little village when I was a girl, and I remember how pretty the church and its stone wall were at one time. I decided to do a small bit of community service to restore what's left of it so people could enjoy this place as much as I once did. The war has been hard on these people and they can't do it themselves. Are you up for a little hard work, Yank?"

They labored diligently for the next three hours with few rest breaks – the brambles and ivy clung tenaciously to the stones, and the wild clumps of grass held tight to all the nooks and crannies; the dirt was wet and heavy. It was well past noon when the job was finally done. By then a small crowd of elderly villagers had gathered to admire the resurrection of the old wall and to thank them for restoring a thing of beauty from its once-shameful state. As he stood back and looked at it, Mitch could understand their pleasure and the comments about how it shone in the afternoon sun like some newly polished gem.

"I think we accomplished something worthwhile," Aynslee said as she placed the wicker basket on the blanket he had spread out beneath a large shade tree on the grounds of the church. "I doubt they could have done it themselves. All the young men are off fighting the war and the older men struggle just to keep the grounds cut back and cleaned up. It made me feel good to see the pride in their eyes at the restoring of another comely part of their much loved village."

"I have to admit it was a morning well spent. Thanks for letting me be part of it."

"Well spent you say?" she replied, unfolding a small white cloth and placing plates and small cups on it. "How so? You've soiled your nice clothes and your hands are blistered."

"Not so much. It felt good to do something constructive rather than destructive for a change." He looked at her out of the corner of his eye and gave a slight smile. "It's also the first time I've tried to do something nice for you that hasn't caused an argument between us."

Her head came up quickly, and she turned in his direction giving him a stern look of disapproval before softening and glancing away. "I suppose you think I deserved that," she said, with an edge in her voice.

"No, I don't. That wasn't directed at you – it was aimed at me. I seem to have this ability to make people angry even when I'm trying to be kind to them. With a little luck maybe I'm beginning to get past that with you – hope so anyhow."

"Honestly, you weren't totally at fault, if that's any consolation."

"Tell me, why did you write that –"

"I packed only two small sandwiches," she interrupted quickly, sounding nervous. "I hope that's enough. But there is also a block of cheese and a box of crackers, plus a bottle of wine from father's locker."

They lingered over lunch and small talk about the village and the history of the little church with its immaculate grounds and cemetery. He realized this was the first time they had ever had a real conversation, and he enjoyed her company. She was as opinionated as Erika, and strong-willed like his mother. In the middle of one of her diatribes, he smiled at the realization and she called him to task on it.

"Making sport of me, Mr. Nolan?"

"I was just thinking how much you're like the important women in my life, that's all."

"How does one take such a comment?" she demanded.

"She takes it well, I hope," he replied in a restrained tone. Taking a deep breath he continued, "Aynslee, I don't know how to say this any other way, but I thought about you a lot these past two months. I shouldn't have but I did. You're special. And now I'm afraid I'll never see you again. I don't have a lot of time. You see, I can't fly in Europe anymore because of the Air Corps rules – once a pilot gets shot down and escapes with the help of the French Underground he can't go back on flying status. It means they'll soon be shipping me back home or out to the Pacific."

"Why can't you continue to fly?"

"They're afraid if one of us got shot down and captured by the Germans or the Vichy, we might compromise the French underground. And a cross-channel invasion is a lot more important than the disposition of a single pilot. I'm going to milk it for as long as I can, but that won't last but a couple weeks at the most." After an uncomfortably long silence he continued carefully. "I know about your loss and I'm sorry."

"You needn't be. Malcolm was a gentleman and a scoundrel," she replied stiffly, lifting her head and jutting out her jaw.

"That seems contradictory."

"Only to you. You Americans have so bastardized the language it's nearly impossible to communicate with you at all. Malcolm was a gentleman solely because he was born to a title and land. By accident of birth he was noble – a gentleman. By actuality of behavior he was a dishonorable scoundrel." She paused and said, "I shouldn't talk of Cateline's father that way."

Mitch remained silent when she had spent herself on the outburst. His father had told him about Malcolm Glendenbrook's death and her mother had intimated the marriage had been less than happy. But he had no idea what to say or feel about her revelation.

Turning quickly and glancing at him Aynslee said, "I'm not much inclined these days to put any faith in the smooth talk of pilots."

"I'm not your average pilot."

"Nor was Malcolm."

"I'm not Malcolm."

"How can I be sure?" she asked tentatively as she cocked her head and looked at him.

"I rode a bicycle five miles and worked for hours clearing away the dirt and weeds from an ancient stone fence – something that was important to you. I've got the callouses and sore muscles to prove it."

"And you think that's enough to convince me?"

"I think it's a start."

"You hope."

"Yes, I do."

Aynslee looked away from him again and hugged her knees close to her chest, rocking slowly as she looked beyond the old church toward undulating fields where a herd of Jacob sheep grazed. "They're ugly things, aren't they?... Those speckled sheep. Speckled is interesting, I guess, but I prefer the more uniform color – the white sheep. Sheep are supposed to be wooly white, aren't they?"

Mitch was puzzled. Why had she jumped so unexpectedly to the subject of sheep? It was almost impossible for him to figure out which direction her mind would go next. "I guess they're supposed to be white," he finally replied.

"When I married Malcolm I expected he was pure and wooly white, but he wasn't. It turned out he was all speckled. I think he may have loved me, but he also loved other women I came to find out. In fact, I learned of it the very evening of the day I met you. Coincidence? Perhaps. When I returned home the next morning and discovered you riding the horse he'd given me, I lost my composure. I wasn't happy with myself for it, and your cheeky manner with me didn't help."

"I didn't know I was being... *cheeky* did you say?" he asked offhandedly, sounding surprised to lighten the moment.

"It's the way you're being now," she shot back at him. "And like the time you took Cateline for a ride in the MG I'd consigned to the back of the stable."

"I was very careful to ask your father's permission."

"Of course you did. But you ignored me when I tried to wave you down and stop you and that other bloke from driving away with my child."

"Just trying to avoid an ugly scene in front of your daughter," he replied, looking into her eyes. "Do you realize we're actually talking to one another for the first time?"

She started to speak but abruptly stopped and gave him a startled look. "Perhaps we are." She cut another piece of cheese and took a sip of the wine. "Who are these other women and why do I remind you of them?"

"You have to understand this is just a first impression – I could be way off."

"For a fighter pilot, you're not very sure of yourself, are you?"

"Only around assertive, pretty women. My sister and mother for starters."

"Should I take that as a compliment?"

"It's the way I meant it. And it's not that I lack confidence. I just don't want to knock that chip off your shoulder again."

"One of your colonial metaphors, I gather," Aynslee said, tossing her head to remove a stray lock of hair from in front of her eyes.

"It means –"

"I know what it means. It's a saying your father uses from time to time, among others."

"I'm glad you told me – so I won't have to translate." He leaned toward her and grew serious, pulling from his pocket the handwritten note she had given him a year earlier. "But you're going to have to translate for me. I've carried this on me since the day you had that sergeant deliver it to me."

She took the card, read it again and looked away. "I was horrid with you that day."

"We both said things we shouldn't have, and it was my fault. I wanted it to happen; I wanted to provoke you – why, I don't know. When I saw you stop at the side of the road and try to wave us down, I knew you'd be angry when we roared past. And you had a right to be."

"I can be very ugly when angry."

"Actually, that's not true. I think you're beautiful when you're angry. Maybe that's why I provoked you with the MG the way I did. The first time we clashed I found you incredibly attractive. Maybe I just wanted to see you like that again and kept poking at you until I got what I was looking for." He stopped and caught his breath, amazed at how much he wanted to know and be with her. "I know you captivated me the very first time I saw you. I felt that same overwhelming attraction every time I thought of you over the years since then – even though I knew I shouldn't. I've never felt like that about any other woman."

Aynslee didn't reply. She looked away across the lawn and past to the church, staring at rolling hills beyond the small village. "I don't know exactly how to respond to you, Mitch. My heart has hardened because of what Malcolm did to it. I don't want it broken again."

He reached across and touched her face. "I promise I'd never do that to you."

"I wish I could believe you."

"My word of honor on it."

"I wonder, after all I've seen in this war, if such a thing as honor even exists any more."

He saw the cautious sadness in her eyes when she glanced at him and quickly averted her eyes and thrust out her chin as if steeling herself.

"I'll make my goal in life to love you and make sure your heart is never again broken. In spite of tension between us, I sense you have feelings for me also. Even that day when you scolded me for exercising your stallion, I was sure there was a spark of... affection toward me. I know I felt that for you."

She would not meet his gaze or respond to his words. He found it impossible to fathom what was going through her mind, but he would not let her walk away again without knowing. This was perhaps his last chance. He had to bring her to a decision – the right decision. "What now, Aynslee? Please, talk to me. Where do we go from here?"

"I don't know. I really don't know." She turned her pretty face and gave him a brooding smile. "I'm really glad you came by and spent last night at the house and the morning here with me. I did want to apologize the day I gave you that note, and now I have. It seems we're perhaps back to square one – like the moment just before you knocked on our door the first time. Perhaps it's best we simply leave it at that. No harm and no acrimony."

"I don't want to leave it there, Aynslee."

"You seem to think there's something more than that. Is there any place for us to go, you and I? I'm not sure there is. And in all honesty, I'm really not sure I want there to be anything else between us. You should go your way and I'll go mine."

"You want me to leave and never bother you again?"

"I want you to get on with your life and let me get on with mine. You seem a nice enough chap but in normal times we would never have even met. I don't dislike you, but I can't say I feel anything for you either." She saw the disappointment in his eyes and regretted she'd said it so tactlessly – especially since she didn't mean it. *He is trying, isn't he? And now he looks so terribly distressed and undone.* She felt sorry for him.

"Perhaps I'm seeking what is normal," she continued. "Nothing in my life these past few years, including you, has been what one would call normal. I simply want to put the past behind and get on with the rest of my life."

Abruptly she stood, and began gathering up the cups and the wrapping paper from the sandwiches, stowing it all in the small wicker basket. He took the hint and folded the blanket, handing it to her. She walked quickly away, down the gentle verdant slope – away from him and the small church.

Watching her, he felt beaten and saddened beyond explanation.

Chapter 40

It seemed all of England was moving south toward the Channel, and had been for days.

All except Mitch Nolan who was driving his jeep counter to the flow along back roads headed toward the American airfield at Cottesmore, a village in the north of the county of Rutland in the East Midlands. It was Mitch's second visit to the tiny town situated twenty miles south of the famous little township of Nottingham to see his brother. Day had already given way to evening twilight as Mitch pulled to a stop at the airfield gate.

It was June 5 and Mitch knew, although he probably shouldn't have, that this was Glenn's last day in England. His father had told him this was it – the invasion – and had sent him on ahead to spend a few hours with Glenn before he boarded the C-47 and took off for France. Mitch also knew more than the average traveler that night about what his brother and the other American paratroopers faced.

Glenn had been posted to company G of the 3rd Battalion in the 505th Parachute Infantry Regiment. It was the most battle-tested regiment in the 82nd, and the only one with combat experience in both Sicily and Salerno, Italy. General Ridgeway had assigned the most critical objective behind Utah Beach to the 505th PIR – to capture and hold the town of Sainte-Mère-Église, sitting on the key crossroads and chokepoint in the road network for enemy forces counterattacking landing beach Utah. Mitch glanced at his watch and guessed that at this moment his little brother was hearing about his mission for the first time.

The young guard at the gate looked at his pass and the orders accompanying it and asked, "Colonel, is that really General Eisenhower's signature?"

"It is."

"You mind if I keep those orders, sir?"

"I do, private. Those orders along with the pass that goes with them get me into and out of a lot of places I need to go. I know you'd like to have the souvenir, but I need to have the access. Sorry."

The guard reluctantly waved him through, and Mitch navigated around the road bordering the airfield inside the barbed wire barrier. C-47s with black and white invasion stripes painted on their wings sat on the main runway, the taxiways and the various ramps clustered around the airfield. He asked an infantry captain for the location of G company and found it several minutes later. Mitch parked the jeep and entered through the main hangar door. An officer was standing on a raised platform in the back of the hangar speaking to hundreds of men sitting on the floor facing him.

"This flag," the lieutenant colonel was saying, pointing to a large Stars and Stripes held by two sergeants, "was the first American flag to fly over Gela, Sicily and the city of Naples. Tomorrow morning, I'll be sitting in the mayor's office in Sainte-Mère-Église, and this flag will be flying over it. I will see you men on the ground there in a few hours." The officer saluted his men and left.

Mitch climbed on a wooden crate next to the wall and scanned the crowd of soldiers exiting the hangar, trying to locate his brother. They saw each other at the same moment and Glenn worked his way through the crowd to him.

"Coming with us?" Glenn asked as they met just outside the hangar.

"Gonna pass this time, little brother. One jump in a lifetime is plenty enough for me. Ask dad about that."

He's coming, isn't he?"

"Two or three hours behind me. He'll be here long before you take-off. How you doing?"

"Good. Real good. No jitters, just raring to go and get this over with."

"Liar."

"Yeah. It's, uh… kinda scary. Wish we could leave right now. Don't enjoy sitting around thinking about it. I don't mind the jumping – actually that's a thrill. It's not knowing what's waiting on the ground. A lot of these guys have two combat jumps behind them, but I can tell they're nervous too, a little." They walked out to the nine Gooney birds lined up on the runway in 'V of threes'. Once there, Glenn placed his rifle on a pile of gear and sat down next to it.

"Is that all yours?" Mitch asked, surprised.

"All hundred and five pounds of it. That includes the parachute."

"And another twenty pounds of stuff in all those cargo pockets in your fatigues?"

"A man's gotta eat and shoot for a good three days once we get there."

Mitch shook his head. His brother couldn't be more than a hundred and thirty pounds and would be carrying something approximating another man on his back, at least for awhile. "It was probably a good idea you shaved all your hair off so you didn't have to carry that, too."

"Not all of it. Still got this nice little Mohawk brush down the middle."

"Your mother would not approve of that as a fashion statement."

"She didn't approve of any of it."

"That's because you're not old enough."

"I will be in five days. You forgot my birthday again, didn't you?"

"I might just surprise you," Mitch said, reaching into the side pocket of his flight jacket and pulling out a photograph. "Here you go, little brother. Happy birthday. Hope it's not too heavy to carry."

Glenn looked at it and broke out in laughter, loud enough that others nearby looked at him. One of them ambled over and sat down. He introduced himself as Earl Wright and asked what all the noise was about.

"My big brother here gave me this for my birthday," Glenn said, handing the picture over. He then reached into his helmet and pulled out a photograph and showed it to him. "A picture I took on my own camera. I gave a framed copy of this to my mother last Christmas. Mitch you keep it. I already have one."

Mitch looked at the pictures side by side and shook his head. "Always liked that picture."

"That's a heck of big fish you boys are holding," Wright said.

"Only for a little while – not more than five seconds after that old man snapped the picture, my goofy little brother threw my fish back. That was the biggest fish ever caught in Long Island Sound and the biggest one I ever caught in my whole life – and I've fished a lot."

"Not exactly," Glenn corrected him. "It was the second biggest striped bass ever caught there. The old man who took the picture still holds the record."

"I should have thrown *you* back in with it."

"Oh, I'd like to have seen that," Wright said. When he laughed it came out as a cackle. "You know that Glenn here is the regiment's lightweight boxing champ, don't you? He whipped the middleweight champ in a fight out behind the barracks when he first got here. I'd think twice if I was you."

Mitch could tell the banter was taking Glenn's mind off the mission ahead and he was glad he'd come to the airfield to see him off. They reminisced for a while about the day they spent together fishing the Sound, recorded now on film. It reminded them both of the times at Lewis and McKinley when they'd fished together. There had been a lot of good fishing in the islands along the beaches and in the mountain streams. It was nice to relive so many of the great old memories.

Glenn filled him in on Erika and this lawyer she'd been dating, observing that he wasn't a bad guy, all things considered. But Ashby let their sister lead him around by the nose and play him like a big fish on a light leader. Still, the lawyer had friends in Annapolis who gave him the use their sailboat for sleeping over on weekends plus the use of a runabout to fish and crab the river and inlets. Glenn proudly told his brother that he'd learned where and how to harvest enough seafood to sell some to local restaurants in Annapolis .

"One of these days this war is going to be over," Glenn observed wistfully at one point. "When it is, I'm going back to what I really love to do. I'm going to be a hunting and fishing guide on the Chesapeake."

Mitch recounted for his brother his many trials and tribulations with Aynslee Glendenbrook over the past four years.

"*You're* having trouble with a girl?! I've got to meet this gal!" Glenn responded enthusiastically. "This I've got to see. Maybe you and Randall B. Ashby have a lot in common." He laughed out loud again, attracting Earl Wright's attention.

"You fellas hold it down over there. Some of us are trying to get some sleep."

Mitch looked at his watch and realized it was almost approaching midnight.

A little while later there was movement around the first three aircraft on the runway. Men were donning parachutes and hanging bags of equipment off their harnesses. Shortly they were being helped aboard three C-47s that had cranked and now finished their pre-takeoff runups. Minutes later they were rolling down the runway one by one and lifting off into the darkness. Five minutes later, complete silence returned.

"Pathfinders," Glenn said. "They jump in ninety minutes before the main body to set up the drop zones and guide the rest of us in."

"It looked like two or three dozen guys," Mitch observed. "That's all? By themselves for a couple of hours? That's crazy."

"I volunteered for Pathfinders but they wouldn't take anybody without a combat jump."

"And you're crazy, too. Man, you are not the same kid I grew up with."

"Maybe I'm just trying to prove I'm not so different from rest of my family. I'm really not adopted like that Monk Moose guy out at Lewis said I was."

"That was Moose Mayer," a voice in the darkness said. "He was a classmate of mine – and he didn't say you were adopted. He thought we bought you from the gypsies."

"Dad! You made it."

"Told you I would. I'd have been here sooner but these back country roads can be pretty darn confusing at night. And I've got a new driver. Did you mail a letter to your mother?"

"I did."

"Got on clean underwear, clean socks and a fresh hankie?"

"What?"

"Trying to think of all the things your mother would ask if she were here," Dave explained to his youngest son. "Did you brush your teeth, wash behind your ears. Did you pack a .45 with two extra magazines and three boxes of cartridges?"

Glenn chuckled under his breath. "I don't think she would have asked that."

"Yeah, but I'm not her. Do you have a sidearm?"

"I wasn't issued a pistol, no."

"Then here, take mine – careful, it's got a round in the chamber. Here's two full mags and four extra boxes of shells. I always carried at least one pistol and that much ammo when going into an attack. You should, too. Don't ever forget that."

"I'll for sure remember next time."

"You probably need this shoulder harness, too. It lets the pistol ride real nice along your side under the armpit. Easy to get to, also. Tell me how you're doing right now."

"I'm ready. Got all my equipment; everything's in tip top shape. I'm a little scared."

"Good. You're about to jump into the belly of the whale, and that's dangerous, so you're smart to be a little scared. Anybody who says he's not is a liar. Stay away from people like that. Don't trust them. I wouldn't let anybody in my boat who wasn't at least a little bit afraid of the whale."

"I know what you mean. Thanks."

"You'll be there in France for a month or so probably. Then you'll be brought back to England for rest and refitting. Nobody's crystal ball is worth a crap now that we're actually going ahead. If I'm right, you'll be coming back about the time I'll be going over. You know how to contact my headquarters outside London. If I'm gone, you might want to go see Henry Smythe-Browne and his wife. They're old friends and would love to have you stay with them."

"I'll keep that in mind."

"I'd suggest you conceal the fact you're related to Mitch if you meet their daughter, Aynslee. Somehow, he managed to pretty much pollute the water for all us Nolans with her."

"I wouldn't say I've polluted the water," Mitch countered sarcastically.

"That's the best metaphor I've got, son. Whatever you've done, you need to fix it."

"I'm working on it," Mitch said.

"Work harder."

"You know, I think I really am adopted," Glenn offered and laughed again. And for the next hour he almost forgot what lay ahead.

It was after midnight when the platoon leader came by and called the roster of the 18 man 'stick' assigned to Glenn's aircraft; his was the next to last called name called. He donned all his equipment and sat down on the runway leaning against the parachute attached to his back and waited until the jumpmaster called their names. One by one each soldier was helped to his feet and waddled slowly to the wide back door of the C-47 to be helped up the ladder and disappeared inside.

When Glenn's name was called, Mitch leaned over and held out his hand and then helped his brother up onto his feet.

Mitch hugged his brother and said, "Godspeed, Glenn. We'll all be praying for you."

"Keep your head down and your eye on the front bead, son," Dave added.

Glenn said nothing as he walked in an ungainly shuffle toward the plane's ladder. With the help of someone already onboard and a ground crewman, he finally got up the ladder and disappeared into the darkness inside. Pretty soon all the planes on the field were cranking; Dave and Mitch walked back to the hangar and watched silently as the multiple dozens of Gooney Birds cranked their engines and pilots lined up for takeoff into the dark night sky.

Mitch noticed the sheet of paper in his father's hand. "What's that?" he yelled to be heard over the loud engine noise.

"Ike's letter to the troops. Every person heading toward France is getting a copy of it and is probably reading it right now. Here, you want it?"

Mitch took the sheet and stepped back into the light of the hangar so he could read.

Supreme Headquarters Allied Expeditionary Force

Soldiers, Sailors and Airmen of the Allied Expeditionary Force!

You are about to embark upon the Great Crusade, toward which we have striven these many months. The eyes of the world are upon you. The hopes and prayers of liberty loving people everywhere march with you. In company with our brave Allies and brothers-in-arms on other Fronts, you will bring about the destruction of the German war machine, the elimination of Nazi tyranny over the oppressed peoples of Europe, and security for ourselves in a free world.

Your task will not be an easy one. Your enemy is well trained, well equipped and battle- hardened. He will fight savagely.

But this is the year 1944! Much has happened since the Nazi triumphs of 1940-41. The United Nations have inflicted upon the Germans great defeats, in open battle, man-to-man. Our air offensive has seriously reduced their strength in the air and their capacity to wage war on the ground. Our home fronts have given us an overwhelming superiority in weapons and munitions of war, and placed at our disposal great reserves of trained fighting men. The tide has turned! The freemen of the world are marching together to victory!

I have full confidence in your courage, devotion to duty and skill in battle. We will not accept less than full victory!

Good luck! And let us beseech the blessing of Almighty God upon this great and noble undertaking.

Dwight D. Eisenhower

"Quite a letter," Mitch observed when he was done reading.

"Six hours ago, Eisenhower was the most powerful man in Europe. Right now he's the most impotent man in the war," Dave told his son. "Since the instant he gave the 'go-ahead' there wasn't a thing he can do. Everything... *everything* rests on the shoulders of privates in landing craft and paratroopers like your brother sitting inside that cramped airplane."

*   *   *

Everybody was nervous and quiet – even the veterans of Sicily and Salerno.

Sitting quietly across from the big door, alone with his own thoughts, Glenn saw hundreds and hundreds of people lined up three or four deep along the sides of the runway. British Army girls, bakers, cooks, Air Corps ground personnel, British soldiers, RAF personnel, US Army troops – no one moved. They simply stared at the planes, offering a silent, overpowering salute, and perhaps a blessing or a prayer. Glenn could feel it – he knew he could. The sound of the engines increased and the jumpmaster closed the cargo door; soon the pilot released the brakes and the plane surged forward.

His breath caught in his throat as he felt the rear of the plane lift slightly as it gathered speed. An eternity later, it seemed, the C-47 was airborne, headed south toward the Channel and beyond that the Atlantic Wall of fortified Normandy.

Some of the troopers in the plane had their eyes closed, while others silently stared straight ahead. Now and then someone would check his watch, tighten or loosen a strap. Stolp was sleeping with his chin resting on his chest, but most were wide-eyed and nervous. Dutch Schultz from New York City was engrossed in counting his beads and saying the Rosary. A few smoked nervously, some chewed vigorously on gum or a toothpick, but there was none of the horsing around so prevalent on their practice jumps – no conversations, no joking, just the constant loud hum of the engines. This was the real thing, and in the subdued red lighting of the cargo compartment that realization showed on every face.

Time wore on so slowly it appeared almost to have stopped. It seemed half his life had been spent in the tiny compartment wedged uncomfortably in between two equally overburdened jumpers.

Glenn checked his watch, a nervous gesture. They'd been in the air only fifteen minutes.

Earl Wright was reading a letter, and next to him his best friend, Kenny Cook read it too, over his shoulder. Wright and Cook had been in the same squad since showing up for parachute school at the Frying Pan area of Camp Benning in the middle of July 1942. Together, they had survived Jump School, the initial formation of the 505th Parachute Infantry Regiment, training in the boondocks of Alabama and North Africa, and two combat jumps. They had saved each other's lives more than once at Sicily's Biazzo Ridge when they had gotten separated from their company and played life or death cat and mouse in a grove of trees for a half hour with two German tanks. They were each other's 'good luck charm' and even during training were rarely separated by more than an arm's length.

The flight wore on.

The jumpmaster – a sergeant name Turnbull – wrestled the door open and the horrendous roar of slipstream and engine noise engulfed the paratroopers inside.

This was the signal – they had crossed the coast of Normandy.

Glenn could see out the door into the dark night. Wisps of clouds, sometimes thick, flew past the opening obscuring the ground as the sergeant leaned out looking for landmarks. He could see two other planes incredibly close, rising and falling as if bouncing on coiled springs. Suddenly the planes veered hard left and disappeared into the clouds; his own banked hard left, then righted, almost throwing him to the floor. *How did Turnbull stay in the plane with that going on?* he wondered. The sergeant never moved, except for his head swiveling, looking for landmarks and occasionally reaching inside to make sure his own static line was hooked.

The red light by the door illuminated and Turnbull moved back inside the plane.

"Stand up!" Turnbull shouted, raising his hands as if signaling touchdown. "Hook up!" Glenn struggled to his feet and hooked the ripcord snap onto the cable running down the middle of the compartment, yanking to make sure it was secure. "Check Equipment!... sound off for equipment check!" The routine for exiting an aircraft had been so ingrained in countless hundreds – or maybe thousands – of repetitions at Benning, he had no need to think. But this time he was concentrating on his every movement as if his life depended on it, knowing it did. Within seconds, the plane started a series of rapid direction changes throwing them against one another and the walls of the fuselage. Glenn could see tracers from the ground going by the open cargo door. The plane surged ahead, then dove, sending them reeling inside. Wright and Cook fell to the floor and were helped up, cussing loud enough to be heard over the engine noise. Now they could hear the explosions of flak nearby, close enough that metal shards rattled loudly against the airplane's skin. Turnbull moved to the door and leaned out again, appearing oblivious to the maelstrom of ground fire.

The C-47 continued juking and alternately diving and climbing. They had been standing up for what seemed like yet another eternity and Glenn felt himself growing tired from the weight of all the equipment. He wondered if he was the only one hoping – praying – the green light by the door would go on allowing him to get out of this wildly bucking airplane.

Abruptly the green light illuminated and Turnbull yelled: "GO! GO! GO!" and troopers began disappearing into the black, tracer-laced void outside the door.

Glenn followed Corporal Fulbrook out the door and felt the prop-blast tear at his arms and at his hands clasped tightly over the small reserve chute on his chest; he felt his jump boots slap together and his elbows tuck tight to his sides as he counted at the top of his voice,,,,, "One-one thousand, two one-thousand…" He forced himself to keep his eyes open and saw his feet below him – only they weren't below but had swung above his head, pointed at the C-47 now seeming to rise above them, drifting away amidst the white searchlight beams and red tracers. His chute opened with a terrible jolt and he heard himself grunt loudly; the plane had been going way too fast and he wondered if he'd torn chest muscles or dislocated a shoulder. His feet swung down through the horizon and he gazed at a boiling, bubbling cauldron of fire and light below as far as he could see.

A few hundred feet to his right a Gooney bird exploded and tumbled from the sky, wing over wing; he saw two others on fire nearby headed for the ground trailing fire and long plumes of smoke. He looked above and saw the canopy fully deployed over him; he reached up and grasped the risers. Looking around he saw the sky filled with parachutes and tiny toy soldier-like figures dangling beneath them. A spewing line of tracers arched up at him and he raised his feet in reflex although the red line seemed to curve away and then ran out. A C-47, with an engine on fire and disgorging jumpers flew beneath him. It looked like the troopers' chutes opened and then immediately collapsed; instantly he thought they must have jumped from only a hundred feet or less in the air. Off to his right front, he thought he could make out a town – Sainte-Mère-Église? Could it possibly be they'd been dropped as briefed? He remembered the complaints from the guys who'd jumped into Sicily and at Salerno about being dropped miles from their planned DZs. The noise around him grew to a horrific cacophony of machine gun, rifle and anti-aircraft artillery fire – he'd never felt so nakedly exposed.

Or as scared.

He saw chutes collapsing below him and realized he was only a hundred feet up, coming down quickly. His mind raced through the pre-landing list as he looked ahead into the absolute darkness and tried to relax his body. *Don't roll; no Jump School landing fall – Wright and the old hands say you'll break a leg with all this equipment strapped on.* Abruptly his feet hit and he fell onto his equipment. Quickly, he got up, collapsed his chute and checked for broken bones. Within a few minutes he had removed the parachute, donned his gear and in utter darkness started in the direction of the rally point with several others. Planes kept droning overhead, troopers were still coming down around him and the sound of guns intensified.

He had cracked Hitler's Atlantic Wall.

And he was still alive.

Chapter 41

The path ran alongside one of the tall hedgerows as they trudged along in darkness, staggering in the soft turf; the low hanging brush over their heads made it seem like a deep, murky tunnel leading nowhere.

Third Battalion had assembled surprisingly quickly in a flurry of shouts and whistles and flare pistol signals that scared Glenn as much as the exit from the C-47. With all the confusion and noise of battle on the ground and in the air, the Germans seemed not to notice. Soon the battalion, with almost three quarters of its soldiers accounted for, set out toward the nearby glow that marked the town of Sainte-Mère-Église. G Company was leading with Sergeant Snyder's platoon out front, and the junior enlisted man, Private Glenn Nolan, walking point.

They encountered a narrow road.

Glenn halted the company column and passed the signal back. Soon, Sergeant Snyder and the battalion commander, Lieutenant Colonel Krause, came forward. They surveyed the situation, sent a squad fifty yards south and another fifty yards north for flank security and were about to cross when an old French man on a bicycle peddled slowly toward them. Glenn walked into the middle of the road and stopped him. The man spoke little English but the battalion commander managed to learn he lived in the town and was fleeing the shooting and a large fire that had broken out in the town's square.

"Let him guide us into town," Krause told Sergeant Snyder. "Hold up as soon as we reach the outskirts and we'll deploy to take the town square and work our way from the inside to flush the Germans out and secure the village." With the old man guiding, Glenn moved slowly through the thick brush along the next hedgerow until they encountered the first of several small houses huddled on the west edge of the town. G Company deployed on line, swept through the cluster of houses and stopped in the shadows at the edge of the town square. A large fire was burning and the townsfolk were engaged in putting it out with a bucket brigade while the fully armed German garrison stood around watching, at the moment oblivious to the American presence fifty yards away.

The roar of engines overhead announced the arrival of another wave of paratroopers and the Germans in the square turned their guns upward and searched the skies. The anti-aircraft firing from inside the town started up again and Glenn watched, enraged as volumes of red and silver tracers ripped through the fuselages of many of the C-47s. Parachutes were floating down directly onto the town and the German garrison troops opened fire on them.

Immediately the soldiers in G Company opened fire on the gray-clad soldiers as the town's inhabitants ran for cover. Glenn took aim on the enemy soldier closest to him and fired, dropping him. The Germans were confused and in some disarray but continued to fire at the descending parachutes. A trooper whose chute had snagged in a tree got shot at point blank range; Glenn was furious and shot the German, and then three more who were firing at Americans descending beneath chutes. Several more troopers got caught on telephone poles or in trees and were shot as they hung there. A trooper came down directly on top of the church at the edge of the square, bounced on the steeply sloped metal roof before his chute draped over the steeple hanging him up on the side of the building in full view of the enemy. Another trooper landed in the square directly in front of the church, shot a German taking aim at the dangling American and was himself immediately shot and killed.

The fire at the far end of the open area continued to rage and Glenn saw a trooper descending and pulled into the center of the flames; he was immediately consumed. A group of three Germans set up a machine gun behind a tree forty yards away and started firing with deadly effect into the sky at descending Americans. The scene in the village square grew more and more macabre as the confusion of battle swelled, backlit by the huge bonfire, casting shadows and framing an eerily lit tableau of men dying by the score.

"Nolan! Wright! Cook!" Sergeant Snyder yelled over the noise. "Get that machine gun!"

Wright and Cook looked at one another and then at Glenn. "What the hell does he think we can do?" Cook asked, looking at the forty yards of open space between them and the gun.

"You guys move left and see if you can get a clear shot," Glenn said over the noise. "I'll work to the right, behind them. Take them under fire and if they move back to cover, I'll have a shot from over there," he said, pointing to a tree. "I'll try to get them to move toward you and you try to get them to move their position toward me. One of us should get a shot. We got to stop them. They're killing our guys like fish in a barrel."

Before Wright or Cook replied, Nolan got up and ran twenty yards and flopped down behind cover and immediately took the machine gun under fire. He could see only one of the Germans manning the gun, but sighted down his rifle, calmed his breathing and fired. The soldier toppled over. His self-congratulations lasted a split second before the machine gun turned and chewed up the ground around him. He low-crawled away as rounds whistled over his head until he found another location, stopped, and took another shot which took out the gunner; as the loader got to his feet to run, Glenn shot him in the chest, toppling him backward. When he finally got back to his original position, Wright just looked at him and shook his head.

The Germans quickly retreated from G Company's fusillade; the Americans finally pushed them south and eventually completely out of the town a half hour later. It was wild and confusing in the dark as German vehicles roared through the town and enemy soldiers suddenly appeared from doorways and behind corners, sometimes as near as arm's length.

Glenn was walking stealthily through a yard behind a small house when he ran into a man, scaring him beyond simple fear – quickly he realized it was a paratrooper hanging by his risers from a tree, swaying, his head slumped against his chest and arms dangling loosely at his side. Glenn felt crushed by the sight, but pushed on. Not far away the platoon came across Germans hurriedly climbing on board a truck. They took the escaping enemy under fire and drove them off in a hail of bullets. Sergeant Snyder stopped the platoon at the southern outskirts of Sainte-Mère-Église and had them take up positions on either side of the N-13 road leading southeast out of town toward Les Forges. The first gliders swooped low over their position as they dug foxholes.

It was 4:00 a.m.

"Where'd you learn to shoot like that, Nolan?" Earl Wright wanted to know as they worked in the dark alongside Kenny Cook to improve their position blocking the road.

"My father… and practice – lots of practice."

"You be more careful," Wright said. "Snyder says I'm responsible for you."

Nolan shrugged and went back to digging, worried that the mines they'd thrown on the road in front of them wouldn't be enough to stop a serious German armor counter attack. The glider arrivals had stopped a while ago and it worried him that none of the promised anti-tank guns had found their way to company G yet. He hoped at least some of them had survived. Thinking back to the training exercises in England and the routine crashes and deaths involved, he didn't hold out a lot of hope for those poor suckers flying them, or the vital cargo inside. He wondered if Snyder or the company commander had thought about sending out a recon team to locate bundles mis-dropped by the Air Corps that might have ammo for the lone bazooka they had in their position.

A few minutes after 5:00 a.m. a German foot patrol came down the causeway and got within twenty yards before the platoon opened fire and swept them off the road. A half hour later another patrol probed their position, this time with reinforcements and a machine gun. The firefight lasted until almost 6:00 a.m. before the enemy retreated. Snyder moved another machine gun next to their hole and sighted it down the road, then sent Glenn along with Marx from third squad back to the first sergeant to pick up ammo resupply. The first sergeant added two men from first platoon and a sergeant to head the detail, sending them to battalion supply located in town center.

The eastern sky was beginning to grow lighter.

Inside the town, German bodies still littered the square and dead paratroopers suspended by their parachutes from telephone poles and the higher trees still hung there as if crucified. It caused his stomach to turn and angry bile to rise up into his throat. Dawn was breaking as the detail trudged by the town hall and Nolan stopped to gaze around at the mindboggling carnage.

"You, soldier!" an authoritative voice called to him. He turned around and saw the battalion commander coming out of the building and motioning him over. "Give me a hand with this." Lieutenant Colonel Krause handed him an old, worn *Stars and Stripes* to hold while he untied the knot of the flagpole's lanyard and lowered the red flag with the Nazi swastika. He unclipped and dropped to the German standard to the ground. He then attached the American flag and raised it over the town of Sainte-Mère-Église. "First flag to fly over the first town liberated on the continent. I told you last night that's what I'd be doing this morning, didn't I?"

"Yes, sir. I remember."

"Something to tell your grandchildren about some day." Krause picked up the Nazi flag, folded it and stuck it under his arm. "What outfit are you in?"

"Company G, sir. Sergeant Snyder's platoon until our lieutenant shows up."

"Then you were among the first soldiers to enter the town."

"Yes, sir. The point man."

Krause's eyebrows went up. "Really. Then you weren't just *among* the first – you were *the* first American here. Tell you what – you take this Nazi flag as a souvenir. The first flag captured by the first soldier into the first town liberated. You really will have something to tell grandkids! What's your name, soldier?"

"Nolan, sir. Private Glenn Nolan."

Krause stuck out his hand. "I'm proud to meet an honest to goodness real live hero, Private Nolan. I'm going to remember this. Hope you will, too. Too bad we're not Marines – we'd have us a dozen photographers around to capture the moment."

Glenn had no idea how to respond and so remained silent. Krause quickly turned and went inside the town hall as Nolan looked around for the ammo detail. Sergeant Gagne probably wouldn't be happy with his lagging behind, and probably wouldn't believe it was the fault of the battalion commander, either. He jogged off in the direction the others had gone and soon caught up with them.

By the time he got back to his position forty-five minutes later, a 57mm anti-tank gun had shown up and was aimed down the road.

"Souvenir?!" Wright exclaimed, taking the flag out of Glenn's hands and unfolding it. "The Nazi flag that flew over this little burg? This ain't right. I got three combat jumps, fought in Sicily, Salerno and now France and the battalion commander gives this little snot-nosed cherry jumper a souvenir like this? That ain't right at all, I'm telling you."

"He's not a cherry jumper any more, Earl," Cook said casually. "Not after last night."

Wright said nothing but glared at the new kid and tossed the flag back at him. Their attention was drawn to the sound of a ferocious fight going on behind them on the north side of the town. German artillery and tanks were working over 2nd Battalion dug in blocking the N-13 highway on the opposite side of Sainte-Mère-Église. It sounded bad even from a mile away.

"They hit us like that down here and we're in big trouble," Cook observed. "We don't have a decent field of fire past two hundred yards for that AT gun."

"That means they don't either," Wright countered. "How long do you think it would take a tank or one of those tank destroyers to move two hundred yards?"

"Twenty seconds at their top speed," Glenn responded. "But we wouldn't have that much time if it was a tank destroyer."

Wright frowned at him. "And you know this how, Nolan?"

"Their armor moves at twenty miles per hour. That means they move about thirty feet a second. Two hundred yards is six hundred feet – that's twenty seconds to cover from that bend to us. Our AT gun would get one shot; two if they're really good, and lucky. We need an outpost around that bend out there to give us more warning and maybe a second shot with the 57mm." Glenn thought about it some more, and then moved to get up from their hole.

"Where you goin', cherry?" Earl Wright asked.

"Talk to Sergeant Snyder. To tell him about our situation. We're not in the right place to hold off a tank attack coming down this road. We have to move up to the bend or back toward town. Right now we're betwixt and halfway between."

"You're going to tell the platoon sergeant and the CO they don't know what they're doing? That's not goin' to make you a lot of friends. Best you sit down and do what you're told. Hell, you got less time in combat than anybody in the whole company."

"I'm going to tell them what it looks like from up here – to me, anyhow." Wright frowned, and Cook shrugged non-committedly.

"You're funeral. Me, I'm going to get some sleep while the getting's good. It's been over twenty-four hours since I last slept and I'm just about wore out." Wright closed his eyes and was soon snoring.

Glenn found his way back to the platoon CP and informed Sergeant Snyder of what he'd observed in front of their position. Together, they went back to the company CP and told the commander, who thought about it for a while. "You might be right, but I can't spare anyone to go on patrol right now. We're at less than half strength and everybody needs some rest."

"I could take a look," Glenn said reluctantly, torn between his gut instinct about their company's situation and his own dilemma. He was certain they had dug in at the wrong spot in the dark not knowing the lay of the land, and that was dangerous for the whole company – maybe the battalion. But he didn't want to risk his life needlessly, or at all, in the process. "It wouldn't take long and I don't think the Germans are that close right now, after we pushed them out of town and beat back their initial probes."

"All right, private," the captain said. "I'll let you do this, just once. You be careful."

Farm fields, orchards, pasturage bound by field stone and earthen embankments taller than a man dotted the land around Sainte-Mère-Église. It was a maze of natural fortifications. Tank movement, except on the road network, would be essentially impossible. These were the hedgerows of Normandy, bordered by sunken cow lanes worn bare over the centuries. He soon realized the enemy could be a few short feet away and he would never know it. It brought out a distinct wariness in his movement, like the times he'd hunted elk in the Canadian Rockies. Infantry could cross this cut up landscape only at great peril. The checkerboard layout of the land would force combatants into close proximity and ambushes at close killing range. This would really get ugly.

Why hadn't this been briefed? he wondered as he stalked along the edges of hedgerows.

He moved as stealthily as he could. Before he knew it he had gone well past the initial bend in the road he'd been sent to reconnoiter, up sunken lanes, across an orchard and through the hedgerows and ditches sprinkled with German units moving toward the town. Glenn carefully and quietly retraced his steps until he was at the corner of the road two hundred meters from his own line. The bend in the road was very slight and hidden from observation behind a small rise. From where he was now, the road toward Les Forges stretched in a long straight line for miles down a slight decline bordered by small rectangular farm fields. The anti-tank gun could cover more than a kilometer from here.

This they could defend.

As he lay in the tall grass thinking about how to describe this position, he saw a column of German tanks led by a half-dozen tank destroyers moving toward him. Their flank security was provided by German infantry in the fields and along the sides of the narrow two lane road. Scouts in gray uniforms preceded the column and he realized that before he could get back to his lines and warn the company commander, the German armor would be well into an attack against his company's current positions.

Without warning, a patrol of six Germans appeared in front of him, stepping out of the brush and onto the road only thirty yards away. Glenn aimed at the soldier giving an order to the others and pulled the trigger. Within seconds, he had fired off a complete eight round clip felling all but one of the patrol. The scene in front of him dissolved into chaos as soldiers on both flanks of the road went to ground and started firing wildly at the top of the small ridge where he lay. The tanks and tank destroyers swiveled their guns and fired at the ridgeline, their engines belching dark smoke as they maneuvered off the road into the surrounding fields.

Another patrol of scouts off to his right were firing at him with long bursts from Schmeisser sub-machine pistols. Glenn shot at a gray-uniformed soldier and the firing stopped. He turned his attention to the left and saw fleeting figures trying to outflank him and work toward his rear. He shot one who went down, then several seconds later another who fled through the trees and the partial concealment of some thick brush.

He was working his way slowly back toward the company positions, firing and moving and hoping his own company wouldn't shoot him as he did. Mortars from somewhere near town center in Sainte-Mère-Église were firing now not far from the top of the ridge providing covering fire as he retreated down the road toward G Company.

Suddenly, he was being pulled into the foxhole by Wright and Cook. He was soaked in sweat and breathing heavily as if he'd run a marathon. The ant-tank gun fired a round, making his ears ring; when he looked up, the first German tank destroyer emerged from the midst of a cloud of white smoke and rolled ominously toward them. German infantry hugged the sides of the road and came on firing continuously. The 57mm barked again and the leading German armored vehicle erupted in flame, exploding one of the American M1 mines on the road. The metal monster lurched to the side and then augured into the ditch a hundred yards from the G Company lines. A second German vehicle appeared and shot a round at the American AT gun. German machine guns raked the 57mm, killing the three-man crew.

"Cover me!" Glenn yelled at Wright and Cook as he leapt from the foxhole and ran across the road to the gun.

He'd never fired a big bore piece like this before, but he'd watched them on the range back in England and thought he could make it work. Not knowing what else to do, he opened the breech and sighted through the the barrel at the German tank as it worked its way around the debris of the first armored vehicle which still burned furiously a hundred yards away. He loaded a round into the breech mechanism and slammed it closed. Glenn pulled the lanyard and his heart sank as the round exploded ten yards in front of the tank. He nervously loaded another round, waited until the tank came closer and pulled the lanyard again.

This time the round pierced the front armor of the mobile German gun and exploded with a roar of detonation and a shock wave that knocked down the gray clad infantry nearby. A blue-yellow flame rocketed upward. A round from another German tank exploded in front of the American gun, lifting it a foot into the air and ripping off some of its armor plate.

G Company rifle fire and machine gun bursts chased the German soldiers back up the incline and left many of them strewn along the road and in the ditches alongside.

Glenn found himself on the ground, barely able to hear but alert enough to know they had stopped this first counterattack from the south. He rolled over on his stomach and vomited before passing out.

Their position was on top of the rise in the hole he'd help Wright and Cook dig. It wasn't much of a position, but it was better than what they'd had to fight from two hours earlier. German artillery and mortars had been shelling Sainte-Mère-Église for the last three hours after G Company had stopped their mid-morning attempt to retake the town from the south.

Battalion had sent another anti-tank gun – one of five that had made it through to the 505th in the first six hours. Colonel Krause had checked the line after the first attack to encourage and thank the company. Glenn had fallen asleep after the colonel's visit, totally exhausted. He was beginning to learn the truth about taking advantage of every opportunity to catch a few minutes of sleep; he'd never been this exhausted in his whole life and it was just the first day of the invasion. It was becoming the longest day of his young life.

Wright shook him awake.

"Captain wants to see you, Nolan."

Glenn rubbed his eyes and stood up in his foxhole. Without thinking, he placed his steel pot on his head and looked up at the company commander standing over him. "Yes sir?!"

"I'm putting you in for an award, Nolan. Wanted you to know. Your early warning on the attack this morning and manning the AT gun might have saved us from having to give the town back to the Krauts. Colonel Krause thinks that's worth at least a Silver Star. Maybe a DSC. Thought you should know. Well done, soldier."

Glenn was still groggy and fought for his balance.

"Thank you, sir." he murmured and put out his hand against the side of the foxhole to steady himself."

"Ain't you glad Nolan's on our side instead of their's, captain?" Earl Wright cackled.

"Won't argue with that."

"Any idea how the landings are going, sir?" Glenn asked, rubbing his eyes again, still drowsy and hoping he could go back to sleep again when the company commander left.

"No word yet but –"

German machine gun rounds kicked up dirt all around them and 82nd troopers dropped to the ground not knowing the location from which the enemy fire had come. Minutes later, the firing stopped and company leaders checked for casualties.

"Come on Nolan, can't sleep while the CO is talking to you." Wright saw Nolan coiled in a fetal position at the bottom of the foxhole and shook him – gently at first, then more roughly when he didn't respond. He turned Glenn over and looked at the large open wound in his chest and the deep gash in his neck, now saturated and oozing blood. "Medic! Medic! Oh damn! Damn... Medic!"

Second platoon's medic ran across the open space and slid into the hole. He ripped open Nolan's fatigue jacket now soaked with blood, pressed a compress against the wound and yelled at Wright, "Keep the pressure on. Keep pressing it! Cook, get a stretcher now! And a vehicle!" The medic constantly kept talking to the young trooper who's eyes looked wide and panicked. "Gonna be all right Nolan. Gonna be all right. Stay with me." The medic opened a packet of sulfa powder and dusted the wound with it, then used a bandage to wrap his chest. In another minute they had him on a stretcher and headed for the battalion aid station in town.

Kenny Cook grabbed Wright by the shoulders. "Nothin' you can do, Earl."

"Damn it, Kenny, I was just startin' to like the kid. That's the problem with these new guys – about the time you get to know 'em a little, they up and get themselves killed."

"He's gonna be all right. Doc said so."

"Doc always says that."

"Yeah, but he's right a lot of the time."

"Did you see the kid's eyes? Did you?! Aw damn, Kenny. The kid's not gonna make it."

Someone yelled "*Incoming!*" and German artillery shells started falling around them.

Chapter 42

Aynslee had finally, and reluctantly, agreed to meet him for lunch at the Ritz Hotel.

Mitch sat at a back corner table of the Rivoli Bar drinking a beer and feeling out of place. The clientele were the richest of the rich – those who had moved out of their mansions into the luxury hotels years earlier when their servants had found better paying jobs in war industries. At the time, it was also conveniently true that the most comfortable air raid shelters for riding out the Blitz were found in such places as the Ritz.

But he also felt conspicuously out of place because as he relaxed in the ornate interior of one of the world's finest hotels, the greatest military operation in history was in progress a hundred and fifty miles away. And while he sat on a plush upholstered chair in a regal hotel sipping a beer, others – like his brother – were doing his fighting for him, flying missions he should be flying and doing the hard, dirty work of winning the war. He felt like a slacker... until he thought of her.

She was easily the most intriguing and perplexing girl he'd ever met – even more than Makara whose behavior appeared, in retrospect, to be bizarre, maybe psychotic. *Who was she really?* he wondered, as he had for months until his return to England. His desire for Aynslee had made the Cairo-based translator a distant and best forgotten memory. He looked down at his watch and saw it was still early. He hoped their time together today would be the catalyst for igniting a lasting and intimate relationship. Lunch, he knew, would be expensive, but he had three months' pay in his pocket. Money was secondary to the goal of impressing this girl with whom he'd become obsessed .

Mitch looked up as an attractive woman in a blue uniform approached and sat down across from him. Discreetly she glanced at the entrance and around the room.

"You're a man of quite predictable habits, Mitch Nolan," the woman said, flashing a radiant smile as she removed her beret. She was gorgeous – a sultry glamor girl not much older than he, in a British SOE uniform adorned with two ribbons and a parachutist badge over her left breast pocket. Her hair was dark, and her eyes smoldering; she fitted a cigarette into a long holder and lit it without asking if he minded.

"I'm certain I don't know you," Mitch said.

"But I know you. And you know friends of mine. It makes a nicely closed loop, doesn't it? Buy me a drink," she told him as one used to giving orders. "I'll have a Pimm's Cup, if the bartender in this place will stoop to making me one. I hear you've been asking after me at the SOE since your return from that appalling incarceration in Spain." The woman blew a cloud of smoke in his direction after he'd ordered her drink. "*Tiercelet* and Christophe send their warmest regards."

His breath caught in his throat. "You're the White Mouse," he said in a low voice.

Again her eyes darted toward nearby tables. "Some call me that."

"What do I call you?"

"You needn't call me anything."

"What if I want or need to talk to you again? Who do I ask for?"

"There won't be a next time. The Maquis are rising up all across France this day and I'll be joining them before midnight. I was curious and wanted to meet you. My people told me about you, and *Tiercelet* was convinced you were who you presented yourself to be. I wasn't so sure. My people have been following you since before you arrived in London and began asking about me. That's how I know about your habits – like being twenty minutes early for appointments and always ordering the same brand of beer in a frosted mug. Habits get people noticed and oftentimes killed. The Nazis have used even more elaborate ruses than a downed American pilot in attempts to capture or kill me. I had to know you weren't simply one more. Once I was certain of your pedigree and intentions, I had to meet you. Tiercelet risked even more than her own life to bicycle from her home to where you were being hidden. It was not like her at all. I was curious to see why she would do it."

"I'm flattered," Mitch replied, trying to remain calm. But this woman had an aura of bristling mystery and an animate confidence unlike anyone he'd ever encountered. Knowing a little of her story from the old Frenchwoman, Margot, and from Christophe, he could now easily imagine how she had earned the fear and respect accorded her by the Germans.

"Flattered? Perhaps you should be. She's remarkable. I know – I trained her." She paused and looked him over, contemplating. "More than simply wanting to meet you, I came to ask an important favor."

"If I can help, I –"

"You can. You know two people about whom I care very deeply – the woman Tiercelet and the man Christophe. They are dearly loved by me, but they have grown careless because of their success. And of course you also know about me. I came to beg for your silence – now and in the years to come. For their protection and my own as well."

"My silence?"

"Yes. The Germans cannot win this war, and some in their highest echelons know this already; more will come to that conclusion soon. The war will end badly for Berlin, but they will not stop eliminating their sworn enemies after the final battle is fought. They hate the Jews and they loathe the Resistance. No matter how long it takes, they will not stop until those they most passionately detest are eradicated. Wars end and people write memoirs and books, make movies to celebrate their victories. I ask you to forget everything you know about us and never share it with anyone." Her drink came and she sipped it before continuing. "Would you do that for us Colonel Nolan?"

"Of course," he replied, not entirely convinced of this woman's story. "I owe you and your people everything for getting me out of France."

She leaned toward him, and pulled him close. The fragrance of her perfume caught his attention as she kissed him. "Thank you... for all of us," she whispered.

Mitch was momentarily flustered. He looked across the Rivoli Bar and saw Aynslee standing just inside the door looking at him. Her eyes flashed at him, and with a sudden quickness she turned and left the room.

"I have to be going," Mitch said quickly, throwing some money on the table and grabbing his hat as he started for the door.

The woman grabbed his arm as she stood and turned him toward her with a strength belied by her lithe, thin figure; she cupped his face with her hands and gave him a quick but passionate kiss. Releasing him she said, "*Tiercelet* asked me to deliver that and to tell you *merci* for a most memorable evening. Now go, and find the girl."

He ran down the long corridor framed by tall columns like some ancient Greek temple. Entering the lavishly decorated lobby, he caught a glimpse of her leaving through a side door. Dodging through the crowded lobby, he found the door, stepped outside and his heart sank as he looked up and down the crowded sidewalks. She was nowhere in sight.

"Yes, I saw her," the doorman replied, when he described Aynslee. "Almost got run over, bolting across the street like she did. Went around that corner there. In a big hurry she was... and not a happy look on her face either."

Mitch dodged around traffic, found the corner and saw her walking briskly across to the other side of the street in the middle of the block. He ran down the sidewalk, crossed over and caught up, grabbing her arm. When she turned on him her face was a mask of anger.

"Aynslee –"

"What a blithering idiot I am! And you – snogging in public with some tart! Right in the middle of the bar at the Ritz."

"What?!"

"Kissing that girl in front of king and country for all to see. How could you?!" She reached up, swiped her hand across his face, and came away with lipstick on her fingertips. She held it close to his nose.

"It's not what you think."

"Oh, of course it's not, and you want to explain – this should be rich. Talk all you want but I shan't be listening to it. What a fool I've been, hoping you were different."

"Do you really think I'd ask you to lunch and bring another girl along? What kind of idiot do you think I am?"

"Now there's the question of the hour isn't it, Yank? Neither of us have enough time before the sun goes down for me to answer that as well as I might. But I'll say this and be done with you: don't call me again. Stay away. I told you once and relented, to my sorrow. There are likely many men I'd consider going out with; however, you are no longer on that list – nor will you ever be." She pushed him away when he reached out to her.

Aynslee turned abruptly and walked away without a backward glance.

*   *   *   *

Two weeks later, as he was processing out with orders sending him to the Pacific, he bumped into Yeager and, as had happened in the Pyrenees, his fortunes changed.

It was mid-morning as he was entering SHAEF Headquarters to leave his father a note when he came across Yeager and another Army pilot leaving the building.

"Nolan!" Yeager said, all smiles. He pointed a thumb at the captain and said, "This here's Fred Glover. He's a bomber guy who evaded from Holland – he got back to England just after we did, and he didn't want to go home either. So we went to together working our way up the Air Corps chain of command, and as Christophe would say, 'voilà'."

"What do you mean – voilà?"

"I mean the two of us are back on flight status here in merry old England. I'm going back to my same squadron at Leiston – three concrete runways surrounded by a sea of mud, with cold and clammy metal huts. But it's home sweet home to me. I felt like a quitter having to go home after a measley half dozen missions while guys like wing man Bud Anderson are already working on their second fifty missions."

"Tell me how you did it?"

"Took charge of my own life, Nolan. And I got a little bit of help from this smooth talkin' college boy bomber guy here. But mostly it just took a little bit of doggedness."

"So tell me how you finally got past the hurdles and who said okay."

"I'm going to leave you two guys alone and get back to my unit," Glover said, shaking Nolan's hand and then Yeager's. "Good luck Yeager. You too, Nolan." He turned and walked away from the American headquarters.

"Okay, Chuck, fill me in on how you did this."

"By being a pain in the ass to the chain of command," Yeager began. "You shouldn't have any trouble with that."

"I'm serious."

"So am I." He grinned roguishly and continued. "I just couldn't see myself going back and becoming a flight instructor for the rest of the war. That's not very impressive, especially if a fellow wants to make a career out of the Air Corps – which I might. But I wasn't thinking about my future really. Guess I was just bein' West Virginia stubborn. I want to stay here and fly and decided to git a little bit brassy with the chain of command. I started with my squadron commander and worked my way up over time through all kinds of colonels and generals here in London until I got to the top man at supreme headquarters."

"You talked to Eisenhower?"

"Himself. Twice."

"That is brassy."

"Actually, it just sort of happened that way. Since I was the first one who ever evaded and got back to London and started talking seriously about staying and finishing my tour, I was sort of an oddity. All those colonels and generals sorta sympathized even though their hands were tied. They kept on pushing me higher up in the chain until there wasn't any further to go."

"So Eisenhower revoked the order and put you back on flight status?"

"Not exactly. He was kinda interested and sympathetic too, but he told me it wasn't his rule. It came out of Department of the Army back in Washington and they'd have to issue the waiver. But, he did promise that he'd look into it. By golly he did, and Washington left the decision up to him. And here I am, on my way back to Leiston to join up with the old squadron and finish off this tour. Heck, I got a whole war left to fight."

"So when did Eisenhower issue this waiver for you and Glover?" Mitch asked, thinking what it would mean if he got back on flight status to finish up his second fifty mission tour. Would he be sent back to Foggia or would he be able to stay in England? His task seemed easier with Yeager having already broken the ice, but going back to Italy wouldn't solve the problems he still had with Aynslee.

"We got orders signed by the general not more than five minutes ago," Chuck replied smiling and waving the sheet of paper in front of him. "I don't know how you're going to work through your chain of command down there in Italy, but you might oughtta get started on it right quick if you want to get back in the game."

"Lieutenant Yeager, you inspire me. I've got a better idea, and I'd like to tell you but I've got to get started right now."

"Good luck friend. Always glad to help out... is that a silver oak leaf on your collar?" Yeager asked, half smiling and half frowning. "If it is, I might know where there's a job you could fit into, flying the Cadillac of fighters, instead of that old twin-engine P-38. My fighter group at Leiston is in the market for a group operations officer and a deputy group commander – each of those are lieutenant colonel slots. Don't know how long they're going to be open. We're down a little on manpower right now, but we're getting boatloads of new Mustangs in – all D-models. It's only gonna be a little while longer before those slots are filled. If you're interested, better not waste any time."

Mitch didn't have to think long about it. "Appreciate that, Chuck, more than you know. Something like that would solve a lot of problems for me. What group is that?"

"The 357th. The Brits call us the 'Yoxford Boys'. It's a little village nearby. Leiston is northeast of here in Suffolk, pretty close to the North Sea coast. Except for cold Quonset huts, you'll like it."

"I'm sure I will. Tell you what – mention my name to your squadron CO, and to the group commander if you can. I'll be in touch with you. And Chuck – thanks again. I'm glad I ran into you. All three times."

"Always thought you had 'lucky' written all over you, Nolan."

Mitch felt the cold chill go up his back and neck. Lucky. For an instant, he felt overpowering sadness. *Man, oh man, Lucky. Why didn't you listen? We could have all made it – you, me, Marv.* He shook it off quickly and took the steps up to the headquarters entrance two at a time.

He checked his father's office, vacant now since the day after D-Day. He was at the new Corps headquarters deep in final preparations for the journey across the channel to join the fighting in France. Mitch went upstairs to the supreme commander's office where he found General Bedell Smith standing outside Ike's door talking to Eisenhower's British driver and confidential secretary, Kay Summersby.

"Kay, General Smith," Mitch greeted them. "I know I'm totally out of line, and I don't have an appointment, but I'd really appreciate just two minutes with General Eisenhower."

"Are you dropping your father's name?" Bedell Smith asked jokingly.

"If it's a help rather than a hindrance, I am. If my ol' man's in dutch with the boss, then I'm here on my own recognizance."

"Spoken like a true Nolan. What do you think, Kay? Can we let him in?"

Kay Summersby was personable and had a delightful Irish accent; there were rumors she and the supreme allied commander were on more than senior-subordinate terms, but that was not his business. His father had suggested to him he always make friends with the woman who guarded the boss's door – whoever the boss was – and he had, for just such a time as this.

"Three minutes, Mitch because I'm feeling generous. But no more. I mean that," Kay warned good-naturedly.

When he entered Eisenhower's office after she announced him, Ike was standing with his back to the door looking at the floor-to-ceiling map behind his desk portraying the known friendly and enemy locations in Normandy. "What do you think Dave? Is there room enough yet to shoehorn your Corps into the line? It still looks a little tight to me, but we have three or four days to decide."

Eisenhower turned and looked startled.

"I was expecting your father. I thought Kay said *Dave* Nolan. Too much on my mind, I guess. I'm not concentrating like I should."

"Sorry to interrupt, general. I won't take long."

"Nonsense. It'll be a welcome respite to get away from the map for a while. In fact, let's do something totally un-military. What say we talk a little baseball? How I'd love to take a few hours one day to shag some flies and hit batting practice. I always enjoyed watching you play when you were in high school. Do you miss it? Andy Fauser always said you were the best catcher he ever saw play."

"I think General Fauser only said that when my father was close enough to hear."

Eisenhower grinned. "He always enjoyed tweaking your dad's nose. Still, I think he may be right. Your senior year in high school at McKinley I recall you hit almost .500. What was your average at West Point?"

"Not quite .400 for the three years I played A-squad ball, sir."

"Both your father and General Bradley would have loved to have had that kind of batting average when they were playing." Eisenhower looked at him over his glasses. "I can tell you've got something more important on your mind, and I'm sidetracking you from it. But honestly I'm doing this to distract myself. So, what brings you here?"

"To make a long story short, sir, I want to get back on flying status in this theater. And the only one who can make that happen is you. I'm asking you to waive the rule for me as you did for Captain Glover and Lieutenant Yeager."

"News really travels fast in this command, doesn't it?"

"I just happened to run into them outside the building. Yeager and I evaded through the Pyrenees together a couple of months back. I want to at least finish the tour that I started."

"You want to stay and continue a relationship with a young English woman you've met."

"Not exactly, sir."

"You want to score at least two more kills so you can surpass the top scoring pilot in the Med. What was his name?"

"Dixie Sloan. But that's not my prime motivation, general."

"But it is a motivation. In fact, your motivation is all those, isn't it? And perhaps more. Ah, to be young again." Eisenhower chuckled softly, as he picked up the phone and pressed one of the buttons. "I'm making this hard for you, aren't I, Mitch?"

"Nothing's too hard if it gets me back on flight status in Europe, sir."

"Kay… that waiver we just gave to the two pilots earlier… I need you to type another for Lieutenant Colonel Mitchell Nolan… Service number? No, I don't, but he'll be out shortly to give it to you. When that's done, I'd like to drive down to Portsmouth to one of the sausage camps and spend time with the troops. Cancel my meeting with Leigh-Mallory or have Tedder cover it for me. Forty-five minutes. Yes." Eisenhower put the phone back on its cradle. "I miss not having Brad and your father around. They were always good tonic for what ails me. I'll tell you another thing I miss. Your mother's grilled fish. She made a wicked Old Fashioned and a terrific grilled filet regardless of the type fish you two boys and your dad brought home. Mitch, those are some of my fondest memories," the Supreme Commander said wistfully.

"Mine too, sir," he replied, taking the hint and standing. He saluted and said, "Thank you for granting me the waiver. I won't let you down, general."

"Nobody in your family ever has," Eisenhower replied, returning the salute as he stood and then offered his hand. "I seriously doubt you'll be the first."

Chapter 43

Mitch Nolan broke out into bright sunshine on top of the overcast blanketing most of northern Europe and felt that old familiar rush of excitement – something he'd not experienced in the three months since last touching the controls in a fighter. This was his element, and now he was back; everything about it felt right...

He'd followed up on Yeager's lead about the two positions in the West Virginian's fighter group. By the time he got there, the operations job, the one he most desired, was already filled. When the group commander learned he'd once commanded a squadron and was willing to take on another fifty mission tour, the slot of deputy commander was his. By the end of June he'd moved into a partitioned room in the commander's Quonset hut at RAF Leiston, given himself a tour of the base and spent the better part of the next week getting acquainted with the three squadrons and the North American Mustang.

It quickly became evident being the commander's deputy didn't require much time or effort. Except for being Colonel Graham's stand-in for briefings at higher headquarters and oversight of the overly large administrative section, there didn't seem to be much demanding his personal attention. This, he decided, was the perfect slot for someone wanting to fly and having the rank to cherry-pick his missions.

The weather over England and the continent had not cooperated the last week of June and the first week of July. He'd spent much of his time in the maintenance sections of the squadrons learning the nuts and bolts of the P-51. His own Mustang arrived the last day of June and he immediately started tinkering with it along with his crew chief, a staff sergeant named "Kit" Kittleson who had been with the group since its inception in December of '42. Kittelson was initially a little put off by a field grade officer insisting on looking over his shoulder but learned the new deputy commander talked the mechanics' language and liked getting his hands dirty. The Group deputy liked to zero his own guns, and helped install the new K-14 gun sight.

He'd had taken *Mitch's Mistress IV* on its first flight July 4.

It was a simple maintenance test flight on a marginal weather day, but he was as eager as a kid on Christmas morning to get back in the cockpit after a long layoff. Although the flight lasted only three hours, it was thrill-packed – beginning with a takeoff more electrifying than it should have been. Yeager had warned him about the torque on the big Rolls-Merlin engine, but it still caught him by surprise, as did the annoying loss of vision straight ahead while taxiing, both wholly unlike the Lightning. But he'd gotten it off the ground and cleaned up for climb. It soon became evident this was a horse of a different breeding.

The Lightning would always be his first love, especially the J-model, but this new mount was intriguingly different – especially at cruise. It was smaller, lighter and felt more nimble. The cockpit layout was simpler and everything from throttles to radios seemed within easier reach and required less effort to locate. The airspeed indicator topped out at 700 – *that's going to be exciting some day*, he remembered thinking the first time he climbed in and familiarized himself with the instrument layout.

High above the North Sea he tried some straight ahead and accelerated stalls followed by a handful of aerobatics – loops, barrel and aileron rolls. Thirty miles offshore, he leveled off at twenty-thousand, rolled it over and plunged straight down, waiting to find the speed at which it began to vibrate – it never did. At ten thousand and well in excess of five hundred mph, the Mustang was as stable and smooth as it was in straight and level cruise. He tried it a second time and was pulling out of the dive at five thousand feet when a call came over the emergency frequency from a B-17 straggler under attack by a pair of Me-110s. He found the bomber trying to fend off attackers forty miles east and charged in, knocking one of the German planes from the sky on the first pass. He chased the other one back to the Netherlands' coast near Amsterdam before sending it down in flames. Flying this Mustang was going to be fun…

Now, as he broke out above the clouds and looked around, he located the large box-like formation of Fortresses thirty miles ahead and a few thousand feet above him. He'd been delayed at a Fighter Wing meeting, standing in for the Group commander and had arrived back at Leiston too late to takeoff with the mission, his first with the new unit. By the time he finally lifted off, he was a good twenty minutes behind and had pushed to make up time. Apparently he had, but where were the rest of the Mustangs?

He scanned the skies but saw no fighter cover. Strange. He did a tight 360 degree turn looking for his group and finally sighted a large formation headed for the bombers, but it wasn't large enough to be the 357th. They were Germans – mostly -109s with a smattering of Focke Wulfs – divided into two distinct flights separated by a few minutes.

The bombers liked to think they could take care of themselves, but that was only marginally true. He estimated the Germans at forty or fifty strong; he was certain the B-17s were sitting ducks.

And he alone was their cover.

Mitch climbed above the flight level of the bombers and placed himself between them and the German fighters coming on them from behind. Looking down his right wing he saw the Luftwaffe planes climbing toward the back of the bomber formation and decided his only option was to attack and try to break them up. He'd create as much havoc as he could until the rest of the group showed up. Turning and heading straight at the lead Messerschmidt, he released his drop tanks and hoped for the best.

The leader of the first flight of -109s flew a plane painted a bright red from the tip of the prop spinner all the way to the cockpit and sported a bright yellow tail. *This guy demands attention – he wants to be seen*, Mitch thought hurtling down toward him. *Maybe if I get him… If I had a Lightning, I could fire from here and hit him with the fifties and the 20mm cannon concentrated in the nose… but you wouldn't be here, Nolan, because this Mustang cruises a good hundred miles an hour faster…*

As Mitch began to fire, the German quickly and easily dodged away and Mitch plunged through the formation going too fast. He pulled a tight, painful high G turn and came back at the formation from the flank just as the German leader began lobbing long range shots at the tail end of the bomber formation.

Nolan fired a burst and saw some hits on the leader who again dodged out of the way of a second pass and latched onto the Mustang's tail as Mitch flashed across the front of the formation a second time. Nolan turned hard left and began a tight roll; the German stayed with him. He then turned back right and rolled over on his back and could see the -109 directly beneath him as they began a turning duel that soon turned to the German's advantage. *This guy is good – really good. Just my luck to run across him on my first mission in a new airplane.*

Mitch leveled and broke out of the turning fight watching the German pull directly behind and close to within two hundred yards. *This is going to be hairy*. Instantly he chopped power and pulled the nose up abruptly, almost vertical and on the edge of a stall, knowing if he did stall he'd fall through and become an easy target. At the first shudder of warning, he kicked in full left rudder which flipped the nose of the Mustang straight down; instinctively, he fired a leading burst at the -109 as the Messerschmitt went by underneath him. He added power to pull in behind the German, fired another burst and saw smoke erupt from the enemy's engine as he started to fall away. Mitch followed him straight down, fired another short burst and saw the 109's canopy come off; the pilot bailed out, seeming to rush upward past Nolan's left wing.

Mitch turned hard and started climbing back toward the bomber formation, seeing now the first Luftwaffe flight had held back, probably to watch their leader dispatch the lone Mustang. Now they were in a confused gaggle circling and heading away from the B-17s. But the second flight continued barreling toward the bombers, seemingly unaware he was climbing up toward them from almost directly below at full War Emergency power. He reached the rear of their formation just as an engine on one of the B-17s ahead started smoking; he continued to a point a thousand feet above and just off to the side of the Luftwafffe formation before initiating a high speed slashing attack at them.

Mitch knocked down the trail aircraft with a short burst from a hundred yards astern, continued to the middle of the flight and knocked down two more in quick succession, one of which exploded in a great fireball in the midst of the enemy formation and caused the rest to scatter. The leader of the second German formation was another hotshot – this time in a plane with a mottled camouflage paint scheme but with a bright yellow nose from the front of the windscreen to the end of the propeller spinner and a bright white empennage. As the planes behind him broke off in twisting, turning maneuvers for self-preservation, the leader pulled straight up into a split S, reversing course and locating the attacker.

As Mitch tore through the formation and out the other side, the leader came around, fired a long deflection shot and got on his tail. Tracers seemed to engulf his canopy and he skidded out of the way, catching a glimpse of the gaudily painted fighter in his rear view mirrors. Mitch did a snap roll and then dove away. *I hope Yeager's right about the Mustang out-performing the-109 at any altitude.*

Soon he found himself desperately trying to shake the Messerschmitt behind him and not having any success. He couldn't out climb the German and was learning he couldn't out turn him either. Every maneuver he tried failed and the enemy in his mirrors seemed to be getting closer to a killing angle on him every time he looked. To add to his growing problems, he was sweating and the oxygen mask kept slipping off his face; he had to keep pushing it back up – an annoyance and a realization he was exceeding 4G in his maneuvers. This couldn't go on for much longer. The German was inching closer and his guns were almost coming to bear. Mitch realized that it wouldn't be long until the enemy pilot had his guns in position to pull a lead, and that would be the end of things for him and his new plane.

His mind raced for a solution – the Nolan roll wouldn't work in a single engine bird, but the trick he'd pulled on Major Broussard in the T-6 at San Antonio would.

With a quick glance at the rear view mirrors, now filled with -109's yellow spinner, he turned as tight as he could with the right wing tip pointed straight at the ground. He pulled the stick hard into his gut and chopped the power, stalling the aircraft. Immediately, he kicked the bottom rudder pedal full forward and pushed the control stick full forward causing his head to hit the top of the bubble canopy. Instantly he centered the stick and looked straight through the windshield at the ground fifteen thousand feet below as the torque of the propeller twisted the P-51; for an instant the Mustang hung suspended in space with zero airspeed.

He knew he'd disappeared from the Messerschmitt's view.

The P-51 fell almost three thousand feet before the Hamilton Standard prop started to bite through the air and the *Mistress* was flying again. As far as he was concerned the Yellow Nose could leave him alone. He certainly wasn't going to go looking for him again. As Mitch started climbing back toward the bombers another -109 flashed across his field of view and he was about to take a quick shot when he realized it was closely trailed by a Mustang with a familiar red and black checkered paint scheme on its engine cowling.

Now as he looked around, the sky was filled with Mustangs and enemy planes tangled in a twisting, turning aerial furball of individual dogfights ranging from just above the ground to contrail level. Airplanes were everywhere, but now a lot of them were friendlies.

Two thousand feet below him a Focke Wulf 190 chased a Mustang just above the clouds.

Mitch rolled the *Mistress* over and dove at the enemy with the advantage of altitude and airspeed. He squeezed off a burst at four hundred yards, missing but surprising the German pilot and causing him to break off his attack and duck into a cloud bank. Mitch followed. *This is crazy Nolan. You looking for another mid-air?* Like a ghostly apparition, the FW-190 filled his gun sight. His tracers arched out and engulfed the entire fuselage of the German fighter instantly producing flames around the engine and a long black cloud of smoke. The plane rolled slowly on its back, headed straight down through the clouds; Mitch fired another burst and his guns went empty just as the German's right wing separated in flames. Nolan pulled up and after a couple minutes of flying instruments he popped out on top of the cloud layer again.

In the freakish way of aerial combat, he was once again alone in the sky asking himself how it was possible that all those aircraft had vanished. Isolated and without ammunition, he turned for home and two hours later arrived back at Leiston.

*　　*　　*

The final frames of the scratchy black and white film flickered and the screen went white in the 357th Group briefing room as the lights were turned on.

"That's all the film from yesterday's mission," Colonel Graham said making his way from the back to the front of the room while the noise and clapping subsided. "As you can see, some of us need a lot of practice with the new gun sight, and everybody except Nolan, Anderson, Yeager and Davis will be scheduled for classes on it. But all in all a good day –

twenty-one kills, eight damaged, and no bombers lost to German fighters. Wing HQ is real pleased and the general asked me to pass along his congratulations for a job well done. No passes to London, though." There was some general grumbling among the pilots and Graham raised his hands for silence. "And it's official – we have our second 357th "ace-in-a-day" – Colonel Nolan. Seems he isn't afraid to fly a plane with only one engine after all. Although he didn't make it on time for take-off, he did manage to get there for the fun and came home early. Good duty if you can find it, I guess. All right, that is all, gents. Enjoy your breakfast."

As the room cleared, Colonel Graham caught Mitch's eye and waved him over.

"Hell of a good day, Mitch." The colonel looked at him out of the corner of his eye. "What's this I hear about your telling Kittelson not to paint any kills on your plane? Something you want to tell me about?"

"Just thought I'd keep this aircraft nice and clean. The Mustang is a pretty bird and I just didn't want to mar the thing." Since the loss of Lucky Lindquist his heart was no longer in keeping score. It seemed immature, even irreverent to the memory of those guys in North Africa and Italy he'd flown with who didn't make it back over the past many months.

"What about that sultry Vargas girl on its nose?"

"Maybe I should take that off, too."

Graham frowned at him and slowly shook his head. "I guess you'll tell me what this is all about one of these days when you're ready. But for now painting the swastika decals on group aircraft is my standing order. And I've got my reasons. Don't buck me on this, Mitch."

"I wouldn't think of it, sir."

"Good. You haven't been around here all that long and I'm sure you're not aware of where this group was and where it is now. We don't have a real long history – we're building it as we go along with good, solid squadron commanders and a cadre of hotshot pilots like Anderson and Yeager, and a few others – like you now. That was a hell of a feat you pulled off. I don't know how you got to the rendezvous point ahead of us, but it's a good thing you did. You gave us six or eight minutes of breathing room."

"The Mustang has outstanding cruise performance," Mitch observed.

"It's some airplane all right, but it still requires a good man at the controls. Yesterday you showed a lot of these new pilots just how good an airplane that is in the right hands." Graham paused briefly, watching Nolan closely. "You see, the Air Corps is turning out a lot of pilots and rushing them here and to the Pacific without all the training they really should have. You got your orientation in that aircraft yesterday on the way to completing your first mission. That's happening a lot in this group right now. Look around at the faces in this briefing room and you'll see a bunch of kids without a whole lot of experience. You're one of the old, old men and you just turned twenty-five."

Mitch grinned. "I've been thinking the same thing myself."

"It's true. In our rush to find and train pilots to man all the aircraft the country is producing, a twenty-one year old is just about average age these days. These young guys need examples to look up to and to emulate. What you did yesterday is now part of the folklore surrounding the 357th. Every kid in here, and every one of them who shows up between now and the end of the war will hear about what you did yesterday."

"I'm not looking for attention – not anymore."

"This isn't about attention or glory. It's about setting expectations and standards. It also tells these young guys that the senior leaders set the pace and can be trusted. That's important. I've seen units where the leadership was not held in high regard and those outfits are worthless. I'm not going to let that happen here. So when a brand-new pilot shows up here, I want him to see your airplane with all those decals and know that he can trust you, me and everyone else he'll be flying with. That's why Kittelson is now painting your airplane." Graham paused to gauge Nolan's reaction. "Your records from 15th Air Force arrived yesterday afternoon. Pretty interesting read. You never mentioned that you had eleven confirmed kills in the Med, Nolan. You should have."

Mitch shrugged and raised an eyebrow. "I thought my personal score was less important than the command time."

"Maybe. Maybe not. I've told Kittelson to go ahead and paint those decals on your plane, too. That makes you a triple ace – a rare bird indeed. Not unheard of in our Air Corps, but uncommon. You know people are going to be watching you now. That may make you a little bit uncomfortable. Tough. I don't think your example will make our pilots foolish or foolhardy. I expect it'll make them more aggressive, which is what I want and need as their commander."

"I understand, sir."

"Good. Now, go back out there and do it again on the next mission." Graham slapped him on the shoulder. "The air war is changing decidedly in our favor. We're just beginning to overwhelm the Luftwaffe with numbers. They're losing a lot of their experienced pilots and from what I see, their replacements aren't quite measuring up."

"I'd have to agree," Mitch replied. The way the German flights had reacted yesterday to his unusual attack had indicated the same thing to him. He couldn't imagine the Luftwaffe he'd encountered in North Africa reacting that way. They were still extremely dangerous, but not overwhelmingly superior as he'd witnessed flying out of Telerghma eighteen months earlier.

"We'll keep pushing them harder and harder until they finally break," Graham said. "Hopefully that's sooner rather than later." He pulled an envelope from his flight suit pocket and handed it over. "This came in for you just as the film started to roll. How does someone like you rate a phone call from Kay Summersby?"

Mitch looked at the note which contained only a phone number, and his heart sank. He knew instantly it was some kind of bad news.

He called the 66th Wing operator from Group headquarters and gave him the phone number. When Kay Summersby came on the line, her nervous tone instantly told him he'd been right – the news was bad.

*　　　*　　　*　　　*　　　*

Erika saw Randall Ashby come out of Senator Payne's office looking distraught and terribly unnerved. There had been a week of closed door meetings of the senator's military oversight committee and neither he nor his young legal counsel had been getting much sleep over whatever news it was they were hearing from the Joint Chiefs. She assumed something must be going terribly wrong with the war effort to weigh so heavy on them both. When she looked through the open door she saw Michelle with an even more panic-stricken expression; the senator's daughter quickly turned away. Whatever it was, she hoped it wouldn't interrupt the quiet little dinner she and Randall had planned that evening – she expected him to propose and had spent the previous week planning her response.

"Erika, the senator needs to see you for a moment," Ashby said, avoiding looking at her.

"You two finally got around to asking someone with an objective viewpoint to help you solve this little problem you've been wrestling with these past few weeks?" she asked, saucily.

"Just come in, please," he replied flatly. "He really does need to talk with you."

His curt response hit a sour note, and she was about to say something but thought better of it. Smiling, she entered and sat on the sofa across the room from the elderly senator who avoided looking at her. Michelle sat next to her and wordlessly took her hand.

"Erika, I… there's some news I need to share with your mother… and with you," the senator finally said after taking a deep breath. "We could use your help when we go to see her. The news is not good."

She gasped and covered her mouth with a hand.

"It's Glenn. I'm afraid he won't be coming home from Europe. I'm sure your father knows by now, but we have to tell your mother."

"No! Not Glenn! It's got to be a mistake. He's just a kid… this will kill her…"

Michelle hugged her close and stroked her hair, whispering softly into her ear.

Chapter 44

The valley was long and narrow, heavily forested and steeply sloped on both the north and south ridgelines. Tanks of the Corps cavalry squadron had chased the panzers into a defile and now the P-47s were pounding them relentlessly. The tactical fighter-bombers were knocking them off one by one while tank destroyers on the ground tore at the remnant.

Dave Nolan, watching the action through binoculars from high ground just to the rear of the leading elements saw two of the fighters pull up from their strafing run as two more swooped in just over his head, their .50 caliber machine guns clattering. From where he stood he could see three tanks burning; the wreckage and German casualties were extensive.

He was amazed at the firepower and resilience of the Thunderbolts. With eight heavy machine guns per plane, they could deal out a lot of punishment on ground targets. Equally impressive was the amount of punishment they could take. Their big air-cooled radial engines withstood almost everything thrown their way. Still, he knew their close support role placed them in great danger and he'd been told it wasn't unusual for a pilot to get shot down in the morning and be back in the cockpit in another plane that afternoon. Flying always amazed and worried him – but what the Thunderbolt pilots were doing sounded categorically suicidal.

He heard his driver, a young buck sergeant named Zimmer, talking on the radio of his command jeep.

"General Patton's looking for you, sir," the driver said, placing the hand mic back in its cradle. "I'll have the coordinates deciphered in a minute."

"Yeah, I know. He's been trying to track me down for a week and a half. I'm not looking forward to it."

Since the *Breakout* from Normandy, Patton's Third Army's race across France had been increasingly rapid and Nolan had been out of touch with his commander for days at a time. George would be unhappy with him, which was becoming increasingly common. But he couldn't complain about the ground XXX Corps had taken – Chateau Thierry, Reims, Verdun. *All the old familiar places from the last time we went to war*, he thought. And now they were only ten miles from Thionville. Two hundred miles in nineteen days. His four divisions had taken more territory in less than three weeks than the Armies of England and France combined had taken in four years during the last war.

It took nearly a half hour to travel the six miles to the small town where they were supposed to meet Patton. The roads were clogged with tanks and trucks lumbering forward loaded down with G.I.s. In every little town, the slow moving vehicles were surrounded by old men and women waving French flags and passing out wine bottles to the Americans. Younger women threw flowers and climbed on American vehicles to give kisses to as many young soldiers as they could reach. Zimmer started to blow the horn to get them all out of the way, but Dave stopped him.

"Every G.I. ought to get the chance to kiss a French woman some time in his life," Nolan said, smiling and looking around. "At least once."

When they arrived at the outskirts of the town Zimmer had circled on his map, they saw a tank pulled off to the side of the road; next to it was Patton's red-upholstered tactical truck with the big mounting ring for his .50 caliber gun. Dave thought it was the first time he'd seen the vehicle when the siren or the multi-toned French horn – or both – weren't blaring.

"Where's the general?" he asked Patton's driver.

"Over there, sir. Under the tank."

A few minutes later, Patton crawled out from under the big metal hull, stood up and watched as the tank crew scrambled aboard, started the engine and drove off with a roar.

"What was that all about, George?"

"Damned if I know. They couldn't get it started so I got underneath and 'encouraged' them. You can bet your ass that by sundown the word will spread to every man in this division about how I helped fix that tank and got it running." He gave a self-gratified smile as he wiped grease from his hand and dusted off his jacket then suddenly turned irritated. "And where the hell have you been for the last week? Nobody in my headquarters seems able to track you down any more. You need to learn how to stay in touch with your superior, general."

"Your orders said –"

"I know what the hell my own orders say, Nolan. Don't think for a minute I'll buy that as an excuse."

"How about XII Corps? Or XX Corps? Are Eddy or Walker any better at being available at your beck and call?"

"What my other corps commanders are doing doesn't have a thing to do with you. And, damn it, Nolan, I ask the questions around here. I'm going to tell you this one time and you get it through that thick Dutchman's skull of yours. I know I gave you latitude, but that didn't include running around the countryside without informing me of your actions and intentions."

Dave Nolan fumed at the rebuke, but held his tongue. He took out his map and spread it over the hood of his jeep.

"Do you know where we are, general?" he asked after indicating to Zimmer and Patton's driver for them to move away, out of hearing distance.

Patton looked at him through narrowed eyes. "Are trying to be funny Nolan?"

"I'm trying to see if you remember this place and what happened here once before. About a mile down this road is the little town called Essy-et-Masserais. It looks pretty much like it did on another September about three decades ago. Five miles behind us, beyond these three ridge lines on the map is where you and I first met and you told me I didn't know how to run my half-assed battalion. It was the first day of the Ste. Mihiel operation and I was out of touch with my higher headquarters and beyond every planned phase line. Remember that? You demanded I continue the attack and forget about my responsibility to communicate with higher headquarters. I think your words were to the effect that if I were under your command and had the enemy on the run and didn't keep on going, you'd relieve me. Communications to higher headquarters be damned. Seems you've changed your tune since then."

Patton stared at him, the color rising in his face. "Are you finished?"

"Not quite. Like I told you on Sicily, you are always within your prerogative to relieve me any time you desire. If my performance doesn't measure up, do it. I'm not here because I want to be. I'm here because I have to be. Now, get rid of me or let me tell you my plans and intentions." *Why was it every interaction with George had to be a knock down drag out bare knuckles brawl?* He was getting tired of it. Maybe he was wearing out and it really was time to get some new blood into the mix. At the moment he really didn't know, and was surprised to realize he didn't much care.

"The matter is closed," Patton declared, still looking harshly at him. "General, you've been under a lot of pressure these past few months. Now, let's look at what you have planned for the next week."

Nolan shook his head and leaned over the map, bewildered as always at Patton's theatrics. In a few minutes, he'd outlined his plans for sending Simpson's division north around Thionville with Mark Hudson's 58th Division frontally assaulting the town to fix the Germans there in place. Collier would send his tank columns on a southerly sweep and then turn northeast toward an objective twenty miles to the rear of the Germans' current position to cut off any retreat.

"It should net us another fifteen thousand prisoners," Dave Nolan said as he finished.

"How many POWs have you bagged so far?"

"Andy tells me the count, as of yesterday, is about forty thousand since the breakout."

Patton's face lit up. "You've done a good job, general. Keep it up. Concerning Fauser — does he continue to operate his still?"

Dave was a little surprised that George knew. "Not since a week before we took Paris. Too much trouble and too little time. He's taken to concocting what he calls a Poor Man's Old Fashioned when he's in need of a drink. That's a mixture of orange marmalade and whiskey. It's awful, but he likes it and I don't mind. I have him under control, George."

"See that you keep it that way."

Two Thunderbolts flew low overhead, one belching smoke as they flew toward the west, away from the front. It made him think about Mitch again as he rolled up his map and watched Patton motor off in his big battlefield wagon.

*   *   *   *

Glenn Miller's Army Air Corps Band was into its second set in the huge hangar at the American bomber base called *RAF Thorpe-Abbotts* by the British and simply Station 139 by American planners and B-17 pilots of the 100th Bomber Group, nicknamed *The Bloody 100th*.

The band and its bespectacled leader were set up on a raised stage on the side of the hangar; a B-17 named the *Gallopin' Goose* with sixteen bombing mission decals on its nose sat in the middle of the building with Army WACs and British WAAFs sitting on the leading edge of the wings, dangling their legs. The music was loud and lively as Miller played his trombone, leading the band in his signature 1940 hit, *In the Mood.* As Americans pilots mingled and danced with the British and American girls, Mitch Nolan decided he'd stay and take part. One way or another he'd find a way to bunk with the bomber crews and return to Leiston in the morning after sleeping off the punch that somebody had obviously spiked.

Colonel Graham, along with his deputy commander, had flown to the base to pitch a new concept to the bomber command. Bomber and fighter group losses were climbing despite the increase in numbers of American fighters assigned as escort. Mitch had a couple of plans he wanted to lay out to the bomber group commander to get his concurrence. Then, if all went well, the bomber group and fighter group commanders could together run it up the line to Jimmy Doolittle at 8th Air Force, and change the dynamic of the air war in northern Europe.

"If I were you, I wouldn't drink this punch if I was planning to fly back to the Group tonight," Mitch said to Colonel Graham draining the last of his glass.

"I take it you're planning to sleep here with the bomber guys," Graham observed.

"Seemed the prudent thing to do. I didn't realize the punch was such high octane until I'd had enough to go over the limit."

"Have you always been so diligent in observing 'eight hours from bottle to throttle', Colonel Nolan?"

"Absolutely!"

Graham gave him a sly smile. He'd learned in the last few months Mitch's use of that word 'absolutely' always meant *absolutely not!* He'd grown to appreciate Nolan's 'work hard and play hard' creed and tonight looked like it was one of his 'play hard' outbreaks. "I'll tell Major Hiro not to schedule you for any missions with the 363rd before noon tomorrow."

"I'm sure he'll be disappointed, sir."

"Absolutely!" Graham replied and laughed aloud. "You behave yourself, Nolan. I always worry about you bachelors around these uniformed gals, especially the British girls."

"You've got nothing to worry about there, colonel. I apparently have some kind of disease or odor that British women immediately sense and dislike. I'll stick with the liquor, the company of pilots and simply enjoy the music and the view tonight."

Mitch wandered back over to the one of the refreshment tables and refilled his glass and took a few small cubes of cheese. As he turned around, a pretty blond WAAF in blue uniform caught his eye and smiled at him. She looked like a grown up Shirley Temple, with a pretty face and long ringlet curls; she filled out the uniform nicely he noticed, as she continued to look at him. When he winked at her, she smiled again, gave him a suggestive come hither stare and winked back. *All right, Nolan, what the heck*, he said to himself and walked over to the end of the table where she stood. He removed his hat and stuck it under his left arm.

"I noticed you were alone," he began, observing she had pretty blue eyes and long eye lashes which she flashed at him. "Since my occupation at the moment is escort duty, I wonder if you might not be in need of my specialty. I'm available and my services are free."

"You're a smooth talker, Yank, but can you dance?"

"Cha-cha, samba, waltz, tango… you name it."

"I prefer slow dancing done very closely," she said flirtatiously, all the more winsome with her British accent.

"I'm your guy." He put the glass down and took her hand. "I have to ask you to excuse me for wearing my hat. I don't want to leave it lying around. Don't trust these bomber guys – one of them might walk off with it."

"So, you don't fly bombers I take it. That means those wings make you a fighter pilot."

"Right you are. My name is Mitch Nolan. And yours?"

"Juliana… Juliana Chilcott. So you fly fighter planes. How intriguing. My best friend is 'arse over tit for a Yank fighter pilot." The expression surprised him coming from the mouth of a cute, seemingly cultured woman. *The Brits have the strangest sayings*, he thought. "She talks of him all the time, but we've never seen 'im. He's a *Moostang* pilot she says."

"A P-51 pilot?"

"That's right – a P-51 *Moostang*. What do you fly?"

"A Mustang, also. There's a lot of us flying them now. What's his name?"

"No idea. We'll ask her before the night's out. Right now I'd like to test your dancing skill," she exclaimed brightly. "I love your American music. What's the name of this song?"

"It's *Moonlight Serenade*."

"I adore it," she said, wrapping her arm around his neck and swaying slowly against him, looking directly into his eyes. "Does it have words?"

"It does."

"Do you know them?"

He sighed, deep in thought then whispered in her ear along with the band's music. "*The stars are aglow, and tonight how their light sets me dreaming. My love, do you know, that your eyes are like stars brightly beaming?... I bring you and sing you a Moonlight Serenade.*"

"Oh my!" Juliana said, giving him a playful look. "He not only dances but he's got a halfway respectable voice as well."

"Only halfway?!" he replied, raising his eyebrows and trying to look offended. "You English girls really know how to hurt a guy's feelings."

"I meant it as truly high praise, Mitch. Most men I know couldn't carry a tune in a gunnysack. But, I must ask, are those truly the words or did you make them up just to make sport of me?"

"No, those are the real words – I swear it. And a gentleman would never make sport of a girl as pretty as you."

"Oh, you are the slick one!" She held him closer, continuing to sway in time with the beat. When the music stopped, she whispered into his ear and kissed his cheek. Looking into his eyes she held on to him until the music started again. "What is this one, my Yank pilot?"

"Stardust. And sorry, I don't know all the lyrics – just a little of the chorus, and I wouldn't dream of burdening you with a chorus sung with my lackluster voice."

"Feelings hurt?" she asked, looking amusingly innocent yet seductive. "I was told you Yank pilots were made of sterner stuff."

"By your friend?"

"By my own observation. You're not the first American I've promenaded with. Perhaps the best dancer – although I haven't seen your jitterbug."

"And you're not likely to, either. I can get carried away and make a public spectacle. I've been told my jitterbugging isn't socially acceptable." He held her close and again whispered along with the tune: *You are in my arms, The nightingale tells his fairy tale, Of paradise where roses grew. Though I dream in vain, in my heart you will remain, My stardust melody, The memory of love's refrain.*

"I'm glad you came to this little party tonight and that you enjoy dancing close," she whispered in his ear then kissed his neck. He realized he was pleasantly relaxed in her company and enjoyed the playful banter and suggestive things she said as they continued to dance together. "I was hoping to meet someone special. Are you special, Colonel Nolan?"

"It all depends on what you mean by special... I'm just a guy who's fortunate enough to fly some of the greatest airplanes in history. No more special than that. I wasn't born on third base with a silver spoon in my mouth."

"Whatever in the world does that mean?"

"It's a baseball analogy."

"Baseball?" She screwed her face into a frown. "Is that the game like cricket."

"Kinda sorta. Only... I don't want to insult your sport. Let's say I wasn't born to land and a title, nor was I raised by a British nanny – that's closer."

"Nor was I!"

"There you go. We have things in common."

"Except for a language!" Juliana looked very directly at him with a surprisingly serious and penetrating stare for what seemed a long while. Finally she asked, "Are you married?"

"No. And why do you ask?"

"Engaged or seeing anyone special?"

"Neither, at the moment. As we say in America, I'm footloose and fancy free. And you? Turn around is fair play."

"No, I'm not married or engaged. Am I seeing anyone special? – that depends on what you do when this evening is over."

He was enjoyably intrigued by her racy insouciance. "Would I be out of line if I asked for your address or a phone number where I could reach you?... in case I remember more Glenn Miller lyrics, or if you might want to hear some from the Dorsey Brothers."

"Aren't you the bright spark? You can take a hint and get right to the heart of the matter, can't you? Yes, I'll give my number. My purse is back at the table. I have a card in it. I'm not usually this quick to give up an address, but you seem a nice enough chap and... well the war and all makes things different. Come, let me introduce you to my crowd. Most of them aren't *too* anti-American," she said playfully.

"My lucky night," he replied, smiling with her and offering his arm.

517

They made their way through the crowd of dancers and arrived near the front of the hangar on the opposite wall from Glenn Miller's band. Juliana held tightly to his arm after almost getting knocked over by a jitterbugging couple. A group of WAAFs stood in a circle in animated conversation but turned and looked as Juliana began introducing him around.

"And this, girls, is my Yank friend, a *Moostang* pilot named Mitch Nolan. Mitch this is Lucy, Abbey, Clarissa, Aynslee, and Nielsa, they are my…"

As Juliana continued to explain the reason they were there as a group and how long they had worked at RAF Headquarters together, the explanation faded away to background noise, and the faces – except for one – went completely out of focus. The skin on the back of his neck felt instantly like prickly heat and his tongue went dry as Arizona dust. He had the sensation of a big wave breaking over him and being tumbled inside a roaring surf.

Aynslee Glendenbrook appeared to be even more uncomfortable than he.

"…and so you're not any longer the only one who knows a Yank pilot, Aynes," Juliana was saying, hanging on his arm. "Is your Yank a singer and a dancer, too, like mine?"

"Are you quite all right, Ayns?" the girl introduced as Clarissa was asking, looking first at Aynslee and then at Mitch.

"Yes, of course. Certainly," Aynslee replied, giving him a forced smile and extending her hand to him. "So, glad to meet you, sir."

"And so glad to meet you… I'm the world's worst on names, so I have to hear them twice and say them back to you. I have Lucy, Abbey and Clarissa – am I right? Yes? Good! Beyond that exceeds what my family calls the *Nolan Law of Threes*." He took a deep breath and hoped his face wasn't as red as the heat he was feeling. "Please give me your name again," he said, still grasping Aynslee's hand.

"The name is Aynslee."

"Aynslee, thank you. Pretty name. And after Aynslee… Nielsa. Is that right? This is a first for me. I think I found the secret to remembering more than three names at a time. It helps that you're all attractive women with equally beautiful names."

"Isn't he the charmer?… for a Yank," Juliana said, holding onto his arm. "And he knows the words to all the music the band is playing."

"So, what do you ladies do at RAF headquarters?" he asked, seeing the still bewildered but hardening look from Aynslee who remained quiet as the other WAAFs engaged him in conversation. They were having a jolly good time, according to Lucy, and they all laughed when he told them in exaggerated seriousness how to tell a bomber pilot from a fighter pilot and why fighter pilots made the best dancers and catches.

"No, it's true," Mitch replied with feigned incredulity when Abbey challenged him. "It's in the face. A fighter pilot is a happy extrovert who loves what he does and knows he's got the world by the tail feathers. But bomber guys are brooders, introverts who are certain that if something bad hasn't happened, it's about to. Honest!" When all but Aynslee giggled, he turned and looked at her. "You don't looked convinced, Aynslee. I'm sure you've noticed in your American friend the truth of what I'm saying."

She chewed absently on her lower lip and glanced away.

"Do me this favor," he said to her. "Allow me the space of two dances to convince you, and if after that I haven't, you win and I'll admit I'm wrong – about everything. Fair enough?" When she hesitated, he said, "Please. Two songs. That's not too much to ask, is it?... Really?"

Finally she shrugged noncommittally.

"Remember, Ayns, he's my Yank," Juliana said, lightheartedly. "I saw him first!"

Mitch looked at her, winked and then led Aynslee onto the dance floor to a place beneath the wing of the *Gallopin' Goose*. He held both of her hands and looked into her eyes, waiting for the the band to start playing.

"So who is this guy you're seeing?" he asked, lightheartedly. "I wonder if I know this *Moostang* pilot Juliana told me about."

"Don't make fun of me," she said quietly. "Oh, Mitch. Surely you can figure it out. I'm not seeing anybody. I made that up to keep from going out and partying with the girls you met from HQ. I wish I'd succeeded tonight. They don't know his name, because he doesn't have one. He doesn't exist." She shivered when he gently placed his hands on her shoulders. "Don't you see?! I can't let you or anyone else... Why did you have to be here tonight of all nights?"

"I have a way of saying and doing the wrong things around you, don't I?"

The band began playing *At Last*. It was a song he knew well and wondered if she did.

At last my love has come along
My lonely days are over
And life is like a song

At last the skies above are blue
My heart was wrapped up in clover
The night I looked at you

"I don't believe in coincidences and I don't believe in luck," he told her as he took her in his arms and felt her stiffen. "Do you?"

"Do you believe in taking no for an answer?" she asked.

"You haven't told me 'no' yet. Not definitively." As she began to reply, he placed his finger on her lips. He took a deep breath and said, "Please. Hear me out, that's all I ask. I fell in love the very first time I saw you – that day four years ago when you opened the door at your father's house. The greatest disappointment of my life was that same night when your father told me you were already married. I honored your marriage to Glendenbrook for as long as he was alive, and for some time after. I never revealed or pressed you about my feelings until much later. If I didn't wait long enough in your mind, I apologize. That didn't keep me from getting to know and like your parents and little Cateline. Tell me how I've wronged you in any of that and I'll make it right."

She remained silent but finally looked up at him. She shook her head slowly, sadly and looked away, saying nothing. When the song ended, Miller announced they were taking a break but would be back for a third and final set in fifteen minutes.

"Take a walk outside with me," he pleaded.

"It's chilly."

"It'll clear your head. And mine."

They walked slowly away from the hangar down a line of parked B-17s – silent, brooding hulks awaiting the dawn when they would each carry ten men and nine thousand pounds of bombs to win the air war and isolate the battlefield on the continent. One in ten of them would not return from their next mission, and it was mathematically impossible for any of them to survive a complete twenty-five mission tour. That was the reason for his trip to the "Bloody 100th" this day. He hoped his plan would improve those numbers and give life to the crews. And now he hoped he could breathe life into his love for this English girl with whom he so desperately wanted to spend the rest of his life.

"What can I do to make you love me as much as I love you," he said as they stopped in the shadow of one of the big Flying Fortresses. The moon was up, almost full, and the sky was surprisingly devoid of clouds. The night was ideal – Glenn Miller's band, the weather, the moonlight. Everything was picture-perfect... and everything was wrong.

"You can't make someone love you, Mitch," she said at last.

"I can try."

"Yes, you can try. She looked away, sighing. "I don't want to fall in love again. I can't."

He thought he could hear her sob and see her body shake. When he turned her around, she seemed to melt into his arms and he rocked her slowly back and forth for a long time. He held her at arm's length and in the moonlight could see the tears trickling down her cheeks. He wiped them away and drew her face toward him, wrapping his arms around her. He placed his finger gently beneath her chin and softly, gradually raised her face.

He kissed her gently. "I love you, Aynslee. I want to spend my life with you."

Immediately, she pushed him away. "Don't, Mitch. Please don't."

"But I love you, Aynslee."

"I don't love you," she said, firmly. "Why can't you understand that?"

"I can't because I don't believe you." He pulled her close and kissed her deeply, aware that before tonight he'd never kissed her even once. She fought him briefly, trying to push him away, slapping at him with glancing blows that bounced off his arms and shoulders and then, knocking off his hat, she ran her fingers through his hair as she pulled his face toward hers. With surprising strength, she pushed him back against the large black tire of the bomber, grabbed his uniform blouse and smothered him with her kisses.

At last, she released his uniform jacket and pushed him away, standing in front of him like some ancient embattled gladiator, her breast rising and falling.

"You must stop doing this to me!" she said to him. "You took advantage of me. Why must all you men take advantage of me?!"

And then she turned and ran toward the big hangar where the Air Corps Band was tuning up in preparation for their final set of the evening.

"Hey!... Aynslee!" he called out, just before she disappeared into the darkness next to the big hangar. "You still owe me a dance!"

Chapter 45

Harrison Reeves sat alone, brooding and drinking in his rambling estate house in Silver Spring, Maryland. It was the first day of spring and the temperature was an unseasonably hot ninety degrees Fahrenheit – a record. He cursed the weather, the good news about the war, his former wife and especially her acerbic father, the senior senator from Pennsylvania. It had been nine months since that old shyster had forced him into retirement from the Army and engineered a divorce from his only daughter that had left him stripped of dignity and half his inheritance. He hated them both with a loathing of Biblical proportions.

She had tricked him into signing a power of attorney and siphoned off half his inheritance over a period of years, placing the money in real estate within a small corporation created and controlled solely by her. He cursed her for her duplicity – after all he'd provided for her over the years. He was still wealthy in his own right but it was the principle of the matter, he repeatedly told himself. And worse, he knew she had invested 'his money' in areas poised to grow exponentially after the war. She owned a mile of Atlantic beach front just north of Ocean City, Maryland, an almost equal frontage on the north shore of Long Island east of Oyster Bay and a few thousand gently rolling acres of farm and grassland surrounding Swan Lake. Thinking about it enraged him.

He was refreshing his drink when the phone rang. He was beginning to feel that pleasant early evening buzz that went along with the daily overindulgence of his predilection for single malt scotch. At first he chose to ignore the interruption, but when it continued well past the norm he finally answered.

"Mr. Reeves, this is nurse MacKenzie at the Capitol Hill Hospice," the voice on the line said. *"I'm afraid I have to inform you of some bad news. About your father, sir. I'm afraid he's passed. It happened only an hour ago, and I have to ask you..."*

He quickly sobered and heard nothing after that.

His father was dead.

Everything else would fall into place after that piece of good news.

*   *   *   *

The religious service for Senator Trenton G. Reeves was held in Baltimore at the historic old St. John's Episcopal Church on Greenmount Avenue. It was a century old but pretty 'English Country Gothic style' building, sure to draw praise from those attending because of its solemn piety and appropriately beautiful trappings. The old stone building had a glorious bell tower and spire; the interior decoration was in the austere Victorian gothic revival style. This was high church and suitable for the religious sendoff of a pretentious agnostic old man like his father who donated large sums to both Catholic charities and Protestant ministries for 'fire insurance' in the event there really was a God, a heaven, a hell or a purgatory. Harrison thought his father might possibly appreciate the irony of all the trappings of a church funeral service conducted by a proper religionist he'd never met extolling his earthly existance.

There was a viewing the evening before at a local funeral home attended by all those who had sought his father's favor in his life and would likely seek the son's favor now that he was gone. The attendance was remarkable, Harrison thought, both in the numbers of people and the positions they held, mostly in government. Now, after the funeral service, there was a catered reception in a large hall just off the narthex.

"Your father was a remarkable man," the Maryland governor told him off to the side of the room not long after the benediction. Davis Landry, a rising star in Maryland's Democratic party, was a handsome man in his mid-forties from Montgomery County which bordered on Washington, D.C. He'd been elected with a significant majority and was well thought of in the state party hierarchy. And, like many of the senior Democrats in Maryland, he was also the beneficiary of significant campaign financial assistance from Senator Trenton G. Reeves. "I think he shaped the political landscape in our nation as well as the state for a generation. Quite possibly more."

"Yes, he certainly did, Davis," Michael O'Dell replied, nodding. "My own father, bless his soul, always said Trenton was a force to be reckoned with. We shall not see the likes of him in our state, or the party, any time soon."

Harrison slowly sipped his drink, thinking how shallow and insipid these people were. "Actually, he made provisions for his legacy to live on."

"How so?" Landry asked warily, casting a circumspect glance at O'Dell who headed up the state's Democratic committee.

"His will entrusts the management of his political trust fund to me as his sole heir under the proviso that his money be spent in furtherance of certain goals and agendas."

"What specifically, Harrison?" O'Dell asked uncertainly.

"Those things he championed throughout his lifetime in the senate. We talked about it at length before his death and he left me with a handwritten document from which to make decisions about the allocation of funds. All Democratic party issues, certainly. And Democratic candidates aligned with his philosophy of governance of course."

"Of course, Harrison," O'Dell replied falteringly. "And he left the decision making to you, you say? With his written guidance?"

"Certainly. He was never one to leave his opinions or his finances up in the air without precise direction. That simply wasn't him." Reeves paused to sip his drink and look slowly around the reception. "As always, he was clear as to his desires for his successor."

"Can you be more specific, Harrison? The state committee has always put great stock in your father's advice and guidance," Michael O'Dell offered, taking a canapé from the circulating hostess.

"More specifically, he desired his legislative agenda in Congress to continue on after his death so the progress made in the last two decades not be impeded. That was his particular directive to me in his last few days as we discussed his legacy. Specifically, he was adamant that I succeed him and fulfill the remainder of his term." Reeves appeared to stare off toward the far side of the room but his real attention was focused on the governor.

"I was unaware of his desire in that eventuality," Landry said after a long pause. "I would have thought since the responsibility to appoint his successor rests with the governor, that he would have relayed his wishes directly to me."

"He was not well in his last days and could barely speak much less write, although he was lucid and very much in control of his faculties for brief periods." Reeves turned his gaze on the governor and stared for several seconds. "Surely you're not questioning my truthfulness or my honor, are you governor?"

"Of course not, Harrison," Landry protested. We've known each other too long for me to start doubting you at this late date. I'll certainly run this by the state party committee per protocol. But I see no issues."

"Nor do I," O'Dell added quickly. "The Maryland Democratic committee will certainly not stand in the way of Trenton Reeves' desires for the furtherance of his or the party's goals. You can most assuredly count on that."

"Thank you, gentlemen. I'm certain my father would be most pleased. I'll check back with you, governor, the middle of next week to work out the wording for your announcement. If you'll excuse me, I see the rector of this fine church and I must offer my sincere thanks for the wonderful homily and the conduct of the service. Excuse me, won't you?"

As Reeves walked away, Landry looked at O'Dell. "Well, Mike, what do you think of that little performance?"

"I think we just got steam-rolled by that son-of-a-bitch. Everything he told us was a lie. His old man hated Harrison's guts and I think we just got a glimpse of why. But Trenton's son now controls about a third of the financing of Democratic office holders and candidates in the state. He knows it, and he knows we know it. He as much as told us the funds will dry up if we don't play ball with him."

Landry nodded. "He's a liar, a cheat and from what we just saw, a highway robber. He's got most of the prerequisites to be a congressman. I guess it's possible we could do worse. How, I don't know. At times like this I despair I've chosen the wrong path for my life."

After speaking briefly with the senior minister of St. John's, Reeves encountered his father's former lawyer and took him aside.

"I appreciate your coming today," Harrison said obsequiously to Arthur Stockbridge, a senior partner at Semmes, Goodall & Taylor, one of Baltimore's oldest law firms. "First, let me apologize for my father's recent decision to cease using your firm's services."

"No apologies needed, Harrison."

"I beg to differ, Arthur. Let me assure you the long, long relationship between your firm and the Reeves family will be reestablished. You have my word on it." Harrison had finessed the firing of Stockbridge's firm before he'd learned of his father's updated will and now realized the necessity of keeping them close and on his side. "Again, I apologize for my father and my family. But I must say he was not in his right mind these last few months. Had he been rational, this unfortunate circumstance would never have come about, I assure you."

Stockbridge nodded slowly and his eyes said he understood.

"I have a copy of his will, which is dated four years ago. Now, however I understand he was thinking of changing it. Would you know about that, Arthur?" Reeves asked, looking casually around as if the subject was mere conversation and of little interest to him.

"He stopped by the office Thanksgiving week with some notes for a rewrite."

"Was it ever finished and signed?"

"Completed, yes. But I don't recall he ever stopped back to review the updates or sign it. It was right about the time of his latest medical episode. You don't have a copy?"

Reeves had run across the rewritten will in his father's home office and the changes had shocked him into action. "I'm sorry I don't," he lied. "He told me in a pique of anger he was going to do something, but honestly I shrugged it off. He'd been having deeper and more frequent episodes of dementia in the last half of the year and I assumed it was that. So the only executed will then is the one dated four years ago?"

"Yes, that's correct," the lawyer said. "You're sure your father was suffering dementia? The last I saw him he was fine, and we had a very congenial chat over a crabcake lunch at Hausner's. He had just donated a Eugene de Blaas painting to the restaurant. Quite nice."

"Sadly, he was lucid at times and could fool even me, however he'd been suffering under delusions for some time. In fact, he was sure you were behind a cabal at your firm to steal his house and his fortune. I'm surprised you and most of his colleagues in the senate didn't see it. But, he always was a pro at hiding his true inner thoughts. As I said, I plan to reinstate your firm as our official legal counsel immediately. From what I can see, it's been some years since your fees have gone up and I propose increasing the retainer for the firm by seven percent and your personal pin money by fifty thousand a year."

"That's more than generous of you, Harrison."

"Not at all, Arthur. You've served our family well and it's only appropriate to recognize that. As the executor of the will, I have some questions. I'll call your office in the coming weeks to review the details of the will. I expect I have some latitude in some areas concerning bequests but I would greatly appreciate your guidance. Wouldn't want to break the law any more than I'd want to circumvent my father's *actual* wishes."

"Of course. I'd be glad to assist any way I can. I'll have my secretary or one of my associates call you this week to set it up. Again, Harrison, my deepest condolences. And thank you for you thoughtfulness in our future relationship."

"It's my privilege. And thank you Arthur, in advance, for your help and wise counsel."

It was approaching dinner time and the reception was breaking up when Trevor Callahan confronted Reeves and led him outside.

"What the hell are you doing, Harrison?" the congressman asked, animated and clearly angry when he was sure they were beyond hearing range. "I just talked to the governor and he says you're replacing your father for the remainder of his term. That's almost five years."

"Yes, I think you're correct, Trevor. Fifty-six months, but close enough."

"We had an agreement."

Reeves furrowed his brow, deep in thought. "An agreement? Concerning what exactly?"

"You know what! About your supporting me with the State party apparatus to replace your father in the senate when he moved on. We talked last spring after the Maryland-Hopkins lacrosse game."

"I remember your asking about it, but I don't recall ever agreeing to such a thing. Good grief, Trevor, I have no say in such matters. I never have."

"You lying son-of-a-bitch."

"You hold it right there, old chum. Impugning my honor is not something I take lightly."

"Your honor? What a farce."

Reeves looked quickly around to ensure they were alone. "Congressman, you should weigh your words very carefully from this point on. I'll forgive you now, but I won't take such slander lightly going forward. I hope you understand my meaning."

"Oh, I get your meaning all right," Callahan replied through clenched teeth. "I don't know why I should be surprised at this. You were the least trusted guy in our class at Gilman – and the least liked. I was hoping you had changed."

Reeves showed his old prep school classmate a churlish smile as he leaned very close. "I never liked you Trevor – not then and not now. You know why? Because you're a whiner and a loser – a guy who never accomplished anything on his own in his entire life. My father – for what reason will always remain a mystery to me and those who know you – put you through Gilman and then bought you your Congressional seat with his money."

"He did that because he liked me. He saw something in me he didn't see or like in you. You were the son he had. I was the son he wished he'd had."

Reeves leaned away and produced his most winning smile. "Perhaps you're right, Trevor. But you were the son to which he left nothing. I'm the son to whom he left everything. And from now on you will see how much you relied on his money and his good offices, because your next campaign will have neither. You'll have a challenger from your own party and *he* will be the beneficiary of the Reeves' family treasure. You're a loser, Trevor, and always have been. Your career is inconsequential, your marriage is train wreck and even when I steered you into a relationship with that Nolan woman you were unable to consummate even that. She was ripe for the picking and yet, to my utter amazement, in almost two years you've failed to get her into your bed."

Callahan stared silently and angrily at Reeves. "I'm glad your wife divorced you and took half your money when she left. Serves you right."

"Trevor, I'm truly surprised. Petulance is unbecoming a United States Representative. Rest assured, I'm not done with her yet… but I will be done with you next fall when you're defeated in the Democratic primary. Until then, you would be wise to stay out of my way. No one ever bests Harrison Reeves. No one."

The thought occurred to him that within a few years he would have enough seniority bought and paid for by his grandfather's railroad and steel money to conduct hearings into whatever he deemed unethical practices involving interstate commerce. He questioned whether or not he could make a case against her, but…

Dave Nolan? Barrett Enterprises and war profiteering? That was a different story.

Chapter 46

SUBJECT: Extract

      Thirtieth Corps Journal Entries – Highlights, Spring Offensive, 1945
      Headquarters, Third United States Army
      General George S. Patton
      Commanding

5 March 1945

XXX Corps continues active defense vicinity of Saarburg with elements of 21st Infantry Division and 15th Armored Division advancing through the west wall seizing the city of Trier. Corps advance during period of 8 – 23 Feb. limited by temporary defensive mission, thereafter constrained by 3rd Army order to limited attacks in support of phase 1 – Operation Lumberjack, 1st U.S. Army. Corps attacked and seized Bitburg. XXX Corps advance since 23 Feb. - 12 miles.

17 March 1945

Corps attack southeast through Hunsruck Mountains continues toward city of Birkenfeld against elements of German Seventh Army – Brandenberger. Isolated pockets of resistance bypassed by 15th Armd. Div. 23rd Inf. Div. N of Birkenfeld. U. S. Casualties (all units assigned XXX Corps) since 11 March: killed (KIA)- 16; wounded (WIA)- 548; missing (MIA)- 6

21 March 1945

Attack continues against light resistance. 15th Armd. Div. now in control of city of Mannheim. 58th Inf. Div. occupies Worms. Parts of German Seventh Army – Brandenberger surrendered after being surrounded north of Brakenfeld by Task Force Simpson (21st Inf. Div. +) – estimated 11-13,000 POW. Advance since initiation of operations on 5 March 45 : 80 miles.

28 March 1945

23rd Inf. Div. seized city of Aschaffenburg (three days house to house fighting). 15th Armd. Div. striking northeast between Frankfurt and Hanau along a 40 mile deep corridor.

4 April 1945

XXX Corps reduced German salient Frankfurt-Limburg-Giessen then continued attack northeast along the left flank of corridor developed by 25th Armd. Div. 29 Mar – 4 April to seize the city of Mulhausen. 23rd Inf. Div. occupied city of Kassel 1130 hrs. 1 April and seized high ground extending two miles north and northeast.

* * * *

Kilroy was working on the finishing touches of his latest dispatch while sitting in the back seat of a jeep outside the old post office building in Mulhausen. After doing an article for the wire services on Bradley, he had wangled a courier flight to the captured airfield just outside the town and there talked his way into a ride to XXX Corps headquarters. No matter what the wire services wanted in the way of the story line, he always found some excuse to return to Nolan's area of operations. The relationship they'd developed first in North Africa and later in Sicily had paid dividends for them both and was one the reporter worked especially hard at maintaining.

He enjoyed the frequent late-night sessions with the general, many of which had nothing to do with the tactical or strategic developments of the war. He found Dave Nolan to be well read, a philosopher of sorts. Most of Kilroy's best pieces could be traced to these informal nocturnal chats and inside information from his staff. Beyond that, Nolan allowed him special status and free access to any place in his Corps area, often providing transportation, an escort officer and paving the way with a quick phone call to ensure cooperation from the units under his command. It had made the job of covering the action on the continent much easier, and his privileged status was the envy of all the other pool reporters he knew. The article he was finishing now, on the massive supply effort using captured German airfields only a few short miles from the front, was one of the many stories the general had put him onto.

He was in the middle of the dispatch, describing how the allies were using converted bombers to shuttle supplies now that targets in Germany were becoming scarce, when Nolan walked down the steps and crossed to the mud spattered Jeep.

"Didn't know you were dropping in," the general said evenly, giving him a stern look. Absent was the usual smile and friendly greeting, and for an instant Kilroy wondered if he'd done something wrong. Even when things weren't going well, Nolan had always been friendly with him.

"Thought I'd stop by and offer you a drink while picking your brain."

"Don't have time. Maybe later." Nolan was clearly agitated. He yelled at his driver, Sergeant Zimmer, to hurry up and looked back at the reporter. "Maybe you should go with me," he said tightly.

Yup, something is definitely wrong, Kilroy thought. He'd never heard the general use that tone with his driver – usually he couched things as requests and treated the young sergeant more like a son than a draftee soldier. There was never any doubt among the troops under his command who was in charge and he didn't have to raise his voice to get done what he wanted accomplish. Except for Bradley, Nolan was the most unpretentious general officer Kilroy had ever run across. He still wore issued clothing – clean but unpressed fatigues, G. I. boots, and a paratroopers field jacket with the big slanted breast pockets. Around his waist a simple web belt with his .45 caliber M1911 in a plain black government issue holster. He'd once heard that Patton had offered to send over his personal armorer to make up a flashier set of sidearms for Nolan, but the general had declined preferring to stick with his M1 and the old pistol with worn bluing and simple wooden grips.

"This isn't gonna be one of those good stories, Eamonn," Nolan said as they started out of town. "The 21st just took a place called Buchenwald, and it sounds damned grizzly. If it's half as bad as what they say… Well, maybe we'll just wait and see. Butternuts can blow stuff out of proportion now and again."

As they drove, Nolan gave the reporter an outline of recent operations since the beginning of April – the drive eastward through cities made famous in the Napoleonic battles. They passed through Erfurt, driving down the narrow rubble strewn streets bordered by devastated buildings. On the outskirts of the town sat a power station, a huge coal and gasworks, destroyed by bombs and battered by artillery; its walls had huge, gaping holes blown in the sides. All that remained of the roof were the steel girders, warped and blackened by fire. Finally they came to Weimar, and just beyond that sat Buchenwald.

"Just how bad is it, Jerry?" Nolan asked Colonel Curtis, a middle aged officer who had been the Jacksonville city manager before the war. He now served as the Corps G-5 – Civil and Military Relations Officer.

Curtis looked warily at Kilroy and said, "It's worse than Simpson reported to General Fauser. Not sure what we have and we might want to hold off opening it up to the press."

"If it's that bad, I definitely *want* the press to see it," Dave Nolan replied. "How many people here?"

"My guess is somewhere around fifteen thousand, sir. It's going to take a while to get an accurate count. I've never seen or heard of anything like this."

"Fifteen thousand? In this little place?"

"Yes, sir. Slave laborers, Jews, political prisoners. Once you see the conditions –"

"Let's take a look, Jerry."

When they passed through the barbed wire fence, he realized that Simpson had indeed understated his findings. A final count three days later would put the exact number of prisoners at over twenty-one thousand. But it was their condition that was worst of all.

The thin-walled barracks were filthy and crowded with narrow bunks four tiers high. There was no bedding or blankets. Those left alive were flesh covered skeletons with shaved heads, ghastly protruding ribs and hip bones, and deep sunken eyes that gazed back at him with the look of the insane. Very few were strong enough to stand or even sit; most were too weak to move and simply lay on the hard slats with their heads resting on filthy shreds of towels folded on top of eating pans. Each time they opened a door to enter another of these hovels, a blast of thick heavy air laden with the awful stench of human feces greeted them.

Curtis showed them other buildings housing incinerators still warm to the touch, and it confirmed the reports what Andy had told him at headquarters. Outside, naked and emaciated bodies lay stacked in piles five and six feet high like jumbled, twisted cord wood. Everywhere was the penetrating smell of burned flesh and the overpowering odor of the dead.

Another building housed a ghoulish laboratory. On the shelves were glass jars containing shrunken heads, diseased lungs, kidneys, and tanned pieces of flesh. They saw all of this in silence, shocked and humbled at the grotesque and mad scene. Finally, unable to bear the macabre sight of the camp any longer, Dave Nolan walked across the open yard and out of the entrance, his face set in hard, cold anger.

"Colonel, you've got one hell of a job ahead of you here," he said to Curtis as they stood beside the Jeep. "I'll tell General Kiel you have priority on food, supplies and personnel to help these people. I'll send you detachments from the engineers and the car platoon, and everybody you want from the med battalion. If you need more doctors than they can supply, let me know and I'll get them for you. That's a promise."

Kilroy leaned against the vehicle's fender, ashen faced and physically sick. He had stopped and dry heaved several times after leaving the crematorium. "What kind of monsters do this?" he asked, wiping his mouth with the back of his wrist.

"Sick, sick people," Nolan replied. "Where the hell were the citizens of the town when this was going on?"

Curtis shrugged. "I've talked to some of them already and they said they had no idea anything like this was happening. They said all they knew was that the SS was running some kind of camp."

"Didn't know?! You can smell the stench of this place for miles. Didn't know?! Well, by damn, they'll know before this day is out, Colonel. I'm going to send a platoon of MPs to round up every last soul in Weimar and herd them through this place. I want them to see every damned detail and then I want them pressed into service as the cleanup detail! And Kilroy – if you're anything more than a half assed reporter, I expect to see this story on every front page of every newspaper and in every magazine in America by the end of next week."

"General, that might not be too wise," Curtis offered. "At least not right now."

Nolan glared at the colonel. "Frankly, I don't give a damn. I want the people of Weimar and the whole world to see the result of *Nazi Kultur*. They ought to know what kind of butchers we're fighting over here. And if they don't like that…" Nolan turned and looked hard at Kilroy. "You guys in the press have a responsibility to put a spotlight on the truth. You owe it to the people in this camp and to the whole world to tell this story completely and graphically and to never let any of us forget. Zimmer, let's get out of here before I turn homicidal."

As the sergeant wrestled with the gear shift and ground it into low, Nolan took one last look over his shoulder at the swastika emblem on a sign attached to the barbed wire fence. He would never forget Buchenwald. Never.

And he hoped the world wouldn't either.

*   *   *   *

The high ceilinged room of the Benedictine Abbey echoed with the sound of his footsteps as Dave Nolan crossed to the mirror and checked the fit of his uniform again. He looked slowly around the room and thought how different it was from the big châteaus in France, or the *Schloss Weissenstein* in Pomersfelden. Now that the crusade was nearly at an end, it seemed almost fitting that his last battle directives should be issued from this Austrian holy place. A crusade? He smiled sadly, remembering Kate Hanley's comment to him at his going away party at West Point a quarter century earlier. *Wonder how Kate is doing? And Doc, too – I wonder if he'll ever get over being angry at me over that slapping incident with Patton on Sicily?*

Dave looked at his reflected image. The short waisted battle jacket fit well – his only compromise with Patton's dress code, aside from the lacquered helmet he would wear today for the first and last time. *Might as well look the part of a general to meet the Russians*, he thought.

Without being asked, Zimmer had scavenged the set of ribbons pinned above his left pocket – six nearly full rows of three, a multitude of colors that was in a glance a snapshot of his life in the service. Wearing them had been a compromise of sorts, too. But he still wore one of the two pairs of field boots that had carried him across Europe this time. They were now a comfortable and meaningful link to his troops.

Andy Fauser threw open the door and entered, followed by Zimmer.

"A right proud haul yesterday and today, blue belly." Lighting a cigarette his old friend added, "About 80,000 of them danged ol' Krauts surrendered. Guess they prefer Uncle Sam to them damned squint-eyed Russians. Division commanders and G-5 are tearing their hair out trying to find holding stations for all of 'em. POWs been the biggest problem on our plate for near to a month."

At least since mid-April, Dave thought.

Patton had shifted his Corps more than 100 miles to the southwest and pointed him south from Nürnberg. As the troops under Nolan's command attacked towards Regensburg and Pascal along the west bank of the Danube, German resistance grew weaker and the lines of prisoners grew longer. They had moved two hundred miles in seventeen days through Bavaria and into Austria. It was time to officially link up with their Russian allies – another unit designated XXX Corps.

"Can I assume the ceremony with Brusilov has been arranged?"

"I reckon so," Fauser replied. "Hell, Davey – never seen such a contrary sort as them Russians since I sold my plow mule before headin' to that Yankee infested rock pile we graduated from. But they said they'd be there to meet you and say howdy in the middle of the bridge like you wanted."

Dave smiled. "Maybe they're not as hard-headed as I thought they were."

The Russian general had insisted that Dave come to his command post on the other side of the Enns River so the Americans could be officially welcomed to Austria by the victorious Russian Army. Nolan had sent the Russian messenger back with a bluntly worded note that both liberating armies would meet on middle ground. Back came the reply that Brusilov would be pleased to meet him on the Russian side of the bridge. Tiring of the game, Dave dispatched Andy to inform the Russian that neither side of the bridge belonged to anybody but the Austrian people, who had suffered more than a half dozen years of Nazi occupation. With that in mind, he proposed to greet the Russian party at the center of the bridge at which time he intended to decorate the Soviet commander with the Legion of Merit, a decoration first awarded to General Black Jack Pershing during World War I. Apparently that did the trick.

Dave and Andy left the Abbey and walked through the streets of Kremsmunster to the edge of the water, then down a narrow dirt road that paralleled the river. A company of Sheridan tanks was spread out along the river bank and a platoon of infantry was waiting for him at the bridge. They stood in formation at ease, smoking and talking quietly among themselves. They reminded him of the battle weary attitude of his company of doughboys when he served in Wild Bill Donovan's battalion so long ago. As Nolan approached, the lieutenant in charge called them to attention and saluted.

"Second Platoon, Charlie company, 3rd of the 427th Infantry ready for inspection, sir."

Nolan returned the salute and then looked beyond the officer's shoulder. "They all look pretty good to me, lieutenant. They look like combat troops instead of parade ground soldiers. Have them stand at ease and smoke 'em if they got 'em." Several matches flared as he looked at their faces. He could tell the veterans, who had seen the action across France, from the new replacements that had flooded in during the last two months. Most of the men who had been with the Corps since the beginning were in their mid 20s but looked older. The newer arrivals were younger by three or four years and hadn't yet acquired that hard distant stare of those who had fought through the French bocage and traipsed across the foggy, snow-covered landscape of Germany. He had been that young once – so long ago that it seemed almost like a previous life. He turned and looked across the bridge at the assembled Russians. Behind him he could catch an occasional snatch of whispered conversation.

"Yeah, that's really General Nolan, you fuzz-faced recruit."

"… wine everywhere. I was drunk for three days back in Montmiral the first time he –"

"You never knew when or where he'd show up. Talked to me in a foxhole one night outside Weisbaden when a sniper shot at us. For a general, he could really shoot the M1."

"… then he grabbed the captain by the stacking swivel and told him not to stop until we got to Berlin. Walked through a wall of machine gun fire and stood up on that hill waitin' for the battalion to catch up…"

Nolan grinned to himself. Legends. How easily erected are our legends. Of course none of it was completely true – just enough of the truth to make it sound plausible, and a healthy dose of imagination to make it exciting; a great adventure. Now that the fighting was clearly coming to an end, the natural release had arrived – and with it the brave war stories.

"You men know what to do?" Dave asked, walking up to the formation. Several nods. "Any questions? Come on, I know there's at least one."

A redheaded youngster wearing PFC stripes spoke up. "Are we gonna get some leave time when this war is over, general?"

"You can count on it. A full limit. Not everybody at one time, but I'd say within a couple weeks you'll be able to. But all of us have to stay tuned and alert until they officially give up. There are always a lot of rumors that float around at the end of a war. So stay alert. Nobody wants to be the last man to die in any war. Keep your head up, and your eye on the front bead." He looked back at the redheaded youngster and a memory surfaced, one he had been able to put in the back part of his mind for a long while. Ed Higgins was a red head, too. "What's your name, soldier?"

"Private Anderson, sir."

"Private Anderson, I want you to promise me you'll keep your head in the game... that you'll stay alive to go home to your mom and dad... and that you'll live a good, long life."

"Yes, sir, I'll do that."

"O.K... guess it's time to meet our glorious allies." He nodded to the lieutenant who called the formation to attention. The group marched to the center of the bridge, halting ten paces from the Russians. Several photographers from the Signal Corps clicked away recording the scene, and a newsreel camera whirred softly in the background.

Brusilov was a short, stocky man with a barrel chest, a shiny bald head and steely blue eyes. He was wearing a high necked tunic covered with ribbons and medals, and riding breeches with shiny black boots. For their part, the Russians appeared coolly suspicious and Dave thought they looked more like adversaries than partners in the conflict against Hitler.

Without any formally agreed-upon ceremony for the meeting, they stood on the bridge gazing at one another. Finally, Dave stepped forward and extended his hand. Before he realized it, Brusilov grasped his hand gave him a quick unexpected kiss on each cheek and stepped back with a broad grin on his face. He said something in his native language and then an interpreter stepped forward to translate.

"General Brusilov welcomes you to Austria which has been liberated from Nazi tyranny by the glorious army of the Soviet Union."

"Tell the general that the U.S. Army is pleased as punch to finally see him here. And tell him we're glad he finally arrived, since we were liberating this country three days before his Corps crossed the Austrian border." *Two can play this game of one-upsmanship* Dave thought. The interpreter glanced warily at his face as he translated into Russian. Before Brusilov could reply, Dave motioned to Andy who came forward and gave him a small black box. "Tell General Brusilov I am pleased and honored to award him the Legion of Merit, commander class, a decoration of the very highest order in the United States Army."

As the soldier translated, Dave pinned the medal on the Russian.

"General Brusilov is very honored, sir. And he now wishes to decorate you with the *Order of the War for the Fatherland*." The Russian's broad Slavic face was still creased with a smile when he finished affixing the medal to Nolan's jacket and spoke to the interpreter." Sir, General Brusilov invites you and the members of your staff to a feast in our Corps headquarters this night at twenty-thirty in honor of XXX Corps."

"The general is most kind. Tell him we'll be there on the condition that he accepts our invitation to dine with us at the American headquarters tomorrow evening." Brusilov nodded happily and shook hands with Nolan when the interpreter relayed this to him.

Dave did an about-face and said, "All right second platoon of C company, I suggest you walk over and meet our friends from the Soviet Union. It looks like we'll be living with them for a long time."

"Ain't you just the smoothest talking thing in the whole cotton-pickin' Third Army?" Andy whispered in his ear. "Pure quill diplomatic magic, ah'd say. Tell me somethin'… they's throwing this party to honor an outfit called XXX Corps – they honorin' themselves or us?"

"Butternuts…"

"Yeah?"

"Don't drink all their liquor. Outside of Arkansas it's bad manners."

Chapter 47

At thirty-eight thousand feet, somewhere between Brussels and Geneva, he was alone with his thoughts. By Army Air Corps decree his war was officially over after this flight, even though the Germans were still holding out – for how long was anyone's guess. But it couldn't be much longer.

Mitch Nolan looked around the sky and felt inordinately melancholy.

The pilots he'd known over the past two years in the Mediterranean and then in northern Europe had all been overjoyed at the prospect of going home at end of their tours. Some, like him, had taken a brief respite of leave and signed on for another stint; no one he knew had gone beyond that.

His official total stood at a hundred and thirty-seven missions, but his own unofficial records exceeded even that. His number of missions and the scorecard of enemy kills had long since become unimportant to him. The only thing of any real importance now had eluded him.

For months he had pursued her with an even greater tenacity than he'd applied to his flying – all to no avail.

Immediately after the evening of the Glenn Miller dance at RAF Thorpe-Abbotts, he had tried to see her again, but through the fall and winter she had been mostly successful in avoiding him. He'd become a semi-regular visitor at her family's estate, having been given an open invitation by her mother and the run of the estate for rabbit and pheasant hunting by her father. Occasionally Smythe-Browne would hunt grouse with him and he'd get the latest news on how his father was doing. Most of the time he'd find himself spending the day with Cateline, teaching her the finer points of horseback riding and taking her on whirlwind tours through the countryside in the MG. She was a remarkably intelligent little girl and he enjoyed the breaks from the routine of duties at Leiston.

But Aynslee kept her distance. Every now and then he'd convince her to go to a show or a dinner, but those evenings were mostly disappointing for both of them. With the advent of spring, he accepted the reality and began to disengage, immersing himself in his flying.

The plans he'd proposed to the Bloody 100th the day of the Glenn Miller show worked well in practice and over time began to lower bomber loss rates. He was realistic enough to comprehend the gradual wearing down of the Luftwaffe by overwhelming Allied numbers was part of the reason, but so was his tactical plan.

The fighter group had begun to range out well ahead of the bombers rather than simply rendezvous and fly close support. The German fighters stayed close to their home bases and usually remained on the ground monitoring bomber formation progress with radar until the last minute before taking off and intercepting them, conserving fuel and making turnarounds faster. A week after the bomber group agreed to the change in tactics, Mitch led two squadrons consisting of sixty planes on a low level penetration of German airspace below radar level. While the box formations of B-17s were still over an hour away escorted by a skeleton squadron, both of the lead squadrons arrived over four different airfields to strafe German fighters on the ground and lingered in the area to catch others from two more airfields as they were taking off. All told, over sixty German planes were destroyed and the bombers got to the target without encountering enemy fighters. The following week the 100th Bomber Group again benefitted from a successful implementation of Nolan's tactic and it became standard operating procedure the following month. Jimmy Doolittle came to Thorpe-Abbotts in mid-November for a briefing and declared it applicable throughout all of the Eighth Air Force.

Winter weather came and blanketed northern Europe from early December until March curtailing much of their operation but Mitch usually got a couple of missions each week.

He realistically didn't consider himself the very best pilot in the Air Corps, but his ego told him he was certainly somewhere close. He'd mastered the two best fighters in the inventory (in his estimation) and had proven himself; dogfighting tested all of a pilot's strengths and had a way of exposing any of his weaknesses. He'd survived multiple dozens of such encounters – except for one. Thinking about it now he cursed the fourth and final German in the fight over Marseille – *the guy should have gone home instead of sticking around after his three buddies got waxed*, he told himself again. He wondered if the pilot had survived the war so far. Probably not. The Americans were too many and had better equipment now.

He missed not being in a front line squadron – he even missed Dixie Sloan… now and then. Dixie had made him a better pilot in North Africa, he had to admit. Sloan was competition, he was gutsy, and he was an example to follow, sometimes. Looking back on the old G-model Lightning he thought of as such a hot machine back then, he was amazed at how sluggish and difficult to fly it was compared to the Mustang and the last two variants of the Lightning. He'd gotten the use of a new L-model just before one of the groups in England phased them out and transferred into Mustangs. What a war machine it was. He wondered how the old 49th Squadron was doing these days. They'd all be brand new faces now – a bunch of young kids getting educated in the school of life and death in a fighter squadron. That was the place where real friendships and real flying happened. He was glad he'd had the experience back then and missed it now. But he'd lost a lot of friends in the process.

Unlike the previous week, the weather was cooperating. He could see the Alps, majestic and glistening white in the sun. It was breathtaking now that he could relax and enjoy the view without concentrating on a disciplined scanning of the sky looking for distant enemy planes.

This day he'd gotten himself assigned as a maintenance spare for one of the squadrons so that if one of their Mustangs developed mechanical problems, he could take their place. They rendezvoused with the bombers over Brussels and was happy to learn nobody had fallen out. Instead of returning to base, he turned south for a final tour of Europe before hanging up his spurs and heading home. *Wouldn't it be funny if one of the remaining few Luftwaffe aces was out on a final hunt and ran across me? Nope – don't need for that to happen, Nolan. This is a pleasure cruise today, friend. Really wouldn't want to get waxed at this late date.*

As he approached Lichtenstein, he could see Augsburg and south of there the Bavarian Alps off his left wing; he thought he could even make out the Brenner Pass. He remembered flying over the Swiss Alps for the first time on a mission out of Triolo. Looking down at the harsh and rugged landscape he thought how little time a body could survive if he went down. Another memory surfaced – Blaxton strafing a petrol wagon on a back road down in a small valley; Mitch had watched it from two thousand feet as he provided cover for the kid. It was only his fifth or sixth mission.

The new pilot had dropped into the valley and lined up on a straight stretch of road, but between him and the petrol wagon coming at him was an old man in a hay wagon slowly making his way, unaware of the P-38 looming behind him. Blaxton slowed as much as he could by dropping his flaps and lowering the landing gear. He'd been sure the kid was going to stall and crash – but he didn't. As soon as the old man passed the petrol truck, Blaxton fired a quick burst and the tank exploded. Instantly he poured on power, raised his gear and flaps and barely made it out of the valley. Mitch could see the old man whipping the horse for all he was worth and he could even see the old man look up as the big Lightning passed directly over, missing him by a few short yards. When Mitch asked him about it later that night, the kid shrugged. "I didn't have anything against that old man and his horse. Just didn't want to hurt him, that's all." Mitch had taken a special interest in him after that. He wondered if the kid had survived his fifty missions. He hoped so.

He turned *The Mistress* – number four, he reminded himself – to the west and headed for Geneva. He'd never been to Geneva and thought he'd like to see it before going home. It was about two hundred miles across the neutral country, and wondered if it was against any international agreements to transit across a declared non-belligerent country in time of war. He really didn't know. He remembered something Churchill said at some point; he didn't know exactly when or the circumstances but he was quoted as saying: *"The hottest place in hell must be reserved for those who, in the face of great moral crisis, maintain their neutrality."* He wondered if he'd said it about Switzerland. Mitch decided he agreed and that he'd buzz Geneva when he got there.

Nolan was at fifty feet of altitude and four hundred miles per hour as he reached Lake Geneva where it became very narrow and funneled down to the city of Geneva itself. He was at rooftop level as he flashed over the city, going too fast to see Saint Peters Church where John Calvin had preached. He thought about coming around for a lower and slower pass, but decided against it. *Better not give anyone a second chance at identifying markings or a tail number*, he thought, and continued into France.

North of Marseille, he thought he located a wrecked P-38 and wondered if it was his lost bird, *Mistress III*. But he couldn't tell. He circled until he was sure he'd found the farmhouse where Margot and Gérard had hidden him, and later Yeager. He did a few low and slow passes, but no one came out to investigate or wave. He was disappointed. He thought about trying to find the path he'd taken through the Pyrenees into Spain but decided against it realizing he'd been exhausted and often delusional during the trek. Spain hadn't been all that cordial the first time and he doubted they'd smile at his violating their border a second time either.

He climbed up to twenty thousand for the trip to Paris. He'd never been there but had seen it from the air a number of times. One more look; maybe take a photograph.

Instantly he thought of Lucky.

He'd kept that memory from his conscious thoughts for a long time. He allowed himself to sift through memories – from West Point, graduation leave, flight school; Casablanca and all his crazy shenanigans flying out of Telerghma. He wondered if he'd ever forget watching Lindquist go down from the flak or hearing his last words over the radio. Such a waste.

When he reached Paris he gave the city more leeway than he had Geneva, before heading out to the beaches at Normandy. Halfway there he decided against it. He couldn't visit the place where Glenn had died. Not yet. Maybe not ever, but certainly not today.

By the time he landed back at Leiston it was mid-afternoon.

He checked in at operations, and learned the word had come down that the Germans were suing for peace. The word was out they would surrender officially in two days and all Air Corps aircraft were grounded until further notice.

He walked back to the hut and began gathering his belongings. Maybe he was one of the lucky ones – going home without doing occupation duty or being saddled with all the burdens of decommissioning units and equipment. That would be a mess. A real mess. And a lot of that nit-picking detail work in a fighter or bomber group would likely fall on the deputy commander. *Somebody's still looking out for you, Nolan. You dodged another bullet.*

The war was over. He had survived. And he would be one of the first to go home.

Then why do you feel so down? he asked himself.

Silence answered as he began loading his footlocker and duffle bag.

*   *   *   *

He awoke the next morning convinced the Russian Army had camped in his mouth with their muddy boots on, and some Viking had left his battle axe planted in his forehead.

It had been a wild party – what he could remember of it.

Like most of the pilots in the Group he had really enjoyed the last few months at Leiston. Winter had been damp and dreary but the coming of spring and the clearing skies lifted everyone's spirits. The announcement of German surrender now seemed almost surreal.

He'd spent most of his military career since graduation flying combat missions. Thinking back on his time with Donald Bennett, flying twin engine Lockheeds across the North Atlantic, he decided that was a combat mission and easily as dangerous as just about anything he'd done. He'd run across Bennett once since then while the Australian was commanding the British Bomber Command's Pathfinder group and they'd shared some memories over a beer.

Now that the war was over, combat flying was a thing of the past, and most of the men and women in the military would go back to the civilian world and get on with the life they had before the war. He realized he had nothing like that to which he could return. He'd been in the military all his life – an Army brat growing up on military posts around the world, a college career of sorts in the military mold and his first and only job was in uniform – shooting down other airplanes. He doubted there would be much of a market for that skill set. They had made the world safe again… and now? All of a sudden, the peace seemed at least as daunting as the war had been and his orders and future were an absolute muddle.

Or were they? He wasn't sure.

But the real question: what does a professional officer do when the war ends? What next? For that question he had no answer, and he wished he could discuss it with his father. *Take it one day at a time, Nolan. If there was ever a time to hurry up and wait, this seems to be it.*

There was somebody who had decided to wait no longer. She showed up the next day.

Cateline arrived just after noon with her grandmother and found him in his hut with clothes strewn on the GI bed and his footlocker open and in a sad mess. The young girl looked around and finally asked, "Is this really where you live? It stinks in here."

Mitch gave her a rueful smile and looked up at Maud Smythe-Browne who shrugged, looking amused. "Out of the mouths of babes," she said and shrugged again.

"So, Miss Cateline, what brings you here?" Mitch asked. "And how did you two get in?"

"It *really* stinks in here," Cateline repeated with emphasis and made a face.

"I wasn't prepared for an inspection or the company of ladies." Mitch tried and failed to hide a smile. "I'll work on it, all right? But the question remains. How and why are you here?"

"I wanted to see where you live," the girl replied very seriously. "And I have a present for you. I think we need to talk, Mr. Mitch. All of us."

"Really?" Mitch replied, trying to keep a straight face. "Did someone put you up to this?"

"It was my own idea," Cateline declared emphatically. "I made you a present last night, but I have been thinking about this for some time." The girl handed over a piece of blue craft paper on which she had glued a hand-written note on white bond. "I hope you like it."

She stood very erect, watching him closely and waiting for him to read the note.

Peace

Peace is green.

It smells like love; It tastes like candy.

It is smaller than God; But it is bigger than the world.

War is its worst enemy; Freedom is its best friend.

Peace keeps hate in its secret place.

Peace's favorite place is heaven; Peace's least favorite place is war.

Peace makes me feel free!

- Cateline   10 May 1945

By the time he got to the last line he could hardly see to read it and turned away to wipe his eyes. "Thank you, Cateline. It's beautiful. I wish people around the world had read your poem before this war got started."

"Mr. Mitch, I wanted you to have that poem because you need peace, too. And my mum and I – we all need peace."

"I couldn't agree with you more."

"Then if you know that, and I know it, and my mum knows, why don't we have peace?"

"But we do have peace… now. They announced it two days ago."

"I'm not talking about that peace," the girl replied. "I'm talking about peace with you and my mum. Every time she talks about you to grandmother she cries. That's not peace! You need to make that stop." She looked at him with the most puzzled look and finally said, "I like you Mr. Mitch, and we have fun together. I don't have a father any more and I need one. I'd like you to be my father. Would you?"

"Cateline!" Maud interrupted. "What on earth, young lady?!"

The seven year old looked frustrated and finally looked at Mitch. "You and my mum should talk. You come see her this Saturday," she declared, and quickly walked outside.

"I don't think I've ever been braced by a seven year old before," Mitch said. "What was that all about?"

"She's a very bright little girl, and she sees a problem for herself – no father, a problem for her mother – no husband, and she sees you as the answer. To a child all things are simple and all problems are easily solved."

"If only the real world worked like that," Mitch said wistfully.

"Perhaps it does in some cases."

"Not in mine – and definitely not where Aynslee is concerned. I've about given up."

"Young man! *About* is different than *wholly*, and you have an invitation from a little girl who will be greatly disappointed if you don't come by this weekend. I've never known you to disappoint her. I'll have luncheon ready for when you arrive. Say around eleven?"

*　　　*　　　*

He was early.

Sleep had been difficult the night before and he'd left Leiston earlier than usual. The roads were no more crowded than usual and he'd pushed the jeep a little faster, probably because he was thinking more about what he wanted to say than he was about his driving. Nothing he dreamed up sounded right to him and by the time he turned into Smythe-Browne's estate he was certain nothing good would come of this visit. For a brief instant he considered throwing in the towel and turning around. In the end, he didn't.

He parked the vehicle out front and walked around behind the house instead of knocking at the front door as he usually did.

He wandered toward the stable and then went inside, stopping to pet the bay mare when she came over and nuzzled his hand looking for an apple. He gave her one he'd taken from the mess hall the night before. When he walked toward the back he was surprised to see the big white back in a stall. Unlike the first time, the animal came to the gate quietly and took oats from Mitch's hand, and allowed his nose to be stroked.

"Well, this is a surprise, big fella," Mitch said. "How did you find your way back here?"

"I bought him back yesterday," a voice from behind him said.

He turned and looked at Aynslee, unable to think of anything to say. An awkward silence lingered between them as he tried without success to find words that conveyed his feelings.

"The man I sold him to said nobody could or wanted to ride him. He's too high strung and with the war on, nobody had the time or patience to try. He seems to remember you, even after all this time. Isn't that strange?"

"I guess it is," he said apprehensively.

"Would you like to ride him again?"

"I'd like that, yes," he said, and quickly added, "but, not now. Aynslee... I had to see you one last time. I came here because –"

"I'm glad you did," she nervously interrupted him. "It's been more than a month."

"I didn't feel welcome."

"My parents like you a great deal, and Cateline absolutely adores you."

"I know."

"The problem is not them of course, is it, Mitch? It's me. And it has been since the day you first knocked on our front door with that silly little story about being an American officer traveling undercover and all."

"I don't for the life of me know why I said that," he offered without thinking, and then reconsidered. "Actually, I guess I do. I can say some really asinine things when disconcerted, and I was definitely flustered when I saw you. You took my breath away and my brain went numb. You can probably tell I'm suffering from that right now, can't you?"

"I felt the same way. And I remember dashing out before I made a complete fool of myself. It was a terrible experience."

"You?..."

"Yes. A married woman, thinking the unthinkable, if only for an instant. It frightened me. I found out later my husband was not only thinking the unthinkable, but acting on it. I was confused. Angry. I took it out on you the next day. I think I've always thought of you in that light, as connected somehow with what went wrong in my marriage. I know that's silly. Every time afterward I did what I could to push you away and hopefully keep you away, thinking if I did, I wouldn't be reminded of all those unpleasant feelings."

"But the note that foggy morning…"

"I realized I was being unbearably ill-mannered for no good reason, and I truly wanted to apologize. I hoped you would write and accept my apology."

"And I never did."

"No, but you showed up again… at about the time I had given up on you and moved on. But you were always the persistent one. You have always confused me with your responses and your timing. And I'm not blaming you. I'm not. I've had bouts of guilt wondering what I did to make Malcolm stray, if I'd been part of the reason he died, even. I've carried around a lot of guilt about him, and I couldn't bear the thought of carrying around any about you."

"How could you be guilty of anything concerning me?"

"I worried about you. Until VE Day, I worried you would be shot down and was afraid of the effect it would have on me. I loved Malcolm, I really did. I hated what he did to me, but I still loved him. I can't explain it." She sighed deeply and looked away. "And I lost him to the war. Since his death, I've hardened myself to him, but I didn't know if I could stand losing two men I loved to the same war."

"You never told me you loved me…"

"I was afraid to. I was always afraid to show my real feelings. It became terribly difficult when you came back to England this last year. Honestly I was afraid of my feelings for you. But for some reason, I'm not afraid any more." She looked at him again; her eyes were full of tears. "How could anyone love somebody like me? My mother thinks I need to see a head doctor. She… Why am I telling you this now? I hadn't planned to. I actually planned to go for a ride and stay gone until you left."

He took a deep breath. "Do you still want to go for that ride… with me?"

"I think that would be nice."

He took her into his arms and hugged her close for a quick moment; when he released her, she held tight.

"I've needed a hug for so long. I really have," she said softly. "A hug says 'I'm here for you, and I care.' It's the best of all silent languages. I know you're here, Mitch, and I know you care about me.

"And I can tell you now, truly – I too care, and I want to be here for you as well."

Chapter 48

"Attention to Orders!"

The clarion-like announcement by the cadet guard from the front of Washington Hall brought silence to the huge West Point mess hall as cadets looked up at the raised granite 'Poop Deck" thirty feet above the floor. The Superintendent stood and came to the microphone.

"We have the privilege of dining this noon with our morning's reviewing officer. Our guest insisted I not spend more than ten seconds introducing him which precludes my reciting his long list of accomplishments and decorations. It also prevents me from telling you he is one of two men in his graduating class to achieve the rank of Lieutenant General or telling you he commanded a Corps in combat." General Wilby turned and briefly looked behind him before again addressing the Corps of Cadets. "Our guest advises me I am already encroaching into the time he has allotted for his one minute speech."

Laughter and clapping erupted in the mess hall, echoing off the four story ceiling.

"As I was saying," Wilby continued, "time precludes me from mentioning he was a two time All-American and a member of the 1914 National Championship football squad or that he lettered in baseball three years as a catcher. Had I the time, I could tell our guest served under General MacArthur when he was the Superintendent of the Academy after World War I, and that much of the land on which you train during the summer was procured by our visitor. Thus precluded from telling you anything about our speaker, I leave it to General Patton, who yesterday sent our guest the following wire from Europe:

Upon your return to West Point I again congratulate you on the outstanding service you provided your country in this latest conflict. As a division commander in North Africa, Sicily and Italy and as a Corps commander in northern Europe, you served long and well. When the history of this great war is written, one of its brightest chapters will certainly be the gallant effort of XXX Corps which you commanded for 278 consecutive days, from the date 3rd Army came ashore on the continent until the cessation of hostilities. In that time, you crossed every major river in Europe, and covered 1300 miles against a determined enemy – an enemy that had conquered France in six days and fought the world to a standstill for five long years. When the final tally was counted, you had captured 426,219 German POWs – the equivalent of 42 enemy divisions – a remarkable feat considering you never had more than four divisions of your own on the battlefield. Of all the Corps under my command, yours has always been the one of which I was most proud.

/*signed*/ George S. Patton, Jr.

"Gentleman of the Corps of Cadets, I introduce to you Lieutenant General David A. Nolan, class of 1916, who returns today from the battlefields of Europe."

The applause started at the back of the three wings when Dave Nolan approached the microphone. As the applause continued, he stood looking around at the cavernous interior of the majestic building taking in the dark wooden wainscoting, tall windows, lofty timbered ceiling and the giant mural covering the entire wall of one of the wings. He held up his hands for silence but it was a futile gesture.

"Take your seats!" he said loudly into the microphone when the noise ebbed slightly. "It is an honor to be with you this day, to be here in this place… to be home. I am unprepared to make a speech because I was told by General Eisenhower when he assigned me this duty that my only responsibility would be to command '*Pass in Review*' and then enjoy the parade."

Ike had called him to SHAEF headquarters a week after the official declaration of the end of the war and told him he was going home. Wilby had requested a senior commander as official reviewing officer for the graduation parade of the class of '45, and the Supreme Allied commander was in a mood to oblige. Eisenhower had decided Andy could finish up whatever needed to be done in dismantling XXX Corps headquarters now that it was no longer needed.

"I'm humbled by your welcome and by the contents of General Patton's telegram. He and I go back a long way and I don't recall ever receiving a kind word from him or hearing him communicate for more than ten seconds without cussing. This is truly a day to remember."

There was an outbreak of laughter and applause.

"One thing you should know about George Patton – it took him five years to get through this school, and there are two lessons to be learned from this. First, you have to examine everything he says in light of that truth. I'm told that just before he graduated one of his classmates accidentally steered him into the library and he was lost for two days because he'd never been in there before." The story wasn't true – it was something he'd made up on the spur of the moment, but most people, including cadets, were amused when the mighty got skewered.

"And the second lesson is that you don't have to graduate high in your class to succeed in the Army. I know that's heresy," he said, turning momentarily to Wilby, "but the truth is most high ranking officers come from somewhere in the middle – or lower. So for those of you waging a losing battle with the academic departments as General Patton and I did, take heart. Trust me, there's hope.

"And hope is the message of this moment in history. We have just won a long and costly war in Europe and I am convinced the defeat of tyranny in the Pacific is not many weeks off. We, your predecessors, have won a war. But your task is far more difficult – to maintain peace. The tyrants of the world can never again be allowed to think that freedom loving people are more willing to compromise than to sacrifice for their human dignity. Keeping the peace will not be easy. Our Army and this institute need the help that only an infusion of youth and fresh ideas can provide. You must guard against inflexibilty and rigid thinking.

"And, you must always and forever honor your commitment to this glorious experiment, this idea called America. You are duty-bound and honor-bound to defend the Constitution of the United States against all, I repeat – all, enemies whether they be foreign or domestic. And this solemn responsibility knows no end date for those who commit to it."

He looked at his watch and then gazed around the mess hall.

"General Pershing once told me that the primary principle and requirement of military communications is brevity. I ask your forgiveness for violating that standard by exceeding my promised time limit by at least sixty seconds. Even so, I ask your indulgance for a few seconds longer because I have one more thing to say… Beat Navy!"

Washington Hall erupted in pandemonium that carried on for many minutes and he was able to slip down the stairs and outside before cadets started piling out of the building.

*   *   *

The sun was down below the horizon and the western sky was a faint reddish-orange. Great, brooding clouds, dark lavender and ringed in gold stretched eastward over Long Island Sound; a light wind, faint and cool, bent the long sea grass at the water's edge washing subtle swells onto the sand below the verdant carpet of grass.

If there's any place in creation that has remained untouched by time and wars, it's here, Dave Nolan said to himself as he sat on the bench at the end of the dock looking out over the water with the onshore breeze in his face. He was deep in thought and for perhaps the first time in his life felt completely adrift.

Dave knew Ike's sending him home so soon was a gift and he had thanked him the day they spent together in the little red school house in Rheims, Eisenhower's last headquarters. It was a strange twist of irony for him to be there. He'd walked the streets hoping to find Nicole Bouvier's little bakery, but it was a hopeless task, he realized. After all these years, much of the city had changed in the three decades since he'd last seen her and besides, she'd moved on with the French underground.

Now, he was free to retire once again from the Army. That was the easy part. Rebuilding his life, especially his marriage, might not be. Their relationship for the last two years had felt more like a long distance pen pal correspondence than a marriage. Would she forgive him and start over? He realized he had asked her to do that so many times over the years she might have legitimately grown weary of it. He wouldn't blame her if she declined and called it quits. Maybe she had already. That was what had occupied his mind all the way back from Europe and remained for him a considerable uncertainty even now.

How did I let everything go to hell so badly between us? he chastised himself for the hundredth time. *I can't blame her for the way I crudded up our life because of this war. Poor gal. She sure got a lousy damned deal when she signed on with me.*

He wondered if she still blamed him for Glenn's death. That had been the most disheartening emotional experience of his life when he'd read the first letter from Denise after their son's death was confirmed. He'd thought it unfair of her, yet he couldn't escape the notion he was at least in some way culpable. Maybe if he'd listened to her and stayed at home running his father-in-law's business operations…

Tomorrow he'd call her and see what, if anything, came of that. Then he'd catch the train to D.C. and see her; maybe things would work out.

From the living room of the cottage Denise saw him through the picture window he'd installed the spring before Mitch's graduation and her breath caught in her throat.

She expected he'd eventually come here after the call from General Wilby's aide a week earlier advising her of his accepting the invitation to review the graduation parade. She had debated meeting him at the academy and in the end decided it would be too awkward. The pomp and circumstance of June Week and the unutterably tedious formalities required for the school to entertain a three star general were too daunting for any quiet personal time.

And they would need time – lots of time. It would be like starting over again in many ways, and she wondered if he'd ever forgive her for things she'd said and done.

She watched him apprehensively as he sat stone still on the narrow little bench at the end of the dock. She remembered with emerald clarity the time he'd come back from the first *war to end all wars* and recalled she had been nervous beyond words then as well. Seeing him now evoked the same seesaw battle of emotions within her. Once again his sudden intrusion back into her life gripped her with animate uncertainty, as it had at the end of the last war.

It took her awhile to find the courage to step outside. *This is going to be thorny. What has happened between us that we became so distant and so much more complicated... how do we set it right?* She paused at the top of the steps and took a deep anxious breath, uncertain about her feelings. As she walked slowly across the lawn with the breeze blowing through her hair she realized her heart was beating rapidly and her breath came in quick little gasps. She paused at the end of the dock, watching him sitting motionless with his arms wrapped around a knee pulled tightly to his chest. Finally she walked toward him and saw him stand and turn to her.

"I knew you'd be here," she said quietly.

"It's the place where my favorite memories live. It was there at the end of the dock you said you'd marry me."

He took her in his arms and held her close, kissing her deeply, passionately, taking her breath away; for an instant she was dizzy, lightheaded. At last he released her and stood at arm's length holding her hands in his.

"I love you, Denise. I always have and I always will. You're still as beautiful as the day we met." He saw she was wearing around her neck the tiny wooden lantern he'd carved for her in Chalons during the last war; slowly he reached out and touched it.

"I started wearing it the day I learned about Glenn." She paused and gave him a forlorn look, the saddest he'd ever seen and it broke his heart. "I'm sorry I wrote that letter."

"You'd lost a son."

"He was your son, too. I should have thought of that before I sent it." She bit her lip and blinked back the tears forming in her eyes. "But now isn't the time to talk about Glenn – I couldn't bear it. In a little while maybe, but not now. We need to talk about us."

"We began our life together in this place; now we have a life to rebuild and a love to rekindle. I want to start here and I want to begin now. Will you...?"

She put her arms around his neck and kissed him. "My soul was wounded when you left and I found it impossible for a long while to forgive you for that. I was wrong. I did some foolish things, selfish things... and I've been miserable because of it. Dave, I –"

He placed a finger on her lips and softly said, "It wasn't your fault."

"That's not the old Nolan sense of responsibility talking."

"The old Nolan has made plenty of mistakes, too." He hugged her close and gently rocked while caressing her hair. "We have to think of the family, not just ourselves. We've all been wounded by the war, and we need to heal. Mitch is making a start in England with Henry and Maud's daughter. Erika's last letter sounded like she's serious about that lawyer – her note said they're looking at engagement rings."

"What do you think about it?"

"I'm not quite ready to let go of my little girl. He's a Washington lawyer! And worse, he's involved in politics. I told her she'd already met the best man she would ever meet in her life, and that man is her father."

Denise's face lit up and she threw back her head, laughing aloud. "You didn't?!"

"I most certainly did." He smiled at her now. "It's so good to hear your laughter again. Nobody sounds as happy as you do when you laugh."

She kissed him again and clung to him. "I have some wine chilled inside, and I just bought a new negligee," she whispered into his ear. "Does any of that interest you, soldier?"

He looked into her eyes and knew the healing had begun.

.

ABOUT THE AUTHOR

Brian Utermahlen is a graduate of the U.S. Military Academy at West Point, NY – Class of 1968, where he was a three year letterman on the Army Lacrosse team.

On active duty as an infantryman, he was an Army Ranger, a parachutist, and a helicopter pilot, serving in Germany, Viet Nam and the U.S.

He is an infantry combat veteran with the 1st Air Cavalry Division in Viet Nam. Following six years on active duty, he returned to civilian life as a manager for the DuPont corporation, Conoco, Inc. and BMC Software. He flew helicopters for 12 years in the Delaware National Guard and is an instrument rated ccommercial pilot in both helicopters and fixed wing aircraft.

He is retired in south Texas where he enjoys shooting sports, hunting and fishing. Along with his wife, Dianne, he spoils three granddaughters – Kaitlyn, Abigail and Megan.

His first novel – *THE HOFFMAN FILE* - was published by DELL, and he is busy editing the third installment of the *PASS IN REVIEW* trilogy - COUNTRY.

The first book in the ***Pass in Review*** series – **DUTY** – was awarded the Bronze Award for 'Best Historial Fiction – 2012' by the Military Writers Society of America (MWSA).

HISTORICAL NOTES AND FOOTNOTES

While the majority of events involving historical figures interacting with the Nolan family, their friends and associates are historically accurate, a few events have been modified or created by the author for dramatic or illustrative effect. The history of WWII is reliable in the detail of well known battles on the ground and in the air. Most of the air actions and many of the characters involved are actual figures and are accurately drawn from Army Air Corps histories.

The meeting between Dave Nolan and Bill Donovan at the St. Regis never occurred in history; however, Donovan was approached by a Canadian in the British Secret Service with a request identical to the one made by Donovan to Nolan – the requester was William Stephenson, now known as the master British spy – Intrepid. Donovan undertook a mission to England in the summer of 1940 as portrayed and for the reasons related in the story. He even stayed at *Claridges*.

Mitch Nolan's adventure flying Lockheed Hudsons from Newfoundland to England in the winter of 1940 is an historical event. Lord Beaverbrook and Australian Donald Bennett are historical figures and the mission and British internal debate are historically accurate.

Most of the individual reactions of people to the bombing of Pearl Harbor are historical.

The ferry flight of P-38s across the southern Atlantic is historically accurate as to flight route, however the timing was altered for the dramatic effect of having Mitch Nolan arrive for the last day of the Casablanca Conference. One of the ferry flight pilots was then Lt. Col. Ben Mason, the deputy commander and later the commander of the 82nd Fighter Group.

One of the women at Casablanca – Aida Gonzalez – is an historical figure who managed the meeting logistics. She was an interpreter at Britain's Cairo Embassy (she did speak six languages). The author had the privilege of meeting her in the late 1990s.

Makara Foulkes, her co-hostess at The Casablanca Conference, is a creation of the author.

Dixie Sloan is an actual historical figure, and for most of WWII he was the leading P-38 ace in the Mediterranean Theater. The author met him the same day he met Aida Gonzalez.

Lucky Lindquist's 'Shiek of Araby' adventure is based on an actual historical incident.

Nancy Wake, the *White Mouse*, is an historical figure. She died in London in August 2011.

Operation 'Cracker Jacks' flown by the Hangmen is based on the historical operation planned by William Dononvan called 'Operation Cornflakes'; it was executed by the 49th FS in February 1945. The mission was led by B.W. Curry who related the events to the author.

LTC Edward C. 'Cannonball" Krause, commander of 3rd Bn, 505th Parachute Infantry Regiment did raise the first American flag on the continent as the sun rose on the morning of June 6, 1944.

HISTORICAL NOTES AND FOOTNOTES
(continued)

Blaxton's rescue of Lucky Lindquist is based on an historical incident in the 82nd Fighter Group involving downed pilot Dick Willsie and his wing man, Flight Officer Dick Andrews. The events were related to the author by Willsie who lived it, and by LTC Ben Mason who witnessed it. The event is recorded in 82nd Fighter Group histories and is known among pilots flying from Foggia.

Lieutenant Bill Chappell ("Flash Gordon") is an historical figure - a legend in the Airborne.

Earl Wright, the squad mate and friend of Glenn Nolan, is an historical figure (as is Kenny Cook). He was in one of the first nine planes over France on D-Day and parachuted into Ste. Mere Eglise as portrayed. He made all four of the 82nd Airborne Division's combat jumps and fought in every engagement in the division's WWII history. He survived the war and never once was wounded.

Co. G, 505th Parachute Infantry Regiment was one of the first companies into Ste. Mere Eglise.

The arguments between Omar Bradley and Trafford Leigh-Mallory actually occurred.

XXXI Corps in England is historical; it was a hoax employed as a ruse of the Allies to mislead German intelligent about the extent of Allied forces and the location of the invasion.

Dave Nolan's commands in North Africa, Sicily, Salerno and Northern Europe are fictional. Nolan's fictional 12th Infantry Division is modeled after the historical 45th Infantry Division. Nolan's fictional XXX Corps performs in actions and across terrain much as the historical XII Corps and XX Corps under George Patton's Third Army in Europe.

Mitch Nolan's escape from occupied France is fictional, however Chuck Yeager's trek through the Pyrenees is historically accurate, including his saving the life of a U.S. bomber crewman. The "bomber guy" was found by Spaniards, nursed to health and returned to the U.S months later.

Chuck Yeager's reinstatement to flying status in Europe is historically accurate as is the way in which it happened. He was the very first pilot to escape occupied France who was allowed to return to flying status in the European theatre. He was also the first "Ace-in-a-day" in the 327th Fighter Group; chronologically it came after the portrayal of that feat by Mitch Nolan.

The Russian Army had a XXX Corps that fought in Austria; the incident portrayed in the book in which a game of one-upsmanship was played by them upon their meeting the Americans at the Kremsmunster, Austria bridge is historically accurate, but Dave Nolan's XXX Corps wasn't there.

The poem – PEACE – was written as a school project in 2010 by
eight year old Kaitlyn McDonald of Friendswood, TX.

Made in the USA
Charleston, SC
21 December 2012